OMNIBUS EDITION: 2

VIETNAM: GROUND ZERO THE HOBO WOODS
VIETNAM: GROUND ZERO SOLDIER'S MEDAL
VIETNAM: GROUND ZERO GUIDELINES

"Which weapon do you want?" Bates asked.

"M-16, I think. And a pistol. I don't suppose I could find a 9 mm Browning." Gerber tossed the laundry bag into the back of the jeep.

"I think it can be arranged," said Bates. "The only thing wrong with those exotic ones is that it's hard to find ammunition."

"I wouldn't call a Browning exotic." Gerber climbed into the passenger's seat.

"Anything that doesn't use .45 or .38 caliber is exotic around here."

"I see the paper shufflers in the World are still directing things. Anyone ever tell them the advantage of fourteen shots without reloading?"

Bates shoved the jeep into reverse, grinding the gears. Then, spinning the wheel, they blasted out of the supply depot in a burst of red dust.

"I doubt it," yelled Bates. "I mean, those are the same guys who have declared the use of the shotgun as too inhumane but have done nothing to stop the use of napalm."

"Yeah," was all Gerber could find to say.

VIETNAM: GROUND ZERO
THE HOBO WOODS

ERIC HELM

A GOLD EAGLE BOOK
London · Toronto · New York · Sydney

ISBN 0 373 62707 6 (Pocket edition)

First published in Great Britain in pocket edition by Gold Eagle 1988

© Eric Helm 1987

*Australian copyright 1987
Philippine copyright 1987
Pocket Edition 1988*

**This OMNIBUS EDITION 1989
ISBN 0 373 57746 X**

8911
Made and printed in Great Britain

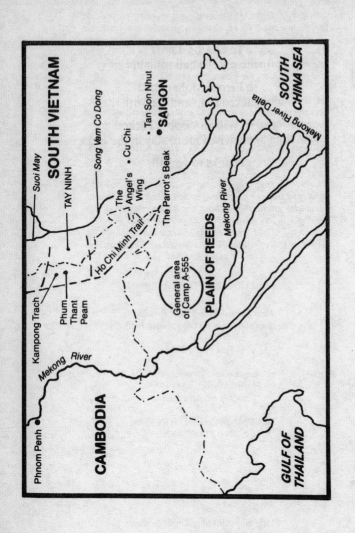

To Sharon Jarvis
who got the ball rolling,

to Feroze Mohammed
who picked it up and ran with it

and to Wilson "Bob" Tucker
who long ago advised me to stay in the game.

Thanks to you all.

VIETNAM: GROUND ZERO
THE
HOBO WOODS

PROLOGUE

THE HOBO WOODS
REGION NEAR CU CHI,
REPUBLIC OF
VIETNAM

Nuyen Van Ti lay in the shallow hole that overlooked the weed- and vine-choked path in the center of the Hobo Woods, watching an American patrol work its way to the north toward the Song Sai Gon. He had been there since before dawn, covered by six inches of moist earth and damp, rotting vegetation; only his eyes were exposed, and there was a small opening for his nose so that he could breathe. Ti had no weapon with him, no equipment. He was dressed in black silk shorts and nothing else. His job was to spy on the booby-trapped trail and report to his lieutenant after the Americans departed.

It was an uncomfortable task. Once his comrades had buried him, he could not move. The stinging rays of the sun, broken and deflected by the scraggly trees and ragged bushes, were absorbed by the earth of his temporary grave, at first not bothering him and then baking him. By midmorning his body was soaked with sweat and he was breathing in short bursts, praying for a drink of water. He wondered why he hadn't been given a canteen with a straw. He had the feeling he was being suffocated, and it was only through tough mental discipline that he was able to remain in place and ignore the dryness building in his throat.

He had spent the morning listening to the American jets and helicopters as they had overflown the spot where he lay buried. There had been a distant rumbling as heavy explosives had been dropped from the planes, and then nearer, louder detonations as artillery had destroyed a small section of the Hobo Woods no more than a klick away. The nearby rattling of the shrapnel against the trees as it had cut through the leaves had scared him. He had feared that the artillery would kill him, but it had fallen without coming very close to him.

Part of the time, to allay his discomfort, he had dreamed of his girlfriend in faraway Ban Me Thuot and the last night they had spent together. He had told her that he was going south toward the delta to fight the imperialist Americans who had invaded their country and who were turning most of it into a wasteland.

She had not argued the point with him, because she worked on the American base at Ban Me Thuot, earning in one month more than her father could earn in a year. The money had allowed her to buy many things that she had only dreamed of. The gifts of the Americans had enabled her to provide much for her family, and although her father resented the newfound wealth from his daughter, he took it, as everyone else in Ban Me Thuot did. Each morning, he, along with a thousand other men, lined up at the main gate to Ban Me Thuot, hoping for a day's employment inside. The Americans didn't realize they were creating enemy soldiers with all their wealth and Ti had realized that he could exploit the situation. He had told his girl's father that the Americans were paying her so much money because they expected more than honest work from her. It had caused trouble in the home and that was what Ti had wanted.

But that last night had been something different for Ti. With the prospect that he was leaving for months or years or maybe forever, she had caved in to his desires. She had sneaked off with him, hiding in the rear of his hootch while he had slowly peeled her out of her clothes. When she was naked, he had licked the sweat from her body, concentrating on her breasts and then her thighs. He had moved slowly, enjoying everything and anticipating the best. Only the thought of his trip had spoiled the pleasure of the night, but he had managed to suppress that by studying her body, feeling the soft skin, tasting her salty sweat and kissing her willing lips.

At first her response had been mechanical and ill-timed, but then she had gotten into the spirit of the act, thrusting herself at him and guiding his hands for her pleasure. She had moaned quietly as he had touched her, the sweat dampening her hair and plastering it to her head. She had spread her legs wide and pumped her hips wildly as the enjoyment had peaked. She had shouted her gratification and glee, forgetting the inhibitions taught to a proper Vietnamese young lady.

Ti felt himself respond to the memories, the thickening at his crotch becoming uncomfortable given the circumstances. He couldn't reach down to adjust himself or to relieve himself. Instead, he forced his mind back to his task.

It was early afternoon when he heard the first American voice in the distance and knew that the enemy was coming closer. For a moment he held his breath, fear invading his body like a disease, but then he remembered that most of the

Americans didn't see what they looked at. A well-concealed trap would be missed by them, and they would never spot his hiding place.

The Americans stuck to the path of least resistance, dodging the thorny bushes and ducking under the clinging vines. There were twelve of them, all wearing sweat-stained uniforms and carrying the black plastic weapon called the M-16. They were walking single file, one man far out in front of the rest.

Somehow the point man missed the trip wire stretched across the trail. He stepped over it and continued to move. His head swiveled from side to side as his eyes searched the vegetation around him. He held his weapon in both hands, the fingers of one curled around the pistol grip and trigger housing. He stopped once, listened and then moved on.

Behind him, one of the men probed a bush with the barrel of his weapon. A big black man passed that soldier, his foot snagging the trip wire, jerking the grenade from the can that held the safety spoon in place. As the grenade pulled free, the spoon flew, and a moment later there was a dull pop like the sound of a light bulb hitting the floor. Red-hot shrapnel sliced through the air, cutting into the trees and the black man.

A scream rose from him as he flipped forward, his hands beating frantically at his back as if to brush off stinging insects gathered there. He was shouting at the men with him, screaming for their help, but they had all disappeared, diving for cover. There were a couple of hasty shots fired at unseen targets and then silence, except for the moaning of the wounded enemy.

Then another American with no weapon, just a green canvas bag with a bright red cross on it, knelt near the wounded man. With scissors, he cut the uniform from the soldier's back, spreading it wide so that he could see the shrapnel damage. It looked as if someone had painted the man red.

The man with the bag dabbed at the blood, wiping it away carefully. He tossed the blood-soaked rag into the bushes at the side and began to shake some kind of powder over the wounds. That done, he taped a transparent material lightly to the man's back and then dug in his bag for a needle so that he could give the wounded black a shot. Ti guessed it was something to ease the pain.

As he completed the treatment, another enemy, a bigger American, came forward and crouched near them. They talked quietly, and although Ti could hear the words, he didn't understand them. Then the others approached, crawling on the ground, probing the trail with their fingers. One of them found a second booby trap and carefully followed the trip wire until he discovered another grenade in the can. He extracted the weapon and tossed it into the trees away from them. It exploded a moment later, injuring no one but scaring a number of birds. They flapped noisily into the air, screaming their fear at the forest around them.

Gently two of the Americans assisted the wounded black to his feet, helping him walk to the north into an open area. All the men spread out, searching for the VC and then sat down to wait as the big man talked on his radio. Ti wished he could hear him now because he would be able to get the American codes, but the enemy soldiers were too far from him.

Within minutes a helicopter appeared. It swooped out of the cloudless sky and touched down in the middle of a clearing nearby. Ti could hear the roar of its turbine engine and the popping of its rotor blades as it leaped back into the sky. They had placed the wounded man aboard the aircraft. The whirlwind of debris, leaves and dried grass slowly fell to the ground. With their wounded friend evacuated, the patrol regrouped and worked its way off the clearing and into the trees.

Although Ti had seen what he had been left to see, he still didn't move. He was enough of a soldier to know that there could be more men behind the first bunch, or that the first group could return. Ti would wait until dark before he extracted himself from his grave so that he could slip into the tunnel system that honeycombed the Hobo Woods and make his report. The officers would be pleased with Ti's good work, even though the news that the Americans were patrolling in the Hobo Woods would be distressing. They would have to be careful as more of the men in their division slipped into hiding there.

1

THE SWAMPS NEAR
FORT BRAGG, NORTH
CAROLINA

It was cold and wet and miserable, and Army Special Forces Captain MacKenzie K. Gerber couldn't figure out how he had allowed himself to be talked into this training mission. There were a dozen men, all of whom Gerber outranked, qualified to stamp through the swamp.

Gerber stopped moving, the clammy, foul-smelling water lapping at his thighs, soaking through the inadequate protection of his fatigues and filling his boots. He listened to the night sounds around him, then reached to the right and touched the smooth trunk of a dead tree, the Spanish moss hanging from its limbs like so much diseased skin. Switching his weapon to his left hand, Gerber pulled his compass from his mud-slimed pocket. He sighted on a distant point of light, checked the dimly glowing dial of the compass and then looked upward through the tangle of leafless branches into the cold blackness of the star-studded November sky.

With great care, he began to move again, rolling his foot forward slowly so that the muck under the water released his boot. He chose an easterly direction, focusing on the dim light that he figured marked an isolated farm or roadside stand. He felt the water move with him, the quiet splashing lost in the night calls of the birds wheeling overhead. Gerber wasn't worried about snakes. It was too cold for them. Too miserable for them.

The water began to drop away, and Gerber scrambled up a slight muddy rise sprinkled with dried grass. He was out of the swamp for the first time in an hour. A gentle breeze reminded him just how cold he was, and he huddled with his back against the trunk of a gigantic tree that dripped Spanish moss and blotted out the sky. Shafts of moonlight reflected on the rippling water of the swamp, dancing gaily, looking almost inviting.

From the east came the drone of aircraft engines. Gerber knew it was the first of the simulated recon entering the tactical zone. He couldn't see the blacked-out shape but could tell from the sound that the C-130 Hercules was approaching. He hoped Sergeant McInnerny had deployed the aggressors near what they presumed would be the drop zone. There were only a few places that a squad could jump into without risking drowning in the swamp or hanging themselves up in the branches of the forest, especially at night. Gerber had ordered McInnerny to cover two of them. Gerber was close to the third.

As the plane neared, Gerber slipped into the swamp again, the water washing around him as he edged his way toward the drop zone. The water closed around his crotch, shriveling his scrotum until he could feel the ache from it. Once he was clear of the overhanging trees, he glimpsed patches of the night sky, blazing with a thousand stars. He heard the engines of the C-130 roll back as the pilot decreased his speed so that the paratroopers could exit. Straining his eyes, he could not see lights from the plane, but as it turned away and the roar increased, he caught the pale reflections of parachutes drifting on a steady breeze. He grinned to himself and eased out of the water, rubbing a hand over his face, which was now covered with mud and disguised underneath layers of camouflage paint. The drop would not be a success.

Free of the water, he crouched near a fallen tree and laid three wet hand grenade simulators on it. Next to them he placed a single flare, then set two spare magazines for his M-16 on it. He was planning a one-man ambush with grenades and flares that would surprise and confuse the parachutists. He hoped that the M-16, dragged through swamp water that was sometimes chest deep, would not jam. He had been careful to keep it out of the water and mud, but he had slipped once, nearly falling.

From the left came a quiet voice, "Captain, I have good news and bad news."

Startled, Gerber rolled away, landing on his side, propped on one elbow and bringing his rifle up to fire, but he could not see a target. As he removed his finger from the trigger, he said, "That you, Tony?"

"Yes, sir," said the voice. Master Sergeant Anthony B. Fetterman seemed to materialize out of the gloom at the base of the tree. He unfolded himself until he was a short, slight black shape against the dark gray of the background.

"Christ, Tony," said Gerber. "You're lucky I didn't shoot you full of holes."

"Had faith in you, Captain. Knew you wouldn't open fire without identifying the target, no matter how surprised you were." He grinned, his teeth flashing in the night. "Besides, you've only got blanks."

Gerber ignored that and turned to the slash of gray that was the intended drop zone. "If you've a few minutes, I'll throw a scare into these guys."

"If you don't mind, Captain, I'll take care of their surprise. While I was waiting for you to finish playing in the swamp, I rigged the DZ with artillery simulators."

Gerber rolled to his hands and knees, crawled to Fetterman, and as he sat down, waved a hand. "Be my guest."

Fetterman picked up the hand-held electrical generator that trailed wires, and crouched near the end of the fallen tree where the roots reached into the night. He held the body of the equipment in his left hand, his right grasping the handle of the crank. Overhead, the parachutists continued their silent descent, barely visible in the light of the half moon. He watched the twelve of them, waiting until each had reached the ground.

With a grin, he said, "This'll wake them up." Savagely he twisted the generator's handle, once, twice, three times. The current surged through the lines, setting off the sequence of simulators.

From his position, Gerber saw the first bright flash, like a giant strobe, and heard the loud, flat bang of the simulator as it exploded. From the center of the DZ came the staccato burst of an M-16 on full automatic, the man outlined by the muzzle-flashes of his weapon. The rest of the squad was standing there, trying to find their attackers, trying to collapse their chutes, and scrambling to bring their weapons to bear on the unseen enemy.

And then it seemed that the whole DZ erupted. Glaring bursts of light ringed the clearing, giving the impression of a well-worn silent movie. The movement of the men took on the jerky motions of old films as they spun, searching for the attackers. In a real combat environment, they would all have died in less than a minute.

Fetterman jerked the wires free from the generator. "That takes care of that."

"I guess it does," said Gerber.

"Now, as I said, I have good news and I have bad news."

"Good news first. Takes the sting out of the bad."

"Yes, sir. Good news is that our orders arrived. Courier brought them to headquarters a couple of hours ago. Special delivery since they were so late. We're on our way back to Nam."

"And the bad?"

"We have to be in Oakland by ten this morning."

Gerber pushed back the mud-encrusted sleeve of his fatigues, peeled the camouflage strip off the face of his watch and saw that it was a quarter of three. "Doesn't give us much time. Not with a four-mile hike to the camp."

"I brought a jeep. I have no great fondness for waltzing through cold, muddy swamp water when I can drive a nice, warm jeep."

"Then lead on," said Gerber.

"What about the men in the DZ?"

"Let them find their own ride."

WITH A GREAT DEAL OF LUCK, a run through Dallas Love Field and a cab driver who knew exactly what he was doing, both Gerber and Fetterman were able to make it to the U.S. Army Processing Center in Oakland, California, by ten the following morning. Since the orders had not been a surprise, Gerber and Fetterman had been packed and ready to go days in advance.

Now they stood at the entrance of an aircraft hangar where there were rows and rows of tables, and nearly a thousand clerks, male and female, civilian and military, circulating. In front of them and in front of the tables were hundreds of men in a variety of uniforms. Sailors, airmen, marines and soldiers stood holding packets of documents while the clerks typed new ones and handed them out. Gerber stared at the mess, at the huge fans blowing across the open floor, at the long banks of lights suspended from the high ceiling of the hangar and at the concrete floor that had been waxed to a dull yellow.

"Looks like a factory," said Fetterman.

"Manufacturing cannon fodder," said Gerber. "Sending the cream of America's youth to do battle with the yellow peril across the big pond."

Fetterman turned to stare at Gerber. "You going to get philosophical on me?"

"No, Tony." Gerber shook his head and added, "Not at all." He sighed. "I suppose we'd better get into one of the lines."

They separated. Fetterman headed off to the section for senior NCOs, and Gerber turned and joined a line of company grade officers. While he was waiting, it suddenly struck him how young most of them looked, as if they should still be in high school or getting ready to enter college, instead of crossing the big pond to Vietnam.

One of the men turned and stared at Gerber's chest where four rows of bright ribbons were pinned. The man was wearing the bars of a second lieutenant, and the bars looked as if he had recently bought them.

"You been there already, sir?" asked the lieutenant.

"Had a tour in '65 and '66," said Gerber.

"What was it like?"

Gerber could tell from the soldier's voice that he was scared. He was a tall thin man with thick brown hair that, contrary to army regulations, touched his ears. He had bright blue eyes, a slender nose and a pointed chin. There was a hint of a mustache on his upper lip, but the hair was baby-fine and almost invisible. Sweat was beaded in his mustache and on his forehead, and it stained the underarms of his tailored, short-sleeved khaki uniform.

"How old are you?" asked Gerber.

"Be twenty-one in March." The lieutenant looked as if he had been insulted.

"What the fuck are you doing here?"

The youth continued to look offended. "I'm preparing to go to—"

"No," said Gerber, interrupting. "What I mean is, why aren't you in college chasing cheerleaders?"

The lieutenant grinned finally. "I think that's why I'm here. I spent too much time chasing cheerleaders and not enough studying. The vulgarities of the deferment system caught me, and here I am."

"Son," said Gerber, suddenly feeling older than his thirty-three years, "if I had a student deferment, I would have been doing my best to protect it."

"Yes, sir," said the lieutenant. "It somehow got away from me."

They moved forward as a first lieutenant took a manila envelope from the clerk and moved to the next processing point. Gerber pulled a handkerchief from his pocket, wiped the sweat from his forehead and looked at the giant hangar doors that were locked, wishing that someone would open them so that the air would have a better chance to circulate. The roaring fans were not up to the task.

To the lieutenant, he said, "I can't tell you what it's like. I have no idea what you'll be doing. But don't worry about it. It's not going to be as bad as you think." Gerber smiled. "It's going to be days of boredom broken up by seconds of pure terror. It's going to be hot and humid, and you're not going to have a solid shit for months."

"Sir?"

"The one thing I remember most is the damned malaria tablets. They do something to the GI tract so that everyone suffers from diarrhea. Not very glamorous, is it?"

"No, sir."

"It's the little things that you miss. Going to the corner restaurant for a pizza because you feel like one. Electricity that lasts all night and television shows that aren't recycled everyday. A hot shower. A hot bath. A girl around who speaks English as a native language. Driving a car and seeing a movie without having to stop every fifteen or twenty minutes for a new reel."

"That doesn't answer my question, Captain."

"What's your name?"

"Boyle. David Boyle."

"Well, Lieutenant Boyle, there's no way for me to answer your question because I don't know what you're going to be doing. You're infantry, so you could end up humping through the boonies, leading a platoon of scared men against Charlie. Or you could end up in Saigon, leading a platoon of unhappy typists against the mountain of paper that drives the American war machine."

"What did you do, sir?"

"I advised the South Vietnamese on ways of killing the North Vietnamese and spent as much time as I could in a bunker." He grinned at the lie.

The line advanced again so that they were near the front. A dozen men had joined them, all of them listening to the conversation, each wanting to ask questions but afraid because it would show emotion. It would show that they were scared, that they were not the John Wayne super soldier of the Saturday matinee.

Gerber knew there was nothing he could say to ease their minds. Each would have to learn about Vietnam in his own way, doing his own job. Of the fifteen or twenty men near him, only two or three would end up seeing any heavy action. Most would find themselves in other military jobs—public relations officers, supply officers, billeting officers, motor pool officers—and never venture outside of Saigon or Nha Trang or Da Nang or their fire support base. Probably the only thing they'd have to worry about would be the random mortar round falling on them. Or the random rocket finding them.

But standing in the line in Oakland, they all wanted to think they would be leading hordes of men into battle to earn great glory. Gerber knew they wanted to believe that Vietnam was a great crusade to save the world from communism. None of them wanted to think that their war year would be spent counting the number of beers sold in the club the night before, although, while they were counting those beers, they would secretly be happy that they had lucked into the soft job. Once safely back in the World, their war year would take on dimension. It would become a thing of great glory to be remembered over beers while others invented bigger lies.

Gerber had only been back for a year, but already he could see the type developing. Soldiers whose chests held the roster medals handed out to everyone who set foot in Vietnam and who had more war stories than any three combat officers. Civilians who hadn't been there, now taking credit for imaginary tours while gullible civilians bought them free drinks.

"David," said Gerber, "there's really nothing I can tell you about this. You'll have to go through it, but within a couple of weeks you'll have your own answers. Just remember that the training you've had is the best in the world. You'll find yourself reacting to situations and later realize that it was the training. And it'll all . . . you'll be home before you know it.'' He had almost said that it would all be over before he knew it.

They had reached the front, and Boyle handed his packet of orders to the clerk, who took three copies and gave the package back. To Gerber, Boyle said, ''Thank you, sir.''

In a few minutes it was Gerber's turn. He gave a copy of his orders to the clerk, a pimply faced man in an ill-fitting uniform with a single ribbon above the breast pocket. The man, whose name was Jones according to his name tag, took the orders, glanced at them, grabbed a form from the stack and asked, ''Is all the information on here correct?'' His voice was high and squeaky and tired.

''Yes,'' said Gerber.

The man rolled the form into his typewriter, a manual job that looked as if it had been used by the Union Army during the Civil War, and copied information from the orders onto it. When he finished with the name, rank, serial number and home of record, he asked, ''You want to leave the beneficiary on your insurance the same?''

For one irrational moment, Gerber thought about changing it to President Johnson. How would the President feel, receiving ten thousand dollars from a GI's death. But that was an emotional response to some of the things he had seen while home, a poor response to the college students who protested the war and the slanted newscasts on network television.

To Jones, Gerber said, ''No, leave it all for my kid brother.''

Jones typed some more, found another form, filled it out and then asked questions that seemed personal to Gerber. The clerk wanted to know Gerber's religious preference and marital status, although the orders contained the latter.

When he finished, he handed the package to Gerber and sent him to the next station in the line.

A bored medical officer in a stained white lab coat sat behind a table and reviewed the medical records. As he flipped through them, he glanced up at Gerber and asked, "You got your shot record?"

Gerber took it out of his wallet and handed it over.

"Uh-huh. You're about due for a couple of boosters." He turned and looked toward a nurse sitting at a table covered with a white cloth and holding an assortment of needles, vials, cotton and small boxes. "Guess these can wait until you get in-country." He stamped one of the forms. "You can go to the next station."

Gerber continued through, had a fat sergeant look at his dog tags to make sure that the information on them was correct, moved to another clerk who logged him in and finally came to a sergeant who told him that he was not manifested through that day and would have to check back the next day before ten o'clock.

"And go through this again?" asked Gerber.

"No, sir. You just come to this station and we'll check the flight manifests. Flights are set by ten, and if you're not booked through, then you return the following day. You have to stay in the BOQ here and leave a number at the desk when you leave the building.

"Thank you," said Gerber. He turned and walked slowly to the front. He found Fetterman sitting there, his eyes closed and his foot tapping in time to some phantom melody. "You about ready, Master Sergeant?"

"Yes, sir," said Fetterman, getting to his feet. "I take it you're not going out today."

"Check in tomorrow is what the man said. First, find a room in the transient quarters, and then, tour San Francisco, I think."

"Yes, sir," agreed Fetterman.

After he had checked in and dumped his gear in the cinder-block room, which was painted a neutral light green and contained a tile floor, two bunks, one dresser and no TV or radio, Gerber headed downstairs to find Fetterman waiting for him again.

"How is it that you get through all this faster than I do?" he asked.

"You'll find, Captain, that the majority of the functionaries we're required to deal with are NCOs. Officers hide in their nice air-conditioned offices and only venture out for lunch, the end of the day or if a pretty lady should stumble into their area. That leaves the NCOs in charge, and we take care of our own."

"Very nice."

Fetterman pushed open the door and allowed Gerber to step into the chill of the autumn afternoon. As he walked down the three steps, Gerber thought about the heat in the hangar. They tried to cool it with giant fans, but no one thought to open one of the big doors to let Mother Nature cool the inside with her natural air-conditioning.

"How we going to get to San Francisco?" asked Fetterman.

As he spoke, a cab slowed near them, and when Gerber moved toward it, the driver stopped. The captain waved a hand, indicating that the answer to Fetterman's question had arrived, then he opened the rear door and climbed in, and the master sergeant followed.

The driver, leaning his right arm on the back of his seat, asked, "Where to, gentlemen?"

"Downtown," said Gerber.

The driver nodded. He pulled back into traffic, drove out the gate and turned west. They crossed San Francisco Bay, and as they entered the city, the driver asked, "Market Street suit you?"

"Market Street will be fine," said Fetterman.

They turned north, and then the driver pulled to the curb. "This be it, gentlemen." He glanced at the meter and told them what the fare was. As Fetterman got out, Gerber handed over the bills and said, "Keep the change."

When the taxi was gone, Fetterman asked, "What's the plan from here?"

"Hell, Tony, I don't know. I suppose we could ease on down to Fisherman's Wharf and look at the water. Smell the dead fish and the salt. Eat seafood."

They walked north from there, looking at the storefronts, the movie theaters and office buildings. There were hundreds of people moving along the streets, some of them dressed in suits and dresses, others in pieces of military uniforms. Cars zipped down the street, weaving in and out of traffic as horns blared and tires squealed.

"Isn't civilization wonderful, Captain?" said Fetterman. He was looking around as if he had never been in a large city before and was taking in all the sights and sounds. "Got to get my fill of it before the trip across the big pond."

As the two soldiers walked out on the wharf, two women, dressed in short skirts and tight blouses, approached. They stopped in front of Gerber and Fetterman, blocking their path. The taller, blonder of the two asked, "You boys looking for a party?"

Fetterman grinned at them. "What did you have in mind?"

"For twenty dollars we'll take care of your immediate needs," she said.

"Well," said Fetterman, "that's very kind of you, but the captain and I were going to find something to eat. We'll buy you lunch if you'd like to accompany us."

Neither woman was sure what to make of that. The blonde stared and then said, "Ah, no, thank you. We've got to make some money first. Thanks anyway."

Fetterman looked crestfallen. "If that's the way you feel about it, but the captain and I were going to find a good restaurant and have a good lunch."

"Really, we have to get to work."

"All right," said Fetterman. "Well, don't forget to write."

The women moved away, angling across the pavement toward a group of four men in army uniforms. The women stopped to talk to them, and Fetterman said to Gerber, "They must feel safe approaching soldiers. Cops on Vice wouldn't be wearing an army uniform. I'll have to remember that if I ever become a cop and get assigned to the vice detail."

"Much chance of that, Tony?" asked Gerber.

"Well, sir, when I was in high school, I would have said that there wasn't much chance I'd become a soldier, so I guess you never know."

Gerber pointed at a restaurant across the wharf from them. "How about there? Looks like it should be expensive. We could drop twenty, thirty bucks on lunch. Maybe a hundred if we worked hard at it."

"Fine with me, Captain."

They crossed the street and entered. There was a man at the door, holding a handful of menus. "Two?" he asked, and then not waiting for an answer, said, "Follow me."

He led them through a huge roomful of people, down a short hallway and into another that had a gigantic window overlooking part of the Bay. There were ten tables, each covered with a pristine cloth, red napkins, a variety of silverware and glasses. The walls were papered with a muted covering, and there were a few seascapes hanging on them.

The only lighting came from the windows. The maître d' gestured at a table and asked, "Will this do?"

"Near the window, I think," said Fetterman.

"Ah," said the man, but before he could protest he felt something being pressed into his hand. Surreptitiously he glanced down and saw the ten-dollar bill. "Please. Over here."

They had the best table in the room. It was situated against the window and gave them a perfect view of the Bay and the city.

When the man disappeared, Gerber asked, "What'd you give him?"

"Ten bucks."

"Bit extravagant, wasn't it?"

"When you consider where we'll be in a couple of days and how many opportunities we'll have to spend money, I don't think so."

A waitress appeared. She was tall and blond, and Gerber wondered where they were all coming from. She could have been the sister of the woman they had seen on the wharf. And like that woman, she was wearing a short skirt, dark stockings and a white blouse. She held a small, wet tray in one hand and asked, "Would you care for something from the bar?"

Gerber was going to decline and then said, "What the hell? I'd like a shot of Beam's Choice, neat, and bring one for my friend."

It took her almost no time to get the drinks. She set one in front of each of them and left.

Gerber picked up his, held it near the window and inspected the almost amber-colored liquor. He nodded toward Fetterman. "To a short, successful tour."

"To a smooth one," said Fetterman.

They drank the liquor, then slammed the glasses on the tabletop. "Now we eat," said Gerber.

When the waiter came, they ordered a variety of foods, including crab, shrimp, and at Fetterman's insistence, some shark. The waiter also suggested salads and baked potatoes, and the lunch turned into a dinner complete with drinks and appetizers.

As they waited for the meal, Fetterman asked, "How did Miss Morrow take the news of our sudden departure? Bet it surprised the hell out of her."

"I didn't tell her."

"Oh?"

"Oh, nothing. Just never got the chance, given the circumstances."

"You could call her now," suggested Fetterman.

"I'll write her a letter from Saigon and explain it. That'll have to do it for her," growled Gerber.

Fetterman wanted to say more but knew Gerber well enough to keep his mouth shut. Instead, he sat quietly, staring out at the Bay, watching the boats and ships, and waited. Finally he asked, "What's the plan after we eat?"

Gerber glanced at his watch. "Getting late in the day. We could sightsee a little more, walk around town, see a movie. Hell, Tony, I don't know."

That was the problem. They were caught in limbo between their existence in the World and that of Vietnam. Nothing to do but wait for their names to appear on a flight manifest so that they could go to Vietnam. Neither of them knew anyone in San Francisco or knew that much about the town. The last time they had flown out to Vietnam, it had been on a military plane from a military base and not this semicivilian operation involving tens of thousands of men.

When the food came, they ate in silence. Each concentrated on his meal rather than worrying about conversation. The food was excellent, Gerber suspected, but he didn't taste much of it. He was distracted by Fetterman's comment about Morrow, distracted by the way the army was plugging people into slots to send them to Vietnam, and irritated at the delay. There had been no need for them to rush to San Francisco to sit around waiting for space on an airplane. Someone at their end, in North Carolina, could have coordinated the activity better so that when they arrived in San Francisco they could have gotten on a plane.

Then he realized that the anger was misplaced. There was no reason to be angry. He was anxious to get to Vietnam and out of the state of limbo. It seemed that this was an opportunity to get his personal life straightened out again. There had been too much turmoil in it since he had returned from Vietnam, not all of it caused by Morrow.

The waiter approached and asked, "Is everything satisfactory?"

"Couldn't be better," said Fetterman. "Great."

"I'd like a beer. Something in a bottle. Anything but PBR," said Gerber.

"Right away, sir."

They passed the rest of the afternoon strolling the streets of San Francisco. Fetterman wanted to find the famed Haight-Ashbury district so that he could see the hippies, but when he found it, he was disappointed. Rather than a hotbed of social concern, he found malcontents who made their social statement by rejecting soap and water. There were men and women sitting on the sidewalk, boys and girls really, who looked as if they were only about one-third conscious. They wore dirty clothes and leather necklaces or colored beads and called one another "Man." It was a depressing sight.

The two men circulated, looking at the boarded-up windows of various failed businesses, the antiwar slogans scribbled on the bare plywood, the free clinics and free lunch centers, and got more depressed. When they came to a bar that advertised Thoroughly Naked College Coeds, Fetterman decided that he had seen enough of San Francisco.

They found a cab and rode in silence back to the army depot. While Fetterman paid the driver, Gerber hurried inside. At the desk, he discovered that someone had goofed and they were scheduled to fly out later that night. "Happens all the time," said the clerk. "That'll be two dollars."

"Two dollars for what?" asked Gerber.

"Two dollars for the room."

"But I didn't stay in it. Only checked in this morning," argued Gerber.

"Doesn't matter. Check out time is two p.m., and it's long after that now. Two dollars."

Rather than argue about it, Gerber paid the man his two dollars, and when Fetterman entered, told him about the sudden change in their flight orders.

Fetterman grinned and asked, "Now why doesn't that surprise me?"

2

THE CONFERENCE ROOM, MACV HEADQUARTERS, SAIGON, REPUBLIC OF VIETNAM

Army Colonel Alan Bates sat quietly in the back of the room, away from the highly polished mahogany table where the important men, both civilian and military, sat, listening to the debriefing of Sergeant Andrew P. Carlson. Bates was a short stocky man with brown eyes and graying blond hair. During the Second World War he had been a paratrooper, jumping into some of the worst fighting of the war. In the 1950s he had joined the Special Forces because he had realized that the nature of war was changing. It had evolved into either a guerrilla-counterguerrilla conflict or it was going to be a total nuclear holocaust.

He picked at one of his fingernails as he listened to the sergeant drone on and on. He looked up. The sergeant was standing at the head of the table behind a lectern, still wearing his jungle fatigues. Once he had gotten in from the field, he had been spirited to the conference room without a chance to shower or shave. His dirty rucksack and weapon were in the corner. His sweat-stained, mud-smeared fatigues contrasted sharply to the creased and pressed khakis worn by most of the military men present.

And to make it worse, the sergeant smelled. A pungent odor from days in the field without a bath filled the room. Bates was familiar with the smell. He had spent weeks in the sweltering heat of Europe or the steaming jungles of the South Pacific where bathing was sometimes a rare event. Bates could tell that the sergeant offended the sensibilities of some of the civilians and was glad. They should have given the man an opportunity to relax before ordering him to the meeting.

Bates looked at the men around the table. One of the civilians, an older man with silver hair and a deeply lined face, had failed to identify himself. The other was Jerry Maxwell, who worked in the local CIA office. Maxwell was dressed in his standard uniform of wrinkled white suit, stained white shirt and dark tie that hung loose.

Across the table were three military officers. The leader, a major general named Davidson, was sitting ramrod straight. He was wearing a fresh khaki uniform with rows of ribbons and a combat infantryman's badge with a star above the breast pocket, jump wings pinned to the flap. Next to him was a brigadier general who wasn't wearing a name tag and whom Bates didn't know. Finally there was another bird colonel named O'Neal. Bates had met O'Neal a couple of times and didn't like the small man. The colonel had black, slicked-down hair, a pencil-thin mustache and a large red nose. Bates had rarely seen O'Neal when he wasn't drunk.

Having finished describing his patrol, including the wounding of one of his men by a booby trap, Carlson was answering questions. Bates was bored with the activity.

Carlson had already given him the information he wanted, but the brass hats had to pretend that they knew what was happening in the field, so they kept asking questions.

"So, you didn't see any enemy soldiers on your sweep?" asked the unnamed civilian. To Bates's surprise, the man had a deep voice.

"We saw no enemy soldiers," repeated the sergeant. "We saw evidence of them. Evidence of quite a few of them. Evidence of recent activity."

The civilian, looking as if he were bored with the meeting, snapped, "What kind of evidence? How many enemy soldiers?"

Carlson turned his gaze on the man and studied him for a moment, as if he had never seen anyone so stupid. He leaned forward on the lectern and said, "With Charlie, you don't see him unless he wants to be seen, or he's attacking you. His squads can pass through an area, leaving as little trace of his presence as a stiff breeze. When you begin to find traces, then you know there are a lot of people."

"Come on, Sergeant," said the civilian, making the man's rank sound as if it were a curse, "you can't expect us to believe that, can you?" He laughed and added, "You people always attach more significance to these field operations than is merited. Always the enemy is right around, about to attack us if we're not ready."

"No, sir," said Carlson, "I don't expect you clowns to believe anything I say, because it's not what you want to hear. But there is evidence of a major buildup of enemy forces in the Hobo Woods. If I were to venture a guess, I would estimate a division at minimum. But then you people in Saigon aren't inclined to believe anything that—"

There was a sound like a pistol shot as one of the army officers slammed a hand on the tabletop. "That will be enough of that, Sergeant," he barked. "You are here to answer questions and no more. Is that clear?"

Carlson turned and looked at General Davidson. "Yes, sir," he said.

"Fine. Then you tell us exactly what makes you think that the enemy is building a force in the Hobo Woods. And I don't want to hear a lot of shit, either."

"Yes, sir. First, there seemed to be more trails. Some of these were new additions, cut through the center of the woods. We could see the new cuts on the bushes and trees where branches had been hacked off. On some of the trails we found sandal prints—Ho Chi Minh sandals made from old tires. I wanted to get a picture to see if we could match the tread with an American brand, but no one had a camera."

"Why not?" asked Jerry Maxwell. It was the first time that he had spoken during the meeting. "If we had those pictures, we might be able to trace the tires."

"Why not?" repeated the sergeant. He sucked in a chestful of air and exhaled slowly. "Well, begging your pardon, sir, but if you had to hump that extra weight through the boonies, you wouldn't be carrying a camera, either. Not when you could carry an extra magazine of ammo or another canteen, something that could save your life."

"Understood. The other evidence?"

"As I said, Charlie is very good about cleaning up after himself. Now we found little things. A bag of rice and fish heads that someone had dropped. A satchel containing a few papers. A few cartridges that were new. The humidity hadn't had time to corrode them. That sort of thing. It suggests a big unit because the smaller ones usually clean up everything."

"Sergeant, a bag of rice could have been dropped by one of our Vietnamese allies."

"Yes, sir, it could have been, but this bag was near the papers that were from a North Vietnamese source. As I said, it was a lot of little things that showed me Charlie was in the area, and in force."

General Davidson glanced at the other men in the room and asked, "Anything else? No? Okay, Sergeant, you may go, and thank you for your time."

"Yes, sir," said Carlson. He moved to his pack, picked it up and started for the doorway.

As he disappeared through it, Bates was on his feet. He caught the man in the hallway and shouted, "Sergeant Carlson! Wait."

Carlson looked less than delighted that a full colonel was shouting at him. Bates figured that Carlson probably thought he was going to be chewed out for his conduct during the briefing. Instead, Bates asked, "Are you sure about the buildup in the area?"

"Yes, sir," said Carlson. "I've been running sweeps through there for eight, nine months, and I've never seen anything like it. We've swept through there and not found anything. Not a blade of grass out of place. Now there are new paths, crushed grass where large units rested, and places where the ground was heavily trampled. This means there are a lot of men there now."

"What makes you think it was Charlie? Could have been our own people or the South Vietnamese doing it."

"The fucking South Vietnamese aren't going to be operating in the Hobo Woods. They're scared of it. And an American operation as large as the one that was run in there would have been news. We would have known about it." Carlson grinned. "And if I didn't know about it, I would have had a ton of evidence. We aren't real good about picking up after ourselves. No, sir, that was Charlie's mess we found.''

"That's fine," said Bates. He clapped the man on the shoulder and said, "You've done a fine job. Now why don't you go get yourself cleaned up, have a steak and catch up on your sleep."

"You mean you're going to do something with the information?" asked Carlson.

"Of course," answered Bates. "I'm not like those men in there. I don't have to keep the ambassador or any politician happy. I can put people into the field."

"Yes, sir," said the sergeant, the enthusiasm unmistakable in his voice.

THE BUS RIDE from San Francisco to Travis Air Force Base was quiet except for the roar of the diesel engine and the whine of the air brakes. Almost none of the fifty military passengers talked. Many of them, still drunk from their travels in San Francisco, slept while the others tried not to throw up. Gerber sat next to the window, watching the darkened landscape slip by. After twenty minutes, he tired of that and closed his eyes.

The bus finally pulled up outside a hangar at Travis Air Force Base, and the driver opened the door. He said nothing. He just waited until the men began getting off the bus. A tired-looking air force sergeant with a clipboard stood near the bus door, pointing at a rectangle of light, and repeated, "Over there. Over there."

Once inside, they were herded along a series of waist-high partitions that led them deeper into the brightly lit building. They finally came to some tables where several men were seated, all of whom looked unhappy about being awake that late at night. Gerber and Fetterman were first in line, and a clerk checked their names off as they reported them.

"Captain Gerber, you'll have boarding pass number one. Please follow the yellow line on the floor into the holding area. Your gear will be transferred from the bus to the marshaling area and loaded on the aircraft. All you have to do is wait until your flight is called and then board."

Gerber took the small card handed to him and slipped it into his pocket. "Thank you."

"Sergeant Fetterman, as senior NCO on the flight, you'll be in charge of the enlisted troops. The NCOs will be responsible for their own file packets, but you'll have those of the E-4s and below."

"Oh, no, he won't," said Gerber.

"I beg your pardon, sir?"

"Sergeant Fetterman is with me, and we have some work to do on the flight. You'll have to assign that task to one of the other NCOs."

"Sir," said the clerk, "you don't understand. The task is generally handled by the senior NCO. All it entails is holding on to the file packets of the enlisted troops, ensuring that they are on the plane after the rest stops, and then handing out the files in Vietnam."

"Fine," said Gerber. "One of the other NCOs can do it quite easily. Sergeant Fetterman is with me, and we have quite a bit of work to do."

"But, sir—"

"I don't think you'll have a problem with that, will you? Finding another NCO?"

"No, sir." The clerk scribbled on a card and said, "Your boarding pass number is two. Follow the yellow line—"

"Thank you," said Fetterman. "I listened to the instructions when you gave them to the captain."

"Of course." The clerk smiled—an evil grin that seemed to hold a trace of irony. "Good luck with your tour."

"Thank you," said Fetterman.

Together they followed the yellow line until they came to a roped-off area with rows of folding chairs. Gerber moved to the front and sat down. They faced a large metal hangar door with peeling paint. On the door was a sign that said Operation By Authorized Personnel Only.

"It wouldn't have been much of a hassle to handle those records," said Fetterman.

"Let one of those other guys handle it," said Gerber. "Most of them will end up at a base camp or fire support base doing nothing anyway, so a little inconvenience now won't hurt them."

"Yes, sir," said Fetterman.

The metal chairs behind them filled up with men, but there wasn't much conversation. Nearly everyone sat quietly, waiting for someone to tell them to board the airplane. All of them looked like condemned men waiting to be told that the chair or the rope was ready.

Gerber wasn't sure why they were quiet. Normally any group of GIs would be playing grab ass all over the place. He wondered if it was because it was late at night, or if it was because of the destination. A tour in Vietnam could take the starch out of anyone's sails.

"Want a Coke?" asked Fetterman.

"Yeah, sounds good."

"Saw a machine on the way in. I'll get us a couple."

"Thanks, Tony."

Fetterman returned a few minutes later and handed a cold can to Gerber. He sat down and pulled the pop top. "You nervous about this trip?"

"Nah," said Gerber. "Just tired after spending all night in the swamp and then all afternoon walking about San Francisco." He smiled and added, "This could give me a chance to get some things straightened out."

An air force master sergeant, dressed in a khaki uniform, his belly hanging over his belt and his bald head reflecting the high-intensity lights overhead, stepped through a doorway. He glanced at his clipboard and raised his voice. "Let me have your attention. In a couple of minutes you'll be boarding the aircraft for the trip overseas. This is a commercial airliner on contract to the U.S. government and manned by a civilian crew. That includes a number of females who are not interested in a lot of fucking around. Please keep that in mind."

Fetterman leaned close to Gerber. "I don't think there'll be a problem going over. Coming home could be a different story."

"We'll be boarding according to the boarding pass number," explained the fat sergeant. "If the men holding numbers one through twenty will follow me, we'll get started."

Gerber and Fetterman stood and walked toward the door. The sergeant checked the boarding pass numbers and marked them off his list. Gerber walked out onto the tarmac, a cool breeze blowing across the airfield. Mounted on the side of the hangar, and at the edge of the roof, were several spotlights that created pools of light on the ground. The aircraft, a TWA 707 sat there, the lights of the cabin on. At the top of the ramp was a stewardess in a dark blue uniform with a short skirt.

Gerber climbed the steps. The stewardess smiled at him and said, "Welcome aboard."

Gerber nodded to her and moved inside. He walked down the narrow aisle until he was about halfway back and then worked his way to a window seat. As he dropped into it, Fetterman sat down next to him.

Neither man spoke. Gerber focused his attention outside where he could see a number of air force vehicles, a dark blue crew van and a pickup truck with a rotating yellow beacon and a sign in the bed that said Follow Me. Several men in fatigues were running around, but Gerber couldn't tell what they were doing.

Behind them he could see a string of lights that marked the taxiway and another that outlined the runway. A jet took off, climbing into the night sky, a bright blue ribbon of flame behind it. Then he turned his attention back to the interior of his aircraft and watched the soldiers enter. They were still a subdued bunch, ignoring the stewardess who hovered about, moving down the aisle quietly and taking the seats that were left. In minutes everyone was sitting, waiting.

As a crewman closed the door, the lights flickered once, and air began hissing out of the vents. Then there was a high-pitched whine as the first of the engines came to life.

The stewardess who had welcomed everyone on board took a microphone from the slot on the bulkhead and said, "Welcome aboard this TWA Airlines flight with a destination of Bien Hoa, South Vietnam. Our flying time will be approximately twenty-two hours with stops in Hawaii and Okinawa."

Gerber tuned her out, not wanting to listen to her instructions about ditching and the use of the oxygen masks. He already knew where the emergency exits were and that the seat cushions could be used as flotation devices.

The aircraft lurched once as the stewardess finished her speech, and they began to taxi. They stopped short of the runway, then taxied onto it. Gerber felt himself pressed into the seat as they began the takeoff roll. As they rotated, lifting into the California sky, Gerber closed his eyes and was asleep in seconds.

WHEN THE PLANE landed in Hawaii about five in the morning, Gerber didn't feel like getting off. He just wanted to be left alone to sleep, but the stewardess insisted that he exit the aircraft. As soon as they were off the plane, Fetterman found a seat. Gerber wandered around, looking at the trees growing inside the lobby, but it was still dark outside, and he saw nothing of Hawaii.

The rest of the trip passed in a haze of half sleep, during which food from box lunches prepared by the air force was handed out by the stewardess. Gerber slept fitfully, the seat becoming cramped and uncomfortable. At one point the stewardess tried to interest them in a movie, but someone in TWA hadn't thought very far ahead. He had scheduled *The Shakiest Gun in the West*. It was not a hit with a planeload of GIs.

They landed in Okinawa and were off-loaded again. Fetterman wanted to head to the 10th Special Forces compound but could not find any transportation. Gerber entered the wooden building that doubled as a terminal for the transients. It was a dirty, dilapidated building that smelled of dust and decay and reminded Gerber of the structures in Vietnam. The afternoon was hot, and two huge fans supported by metal posts roared near the doors, trying to create a breeze that would cool the interior. Gerber sat near one of them, the wind from it rippling his hair, and went to sleep. Fetterman shook him awake when it was time to board the plane.

As they sat down and belted in, Gerber said, "Don't know why I'm so tired. Can't seem to stay awake."

"Makes the trip shorter if you can sleep through it," said Fetterman. "Besides, chasing the sun the way we are is hard on the body. If you were awake long enough to look around, you'd see that nearly everyone is sleeping most of the time."

Gerber nodded and went to sleep. He opened his eyes once and looked out. Through the clouds below he could see the blue of the Pacific Ocean. He glanced at his watch, but it was still set on North Carolina time, and he had no idea what time it actually was or how much longer they had to be in the air. He felt wide awake, but his eyes burned as if he had been up for hours. In seconds he realized that he had closed his eyes. He snapped them open, determined to stay awake for a while, but the next thing he knew, the stewardess was announcing that they would soon be descending on approach to Bien Hoa.

Looking out the window, he noticed that the deep blue of the ocean gave way to a lighter color as they approached Vietnam. Far below, the coast slipped under the airplane, and he knew that he was now over Vietnam.

Suddenly it felt as if they were falling out of the sky as the pilot began a rapid descent toward Bien Hoa. That was to give the enemy no time to set up to shoot at them. The plane roared out of the sky, hit the end of the runway, bounced high and touched down. The engines roared as the thrust was reversed to slow the aircraft, and as he was thrown forward against his seat belt, Gerber could imagine the pilot standing on the brakes.

They taxied off the runway, and the jet jerked to a halt. One of the crewmen opened the door as mobile steps were pushed against the fuselage. The heat and humidity flooded into the interior, overpowering the air-conditioning, and Gerber recognized the smell of Vietnam. He coughed as he breathed deeply. As he stood to exit, he felt the sweat pop out on his forehead and begin to trickle down his sides.

Fetterman looked back at him. "Ah, home at last."

"Not very funny, Tony."

"Wasn't meant to be."

At the bottom of the steps they were met by a short sergeant in faded, sweat-stained jungle fatigues. There were large damp rings spotted with salt under his arms, and the collar of his uniform was wet. He wore a helmet and flak jacket that barely concealed his belly. Slung low under his stomach was a pistol belt that held a .45. Like all the other sergeants Gerber had seen recently, he held a clipboard.

"If you men will move along to the hangar, we'll get you an in-briefing." He pointed at the open doors across the tarmac where rows of seats were visible.

Gerber walked toward the hangar, the late morning sun beating down on him with a strength that it lacked in the World. He stopped at the door and looked to his left, where there were several two-story buildings, each with a wall of green rubberized sandbags four or five feet high next to it. The corrugated tin roofs glowed yellow in the sun, and there were sandbags scattered across them.

The interior of the hangar was a duplicate of those in the World. It had concrete floors that had been waxed heavily, high ceilings that could accommodate planes with tall tails, beams and bracing that weren't disguised, just painted a pale green, and dozens of lights that were blazing. Near the door was a roped-off area with folding chairs set up inside it. In one corner was a map of South Vietnam divided into the four tactical corps areas. Behind it was the South Vietnamese flag, a yellow banner with three red stripes across it. In the other corner was the American flag. Surrounding the area were several giant fans blowing the warm air at the chairs.

Gerber sat in the front row. He could see a line of palm and coconut trees two or three hundred yards away. A truck roared down a dirt road, kicking up a cloud of red dust. Above it a partially overcast sky boiled, threatening rain in a couple of hours.

When everyone who had been on the plane had found a seat, the sergeant with the clipboard moved to the front. He leaned over, set his clipboard on the floor and dropped his helmet on top of it. Then he stripped off his flak jacket and tossed it aside.

"Welcome to Vietnam, gentlemen," he said. "For the next twenty-five, thirty minutes, I'm going to give you the orientation lecture on what you can expect. When I'm finished here, we'll all climb on buses and drive over to the 90th Replacement Battalion and begin the in-processing. Now, how many of you are on your second tour?"

He waited, counted hands and said, "Then you don't have to listen because you know the score. Just sit quietly, and we'll get this over as quickly as we can."

Taking the sergeant's advice, Gerber tuned him out. He heard only some of what the man said, including the standard joke about the snakes of Vietnam. Ninety-nine percent of them were poisonous, and the other percent would swallow you whole. He listened as the men were cautioned about the varieties of venereal disease and told to respect the customs of the Vietnamese people because they were guests in the country.

When the sergeant finished, he directed them to the buses that had pulled up outside. Gerber led the way out and climbed on the first bus. They were sixty-passenger jobs, painted a dark green with huge screens across the windows. An armed MP stood next to the driver.

"Won't keep the bugs out," said one of the men.

"Supposed to keep the grenades out," said another.

"Yeah. Now they tie fish hooks to them so they hang outside the windows and you can't get to them," said someone else.

Gerber sat in the front seat. Fetterman joined him. He looked happy, as if he had just arrived home. There was a smile on his face, and his eyes seemed to sparkle.

As the last man got on the bus, it rumbled to life. The driver slammed into gear, and they started with a lurch and the stink of diesel smoke, bouncing forward along a rutted path that masqueraded as a road. There were deep pools of bloody-looking water lying across it.

They came to a gate and turned onto a paved road. Vietnamese walked along the side of it—men and women dressed in black pajamas, carrying everything they owned. Most kept their heads down, watching the ground in front of them as if they were afraid of inviting the wrath of the Americans on the bus. A few cars, mostly old and dented, whipped by them. Bicycles and Lambrettas filled the road.

They passed through a village made of mud hootches with tin roofs. Some of them looked abandoned while others had signs in Vietnamese and English announcing the Texas Laundry or the California Bar or the Colorado Souvenir Shop. GIs crowded around some of them. Vietnamese women dressed in short skirts and tight blouses hovered around the crowd.

Ten minutes later they entered the base at Long Binh and jerked to a stop. Without a word from anyone, Gerber and Fetterman got off and were met by a sergeant who pointed at a bunker.

"We'll get organized over there," said the sergeant. "I'll get everyone headed in the right direction."

Gerber stopped at the side of the bunker, a gigantic structure that was hidden behind the rubberized sandbags that were becoming a common sight in Vietnam. From the top sprouted a dozen radio antennae.

"Jesus, Tony," Gerber said, "I'm tired. How about you?"

"I could use ten or twelve hours of sleep myself."

The rest of the men straggled off the bus, fanning out as they moved toward the bunker. As they approached, Gerber heard a distant pop and recognized the sound immediately. One of the men dived to the ground yelling, "Incoming! Incoming!"

There was a scramble as the men tried to find cover. They didn't know whether to try to get into the bunker, head for the trees near them, dive back into the bus or roll under it. The faces of some were drained of blood as the first rounds exploded into a cloud of black smoke and a fountain of red dirt a hundred yards away.

Gerber crouched next to the sandbags and watched. There was a second rattling whir, followed by a closer detonation, and a few seconds after that, another. Gerber dropped to his stomach, his eyes on the line of explosions coming at him. There was a snapping sound near his head, and a dull impact as hot metal ripped into the sandbags.

A siren went off, the wailing building and dropping. A few men scrambled from buildings nearby, running for bunkers tucked between the structures. One man slammed on the brakes of his truck, jumped from the cab and rolled underneath it.

Fetterman was kneeling against the wall of the bunker grinning. "Nice of them to arrange the fireworks display for us," he said when Gerber glanced at him.

When there were no further pops and no more mortar rounds dropping on them, Gerber got to his feet, brushing the dust from the front of his khaki uniform. "I could have done without this."

A second siren, sounding like a car horn, went off, signaling the end of the mortar attack. The sergeant who had been leading them raised his voice for everyone's benefit. "Just some harassing fire. Charlie's been doing that more and more lately. Gives us something to worry about."

"Jesus," said one of the men as he crawled from under the bus. The front of his uniform was torn, his ribbons hung by one corner over his breast pocket, and there was a smear of grease on his shoulder and arm. "Been in fucking Vietnam for an hour and they've already started shooting at me."

There was a bark of nervous laughter from some of the men, and one of them said, "I don't think they were shooting at you particularly."

"Close enough for government work," he said.

Gerber turned away from the FNGs as a man exited the bunker. He was a short stocky man with blond hair that was graying at the temples. He had brown eyes separated by a long pointed nose. His eyebrows were lighter than his hair and nearly invisible against the tanned skin of his face. He stopped, stared and said, "Welcome to Vietnam, Captain."

"Alan Bates, you old son of a bitch," said Gerber.

Bates touched the black eagle on the collar of his jungle fatigue jacket. "Colonel Son of a Bitch to you, Captain."

Gerber came to attention, snapped off a salute that would have made a parade ground instructor happy and then grabbed the proffered hand, pumping. "Damn, it's good to see you again. Thought you'd be home, retired as a full bull, planting flowers and telling lies."

"Got the eagles," said Bates, "as you can see, but I was told that I had a chance for the star if I hung on. Another tour in Vietnam would do it. Be brave and don't fuck up is how they put it."

"What are you doing here? At Long Binh?"

The grin deserted his face. "Bad news, I'm afraid. I was sent up here to claim you and Sergeant Fetterman. I don't suppose either of you has a preference for assignment on this tour, do you?"

"Hadn't thought about it," said Gerber. He stepped rearward and let several FNGs pass. The back of one man's uniform was covered with grease from the undercarriage of the bus. Another had a scrape on his arm that was trickling blood, which he had already smeared on his khakis. Several of them looked as if they were about to pass out.

"Well," said Bates as the last of the FNGs disappeared into the bunker, "the big push is SOG, Studies and Observations Group at MACV. They're looking for people. You could live in Saigon and work out of any of the camps you wanted to. Besides, you're getting too senior to operate as a detachment commander. Why aren't you a major?"

"I'm on the list, but the orders haven't caught up with me yet."

"I'll check into that." Bates looked over Gerber's shoulder and saw Fetterman. "Didn't mean to slight you, Tony. How you doing?"

"Just fine, Colonel."

"Listen," said Bates, "you can go on in there and take whatever assignment they come up with for you, then report to Nha Trang for potluck again, or you can come with me and let me grease the wheels of the big green machine."

"Tony?"

"Hell, Captain, if we let the army decide, we're going to get fucked. You know that. Let's see what Colonel Bates has to offer."

"There you have it, Colonel," said Gerber.

"Then grab your gear. I've got a jeep parked around here somewhere, if Charlie hasn't blown it up with his mortars. We'll run down to Saigon and check in there. I'll get your orders cut."

"Why don't I check with the bus driver and see what they did with our luggage?" suggested Fetterman.

"And I'll go get the jeep," said Bates.

Twenty minutes later they were on the road, a divided highway that led from Long Binh into Saigon. Gerber, sitting in the front seat, one foot propped up on the dashboard, shouted over the sound of the rushing wind, "It's just like we never left."

"Closer than you think," said Bates. "Captain Bromhead is back, with a detachment up in the central highlands. Noticed a couple of other former members of your team are in-country. Tyme is in Nha Trang. So is Galvin Bocker."

Fetterman leaned forward so that he was almost between Gerber and Bates. "What's all this Studies and Observations Group shit?"

"As you know," yelled Bates as he downshifted, dodged an oxcart and then accelerated, "we're running recon and intelligence operations throughout the south and into Cambodia and Laos. We need all the experienced troops we can get. Too many people on their first tours are gumming up the works." Bates glanced at Fetterman and then back at the road, "Hell, Tony, it'll be better than living in the field all the time. While you're here, you can take advantage of all that Saigon has to offer. You can live downtown if you want. Set yourself up with a nice arrangement."

"I'm not suggesting that I don't want the assignment," said Fetterman. "I was just wondering if things had loosened up any. You remember that one of the last cross-border ops that we ran resulted in a great deal of trouble for everyone. Trials and charges and the like."

"These are sanctioned at the highest levels, if that's what your concern is. We don't do anything without authorization. Your butt is covered."

"Sounds like great fun," said Fetterman.

"Glad to hear you say that," said Bates, "because I've a team going into the field in about an hour and would like you to go with them. They're looking into a couple of things for me, and I'd feel better if you were there with them."

"Christ, Colonel," said Gerber, "you don't fuck around, do you?"

"No time." He shot a glance at Fetterman. "If that's too quick for you, I can arrange something else."

"Oh, no, sir," said Fetterman. "If I can draw a field issue, zero my weapon, I'll be set to go. Never did like screwing around in the rear areas when there was a job to do."

"Everything you need is at our base of operations. You'll have to zero the weapon in the field. There won't be time before. We can pick up the rest of your team and head out to Tan Son Nhut so that you can catch the chopper."

"And what do you have for me?" asked Gerber.

"Once we get rid of your sergeant, we'll get you briefed on the overall picture—Project Delta and some of the operations we've run off the Delta concept. When you're up to speed on them, and have your major's leaf in hand, we'll get you the operational command of an AO."

"Great," said Gerber. "In-country two hours, been mortared once already and now you're sending us out to fight the war, and we haven't even processed in."

"Yeah," said Bates, grinning. "No time to fuck around."

3

TAN SON NHUT
INTERNATIONAL
AIRPORT, SAIGON

Bates had parked the jeep outside the fence that led into The
World's Largest PX and Hotel Three. Fetterman, now
wearing brand-new jungle fatigues that contained no patches
and no insignia, leaned over so he could retrieve his recently
issued equipment. He backed up against the rear of the jeep
and slipped into the shoulder harness, tugged at it until the
rucksack, loaded with more of the new equipment was seated
on his shoulders, and buckled his pistol belt. The issue knife
looked dull, and they had only given him one canteen. He
had asked for extra ammo and had been told that standard
issue was two hundred rounds, ten magazines. Bates and
Gerber had stood by watching and smiling.

"You can get set up properly with a decent field issue on
your return," said Bates.

Fetterman stood quietly for a moment, studying the pile
of equipment, and then said, "I think I'd prefer to wait a day
or so, Colonel. Give me a chance to find my own gear, zero
my weapon and get acclimatized."

"This is only for a couple of days, Tony. Won't be so bad. Besides, with the big American base at Cu Chi, you're only ten minutes away from help now. They've got several aviation units there, artillery, jeeps and trucks and even tanks. Not like the old days when help was hours away."

"If you've a real problem with this, Tony," said Gerber, "just back off."

Fetterman looked from one man to the other. "No, sir," he said. "I just wish I could go into the field a little better prepared for it. Hell, I haven't even met the men I'll be working with."

"You'll meet them in a few minutes."

As Fetterman took the rest of the gear out of the jeep, he said, "I expect a few rewards for this. A thick steak on my return, purchased in a restaurant and not a club. And a bottle of Beam's."

"Anything you say, Tony," said Bates. "I appreciate your cooperation, since you've only been in-country for a couple of hours. I know this is a lot to ask."

"Yes, sir, it is," agreed Fetterman.

They walked past the guard, an air policeman wearing a white hat and white pistol belt. He looked uncomfortable in his gear, as if he felt like the world's biggest target with the kill zone clearly marked in white so the enemy could spot it easily. He saluted the officers as they approached and opened the gate for them.

"God, this place has changed," said Gerber. He was looking beyond the guard at a PX that held a movie theater, the smell of popcorn drifting on the late afternoon breeze. A line of men waited for the ticket booth to open. They were dressed in fatigues and khakis, looking like the soldiers from a base in the World, not the war zone in Vietnam.

As they walked past the PX and theater complex and approached Hotel Three, Gerber saw more changes. The terminal had been rebuilt and improved. There was a tarmac strip in front of it, six concrete rectangles that were the landing pads for helicopters south of that and a long grass field where more helicopters were parked. Two men in jungle fatigues worked near a high chain-link fence topped with barbed wire, pulling weeds and trimming the grass.

"There's still a war on, isn't there?" asked Fetterman, studying the changes as if he disapproved of them, or as if he felt that the purpose of sending troops to Vietnam had been lost in the shuffle.

"Yes, Tony," said Bates, "it's been chased from around here. Rockets or mortars once in a while, but most of those are directed into the city to panic the civilians. Little happening around here. Everyone seems to take this as another assignment and fuck the war."

"Good attitude," said Fetterman. "And what happens when Charlie storms the wire?"

"There'll be enough men like you around to repulse the initial assault so that we'll have time to bring in some combat troops. Not to mention army helicopter gunships and air force fighters."

A man dressed in faded, sweat-stained fatigues approached them. He wore jungle boots, the toes blackened but not shined. He carried an M-16 and wore a .45 at his hip. There were three canteens on his pistol belt, and even in the heat of the afternoon, in the relative safety of Saigon, he wore a flak jacket, although the front was not zipped. A stained and dirty green beret sat on his head.

"Sergeant Fetterman?" he asked as he came up. He neglected to salute, having been told that saluting on the flight line wasn't done. People had to watch for operating aircraft and flying debris.

"I'm Fetterman. This is Colonel Bates and Captain Gerber."

The sergeant nodded. "I know Colonel Bates. Glad to meet you, Captain," he said, holding out a hand. "My name's Guerrero. Arturo Antonio Lopez Guerrero."

Gerber shook hands with the man. He was big, with broad shoulders and a huge chest. He had light brown hair, blue eyes and a permanently sunburned complexion that didn't look Spanish. Gerber asked him about it.

"My father's wish," he said. "My mother was French and acquiesced to his desires."

"Acquiesced?" repeated Gerber.

"Yes, sir. Some of us enlisted pukes managed to attend college before we saw the light and joined the army. Learned some big words."

Fetterman nodded. "How's the squad look?"

"If you mean militarily, a little less than perfect. Somewhat ragged around the edges. But they're all experienced, with seven, eight months in the boonies."

"Okay," said Fetterman, looking at Bates. "This may not be the boondoggle that it seemed in the beginning." He turned his full attention back to Sergeant Guerrero. "What's the op look like?"

"Pretty standard," said Guerrero. "No real intel of enemy activity in the area, but then, intel hasn't really been in the area." He glanced at Bates.

"I've gotten some information that the enemy is building up a large force in the Hobo Woods. I think the intel is good enough to warrant your little op," said Bates.

"Once we get into the chopper," said Guerrero, "I'll show you a map of our AO and suspected enemy locations on it. You can take it from there."

"Not much briefing time," said Fetterman.

"Shouldn't need that much, Sarge," said Guerrero. "You're familiar with the way Charlie operates. That hasn't changed. You've just got more NVA to contend with, and some of those boys have been well trained." He grinned. "Others were handed a rifle and pointed south."

"If you're satisfied, Sergeant Fetterman?" said Bates, making it sound like a question.

"Yes, sir. Seems as if it's a very good team. We're just on a recon, right? Not supposed to make contact with the enemy."

"That's right, Tony," Bates agreed. "A sneak-and-peek. We don't want Charlie to know that we're operating in his AO or that we have the information you'll undoubtedly obtain."

Fetterman took a deep breath and blew it out slowly. "If someone will provide me with a spare canteen, some extra ammo and the beans and franks from the C-rations, I guess I'll tag along."

"No problem," said Guerrero. "We've got about four times the ammo the army thinks we'll need. And we combed the C-ration boxes, throwing out the ham and lima beans and the scrambled eggs. Only brought the good stuff."

"Well then," said Fetterman, "I guess my last objection has been overruled. Be back in a couple of days."

"I'll meet you then, Tony," said Gerber, "and we'll make Colonel Bates buy you that steak."

"Thanks." He touched Guerrero on the shoulder. "Lead on, Macduff."

Bates and Gerber watched them walk across the grass to the helicopter and climb into the cargo compartment. One of the crewmen leaped out, ran to the rear of the chopper and untied the hook that was holding the rotor blade in place. As soon as the blade was free, there was a whine from the turbine as the pilot cranked.

When the chopper picked up to a hover, the rotor wash whipped across the grass, flattening it, and Bates and Gerber retreated. They walked past the PX, out the gate and down the street, which was lined with two-story buildings, palm trees, bushes and small, manicured lawns. They came to the officer's club and entered.

In the year that Gerber had been in North Carolina, they had expanded the club and redecorated it, but it had not changed significantly. There were still the boxes for weapons lining one wall of the entrance. The main dining room was larger than Gerber remembered. Although the bar still dominated one wall, there was still a stage tucked into one corner and black velvet paintings on the paneled walls. It seemed that more tables had been crammed into the dining area, and the dance floor had shrunk. Opposite him was the door with the sign General Officers Only above it.

Bates led Gerber into the crowded dining room. There were dozens of men and women, many in uniform, both fatigues and khakis, and a few wearing civilian clothes. Bates worked his way around the tables, found an empty one and dropped into one of the chairs.

"You want to eat?" asked Bates.

"Not really," said Gerber. "I'll take a beer, though."

Bates signaled a waitress, a Vietnamese girl who could barely speak English, but Bates managed to order a beer for Gerber and a Scotch for himself.

As the waitress vanished, Gerber leaned on the table and said, "That was a pretty dirty trick to pull on Tony. Gives him no chance to adjust to being in Vietnam."

"Wouldn't have done it if I didn't think he could handle it. Hell, Mack, that's what happened to our troops in the

Second World War. One day they're sitting on a ship playing cards or dice, reading books and writing home, and the next they're running across a beach with the enemy trying to shoot them."

"Yeah, but they also knew what was happening. They knew that one minute they would be in the relative safety of the ship and the next running across that beach you mentioned. Sergeant Fetterman expected a week of orientation briefings."

"Okay, Mack," said Bates, holding up his hands as if surrendering. "I agree that it wasn't fair, but then much in the army isn't fair. He could have backed out if he'd really wanted to. I watched closely to make sure that he wasn't going into this thing because a colonel said he had to. His arguments were only halfhearted. I think Sergeant Fetterman appreciated the fact he didn't have to spend that week getting his Vietnam orientation."

Gerber couldn't help laughing. "I think you've got it right there."

Before he could say more, there was a shout behind him, an excited feminine voice that yelled, "Mack Gerber! You're here! In Vietnam!"

Gerber turned in his chair, and looked over his right shoulder at the bar. Standing surrounded by a number of men and women in civilian clothes was Robin Morrow. She was a tall, slender woman with long blond hair and bright green eyes. Dressed in baggy khaki pants and a man's shirt she had a camera slung around her neck.

Gerber stood as Morrow began to advance on him rapidly. There was a big grin on her face, and her eyes seemed to sparkle. As she got closer to him, the glow faded. It seemed that she suddenly remembered that she had to be reserved because people were watching, or that she didn't know what

Gerber's reaction would be. She slowed as she came forward, her hand extended, and said, "Glad to see you again."

Taking her hand, Gerber said, "Nice to see you. Haven't talked to you in what, six months?"

"Closer to seven, but then, who's counting?" She glanced at their hands, hesitated and pulled hers free. "So," she said a little too cheerily, "what brings you here?"

"The war," said Gerber. He realized they were talking as if they were acquaintances and not people who had been close once. He was uncomfortable under her stare but didn't know what to say to her, or how he should say it. He dropped his eyes and repeated, "Nice to see you."

"Are you stationed here? Here in Saigon, I mean?"

He shook his head. "I'm not really assigned anywhere at the moment. I'm working on getting assigned. I've only been in-country for a couple of hours."

"Well," she said brightly, "can I buy you a beer or something?"

Gerber jerked a thumb over his shoulder and said, "I'm with Colonel Bates. You want to join us?"

She turned and looked at the people she'd been with, a group of civilians who were now watching them. She shrugged and said, "I'm with them."

"You working in Saigon?" he asked.

"In the bureau here, yes. You can contact me there or leave a message, if you want."

"Tell you what," said Gerber, glancing at Bates, who was grinning at him, "when I get set and learn what's going on, I'll give you a call."

"You do that." She kept her eyes on him, as if waiting for something more. "I guess I better get going."

"Listen, Robin, it was really good to see you again. I'll call, I promise."

"Yes, do." She reached out and touched his arm. "Maybe I can con you into buying me a dinner."

Gerber realized that he had been in-country for only a couple of hours and already had two dinner dates. One of them, with Fetterman and Bates, wasn't much of a date. The other, he feared, was one that could grow into something more than a date. "Sure," he said. "I'll buy you dinner, and you can tell me how the war is really going."

"Sounds good." There wasn't anything else to say, but she was reluctant to leave. She stood silently, looking at him, her eyes darting, searching his face for something more than was being said.

"I'd better get back to the colonel," said Gerber, suddenly uncomfortable in the situation.

"Yeah. My friends will wonder what I'm doing. Probably think I'm developing a source." She smiled at him, stared into his eyes for a moment and then glanced away.

Gerber retreated a step and turned toward the table, his eyes on her. "I'll call you in the next couple of days."

She could think of nothing else to say except, "Okay." She returned to her friends at the bar.

As Gerber sat down, Bates said, "I don't believe you. In-country for only a few hours and already you've found a girlfriend. You're unbelievable."

"I don't think Robin counts as a girlfriend anymore."

"No, and Vietnam doesn't qualify as a war."

FETTERMAN SAT in the cargo compartment of the UH-1D helicopter, studying a map that Guerrero had handed him. He glanced up from it, at the backs of the pilots' helmets, at the instrument panel visible between their seats and at what lay outside the windshield. Ahead of them were clumps of palms that hid small villages. He could see sunlight flashing from the tin roofs.

It was as if he had never left Vietnam. The past year seemed unreal, somehow, as if he had never been in the World, or in North Carolina. Fetterman turned and looked out the cargo compartment door. The ground below was a deep, dark green. Rice paddies spread from the clumps of trees northward, disappearing in the distance. Workers in the paddies were wearing the conical straw hats that were so much a part of the Vietnamese wardrobe.

Fetterman could smell the air being blown into the chopper. He breathed in deeply, surprised at the purity of the air now that he was away from the big cities of the United States. A dozen impressions, a hundred, came at him with a vague sense of déjà vu.

He looked at his companions. He wasn't worried about Guerrero. The sergeant had already shown that he had something on the ball. The way he carried himself, the equipment he had, all pointed to a combat veteran. And his companions seemed to have the same sense. Although they each wore a green beret, it didn't mean what it once had. Training requirements had relaxed with the big buildup in Vietnam. Thousands of warm bodies were needed, and if the training suffered, then the men at the top didn't mind that much. After all, it wasn't their lives on the line.

No, the green beret didn't mean what it once had, but these men had been in Vietnam for several months. And more importantly, each of them had a steel pot with him. That proved they knew what they were doing. The brass in Saigon wouldn't be caught dead in a steel pot, but combat soldiers knew the advantage of it.

Each of the men had several canteens and all the extra ammo they could carry, and Fetterman was sure that if he looked into their rucksacks, he'd find only essential equipment. None of the trash the FNGs carried. No paperback novels or transistor radios or stationery to write home.

Although he didn't know these men, his first impressions of them were favorable as they had been introduced to him. First was Staff Sergeant Larry Long. An old man of nearly thirty-two, Long was tall and thin with extremely wide shoulders and long arms. He had a gaunt face that looked almost emaciated. Dark circles lined his brown eyes. He watched the ground outside the helicopter as they flew along.

Sitting next to him, in the center of the troop seat so that he was resting against the transmission wall, was Sergeant Jason Carlisle. He was shorter than Long and stockier. He had a round face that was burned dark by the tropical sun. And he was younger. Fetterman guessed that Carlisle couldn't be much over twenty. He had thick hair and looked as if he needed to shave twice a day to meet army regulations, and it appeared that it had been two days since he had shaved last.

The last of the men was Sergeant Nolan. He was sitting on the cargo compartment floor, his back against the fuselage frame so that his feet dangled out of the chopper. He, too, was a young man. Big and blond, he reminded Fetterman of Sam Anderson. He had a light complexion even after all his time in Vietnam. In one hand he gripped his M-16, and with the other he was unconsciously stroking the plastic butt of his weapon. He had not said a word when he was introduced. Instead, he had studied the bright green fatigues that Fetterman wore, as if sizing him up. Fetterman hadn't minded the scrutiny since he'd been doing the same thing.

As he looked at them again, Fetterman decided they were a good team. The little things were there, little things that told him these men were survivors who knew their business.

He turned his attention to the map Guerrero had given him a moment earlier. He folded the map so the Hobo Woods showed and pointed to an *X* marked on it.

"Site of an NVA district headquarters, which we found about ten months ago," Guerrero informed him. "Lots of documents and plans for the future. Lots of medals and promotions out of that for our boys. Brass in Saigon was really impressed. They had a lot of stuff to show TV boys so that it looked good on the news at home." Guerrero pointed to the Hobo Woods and asked, "You familiar with this area?" He had to shout over the noise of the engine and the rushing of the wind.

"Somewhat," responded Fetterman. "Didn't do much on the ground around here. My camp was farther to the west and south of Highway One."

"Our AO isn't triple-canopy jungle. In fact, it's not actually jungle at all. More of a forest than a jungle. Laced with trails."

"Only problem I have," said Fetterman, "is that I haven't zeroed my weapon. I'd like a chance to do that."

"Could be a problem," shouted Guerrero. "Once we're on the ground, we're supposed to fade into trees. Besides, most jungle fighting is done within ten feet of the enemy. You don't have to aim. Just point and shoot."

The crew chief leaned around the transmission wall of the helicopter, pulled the boom mike down out of the way and shouted, "Be about ten minutes. Get ready."

Fetterman watched the men take off their berets, roll them, then stuff them into their pockets. One by one they put on their helmets, buckling the chin straps so that they wouldn't lose them when they leaped from the chopper.

Each man checked the magazine in his weapon and then chambered a round. All weapons were pointed upward in case there was an accidental discharge.

There was a change in the noise coming from the aircraft's engine, and they began a rapid descent. Fetterman felt a curious sensation in his stomach. He sat up straighter, touched the safety on the side of his weapon and wished that he had his old M-3 grease gun.

They were suddenly racing along the ground, bouncing up and over trees, around others and then diving until they were only two or three feet high. Fetterman grabbed the edge of the troop seat, holding on. He glanced at Guerrero who was grinning from ear to ear.

Guerrero saw Fetterman staring at him and whooped, his voice piercing through the noise of the straining engine and thundering rotor blades.

The nose of the aircraft popped up, and the chopper rolled over on its side as the pilot sucked in an armload of pitch. Fetterman felt himself forced down on the troop seat, and then the chopper righted itself and settled to the ground.

At that instant, Guerrero dived out the door, followed by his men. He crouched near a dry bush, his weapon pointed at the tree line. Then Fetterman dropped to the ground. Behind him, the chopper lifted off in a swirling cloud of red dust and dried grass. As it disappeared over the tops of the trees, Guerrero and his men were on their feet, running for the cover of the tree line. Fetterman was right behind them.

They fanned out, dropping to the ground. Fetterman crouched near a dead tree, his weapon ready. His eyes raked the trees, bushes, vines and ground around him, taking it all in. It had been a year since he had done it for real, and yet it seemed to be only hours. Senses that had been dulled by the noise, the sights, the smells of the World suddenly became sharp. He could hear the scramble of tiny feet on the dried leaves as a beetle hunted for food. He turned his head slowly toward the sound and picked out the dung-colored beetle in its dried, tanned surroundings.

Guerrero got to his feet and made a gesture, and Long hurried forward to take the point. Fetterman could hear his feet as he moved, although the man was walking quietly, placing each foot carefully. It was all coming back to Fetterman in a rush. Things that had been second nature in Vietnam but forgotten in the World were suddenly with him again.

One by one they got up and began working their way deeper into the trees. Fetterman followed, taking a position in the middle of the formation. He felt the sun on his back, burning through the material of his fatigue jacket. Sweat popped out on his forehead and trickled down his sides. He was suddenly hot in the humidity of the tropics, and he loved it.

For an hour they worked their way through the trees, avoiding the paths and skirting the clearings. There were areas that had been shattered by bombing. Giant craters blocked their path a couple of times. In other places the trees and bushes and vines had been blown around until they had formed a nearly impenetrable barrier. Guerrero called a halt once, and they filled their canteens from the water at the bottom of one of the craters.

The one thing that Fetterman noticed was how quickly they could move through the Hobo Woods. In some places in the jungle it could take an hour to move fifty yards. In the central highlands, the jungle was such a tangle that the only way to make any progress was to crawl. But here the vegetation was too thin to inhibit them, just scraggy trees, bushes and light brush. Their pace was rapid and quiet.

They moved deeper into the woods, leaving the trails behind. Although Guerrero and his men had machetes, they didn't use them because they didn't want to leave any sign of their passage. The pace slowed but was still steady.

After an hour of that, Guerrero held up his hand. Without a word from him, the men spread out, forming a loose circle so that they were protecting one another. They went to half alert. Fetterman kept watch on the patch of woods in front of him while Carlisle, on Fetterman's right, dug into his rucksack for something to eat.

As the sun died, Guerrero made his way around the tiny perimeter, talking quietly with each of the men. He stopped next to Fetterman and said, "I think, after dark, we'll move farther to the north and hole up to watch. Stay in place for a day, maybe two, and then extract if we've seen nothing. If something interesting pops up, we may pull out earlier."

Fetterman nodded to indicate that he had heard. Although lying in the stinking mess that made up much of the floor of the woods around him wasn't a pleasant thought, Fetterman was happy about it anyway. It meant that he was back in the action.

4

THE MACV
COMPOUND SAIGON

After he had dropped Gerber off at the transient quarters at Tan Son Nhut, Bates drove through Saigon, heading for MACV. He purposely drove through the heart of Saigon because he wanted to see the noise and the lights and the people. It was as if he couldn't believe that it could exist and had to reassure himself it wasn't some kind of garish nightmare.

He slowed as he came to the crowded sections, the bars alive with neon and loud rock music. Outside on the sidewalk stood hundreds of people. Americans in jungle fatigues, khakis or civilian clothes stood talking with Vietnamese women, most of whom were dressed in short skirts and revealing tops.

The scene stretched as far as he could see. The only changes were the colors of the lights and the type of music. A few of the clubs featured country and western.

Bates slowed and stopped for a red light. The heat and oppressive humidity of the night wrapped itself around him. He felt the sweat trickling down his sides. In front of him was a jeep holding two American MPs from the 716th MP Battalion. Bates knew because they were wearing the shiny black helmets with the large white 716 on them.

They turned a corner, disappearing down a street that was rocking with noise. As Bates crossed the intersection, he saw a group of people, men and women, civilian and military, American and Vietnamese, standing in the street watching something.

Bates continued on, swerving around the street barricade that contained one of the White Mice who was trying to direct traffic. Nearly everyone ignored him. The Lambrettas and motor scooters shot around him, weaving in and out of the traffic. These were driven by young Vietnamese men with slicked-down hair and tight-fitting clothes. They were called cowboys, and on the scooters behind most of them were young Vietnamese girls in skirts so short that nothing was left to the imagination. The Saigon cowboys were gaining the reputation of a street gang. There had already been fights between them and GIs.

Suddenly depressed, Bates worked his way through the traffic. The whole Vietnam experience was getting to him. Hundreds of thousands of Americans in Vietnam, most of them doing an unimportant job so that a tenth of their number could hump the boonies. Money thrown away because no one cared enough to watch it. Regulations ignored because it was a war zone so that if something went awry, it could be explained away as a combat casualty and all would be forgiven.

Bates wished he hadn't driven downtown. He couldn't stand the sight of GIs racing around wearing civilian clothes and driving army jeeps. He couldn't stand the sight of drunken soldiers sitting on the sidewalk or throwing up in alleys. He couldn't stand the sight of hordes of people who violated the laws as if there were no tomorrow.

As he turned onto a darkened palm-lined street, he wondered what would happen to all these people if the Saigon government lost the war. Would they be able to adapt to the Communist government, or would they perish in the transition? Then he wondered if anyone anywhere thought about them—the few million people who lived on the edge of disaster. A Communist takeover would be such a radical change that they probably wouldn't survive it, and since they weren't the nice people, or the government employees, but the bar owners and hustlers and prostitutes, no one would miss them.

In the distance the subdued lighting of the MACV compound appeared, and he realized that it had been a mistake to drive through Saigon at night. It had been too depressing, especially when he remembered that he had men in the field, maybe dying to protect the decadence of Saigon.

As he pulled into the parking lot, he smiled to himself, but not because he had thought of something funny. It was the irony of his depression over the decadence. He was fighting communism, which was fighting the decadence of the West. He got out of the jeep and decided it wasn't just ironic; it was sickening.

The guard at the gate waved him through, and he walked rapidly toward the doors. Inside, he was further depressed by the air-conditioning. Somehow it didn't seem right that the generals and colonels should be importing air conditioners for their comfort when there were so many things the men in the field couldn't get. He forced the thoughts from his mind as he climbed to the second floor, walked down the hallway and stopped outside General Davidson's office.

Instead of knocking, Bates entered, and found a solitary clerk sitting on the settee, which was pushed against the side wall. He was reading a paperback. When the clerk saw Bates, he leaped to his feet and asked, "May I help you, sir?"

Bates faced the soldier. He was a young man and wore spit-shined boots, creased jungle fatigue pants, an OD green T-shirt that was spotless and ID tags that hung around his neck in the fashion of TV soldiers. Bates stared into the brown eyes that reminded him of a basset hound and said, "I'm here to see the general."

"You're Colonel Bates?"

"Yes."

The clerk turned and set his book down so he wouldn't lose his place. "The general is waiting."

Together they moved to a second door, a massive wooden affair that would have graced the White House. The clerk opened it, stepped aside and announced, "Colonel Bates."

Davidson stood and waved him in. "Welcome, Colonel."

The interior was colder than the outer office, but it wasn't the icebox that Billy Joe Crinshaw had lived in when he had been at Tan Son Nhut. The room was bright, but there were thick blackout curtains over the windows to mask the light. And unlike his own office, which was paneled in a haphazard fashion, this one was covered with rich dark mahogany.

In one corner of the office was a grouping of brown furniture that was a conference area. A lush green plant was suspended from the ceiling, the vines hanging down and brushing the floor. Davidson came from behind his ornate desk and held out a hand.

As they shook hands, Davidson guided them to the conference area and said, "Please, Alan, have a seat."

Bates nodded and dropped into one of the high-backed chairs. He leaned forward, was about to speak and then stopped. He waited for Davidson.

"It was good of you to come over during off-duty hours, Alan," said the general.

"Well, General, I guess we're never actually off duty over here."

"No, that's true." Davidson reached for a small wooden box that was sitting on the edge of the table between them. As he opened it, he held it up and asked, "Cigarette?"

"No, thank you, General."

Davidson took one out, then felt for a box of matches in his pocket. When he had the cigarette going, he shook out the match and tossed it on the carpet. "Vietnamese expect us to be sloppy. If we're not, then they believe that we think they aren't capable at their jobs."

Bates nodded, not sure that he believed that. He glanced at the captured weapons mounted on the walls like so many game fish. If Charlie ever raided MACV Headquarters, he could restock a battalion with all the weapons hanging on the walls of the offices.

For a moment, Davidson puffed on his cigarette, letting the blue smoke ring his head. Finally he leaned forward and tapped the ash into the bottom of a 40 mm shell set there for just that purpose. "You know why I've asked you to come in?"

"No, sir, I don't."

"Good," said Davidson, grinning. "It's always a plus to keep your subordinates guessing. No, actually, I wanted to discuss these operations of yours into the Hobo Woods."

"Yes, sir," said Bates, surprised.

"Wanted to fill you in on the big picture. The whole situation, as it were."

Bates was sure he was expected to make some kind of comment but wasn't sure what it should be. Instead, he sat quietly, waiting.

"Situation back in the States isn't good," said Davidson, waving his cigarette as if it were some kind of magic wand. "Not good at all. People protesting in the streets, burning ROTC buildings and draft cards. Thousands of them shouting, 'Hell, no, I won't go,' as if we'd want them. A real field day for the news media, I might add." He stopped talking, puffed on his cigarette and continued. "A very unhappy home front. You see where I'm going with this?"

"No, General, I don't."

"No? Then I guess I haven't made it very clear. Well, let me say this. The feeling in Washington is that we've got to lay low over here. Take things slowly and don't push for a confrontation with the enemy. The last thing the administration wants right now is a pitched battle with the VC and the NVA. You see that?"

Bates let his eyes drift to the ashtray, then he glanced back at Davidson. "I don't want to seem obtuse, General, but I'm afraid you lost me at one of those turns."

"Yes, well, a big battle now would capture all the headlines. A big battle would undercut our contention, or rather the administration's contention, that the war is winding down, that the VC have lost their will to fight and their ability to fight. Now, if suddenly there's a large-scale battle, the media is going to question us about it. You see that, don't you?"

"Yes, sir, I see it perfectly." All too perfectly, he thought.

"Now, I know you've one team in the Hobo Woods and that another was in there and found evidence of a large-scale enemy buildup."

"Correct," said Bates. He didn't know if the general wanted him to speak, but he felt the need to.

"And I have no problem with that. Let's just hope that those men don't find the NVA or VC division that some of your people think is hiding in there."

"If they do, what's our response?"

"Right now there is no NVA division in the Hobo Woods. Your team won't find evidence of it. You can continue to search the area, but I don't want to have your people make contact. Do you understand that?"

"Yes, General," said Bates. He understood all too well. The Saigon brass was sticking its head in the sand again so it wouldn't upset the men in Washington, the men whose lives weren't on the line.

"If, by chance, contact is made, the men will be extracted. They'll break contact with the enemy unless it's a small unit that can be quickly and quietly eliminated. Is that understood?"

"Yes, General."

Davidson leaned forward again and stubbed out his cigarette. "I know this is a hell of a way to fight a war, dodging the enemy, especially when we have the upper hand, but this isn't a real war. It's not one fought to preserve the United States. It's a political exercise." He held up a hand to stop Bates's protest. "To the men in the field, it's a war. I know that. But, until the crisis at home is resolved, we're going to have to play it close to the vest."

"Yes, sir."

Davidson stood. "I knew I could count on you, Alan." He smiled. "And I know that if we decide to wage this war properly, we'll be able to overwhelm the enemy in a matter of months. That's why we can play these political games. Militarily we can win whenever we decide to."

"Yes, sir." He was sick to his stomach. After the ride through Saigon, this didn't help his depression. The only solution seemed to be a bottle and a night's sleep.

He was going to leave, but he couldn't help himself. "It's too bad that men have to die so that the administration won't be inconvenienced."

"You know it's not as simple as that," said Davidson quietly.

"Yes, General, but that doesn't make it any easier for the men in the field."

"No, it doesn't. But this is only a temporary setback. In a few weeks we'll be able to operate the way an army is supposed to fight. Now, I'll let you get out of here. Just remember what I said."

Since there was nothing that he could do about it, Bates said, "I'll remember, General." With that he got out.

IT WAS A QUIET NIGHT. Fetterman lay under the rattling leaves of a dying bush and watched the open ground in front of him. He lay as quiet as death, listening to the calls of the night creatures as they searched for one another. He heard the light step of a huge cat as it worked its way through the vegetation. There was a scrambling as monkeys climbed the stunted trees. Not far away was the rustling of a snake as it wound its way through the bush.

After midnight the light breeze died, and with it, the sounds around him. There was the occasional pop of distant artillery or the roar of a jet as it raced overhead or the insistent buzz of the turbine engine of a Loach as the pilot searched for the enemy. As the wind dried up, the insects swarmed around, drawn by the odor of sweat and the taste of salt. Fetterman didn't slap as the mosquitoes attacked him. Instead, he pushed his face into the mud and smeared it on his skin. He did the same with his hands until he was covered. The mud might not stop the insects, but it made it harder for them to attack.

As he lay motionless, listening and watching, he felt fatigue creep up on him, almost overwhelming him before he was aware of it. Normally, in an ambush patrol at night,

Fetterman would be up on one knee so that sleep would be impossible, but this was not an ambush. The enemy was not supposed to find them, so Fetterman was lying prone, his arms in front of him, holding his weapon as he watched. It would be so easy to lay his head on his hands and catch a few minutes of rest.

It was a tempting thought, but Fetterman ignored it. He knew that it was the kind of mistake that could kill as quickly as stepping on a land mine. He had to remain alert and that meant concentrating on the task at hand. It meant not thinking of clean sheets and a comfortable bed or the warmth of a woman next to him. It meant not thinking of the trip through San Francisco or worrying about being sent into the field within an hour of landing in Vietnam. It meant keeping his eyes open and searching the forest around him. It meant watching the ground, memorizing the positions of the bushes and trees in sight and not be fooled by the shifting shadows caused by the breeze and the moon. It meant, simply, remaining alert for the enemy.

At about three in the morning, the moon disappeared and the artillery fire seemed to come closer. Fetterman recognized the rumbling of thunder, and in seconds the woods were alive with the sound of frying bacon. The half-light that had been filtering through the trees vanished in a sheet of impenetrable gray.

Fetterman used the cover of the rain to shift around and bring his weapon under his body where it was protected from the worst of the rain. Like almost everyone, he had left his poncho behind because it added weight to the pack and was almost useless in wet weather. Even worse, it was made of plastic that didn't allow air to circulate. Within minutes of donning it, you felt as if you were standing in a steam bath, the warm, wet heat sucking the life from your body.

He took a drink from his canteen, draining it so that the water wouldn't slosh around if he was forced to move during the night. He had one other, scrounged from one of the men with him.

The rain ended twenty minutes later, but the water dripping from the trees and bushes made an audible hiss that drowned out the noise of the animals and the enemy.

Fetterman was now soaked to the skin, his fatigues a clammy, soggy mess that only underscored the miserable conditions. He felt like smiling. This was something that the civilians could never understand—the joy of lying in wait for the enemy in wet clothes. The early morning breeze that sprung up did little to dry him; it merely sent a chill through the air to add to the sensations.

As the sun came up an hour later, Fetterman caught the first whiff of rotting flesh. He turned his head slowly, sniffing at the breeze. He knew the smell indicated bodies near him. It was a stench that once encountered was never forgotten. He had breathed it within a day and a half of his landing at Normandy in France; it was a smell he had become familiar with in a dozen locations around the world.

A few minutes later Guerrero appeared, crawling toward him. Guerrero's uniform was wet, slimed with rust-colored mud that looked like bloodstains. There was dark stubble on his face, black circles under his eyes and smears of mud on his cheeks and forehead. When he was close, he pointed to the west and whispered, ''Can you smell it?''

Fetterman nodded.

''Then I suppose we should check it out.''

''We're supposed to find the enemy, and that might be a quick way to do it.''

''Yeah,'' agreed Guerrero. ''Let's slip back, have some breakfast and then go searching.''

Fetterman eased himself out of his position, sliding deeper into the trees, using his free hand to spread the dead leaves, broken twigs and other debris over the area to disguise his hiding place. He moved slowly, his muscles stiff from the forced inactivity. It was a sign that he wasn't quite in the shape he had thought. During the night, he should have done more to keep his muscles from tightening.

Half of them ate a cold meal of C-rations while the other half watched for the enemy. Fetterman finished a can of peaches, one of white bread that had the taste of compressed cardboard and some boned turkey. When everyone had eaten, they crushed the cans and then buried them two feet deep to deny them to the enemy.

As they moved to the west, the odor became stronger. Fetterman tied his handkerchief around his face and wished that he had some gasoline. A drop of gas would paralyze the sense of smell; it was becoming obvious that the men they searched for had been dead for a long time in the tropical heat.

They cut back and forth, moving northwest and then southwest until they came to a wide path that had been paved with bamboo matting. Fetterman crouched at the edge and peered down it. It ran through the thickest of the undergrowth, which had been hollowed out so that it was a living tunnel. From the air it would be invisible and from the ground almost impossible to detect unless they tripped over it. The men who used it would have to crawl along it. It was a beautifully engineered expressway through the heart of the Hobo Woods.

As Fetterman knelt there, he realized that the odor was filtering down the trail. He glanced over his shoulder at Guerrero, who was squatting near the base of a rough-barked tree, facing the other direction.

Fetterman retreated and crouched near Guerrero. "The trail is unbelievable. I think if we follow it we're going to find the dead men."

"You think that's wise? Following an enemy trail, I mean?"

"I think if we move along it carefully we'll be all right. Charlie isn't going to want to run into us. From the stench, I don't think we've far to go."

"You want to stay on point?"

"Hell, I'm not happy unless I'm on the point. Might suggest that we put out flankers, though. That way, if we get into trouble, we can probably shoot our way out of it."

"Give me two minutes. I'll get the men ready and then follow you."

Fetterman counted off the minutes and then saw Guerrero approaching. With that, Fetterman reached out and forced his hand through the vegetation so that he could enter the trail. He got down on his stomach, eased forward and studied the ground around him. With his right hand, he felt the mat. It was a woven pad of thin bamboo strips. He pressed on it, but there was no give. It seemed that the ground had been rolled and hardened before the mat had been spread on it. His analysis of an expressway hadn't been far off the mark.

He crawled forward and turned to the north. For a moment he lay on the bamboo, his face pressed against it. It seemed to be cool, and there was a slight odor of fresh dirt coming from it, but then that was overwhelmed by the stink of the dead. Fetterman took a breath and forced himself to his hands and knees so that he could advance.

Fifty meters ahead of him, the trail jogged to the right. Fetterman worked his way to that point, hesitated for a moment, listening, and then edged forward. Twenty-five or thirty meters in front of him, he saw the bodies of the dead. Bloated bodies were scattered on the ripped and blackened bamboo.

GERBER WAS AWAKENED by someone pounding on the flimsy wooden door of the room he had rented in the transient quarters at Tan Son Nhut. It was a dirty, tiny room with a metal frame cot, a paper-thin mattress, a scarred chest with a broken drawer and an overstuffed chair marked with cigarette burns. A ceiling fan rotated overhead, and the open window had venetian blinds that banged with the gusts of wind.

The banging on the door had startled Gerber. He sat up in bed, his heart pounding and his stomach fluttering. For an instant he didn't know where he was, then the vestiges of sleep and jet lag fled.

"Just a minute," he called, annoyed. Then he asked, "Who in the hell is it?"

"It's Colonel Bates. Open up."

Gerber ran a hand through his thick hair and then forced himself to his feet. The inside of his mouth tasted like someone had walked through it with muddy shoes. He grabbed his pants from the chair, climbed into them and fastened the button, but he didn't bother to zip them up. Scratching his stomach and yawning, he opened the door.

"Come in, Colonel."

"Christ, you look horrible. All this from a little drink last night?"

Gerber turned and walked back to the bed. He sat down, pulled a dirty sock from his shoes and worked it onto his foot. "Thanks," he said. "Appreciate your concern."

Bates entered the room, moved the khaki shirt from the seat to the back of the chair and sat down. "Just don't remember you taking so long to come to."

"Look, Colonel, about two days ago I was in a swamp in North Carolina playing at war. Today I'm twelve thousand miles away in a real war. My mind and body haven't adjusted to it yet."

"Sorry, Mack, didn't mean anything by it." He looked at his watch. "I wanted a chance to brief you before you catch the courier flight to Nha Trang."

Gerber held up a hand. "Wait a minute. What's this about going to Nha Trang? I haven't even drawn my field gear yet."

Bates clapped his hands and rubbed his palms together. "We'll take care of that this morning, then head over to my office and let you take a look at a few afteraction reports so that you'll know what's going on."

"And what about Tony?" asked Gerber. He bent over and searched for the other sock.

"As soon as Sergeant Fetterman returns from his mission, I'll get him north to meet with you. He'll have a better idea of what's going on with this mission under his belt."

Gerber located his sock, put it on and then slipped his feet into his shoes. He stood up and realized that he didn't feel rested. He was still tired, and his head hurt. It felt like a hangover, but he hadn't had that much to drink. Gerber didn't think it was fair that he felt so bad and hadn't had the fun to go with it.

He reached around Bates and got his shirt. He held it up and examined it. As he put it on, buttoned it and tucked it in, he said, "Since you've insisted on getting me up at the crack of dawn, the least you can do is buy breakfast."

"Well," said Bates, "it's not the crack of dawn. More like the crack of ten in the morning. There isn't time for breakfast now, but if you come over to my office, I can promise coffee and maybe a few doughnuts."

Gerber looked around the room, as he felt his chin. "I should shave."

"Shave later. We've work to do."

Gerber spotted the bottle of Beam's sitting on the dresser and snagged it. He opened it and tilted it, drinking in a mouthful and gargling. There was no place to spit, so he swallowed it. He grinned at Bates. "My breath may not be fresh, but it probably smells better than it did."

They left the billeting area and walked to the jeep that Bates had signed out of the motor pool. Bates climbed behind the wheel and unlocked the chain that held the steering wheel in one position. He dropped the chain to the floor, started the engine and yelled, "Got a new office since you were here last time. I've moved over to the MACV compound."

"Great," said Gerber. "A drive through Saigon without a weapon. Everything seems to be breaking my way."

"It's not quite as bad as it once was. The MPs and White Mice frown upon combat soldiers carrying weapons in Saigon. Think we'll be out shooting one another full of holes."

Gerber didn't respond. He sat back and watched. They left Tan Son Nhut and headed east. They didn't penetrate the downtown section of Saigon but remained on its fringes. There were still hundreds of vehicles crowding the streets. Bicycles and Lambrettas were the most numerous, and there were quite a few army trucks and jeeps. There seemed to be more cars than Gerber remembered. Most of them were old and looked as if they had been painted four or five times. Some were hybrids, with the front of a Ford grafted on the rear of a Chevrolet or Dodge.

They continued until they reached the MACV compound. Bates pulled into the new lot, a level area of red dust that was marked by metal posts and a length of chain. He parked in an empty spot, shut off the engine and hopped out.

"We'll head on in."

For a moment Gerber stood and stared. It was the same building he remembered from his last tour. There had been improvements to it, though. Now there was a larger flagpole in front with a small garden of brightly colored flowers around it. There was also a concrete sidewalk that led to a set of double glass doors.

As they approached, Gerber noticed air conditioners sticking out of some of the windows. "I thought the building was air-conditioned," he said.

"Is," confirmed Bates, "but the air-conditioning plant on the roof is getting old and breaks down periodically. You wouldn't want some general sweating all over his stars, would you? Might rust them."

Bates grabbed the door handle and gestured Gerber through. They entered the building. Gerber noticed the air inside was cooler than outside, and for the first time since he had gotten off the plane he felt cold.

They turned right and walked down a tiled hallway that looked as if it needed to be swept and then waxed. The walls were covered with posters and bulletin boards. There were notices about the joys and sorrows of contact with the local female population. There were directives on the use of gas masks and how to care for the M-16. There were signs telling soldiers how to wear a uniform and others telling them that they were authorized to wear jungle fatigues only in the field. Gerber ignored them all.

Bates stopped in front of his office, took out his key and unlocked the door. He glanced at Gerber. "You wouldn't believe the pilfering that goes on in here. Can't keep a pen or paper if it's not under lock and key."

"Viets taking it?" asked Gerber as he entered.

"Shit, no. It's the goddamned paper pushers. Steal everything in sight if given half the chance. I suggested that we send anyone caught stealing into the field for six months, but that idea was shot down. Most of the people in here have some kind of pull so that they don't end up in the field. Father's a senator and has a kid in Vietnam so that he's sharing the grief of thousands of other families. Except those families have sons and fathers in the bush and the senator's kid is sitting here."

The interior of the office was dark. Plywood, stained by using a blowtorch to bring out the grain and then varnished, paneled the walls. There was dirty green tile on the floor, a single metal desk painted battleship gray, a couple of chairs and a coffee table.

Bates opened the inner door and snapped on the lights. "Let's talk in here. Have a seat."

Gerber entered, slipped into one of the two chairs facing the desk and looked at the Spartan furnishings. He saw a functional desk, functional metal chairs and a metal bookcase holding a dozen black loose-leaf notebooks, each with a white label on the spine to identify it. There were no pictures on the walls, no captured weapons and no cute signs that some of the Saigon high-rankers were fond of.

To one side of the desk was a two-drawer file cabinet with a combination lock on it. Bates crouched in front of it, spun the lock and pulled open the top drawer. As he rummaged through it, he spoke over his shoulder. "I've got some reports here I want you to look at. Most deal with Project Delta. Delta's not all that classified, but we don't go mentioning it to the press or anything like that, and of course, these reports are all classified."

Bates stood up and pushed the drawer closed with his knee. He handed a number of file folders to Gerber. "That should keep you busy for a while."

"What about the coffee and doughnuts you promised?"

Bates dropped into his chair. "You want me, a full colonel, to go out and find you, a captain, some coffee and doughnuts? Is that right?"

"Only because you promised."

Bates stood. "Okay. Okay. I'll see what I can do. Don't take those documents out of this office, and I've left my safe unlocked, so you'll have to remain here."

"Uh-huh," said Gerber. As Bates left the office, Gerber examined the top folder. It was dated January 1966, with the subheading Operation 2-66. Gerber opened it and read carefully.

It told of a reconnaissance made by a six-man team of American Special Forces NCOs under Sergeant First Class Frank R. Webber, Jr. They had scouted several trails on January 28 when they had been spotted by several Vietnamese woodcutters. Fearing the worst, Webber had led his men to higher ground where they had dug in for the night. The next morning heavy fog and a persistent rain had made travel through the thick undergrowth difficult. In some places it had been so bad they had been forced to crawl through it on their hands and knees. By noon they had reached a small clearing laced with small trees, a cluster of bushes and broad-leaved ferns. Webber had ordered the men into a defensive ring so that they could discuss the next move.

There had been a sudden burst of machine gun fire that had ripped through the jungle. Jesse L. Hancock had dropped, dead before he'd hit the ground. George A. Hoagland and Marlin C. Cook had been hit and had fallen, as had Webber.

The wounded men, and those not hit, had tried to return the fire, but the jungle was so thick they'd had no idea where the VC were hidden. Cook, paralyzed from the waist down, had rolled to his stomach and shot into the vegetation. Charles Hiner had sprinted from cover, dived close to Cook and jerked the radio from his rucksack. He had scrambled to an outcropping of rock, pulled the antenna up and began calling for assistance.

Donald Dotson had jumped up then and tried to run across the clearing to help. He had been shot in the chest and killed.

Hiner had succeeded in contacting a helicopter, and his emergency message had been relayed to a forward air controller. Hiner, yelling over the radio, had told them to strafe his perimeter. As the helicopters had begun to work the tree lines, their 2.75-inch rockets and 7.62 bullets from M-60 machine guns tearing into the heavy foliage, the VC firing had tapered off, becoming sporadic.

Webber, his arm shattered by the VC bullet, had crawled into the clearing and dragged Cook to the rock where Hiner was crouching. By now, Hiner, too, had been wounded. The helicopters had continued to strafe, and a stray round had hit Cook, killing him instantly.

Only Webber and Hiner had still been alive at that point, but both were weak from loss of blood. Although Hiner had kept passing out, he'd heard the request of the rescue party to throw smoke. Within minutes, the rescue team had been there, and rope ladders had been used to extract the two wounded men and the four dead.

Gerber closed the folder and looked up as Bates entered the office carrying a couple of cups of coffee and a bag of doughnuts. He waved the report at the colonel. "Jesus H. Christ."

Bates set the coffee on the desk and then walked around to sit down. "Hell of a thing, isn't it?"

"Makes my blood run cold. The information they gather worth the risk?"

"Wait till you read some of the others before you ask that." Bates opened the bag and took out a doughnut dripping strawberry jelly. He pulled open a desk drawer and took out a blank piece of paper to use as a plate. "Let me say this first, though. Most of the information these guys get is lost in the bureaucracy here and in Nha Trang. It's one of the reasons I want you to take this job."

Gerber put the folders on the floor near his feet and grabbed one of the coffee cups. "The army writing style can make nearly anything boring, but even with that—"

"I know what you mean, Mack. But read on."

Gerber sipped his coffee and then set the cup on the desk. He pulled off the top folder and opened it. It detailed Operation 10-66 in War Zone C and was a combined op with the 196th Light Infantry Brigade.

At that time, Major Robert E. Luttrell, the commander of Detachment B-52, had been airborne when he'd spotted a red panel and smoke and had seen a signal mirror flashing at him. Luttrell had called for helicopters, and as the choppers had arrived, Sergeant Timothy O'Connor had run from the jungle under heavy fire, carrying the seriously wounded Johnny Varner. He had left Varner in the open to be picked up and then run toward Sergeant Eugene Moreau, who was on the ground and appeared to be dead. Then O'Connor had been hit and gone down.

As automatic weapon fire had raked the landing helicopter, a wounded LLDB sergeant had crawled into the chopper. Once he was on board, the helicopter had taken off, carrying him and Sergeant Varner to safety.

Shortly after that, another wounded LLDB sergeant had been spotted and extracted. After dark a ranger battalion had swept through and collected the bodies of Sergeant Moreau and LLDB Corporal Mo.

Gerber looked at Bates, who sat with his feet up on the desk, drinking his coffee and trying to prevent his doughnut from dropping jelly on his uniform. The Special Forces Captain flipped the page and saw the results of the patrol. One American SF soldier killed and another four wounded. But the men had provided information about an extensive trail system leading from Cambodia into Tay Ninh Province. Later patrols had reported extensive bomb damage from air strikes directed against the trail system discovered by the Special Forces sergeants.

Gerber decided that he wanted to see something a little more recent. He studied the folder tabs and found Operation Alamo, which had been finished only a few weeks earlier.

Most of the operation had been conducted in the Song Be area and had uncovered a number of enemy base sites, ammunition and weapons caches, hospitals and food supplies. Various raids and air strikes had been directed at the area, using the information gained by the twenty-seven patrols.

Gerber made his way through the files and found references to Projects Omega and Sigma. Operating in the First Field Force and Second Field Force tactical areas in northern South Vietnam, there were counterparts to Project Delta. The results of the long-range capabilities there were similar to those in Three and Four Corps. The enemy and his bases were discovered with the same regularity in the north as they were in the south.

When Gerber finished the files, he picked them all up, straightened them and set them on Bates's desk. He grabbed his coffee, found it cold and put it back.

"Well," said Bates.

"Interesting," responded Gerber.

Bates sat up and looked at the younger man. "I've shown you that material to demonstrate the changing role of the Special Forces in Vietnam. When you were here before, the rule was that we were advisors. We trained, we educated and we assisted, but we did not engage in a combat." Bates smiled and held up a hand. "I know we did get into fire-fights, but we weren't supposed to. Now that charade is over. We're running combat operations without benefit of the ARVN."

"Well," said Gerber, "that's one thing."

"The other is that we've been stripping the A-Detachments to find enough men for the recon teams. Now, with the commander of the B-Detachment DEROSing, we need someone to take over his job. I'd like you to do it."

Gerber sat staring at the file folders for a moment. "I didn't expect to get another A-Detachment."

"Then you'll do it?"

"How big an area does that cover?"

"Project Delta operates throughout South Vietnam and confidentially, Cambodia and Laos. And as of the first of November, both Omega and Sigma are being directed through MACV-SOG, here in Saigon."

"Colonel, I've been in the army for fifteen years, and this is the first time I've been interviewed for a job. Normally someone hands me a mimeographed set of orders, and I do what I'm told to do."

Bates opened the middle drawer of his desk. "You mean like these?"

Gerber took the package. "Exactly like these."

"If you want the job, I'll sign them, have them approved and you'll have the command inside of three days."

"And Sergeant Fetterman will be assigned to me?"

"I'll have the orders cut this afternoon for him. You've got a top-notch sergeant major assigned there already, though."

"But there's no one as good as Fetterman, and you know it." Gerber grinned. "How many men do you know have been captured by the VC and escaped within a couple of days to lead the rescue operation?"

"You'll have to break the news to Sergeant Santini."

"I'll give him an option and tell him it's no reflection on him. I'm just bringing in one of my own people, or make Sergeant Fetterman the Operations NCO, which he'd probably prefer anyway."

"Then you'll do it?"

"Of course. Was there ever any doubt?"

5

THE HOBO WOODS

The stench from the corpses threatened to overwhelm Fetterman as he crawled closer. They had been dead only two or three days, but the decay had been accelerated by the tropical heat and humidity. Fetterman felt his stomach flip and thought for a moment he was going to vomit. He forced himself to swallow and tried to breathe through his mouth, but the air was so thick with death that he could taste it. He hesitated, waiting for Guerrero, and when the sergeant was close, whispered, "Give me a cigarette."

Guerrero's first instinct was to say they couldn't smoke in the field, but he held his tongue. Silently he fingered a cigarette from the plastic pack in his side pocket and handed it to Fetterman.

Fetterman took it, crumbled it and stuffed the tobacco in his mouth. He chewed it rapidly, mixing his saliva with the tobacco and then pushed the soaking mass into his cheek with his tongue. The nicotine paralyzed his taste buds and affected his sense of smell, killing some of the odor of the dead men.

The closest man didn't seem to have a mark on him. His body was swollen because of the internal gases. The skin of his face and hands were stretched tight, making it look like a bad plastic imitation. The buttons of his shirt over his belly had popped free, revealing his grotesque stomach. Lying near one outstretched hand was an AK-47 that had a piece of shrapnel sticking through the stock.

Fetterman examined the collar tabs of the uniform, but there was nothing distinctive about them. He worked his way around the body. The next corpse was riddled. There was not the same degree of bloating because of all the holes in the stomach and chest for the gases to escape. The flesh hung from the bones, looking like rotting cloth. White bone gleamed in the sunlight that filtered through the vegetation. There were rust-colored stains on the bamboo near the body where the blood had flowed. Near the pistol belt was a large wound that revealed the intestines, and from that cavity came the buzzing of tens of thousands of flies. The inside, a dark mass, seemed to vibrate with activity.

Fetterman worked his way around that body and came to the crater left by the artillery round. It had ripped through the covering vegetation, torn up the bamboo matting and blackened it. Lying in the bottom of the crater was a single boot with the foot still in it. It appeared to be an American combat boot and had probably been stolen from a dead American.

On the other side of the crater was a body missing both legs. Large pools of blood had flowed from the stumps, leaving a sticky mess buzzing with feeding black flies. Next to it was a fourth dead enemy. He was lying on his side, his knees drawn up and his hands wrapped around a lump of blackened, rotting flesh that had been his intestines. It was obvious he had died trying to push them back into the cavern of his belly.

Fetterman moved past the stinking, decaying dead men, parting the vegetation. On the other side of the living wall, he glimpsed several enemy bodies, but the flankers were approaching them.

The last body on the trail was missing its head. It had been severed near the Adam's apple with one clean cut. The dead man was lying on his back and was propped at a strange angle because of the rucksack he wore. Fetterman pushed him over and opened the pack, which was stuffed with documents. Some of them were stained with blood.

He flipped through them quickly but couldn't make out much from them. During the past year, Fetterman had learned to speak some Vietnamese, but he hadn't learned to read it. He tried to sound out a few of the words, but the Vietnamese language was made up of so many words that sounded alike that it was hard to understand it, let alone read it. The variation on the inflection of a word might be enough to change the meaning radically.

Stuffing the documents into the sack, he used his knife to cut it from the dead man's shoulders. He noticed the soldier was wearing a pistol, which meant he was an officer. Fetterman took the weapon, pulled the collar insignia from the uniform, then pushed forward, away from the dead.

He moved ten yards down the trail and cut his way clear of it. Outside, the air seemed to be cleaner, fresher. He spit the tobacco out, washed his mouth out and spit out the water. He then took a deep drink and thought he could taste death in the water.

Moments later Guerrero joined him. "What'd you find?"

"Lots of documents, but I don't know how important they are. Could be a complete listing of everyone in the area, or it could be the man's collection of poetry."

"You think this is worth going in?"

"Well, Sergeant, we have two choices. We can take it in or call for a chopper to come for it, although, if we remain behind, we'll be compromised. Charlie will have to know that we're here."

There was a sudden burst of fire—the quick hammering of a single assault rifle on full-auto. Guerrero's chest exploded into a sea of crimson. He stood still for a moment, as if balanced on two poles instead of standing on legs, and then fell.

Fetterman dropped to the ground beside him and reached to check the pulse. He didn't expect to find one.

There was a detonation behind him, a grenade thrown by the enemy. The shrapnel ripped through the thick vegetation. Fetterman rolled to the side as another grenade blew up near Guerrero's body, lifting and flipping it.

Firing broke out around him. He could hear the M-16s of the team firing single-shot as the enemy opened up with everything he had. There was the chatter of the AKs and the slower pulsing of an RPD. The air was suddenly filled with explosions, shouts, screams of terror and the hammering of weapons.

For a moment Fetterman lay still. In the sunlight of the Hobo Woods it was hard to see the muzzle-flashes. He let his ears direct him, turning his head slowly. Through the shafts of light penetrating to the ground, he could see the smoke from gunpowder, a blue haze that drifted on the breeze. Then, near the base of one tree, he saw the glint of a machine gun barrel.

Fetterman couldn't use his weapon because that would give away his position. Instead, he jerked a grenade free of his harness, pulled the pin and let the safety spoon fly. A moment later he lobbed it at the suspected machine gun nest. The grenade exploded in the air, raining deadly shrapnel from a black cloud. There were screams of pain from the enemy and then moans as the men died. The machine gun fell silent.

Suddenly everyone stopped firing. Then came a low moan that built slowly like the rising of a police siren until it was a wail of pain that cut through the woods like a knife. A voice shouted something in Vietnamese, and a shot cut the cry off abruptly.

In the lull, Fetterman crept to the rear and slipped onto the trail. As he passed the bodies, he heard the firing break out again, M-16s against AKs and SKSs, a yammering of weapons, the bullets fired blindly at the unseen enemy, rounds snapping through the bushes and slamming into the trees, raining bark and bits of leaves on the combatants.

Once on the clear trail, Fetterman got on his hands and knees and crawled rapidly away from the ambush. When he was sure that the firefight was going on to the east of where he was, he cut his way through the tangle of woven bush and vines. He circled until he was at the rear of the enemy formation. Through gaps in the trees and bushes, he could see one man kneeling with his AK-47 and firing into the woods around him. The enemy was like an automaton. He held his weapon above his head, fired the magazine, lowered it and reloaded. Then he burned through the fresh magazine.

Fetterman aimed carefully and squeezed the trigger of his own weapon. There was a slight recoil from the kick as the rifle fired. The VC never knew what hit him. His head exploded in a splash of blood and brains. He fell forward, his weapon dropping to the ground in front of him.

The firing suddenly seemed to be tapering off. Fetterman heard someone crashing through the woods, running from the fight. A man in black pajamas appeared, leaped over his fallen comrade without a thought and charged Fetterman.

The Special Forces sergeant didn't blink. He could see the panic in the enemy's eyes. The man had lost all sense and was running for safety. He was not thinking or acting like a soldier.

Fetterman raised himself to one knee, aimed and fired. The first round caught the man in the shoulder, spinning him. The force of the impact caused him to throw his weapon away. He didn't care and didn't seem to notice the wound. He changed direction and kept running.

Fetterman put a bullet in the man's spine. The slug lifted him from his feet as if he had been hit with a sledgehammer. He threw his arms out, as if to break his fall, and then landed on his face. He didn't move.

A third VC rushed out of the woods. He came at Fetterman, screaming almost incoherently. He was pulling on the trigger of his weapon, jerking it around, as if trying to throw the bullets. There was a trickle of blood on the side of his head.

Fetterman remained calm. He raised his own weapon, aimed at the enemy's chest and squeezed the trigger. The bullet punched through the man, killing him. He staggered two steps forward and collapsed, tossing his rifle out so that the bayonet buried itself in the soft earth.

Around him, the firing became sporadic and then stopped altogether. Fetterman got to his feet and worked his way toward the first man he had killed. As he approached the dead man, he could see a small entrance wound in the side of the head, near his left ear. There was a ragged, bruised hole with only a trickle of blood. Fetterman noticed a short stubble of hairs there, as if he had been given a razor haircut recently. In the American army that was called white sidewalls. Although the man was wearing black pajamas, it meant that he was probably Main Force NVA. An interesting bit of intelligence.

Fetterman checked the body. As he lifted the shoulder, he saw the exit wound. A fist-sized hole had been blown in the enemy's head, and a green-gray substance was seeping out. Fetterman ignored it and picked up the weapon that was a foot from the man's hand.

As he worked his way toward his own men, he saw Carlisle crouched over the body of an NVA soldier. That man was in dark green fatigues. Fetterman moved toward him, and when he was close, asked, "We got security?"

"Sergeant Guerrero will see to that."

"Sergeant Guerrero is dead. I want security out now. You find one of the other men and establish it. I'll check the bodies for documents."

Carlisle looked angry for a moment, as if thinking Fetterman was the FNG and had no right to give orders. Then he nodded and headed off into the trees.

Fetterman located seven bodies, including three around the smoking remains of the RPD. He checked them all for documents, cut the collar tabs and insignia from the uniforms and took all the weapons. When he finished, he found the body of Sergeant Guerrero and carried it into the open.

Sergeant Long approached him and asked, "What do we do now?"

"I think it's safe to assume we've been compromised. We call for extraction and report our findings to Colonel Bates. He can get the documents translated and tell us the significance of Main Force NVA dressed in black pajamas."

"You sure about that?" asked Long. "Sure that they're Main Force NVA?"

"Unless they've radically changed in the past year, I'm sure. Check the haircuts on these guys. It's a kind of status symbol. I don't think the Communists realize we know about it. Gives us an edge."

"Okay," said Long. He crouched and slipped his ruck-sack from his shoulders. He took out the radio, pulled the antenna up to activate it and began the ritual for extraction.

Fetterman watched the men work. He had to admit they were good. Except for that one botch when they'd expected Guerrero to get security established, he couldn't fault them. They had done what they had to do without an order from him.

GERBER STOOD in the supply depot as he was issued his field gear. It was a massive warehouse-type building with few windows but nearly a dozen huge fans blowing along its length. Gerber was waiting in front of a long, battered, waist-high counter while the NCOs dressed in dirty, baggy fatigue pants and torn OD T-shirts threw the gear onto the counter. A third sergeant marked the items off a list.

They gave him a laundry bag and began to stuff it with jungle fatigues, jungle boots, a canteen, entrenching tool, pistol belt, rucksack, underwear, socks and a variety of other things, all of which were colored OD green, including the bath towel. When the supply sergeant finished, Gerber dropped the laundry bag on the floor and asked, "What about a weapon?"

"You get that from your unit. I don't issue no weapons to nobody."

"Thanks. Don't I have to sign for any of this stuff?"

The supply sergeant picked up the well-chewed butt of a thick cigar and stuck it between his stained teeth. "This shit is all expendable. No one gives a shit how much of it you get. When you go home, you take it with you. The more of this shit you move out of here, the less of it I have to fuck around with. You got a problem, you gotta talk to the major, and he ain't here. He ain't ever in."

"Marvelous." Gerber hefted the bag, slung it over his shoulder and left. Outside, he stopped and blinked in the bright tropical sunlight. He raised a hand to shade his eyes. Bates and the jeep roared up a moment later and slid to a stop.

"Got it, I see," Bates said.

"Yeah. Got it. Didn't give me a weapon, though," said Gerber, climbing off the loading dock to the dirt street below him.

Bates nodded. "What do you want?"

"M-16, I think. And a pistol. I don't suppose I could find a 9 mm Browning." He tossed the laundry bag into the rear of the jeep.

"If you want one, I think it can be arranged. The only thing wrong with those exotic ones is that it's hard to find ammunition."

"I wouldn't call a Browning exotic." Gerber climbed into the passenger seat.

"Anything that doesn't use .45 or .38 caliber is exotic around here."

"I see that the paper shufflers in the World are still directing things. Anyone ever tell them the advantage of fourteen shots without reloading?"

Bates shoved the jeep into reverse, grinding the gears. He turned and watched as he backed up. Then, spinning the wheel, he slammed it into forward. They blasted out of the supply depot in a cloud of red dust.

"I doubt it," yelled Bates. "I mean, these are the same gentlemen who've declared the use of a shotgun as too inhumane but have done nothing to stop the use of napalm."

"Yeah," said Gerber, shouting over the noise of the wind. "Say, what the hell's the big hurry?"

"Thought you'd want to get changed before your trip to Nha Trang, then I've got to find you a weapon."

They headed back to the MACV compound, left the jeep and went inside. Bates pushed through his outer office and, ignoring the sergeant who sat there, entered the inner office.

"Why don't you get changed, and I'll go to the arms locker for an M-16. This won't be your issue weapon, just a temporary loan. You'll have to sign a hand receipt for it."

"Fine," said Gerber.

An hour later Gerber found himself sitting in the rear of a C-130 as it roared down the runway at Tan Son Nhut. Around him were forty other soldiers, most of them wearing brand-new jungle fatigues and looking as if they were about to die. From the evidence in the interior of the plane, Gerber felt they might be right. It was a stained, dirty mess and seemed to be overloaded.

Once they were airborne, Gerber closed his eyes and went to sleep. It wasn't easy in the crowded Hercules, the men jammed shoulder to shoulder, but he still hadn't shaken the effects of jet lag. He dozed, in and out of consciousness, never really waking up, but sometimes aware of all that was going on around him. The nap didn't help.

They finally landed at Nha Trang, the plane diving out of the sky to land roughly, bouncing several times just as the commercial jet had done when he'd arrived in-country. Gerber was thrown around the interior of the C-130, restrained by the seat belt cutting across his lap. The aircraft rolled to a halt, but the engines weren't shut down.

The loadmaster stood near the exit at the front and shouted over the roar of the engines, "Please exit the plane here. Do not walk under the wings, and stay away from the spinning propellers. They'll chop you up in seconds."

Gerber got to his feet, collected his weapon and made his way out of the aircraft. As he stepped onto the tarmac, he glanced to the north and saw the 8th Field Hospital. It reminded him of Karen Morrow, and he felt a cold hand on his stomach. He remembered the nights he had spent there with her. He also remembered the nights he had expected to stay with her only to be told that she was too tired or too sick. He tore his eyes away from the hospital and saw a Special Forces sergeant hurrying toward him.

"You Captain Gerber?"

"That's right."

"Sergeant Santini, sir," he shouted, glancing at the noisy engines of the plane. "The major sent me to collect you. Thought it would make a good impression on you and then you wouldn't fire me."

Gerber studied the man as they hurried toward his jeep. Santini was a small man, almost in the mold of Fetterman. His faded fatigues had been ironed recently. The sleeves were rolled halfway between the elbow and the shoulder as regulations demanded. The sergeant wore a pistol belt with a .45 attached near the small first-aid kit. A combat knife hung on one side, with a canteen near it.

Santini's face was clean-shaven. His eyes were brown, and he had heavy eyebrows. The man's thin face had a pointed chin and nose, and his dark complexion was probably the result of heredity and the tropical sun. Under his beret, there was thick black hair that had been cut very short recently. Gerber could see a difference in the skin that was now exposed to the sun. He grinned at that. It meant that Santini might actually be worried about his job.

"My jeep, sir," said Santini, gesturing at a vehicle.

The jeep had been waxed to an incredible shine, and the top was up. It wasn't a standard field vehicle but one that had been modified for use by the brass in Vietnam. Gerber wasn't sure that was a good sign. Santini had a green beret and jump wings and even a pathfinder badge, but he was beginning to look like a garrison trooper.

"Been here long, Sergeant?" asked Gerber.

"In Nha Trang or the Nam?"

Gerber flinched at the term. He knew of no combat soldiers who referred to it as "the Nam" except when mimicking the news media, but he had been home for a year. It might be common jargon now.

"Vietnam," said Gerber.

"Nine months. Did some work with recon and of course was in the field with B-52. Got this plush assignment when I broke my ankle jumping from a helicopter." Santini shot Gerber a glance from hooded eyes. "No, I didn't get a purple durple. I did it coming in, not going out. Medics laughed themselves sick, as did my team. But now they're out in the boonies and I'm here at the Neptune Club in the evening sucking down beer and eating steaks."

They roared to the west, off the airfield, turning toward the 5th Special Forces Headquarters. Santini turned and backed his jeep into the slot that had been left for it. Gerber studied the single-story building. There was the standard corrugated tin roof on it, and all the windows were protected by shades that stuck out at a forty-five-degree angle. They let in the light but kept out the rain and the direct rays of the sun. Over the double doors was a huge sign that said Headquarters, 5th Special Forces Group (ABN), 1st Special Forces.

"Major Madden is waiting in his office for you. Please follow me."

They entered the building and worked their way down the hall to an open door. They entered, and Santini waved at the clerk who was typing on an old manual machine and appeared not to be making much progress. Santini walked past the beat-up desk, opened another door and stepped out of the way.

Gerber entered, and the man sitting behind the desk stood. He was a thin man with a receding hairline. He had a thick black mustache in contrast to his thinning, graying hair. Sweat stood out on his forehead and stained the underarms of his fatigues. He wiped the sweat from his face and rubbed it on the front of his fatigue uniform.

"You Gerber?"

"Yes, sir. Major Madden?"

"Correct. Grab a seat. Andy, why don't you scare up some coffee for us. That okay with you?"

Gerber dropped into the offered chair. "Prefer a Coke if there's a cold one around."

"Andy. Find us a Coke," Madden said, sitting down. "I've only one question for you," he said to Gerber when the sergeant left. "How come they're sticking you into this job when you're only a captain? TO&E calls for a major."

"I'm on the promotion list. I'm probably the senior captain in the entire U.S. Army and possibly the entire free world. Any minute now I'll blossom into a major. And I have no idea why I've been dragooned into this."

Gerber looked around the room. It was as Spartan as the office used by Bates. A Special Forces crest of crossed arrows and dagger hung on the wall with the Latin *De Oppresso Liber* under it.

The walls were made of thin plywood and painted a light, sickening shade of green. A bamboo mat sat on the floor, which was also plywood. There was the standard military gray desk, a couple of metal folding chairs and a beat-up settee with mismatched cushions. On the wall behind his head, across from the windows, was a framed citation for the Vietnamese Medal of Honor. Although it was the highest award of the South Vietnamese government, it meant very little to the American army. Gerber figured it was there to appease the ARVN and not because Madden was impressed with it.

"You've had one tour?" asked Madden.

"Yes, sir. Worked with an A-Detachment on the border between Three Corps and Four Corps, near Cambodia. Built it from nothing in an effort to slow down the cross-border resupply of the VC by the NVA."

"You do any good?"

Now Gerber smiled. "Forced them to find an alternative route for a while. Afraid there were so many holes in the border they got the stuff in anyway."

"Okay, Captain. You've probably figured that I've read your file. Hell, I'd be derelict in my duty if I hadn't. I'm turning a reasonably large, complex organization over to you. It does a dangerous mission, and we've had more than our share of casualties in the past year." Madden tented his fingers under his chin and stared at his desk. "What I'm saying is that I don't want to turn this over to a bureaucrat, someone who is more interested in how things look on paper than in results in the field."

"Well, if you've read my file, you know that I've spent my share of time in the field. And my share of time fighting with the bureaucrats."

The door opened, and Santini entered with a cup of coffee and a can of Coke. There were beads of condensation on the can. Gerber accepted it gratefully and popped the top. He drank from it and said, "Thanks, Sergeant Major."

Santini retreated, closing the door behind him. When he was gone, Madison said, "Final say on who takes over for me is my duty. Bates has been on the horn giving me all the poop.

I wanted a chance to look at you. I think you'll do.'' he grinned and reached across the desk to shake hands. ''Welcome aboard, Captain.''

Madden spent the better part of two hours telling Gerber everything he had read in the files that morning. Then Santini entered and reminded the major about the four-thirty briefing with the general at Field Force Victor Headquarters. Madden got to his feet and asked Gerber, ''How long you going to be here, in Nha Trang?''

''Wanted to get back to Saigon tonight. Got a man in the field.''

''Stay the night and we'll have breakfast. Then you can catch the flight to Saigon and be there by dinner time.''

Gerber nodded. ''Fine. If you'll excuse me, I need to arrange for billeting and get over to the PX to buy a razor, toothbrush and a dirty magazine.''

''Billeting's no problem,'' said Madden. ''At the worst, we can put you up at the Recon School. If that doesn't suit you, we'll take you downtown to the Nha Trang Hotel. Sergeant Santini will see that you have transport.''

''Okay,'' said Gerber.

They left the office, collected Sergeant Santini and exited the building together. No sooner had they stepped out, when Gerber heard his name called by a feminine voice. As he spun around, a human bundle launched itself at him. He caught her as she wrapped her legs around his waist and her arms around his neck and began kissing him rapidly.

Madden took a step back, surprised, watched the scene and then asked deadpan, ''Have you two met?''

Gerber slowly extricated himself. He held the woman at arm's length. ''Kit?''

She was dressed in American jungle fatigues. The shirt was open, revealing the OD T-shirt she wore. Her long black hair hung free to her waist. She had the classical oval face of the Oriental except that it was on the thin side. She had blue eyes that looked violet in a certain light; they were a legacy from her father.

"You came back," she said breathlessly. "I knew you would."

"Major Madden, this young woman is a former VC who—"

"I know who she is," said Madden. "I just didn't know that you knew her. It's apparently one of our worst-kept secrets."

"We worked together once," said Gerber. "She operated from my A-Detachment."

Madden glanced at his watch, holding his fist up in front of his face so that he could look at the underside of his wrist. "I'd love to stand here and reminisce with you, but I have generals to brief and colonels to fight with."

"Go ahead, Major," said Gerber.

"Yes, go ahead, Major," said Kit. "I will take care of Mack Gerber."

Madden started for his jeep, then stopped and turned. He watched for a moment and then continued on.

"Kit," said Gerber, "I have to get checked in here. I've got things to do."

"I have nothing to do," she said. "I will go with you."

Now Santini laughed. "Don't look at me, Captain. Your lady friend can get you around." He tossed the key for the jeep to Gerber. It wasn't for the ignition, but for the padlock that held the chain wrapped around the wheel so that the vehicle couldn't be stolen. "You take the jeep. Bring it back here when you're finished."

Kit grabbed Gerber's hand. "Come on, Mack. I'll take you around. We'll go downtown, find a hotel and get a drink."

Still smiling, Santini said, "The King Duy Tan Hotel is on the main drag and close to the beach. Might be your best bet." He turned, heading for the headquarters, chuckling to himself and shaking his head.

"Kit," said Gerber, "I've got a lot to do. It'll be boring for you. Why don't I meet you somewhere in a couple of hours and we'll go to dinner or something."

"No," she said. "I'll go with you now. I don't mind waiting. There is nothing for me to do around here."

Gerber shrugged helplessly. "Come on, then." He pointed to the jeep. "Hop in."

IT TOOK FETTERMAN and the Special Forces NCOs two hours to hack their way through the tangle of bush, vine and stunted trees on their way to the LZ. The canopy, only fifteen or twenty feet over them, was broken and spotty. The afternoon sun blazed, baking them under its relentless rays.

As they chopped their way to the north, Fetterman realized just how tired he was. He felt the strength in his arms diminishing and had difficulty swinging the machete. He turned the point duty over to Long and took his place carrying the makeshift stretcher holding Guerrero. All he had to do was move his feet, and he found that easier.

They burst out of the woods into the clearing with almost no warning. Immediately they turned and stepped back into the protection offered by the trees. Once they had set down the stretcher and established security, Fetterman used the hand-held URC-10 to make radio contact with the helicopter pilot.

"Crusader One Two, Crusader One Two, this is Capital Team Five."

"Roger, Five, go."

"We are at the lima zulu. Lima zulu is cold. Are you in-bound?"

"Understand you're at the lima zulu. We are ten out. Will you throw smoke?"

"Throwing smoke," said Fetterman. He looked at Long, who held the smoke grenade in his hand. "Do it, man," Fetterman ordered him.

Long pulled the pin and tossed the grenade toward the center of the LZ. It began to billow bright green, the cloud swirling about in the light breeze.

"ID green," said the pilot.

"Roger, green." Fetterman still hadn't seen the helicop-ter. Then, in the distance, he heard the distinct popping of the rotor blades. The chopper appeared a moment later, at first looking like a huge insect coming at him. When it was close, it dived out of the sky and flared thirty feet in the air so that it was nearly standing on its tail. As it began to sink, the nose dropped so that the skids settled into the grass, the front of the helicopter over the smoke grenade.

Without a word, Long and Carlisle grabbed the stretcher, running into the open toward the helicopter. Fetterman hesitated, waiting for the last of the men to move. Once they were in the clearing and in front of him, he abandoned his position, sprinting through the knee-high grass, his head bowed as if running into a strong wind. He leaped over a twisted, rotting log, and as he scrambled into the cargo compartment, the door guns opened fire.

The pilot had turned in his seat, looking into the rear. When he saw Fetterman's raised thumb, he pulled pitch, lifting the chopper out of the grass. He kicked the pedals, spinning the aircraft, and took off the way he had come in. The door guns kept firing, putting a steady stream of ruby-colored tracers into the trees in case there were any VC in the area.

As they crossed the tree line, the door guns fell silent, and the two crewmen looked around the transmission from their positions in the well. Neither of them came forward to joke with the SF men. They looked at the body, at the bloodstains on the front of the uniform and at the bullet holes in it and stayed where they were.

Fetterman took a deep breath and leaned back against the soundproofing that masked the transmission wall. He shut his eyes and breathed in the air of Vietnam. He was sorry that Sergeant Guerrero had died. He seemed to be a good soldier who knew what he was doing. Fetterman hoped the documents and intelligence they had was worth the sacrifice.

6

HOTEL THREE, TAN SON NHUT INTERNATIONAL AIRPORT, SAIGON

The chopper carrying Fetterman and the survivors of the team stopped once at Cu Chi for graves registration. Both Long and Carlisle protested, claiming that Guerrero's body should be taken to Saigon, but the aircraft commander refused. His orders were to drop the body at Cu Chi so that the press, which swarmed all over Tan Son Nhut, would not see the dead American brought in. The AC said that arrangements to ship Guerrero to Saigon would be made by graves registration. It would delay the process by a few hours and prevent the media from swooping down on them like so many vultures.

The stop, on the south side of Cu Chi near the evac hospital, was short. The aircraft landed far enough away from the emergency pad so that the men being carried in for treatment wouldn't see the bodies. Almost as the skids touched the PSP, two men, both wearing fatigue pants and sweat-soaked OD T-shirts, ran from the double wooden doors in the corrugated Quonset hut and reached into the cargo compartment. As one of them snagged the end of the makeshift stretcher, Fetterman got a good look at him: a tall, thin man whose skin seemed bleached to an unnatural white as if he had been standing too close to a vat of chemicals. He had bony arms and was almost completely bald. His eyes looked as if they had sunken into his skull, and when he smiled, his skin seemed to pull off his teeth. It made him look like a skull trying to grin.

Without a word, they reached in for the stretcher, but Nolan grabbed it, stopping them. He stared down at the bloodied body, the shirt soaked black. His lips moved silently and then he rocked back on his heels, staring at the top of the cargo compartment, blinking his eyes rapidly.

The graves registrations men waited patiently, and when Nolan finished, they pulled the stretcher out of the chopper and took Guerrero's body into the building. As the pilot started to suck in some pitch, Long touched Fetterman's arm. "Shouldn't we go with him? Make sure they treat him right."

"No," said Fetterman. "Sergeant Guerrero is dead, and there's not a thing we can do for him, but the information we have might save some lives. Right now our job is to get into Saigon with it. Once it has been passed along, we can say a few words about Guerrero."

Long seemed to accept that. He sat back on the red canvas troop seat and stared at the gray metal deck of the cargo compartment.

They took off, climbing to the south, away from the perpetual cloud of smoke and dust that marked Cu Chi, and crossed Highway One. A pilot had once told Fetterman that helicopters followed the rules of the road. In other words, those heading east flew along the south side and those going west took the north side, just as cars and trucks did on the highway.

As they neared Saigon, they descended so that they were only a couple of feet above the ground. They flew through a gap in the tree line and popped up to five or six hundred feet. To the left was the sprawl of Tan Son Nhut, the runways and taxiways easily visible. On the east side of the field were several giant hangars, a couple of them with sandbagged revetments in front of them guarding camouflaged fighter planes, others with commercial aircraft parked nearby. Closer in, almost under the helicopter, was Hotel Three.

They worked their way around the traffic pattern, staying away from the buildings. Finally the chopper touched down on one of the cement pads, and as it settled and the AC rolled the throttle to flight idle, a sergeant came running from the terminal waving his hands. He headed for the aircraft commander's door, stepping up on the skid so that he could yell in at the pilots.

"You can't land here," he shouted. "VIP only."

The AC stared at him and then tapped the side of his helmet to indicate he couldn't hear.

Fetterman hopped out and reached in for his rucksack. He held his M-16 in his left hand, and as he turned, the NCO yelled, "You men are not authorized to disembark here. I just won't have it."

Fetterman shouldered his pack and stood there waiting for Carlisle, Long and Nolan. Once they had all their equipment, they headed for the gate at Hotel Three, trying to ignore the fat, obnoxious sergeant. The man chased after them, grabbing Fetterman by the arm.

Fetterman swung around, his right arm snapping up so that it slammed into the NCO's hand, knocking it away.

Surprised, the NCO stumbled back a pace. His face grew red, and he screamed, "I told you men that you couldn't get off here. I will not have you violating our written directives." He glanced at Fetterman and then backed away as if he had seen something that frightened him badly.

Once outside the Hotel Three compound, standing on a peta-primed road, Fetterman asked, "What do you normally do about transportation?"

"We normally use the phone in the terminal to call for it," said Long, grinning, "but after you chased their sergeant away, we didn't think it wise to ask to use the phone."

"Then how about this," said Fetterman, "I'll buy the beer at the NCO club while one of you phones for the transport. By the time it arrives, we'll have washed most of the dirt out of our throats."

"Yeah," said Carlisle. "I like that plan."

Within an hour, after drinking a quick beer in the club and then rushing out for their jeep ride, they were at the MACV compound, sitting in a small conference room in the basement, just down the corridor from the CIA office occupied by Jerry Maxwell. It had been Maxwell who had signed them through the metal gate guarded by a military policeman. The Company operative had then escorted them to the cinderblock conference room and told them to wait there.

The room was cold. In the middle of it stood a table surrounded by six chairs and another half dozen along one wall. At the center of the table was a pitcher and four glasses, but no water. There were a couple of ashtrays, a notepad left from the last meeting and a broken pencil.

The walls held nothing other than a single poster showing a GI in combat gear and wearing an M-16 strapped to his back, skiing down a mountain that was lush with jungle vegetation. Under it was the legend Ski Vietnam.

The floor was waxed concrete and without the benefit of any kind of carpeting. Not even a bamboo mat. It looked more like an interrogation room than a conference room.

Fetterman dropped his rucksack in the corner, set his weapon against it within easy reach and sat down at the head of the table. He watched Long and Carlisle mill around and gestured at the chairs. "You might as well make yourselves comfortable." Nolan had already dropped into one of the chairs along the wall.

Before either Long or Carlisle could sit, the door opened and Colonel Bates entered. Fetterman got to his feet, assuming a relaxed position of attention, and waited.

Bates took the chair at the other end of the table, waited while a captain and a sergeant entered, then said, "Let's be seated." When everyone was comfortable, he said, "This is Captain Davis, my S-2, and his NCOIC, Sergeant Landon. These gentlemen may have a few questions to ask you."

Fetterman nodded and studied the two men. Both wore starched fatigues, and there was no evidence that either had been out in the heat of the afternoon. No sweat stains or salt rings. Just fresh uniforms that might have been put on only moments before. Davis had short black hair and was unusually pale. He had water-colored eyes, a big nose and ears that stuck out like open doors on a car.

Landon was bigger than Davis. He had light hair, dark eyes and a massive chin. There was a scar on his cheek that was dimpled like a bullet hole. He took a steno notepad from the side pocket of his fatigues, set it in front of him and opened it. He nodded to indicate that he was ready.

"Go ahead," he said.

Fetterman glanced at Bates, who nodded once. With that, Fetterman began his narration, telling Long, Nolan and Carlisle to interrupt if they had something to say. He talked about everything they had seen and felt and heard. He described finding the bodies, the search and then the ambush that had killed Sergeant Guerrero. He went into detail about the ambush, describing the tactics used by the VC, the weapons they carried and the fact that they were backed by a Russian RPD. It was a well-equipped squad with complementary weapons, not the ragged mix that was normally associated with the VC.

When he finished, Davis asked, "What happened to the documents?"

Fetterman slid his chair back, stood and stepped to his rucksack. He pulled the documents out and tossed them onto the table. "I've looked through them," he said, "but I can't make out anything. Reading Vietnamese isn't my strong suit."

"Uh-huh," mumbled Davis. Pulling the package close and spinning it, he began to leaf through them. Shaking his head, he said, "Not much here. Fairly standard stuff."

"One thing that bothered me," added Fetterman, "was the one guy we killed who had the NVA haircut. He was outfitted like a VC, and I don't remember those guys ever doing anything like that. Dressing as VC."

"Sometimes they do," said Davis, still reading the documents.

Now Landon spoke up. "You sure he was NVA?"

"Unless they've changed the way they work in the past twelve months," said Fetterman, "I'm pretty sure. Noticed his haircut first. Standard NVA. Then his hands. They were too soft. He wasn't a rice farmer."

"Captain," said Landon, "I think Sergeant Fetterman may have something here."

"What?"

"NVA masquerading as VC. Be a good way to infiltrate a large force into the area without us being aware of the buildup. We keep finding VC, but no NVA, so we're not too concerned."

"I don't know," said the captain. "That's a pretty flimsy theory to be constructed on an observation by a man who hasn't been in Vietnam for a year. You *did* say you just returned, didn't you, Sergeant?"

"Yes, sir, I did. But I didn't turn my brain off for the year I was in the World. I've kept up with the intelligence reports."

"Yes," said Davis, returning to the documents.

Bates spoke up. "Anything else?"

"I was surprised that those guys jumped us in the middle of the day," said Fetterman. "Another sign of their growing boldness?"

"Hello!" said Davis. He looked up and searched each of the faces. "I think we have something here, gentlemen." He read a few more lines of the document, flipped the page and added, "Sergeant Fetterman, I apologize for my ill-advised remarks. Seems that the NVA is infiltrating a large number of people into the Hobo Woods. I've found an order dictating this new policy, and it's signed by an NVA general and countersigned by COSVN. That's the major enemy headquarters in this region. There is a pay roster attached, which indicates a regiment has been deployed."

"This means?" asked Bates.

"It means that there is a major buildup." Davis grinned as he continued to search through the documents. He pulled one out of the stack and said, "In fact, I have a complete order of battle here. If we can confirm these units, then we've got some people in the Hobo Woods who haven't been there before."

Fetterman nodded knowingly. He reached into his pocket and pulled out the collar tabs and unit insignia he had taken from the uniforms. He tossed them on the table, watched them slide toward Davis and then said, "I thought you might want some confirmation. How's that?"

Davis picked up a collar tab and turned it over in his hand. "All NVA wear these." Then he examined one of the insignia. "But then, this identifies the unit." He nodded his approval. "Well done, Sergeant."

"I have one question," said Fetterman. "What are you going to do with this information?"

"Well, we'll get a report typed up and forward it to Nha Trang. They'll process it and develop a search-and-destroy mission from there. Probably deploy a battalion from Cu Chi, Tay Ninh or Dau Tieng."

"How long?" asked Fetterman.

"Week. Ten days. Hard to say," said Davis. "Depends on their commitments."

"Just as I thought," said Fetterman, his voice sounding tired. "Sergeant Guerrero died to get that information. It would be a crime if that information is allowed to deteriorate through a lack of action."

Davis assembled the documents into a neat pile, grabbed the insignia from the dead men's uniforms and touched Landon on the shoulder. The sergeant flipped his notebook closed and said, "We'll be in touch if we have any additional questions about the mission."

Both got to their feet. Davis turned to Bates and said, "If you'll excuse us, Colonel, we'll get to work on deciphering the rest of these documents."

"By all means."

When they had closed the door, Fetterman asked, "You're not going to let this evaporate like that, are you?"

"No, Tony. As soon as I can get Mack back from Nha Trang, we'll get a mission into the Hobo Woods. Be a day before Davis and his people sort through that material, and it might pinpoint a location for us. Three days at the most before we go in, but probably a lot less. We'll act before this information becomes useless."

GERBER SAT SWEATING in his jeep outside the PX and tried to decide what to do about Kit. He had met her prior to a mission into Cambodia. A former VC who had defected, she had come over to the side of democracy. Her real name was Brouchard Bien Soo Ta Emilie, although everyone he knew called her Kit because she was a Kit Carson scout.

"You going to wait out here?" asked Gerber.

"No, I will come inside with you."

Gerber shrugged and got out of the jeep, taking his weapon with him. He stopped at the door and waited. Together they entered easily because there was no ID check. The management, meaning the Army-Air Force Exchange Service, assumed that anyone who was on the military base at Nha Trang would have exchange privileges.

It was like a hundred other PXs in a hundred other locations: stereos and cameras and televisions and fans; racks of clothes and racks of books; shelves of food and a thousand other items. Dozens of soldiers were circulating in the aisles, studying the displays. Many of them carried weapons. Twenty or thirty Vietnamese women worked as clerks.

Kit dragged Gerber to an aisle where there was a variety of women's clothing in small sizes that was obviously there for the men to buy for their Vietnamese girlfriends. A couple of the clerks were pawing through a heap of lacy garments, searching for something new.

"You buy me what you like and I'll wear it for you," said Kit.

"I don't know," said Gerber.

She dug into a pile of blouses, holding one of them up in front of her. "You like this?"

"It's fine."

"You don't have to buy it," she said. She set it aside and looked at the dresses and skirts. She chose one, then pulled a second from the hanger. Holding it against her waist, she checked the length and then grinned at Gerber. "It's pretty short. What do you think?"

Gerber pretended to study the problem. "It looks just fine."

But his mind was elsewhere. He couldn't believe it, but it was happening all over again. Many men joined the army to get away from women, but Gerber wasn't having that kind of luck. He had left Vietnam a year ago, figuring that his problems with women would be over. Now, after twelve months, all the problems were resurfacing. All he needed to make the circus complete was for Karen Morrow to arrive on the scene. At least that was one woman he wouldn't be running into.

It wasn't that he didn't like Kit. She was an extraordinary woman. They had spent some interesting nights together, not the least of which had been in the field in Cambodia as they'd spied on the Ho Chi Minh Trail. Gerber didn't want to respond to her as a lover, because he didn't want to lead her on. And yet, he found himself responding to her enthusiasm, responding to her because she was a woman, and that was the last thing he wanted to do.

She leaned close, her breath hot and sweet, and whispered. "I'm not wearing any underwear. Too hot in fatigues." She glanced up at him, her eyes wide in innocence.

The line drove a spike through Gerber's heart. He suddenly remembered another lady who had been in Nha Trang at the time, saying the same thing to him. She hadn't been worried about the heat, but the results had been the same. No underwear.

"Maybe I should take you back to your quarters," said Gerber.

Misunderstanding him, she said, "Maybe you should. I have no roommates this time."

Involuntarily Gerber retreated a step, holding up his hands as if surrendering. "No. No, you don't understand. I meant for you to go back there. Not me. Just you."

"Not on your life, Mack Gerber," she replied quickly. "If I buy these clothes, then I expect you to buy me a nice dinner." Her smile turned impish. "And even if I don't buy them, I still expect a dinner."

Gerber realized he was beaten. He also realized that he was on shaky ground. She could choose to misinterpret everything he said. Rather than fight it further, he said, "Let me get some shaving gear so that I can clean up, and we'll go to dinner. And I want to swing by the SF Headquarters and let Sergeant Santini know where I'll be in case someone needs to find me."

She took his hand. "That's a wonderful plan. I like it."

Within an hour, they were standing in the lobby of the King Duy Tan Hotel. Gerber was in a fresh set of jungle fatigues, and Kit was wearing the short dark skirt and white blouse she had bought, with a red tie at the throat. Gerber left her standing near a couple of wing chairs while he registered for the night. The clerk, an old Vietnamese man who could barely speak English, didn't bat an eye when Gerber picked up the rifle he had leaned against the front desk.

Then, rather than heading upstairs, Gerber took Kit into the dining room.

It was a huge hall with ten-foot-high windows and large chandeliers. There were twenty-five or thirty tables, each with a white linen cloth and a place setting of silver and crystal. Red napkins and bright flowers added a touch of color to the room. At one end of the hall there was a raised dining area and French doors that looked out on Nha Trang Bay. The whole place smacked of wealth, and so far it seemed to be undamaged by the war. Gerber noticed a couple of freshly patched places where the paint didn't quite match the rest, and there were a few windowpanes that looked cleaner than the rest.

The maître d' intercepted them, looking down his nose at Gerber's fatigues and M-16 and Kit's clothes. In French, he asked, "Two for dinner?"

Gerber nodded and responded in English, "If you have a nice table."

The maître d' took them toward the rear of the room, near the doors that led into the kitchen. He pulled a chair out for Kit, but Gerber refused to sit. The captain stared at the man and said, "I believe we'd be happier near the balcony."

"Those tables are reserved."

"Ah," said Gerber. He put a hand in his pocket, took out a bill and moved closer to the man. He slipped the bill into the man's hand and asked, "Why don't you see if there's a reservation for Gerber?"

The maître d' went to the front door, checked his book and surreptitiously looked at the bill Gerber had given him. A smile broke out on his face, and he hurried back. "Please forgive me, sir, I have made an error. Come with me."

They took a table near the window where they could look out on the darkening of the bay and the deep purple clouds that hung over it. A couple of sampans were visible, and a navy patrol boat cut across the dark blue of the water. In the distance Gerber could see a destroyer on picket duty. He watched them for a moment and then turned his attention back to Kit.

"So, how have things been going for you?" he asked.

She shrugged. "They are fine. We have made a big dent in the Vietcong. Stopped them many times. Killed many of them in battle. But I do not want to talk about the war."

"What would you like to talk about?"

Before she could answer, the waiter arrived and handed them menus printed in both Vietnamese and French. As he turned to leave, Kit leaned across the table and said quietly, "I can translate for you."

Gerber smiled and said in French, "There is no need. I can read enough French to find something to eat."

"Of course."

They spent a few quiet minutes studying the menus. Gerber was glad for the diversion, because he still wasn't sure how to react to Kit. His whole attitude had been directed by outside circumstances and influences from the time he had met her in Saigon. Initially he had been unsure of how much to trust her because she had been a VC and then later he had almost been afraid of her because of her obvious interest in him. All of that had been complicated by the Morrow sisters and the war.

While she read her menu, he took a moment to study her. She was indeed a beautiful woman. Slight and delicate, she still somehow radiated strength, and her long black hair was silky as it cascaded down her back or brushed her eyebrows in heavy bangs.

She had lied to him on a couple of occasions, but they had been lies born in the violence of war and were not meant to be deceitful. She was a sincere, intelligent woman who was as brave as any man and more ruthless than most. Looking at her, he felt his affection for her build and wondered at his automatic resistance to it. If she suggested a trip back to her quarters, or a drink in his room after dinner, it might be something to consider.

He let his eyes fall back to the menu and thought about Karen and Robin Morrow. Both were women who claimed they loved him. Robin's love seemed to be real, while he was never sure what Karen was thinking. Sometimes he felt as if he was just another conquest for her, as if she was trying to see how many men she could catch before discarding each of them.

It was something that he wasn't going to resolve in a few minutes. Maybe the year in Vietnam would give him some clue about Karen, or about Robin. The only thing he could be sure of was that he didn't have to solve the problem in the next five minutes.

As they set the menus aside, the waiter returned for their orders. Gerber asked for a Beam's neat, and Kit ordered a Bloody Mary. Before the waiter could get away, Gerber ordered a rare steak, baked potato with sour cream, chives and butter, and blue cheese dressing on his salad. Kit ordered fish.

The waiter left, and moments later a waitress brought the beverages, set them on the table and vanished without a word.

Gerber grabbed his, drank half of it in one hasty gulp and said, "Never get over how smooth that is."

Kit sipped hers and set the glass down. She leaned forward, both elbows on the table. She had failed to button the top of her blouse, and as she leaned toward him, Gerber could see the top of her breasts. He pulled his eyes away and looked at her face. She was smiling at him.

"You know, Mack Gerber," she said, "I missed you while you were home hiding from the war."

Gerber's first reaction was to deny he was hiding from the war, then he realized she was teasing him. He thought of a dozen responses, but decided against all of them.

"I would like a chance to visit the United States," she said. "Maybe you could take me there for a visit sometime. A short visit."

Trying not to commit himself to anything, Gerber said, "That might be possible."

"Good." She turned so that she could look at Nha Trang Bay. Now it was almost completely dark. A few lights flickered—a couple of them were the navigation lights of American vessels—but almost everything else was dark. Everyone had learned that to burn a light after nightfall was to invite attack.

The salads arrived, and they began to eat. Kit kept stealing looks at Gerber, who was doing his best to ignore them. He knew that he had made a mistake by allowing her to rope him into the dinner, but he hadn't seen an easy way to get out of it. An ambush, an assault on his camp, or a mortar attack, he could deal with, but a woman who wanted to have dinner with him was another matter.

They finished the salads, and the main course arrived. As the waiter withdrew, Gerber caught a flurry of motion out of the corner of his eye and saw Sergeant Santini hurrying toward him. Santini carried an M-16 and an overnight bag. He ignored the maître d', who was trying to intercept him.

He stopped next to Gerber, nodded at Kit and then put his lips close to Gerber's ear. "Call from your Sergeant Fetterman in Saigon. Your presence there is requested immediately."

"He say what it was about?"

Santini straightened. "No, sir. I have a jeep outside to take you to the base."

"I've one, too."

"Yes, sir."

Gerber looked at the steak that had been set in front of him—a thick T-bone running with juice, and next to it, a baked potato with steam curling above it. He snatched his napkin from his lap, patted his lips and tossed it aside. "That's it then."

Santini stepped back as Gerber stood. The sergeant said, "Courier plane will be leaving in twenty minutes. You're manifested through."

"Kit, I'm sorry," said Gerber. "I have to leave."

She nodded. "That is all right. I understand the nature of your business, but only if you promise to buy me a dinner another time."

"Of course," said Gerber. "Another time. Sergeant Santini, have you eaten yet?"

"No, sir."

"Then why don't you have a seat and finish my meal? You can drive Kit back to the base."

Santini moved so that he could sit down. "This may be a little more expensive than I'm used to."

"No problem," said Gerber. He took several bills from his pocket, checking each one carefully. In accordance with military regulations, he had changed all his American money for MPC, the so-called Monopoly money used by the U.S. armed forces in Vietnam. He handed Santini forty dollars. "You pay for the meal and buy Kit an after-dinner drink. Oh, and you'll need to check me out of the hotel. Since I haven't even been to the room yet, there shouldn't be any trouble with that."

"Yes, sir," said Santini. "I'll take care of it."

"Thanks."

Before Gerber could get away, Kit stood and grabbed his sleeve. She turned him and brushed his lips with hers while she clung to him, pressing herself against him. "You owe me one dinner, Captain," she said seriously. "And I will go to Saigon to collect it. You remember that."

"I will," said Gerber. "Now please sit down and finish your meal, then Sergeant Santini will drive you home."

"Yes, sir," she snapped.

Gerber turned and hurried from the hotel. He climbed into his jeep, and in minutes he was at the terminal at Nha Trang. A Special Forces sergeant was standing by. When Gerber appeared, the man came forward and asked, "Are you Captain Gerber?"

"Yes."

"Come with me please, sir, and we'll get you on the plane immediately."

In less than ten minutes, Gerber found himself strapped into the rear of a Hercules C-130. He had no idea why he had been summoned to Saigon with such haste, but knew if Fetterman wanted him, it had to be important. Fetterman wouldn't have called otherwise.

7

TAN SON NHUT
INTERNATIONAL
AIRPORT, SAIGON

It was a scene out of an adventure movie. As the plane rolled
to a stop, two jeeps, one of them with a red light rotating on
a roll bar behind the driver, roared around a corner. They
approached the C-130, halting near the nose as the pilot cut
the engines and the noise died. The loadmaster, a young staff
sergeant, told everyone to stay put and then escorted Gerber
to the front of the aircraft so that he could get out.

Almost as his foot hit the tarmac, one of the men in the lead
jeep was rushing toward Gerber. The driver threw him a salute and announced, "We're supposed to escort you to a
meeting."

"It's after midnight," said Gerber.

"Yes, sir. Please follow me."

Gerber shrugged and climbed into the rear of one of the
jeeps. As he sat down there was a grinding of gears, and they
took off with a squeal of tires. These were not standard-issue
jeeps.

They raced off the tarmac between two hangars, one of
them belonging to Air America, and then turned east. They

left the airfield proper, entered the base itself, and without slowing for either air police or checkpoints, drove straight for a building that Gerber was familiar with. He had watched two of his men undergo court-martials in it, had met Kit in it, and now was being taken to it again. He was not pleased.

The jeep pulled to a halt in a parking lot that was covered with crushed gravel and free of potholes. A length of white chain was draped between three-foot-high logs set on their ends to create a fence.

"Thought we'd be going over to the MACV compound," said Gerber as he climbed out of the jeep.

"No, sir. Colonel Bates moved the operation over here. Closer to the flight line and heliport. We can get out of here faster than over at MACV."

One of the men escorted Gerber to the concrete sidewalk, past the flagpole surrounded by flowers, to the double doors that led inside. The bullet hole that had been in one of them when Crinshaw had commanded had been repaired by the new CO, and Gerber took that as a good sign.

They hurried along the dark corridors, the only light coming from exit signs above the doors, and nearly ran up a flight of stairs. On the second floor there was more light, most of it coming from the open door of a conference room.

The man pointed at the open door. "You're wanted in there, sir."

"Thank you," said Gerber, nodding. He walked down the hallway, his footsteps echoing off the cinder-block walls. When he reached the door, he stopped and glanced inside. It was a typical conference room with a table holding water glasses and a pitcher, chairs, a blackboard and a covered easel. Bates stood with his back to Gerber. There were three men whom he didn't recognize and, of course, Fetterman.

"Tony," said Gerber as he entered.

"Captain."

Bates turned. "Sorry to drag you back like this, but we've hit on something that's too important to ignore. If you'll grab a seat, we'll get started." He dropped into his chair.

Fetterman pointed to the other men. "Captain Gerber, this is Sergeant Long, Sergeant Carlisle and Sergeant Nolan. They were on the patrol with me."

"Nice to meet you." He shook hands with the men, leaning across the narrow mahogany table. Then he glanced at the file folder in front of him. There was a bright red Secret stamp at the top and bottom.

"About two hours ago," said Bates, "my S-2, on reading some of the documents found by Sergeant Fetterman, realized that we have a massive buildup of enemy forces in the Hobo Woods. This all confirmed what Sergeant Fetterman and his patrol had reported. In fact, confirmed something we've suspected for the past few weeks."

"Two hours ago," said Gerber, "I was already on the airplane heading back here."

"Well, yes," said Bates, grinning. "Let's just say I had more faith in Sergeant Fetterman than some of the brass around here who don't know him."

"Ah." Gerber glanced at Fetterman, who sat smiling like a skinny version of Buddha.

Bates stood and moved to the covered easel. There were no markings on the cloth draped over it. He picked up a pencil to use as a pointer and snatched the cloth away, letting it drop on the floor. Underneath was a map. "Here at Cu Chi is a major American base. It houses a number of aviation units, the 12th Evac Hospital and two brigades of the 25th Infantry Division. Due north of there, near this bend in the Saigon River that the pilots have dubbed the Mushroom, is the Hobo Woods. As you men know, it isn't a real jungle environment, but more like a forest you'd find in the World."

"Interesting, Colonel," said Gerber, "but?"

"But," said Bates, "the information is that the north section of the woods, closest to the river, is being used as a staging area. Although there have been no movements of the VC and NVA along the river, we assume they'll be using it to send their forces to Saigon when they're finally ready to make their strike."

"But we're not going to give them the chance," said Gerber, anticipating.

"Right," said Bates. "Now I've coordinated with the 1st Aviation Brigade and the 25th Infantry Division. We have helicopters and ground forces that will be ready for pickup tomorrow morning at 0600 hours."

"Moving kind of fast, aren't you?" asked Gerber.

Bates put the pencil in the tray on the easel and sat down. He stared at the younger man and said, "Intelligence of this nature is a highly perishable commodity. What is true today may not be true tomorrow. Right now we know where the enemy is, we know which units are there and we have the resources to disrupt him. Sergeant Fetterman and his friends here can lead the infantry to the VC."

Gerber looked at Fetterman again. "How much sleep have you had since we arrived in Vietnam?"

"Enough, Captain. Slept in the field, and I've grabbed a few hours since we came in."

Bates took over again. "Tony, why don't you show us the areas of your patrol and the possible LZs?"

Fetterman got up and stepped to the map. "We landed in a small clearing right here. It wasn't large enough to put in more than two or three ships. Extraction was made here, north and west of the first LZ. That was a small clearing that might take five choppers, but it would be a tight squeeze." Fetterman nodded at the table. "Aerial photos and Sergeant Long's experience show there are two good LZs in the vicinity that we could use."

"Captain, do you have any questions?" asked Bates.

Gerber stood and moved to the map. He examined it closely. There were several plantations, a couple of small villages south and west of the woods and a road that bordered the northern edge. There was an ARVN base at Trung Lap and an indication that there was a helicopter landing area available at Ben Suc near the Mushroom. "What are we using for a staging area?"

Bates opened his file folder. "We can use the airfield at Cu Chi, Trung Lap or Dau Tieng. POL is available at Cu Chi and Dau Tieng. Additional troops are available at Dau Tieng if we find that we need them."

"How many lift companies?"

"We have the Hornets at Cu Chi, the Crusaders out of Tay Ninh and ten ships from the Little Bears on standby. Only the Hornets will be involved in the initial insertion. The other aviation assets are committed to another operation but will be available to us about noon."

Gerber nodded. "I suppose we can count on arty support out of Cu Chi?"

"For the initial assault, yes. That's been coordinated. There is also support available from Fire Support Base Pershing. That gives you eighteen tubes. Twelve 105s and a battery of 155s."

"Sounds like this thing has been well organized," said Gerber. "What the hell is my role?"

Bates grinned. "Sergeant Fetterman, Sergeant Long and Sergeant Carlisle will be the scouts for the three lift companies being used. Sergeant Nolan will remain here to coordinate. Fetterman will take in the first bunch. Your job is Ground Mission Commander.''

"I have no experience for that," said Gerber.

"Then it's time you got some," responded Bates. "Since you're taking over for Major Madden, you'll need to gain some experience as the Ground Mission Commander. Instead of controlling the platoons of a company, you'll be in charge of the companies. Now, do you have some idea of how you'd like to deploy your forces?"

"Tony," said Gerber, "you've been there. What's your recommendation?"

"I'd put one company in here," he said, circling an area of the map. "I'd reinforce them with two platoons from another company and then drop two platoons here near the river as a blocking force. If they attempt an escape, I believe they'd try to move in that direction."

"Okay," said Gerber. He turned to Bates. "I've a couple of questions for you. One is recon of the area. There be a chance for that?"

"You're Ground Mission Commander," said Bates. "What do you think?"

"I think I'd like the C and C available forty-five minutes to an hour before the assaults go in so that we can have a visual recon of the LZs."

"You think that's wise? Might give away our plan," Bates commented.

"Yes, sir. I think it's wise. We'll only take a quick look at the important LZs, and we'll also examine a few we're not going to use. Hell, Colonel, an arty prep's going to alert them anyway."

"Good point. That's one question. Your second?"

"I know nothing about these soldiers. Who are they?"

"Most of them have been working search-and-destroy and combat assaults for six, seven, eight months. They're an experienced group. Not as good as our own men, but reliable soldiers. Only a few FNGs in the bunch. All good troops from the 25th Infantry Division. I don't think you'll have any complaints about them."

"Somebody worked out a schedule of events yet?" asked Gerber.

"We'll be in the field from just after sunup and out before sundown," said Bates. "I don't want that kind of force in there after dark, not until we know more about it. That's, of course, if we haven't made contact. In the event that we've found the enemy, then we stay until we've killed them all or pushed them out of there."

"Call signs?" asked Gerber.

"The SOI has them for all the units, plus their normal company fox mikes and uniforms. You'll be Dracula Six. Sergeant Fetterman will be Dracula Five. Long will be Dracula Seven and Carlisle will be Eight. Nolan will be Two."

Gerber pulled a yellow pad from the file folder and started making notes. He wrote rapidly, read it over and said, "Here's what I want. First, I want Tony to go to bed." He looked at the master sergeant. "You can catch a flight out of here as late as five-thirty and still be at Cu Chi in time. Then I want to coordinate with SF HQ in Nha Trang. If possible, I'd like Sergeant Santini here to help coordinate. I'll want a flight out of here about four o'clock so that I can link with the people at Cu Chi."

"You've got it all," said Bates.

"Then let's get at. Where are we going to be while here?" asked Gerber.

"We can use this conference room as a CP until you leave, if that's what you want."

"Good," said Gerber. "And how about some coffee?"

Long stood. "I don't have anything else to do right now. I'll see about it."

Gerber clapped his hands. "Let's get going."

BY TWO, GERBER felt satisfied that everything that had to be done had been done. He rocked back in his chair and laced his fingers behind his head. Taking a deep breath, he glanced at the ceiling. His eyes burned from a lack of sleep and his body ached, but he felt good. Back in Vietnam for less than a week, he was already involved in an important operation, a mission that could hurt the enemy, maybe cripple the VC.

There was a tap at the door, and Santini, dressed in jungle fatigues, stood there. He smiled as if he had caught Gerber screwing off and said, "Mind if I join you?"

"No, come on in." Gerber dropped his feet to the floor. As he stood to move to the coffeepot that had been brought in by Long, he saw Kit. "What the hell?"

She had changed from her civilian clothes to tailored jungle fatigues that fit her almost like a second skin. "I came to scout. Major Madden thought that I might be able to help."

"Uh-huh," said Gerber.

"You are not happy to see me?"

Gerber turned his back and poured a cup of coffee. He added sugar, which he normally didn't use, stirred and then returned to his seat. All the while Kit watched him, waiting for a response. Finally he said, "I'm happy to see you. I just don't think you'll be needed for this mission."

She entered the room and sat opposite him. Her gaze fell on the map, which had remained uncovered. There was nothing marked on it, except one black circle around the primary landing zone.

"I was with the VC in there. I know where everything is. I can help you find them."

For an instant, Gerber was going to cover the map, but then thought better of it. Even if Kit was a double agent, there would be no way for her to communicate the information to the enemy. The mission was scheduled to begin long before that could happen.

"We don't need a guide for this one. We know where we're going, and we don't plan an extended search-and-destroy."

"But I can help."

Gerber set his coffee cup down and searched her face. He wondered why he was reluctant to take her on the mission. There were services that she could provide, especially if she had been in the area before. She had proved herself on his last mission in Vietnam. But still there was a doubt, a doubt that was more than a suspicion that she might still be VC, a doubt that his feelings for her might run deeper than he cared to admit.

He shot a glance at Santini, who stood near the coffeepot holding a steaming cup. Santini shrugged as if to say it wasn't his business.

At that moment Sergeant Nolan returned, escorting Jerry Maxwell. The CIA agent stopped at the door when he saw Kit. It was as if he had walked into a solid barrier. Nolan chose to ignore the situation. He flopped into a chair at the end of the table and said, "Think that covers it. Chopper will pick you up at Hotel Three in little more than an hour. You can operate from it like it was a C and C. Hornets will put up a second ship about dawn with more command and control functions. That means they'll have Hornet six and some colonel from the 25th."

"Good," said Gerber. "Who's going to be standing by if we need them?"

"Company from the 25th at Cu Chi. Their area is near the runway, so they'll be held in the company area."

"Okay, how about this?" asked Gerber. "After we all get off, you see about flying Kit out there and having her link up with their company commander? She might have some intel we could use if we find anything."

"No problem," said Nolan. "Take care of it as soon as I finish my coffee."

From the door, Maxwell said, "Captain Gerber, may I have a word with you?"

Gerber got up, touched Kit on the shoulder and then moved to the hallway. Maxwell was standing with his back to the wall.

"I can't believe you're going to take that former Vietcong on this mission," he said.

Gerber rubbed a hand over his face. Once again he realized how tired he was. "Jerry, I don't believe you. I've been gone for a year. Haven't seen or heard from you in all that time, and the first thing you do is start giving me instructions. No 'Good to see you again, Mack.' No 'How are things in the World?' Just an expression of disbelief."

"I don't have the time to stand here and exchange pleasantries with you, not when you're allowing a security risk access to information about an operation." There was anger in his voice.

"Well, then," said Gerber, raising his voice. "I don't think there is a way for us to be compromised. She wouldn't have the time to pass the intelligence."

"Captain, within an hour of the massacre at the Little Big Horn, Indians a hundred miles away knew about it. I think the VC have a better communication system."

"Look, Jerry, the last thing I need right now is to get into a long conversation about this. She's not going to be out of our sight long enough to do any damage. When this is over, we can talk about it if you want.''

''Okay, Mack,'' he said. Finally he smiled and added, ''So, how have you been? How were things in the World?''

''Mr. Social Director,'' said Gerber. ''I've been better, and things were great in the World.''

''Mack, I didn't mean to jump on you. You've had a year off, but I've been here the whole time.''

Gerber was still annoyed, but he suddenly remembered that if it hadn't been for Maxwell, he might have been killed on a mission in Cambodia.

''Sorry, Jerry,'' Gerber said, then turned and entered the conference room to begin the wait.

AT FOUR-THIRTY Gerber was standing outside the terminal, under the tower at Hotel Three, watching as a chopper made its final approach. It landed on one of the VIP pads, but there was no sergeant in the terminal to rush out and complain. Gerber nodded once to Bates, then grabbed his rucksack and weapon.

''Mack,'' said Bates, ''one thing you should know. We've got to keep a low profile on this.''

Gerber had been about to rush to the chopper. He hesitated and looked at the colonel. ''Low profile? What the hell are you talking about?''

''It's too long to go into here and now. Let's just say that a lot of people would be very unhappy if this turned into a major conflict.''

''Colonel, that makes no sense at all.'' Gerber suddenly felt hot, as if it were noon rather than an hour until dawn.

''Mack, the political situation is such that no one wants to see a battle on the six o'clock news. We can go in and search for the enemy, but if you find a large force, I want you to withdraw, and we'll call in artillery or air strikes. Deal with them that way rather than with infantry.''

Gerber shook his head. ''Then what's the point of putting anyone in? Why not call in your air strikes from here?''

''Because I don't want to go blowing up the Hobo Woods if there are no targets. Think about this as a recon in force. You find the enemy, you fall back and let the flyboys and cannon cockers do their job.''

''This is the most fucked-up thing I've ever heard. Go look for the enemy but don't find him.''

''Of all the men I know in Vietnam,'' said Bates, ''I thought you were the one who would understand.'' He looked past Gerber at the helicopter that stood on the concrete pad, the rotors spinning and the engine roaring. Beyond that was the airfield at Tan Son Nhut, quiet for the moment.

This was something he had never expected from Bates. The colonel wasn't the kind of man who would throw others to the wolves for his own career. It was the last thing Gerber expected to hear him say—warning him about possible career consequences.

''A star that important to you?''

''You know better than that. If it was, the intel would be on its way to Nha Trang and all of us would be in bed right now. No, the star isn't that important.''

''Okay, Colonel,'' said Gerber. ''I'll do what I can to avoid a fight.''

''Thanks, Mack. Good luck.''

''Thank you, Alan.'' Gerber turned and ran toward the chopper, his head bent low.

As he climbed in, the crew chief handed him a flight helmet that was plugged into the chopper's intercom system. Gerber dropped his steel pot on the troop seat beside him.

He put on the helmet, pushed the boom mike around so that it was only a fraction of an inch from his lips and reached for the hand-held switch. He depressed the button and said, "I'm ready."

The AC turned in his seat. "You're Captain Gerber, aren't you?"

"That's right."

"Yeah. I thought you had to be. What other nut would be running around out here this late at night."

The roar from the engine increased, and the chopper picked up to a hover. Gerber glanced out the cargo compartment door, and in the half-light of the helipad he saw a figure run up to Bates—a small, slight woman with a camera around her neck. She pulled her boonie hat from her head and let her light-colored hair spill around her shoulders. Gerber couldn't figure out how Robin Morrow had found them, but knew Bates wouldn't be happy about it. The last thing he wanted was a reporter dogging his footsteps.

Then, over the earphones of the helmet, Gerber heard the pilot say, "Saigon Tower, this is Hornet zero seven three, ready for south departure, Hotel Three."

A tinny voice speaking barely intelligible English said, "Clear for takeoff."

The pilot dumped the nose, and they began the climb out. As they passed over the fence that marked the edge of Hotel Three, Gerber looked back and saw Bates and Morrow, now little more than dark shapes, standing close together. He hoped Bates could talk his way out of it. If he didn't, his star was definitely gone.

A voice on the intercom dragged Gerber's attention away from the problem on the ground. He heard the AC explaining the radio and flight procedures to the Peter pilot. "Normally you'd contact the tower here at Hotel Three, except at this time of the day it's shut down, so you have to alert Saigon Tower. If we were into flight following, we'd call Capitol Control. At least they're all Americans and you can understand them."

They turned west and finished climbing, leveling out at fifteen hundred feet. The AC said, "You've got it."

The pilot responded, "I've got it."

As the AC released the controls, he turned in his seat. He used the floor button for the intercom and asked, "What's the plan, Captain?"

"How much do you know?"

"Got a briefing in our Ops before takeoff. They said we'd be operating as command and control for two lifts into the Hobo Woods."

"Exactly. We might be required to land in the LZ, depending on the circumstances."

"That's no problem. You call the shots on that."

"Good."

"One thing. Before we head out to the Hobo Woods, we'll want to stop at POL at Cu Chi to top off the tanks."

Gerber pushed the button, but someone else said, "ADF."

"What's that?" asked Gerber.

The AC smiled. "Our navigation aids cover the commercial broadcast bands. We usually have AFVN tuned in because most of the time we're not traveling that far. We navigate by dead reckoning instead of using all this extra shit hung in here. When someone says ADF, it means there's a good tune on the radio."

"That's a real valuable piece of information to have," said Gerber.

The crew chief came out of his well and reached for the radio control head hidden among the soundproofing in the roof of the cabin behind the pilot's head. He flipped one of the microswitches, then held up a thumb. Gerber could hear the Beatles singing in the background.

For a few moments no one said anything. Gerber looked out of the cargo compartment door and was surprised to see how dark it was. There were virtually no lights on the ground. Silver ribbons marked the canals and rivers while black threads signified the few roads. Then, off to the north, he saw a pool of light that indicated the American base at Cu Chi.

They entered the traffic pattern and landed on one of the dozen or so concrete pads next to a refueling point. Without waiting for shutdown, the crew chief leaped out and ran to the metal pole, which had an oversized nozzle stuck in its top. He swung the long, thick hose forward and dragged the nozzle to the chopper. The door gunner had already gotten out to push the cargo door forward so that they could begin refueling.

Gerber watched the aircraft commander climb out. The man was dressed in jungle fatigues and wearing a ceramic plate that protected his chest. The pilots called them chicken plates, but Gerber knew two or three pilots who would be dead if they hadn't been wearing the plates. One man had taken two AK-47 rounds in the chest that the armor had stopped, and although he had been badly bruised, he could now laugh about it.

The other thing Gerber noticed was that the man was wearing an old West type holster with a long-barreled .38 in it. There were even bullets stuck in the loops on the back of the holster belt in imitation of John Wayne.

As he passed the cargo compartment, the pilot grinned and then unzipped his fly. Gerber watched the man urinate on the rear of the skids for a moment and wondered if there was any significance to the act.

A few minutes later they lifted off, climbing out over part of the darkened city of Cu Chi, which was little more than a collection of broken-down mud hootches with tin roofs. They looped around the southern edge of the camp, along Highway One, before breaking to the north and west. Off to the east, the sky was starting to gray and the stars were beginning to fade. Gerber could make out things on the ground now: hootches stuck into groves of palms or in the middle of rice paddies.

"Okay, Captain," said the AC. "We're getting close. What do you want to see?"

"Has anyone given you a list of the LZs yet?"

"I have a couple marked on my map." He bent over and pulled an acetate-covered map from a pouch on the rear of the console between the pilots. He handed it to Gerber. "Got them circled in black."

Gerber studied the map in the dim red light of the cargo compartment. He cross-checked them with the LZs designated on his own map. As he handed the map back, he said, "Yeah, you've got them right."

"Okay. What I want to do is fuck around up here for a while, letting it get a bit lighter. Then if you want we can fly over the Hobo Woods at altitude, giving you a chance to see the LZs. After that we can drop to treetop level and fly by, but I don't recommend that action."

"You worked this area before?" asked Gerber.

"We've been in and out all over this place."

"Then you've seen the LZs?"

"Oh, yes, sir. Been into a couple of them. There aren't that many places to land around here. Charlie knows it, too, and sometimes surrounds them in case we decide to make a landing. There are abandoned bunker complexes around them that Charlie can slip back into, and I think there are tunnel systems, too.''

Gerber didn't like that information. He wasn't surprised by it, because it made good sense. The VC would know that the helicopters needed to land, and if there were only a limited number of landing sites, Charlie could build bunkers around them and mine them. That was the reason for arty preps, gunships and full suppression—keep Charlie's head down long enough to establish an airhead.

''If you're ready, Captain, we'll make the first pass. Look out to the left and you'll see a hole in the tops of the trees. That's the first LZ.''

Gerber slipped to the left so that he could look at the ground. The sun was peeking over the horizon, but the ground was still wrapped in shadows. There were patches of black and dark grays, and Gerber couldn't see any detail. He couldn't see what the terrain of the LZ was like, if there were any logical rally points or if there were any strongpoints for the enemy to use for attacks against them.

''Can't see anything,'' said Gerber.

''All right, Captain,'' said the AC. ''We'll pull back and try again in a few minutes.''

They broke to the north and crossed the Saigon River, taking up a wide orbit over a rubber tree plantation. Rows and rows of trees were planted close together; they had a symmetry that defied nature.

For ten minutes they orbited in silence. Finally they turned south again, and the AC asked, ''You ready now?''

''Let's get it done,'' said Gerber.

They crossed the river and the edge of the Hobo Woods. ''Coming up on your first LZ.''

This time Gerber could see the ground. The LZ was fairly flat and covered with tall grass. There were bushes scattered around that would provide concealment for his men. The few trees that had been growing in the middle of the clearing had long since been knocked down by artillery or bombs. That would also give his men some protection.

They broke away from the LZ and crossed the Hobo Woods. They turned north, and the AC said, "Blocking force goes in here."

This LZ was smaller and rougher. At one end were the remains of a hootch, the roof caved in and one mud wall collapsed. A tiny stream bisected the LZ.

"You have any trouble landing in there?" asked Gerber.

"Five ships max," said the AC. "Have to break the flight into two platoons to do it, but it won't be a problem unless we hit stiff resistance."

"Okay," said Gerber. He kept his eyes on the ground. "What else do you want to show me?"

A klick away, they circled an area that didn't look much like an LZ. The AC said, "Looks deceptive from the air, but we can get six, seven ships in there. We have to scatter them around, and that sometimes makes unit integrity hard to maintain, but Charlie doesn't expect us to use it. Might be able to sneak someone in there."

"I'll keep that in mind."

"We've got to get out of the area now," said the AC. "Arty prep will be starting in about five minutes. If we orbit north of the river, we won't be fouling any gun target lines and we won't get hit by a stray round."

As they banked to the right, Gerber glanced at his watch. In twenty minutes the first of the troops would be on the ground.

8

CU CHI, RVN

Fetterman stood on a strip of asphalt that paralleled the runway, some of the men milling around him as the sun began to rise. There were eight soldiers near him, all dressed in jungle fatigues, wearing rucksacks and steel pots and carrying weapons. Two of them had M-79 grenade launchers, and one carried an M-60 machine gun, the ammo draped around his body. Two wore radios strapped to their backs, the whip antennae waving above their heads.

The rest of the company was divided into groups of eight each for ten aircraft. They stood around, sticking close to one another and checking one another's equipment. Fetterman sought out the company commander and asked, "You familiar with the Hobo Woods?"

"Been in there a couple of times," said the CO, a captain who wore a boonie hat underneath his helmet. Fetterman took in everything about the officer. He carried a CAR-15 instead of an M-16. His uniform was starched and looked as if it had been pressed recently. There were the beginnings of sweat stains under the arms, which indicated that the morning was going to be hot and humid.

Fetterman wasn't sure he was pleased with the idea of going into combat with this man, but decided to give him the benefit of the doubt. A starched uniform and an affinity for a glamour weapon did not mean he would be a bad soldier.

There were things Fetterman wanted to say to him, questions he wanted to ask, but he held his tongue. The officer either knew his job or he didn't, and it made no difference what Fetterman did at this point. He couldn't get a new company commander to take over before the helicopters arrived and he couldn't teach this one how to survive in the field in so short a time. Suddenly Fetterman wished he had insisted on using a Special Forces Mike Force instead of American infantry. With a Mike Force he would have been dealing with a known quantity. With these men, he had an unknown. By and large, the American infantry was far superior to anything the Viets could muster, but Fetterman just didn't know about these soldiers.

The popping of rotor blades and roaring of turbine engines announced the arrival of the helicopters. In the early dawn light the choppers were little more than dark shapes swooping out of the sky, dim red and green lights winking on their sides and a bright red one rotating above the turbine. A beam stabbed out from the landing light of the lead aircraft, and one of the men from the first load ran to the center of the assault strip. He held a strobe in one hand to direct the landing aircraft, the blinking light looking like the muzzle-flashes of a weapon.

The flight shifted into a trail formation and descended. The choppers flared as one, the rotor wash pushing out in front of them in a swirling windstorm that tore at the uniforms, equipment and packs of the waiting soldiers. Paper, dirt and debris were picked up and blown around. Men ducked their heads, and those wearing boonie hats held on to them. The dust storm increased as the ten choppers landed, and for a moment they were lost behind the cloud of spinning, blowing earth.

As Fetterman ran toward the lead ship, there was a crash behind him. He knew it was the artillery at Cu Chi firing its first volley. He heard the rounds roar overhead but didn't hear the impact seconds later. At the lead chopper, he stopped and turned, watching the men. Those who had been wearing boonie hats replaced them with helmets. They formed lines near the cargo compartments of the choppers and then one by one climbed in.

In almost no time the helicopters were loaded, the men sitting on the troop seat or the floor of the cargo compartment, some of them dangling their legs outside like kids on a dock. A few checked their weapons, while others closed their eyes to catch a final few minutes' sleep or because they were frightened by the prospect of flying in the open cargo compartments. Many of them had red plastic caps fastened over the flash suppressors of their weapons. Before firing the rifle they would have to remove the plastic, which had been designed as one more safety feature.

After Fetterman climbed into the lead chopper, he was handed a set of earphones with a boom mike. The crew chief indicated that Fetterman was to put them on. The man then flipped the switch on the comm control to the number one position so that Fetterman was in communication with Gerber in the C and C aircraft.

"Dracula Six, this is Dracula Five," said Fetterman.

"Roger, Five," answered Gerber. "Say status."

"We're loaded and ready to go."

"Roger, Five."

A moment later the chopper lifted off the ground and executed a slow pedal turn to the left so that the AC could look at the flight behind him. Over the radio Fetterman heard someone say, "You're loaded with ten."

As the aircraft turned again, facing north, the AC said, "Roger. Lead's on the go."

They took off, the lead chopper hovering slowly down the assault strip and lifting gently into the brightening sky. Over the radio came the message, "You're off with ten."

"Roger. Ten."

Fetterman leaned forward so that he could look out the windshield of the aircraft. The ground, no longer hidden by a veil of darkness, was spread out in front of him. Orange sunlight reflected off the tin roofs of the hootches scattered throughout the area.

"Lead, you're joined with ten."

"Roger. Rolling over to eighty knots. Come up a staggered trail."

Fetterman hesitated a moment and then pushed the button for his mike. "Dracula Six, this is Dracula Five. We're off."

"Roger, Five," said Gerber. He used the intercom to relay the message to the AC. "Flight's off."

"Lead already told me," he said. "Arty prep should be started by now."

Then, over the radio came, "Lead, you're formed in a staggered trail."

Gerber glanced out the left side of his aircraft, looking back toward the Hobo Woods as the center of the LZ erupted into mushrooming clouds of black and brown and silver. For a moment it seemed silent, calm on the landing zone, and then it blew up again. Smoke drifted to the east, showing them the wind direction. And then they turned so that the LZ was momentarily invisible. As they rolled out, Gerber saw flashes of orange and yellow and puffs of white as the artillery switched from HE to antipersonnel and smoke. Gerber knew the last rounds were used to detonate any land mines or booby traps that the HE might have missed.

On the radio he heard, "Last rounds on the way."

"Lead, last rounds on the way. Start inbound," ordered the AC in the Command and Control aircraft.

The unidentified voice of the lead pilot came back with, "IP, inbound."

"Lead, this is Hornet Eight Six. Do you have me?"

Although Gerber couldn't see it, he knew the gun team leader, Hornet Eight Six, was breaking in front of the flight to lead them into the LZ. As they passed over it, he would have his crew chief and door gunner toss smoke grenades from the cargo compartment to mark the LZ and touchdown spot.

"Roger, Eight Six. I have you."

Gerber keyed his mike and said, "Dracula Five, this is Six."

"Go, Six."

"You're inbound. Still no reports of enemy activity at the lima zulu. Once you're on the ground, you will move directly to the north."

"Roger, Six."

"Flight, come up a heavy right," said Lead on the fox mike.

A moment later. "You're in a heavy right."

From the C and C came the radio call, "Last rounds on the ground. Flight, you'll have full suppression. Repeat, you'll have full suppression."

"Roger, full suppression," said one of the pilots.

Gerber hadn't seen the final artillery shells hit, but knew that one of the others had. They would not cross the gun target lines without being assured that all the rounds had detonated. The last thing any of them wanted to do was fly into an artillery barrage.

With that call, Gerber's aircraft broke orbit and headed south. By sitting up straight, Gerber could see the LZ through the aircraft's windshield, now marked by a dissipating cloud of dust and smoke. Far to the south and east, Gerber caught a flash of light from the fuselage of one of the Hueys as the flight approached rapidly.

"Lead, we're about a klick out," said the gun leader.

"Roger."

Two more aircraft appeared below the flight, racing along the tops of the trees, their skids almost in the scraggy vegetation. Gerber knew those gunships would strafe the edges of the landing zone to protect the flight.

At that moment, the lead gunship dumped its nose and dived for the ground. The chopper's pilot flew over the LZ, and as he hauled back on the cyclic to begin his rapid climb out, two smoke grenades tumbled from the rear, trailing purple tails.

"ID purple," said the lead pilot.

"Roger, purple. Land twenty meters south of the smoke."

"Roger that."

For an instant longer everything remained quiet. There was no chatter on the radios. There were no artillery rounds detonating. It seemed to be a calm, peaceful morning with patches of white ground fog lying near the river and among some of the trees of the Hobo Woods.

And then the LZ exploded again. Flashes of flame burst from the trees as the enemy, who had been lying in wait, opened fire.

"Chock Three's taking fire on the right," radioed one of the pilots.

Along the side of the flight, the door guns began to shoot. Three-foot-long tongues of flame leaped from the barrels. Ruby-colored tracers danced over the ground, disappearing among the vegetation.

"Flight's taking heavy fire from the right," said the icy voice of a different pilot.

"Flight's taking fire from the front," reported the lead pilot.

"Chock Four going down."

"Roger, Four," said the AC in Gerber's chopper.

It seemed that the whole of the Hobo Woods had come alive and that everyone there had some kind of weapon. The shadows twinkled as the enemy fired. Emerald tracers flashed toward the flight, some of them passing through the thin metallic skin of the chopper tail booms in showers of bright sparks. There were puffs of smoke as RPGs ignited and then detonations of black as they exploded.

"Eight Six. Eight Six. I have people in the trees," called one of the gunship pilots.

"Get them! Get 'em!"

"Rolling in."

The flight crossed the tree line, settling toward the ground. The gunships started their attack, their rockets firing and exploding in the forest. There were bright orange flashes and clouds of dirty brown smoke that seemed to strip the branches from the trees.

At that moment, there was a fireball in the center of the flight. A few of the choppers dodged right and left, diving for the ground to avoid the burning wreckage that had plunged to earth. Black smoke poured from it as flames shot into the sky. There was a single explosion as the fuel cells went up in a rolling ball of orange and yellow.

Over the radio came a dull monotone. "Chock Five exploded. I say again, Chock Five exploded." It sounded as if the man was reporting an everyday event.

Hornet Eight Six broke around, cutting back to the south so that he could see the wreckage. There was no movement near the helicopter.

"Ah, Three Seven, this is Eight Six. I see no movement near Chock Five. No survivors."

"Roger, Eight Six."

The rest of the choppers began to settle to the ground. The landing zone was alive with fire, door guns hammering at the base of the tree line. The M-16s of the grunts opened up from the cargo compartment doors. Some of the men had moved out onto the skids, hanging on to the legs of the troop seats, watching the ground come up under them. A couple of the choppers bounced in the rough landings, but as the skids skimmed the grass, the men leaped from the choppers, rolling for the little cover available on the landing zone. The sound of the firing seemed to penetrate the noise of the helicopter's blades and turbines, rising into the morning sky.

"Chock Seven is going down."

"Lead, this is Chock Eight. I'm breaking out. Four dead on board."

"Flight's taking fire on the left."

"Trail's taking fire from the right and left."

"Chock Nine is going down."

"Christ, Charlie's all over the fucking place."

"Flight's taking RPGs."

"Roger, I see them."

"Lead, you're down in the LZ and unloaded," said the pilot in Trail.

"Lead's on the go."

"Flight's taking heavy fire from the left."

"Lead, this is Trail. You want me to pick up the downed crews?"

"Negative."

"Chock Two is going down." In the background the two M-60 machine guns hammered away as the crew chief and door gunner tried to protect the chopper.

Suddenly there was silence on the radios. From his position in the C and C just fifteen hundred feet above the LZ and less than half a klick away, Gerber could see the destruction of the flight. There were fires burning brightly, the black smoke towering above them. Men were running around shooting into the surrounding forest. Tracers ripped into the enemy positions. Grenades exploded near the trees and more across the LZ as the VC retaliated. Tiny, almost innocuous-looking puffs of white, gray and black smoke, which hid the deadly shrapnel, dotted the LZ.

The remaining helicopters lumbered into the air, trying to maintain some semblance of formation. The door guns, which had fallen silent as the grunts had jumped into the LZ, opened fire again, raking the ground under them as the door gunners tried to get even.

"Lead, you're off with four," radioed the trail pilot, his voice hushed, as if awed by the situation. "Fire received all around." There was a pause and then, "My God, we've only four left."

AS THE LEAD HELICOPTER touched down, the world around it blowing up, Fetterman leaped from the cargo compartment into the knee-high grass. He took one running step and then dived for the ground. He rolled to the right, his weapon aimed at the tree line, which seemed to be alive with VC. Bullets snapped in the air over his head, cutting through the vegetation around him, and he heard them slam into the side of the aircraft.

Fetterman looked to the left and saw a soldier standing near him. The man's chest exploded, the blood splattering from his back, spraying the side of the helicopter. He threw his hands up, tossed his weapon into the air and fell forward. He landed with his face turned toward Fetterman, the unseeing eyes staring at him.

Fetterman tried to get up, but the enemy fire intensified, forcing him back to the ground. Then from behind came a gigantic roar as one of the choppers blew apart, showering the LZ with shrapnel, engine parts and red-hot debris. There was a grisly rain of body bits as the twelve men on the aircraft died. One leg, the thigh ripped and bloody, landed near Fetterman. It still wore its boot, which had held its brush shine.

Seeing the antenna of the RTO off to the left, Fetterman began to crawl toward it. He heard the lead chopper lift off, felt the wind of the rotor blades wash over him as they bit into the air, but realized that too many aircraft were left on the ground. Two of them were burning ferociously, the ammo for the door guns cooking off in a series of pops and snaps that sent the burning tracers tumbling through the sky. One of them was bleeding flaming JP-4 onto the ground, setting the grass and bushes ablaze, obscuring the southern end of the LZ with thick, choking black smoke.

As Fetterman reached the RTO, he found the company commander. He hadn't lasted very long. He had a neat round hole in his forehead. It looked like a black, bloodless third eye. His head was cradled in his helmet, which was filling rapidly with his blood.

The RTO was hugging the ground, as if he was trying to crawl into it. The side of his face was pressed to the dirt, and his eyes were shut as his mouth moved in silent prayer.

Fetterman grabbed the handset, blew into the mike twice to make sure the radio was working and broadcast, "We are taking heavy fire from the whiskey side of the lima zulu. Enemy is entrenched in bunkers. Sporadic fire from the north and the east."

"Roger," said a voice. Behind it was the popping of rotor blades and the firing of a machine gun.

Fetterman turned and tried to figure out what was going on around him. Each of the aircraft still in the LZ was empty, the flight crews and the grunts having abandoned them. Inside the burning cargo compartment of one, he could see a single man sitting on the disintegrating troop seat, the skin and fatigues burned away from his knees, which were showing the bone. There was a snap, like wood popping in a hot fire, and the head toppled from the neck.

Dragging his eyes from the grisly scene, Fetterman stared at the radio strapped to the RTO. The man had grabbed the whip antenna and was holding it so that it wouldn't stick into the air and give away his position. It was the only smart thing the RTO had done.

To Fetterman's right and left grunts fired their weapons. One or two burned through the magazines as quickly as they could while others cranked off shots one at a time. Scattered around were the bodies of the men who had not survived the combat assault. Some of the corpses were missing hands or feet or legs. Many of them had been killed when they had jumped into the grass.

The firing around him seemed to intensify as the enemy poured everything they could into the LZ. Machine gun bullets ripped up the ground or tore into the shattered helicopters, rocking them. For an instant Fetterman wondered if the mission had been compromised in some way, but the explosions of Chicom grenades and the pulsing of the automatic weapons drove the thought from his mind.

Fetterman wanted to assault the tree line. He knew they had to attack the VC in their bunkers to break up the integrity of the enemy, but the fire coming from the tree line was too murderous. If he didn't act soon, they would be overwhelmed. But if anyone stood, it was immediate death.

Then the gunships rolled in, firing rockets. At the very edge of the tree line, almost hidden in the verdant growth, a series of explosions walked slowly north. The fireballs destroyed trees and collapsed the bunkers, but it didn't slow the shooting. Emerald tracers from .51 caliber machine guns raked the LZ, bouncing around like giant green softballs. More tracers from the yammering .30s swarmed from the forest like angry bees. And then mortar rounds began to rain down, blowing up soggy chunks of damp ground in geysers of water and dirt.

At that moment, the situation began to deteriorate rapidly. More firing erupted on the northern edge of the LZ and then on the east as the enemy there realized there were men still on the ground. A deadly cross fire was woven like a net above the landing zone, and the men tried to dig themselves into the earth. They could not move because movement brought a dozen weapons to bear. Shooting from the Americans tapered off as they emptied their rifles and then refused to reload them.

One sergeant shouted at his men and crawled around, slapping at them. He kicked a soldier in the side of the head, knocking his helmet off. The man, who had been lying facedown, looked up and then raised his weapon. He fired it into the trees, the ruby tracers smashing into the front of a bunker but doing little damage. When it was empty, he dropped it and covered his head with both hands.

Fetterman keyed the mike again and said, "Dracula Six, this is Dracula Five, I have a fire mission for you. Will you relay?"

"Roger, Five. Say status."

"We're pinned down, taking heavy casualties. Cannot move off the LZ. I say again, we're pinned down."

"Understood," said Gerber on the radio. "Tell me what you need."

"Enemy is in bunkers all around us. Dug in good and deep. We need to have it on them. We'll need HE to dig them out."

"Roger," said Gerber.

The air at that moment was filled with shouts and bugles and whistles. The firing from the enemy remained at a high level, keeping the Americans pinned down. And then on the north, the first of the enemy soldiers appeared. The plan seemed to be to overrun the landing zone, killing all the Americans before they could get organized.

Fetterman tossed the handset at the RTO, who still hadn't moved. He grabbed his M-16 and began firing at the massing men. He screamed at the others, "Open fire! Open fire! Open fire!"

GERBER FELT THE BLOOD drain from his face as he listened to the radio transmissions from the flight and then from Fetterman. Men were dying quickly in the LZ, much more quickly than anyone had anticipated. Gerber was amazed that the voices of the pilots were so calm as they reported the destruction of aircraft and the deaths of their fellow soldiers.

He used the radio to contact Cu Chi arty and told them he had a fire mission: enemy in bunkers firing on American troops in the open. He needed HE to blast them out and give his men an opportunity to advance. The rounds would be dropping danger close, and he would spot.

He hit the button for the intercom and said, "We've got to get a second lift in there."

"Negative," said the AC. "Can't. We don't have the aircraft."

"We've got over a hundred men down there!" insisted Gerber.

"Captain, I'm not refusing to do it. I'm telling you we can't. We've lost over fifty percent of the helicopter assault force. We try to go in again and we'll lose everything else. It's too hot."

"If we don't move," said Gerber, "those men on the ground will die."

"Look, I'm trying to find replacement aircraft," said the AC. "We were told there wouldn't be other companies available until noon. Right now operationally we have ceased to exist. Too many helicopters have been shot too full of holes. We're pulling in everything we have."

"Can we evacuate the LZ?"

"Same problem. We'd never get the choppers out even if we had the aircraft to do it."

Over the radio came, "Shot over." It was the artillery officer at the base camp announcing that the first of the spotting rounds was on the way.

"Shot out," Gerber answered, the irritation unmistakable. He wanted to work out the helicopter problem, but needed to spot for the artillery. One more thing to do. He turned on the troop seat and looked out the cargo compartment door. He saw the fountaining explosion of the willie pete marking round.

"You're on target!" he shouted. "Fire for effect."

"Rounds on the way."

While he was watching the artillery do its work, he heard the AC on the radio talking to flight lead, giving them orders to pick up the blocking force at Cu Chi and transfer them to Trung Lap. He called Hornet Operations, telling them of the disaster on the ground and requesting the spare, the backup spare, the maintenance aircraft and anything else that was flyable. He didn't care where they got them, but they needed more aircraft immediately. And then he told the operations specialist to get on the horn and find more infantry troops. They were going to need everything they could get.

At that moment, another voice broke through the chatter on the radio. It was a young voice filled with fear. In the background Gerber could hear the intense firing that was rocking the LZ.

"We have wounded all over the fucking place!" the man shouted. "We need a Medevac. We need lots of them. We need help or we're all going to die."

Gerber hit his mike button and asked as calmly as he could, "Where are you?"

"In the fucking LZ, stupid! Jesus Christ, what the hell do you expect?"

Gerber was utterly helpless. He knew how the men on the ground felt. Their world had turned to shit, and there was nothing they could do about it. Most were trying to survive from one minute to the next, figuring they were about to die anyway. And each of them believed that anything they requested should be granted immediately. They were the ones who were pinned down and they were the ones who were dying.

The C and C turned again, and Gerber had to slide across the troop seat to look out. He saw the first of the artillery rounds erupt in the trees on the western side of the LZ. Two of them were long, landing fifty yards behind the bunker line, but the others fell among the enemy. The air around them was filled with flying debris, smoke, dirt and falling trees. But it did nothing to slow the enemy fire. Gerber could still see the muzzle-flashes of the enemy's weapons, the tracers slashing into the American position.

"Where the fuck are the choppers?" wailed the voice on the radio. "Get us the fuck out of here."

"Dracula Five, this is Six."

There was a moment's hesitation, and in that one moment, Gerber's imagination ran wild. In his mind he could see the dead, ripped body of Fetterman. But then came the answer.

"Go, Six."

"Say status."

"Fire from west is still intense. Artillery on target. Keep it coming."

FETTERMAN HAD NO SOONER made that last transmission when the VC and NVA who had been on the northern edge of the LZ attacked. They ignored the artillery rounds falling on their comrades in the bunkers on the west. They ignored the withering fire now coming from the Americans trapped on the LZ. They ran from the trees, their weapons at their hips, shooting as fast as they could pull the triggers, shouting and screaming.

An M-60 in one of the crashed helicopters opened fire, stitching the lead element with ruby tracers and hot lead. A dozen of the enemy fell. Then others dropped to their knees, their rifles at their shoulders, firing at the man in the chopper. The thin metal of the fuselage was pierced, and the Plexiglas in the windows shattered. Bullets tore into the soundproofing on the transmission wall, and the fuel cells were holed, leaking the volatile JP-4 into the LZ. But the man didn't stop shooting. With his left hand, he dragged the linked 7.62 ammo out of the can, feeding it into the weapon. His right held down the trigger so that he was firing one long, continuous burst. The barrel began to glow pink, but the man didn't let up. He poured fire into the enemy, thinning their ranks.

Suddenly he was hit in the shoulder. As he spun, a second round caught him in the back, punching through his body and hitting the chest protector he wore. That deflected the round, which ricocheted into one lung, lodging there. He dropped to the seat behind his weapon, coughed up a gout of blood and toppled lifeless to the dirt of the LZ.

But his bravery had slowed the enemy assault. Fetterman crawled to a palm log and pushed the barrel of his weapon over it. Carefully he aimed at the closest enemy soldier and squeezed the trigger. The round hit the man in the throat, nearly blowing his head off.

He aimed again and fired again. A VC staggered, spun and then fell. Fetterman kept shooting, watching the enemy soldiers die one by one. He saw blood spurt as the round struck, saw dust fly from the uniforms under the impact of the bullets, saw men collapse and heads fly apart, scattering bits of bone, blood and brain.

Around him the Americans began a steady resistance. One old sergeant ran around the LZ in a crouched position, forcing the men to use their weapons. He directed their fire, pointing to the enemy and ordering his soldiers to kill them. He organized the grenadiers so that they began a barrage of 40 mm grenades that landed among the attacking Vietcong, shredding them.

The increased intensity of the fire forced the enemy to retreat. They scrambled for the safety of the trees as more of the Americans brought their weapons around, firing at them with M-16s and M-60s and tossing grenades to reinforce the damage done by the M-40s.

As the enemy disappeared, leaving the bodies of their dead behind, the Americans turned their attention to the bunker line on the west. Artillery rounds were still falling there. The roaring of the shells as they passed overhead split the morning and were punctuated with detonations that shook the ground. They could hear the shrapnel ripping through the trees, tearing at them and shredding them. Fountains of earth, dirt and debris splashed into the air, but the enemy fire didn't seem to waver. The machine guns kept hammering and the AKs kept firing, holding the Americans on the LZ.

Fetterman turned and looked at the wreckage of the choppers behind him. The fires had burned themselves out, and the flaming fuel had ignited the wet grass and rotting vegetation on the ground. Near one of the downed choppers, Fetterman could see the blackened corpses of the crew, their bodies still smoking.

Firing erupted behind them then as the enemy in the bunkers on the east side of the LZ started shooting. Fetterman crawled toward one of the wrecked choppers and used it for protection. He watched for the muzzle-flashes and shot back at them. The men around him did the same until they were all shooting as fast as they could, burning through the ammo in sheer desperation.

9

TAN SON NHUT, SAIGON

In the conference room that had been made a temporary command post at Tan Son Nhut, Colonel Alan Bates listened to the growing disaster on the ultrahigh frequency radio that Sergeant Nolan had found and brought in. Nolan had spent an hour running wires to the antenna system on the roof of the building, but when he was finished they had communications with Gerber and Hornet Three Seven, who were in the Command and Control aircraft. They couldn't read the fox mike transmissions, but Bates hadn't been worried about that. After all, it was just a recon into the Hobo Woods to establish the presence of enemy soldiers operating there.

During the initial assault, Bates had heard virtually nothing. Now he sat quietly, staring at the glowing lights on the UHF radio control head and tried to will it to speak. Kit sat on the edge of her chair, her elbows on her knees and her head down, as if concentrating on a weighty problem. Both Nolan and Santini stood near the coffeepot, gulping down the muddy liquid as if it were ice-cold beer.

The first indication that something was terribly wrong was when Gerber came on the UHF and said, "Crystal Ball, Crystal Ball, this is Dracula Six."

Not liking the urgency in Gerber's voice, Bates leaped from his chair and snatched the handset from the side of the radio. "This is Crystal Ball. Go."

"Roger," said Gerber. There was a moment's hesitation, as if Gerber was trying to phrase his request properly, and then, "Be advised we have encountered stiff resistance. There was a large enemy force waiting for us. Request additional airlift support and ground support. Need Medevac and guns."

Bates stood staring at the radio, the sweat suddenly popping out on his forehead. He swiped at it with the sleeve of his uniform before he spoke again. "Understand. Will advise ASAP."

"Roger," said Gerber, his voice almost inaudible because of the rotor blades popping in the background. "We have stepped into it. The stars are not with us."

"Roger," said Bates. "Message received." He glanced around, pulled up a chair, then collapsed into it. The line about the stars could only be a reference to the conversation they had had prior to Gerber getting on the chopper. It told Bates that the situation on the ground was desperate. They had a large-scale fight that would undoubtedly draw media attention, the very thing he had been warned against.

Feeling that he had made a mistake, he turned and looked out the window, studying the clouds boiling in the western sky. He dreaded the next move but knew it had to be made. It would be bad enough informing the deputy assistant commander at MACV, General Davidson, of the problem, but if Creighton Abrams, or Westmoreland himself, heard about it through the grapevine or because some overzealous reporter told him, Bates could kiss his chance at a star good-bye.

"Santini," he said tiredly, "get on the horn to your boss and see if there's a Mike Force available." Bates was thinking that the American media wouldn't be interested in the movements of a battalion of South Vietnamese or Montagnards. They might be able to disguise the rescue operation that way.

"I think," said Santini, "we've got a Mike Force at Moc Hoa. Crusaders out of Tay Ninh could pick them up and transfer them into the Hobo Woods."

"Good." Bates began to brighten.

"Colonel," said Kit. "I could go as scout. I can lead them to the right place."

"No," countered Bates. "I don't think that's going to gain us anything. Hell, we can find them easily enough without a scout. It's not like they're hiding from us."

Kit was on her feet. "But I know the area. I can help them avoid ambush."

Bates shot a glance at Santini. The sergeant's eyes were darting from Kit to Bates. "The Mike Force won't need the help, but if you're going to send in some American units, she might be helpful."

"Nolan, I want you to call the brigade commander of the 25th and see what he has to commit to this. If we have the aviation assets to get Kit out to Cu Chi, then she goes in with them."

"And me?" asked Santini.

"You work with the Mike Force. I think you'll be more valuable here as a liaison."

"But, Colonel—"

"No," snapped Bates. "I want you here. You coordinate with the CO out at Moc Hoa and with Madden up at Nha

Trang. Once we get this organized, then we might shake you loose.''

"Yes, sir."

Bates pulled back the sleeve of his fatigue shirt and looked at his watch. "We have thirty minutes to get all this started. You men know what to do."

He stopped talking for a moment, a pensive look on his face. Santini and Nolan would be able to coordinate the rescue. They couldn't authorize it because that was Bates's job. But he had to see Davidson, at best, or Abrams, at worst. It was something that had to be done because if he didn't, neither officer would accept excuses.

That was typical of the military, he thought. Right in the middle of a big operation with the world turning to shit, and he had to drop everything to report to his superiors. Luckily both Santini and Nolan knew what to do. Bates could get his deputy, Major Quinn, to come up to supervise the preparations. There was actually nothing Bates could do for thirty or forty minutes anyway.

Bates spun and grabbed the handset of the field phone. He cranked it, waited and cranked again. When the clerk answered, he said, "Connect me with MACV Headquarters, Major Quinn's office."

"Yes, sir. Wait one."

A moment later came a voice that sounded as if it was coming from the other side of the universe. "Quinn."

"John, this is Alan Bates. I want you over here now."

"Over there being the conference room, I take it."

"That's right," said Bates. "You have fifteen minutes."

"Yes, sir."

Bates cradled the handset and turned to Santini. "I'm going over to MACV. I'll have a radio in the jeep set on 62.50. Anything happens, anyone gives you a ration of shit, you call me. I'll take care of it. One thing, though, you are not authorized to initiate the mission without talking to me."

"Understood, sir."

"I'll be either in General Davidson's office or in General Abrams's office. Something happens and you need me, you call. We'll smooth the ruffled feathers later."

"Yes, sir."

Bates forced himself from his chair and left the conference room without looking back. Outside the building he climbed into his jeep and leaned into the rear to turn on the radio mounted there, making sure it was set on the proper frequency. Then he unlocked the steering wheel and started the engine. Without paying attention to his surroundings, to the heat or sun, he drove through the gate and out into Saigon on his way to MACV Headquarters.

He left the jeep in the parking lot and walked to the gate, nodding at the armed MP stationed at the entrance to the building. For a moment Bates hesitated in the hallway, studying the bulletin boards with their posters dictating various military policies. He examined the one showing the officer ranks of all the services, noticing again there was a difference between the insignia worn by the navy and marines and the army and air force. Standing there, he realized he was delaying the meeting.

He climbed the stairs, feeling like a doomed man. He stopped in Davidson's office, only to be told the general was in a meeting with General Abrams. It was as if someone had asked Bates for the worst thing and then arranged it. It was bad enough having to face Davidson.

Bates left that office and turned down the hall, trying to remember what he knew about Abrams. General Creighton W. Abrams had taken over as the deputy in July. Already Abrams had developed a reputation as a man who hated the

Green Berets. He didn't believe there was a place in a real military organization for the dirty renegades who inhabited the Special Forces.

He walked down the second-floor hallway past hustling men and women, both Americans and Vietnamese who worked there. Bates took off his beret, rolled it up and jammed it into the side pocket of his jungle fatigues where it wouldn't be obvious. Outside the oak door that led into Abrams's office, he hesitated again, wondering if he should have changed uniforms, shaved or taken time for a haircut. Sometimes the brass had a habit of focusing on the trivial and ignoring the important. Bates had heard it described as being so busy stomping on the ants that you forgot about the elephants.

Bates sucked in his stomach and threw back his shoulders. There was nothing he could do about the sweat stains on his uniform or the gray-black stubble on his face. All he could do was hope that Abrams would be more concerned with the situation developing in the Hobo Woods.

He opened the door and stepped in. His first reaction was a feeling of déjà vu. The interior was as cold as the inside of a meat locker. Air conditioners built into the walls poured out frigid air. There were three clerks, two American males and one Vietnamese woman. A major sat to one side at a huge desk, working on a pile of papers. He had three in-out baskets on the corner of his desk, several black loose-leaf notebooks and an ornate pen and pencil set.

Bates ignored the others, his attention on the busy major. He stepped to the man's desk and said, "I have to see the general."

Without bothering to look up, the major said, "Oh, you do, do you?"

"That's right, Major," snapped Bates.

Now the major looked up. He was a young man with dark hair, light skin and dark brown eyes. He sat up straight and blinked rapidly, as if he had just left a cave and walked out into the bright morning sun.

"I'm sorry, Colonel," said the major. "I was expecting someone else. The general is busy right now. He's in a meeting with General Davidson."

"I'm sure he is," said Bates, "but you had better announce me because if you don't, we're both going to be in the shit locker. And I do mean shit."

The major stood, revealing that he was a short man. His fatigue uniform hung on him, and Bates wondered if he had been wounded recently and was given the job of aide while recuperating.

"Who shall I say is calling?" asked the major.

"Bates. Colonel Alan Bates."

"Yes, sir. Please wait right here." The major turned and knocked twice on the door before opening it. He disappeared inside and closed the door. Bates could hear nothing from the office.

Generals sure lived better than the rest of us, thought Bates as he looked around. The walls were paneled and held the standard captured weapons, including an RPD, an RPG-7 and an AK-47. The desks for the staff were wooden, and there was carpeting on the floor rather than the dirty bamboo mats that the rest of the troops had to live with.

Before he finished his survey, the door opened and the major said, "The general will see you now."

Bates turned and moved toward the door. As he passed the major, the man whispered, "Don't forget to report in a proper military fashion."

Bates entered the office, focused his attention on the general and moved across the plush carpeting to stand directly in front of the huge ornate desk. He stood at attention and saluted, saying, "Colonel Alan Bates requests to speak with the general."

Abrams was a burly, graying man who had, as a lieutenant colonel, led a tank battalion to the relief of Bastogne in the Second World War. He sat behind his gigantic desk and worked on a report. Finally he glanced up and tossed a salute at Bates.

"What can I do for you?"

"General, I thought I had better report that we've had some bad luck on an operation we're running in the Hobo Woods near Cu Chi."

Abrams jammed his pen into the holder and rocked back in his leather chair. He laced his fingers behind his head and said, "Go on."

"Yes, General. It seems that an airlift company we inserted on a recon and sweep has run into a large force of VC and NVA. At the moment, our people are pinned down in the LZ. We've countered with artillery and are trying to arrange reinforcements."

Abrams sat forward and leaned both elbows on his desk. "Casualties?"

"No reports yet, but I believe about half the helicopters were shot down on the first lift."

Abrams slammed a hand to the desktop. "Jesus H. Christ! I told you people to watch your step. The last thing we need now is a lot of adverse publicity. I told General Davidson to tell you that." Abrams shifted his attention to Davidson. "You did mention this to him, didn't you?"

For the first time Bates became aware of another man in the office. He glanced out of the corner of his eye and saw Davidson sitting to one side.

"Yes, General," said Davidson. "I briefed Colonel Bates on the entire political situation."

"General—" started Bates.

"Listen to me, Colonel," snapped Abrams, cutting Bates off. "I want you to understand the big picture."

"I know the big picture."

Abrams started to rise and then dropped into his chair. Quietly, almost calmly, he asked, "Are you trying to provoke me?"

"No, General."

"Then you shut up and listen. That's your only job at the moment. You listen and I'll talk. I don't want to hear a word from you. You understand that?"

"Yes, General."

"We've been trying to avoid a pitched battle with the VC and NVA for the past few weeks because of the political climate in the States. Two, three weeks ago, fifty thousand people were marching around the Lincoln Memorial, chanting. People are beginning to riot in the United States, and the Administration has wanted the news from here to take on a more positive note. You understand that?"

"Yes, General," said Bates. He had not moved since Abrams had slammed the desk. The interview was taking the path that he had feared.

"Now, how can we say that the war is going well if you come in here and tell me that you have men pinned down in an LZ? How can we say the war is going well with helicopters shot down all over the place. How many men are trapped in there?"

"No more than a hundred and twenty," said Bates.

"No more than a hundred and twenty," mocked Abrams. "A hundred and twenty. Christ, Colonel, if we don't get them out of there, it's going to be front-page news all over the fucking country. The President is not going to like the negative press about this.''

''Yes, General. I've authorized the CO of the Third Brigade, 25th Infantry to reinforce. I'm trying to get a Mike Force out of Moc Hoa into the Hobo Woods.''

''More of that Green Beret nonsense,'' said Abrams.

Bates chose to ignore the remark. He said hastily, ''My thinking was that to reinforce with a Mike Force might keep the media from learning too much about the operation.''

''Colonel, you've missed the point,'' said Abrams. ''Get those people out of there. Get them out now. I don't care how you do it, but I want everyone withdrawn and I want it now. No more troops committed to the battle, everyone out. Period. And then we can figure out what to do with you for this world-class fuck-up. Now you get out of my office and don't come back until you've resolved the situation.''

There was no response that Bates could make other than, ''Yes, General.'' He saluted and got out.

''LAST ROUNDS ON THE WAY. Tubes clear.''

Gerber keyed his mike and rogered the call. ''Understand.'' He looked out the cargo compartment and saw the final detonations of the artillery, mushrooming explosions that sprayed dirt and debris into the air. The dust hung over the LZ now like the remains of an early morning fog. In the bright sunlight, the shadows were dancing across the landing zone as the men scrambled for cover or fired at the enemy when there was a target.

When the dust cleared and the smoke dissipated, Gerber could make out the remains of the five choppers. One of them lay on its side, the cargo compartment yawning at him like the mouth of a sleepy giant. Two others were little more than smoking, blackened shells. Another sat on its skids, looking almost undamaged, except that the main rotors were hanging from the mast and touching the ground.

Over the radio came another frantic cry. "We have wounded! They're going to die! We've got to get them out! Get us a Medevac now!"

Gerber listened as the pilots in his chopper discussed it on the intercom. One of them said, "We might be able to get in and out before Charlie knows we're there."

Gerber pressed the button for the intercom. "If you're hesitating on my account, don't. You think you can get the wounded out. Let's do it."

"Yes, sir."

Gerber keyed his mike and said, "Dracula Five, this is Dracula Six."

"Go, Six," said Fetterman immediately.

"Can you give covering fire? We're going to try to evacuate the wounded."

"Roger, Six. Say the word."

"Open up with everything you have in six zero seconds." Gerber glanced forward and saw the aircraft commander hold up a thumb.

"Understood."

At that moment, the chopper broke down and away from the LZ. Gerber lost sight of it as they dived for the trees. They turned in a steep circle, gravity forcing him down in the seat, making him uncomfortable. They rolled out, heading south. Gerber searched the Hobo Woods through the windshield, marking the cloud of dust and smoke that hung over the LZ. They were racing straight for it.

As they got close, the VC opened fire. The first rounds caught them in the nose, and the pilot lost control. The windshield disintegrated, and the instrument panel blew apart. The chopper began a slow roll to the right, losing the little altitude it had gained. Gerber was thrown against the transmission wall with enough force to stun him. His left hand snaked out and grabbed the edge of the seat, securing himself there.

At that moment, the crew chief grabbed his M-60, but the force of the roll threw him against the bulkhead. The AC hit the mike and said, "Three Seven's taking fire and going down."

Gerber was staring at the deck of the cargo compartment when a portion of the metal exploded. Four rounds burst through, leaving gaping holes.

The aircraft then settled into the trees as the pilots fought the controls. The rotor blades shattered into clouds of splinters and dust as they hit the hardwood teaks and palms. The AC crushed the plastic grip on the cyclic as he keyed the mike and shouted, "Three Seven is going down."

The chopper crashed through woods and out into the open of the landing zone, hitting with its nose low. It bounced once and flipped on its side, stopping near the tree line. Fuel bubbled from the smashed tanks.

The shooting seemed to increase then. Hundreds of rounds were fired from everywhere, slamming into the helicopter. Stunned, Gerber tried to sit up and then felt hands grabbing at him. He shoved them away, momentarily unaware of what was happening around him. Then he recognized one of the faces peering down at him.

"Get me out, Master Sergeant," he yelled.

As they dragged him from the broken chopper, he saw that the aircraft commander had been killed in the crash. His blood had splattered the shattered remains of the windshield and instrument panel in front of him. He was slumped sideways in his seat, his head at an unnatural angle, his blank eyes staring at the greenhouse.

Once clear of the downed chopper, the men dropped into the grass, hiding. Gerber dived shakily to the ground near Fetterman and asked, "What's your situation?"

"Getting grim. Artillery held them up, but they're beginning to taste victory. And we're running low on ammo. I think we could punch out of here, but that would leave the majority of the wounded for the VC."

There was an explosion near them. A black cloud sprang up, masking part of the tree line. Gerber covered his head with his arms and listened as the dirt clods from the detonation rained down on them. He felt them pelting his back. Not hard enough to hurt, just hard enough so that he knew they were there.

"How many wounded?" he asked.

"We'd have to leave fifteen, maybe twenty," said Fetterman. "A couple of those are critical."

"No way," said Gerber. "You still got a working radio?"

"Yes, sir. One, anyway." He glanced at Gerber and grinned. "What the hell did you think you were doing, anyway?"

Gerber noticed the dirt smeared on his face and the look in his eyes. Fetterman was tired, and the strain had added years to his face. Now Gerber grinned and said, "We were going to Medevac the more seriously wounded."

"Yes, sir. You sure fucked it up."

BATES COULDN'T BELIEVE IT. He had stopped by his office and found thirty reporters in it, each of them shouting at the clerks, demanding to see the colonel. They were screaming that the public had a right to know and demanding that someone answer their questions immediately before the afternoon plane took off or they missed the satellite feed. Bates looked at his clerk, who shrugged and then disappeared through the open door.

The colonel held up his hands and shouted, "If you'll all calm down, I'll try to give you something!"

"Something, my ass, Colonel!" shouted a male voice. "I want to know what the fuck is going on."

"May I have your name and affiliation?"

"Ralph Richards, CBS."

"Mr. Richards, right now we have a company in contact in the Hobo Woods."

"Could you elaborate?" shouted an impatient female voice.

Bates pulled a handkerchief from his front pocket and mopped his face with it. "Your name?"

"Ellen Cain."

"Elaborate," repeated Bates. "All right. We have approximately one hundred and twenty men in heavy contact. As of this moment, we have very little information, except to say they are holding their own under adverse circumstances."

"What sort of circumstances?" asked a different male voice.

Bates was going to ask for a name but knew it wouldn't do any good. The reporters had the scent of a story, and there would be no stopping them. "I understand a number of helicopters have been damaged by ground fire."

"By damaged, do you mean shot down?"

Bates turned, searching for the questioner, but was confronted by a sea of faces. Most of them had microphones in one hand, which they shoved at Bates. A few were scribbling down everything that was said. Bright lights blinked on and off as the TV people tried for some film that would look good on the evening news.

"I mean damaged," Bates finally said.

"Colonel, you're being very vague. Does that mean the men have been wiped out?"

"Christ, no!" said Bates. "It means I'm not in touch with the men in the field—"

"Then they have been wiped out!" shouted someone.

"No!" snapped Bates. "It means the men in the field have other things on their minds right now. They're busy coordinating with the reinforcements, artillery and air strikes. We've been giving them a free rein, so our information is sketchy. Coordination is being handled at another location, not here. That's why I'm not in touch with them."

"May we have that exact location?" said an impatient male voice.

"No," said Bates. "The men there have more important things to do." The instant he said more important, he wished he had bitten his tongue. The press liked to be thought of as an important arm of democracy, not something to be put up with.

Apparently the reporters were willing to overlook the slight. One of them, shouting above the others, demanded, "Given the political situation at home, how do you think this will be received in the White House?"

"The political situation in the United States is the least of our concerns."

That brought a clamor from everyone as they all screamed questions at Bates. He stared at them, thinking of jackals after the lions had finished their meal. He stepped back and sat on his desk, wondering if he should shoot two or three of them.

When they quieted down, Bates began, "What I meant by that is we're concerned about our soldiers first. The political climate in the United States can wait until this situation has been resolved.''

"From your tone,'' sounded one of the women, "I assume this is developing into a defeat for the United States and its policies in Southeast Asia.''

"Christ!'' said Bates. "The only significance is that we have a stand-up fight with the VC and NVA. What we—''

"Can you prove that allegation?''

"Allegation?'' asked Bates.

"That there are members of the North Vietnamese army engaged in this conflict. I understand the NVA, while advising some of the local popular troops, aren't actively involved in the actual fighting.''

"What the hell kind of bullshit is this?'' asked Bates. "The NVA has been fighting alongside the VC for years. It's only members of your profession and the Communists in North Vietnam who deny it.''

"Then you have no proof?'' said the man.

Bates stood up. "That's all I have to say. When we have more information, I'll make sure you're briefed.''

"Colonel!'' shouted the man. "We'd like permission to go with the troops into the combat zone.''

"No,'' said Bates.

"You afraid of what we'll see?''

"No,'' said Bates. "Believe it or not, I'm afraid one of you might get injured or killed. Right now that's all we need—a dead reporter.''

"I'll take that chance,'' said one of the men.

Bates stared at the man, shook his head and then shouted, "Sergeant Benner, I want this place cleared.''

The reporters began screaming their questions again. Dozens of questions about the operation, about the policies, about the weapons, about the political climate filled the air. Bates responded by calling for the military police. As the black-helmeted men entered the office, the reporters filmed them and then began to reluctantly give ground.

As the MPs grabbed the arm of one woman, she shouted over the noise, "Alan Bates!"

He saw Robin Morrow being pushed toward the door by an MP. He snapped his fingers. "Sergeant, I'll talk to her."

That brought a storm of protest from the others, but the MPs ignored it, pushing them into the outer office. As the last of them disappeared and the door was closed, Bates said, "I hope you're not here as a reporter expecting me to give you something that I didn't have for the others."

"No," she said. "I wanted to know where Mack is."

Bates rubbed his face with both hands. He studied her for a moment, taking in the light cotton dress that she wore. Her hair hadn't been combed recently, there were dark circles under her eyes, and perspiration dotted her forehead.

"Listen, as far as I know, Mack is safe. Yeah, he's involved in that mess, but he's Ground Mission Commander—"

"Which means?" she asked. Her voice was quiet, subdued, as if she was frightened.

"It means he's in a helicopter over the battlefield, coordinating the activities."

"And Sergeant Fetterman?" she asked. "Is Sergeant Fetterman with him?"

"No, Robin. Sergeant Fetterman is on the ground."

He watched the blood drain from her face. It was an incredible thing, to see her suddenly turn pale.

"Then Mack's on the ground, too," she said. "He won't leave Sergeant Fetterman there alone. Somehow he'll end up on the ground with Fetterman."

Bates moved to her and took one of her hands. He studied her eyes for a moment, saw them fill with tears and said, "Don't worry, Robin, it's not that bad. Besides, we're going to pull them out. Orders."

She shook her head as if she didn't believe it. "Can I stay here?" she asked.

"As long as you want," said Bates, "but I'm going to have to leave you. I've things to do."

"That's all right. I'll be fine."

Bates pulled his hand free and moved to the door. He stopped, looked at her and then left. Benner had gotten the reporters out of the office, but Bates could hear them in the corridor. To Benner he said, "Get me a chopper. I'm getting the hell out of here."

"Yes, sir. Where are you going?"

"I'll stand by at Cu Chi, coordinate the effort from there and worry about the reporters later." He glanced at the sergeant and added, "You tell no one where I've gone with the exception of the commander or Abrams. He may want to talk to me."

"Yes, sir."

"And one more thing, don't talk to anyone you don't know. We've got so many reporters running around here now that you can't trust anyone." Bates shook his head. "I think I've already given them more than enough copy for one day."

"I understand," said Benner.

"I hope you do, because I have a feeling that things are going to get worse before they get any better."

10

THE HOBO WOODS

Gerber lay in the deep grass, fifty or sixty yards from the wreckage of his chopper. The firing from the woods surrounding him had tapered to sporadic shots. A single machine gun kept a steady stream of bullets crisscrossing above them. Around him the air was filled with the cries and moans of the wounded as three medics crawled from one injured man to the next. Fetterman was lying on his back by a palm log, working to load an M-79 grenade launcher. When he had it ready, he fired it over the tops of the downed helicopters.

For a moment everything was held in stasis. Trapped in the center of the landing zone, the Americans couldn't move in any direction. The enemy, secure in their bunkers and protected by the foliage, weren't going to mount an immediate attack. They shot when they had a target to remind the Americans they were still there.

Spotting one of the RTOs, Gerber began crawling toward him. As he approached, he heard over the radio, "Hornet Three Seven, this is Hornet Six. Say location."

When the RTO didn't move, Gerber grabbed the handset and said, "Hornet Six, this is Dracula Six. Three Seven is down in the LZ."

"Roger, Dracula Six." Gerber had a feeling that Hornet Six was not surprised by the information.

Gerber was about to request reinforcements, instructing they be put into the closest landing zone and march toward the rear of the VC bunker lines, but firing erupted again. The air was split by thousands of rounds. The Americans began a scramble to return fire, adding the hammering of their assault rifles to the cacophony. There were two explosions as grenades detonated. Fetterman rolled to his stomach, tossed away the high explosives and jammed a canister round into the chamber. He snapped the grenade launcher shut and waited.

The bugles sounded again, and there was a rising shout that turned into a cry of anguish. Fifty VC rushed from the woods, screaming and firing or waving their machetes above their heads as if waiting for a chance to chop through the Americans.

No one had to give a command to fire this time. The trapped Americans began to shoot as soon as they had a target, their ruby-colored tracers looking small and almost harmless in the bright late morning light. The red tracers crisscrossed with the green used by the VC as the firing increased until it seemed to be one long, sustained burst.

This time there was no hesitation by the enemy. They charged out of the trees, racing across the open ground until they were among the American positions. As the first men stood to fight, they were shot down, but then the two forces became mixed and the fighting was suddenly hand-to-hand.

Gerber was on his feet as one of the Vietcong ran at him, a machete held high. The man took a swipe at Gerber with enough force to decapitate him, but Gerber blocked the swing with his M-16. The machete smashed through the plastic stock, shattering it. Gerber thrust outward with his broken weapon, twisting the enemy's blade away from him.

He leaped back, and the VC came with him. Gerber turned to the side and aimed a kick at the enemy. The tip of Gerber's steel-toed combat boot caught the man in the crotch and lifted him off the ground. The soldier shrieked in pain as he fell to the earth.

Gerber spotted an abandoned M-16 and picked it up. As another VC came at him, Gerber aimed and pulled the trigger, but the weapon failed to fire. He worked the bolt, but that, too, was jammed and wouldn't budge.

He flipped the weapon around, holding it by the barrel, and swung it at the soldier. The light plastic stock slapped the VC on the side of the head and bounced off. Gerber jumped forward, jamming his forearm under the Vietcong's throat. He smashed the man's voice box and crushed his trachea. For an instant the VC fought Gerber, swinging a fist at him and catching him under the eye. Gerber staggered backward, his cheek swelling immediately.

The enemy soldier suddenly realized he couldn't breathe. He dropped to his knees, his face turning red and then purple. As he toppled on his side, his fingers clawed at his throat, leaving ragged, bloody welts. His eyes began to bulge, turning crimson as the capillaries ruptured.

After making sure the soldier was dead, Gerber worked at the bolt of the M-16. He dropped the magazine free and saw that a round had not seated properly. There was no time to fix it, and Gerber threw the weapon into the bushes.

He turned in time to see another VC rushing him. The man had his head down, as if watching his footing. The bayonet of his weapon was extended. He tried to impale Gerber, but the Special Forces captain grabbed the barrel of the AK-47. As Gerber jerked upward, the soldier pulled the trigger. A stream of shots cut through the air harmlessly, but the heated barrel scorched Gerber's palms.

The VC tried to wrench the weapon out of Gerber's hand. Gerber let go and snapped his elbow back, slamming it into the Vietcong's face. The nose shattered, spraying blood. The soldier dropped to his knees, and Gerber smashed the heel of his hand into the man's nose, splintering bone and driving them into the brain. The Vietcong died without a sound.

Around him the fight raged on. Men struggled with one another until one or both collapsed into the dry grass or onto the muddy earth. There were cries for help, screams of pain, shouts of anguish. The firing was sporadic between the clash of rifle barrel against bayonet and machete. Gerber ducked like a quarterback trying to shed a blitzing linebacker as a VC tried to knock him to the ground. The man fell, and Gerber's foot shot out, slamming into the base of the enemy's spine, snapping it. Then the American brought his heel down on the man's throat, and the VC died.

As Gerber dived for cover, a bugle sounded, was answered by another and another and was joined by a whistle. Gerber expected a fresh assault, but the enemy soldiers tried to disengage. The Americans kept the fight going, stabbing, punching and shooting. A few of them managed to break contact and tried to flee to the trees, but were cut down.

Slowly the intensity of battle tapered off as the two sides separated. The Americans fell to the ground as soon as they had driven off the attacking enemy. Firing from the bunkers erupted, but it was strictly for effect and to cover the retreat.

Gerber crawled toward the radio. He found Fetterman lying next to it, blood on his face and sleeve, but not badly hurt. Near him were the bodies of seven VC and NVA soldiers.

"You okay?" whispered Gerber.

"Fine, Captain." He grinned. "That was a mite closer than I care for."

Gerber nodded and grabbed the radio handset. He keyed it and said, "Hornet Six, this is Dracula Six."

"Go."

"Can you get us a Medevac?"

"Negative. Firing is too intense. Medevac would never get out of there."

"Say status of reinforcements."

"We have one flight airborne and on the way to pick up troops."

"Roger. Do you know the LZ a klick and a half from the Saigon River?"

"Roger that."

"Can you put the people into it and let them come to us? Break the ring?"

"Roger. As soon as we get them picked up, we'll get them there."

Gerber was going to say more, but the air was split by the roar of jet engines as two F-4 Phantoms screamed overhead, no more than a hundred feet off the ground. They climbed rapidly, turned and called, "Dracula Six, Dracula Six, this is Cobra One One. I have two fully loaded aircraft."

"Say ordnance."

"Roger. Have high explosives and napalm and 20 mike mike."

Gerber looked at Fetterman. "If we have them hit the western edge of the LZ, you think we can mount an assault on it? Get the fuck out of the open?"

"The flyboys do enough damage," said Fetterman, "we should be able to dig the VC out."

"Okay," said Gerber. He keyed the mike. "Put it on the western edge of the LZ, about five meters into the trees, south to north. Break to the west. HE and then napalm."

"Roger."

The roar of the jets faded for a moment, and then suddenly they blasted out of the south. The bombs fell from the aircraft as they dived at the ground, and an instant later the ground shook and the air vibrated. The explosion, near the center of the bunker line, just a few meters into the trees, erupted into the bright blue sky. The fountain of black dirt climbed nearly a hundred feet high.

That was followed immediately by another bomb detonation that threw so much debris into the air the men in the LZ lost sight of the bunker line and forest. The concussive force of the explosions washed over them, driving them down. A few of the Americans began to bleed from the nose and ears because the heavy bombs were falling so close.

Moments later the jets returned. This time twin canisters tumbled from under the wings. They bounced through the vegetation and then erupted into orange flames and black smoke. The heat from the napalm flooded into the bunkers and bled into the LZ. The Americans felt it and welcomed it. A quiet cheer rose from a dozen throats and then bubbled up until the men were screaming their pleasure.

As the heat began to dissipate, the jets rolled through again, their cannon firing 20 mm exploding shells into the smoking, burning hell they had created. The trees, bushes and vines collapsed under the onslaught. The ground seemed to boil with the activity.

Over the radio, Gerber heard the jet pilot break off, claiming they had expended their ordnance. With that, Gerber was on his feet, an M-16 in his hand. He waved at the trees and bellowed, "Follow me! Follow me!"

Almost as one, the Americans were swarming into the tree line, screaming and firing as they penetrated the ruined bunker line. Gerber crashed through the trees, his forearm up to protect his eyes. There were shouts around him, rebel yells bubbling from the Americans as they attacked.

Alone in front of the charge, Gerber leaped to the sloping top of a smoking bunker. As one foot slipped, he sprung again, landing behind it. Two VC appeared in the lopsided square of the door, fighting each other to get out. Gerber triggered his M-16, pouring a burst into the structure. There was a piercing scream of pain and then silence.

Before he could toss a grenade in, an NVA soldier rushed him. Gerber parried the thrust of the bayonet, forcing the weapon to the side. He kicked out, hitting the enemy in the knee. There was a pop of bone as the man fell to the left. Gerber put one round in the soldier's back. He was rewarded with a jet of blood as the man died.

He turned and saw a single VC running for the trees, fleeing for his life. He had thrown away his weapon, his helmet and his web gear. He was a lone man, in black shorts, the sunlight glistening on his sweaty body. Carefully Gerber took aim and fired. The impact seemed to lift the man a couple of feet into the air, then he dropped to the ground.

The battle ended quickly. The Americans fanned out, searching for the VC and NVA, but there weren't many left. They found some dead enemy soldiers—blackened lumps that bore no resemblance to human beings, smoking remains that stunk like burned pork.

Firing broke out from the north side of the LZ as the enemy there began to shoot. But now Gerber and his men had gained the protection of the trees. They returned the enemy fire, shooting at anything that moved.

Fetterman was yelling for the men to form a skirmish line. He dropped men from it to guard their rear. He shouted at them to hold their position there as he climbed into the smoking remains of a bunker. The palm logs that had protected it were overturned and burning. He spotted a trapdoor that hadn't closed properly and emptied a magazine into it. As he kicked the remains out of the way, he grabbed a grenade and dropped it through. A second later there was a muffled detonation, and smoke poured from the tunnel entrance as it collapsed.

He leaped clear and found Gerber with the RTO, talking rapidly to the pilots of the choppers.

Gerber gave the handset to the RTO. "We're off the fucking LZ."

"Yes, sir," responded Fetterman. "I just wish I didn't feel like we had jumped from the frying pan into the fire."

BATES SHOOK THE PRESS at the MACV compound and rushed back to the conference room at Tan Son Nhut. There he told Quinn that he was going to Cu Chi. When Quinn protested, Bates pointed out that he had been ordered to extract the men in the field and that he was going to supervise the operation. He told Quinn to cancel the Mike Force and then turned to look at the others. Both Kit and Santini had leaped up and demanded that they go, too. Bates, forgetting his earlier orders, had no real objection and told them to come along.

The chopper stood waiting at Hotel Three. This time there was no complaint from the sergeant in the terminal because Bates had the highest clearance. Abrams wanted the problem resolved, and a single call had cleared the way.

Bates, holding down his green beret on his head, ran across the grass and tarmac and leaped into the cargo compartment. He held out a hand to Kit and nearly jerked her arm from the socket as he pulled her up into the chopper. Santini was last, and the pilot pulled pitch even before he climbed on. In seconds they were out of the traffic pattern and heading northwest.

At Cu Chi they landed on the helipad belonging to the Black Barons. Bates got off, leaving Santini and Kit on board with instructions to find the rescue companies and join them. They were assembling on the assault strip near the runway.

Now Bates stood in the TOC of the 269th Aviation Battalion at Cu Chi. Radio operators and clerks were scurrying around. It was dim and dirty in the heavily sandbagged bunker. A chart on one wall showed suspected locations of the enemy forces. The commanding officer of the battalion, Lieutenant Colonel John Wetzel, was studying it carefully.

"I can bring in the Crusaders from Tay Ninh," he said. "That'll give us about twenty to twenty-five lift ships and three heavy gun teams." He looked at Bates and added, "If you want anything more, you'll have to coordinate with the commander of the Little Bears."

"You can take eight Americans on each helicopter?" asked Bates.

"In a pinch, with luck, ten. Since we're working close to Cu Chi, we don't need the fuel, so we can compensate for the weight that way."

"Two hundred men," said Bates.

"Two hundred, two fifty. Something like that," Wetzel said, "And I've talked to the CO of the 25th. He's got the men standing by on the assault strip. There's a company on standby at Trung Lap and a third at Dau Tieng. The only thing we have to decide is where to put them. And we have one company airborne now."

"How did you get this done so fast?" asked Bates.

"Hell, Colonel, I've got men down there, too. As soon as I realized what was happening, I started arranging for the infantry and trying to locate more aircraft. Now I've got to decide where to put them."

"Didn't Hornet Six have some thoughts on that?"

"Yes, sir. Said your man on the ground requested they use other LZs and work their way toward them."

"We've got to get those people out of there," said Bates.

"Out?" asked Wetzel. "We need to reinforce. We've got an opportunity to—"

Bates shook his head. "Orders are to get them out. As quickly as possible."

"But—"

"No buts, Colonel. These orders come from the top. We have to be careful on the deployment of the new forces and organize it so that they're out of there by dark."

Now Wetzel shook his head. "I don't believe it. We spend weeks searching for the enemy, and when we finally make contact we're ordered out."

"Those were my feelings, but they're not worth shit. We've got our orders." Bates looked at his watch and then confirmed the time with the clock on the wall. "How soon before we can get this show on the road?"

Wetzel moved to the map and checked it carefully. He looked at the LZs. "Twenty minutes at the most."

WHILE FETTERMAN WORKED his way up and down the captured bunker line, setting the surviving men in position to cover an assault from any direction, Gerber crouched near the smoking stump of a tree with the radio. He was on the frequency being used by the assault helicopter companies.

From the distant choppers came the disembodied voices. "Hornet Six, this is Lead."

"Go."

"IP in bound."

"Roger, Lead. Stinger Eight Six, you have the flight in sight?"

"Flight in sight."

Since he had watched a similar operation earlier, he knew exactly what was happening. The gunship was setting up to lead the flight into the landing zone while the other members of the team raked the tree lines with machine gun and rocket fire.

On the radio came, "On final."

There was the sound of machine gun fire behind the voice, but Gerber knew it was the door guns on full suppression. There were none of the other calls that suggested the flight was taking fire. And then there were several drawn-out moments of silence before, "Lead, you're down with ten. Negative fire reported."

"Roger."

"You have ten unloaded."

"Lead's on the go."

"Lead, you're off with ten. Negative fire."

"Flight, come up a staggered trail."

When that was done, Gerber keyed his own mike and said, "Hornet Six, this is Dracula Six."

"Go."

"Be advised we now hold the west side of the lima zulu. Have your men sweep south toward us."

"Understood. I will relay the message."

Gerber stood and moved along the bunker line. He avoided the areas of the worst damage, places where the earth still smoked, where embers glowed red and flames danced. In some spots 20 mm cannon had turned the earth up as if it had been plowed. Some men, using their entrenching tools, worked feverishly to dig out the collapsed bunkers, throwing the debris out and repairing them quickly.

Then, to the north, he heard an outbreak of firing—small arms punctuated by mortars and grenades. He turned to look but could see nothing. Fetterman appeared at his side. "Sounds like the reinforcements are being ambushed."

"Figured as much," said Gerber. "But that draws the pressure away from us. They've got all the support they can use. Now, if we can get a couple of other lifts in, we can spread the enemy out and deal with him piecemeal."

BOTH BATES AND WETZEL were standing in the TOC staring at the radios, listening to the combat assault being flown. There was nothing for them to see other than the glowing lights that indicated the radios were working, and the VU meters with their dancing needles.

Crowded around them were the men who normally inhabited the TOC, the clerks, the RTOs, the operations specialists. These were the people who handled the routine traffic of the day-to-day operations. Rarely were so many other members of the battalion involved in a hostile action. When it happened, it usually happened fast and the losses did not approach fifty percent. The morning's assault had been such a disaster that the men, normally making jokes about all the glory and medals gained by the flight crews, were quiet, listening to the radios. A somber mood hung in the TOC like a bad smell.

Wetzel took to pacing in front of the radio, his arms folded across his chest, one hand on his chin. Each time he passed the radio, he glanced at it, stopping only when there was a transmission.

Finally, hearing that the flight was out of the landing zone and there had been negative fire so far, Wetzel could stand it no longer. He looked at Bates. "You up to doing some flying?"

"What?" asked Bates.

"My helicopter. I've got enough communications gear in it to cover all the bands that everyone will be using. Hell, I think I could call the fucking White House if I wanted. We can get a look at the battlefield."

Bates hesitated. He didn't like the idea of crowding the skies with choppers carrying sightseeing brass. From the afteraction reports he'd read, he knew it created a problem. A unit makes contact, and everyone with a chopper and a radio arrives on the scene, although they have nothing to contribute.

"Look," said Wetzel, "we can get a better feel for what's happening on the ground, and we'll be in a position to Medevac wounded if that's needed."

"Okay," said Bates, nodding. "Okay. Let's do it." He felt a sudden rush of adrenaline. He wanted to sprint from the TOC and run out to the helipad where the chopper waited. Instead, he moved to retrieve his flak jacket and his weapon. He picked them up, slipped into the jacket and exited with Wetzel.

As they entered the bright sunlight, Wetzel turned to look at Bates, shrugged once and then took off at a run. Caught by surprise, Bates stood flatfooted for a moment and then raced after Wetzel.

They ran between a couple of sandbagged buildings and passed by one made of corrugated tin with a fancy entrance, marking it as the mess hall of the 269th. In front of it was an open area where two Huey helicopters stood. On the door was a white peace symbol and the words Peace Maker. As they approached, the crew chief leaped from the cargo compartment to untie the rotor blade.

"You can fly, can't you?" asked Wetzel.

"'Fraid not."

"Well, sit in the front anyway and don't touch anything." Wetzel opened the door on the right side of the chopper and then ran around to the left.

As Bates climbed in, the crew chief slung the blade around so that it was perpendicular to the fuselage. Wetzel took the ceramic chicken plate handed to him by the door gunner, put it on and crawled up into the chopper. He eased himself into the pilot's seat, put on the shoulder straps and threaded the seat belt through the loops at the ends. He buckled in, leaned over the console, rolled the throttle to the flight idle detent, slipped it back to the down side and then said, "Shit."

He sat up and flipped the switches on the panel over his head, turning on the generator, the start generator and the main fuel. With one gloved hand, he brushed the circuit breaker panel and pulled one of them out. He grinned at Bates. "Usually have a Peter Pilot do this. All I have to do is kick the tire and light the fire."

Finally ready to start, he yelled, "Clear," heard both the crew chief and gunner respond and pulled the trigger on the collective. There was a whine as the turbine began to wind up and the rotor blades began to slowly rotate, picking up speed as the noise grew to a roar.

Bates watched the instruments in front of him, the needles bouncing wildly and then settling down in the areas marked in green. After thirty or forty seconds, Wetzel sat up and pointed at the flight helmet hanging on the back of the armored seat.

Bates turned and put it on. He twisted the boom mike so that it touched his lips. He let the chin strap hang down, suddenly feeling like John Wayne. Using the knob on the front of the helmet, Bates lowered the visor.

Over the intercom he heard Wetzel say, "I'm turning on all your radios so that you can hear everything that is happening." He pointed at the control head on the console. "The first position is for the fox mike, second the uniform, and we don't bother with the other two. If you need to transit, you'll have to move that control knob, otherwise you'll be on the intercom."

"Got it," said Bates.

Wetzel grinned. "That means you have the controls of the helicopter, so don't say that unless you plan to take over the flying duties."

"Oh."

"Okay, I'm going to make contact with the tower and then we'll be out of here."

"That's great," said Bates, not really sure that it was.

11

THE ASSAULT STRIP
CU CHI

Kit and Santini slowly approached the grunts sitting on the ground near the assault strip. Most of them were talking quietly. They were aware of the problems in the Hobo Woods and knew they were going to be put into an LZ that would probably be hot. Each of them knew the chances of surviving the initial assault in such circumstances were fairly small. Each was secretly glad he wasn't a helicopter pilot who was forced to sit up front surrounded only by Plexiglas and looking like the biggest target in the whole world.

Near the center of the group, Santini saw a man kneeling near an RTO. A second man stood next to them, holding a map so the kneeling man could see it.

Santini touched Kit's shoulder lightly. "That should be the company commander. We'll go tell him we're here."

Kit nodded but didn't say a word. Secretly she knew the Americans would resent her presence. They were watching her as if she were a brightly colored serpent. Each of them would be waiting for her to turn on them. That was what separated Gerber from the rest of the Americans she knew.

Although he might believe the same thing about her, he hid it very well. She wasn't sure what his attitude was.

Santini stopped directly in front of the kneeling man, saw there were black captain's bars pinned to the collar of his dirty sweat-stained fatigues and knew he had guessed right. He waited until the officer gave the handset back to the RTO and then said, "Captain, I'm Sergeant Santini. I've been sent to help out."

The captain pushed his helmet back so he could see Santini. "Help out how?" He was a slight man with deeply tanned skin, a narrow face and almost nonexistent eyebrows. His eyes were washed out, almost lacking in color. He had a pointed chin with a puckered knife scar on it.

Santini jerked a thumb over his shoulder. "I've a scout who is familiar with the Hobo Woods."

The captain turned to stare at Kit. He nodded once. "How come she knows so much about it?"

"I didn't say she knew a lot about it, only that she's familiar with the area. She's volunteered to help us once we get there."

"Okay, Sergeant. Tell you what. I'll put you and your friend on the lead bird. Once we're on the ground, you can run around and see if there is anything you can do to help."

"Yes, sir."

"Other than that, you and your friend stay the fuck away from me. I don't want you stumbling all over me. You got that, Sergeant?"

"Yes, sir."

"Now get the fuck out of my sight."

Santini moved to the rear and said to Kit, "We're all set now."

"Sounds like he was delighted to have our help," she said quietly.

"Don't worry about it. He's got a lot on his mind, and we've just added one more thing. He'll come around once we're on the ground and he has a chance to see how valuable you can be."

Before she could answer, they were interrupted by the approaching helicopters. They hovered from the active runway in a swirling storm of dust. As they touched down on the assault strip, the grunts swarmed onto them, and in seconds the choppers were ready for takeoff.

THE FRANTIC ACTIVITY had slowed as the Americans cleared the damaged bunkers of debris and established a line of defense. It was a short line, anchored on one end by two M-60 machine guns backed by an M-79 grenade launcher, and on the other by a single M-60 and four M-79s. The badly wounded were in the center of the line, set in a crater that had once been a large bunker, where they would have the best protection.

The walking wounded, the men who were not badly injured, were scattered throughout the line to provide additional support.

Gerber, and the PRC-25 taken from the body of the RTO, were near the center of the line in another blackened bunker. The logs that had roofed the bunker were now stacked around it, providing added protection. Wisps of blue smoke curled from the ends of the palm logs.

Gerber had set the radio in one corner, the antenna sticking above the ground. He had turned the volume up so he could listen to the various helicopter and infantry companies as they moved into the area. Apparently Hornet Six had gotten one lift company into the air and another was about to take off. All that had happened during the air strike and the assault on the bunker line.

As far as he could tell, other infantry companies had been lifted from Dau Tieng to Trung Lap at the edge of the Hobo Woods and were standing by there. Still others had been marched to the assault strip at Cu Chi where they waited for pickup, and more were standing by at Tay Ninh in case they were needed. Gerber had even heard that one armored infantry company was racing along Highway 237 where it would stand by to lend support if the infantry couldn't punch through.

In the distance, he could still hear the firing of the company that had landed in the LZ closer to the Mushroom, but it had tapered significantly during the past twenty minutes. Closer to him, Gerber had only heard an occasional shot, sometimes a burst from an M-16 or an AK-47. Gerber suspected the majority of the NVA and VC had broken off and were now fighting with the relief company. If he hadn't been responsible for protecting the wounded, Gerber would have assaulted the rear of the enemy.

Now, on the radio, he heard, "Hornet Six, this is Crusader Lead."

"Go, Crusader Lead."

"I have taken up an orbit in the vicinity of Ben Suc," said the pilot.

"Understood. Hold there."

"Roger."

A moment later came the message, "Hornet Six, this is Hornet Two Six. I am on the ground at Trung Lap and loaded. Ready to take off."

"Roger, Two Six. Wait one."

There was a hesitation, then a new aircraft joined the parade. "Hornet Six, this is Smoky. We're in the AO."

"Roger, Smoky."

"Say instructions."

"Point man is down in the area of the Mushroom. Can you cover him?"

"Roger."

There was a moment's silence while the smoke ship communicated with the rescue force on the ground and the gun team working with the grunts. From them he received instructions and coordinates. Then came the call, "Smoky's rolling in."

Again Gerber was left with his imagination. He had seen the smoke ships work before. They were Hueys with rings attached to the exhaust. Oil was injected into the stream of hot gases, which caused them to smoke heavily, laying a thick white cloud into the trees or at the edge of a landing zone and covering any movement made by the ground troops and the landing helicopters. The smoke screen only lasted for a minute or so, but for that minute it provided some protection for men or aircraft caught in the open.

"You ready for your run, Smoky?"

"Roger, Eight Six. I'm rolling in now."

Behind the sound of the voices was the hammering of a machine gun.

"Smoky, you're taking fire from the rear."

"Roger, got it."

"Ah, Smoky, there's a bunker sitting twenty or thirty to the west. Do you have it?"

"Roger."

"Point man is lying there. Can you cover so someone can get to him?"

"Rolling around again," said Smoky.

There was silence on the radio. Gerber turned his attention to the LZ in front of him. There was no movement. He could see bodies scattered around it, the wreckage of the choppers that were no longer burning and the equipment that had been dropped. Rifles, bayonets, rucksacks, helmets, knives, canteens and entrenching tools littered the landing zone so that it looked like a dumping ground.

Over the radio came, "Smoky, they couldn't get to him. Can you make another run?"

"Roger."

"Eight Four, this is Eight Six. Hose down the tree line to the south, but do not cross the stream. We're taking some sporadic fire out there."

"Roger."

"Hornet Six, have the ground troops pull back until Smoky's made his run."

"Roger."

"Hornet Six, this is Two Six."

"Go."

There was a squeal as two or three men tried to use the same frequency. When it died, Hornet Six said, "Say again, Two Six."

"Roger. We'd like to take off."

"Negative. Hold there. We have artillery going into your LZ in one minute. Wait for instructions."

Then it seemed that everything disintegrated. A shout came over the radio. "Smoky, we've got a fifty. Break right!"

"Breaking right!" In the background came the sound of machine guns firing.

For a moment there was silence, and Gerber wondered what was happening. He turned so he could look at the radio, almost as if willing it to speak to him, and then glanced back into the center of the landing zone.

Finally there was, "I think that's got him. Smoky, can you make another run?"

"Christ," was the response. "I've smoked the whole damned grid square."

"We need smoke in front of the bunker."

"I was doing pedal turns over it," came the reply. "What the hell do you want?"

Before he could answer, someone broke in and said, "ADF."

Gerber snapped his head around to stare at the radio. It seemed incredible to him that anyone would say that in the middle of everything else that was happening.

Then, as if no one had heard, Eight Six said, "Smoky, make your run."

"Roger."

And then, "They've got him. Eight Four, hit the fucking bunker now."

For some reason Gerber felt like cheering. The whole thing had been like listening to a story on the radio, but instead of being fiction this had been real.

At that moment artillery began to fall to the east. He couldn't see the explosions because of the trees, but he could hear the rounds landing, feel them through his feet.

From the radio came, "Hornet Two Six, this is Hornet Six. Take off to the south and stay south of Trung Lap. I'll want you at the IP in two minutes."

"Roger."

"Crusader Lead, this is Hornet Six. You'll be landing in three minutes."

"Roger."

Gerber grinned then. In less than five minutes the world was going to turn brown and smelly for the Vietcong.

WETZEL AND BATES ORBITED west of Trung Lap, away from the Hornet flight, watching the show in the Hobo Woods. From their position and altitude they could see the smoke ship making its numerous runs until the whole damned grid square, indeed, looked as if it had been smoked. The dirty white cloud settled slowly to the ground to cover everything, masking the grunts as they plunged into it to rescue the fallen point man. Although Bates and Wetzel couldn't see the rescue, they saw the green tracers lancing through the cloud and the ruby ones fired in return. Moments later they saw the men, hunched over, run from the smoke, dragging the wounded man with them.

As soon as they were clear, another helicopter swooped in and landed behind another veil of smoke to pick up the wounded man. Within seconds the dust-off ship was out of there, racing low level for the 12th Evac Hospital at Cu Chi.

With that taken care of, the arty prep started. Bates had the best seat in the house. Although he couldn't see the guns that were firing, he could see the spectacular results. The center of the LZs seemed to explode. Fountains of black, brown, gray and silver erupted into the sky and then slowly fell back to earth.

Over the radio came, "Last rounds on the way."

Wetzel turned his aircraft east and joined the rear of the flight, staying a half klick behind them. He had no plans to land, just watch.

Then there was, "Last rounds on the ground."

From there it was a normal combat assault. The gunship appeared to lead them in. Two more joined them on the right and left flank, and as the first ship flew over the LZ to drop its smoke grenades, the others began to fire rockets into the trees. Each of the door guns opened fire, raking the base of the tree lines that bordered the landing zone.

As they got closer, flickers of light—the muzzle-flashes of AKs and RPDs—appeared in the shadows of the forest. The red tracers of the door guns and the orange detonations of the rockets' warheads slammed into the enemy positions, silencing some of them.

Wetzel broke away from the flight as it passed over the edge of the trees on its approach. Bates twisted in his seat, looking back at the landing zone. He saw the aircraft touch down, the grunts leap from each side of the cargo compartments and then dive for cover.

"You're down with ten. Fire from the right," said the pilot in Trail.

"Roger. Lead's on the go."

As the choppers lifted off, the grunts were on their feet, firing their weapons and charging into the trees. For a moment there was return fire and then almost nothing. Bates could see men running through the trees, dodging for cover as the Americans gave chase.

"Lead, you're out with ten."

"Roger."

A moment later, Lead radioed the Command and Control and told Hornet Six that the grunts were on the ground and the flight was out. As he finished his transmission, Crusader Lead made the same call. Hornet Six, using a UHF frequency coordinated with Cu Chi and Dau Tieng, ordered the armored infantry, two companies with APCs, to begin the sweep to the north.

Bates looked at the map spread out on his lap. Gerber's LZ was near the center of the Hobo Woods. The company originally intended to be a blocking force, the one with the wounded point man, was on the north and again sweeping south. The Hornets had just put a company in on the southeast, and the Crusaders had gone in on the east. Now the armored cavalry was moving north. It all had the look of several hammers coming down on an anvil, and that anvil was Gerber's tiny force defending a series of bunkers taken from the VC.

KIT SAT ON THE EDGE of the troop seat, looking at the ground as it flashed by below. Santini sat beside her, a hand on her shoulder as if holding her in place. The grunts on board were either studying the ground or checking their weapons. Almost none of them were paying attention to her.

She held an M-1 carbine, a weapon that had been used in the Second World War. She had only two spare magazines, but she didn't plan to use it that much. Her main concern was to get the company moving toward the landing zone where Gerber and his men were trapped.

Far out to the west was an area that was first rice paddies, then woods and finally a single open area that was going to be their landing zone. It was a klick from the one used by Gerber, and as she stared at it, the ground exploded. Geysers of dirt erupted and then cascaded back. There were black, brown and silver jets climbing upward and raining down.

Around her, the men had shifted so they could watch the arty prep. The chopper banked, and then the crew chief yelled at them, "We're on our way in. Get out quickly."

One of the grunts leaned around her and shouted, "Is the LZ hot?"

"Negative," yelled the crew chief. "Last reports are that it's cold, but be ready."

Santini squeezed her shoulder. When she glanced over at him, he smiled, then leaned toward her so that his lips were near her ear. "Couple of minutes."

She wasn't sure what he had said but nodded her agreement. This wasn't a situation she liked, heading into combat with men she didn't know and who didn't trust her. But then, it was the only way she could get into the action, and she might be able to find a quick way to get them to the LZ where Gerber was trapped. She might be able to keep them from walking into danger.

To the right, slightly below her, she watched another helicopter approach and fall into the formation. It seemed to surge ahead and then the nose dumped. Puffs of smoke appeared at the rear of the pods, and orange fire jumped from the front as the rockets were fired. Kit didn't see where they hit because they landed too far ahead of the chopper.

Suddenly her helicopter seemed to drop out of the sky as the door guns opened fire. Streams of red tracers danced into the forest at the edge of the LZ, but there was no return fire. The ground rushed up, and they were thrown back and then forward as the chopper hit the ground. The door guns fell silent, and the skids touched the soft earth. Kit leaped into the tall wet grass, fell to her knees and ducked her head, waiting.

A moment later a rush of wind tried to push her to the ground as the helicopters lifted. As they crossed the tree line, their door guns opened fire, tongues of flame lashing at the vegetation.

And then it was silent in the LZ. She couldn't hear well now that it was quiet. The roar of the turbines and the hammering of the guns still echoed in her head. But the men were on their feet, sweeping out of the sunlight of the landing zone, entering the shadows of the forest, fanning out, and then coming together as they began to push toward the trapped men.

GERBER SPENT THE AFTERNOON waiting for the reappearance of the VC. For an hour he could hear the sound of gunfire around him, the noise getting closer. The radio kept him advised of the progress made, and although they had been taking sporadic fire for most of the afternoon, there hadn't been a rush of the enemy to try to dig them out.

Gerber leaned against the crumbling, blackened earth of the bunker, watching the landing zone. He heard a noise to the side and glanced at Fetterman as the sergeant slipped into the bunker with him. Fetterman's uniform was now covered with ash, and it was almost impossible to tell the original color. His face was smeared with dirt, except for a single white patch near his right eye where he had rubbed away the dirt and the sweat had dripped from his hair.

"Captain," he said, "I think we've got a problem."

Gerber couldn't help grinning. "Just one, Master Sergeant?" he asked.

"Just one of importance. I've been working my way through here, and it doesn't seem the flyboys killed enough of the VC. There was a sizable force in here, and when we attacked, it took very little effort to push them out."

"The point."

"The point, sir, is that I think this place is honeycombed with tunnels, just like that complex we found about a year ago before our trip to Hong Kong."

Gerber dropped his eyes and searched the floor of the ruined bunker. There was nothing obvious about it: torn-up bamboo matting, broken and splintered logs that had been used to cover it and hold back the dirt sides and quite a bit of debris from the bombing and napalm.

"You're suggesting?" said Gerber.

"I'm suggesting that the majority of the enemy we were facing escaped into the tunnel system, that they're all safe underground."

Now Gerber stared at the bunker floor as if it had suddenly come alive and was crawling with snakes. "We're going to have to dig them out."

"I suggest we search the bunkers for the bolt holes and trapdoors and drop grenades down them. We'll collapse some of them that way."

"But we won't seal them in," said Gerber.

"No, sir. We'll just keep them from popping up in the middle of us right now."

"You know what this means, don't you?" said Gerber. "We've got to get out of here by dusk or the VC are going to slip in among us and start cutting throats."

"Yes, sir," said Fetterman. "That's exactly what it means."

AGAIN, AS HAD HAPPENED so often earlier in the day, the artillery at Cu Chi and two fire support bases began to drop rounds into the center of the LZ. When it ended, Wetzel and Bates saw the gunships begin their run in.

Bates glanced at the clock in the center of the instrument panel. It was now 2:00 p.m. Bates couldn't believe it. Time seemed to have stood still. The sun was beating in through the Plexiglas of the helicopter, heating the interior so that he was bathed in sweat. He had hoped they would be cool once they reached altitude. Everything swirled around him, the heat, the crawling of the second hand on the clock, the radio calls and the firing. With all that he was convinced it should have been later in the day, and yet when he thought about it, he realized it couldn't be.

He touched the mic button near his foot. "How fast can we get all those people out of there?" he inquired.

"You've four companies on the ground or about to be on the ground," said Wetzel. "If there is no resistance in the LZs, we could have them out and back at Cu Chi in less than an hour."

"And if it's hot?"

"Christ, Colonel, who can say? It depends on the enemy and what he does."

"But we've got to get them out by nightfall."

"Why? We can resupply them so they can remain in the field. That's no problem."

"Colonel," said Bates, "I have been ordered to make sure that everyone is out of there by midnight. I was ordered not to commit any more troops to the battle, just to get the men in contact out of there."

"That makes no sense." Wetzel's forehead was creased into a frown.

"Doesn't have to make sense," said Bates, "because those are my orders." He hesitated and then added, "From the highest level. The very highest."

Wetzel looked at him and then back out the windshield of the aircraft. "I understand."

12

THE HOBO WOODS

For an hour Gerber listened to the sounds of the firing as it came closer and closer. At first it was something at the edge of his hearing, dull pops and snaps that suggested a fire-fight. Then, as the rescue teams pressed nearer, the shooting between the forces defined itself.

Four columns were approaching. The one from the north that landed first had been momentarily pinned down by an ambush but was now on the way again. Most of what Gerber could hear was coming from that direction. The two to the east were meeting little resistance. Finally there was the armor company coming up from the south.

As those fights built and then waned, Gerber realized the sniper fire they had been taking for an hour had stopped. The enemy, realizing that more Americans were on the way, had suddenly faded from the landscape. Gerber worked his way up and down his line, checking the bunkers and warning his men about the trap that Fetterman had discovered.

Then, in the trees on the opposite side of the LZ, almost hidden behind the wreckage of the helicopters, he saw more of the enemy. They were moving through the trees, dodging in and out of view. Around him, the Americans began to shoot as the targets exposed themselves. At first it was single-shot, one man firing the moment he saw something. Gradually it grew into a continual rattle of small arms.

All around him the men were shooting, some of them on full automatic. There was a ripple of firing to the right and left. Across the LZ, the vegetation vibrated with the impact of the rounds. Bark and leaves stripped from the trees floated to the ground.

There was very little return fire. An enemy soldier ran from the tree line and leaped into the rear of one of the downed helicopters. It looked as if he was trying to pry something from the inside of the cargo compartment. Gerber didn't care what he was doing. He shot him once, watched him drop into the grass and then fired again as the man tried to escape.

And then, for an instant, there was a pitched battle. The enemy on the opposite side of the LZ turned their weapons on the Americans, firing everything they had. RPDs ripped through the afternoon, kicking up huge gouts of dirt. AKs rocked the bunker line, forcing the Americans to dive for cover. Grenades were thrown but fell short, exploding one after another until the opposite tree line was obscured by the drifting dust and dirty smoke. The smell of cordite hung heavy in the air.

Just as suddenly as it had begun, the firing ceased. One moment the enemy was running through the trees, firing, yelling, screaming, and the next, he was gone, as if he had vanished into thin air.

Gerber realized what had happened and yelled, "Cease fire! Cease fire!"

The rattling of the weapons tapered off and then fell silent. Gerber changed magazines, keeping his eyes on the other side of the LZ. He waited, listening, and finally saw a flash of movement. He aimed at it but didn't shoot. Instead, he lowered his weapon.

There was a sudden burst of static from the radio, and the newly appointed RTO said, "Captain Gerber, there's a message for you."

Gerber took the handset, consciously stopped himself from blowing into the mike and said, "This is Dracula Six."

"Roger, Dracula Six, this is Green Giant Six."

"Go, Green Giant."

"Be advised that we have pushed the Victor Charlie to the edge of your lima zulu. Contact with the enemy is now broken."

"Roger."

"In six zero seconds we will enter the lima zulu. Please hold your fire."

"Roger," said Gerber. "Can you throw smoke?"

"Smoke out."

"ID yellow."

"Roger, yellow."

"Wait one and then come ahead." To the men near him, Gerber called, "Hold your fire. Reinforcements have arrived. Spread the word." He heard the men passing the instructions up and down the bunker line.

Then, in the trees on the other side of the landing zone, he saw more movement—shadows and shapes flashing among the trees as the men there moved east. A moment later a shape burst into the landing zone, and Gerber saw that it was an American soldier.

"Don't shoot," Gerber ordered again, just to be sure. "They're Americans."

For a moment time seemed suspended. Gerber was convinced, in that moment, that both sides would open fire. But it didn't happen. Instead, there was a single cheer from one of the men in the bunkers, and then another as they realized that one of the columns had punched through to them.

Slowly the men came from their defensive positions. One by one they entered the LZ again. A few of them rushed across it and leaped into the woods on the other side.

Gerber followed them and ran into the trees. Almost directly in front of him, he spotted Santini. As he moved toward the Special Forces sergeant major, he asked, "What in the hell are you doing here?" Before Santini could answer, Gerber heard a feminine voice to his right. He spun at the sound of it. "Kit?"

She grinned at him. "I have come to collect on the dinner you owe me. Last time you ran out on me."

Gerber noticed that several of the Americans were laughing at him. He didn't like talking about personal problems in the middle of the damned jungle, or rather the damned woods, especially when there had been enemy soldiers all over the place only moments before.

"Glad you could make it," he said.

Kit moved closer. "Do not let your enthusiasm run wild with you, Captain."

Before he could respond, more of the men were sweeping through on line. To the right, he caught a glimpse of a waving radio antenna and hurried toward the man walking near the RTO.

"Glad you made it, Captain," said Gerber as he approached.

"Glad you were still alive," said the man.

IT TOOK THEM TWO HOURS to sweep through the surrounding forest. While they were clearing it, Medevac choppers came in to take out the wounded. Resupply choppers landed, bringing more ammo, fresh water and medical supplies to be used on the men not seriously wounded. A Chinook took out one of the lightly damaged helicopters, the crew rigging it so it could be slung from the landing zone. The other downed choppers were rigged with explosives so they could be destroyed.

Around them, as the other columns worked their way toward the LZ, Gerber and his men could hear the sporadic bursts of AKs, M-16s and RPDs. Throughout, grenades punctuated the fighting, which was always brief.

Gerber and Fetterman, using the fresh troops of Green Giant Six, put security patrols out, but the men made no contact. Finally the sporadic shooting to the north tapered off to nothing. Moments later the column entered the landing zone, bringing the number of Americans there to nearly three hundred.

Within minutes they could hear the rumbling of the APCs as they pushed their way through the light growth of the Hobo Woods, crushing the skinny trees and scraggy bushes beneath their tracks. They halted fifty to sixty yards to the south and set up their own perimeter, but a patrol made its way into the LZ.

The men worked their way around the landing zone, searching the bunkers on the north and west for weapons, documents and bodies. They destroyed whatever they found.

Gerber took the opportunity to use the radio. "Hornet Six, this is Dracula Six."

"Roger, Dracula Six. Go."

"Can you coordinate for a resupply, bringing in more ammo and water? We plan to remain here and sweep to the west tomorrow."

"Dracula Six, this is Black Baron Six. Be advised that I have Crystal Ball in orbit with me," interrupted a new voice.

Gerber looked at the radio in surprise. "Roger, Black Baron. Can you relay to Crystal Ball?"

"Dracula Six, this is Crystal Ball."

Gerber was tempted to shout a hello at Bates, but knew it wasn't proper military procedure. Instead he asked, "Did you monitor my transmission?"

"Roger. Be advised that airlift is inbound your location."

"Understand airlift?"

"Roger. You will arrange the ground forces for immediate extraction. Do you copy that?"

"Roger," said Gerber. He frowned at the radio. There were a dozen questions he wanted to ask, none of which he could transmit. He keyed the mike, hesitating before he spoke. "We'll be ready for extraction."

He turned and saw Fetterman standing near him. "What the fuck gives, Captain?"

"Haven't the foggiest, Tony. Form one of the companies on the western side of the LZ for extraction. Have them stand in the trees to give the choppers all the room they can. And have one man stand by to act as guide for Lead." Gerber almost told Fetterman about the discussion he had had with Bates, almost told him about Bates's warning to avoid a major firefight. He had hoped the circumstances would take care of the problem. Apparently that hadn't happened.

"Yes, sir," said Fetterman, interrupting his thoughts.

"You talked to the engineers?" asked Gerber, dragging his mind back to the LZ.

"Yes, sir."

"They rig those choppers with a delay fuse so they'll blow as we get out of here?"

"I don't know, sir. I'll find their NCO and tell him that's what you want."

Gerber stared at the grimy master sergeant for a moment. Fetterman's uniform was now completely black with dirt and ash. There were sweat stains under the arms and down the front. One sleeve was ripped away showing the almost pristine whiteness of a bandage wrapped around his left forearm. Even in that condition, Fetterman looked happy.

"It was a close fight, Tony."

"Yes, sir." He laughed once. It was almost a snort. "And they're pulling us out before we can follow up on it. Just like they did a year ago."

Gerber turned and raised a hand to his forehead and stared toward the sun, ignoring the remark. Suddenly he realized how tired he was. It hadn't been an easy day. "We've got a couple of hours of light left. Guess they want us out of here before dark."

Now Fetterman shook his head, almost in disbelief. "Damned brass can't figure out that we should operate in the dark, just like Charlie. We'll never win this damned daylight-only war."

"Ours is not to reason why," said Gerber.

"A great philosophy for the Light Brigade in Crimea. Not so great for the U.S. Army in Vietnam."

"But orders are orders."

AN HOUR LATER Gerber and Fetterman, still dressed in the dirty wet uniforms they had worn in the field, were sitting in the mess hall of the 269th Combat Aviation Battalion at Cu Chi. Bates, in a fresh uniform, was with them, sipping coffee from a chipped mug.

The mess hall was certainly better than anything he had seen in a while. It was completely enclosed by dark paneling. Since there were no windows, it was artificially lit and air-conditioned. Apparently the CO of the 269th didn't have the pull the generals did; he had two large fans, one in each corner near the "head" table to help with the cooling.

Except for the head table, which was covered with a clean white cloth, and place settings for seven officers, the rest of the room was filled with four-man tables. They didn't have cloths or place settings.

Gerber, anger etched on his face, leaned forward, resting his left hand on the table and ignoring his surroundings. With his index finger, he tapped the table for emphasis. "I'm telling you exactly what happened. They bolted underground. Those men are still there. When we started getting the upper hand, they split."

"And I'm telling you it makes no difference. We ignore it," said Bates.

"Colonel." Gerber's voice rose. He glanced around and saw some of the others staring at him. He lowered his voice to a whisper. "There's a full division hidden out there. You know it. I know it." He pointed to Fetterman and added, "He knows it, too. A full fucking division."

"Mack, I don't know how to make this any clearer to you. We aren't going to do anything to disturb that division right now. We know it's there and we'll keep watch—"

"And do what?" demanded Gerber. "Move our pins around on our fucking maps? Tell the generals the 9th NVA Division is still hiding in the Hobo Woods, so we don't want to do anything to disturb them?"

"Right now," said Bates, realizing he was beginning to echo the arguments given to him by both Abrams and Davidson, "that's all we can do. The political climate is completely wrong."

Gerber slapped the table with his hand. "Shit!"

"Mack, I know how you feel, but right now that's all we can do. I told you that this morning. I told you we weren't allowed to get involved in a large-scale fight. You have no idea what the political repercussions of that fight are going to be. Now just sit back and watch."

"What do we do if the enemy decides he doesn't like it in the Hobo Woods anymore? What if he decides it's nicer at Cu Chi or Saigon or Vung Tau?"

"We'll cross that bridge when we come to it. We'll let Abrams and his boys cross that bridge when they come to it. Hell, Mack, look at the facts." Now Bates leaned forward and lowered his voice. "If Charlie had that full division in there, he could have overwhelmed your little command in a matter of minutes even with the reinforcements."

"That's a load of crap," said Gerber.

"No," said Bates. "It demonstrates that Charlie doesn't want a stand-up fight with us unless he thinks he can win it quickly with little damage to his own side."

"Fine," said Gerber. "And we don't want a stand-up fight because the time is wrong politically. I have an idea then. Why don't we all go home until somebody decides it's time to fight the war?"

"There are things operating here that you don't under-stand or don't know," said Bates.

"All I know is we had a chance to inflict some damage on the enemy but had to let them go. We had them in the open, willing to fight, but rather than stay in place and chase them down, we withdrew from the field."

"Politically it wasn't the right time." Bates felt sick hav-ing to say that.

"You know, during the Indian Wars, the U.S. Army claimed victories because they held the ground after the battle was over. At Rosebud they were mauled but called it a victory because they held the ground. Using that standard, the VC won today. They held the ground.''

''That's not fair, Mack, and you know it,'' said Bates. ''You know this situation was out of my hands.''

''All I know is,'' said Gerber, ''we had a chance and you boys blew it.''

13

THE OFFICE OF GENERAL CREIGHTON W. ABRAMS, MACV COMPOUND, SAIGON

Bates, Gerber and Fetterman stood in General Abrams's outer office. The clerks scurried around, each carrying a file folder, stack of papers or mimeographed orders. They ignored the three men who were still wearing sweat-stained jungle fatigues, which were covered with dirt and mud. Gerber wished he could have escaped to Nha Trang the way Santini and Kit had done after the airlift to Cu Chi. After ten minutes, the major opened the door to the inner office.

"You may come in now."

They entered and stood at attention, waiting for Abrams to acknowledge them. Slowly he placed his pen in its holder, folded his hands and said, "I've asked Major McBane to remain and take notes. His record will be useful if there are any repercussions from this meeting."

Bates shook his head. "I believe we've handled the situation in the proper fashion."

Abrams interrupted by holding up a hand. "Proper fashion would not involve stories on the six o'clock news. Proper fashion would be low key so that no one knows about it."

Bates decided to risk an interruption. "But we've discovered that the units engaged in the battle were from the 9th NVA Division along with elements from several VC regiments and a couple of independent battalions."

"*Colonel* Bates, and I stress the rank because I don't think you'll be moving up in grade after this mess. Colonel, the point is that it makes no difference what you believe. The point is that the media learned of the battle. Now I'll grant they have no idea about the size, but that, too, makes no difference."

Abrams picked up a file folder, the top and bottom stamped Secret, and said, "I see that you involved two assault helicopter companies, the Hornets and the Crusaders, and one heavy lift company, the Muleskinners. There were four companies of infantry, an alert to a Mike Force battalion at Moc Hoa that you had the sense not to deploy and an armored cavalry company." Abrams glanced up from the notes. "My God, man! What in hell were you thinking about?"

There was silence for a moment, and Bates wondered if he was supposed to answer. When Abrams continued to stare, he said, "We put the men in to recon the area, checked out the intelligence they were getting. When they got into trouble, the only thing I could do was help them. A massacre would be worse than a pitched battle."

Gerber could stand it no longer. He interjected, "A pitched battle until we decided to cut and run."

Abrams turned his glare on Gerber. "You like being a captain? I can arrange it so you retire as a captain. Now you keep your mouth shut until I ask you something."

"Yes, General."

He turned his attention back to Bates. "Now, Colonel, I'm sorry you saw fit to ignore my directives—"

Again Bates interrupted. "Excuse me, General, but I didn't ignore them. We couldn't sacrifice the men on the ground."

"That's splitting hairs, and you know it," said Abrams. He stood and moved around so that he was closer to the three men standing in front of him. It was almost as if he was closing with the enemy.

"Now," said Abrams, leaning against his massive desk, "you were told to stay out of the Hobo Woods. You saw fit to put people in there—"

"As a recon," Bates protested, realizing he was tramping on military courtesies.

"Goddamn it!" roared Abrams. "You put people in there and then reinforced them when we needed a low profile. You refuse to understand that point."

"Yes, sir," said Bates.

Abrams rubbed a hand over his face and dried it on the chest of his starched jungle fatigues. "I'm tired of all this," he said. "Bates, you've had it. As soon as I can get the orders cut, you're gone. No star and a bad OER. You can protest the OER, but it'll sink the chances of you ever getting that star."

He turned his wrath on Gerber. "Captain, I don't know what to make of you. You've either fucked up with the best or you've pulled off one hell of a defensive maneuver, getting that company off the LZ. Custer didn't make it out. You did. That should say something."

"Yes, sir."

"I understand you're supposed to replace Major Madden up in Nha Trang. I believe I'll think about that for a bit. As of now, you're assigned to Saigon. I'll work out the details with the Special Forces. You stay where I can find you and let you know what you'll be doing."

"Yes, sir."

"Sergeant Fetterman . . . I'm not sure why you're even here."

"Because you requested my presence," said Fetterman calmly.

"Yes, that I did. I guess I just wanted to see the man who set this whole ball rolling. Quite a feat."

"Thank you, General," said Fetterman.

"I'm not convinced I meant that as a compliment," said Abrams. He was quiet for a minute and then said, "The various orders and documents will be prepared within a week. In that time, I don't want to hear anything about you people or from you people. You got that?"

"Yes, sir," said Bates.

"Now get out."

They passed through the outer office and stopped in the hallway. Gerber turned and stared at Bates. The older man was pale, as if he had just been informed of a death in the family. His face was so white it looked like a mask.

"You okay, Colonel?" asked Gerber.

"Just a little light-headed," he said. "After that, who wouldn't be?"

Fetterman pointed. "There's a dayroom down here."

"Right," said Gerber. He took the colonel's elbow and guided him into the room. There were three clerks in it, sitting at a card table. "You men excuse us for a moment?"

One of them turned to protest, saw the look on Bates's face and said, "Sure thing, Captain."

Gerber steered Bates to the couch against the wall. It was a new piece of furniture, nearly seven feet long in rusts and golds. Already there was a stain on one of the arms where someone had spilled a cup of coffee.

"Shit," said Bates, "I knew I wasn't going to get the star. I don't know why I let myself hope."

"Look, Colonel," said Gerber, "you did the right thing. You acted like a soldier. You merely forgot that it isn't soldiers who are in demand today. It's managers and politicians. Soldiers are the grunts in the field getting their asses shot off."

Bates looked at Gerber. "Thank you, Mack. I understand, but it doesn't make it easier."

"So you're going home. Why worry about that?" said Fetterman. "About ninety-nine percent of the men here would pay for the privilege."

Bates smiled weakly. "You cut through the shit, don't you, Tony?"

"I just see things differently than you do. My perspective from the depths of the enlisted ranks."

There was a tentative knock at the door, and they all turned to look. Robin Morrow, dressed in jungle fatigues, a camera hanging around her neck and her blond hair hanging in her eyes, asked, "Can I come in?"

Gerber turned to Bates, who nodded. "Come ahead, Robin," said Gerber.

She stopped near him, looking down at him. For a moment she was silent. Then she asked, "You okay?"

"I'm fine." Gerber shot a glance at Bates, picked up the almost imperceptible shake of his head and added, "We're all fine. You?"

"Just great. Love to sit in offices and be forgotten. Does my heart good."

"Yeah, Robin," said Bates, "I'm sorry about that. I got swept up in the circumstances."

"Wouldn't be so bad," she said as she sat down on the arm of the couch, "if I had something to give my publisher. Everyone thinks I got the inside story. Won't believe you all left me sitting there, alone, with nothing."

Gerber realized he had a golden opportunity to blow the whistle. He could tell Robin what had happened, and she would see that it would get printed. Hell, it wouldn't be the first time he had used the press to get something accomplished, get the real story out and protect the people who were caught in the middle.

He felt a pressure on his arm and turned to look at Bates again. It was almost as if the colonel had read his mind and was telling him to forget it. If the story wasn't spread all over the papers, they might be able to salvage something from it. Abrams might forget about it if the media didn't suddenly appear with a great deal of information about the Hobo Woods. That was the real problem—the possibility of adverse publicity. Without it, the whole thing might blow over.

"Not much to tell," said Gerber, focusing his attention on Morrow. "A little contact and then the enemy broke it off. Wasn't even worth the effort to chase him."

"That why everyone was jumping through his ass a couple of hours ago?" asked Morrow suspiciously.

Now Fetterman broke in. "You know how these rear area types are. Get confused and excited about all the wrong things. Run off in twenty different directions without knowing what they're doing half the time."

Robin looked from face to face. "You all going to stand by that story?"

"Tell you what," said Bates, some of the strength returning to his voice, "why don't we go find us some civilian clothes and head into Saigon to get drunk. That's something I think we all could stand."

"I might remind you," said Fetterman, "that you promised me a dinner. I would like to collect before you slide back to the World."

Bates forced himself to his feet. "Then let's do it. And I'll buy. I owe you guys that. And you, too, Robin. That's the least I can do for forgetting you."

"Good," said Gerber. "Sounds real good."

As they left the dayroom, Fetterman touched Gerber's sleeve, and when the captain looked at him, he grinned and said, "Well, sir, we're back."

GLOSSARY

AC—Aircraft commander. The pilot in charge of the air-craft.

AFVN—U.S. armed forces radio and television network in Vietnam. Army PFC Pat Sajak was probably the most memorable of AFVN's DJs with his loud and long, "GOOOOOOOOOOOOD MORNing, Vietnam!"

AK-47—Soviet-made assault rifle normally used by the North Vietnamese and the Vietcong. AO—Area of Operations.

AO DAI—Long dresslike garment, split up the sides and worn over pants.

AP ROUNDS—Armor-piercing ammunition.

ARVN—Army of the Republic of Vietnam. A South Vietnamese soldier. Also known as Marvin Arvin.

BISCUIT—C-rations.

BODY COUNT—Number of enemy killed, wounded or captured during an operation. Used by Saigon and Washington as a means of measuring progress of the war.

BOOM-BOOM—Term used by Vietnamese prostitutes to sell their product.

BOONDOGGLE—Any military operation that hasn't been completely thought out. An operation that is ridiculous.

BOONIE HAT—Soft cap worn by the grunts in the field when they were not wearing their steel pot.

BUSHMASTER—Jungle warfare expert or soldier skilled in jungle navigation. Also a large deadly snake not common to Vietnam but mighty tasty.

C AND C—Command and Control aircraft that circled overhead to direct the combined air and ground operations.

CARIBOU—Cargo transport plane.

CHINOOK—Army aviation twin engine helicopter. A CH-47. Also known as a shit hook.

CHOCK—Refers to the number of the aircraft in the flight. Chock Three is the third. Chock Six is the sixth.

CLAYMORE—Antipersonnel mine that fires seven hundred and fifty steel balls with a lethal range of fifty meters.

CLOSE AIR SUPPORT—Use of airplanes and helicopters to fire on enemy units near friendlies.

CO CONG—Female Vietcong soldier.

DAI UY—Vietnamese army rank the equivalent of captain.

DEROS—Date of Estimated Return from Overseas Service.

FIVE—Radio call sign for the executive officer of a unit.

FOX MIKE—FM radio.

FNG—Fucking New Guy.

FREEDOM BIRD—Name given to any aircraft that took troops out of Vietnam. Usually referred to the commercial jet flights that took men back to the World.

GARAND—M-1 rifle that was replaced by the M-14. Issued to the Vietnamese early in the war.

GO-TO-HELL RAG—Towel or any large cloth worn around the neck by grunts.

GUARD THE RADIO—Term meaning to stand by in the commo bunker and listen for messages.

GUNSHIP—Armed helicopter or cargo plane that carries weapons instead of cargo.

HE—High-Explosive ammunition.

HOOTCH—Almost any shelter, from temporary to long-term.

HORN—Term that referred to a specific kind of radio operations that used satellites to rebroadcast the messages.

HORSE—See *Biscuit*.

HOTEL THREE—Helicopter landing area at Saigon's Tan Son Nhut Airport.

HUEY—UH-1D helicopter.

IN-COUNTRY—Term used to refer to American troops operating in South Vietnam. They were all in-country.

INTELLIGENCE—Any information about the enemy operations. It can include troop movements, weapons capabilities, biographies of enemy commanders and general information about terrain features. It is any information that would be useful in planning a mission.

KA-BAR—Type of military combat knife.

KIA—Killed In Action. (Since the U.S. was not engaged in a declared war, the use of the term KIA was not authorized. KIA came to mean enemy dead. Americans were KHA or killed in hostile action.)

KLICK—A thousand meters. A kilometer.

LIMA LIMA—Land Line. Refers to telephone communications between two points on the ground.

LLDB—Luc Luong Dac Biet. The South Vietnamese Special Forces. Sometimes referred to as the Look Long, Duck Back.

LP—Listening Post. A position outside the perimeter manned by a couple of people to give advance warning of enemy activity.

LZ—Landing Zone.

M-14—Standard rifle of the U.S., eventually replaced by the M-16. It fired the standard NATO round—7.62 mm.

M-16—Became the standard infantry weapon of the Vietnam War. It fired the 5.56 mm ammunition.

M-79—Short-barreled, shoulder-fired weapon that fires a 40 mm grenade. These can be high explosives, white phosphorus or canister.

MACV—Military Assistance Command, Vietnam, replaced MAAG in 1964.

MEDEVAC—Also called Dust-Off. A helicopter used to take the wounded to medical facilities.

MIA—Missing in Action.

NCO—Noncommissioned officer. A noncom. A sergeant.

NCOIC—NCO In Charge. The senior NCO is a unit, detachment or a patrol.

NEXT—The man who said it was his turn next to be rotated home. See *Short*.

NINETEEN—Average age of combat soldier in Vietnam, as opposed to twenty-six in the Second World War.

NOUC MAM—Foul-smelling sauce used by the Vietnamese.

NVA—North Vietnamese Army. Also used to designate a soldier from North Vietnam.

PETA-PRIME—Tarlike substance that melted in the heat of the day to become a sticky black nightmare that clung to boots, clothes and equipment. It was used to hold down the dust during the dry season.

PETER PILOT—Copilot in a helicopter.

POW—Prisoner Of War.

PRC-10—Portable radio.

PRC-25—Lighter portable radio that replaced the PRC-10.

PULL PITCH—Term used by helicopter pilots that means they are going to take off.

PUNJI STAKE—Sharpened bamboo hidden to penetrate the foot. Sometimes dipped in feces.

RPD—Soviet 7.62 mm light machine gun.

RTO—Radio Telephone Operator. The radio man of a unit.

SIX—Radio call sign for the unit commander.

SHIT HOOK—Name applied by the troops to the Chinook helicopter because of all the "shit" stirred up by the massive rotors.

SHORT—Term used by everyone in Vietnam to tell all who would listen that his tour was almost over.

SHORT-TIMER—Person who had been in Vietnam for nearly a year and who would be rotated back to the World soon. When the DEROS (Date of Estimated Return from Overseas) was the shortest in the unit, the person was said to be next.

SKS—Soviet-made carbine.

SMG—Submachine gun.

SOI—Signal Operating Instructions. The booklet that contained the call signs and radio frequencies of the units in Vietnam.

SOP—Standard Operating Procedure.

STEEL POT—Standard U.S. Army helmet. The steel pot was the outer metal cover.

TEAM UNIFORM OR COMPANY UNIFORM—UHF radio frequency on which the team or the company communicates. Frequencies were changed periodically in an attempt to confuse the enemy.

THREE—Radio call sign of the operations officer.

THREE CORPS—Military area around Saigon. Vietnam was divided into four corps areas.

THE WORLD—The United States.

TOC—Tactical Operations Center.

TOT—Time Over Target. It refers to the time that the aircraft is supposed to be over the drop zone with the parachutists, or the target if the plane is a bomber.

TWO—Radio call sign of the intelligence officer.

TWO-OH-ONE (201) FILE—Military records file that listed all of a soldier's qualifications, training, experience and abilities. It was passed from unit to unit so that the new commander would have some idea about the capabilities of an incoming soldier.

VC—Vietcong, called Victor Charlie (phonetic alphabet) or just Charlie.

VIETCONG—Contraction of Vietnam Cong San (Vietnamese Communist).

VIET CONG SAN—Vietnamese Communists. A term in use since 1956.

WHITE MICE—Referred to the Vietnamese military police because they all wore white helmets.

WIA—Wounded In Action.

WILLIE PETE—WP, white phosphorus, called smoke rounds. Also used as antipersonnel weapons.

XO—Executive officer of a unit.

ZAP—To ding, pop caps at or shoot. To kill.

ZIPPO—Flamethrower.

Gerber opened the
Stars and Stripes

As he looked at an inside page, he felt his stomach turn over. Smiling out at him was a picture of Sean Cavanaugh, looking as if he had just escaped from high school. Gerber stared at the youthful face, short hair and the white shirt and dark tie. He thought of the young man who had evaded the draft by volunteering for active duty in the Army and found himself in Vietnam before anyone in the World knew where in hell it was.

Below the photo of Cavanaugh was another of two people. The captain had thought of Cavanaugh's parents as elderly, but this couple didn't look old. They looked miserable. The woman was holding a handkerchief to her face as the man, his face contorted in anguish, accepted the Congressional Medal of Honor from the President.

A scrap of powder-blue cloth, Gerber thought, sprinkled with white stars, and an iron wreath with a star in the center and the word Valor engraved on it.

Certainly not worth a son.

VIETNAM: GROUND ZERO
SOLDIER'S MEDAL

A GOLD EAGLE BOOK

London · Toronto · New York · Sydney

ISBN 0 373 62705 X (Pocket edition)

*First published in Great Britain
in pocket edition by Gold Eagle 1988*

© Eric Helm 1987

*Australian copyright 1987
Philippine copyright 1987
Pocket Edition 1988*

**This OMNIBUS EDITION 1989
ISBN 0 373 57746 X**

8911
Made and printed in Great Britain

AUTHOR'S NOTE

The report of the NVA attack on Special Forces Camp A-102, March 9-10, 1966, is based on official U.S. Army and U.S. Air Force records and after-action reports. Major Bernard F. Fisher, USAF, was awarded the Congressional Medal of Honor for his heroism at Camp A-102 on March 10, 1966.

New U.S. Special Forces Camp A-555
(Triple Nickel)

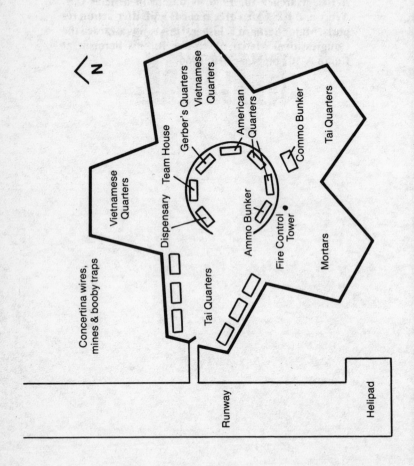

VIETNAM: GROUND ZERO
SOLDIER'S MEDAL

PROLOGUE

U.S. ARMY SPECIAL FORCES CAMP A-555 NEAR THE CAMBODIAN BORDER IN THE THREE CORPS TACTICAL OPERATIONAL AREA, RVN 1966

Army Special Forces Sergeant Sean Cavanaugh fell against the rear of his foxhole in Listening Post One and stared at all the fucking dead men lying in the short elephant grass and in the rice paddies near him. From the direction of the camp three hundred meters away, he could hear the rattle of small arms fire, the crash of mortars and the bang of grenades. Above the camp he could see the flares hanging beneath their parachutes as they drifted toward the ground, a line of smoke describing their path through the sky. With his right hand he grabbed the heavy PRC-10 to request support from the camp's mortars, but the radio had been so shot full of holes that it was useless, and the field phone had disappeared in a grenade blast that had wounded Sergeant Luong and killed Corporal Lim.

The last of their ammo had been used during the attack when the fighting had degenerated into a hand-to-hand conflict, and Cavanaugh and his tiny command of armed strikers had been forced to use their worthless rifles as clubs.

Now Luong was struggling to pull the equipment away from a dead VC. Grunting with the effort, the wounded sergeant tried to free the pouch that contained extra magazines for the AK-47 that he had already taken. He dropped the used clip from the weapon and slammed a new one home as the enemy reappeared in the flickering light of the distant flares and ran toward him across the open ground.

When Cavanaugh saw them coming, he picked up his carbine, but it was empty, and he had no spare ammo for it. Clawing at his holster, he drew his .45 and fired rapidly onehanded, the weapon jumping with the recoil.

It was as if the enemy had suddenly sprung from the ground. At first there was no sound, but then a noise began, a low growl that built slowly until it was a roar. The VC began shooting, firing their weapons as they ran, trying to cut down the defenders of the listening post.

As one of the enemy reached the edge of the foxhole, Cavanaugh fired a last time, his pistol only inches from the VC's stomach. The man dropped as if he had been poleaxed, but another materialized right behind him, leaping across the body and colliding with Cavanaugh. They fell together, rolling over in the confined space of the hole. Cavanaugh kicked with his right leg, twisted his body and found himself facing the enemy. He swung with the empty pistol and felt it connect, shattering the bones of the VC's face. Cavanaugh scrambled closer, grabbed the man around the neck and squeezed as he hit the enemy again with the pistol. He heard a sharp crack as the skull caved in, and the man slumped lifeless to the ground.

To his left he saw Sergeant Luong struggling with a VC. The enemy kicked out, knocked Luong to the ground and drove his spike bayonet through the young Vietnamese's side. Luong suddenly sat up and grabbed his attacker around the throat, pulling him forward, squeezing as he hit him in the face with his fist. The two fell back to the ground.

Cavanaugh tossed away the useless pistol and picked up his carbine, swinging it like a baseball bat. He knocked one man off his feet and smacked a second in the head with such force that the wooden stock splintered. As a third man leaped at him, Cavanaugh dropped the rifle and grabbed his entrenching tool, chopping with it as if he was clearing vines from a jungle trail.

Unaware that a growl was bubbling in his throat, that all the RFs with him were dead and that the VC were trying to escape, he kept swinging the tool. He smashed the blade into the side of a VC, knocking him to the ground. Then, screaming, he hammered the fallen enemy. The sergeant leaped to his right, balanced on the balls of his feet, his knees flexed, his head swiveling right and left, looking for more of the enemy. But they were suddenly gone, as if the ground that had given them birth had swallowed them again.

For a moment Cavanaugh stood there, his eyes shifting from one body to the next, watching them, waiting for them, as a light mist seemed to drift out of nowhere, hiding some of the dead. Cavanaugh fell back against the side of the foxhole, his breath rasping in his throat, the sweat trickling down his face to stain the collar of his torn and dirty fatigues. He listened, but the night was suddenly quiet as even the sounds of the firing from the camp died away.

Then out of the darkness he heard a moan, a single low cry of pain. When he looked up, he saw one of the enemy soldiers standing there, a gaping wound in the side of his head glistening wet and red in the moonlight and the flares. The man seemed stunned but stumbled toward Cavanaugh, who felt fear knot his stomach.

Around him more of the enemy were coming to life. Men missing hands or feet or legs. Men with uniforms ripped by bayonets and knives, with wounds in their stomachs and chests and entrails hanging from their bellies. Men who had been dead moments before now with new life breathed into them, coming at Cavanaugh, who stood helpless, holding the entrenching tool in one hand and the broken carbine in the other.

"No," he shouted. "You're dead." He tried to take a step back, but there was nowhere for him to go. Under his breath he mumbled, "No, not again."

Suddenly he was awake, sitting on his bunk, his back pressing against the wall of his hootch. His OD T-shirt was soaked with sweat. Cavanaugh could feel it crawling down his back and dripping from under his arms. He lifted a trembling hand to his neck and rubbed the back of it, surprised at how wet it was. His mind flashed to the walking dead men, the corpses from the battlefield that haunted his sleep, and suddenly he had to stand up, to move somewhere, as if the very act of moving would take his mind off the horrors that were there.

He stopped in front of his metal locker, opened the top drawer and felt under his clean uniforms for the bottle he had stashed there. Army regulations prohibited enlisted men from having alcoholic beverages in their quarters, but Captain Gerber winked at such things. The Special Forces rarely followed all the Army's regulations.

Cavanaugh pulled the cap from the whiskey bottle and drank deeply, feeling the liquor course down his throat and pool in his stomach, spreading liquid fire. He exhaled through his mouth and took a second deeper drink. This time he rocked back on his heels and looked at the hootch's rafters, at the screen there and the light filtering through it. To his right the gentle rise and fall of the chest of the form on the cot told him that Sully Smith, another of the team's

NCOs was still asleep. Cavanaugh grinned to himself. Since Sully was asleep, it meant that Cavanaugh hadn't cried out as he sometimes did. He took a third pull and felt his hands steady and the sweat begin to evaporate.

Glancing again at the sleeping Smith, Cavanaugh capped the bottle and tucked it away. The sergeant stood and moved back to his cot, then sat down. He rubbed a hand through his close-cropped hair and sighed. He was getting better. Now the dream only came two or three times a week. Immediately after the battle to defend the listening post, he had had the dream every night, sometimes twice a night, and it had been so frightening that he had tried to stay awake twenty-four hours a day. Now with the booze it was something that could be controlled. He didn't lie awake for hours shaking but only until he could get to the bottle. He wasn't sure whether the booze stopped the anxiety or if it was the act of getting it. Drinking water or tomato juice or smoking a cigarette might have done it. Anything that took a little time and gave him an immediate goal. Something to do.

Cavanaugh lay back with his hands under his head and stared up at the silk from a parachute flare that was draped over the rafters of the hootch. Dirty white silk that hid the tin of the roof and was a standard interior decorating item in South Vietnam. Hanging through the middle of it was a ceiling fan that spun slowly, stirring the fabric and the air.

Cavanaugh concentrated on remembering everything he could about flying saucers, a subject that had interested him since he was a kid. He could barely wait for morning, for the opportunity to get up and out and do something else. He didn't want to tour the defenses or check on the status of the strikers in the bunkers and on guard because the captain would notice that and wonder why he was out every other night doing it. It wasn't normal, and Cavanaugh knew that the last thing he wanted was to appear abnormal.

1

SPECIAL FORCES
CAMP A-555 NEAR THE
CAMBODIAN BORDER

After a long hot night spent sweating under the mosquito netting of an Army cot and listening to the quiet squeak of the ceiling fan as it slowly spun, Sergeant Sean Cavanaugh was ready for the patrol to begin. One hour before sunup he had gotten out of bed and searched through the metal wall locker where he stored his uniforms, gear, civilian clothes and, against Army regulations, his space ammo. He had done it by touch, feeling the coarse fabric of his jungle fatigues, the rough hardness of the web gear and the cool smoothness of his M-14

Like a man with arthritis, he moved slowly, trying to dress noiselessly and wondering if he should wear the thick OD socks the Army issued. During long patrols the socks tended to slip and rub against the foot and ankle, causing blisters. He sat on his bed, staring at the dark shape of his naked foot outlined against the light plywood floor, and thought about it. Finally he tossed the socks back into the locker and pulled on his newly issued jungle boots with their green nylon panel along the ankle.

When he finished dressing, he grabbed his web gear, pistol belt and spare canteens from his locker, shouldered his weapon and carefully latched the metal doors. As he stepped toward the entrance of the hootch, he glanced back at Sully Smith, who slept on, a dark, almost invisible shape concealed by the wispy green mosquito netting. Cavanaugh flipped him a salute and walked out into the muggy heat of the Vietnamese morning.

The sergeant stepped down into the red dust of the compound and hesitated. When he had first returned to the camp, he had told Fetterman that it looked completely different. Then he learned that it *was* different. Almost the entire camp had been burned to the ground and then rebuilt. Next to his hootch were two more like it. They were frame structures, the bottom half covered with unpainted, overlapping one-by-sixes that looked like clapboards; the top half of each hootch was screened with wire mesh to allow any breezes to pass through. The roofs were covered with shiny corrugated tin that was supposed to reflect the sun's heat. But the tin rusted quickly in the wet Vietnamese environment so that the roofs took on a golden glow in the daylight.

Across the compound were more hootches for the officers and the team sergeant. The team house, a long building used as a mess hall, rec room and briefing room, also squatted there. Next to it was the commo bunker, obvious because of the antennae sprouting from it like the whiskers of a cat, then the dispensary, a heavy sandbagged structure, one of the ammo bunkers, a weapons locker and the supply room. All this was crammed into the redoubt, an earthen breastwork that was five feet high and topped with barbed wire. Outside was the rest of the camp: the mortar pits, the hootches for the strikers and their families, the fire control tower and a line of bunkers that surrounded the camp, giving it a star-shaped look from the air. The runway and main helipad were outside the six strands of concertina wire, rows of claymores and booby traps. There was a secondary emergency-use helipad that was inside the compound but outside the redoubt.

Cavanaugh settled his boonie hat on his head, slipped into his web gear—the giant Randall combat knife was taped upside down to the left shoulder strap—and headed for the team house. The knife was a replacement for the one he had lost during the defense of the listening post, paid for by the members of the team as a "welcome home" present. They had mail-ordered it from Ironmonger Jim of Anoka, Minnesota. Cavanaugh had accepted it quietly and then spent the better part of two days sharpening it until it could slice easily through the toughest material or the softest flesh. He had blackened the blade so that it wouldn't flash in the sunlight or glint in the moonlight.

He entered the team house and saw Captain MacKenzie K. Gerber sitting at one of the six square tables that were already set for breakfast. The tables occupied the front two-thirds of the hootch. A bar separated the back third from the area where the tables were. Behind the bar was a stove, an oven and a storage area for canned foods. A single Vietnamese woman worked back there, preparing the morning milk by mixing cool water with powdered milk. To the left of the entrance as one came in were the remains of the old refrigerator—the plug had melted in the fire when the old team house burned—and a new refrigerator that seemed to have taken on the personality of the old one. It rarely worked and, when it did, froze everything solid.

Gerber was reading an overseas edition of *Time*, turning the pages as if the whole issue disgusted him. He glanced up at Cavanaugh and greeted him. "Morning, Sean. You're up early."

"Yes, sir," Cavanaugh replied, slipping into a chair near Gerber. "Got a patrol this morning."

Gerber flipped the magazine closed and set one hand on the back cover. "It's still early. And you don't have to bring all your equipment with you."

"I know, sir, but Sully was asleep and I didn't want to wake him." Cavanaugh unbuckled his pistol belt and grinned sheepishly. "Besides, this is my first patrol since I returned, and I guess I'm a little nervous about it."

"No reason to be nervous, you've done it all before." Gerber got up and moved to the coffeepot for another cup.

Cavanaugh stood and slipped out of his gear, piling it on the floor next to his chair. He walked to the bar, grabbed one of the individual boxes of Kellogg's Corn Flakes and a pitcher of milk, the sides of which were beaded with sweat. Ice cubes in the pitcher clinked against the metallic sides as Cavanaugh returned to the table.

As he sat down, Sergeant First Class Justin Tyme, the light weapons specialist, entered. Tyme was a tall, slender, sandy-haired young man who was normally quiet and seemed to be overly serious at times. Unlike Cavanaugh, he wasn't wearing his full field pack. He was dressed in jungle fatigues that were clean but not starched, and he hadn't bothered to tie the laces of his boots. He nodded at Gerber, who had returned to his chair, then waved at Cavanaugh. Tyme collapsed into the chair nearest the door, rubbed his face with both hands and said, "I'm not ready for this. Let's take the patrol out about noon, or better yet, about five."

Cavanaugh set his cereal and milk on the table and sat down. He pushed the perforations on the front of the small box, spread open the flaps and dumped the contents into his bowl. He splashed milk on the cereal, sprinkled it with lumpy sugar and began to eat.

Tyme watched Cavanaugh, then glanced at Gerber. "Any orange juice this morning, Captain?"

"I think we have some Tang."

"Christ, that's not orange juice, that's colored water."

"Then no," said Gerber, "we don't have any orange juice. We have some lousy coffee and some powdered milk and about half a case of warm beer."

Tyme rubbed his eyes with his hand and then, without looking, gestured at Gerber. "I'll take one of the beers."

"Before the patrol?" asked Gerber.

"Yes, sir. Unless you object?"

"No, Boom-Boom," said Gerber, "I don't object to a single beer, although I'm not convinced it's the best eye-opener."

"It's better than Tang."

Gerber got one of the beers out of the refrigerator and set it in front of Tyme. "I'll give you that." He turned his attention to Cavanaugh, who was hunched over his bowl. "I'll see you two at the gate before you leave."

As Gerber left the team house, taking his coffee with him, Tyme picked up his beer and moved to the table where Cavanaugh sat. He took a deep drink and made a face at it. "I wish we could get some real orange juice in here."

"Yeah," said Cavanaugh, "it's a little early in the day for beer."

"Sometimes that's all there is to drink. Powdered milk and powdered orange juice and powdered eggs—none of it tastes real. And shit, in Saigon they're probably dining on real eggs and real steaks and telling the press that war is hell."

Cavanaugh dropped his spoon into his bowl and pushed them away. "I'll meet you at the gate," he said, making it sound more like a question than a statement.

"Sure." Tyme nodded. "Make the equipment check. Make sure they all have the ammo they're supposed to carry. Sometimes on these routine patrols they leave the ammo back. Don't like humping it through the jungle."

"I know my job," snapped Cavanaugh.

"I'm sure you do," said Tyme. "It's just that you haven't been out here for a while."

Slowly Cavanaugh got back into his gear. He adjusted the shoulder straps until they rested comfortably on his shoulders, buckled his pistol belt and walked to the door. For a moment he stared out, looking into the deep blue of the sky overhead. Back to the west was a line of black clouds that suggested afternoon storms. As he left the building, he said over his shoulder, "Meet you at the gate."

Since the camp had been destroyed during the fight to recapture it and since it had been redesigned afterward, the gate was now on the west side about a hundred meters from the runway. Two large bunkers that housed heavy machine guns, two .30-caliber machine guns and 90 mm recoilless rifles guarded the flimsy gate and graded road that led to the Triple Nickel. Immediately inside the gate was a low wall of green rubberized sandbags that could be used as an additional machine-gun nest if the enemy was getting too close.

Most of the Vietnamese strikers stood near the low wall, their packs on the ground at their feet, their rifles stacked nearby. A couple of them sat staring at the ground or talking to one another. Cavanaugh approached them slowly, cautiously, wondering if any of them remembered him or if they blamed him for the deaths of the RF strikers during the defense of the listening post. He could see nothing in their eyes that suggested they knew what had happened, or maybe it was just something in their past and they assigned no blame for it.

He leaned his rifle against the sandbags and said, "Let's get this show on the road."

The Vietnamese responded slowly, getting to their feet and helping each other seat the packs on their backs. They all picked up their weapons, a collection of rifles from the Second World War and Korea with a few of the new M-16s thrown in, and formed a ragged line facing away from the sun.

Cavanaugh wiped a hand over his face, which was sweat damp in the early morning heat. He moved down the line, checking the packs, looking for the food rations of cooked rice and fish heads. He had to make sure that each man was carrying his allotment of spare ammo, that each had his share of the squad equipment—spare ammo for the M-60 machine gun, extra rounds for the M-79 grenade launchers and extra batteries for the radio.

Moments later Tyme approached from the redoubt. He walked up to Cavanaugh and put a hand on his shoulder. "We about ready to bug out?"

"They're all set," Cavanaugh told him. "Want me to check your pack?"

"Take a look if you want," said Tyme, "but shit, Sean, we're only going to be out twenty-four hours. I can carry everything I need for that in my pockets."

"Just a thought."

Tyme turned to watch Gerber as he came toward them. No one saluted because saluting only identified the officers for the enemy.

When he was close, Gerber asked, "You ready?"

"Yes, sir. Everything's set."

Gerber glanced upward, noticing that there were only a few wispy clouds directly above him, ignoring the black ones to the west. "Let's watch the pace," Gerber warned them, "it's going to be hot and miserable out there."

Tyme wiped his face and then rubbed his hand across the front of his fatigues, leaving a ragged stain. "Yes, sir, it sure is. Anything else?"

"Not that I can think of." He moved closer to Cavanaugh. "Sean, you've been out of this for quite a while. Don't be afraid to say something to Justin if you're not used to humping in the bush."

"No problem, Captain," said Cavanaugh. "I spent some of my time in Saigon working out. I can handle it."

"Okay," said Gerber. "Have fun, then. I'll see you when you get back. Good hunting to the both of you."

Tyme nodded to one of the Vietnamese. "Hanh, take the point. Move on out for about two hundred meters and halt."

Hanh shrugged and trotted through the gate and down the rough red dirt road that led to the runway. He crossed it and stepped onto the new shoots of elephant grass growing up through the thin layer of ash.

Gerber stood watching as the rest of the twenty-man patrol exited the camp and crossed the runway, heading to the west. He put a hand to his eyes to shade them and then turned at a noise beside him.

"They get off?" asked Master Sergeant Anthony Fetterman, the team's operations sergeant. He was a small man, both short and skinny, and looked as if a stiff breeze would blow him over, yet he had a strength that surprised and amazed the rest of the men on the team. He had a dark complexion and claimed to be part Indian, sometimes Aztec, sometimes Sioux and sometimes Cherokee.

"Yeah, they got off," responded Gerber. "Just left. Be out of sight in the trees in ten, fifteen minutes."

"Cavanaugh went out?" asked Fetterman.

"Yeah," said Gerber. "Cavanaugh went out."

"Good. We need to have a talk about him, and I figure'd it would be easier with him off the camp for a while."

TYME WATCHED THE POINT MAN cross the runway that had been sprayed with peta-prime, and then followed with the patrol. They entered into an area where the grass had burned off, the tiny green shoots pushing up through the black ash and red dust. The strikers kicked up tiny clouds of ash and dust that seemed to hang in the air with no breeze to stir them.

The column moved across the open ground, trying to reach the trees before the sun climbed high and baked them with its merciless heat. Tyme could see their path behind them, a wavering line of red in the nearly unbroken field of black and gray and green.

Up ahead a finger of jungle reached toward them. At first it was little more than a few bushes and a couple of trees, but it widened rapidly into a deep green belt of coconuts, palms, teak and mahogany that stretched skyward. The broad leaves of the trees were interwoven in a canopy that shaded the ground and stopped the rain. If they could reach it before the sun got too high in the sky, it would make travel a little less difficult. It would still be hot and humid, almost like hiking through a steam room, but the sun wouldn't sap their strength like an energy vampire.

Tyme was already sweating when they entered the jungle. He could feel it on his back and under his arms. The go-to-hell rag around his neck absorbed some of the sweat, but not enough to make him comfortable. Tyme wiped his forehead with the sleeve of his jungle jacket and wished that it would snow. Just once and for only an hour or so. The constant hot weather was getting to him. Vietnam was a land of seasons. Two of them. Hot and dry, and hot and wet. He wasn't sure which season he was in, however, because it had rained heavily the day before.

In the jungle the patrol slowed, walking carefully, each man watching the ground around him for signs of booby traps or ambushes. They had found a game trail that looked as if it hadn't been used by anything for a while. The growth wasn't nearly as thick as it was in the surrounding jungle, and Hanh was able to make his way through it without using his machete. The strikers and the Americans stepped over fallen palms, pushed branches out of the way, tried to avoid the brambles of the wait-a-minute vines. Slipping through the jungle, the idea was to leave no clue that they had been there, but to look at the ground, searching for hints that Charlie might be near. Charlie was as good as they were, however, sometimes better at concealing his movements.

Tyme glanced up then, and through the breaks in the vegetation, he could see the strikers leaping from the trail, taking up firing positions, facing right and left so that they were guarding each other's backs. They crouched among the bushes and grasses, their rifles held ready, watching the jungle for hostile movement as they had been trained to do. Cautiously, Tyme made his way to the head of the patrol where he found Cavanaugh lying on his stomach, his rifle out in front of him, his chin nearly on the ground as he stared straight ahead.

Tyme approached him, knelt and said, "What you got?"

Cavanaugh turned his head slightly so that he could look back over his shoulder. He grinned at Tyme. "Trip wire. Step back a couple of meters, and I'll see what it does."

Tyme backed off and watched as Cavanaugh reached out with his M-14. Then he pulled it backward until the wire was against the weapon's forward sight. He jerked it once and dropped the rifle to the ground.

There was a popping of vegetation as if something large was crashing through the jungle. An instant later there was a whoosh as a small tree that had been bent back was suddenly freed; it swept across the trail and smacked into the trunk of a large palm. Tyme could see that a dozen sharpened bamboo stakes had been driven into the palm by the force of the impact. They were about knee-high and designed to take out one or two strikers on patrol, maiming but not killing them. The philosophy behind the booby trap was that a wounded man required two other patrol members to carry him to safety, but a dead man was just dead.

Tyme stood and looked at the trap again. Ingenious in design and use of local flora. He wasn't sure that he liked the way Cavanaugh had triggered it, although no one had been hurt by it.

Cavanaugh climbed to his feet and brushed the dirt and dead vegetation from the front of his fatigues. "That takes care of that. Ready to move out?"

"Let's give the men a break," said Tyme. "We've been at it for better than an hour."

"Fine with me." Cavanaugh stepped off the trail and into the jungle, almost disappearing into the vegetation. He crouched and took a drink from his canteen, then poured some of the water on his go-to-hell rag. Draping it over his head, he let the evaporation of the water cool him.

Cavanaugh dropped his pack, rummaged through it until he found the pound cake from one of the C-ration meals that he carried. He opened the tin with his P-38, got the cake out and ate it quickly. He took another drink from his canteen, draining it, and then sat back to look at the tiny patches of sunlight that managed to find their way through the thick foliage. On the branch of a small bush, he saw a spider spinning a complex web that seemed to fill one patch of sunlight.

When Tyme passed the word for them to saddle up, Cavanaugh slipped on his pack, adjusted the shoulder straps until it rode high on his back and then smashed the spider's web with his boot, crushing the insect before he stepped onto the trail.

Moving into thicker jungle, they were forced to follow the trail more closely because of the tangled vegetation. Vines clogged the undergrowth like a net strung between the trees. The canopy, now three layers thick, kept the sun from penetrating to the jungle floor. They were wrapped in a continuous twilight with deep black shadows that shifted in the light breeze. Instead of cooling them, it only reminded them of the muggy heat. Far overhead they could hear the rumble of thunder and knew that it was raining. They could smell it, the fresh, clean odor brought by the breeze, and they could hear it falling into the trees above them, although the water didn't reach the ground yet.

As they continued to move, the rainwater trickled down the trunks of the tall hardwood trees and fanned out onto the broad leaves of the bushes before dripping onto the soft earth of the jungle floor. The men nudged the bushes forward, then let the branches slap back, hitting the others behind, covering each with the moisture that was now seeping into the jungle. They looked as if they had been standing in an open field in the storm. Even though they could now tell that the rain above them had slowed, they knew that the water would continue to seep through the vegetation for hours.

The patrol halted again, and Cavanaugh moved forward slowly, using the undergrowth and trees for cover until he found Tyme crouching at the edge of a clearing. There, uprooted trees, broken bushes and a thick growth of elephant grass had taken root on the sides of a gigantic bomb crater. Before he could say a word to Tyme, he noticed a slight movement in the vegetation on the other side of the crater. A single VC, dressed in black pajamas but wearing Khaki web gear and carrying an old bolt-action rifle, was moving through the clearing slowly, watching the ground near his feet.

"Do we take him?" Cavanaugh whispered.

"Not yet," answered Tyme. "Let's see if there's anyone behind him."

Cavanaugh slipped off the safety of his weapon and aimed at the enemy, tracking him as he progressed across the clearing.

"Don't shoot him," warned Tyme.

"I'm not planning on it," Cavanaugh replied. "I'm just keeping him covered." His weapon didn't waver from the VC.

The man walked into the trees and then reappeared, his shoulders hunched against the light rain. He moved to the edge of the crater and looked down into it, as if he had found something fascinating in the bottom of it. He reached back toward his hip and then seemed to look right at Cavanaugh and Tyme.

Cavanaugh didn't hesitate. He pulled the trigger of his weapon twice and watched as the enemy soldier was slammed backward violently, one hand flung in the air, the other clutching his rifle in a death grip. The man disappeared into the grass, rose slightly as if to look at his killers and then fell back out of sight.

"What in the hell did you do that for?" snarled Tyme.

"He saw us. He was going for a grenade."

"Christ, Sean, we could have captured him. You didn't have to shoot him."

"I thought he was going for a grenade."

"Okay." Tyme pointed to three of the strikers behind them and indicated positions for them. Then, moving slowly, Tyme got to his feet and entered the clearing. He skirted the edge of the crater, looked at the clear water that filled the bottom and then approached the dead soldier. He stepped on the hand that still was clutching the rifle and bent over to jerk it free. With his foot he rolled the body over, saw the two bullet holes in the chest—neat, circular holes in the man's black pajamas, the edges glistening bright red. Near his hip the VC carried two hand grenades and a canteen. Tyme looked at the grenades, the canteen and the water in the bottom of the crater. Cavanaugh could have been right. Or the man might have been about to refill his canteen.

Tyme shrugged, pulled the web gear from the body, checked for documents and insignia that would give Kepler and his intelligence boys something to work with.

"I think we might as well head back to the camp," said Tyme when he reentered the trees.

"Let's see if this guy had any friends," said Cavanaugh. "We might be able to get a couple more."

"I doubt it. If he had any friends, they would have scattered by now. Searching the jungle won't do us any good. Besides, I've seen all I was supposed to. Sean, why don't you take the point."

"You're the boss," Cavanaugh said, but he didn't ask for a direction of march. Instead, he began to backtrack, following the same path that they had used to get to the clearing.

GERBER AND FETTERMAN were going to have their talk in the team house after they had finished their checks of the camp's defenses to make sure nothing had happened to them during the night, but Sully Smith was there eating his lunch. Gerber stopped in the doorway and turned to look at Fetterman. "Let's go over to my hootch."

They crossed the compound and entered the small structure. It was similar to the two- and three-man hootches used by the others, only smaller. Gerber had his Army cot shoved against one wall under the off-center ceiling fan. Next to the bed was an old ammo crate, which had been turned on end to serve as a nightstand. Near the door was a small Army field desk that could be folded into a cube about two feet on each side. When opened and assembled, however, it was a moderate-sized desk painted a sickening green. A metal folding chair sat behind it while two more occupied the space in front of it. The furnishings weren't quite as nice as the ones Gerber had had before the camp was burned.

"Take a seat, Tony," he said. He pulled a bottle of Beam's out of the desk's bottom drawer. "You want a touch?"

"Not now, Captain. It's a little early."

Gerber smiled and put the bottle away. "Don't let it be said that I wasn't the gracious host. Now then, what do you have on your mind?"

Fetterman crossed his legs and ran his thumb and index finger along the crease in his jungle fatigues. He studied his uniform intensely for a moment and then asked, "Are you aware that Cavanaugh has been having nightmares?"

"I think that's to be expected," said Gerber, "given the circumstances."

"Yes, sir. But they've continued. I've seen all the classic signs. He's the last one to leave the team house, usually the first one up, looks tired, and I've seen him out inspecting the bunker line at night when it's someone else's turn to do it."

"I know that," said Gerber, nodding. "Saigon advised me of it, but they also pronounced him fit for duty. They should know what they're doing. Besides, he asked to come back here."

Fetterman smiled. "I don't know why you would think that Saigon knows what it's doing. I know I don't trust those doctors. Hell, Captain, they're a bunch of college boys who've never been out in the real world. What are they, twenty-six, twenty-seven years old and given commissions as captains and majors because they've spent eight, nine, ten years in college? They blow into Vietnam and pretend they understand the stress of combat based on the Saturday afternoon matinee."

"I would think they're qualified to practice medicine," said Gerber.

"I do, too, sir. But they don't understand the nature of combat. How could they? They've never been in it. They see it in the movies and think of it as something adventurous. People die, but they die cleanly. Little, neat holes in a shirt with a little fake blood splashed around, and in the next feature the guy is up and around again. They know about the clichés, but they don't know the business. They've never seen a man killed in battle, his uniform soaked in blood, with the top of his head missing, or an arm, or all his guts stacked on his chest."

"There a point to this, Tony?"

"All I'm saying, sir, is that you've got a bunch of doctors in Saigon who don't understand that we have to work closely with the men here, get to know them, and who don't understand that Sean should be home chasing cheerleaders, not defending a listening post to the last round of ammunition and the last of the men under him. They think they know about the trauma of combat, so they pronounce him fit for duty."

Gerber nodded and reopened the desk drawer to get the bottle. He opened it and took a drink, feeling the liquor burn its way down his throat, before handing it to Fetterman. "You building up to something, Tony?"

"Just that I think we should watch Sean carefully. You didn't see him when I found him. Just sitting there holding that broken carbine and blood-covered entrenching tool, the bodies of the strikers lying next to him and the LP surrounded by sixty, seventy dead VC. Real dead men. Not the Hollywood variety. Real blood soaking and staining the grass and the buzz of the flies. That's what's always missing in the movies, the sound of the flies."

Gerber stretched his hand out to Fetterman, who still had the bottle. The captain took a last drink before corking it. "No, I didn't see him there, but I did see him in the hospital. I did talk to the college boy doctors, and although they may not understand combat, they do understand the nature of the human mind. They told me that Cavanaugh feels guilty because he survived and all the men around him died. He feels he should have died with them, that he let them down by not doing so."

Fetterman started to speak, but Gerber held up a hand to stop him. "Yes, that's pretty standard, and you don't have to go to school for ten years to know that, but what you don't know is that the Army contributed to that feeling. You, Bromhead, me, everyone here thought that we should get Sean the Medal of Honor. That was one piece of impressive fighting, but there were no other survivors. We couldn't prove that Sean had been brave. You know it and I know it, but we couldn't prove it. The Army isn't going to accept our speculation that Cavanaugh set up the defense because if he hadn't, they would all be dead, including him, and there would have been no enemy bodies around his position when we found it."

For a moment Gerber stopped talking and looked out the door at the bright afternoon sunlight and the red dirt of the compound and part of the redoubt. "So we couldn't get him the Medal of Honor no matter how much he deserves it," he continued. "The regulations worked against us. Then we had Crinshaw sitting in his office in Saigon not wanting to do us any favors, so he made sure that anything we put Cavanaugh in for was downgraded, and so on. By the time the award was approved, it was just a regular medal, nothing great, and Cavanaugh took that to mean that the Army disapproved of his actions."

"But that's just—" Fetterman began.

"Ridiculous," Gerber finished for him. "Of course, but Sean, being as young as he is, doesn't understand the politics that go on in the Army. Crinshaw doesn't want us to look good because he believes that makes him look bad. He isn't concerned with the emotional state of a nineteen-year-old kid. So Cavanaugh sees the reduction of his award from what should have been the Medal of Honor as proof that he's no good. Shit, Tony, we should have put him in for it, anyway, even if there was no way he could get it."

"Yes, sir," agreed Fetterman. "It looks good in the record, even if the award isn't made."

"So what you don't know is that the Army doctors asked me to let him come back out here, nightmares and all. It wouldn't look good in his record if I had turned him down because of what had happened."

Fetterman got to his feet. "I understand that. But it wouldn't look good if he's marked down as KIA. Especially if you have to mark Boom-Boom KIA, too."

Gerber didn't move. He stared at Fetterman for a moment. "I'm aware of that. But I'm aware that we owe Sean a debt, as well. We'll just have to watch him closely until we're satisfied that the problems have been resolved."

"Yes, sir."

2

OUTSIDE THE MAIN
GATE OF CAMP A-555

Sergeant Sean Cavanaugh halted the patrol shortly before dusk about four hundred meters from the main gate. Using the PRC-10, he alerted Bocker, who had the radio watch, that they would be coming in and would pop smoke, selecting yellow because the bright color would be easier to see in the fading daylight than one of the darker colors. As soon as it was acknowledged, Cavanaugh waved the patrol forward. They crossed the airstrip again, trying to avoid stepping in the pools of peta-prime, and entered the camp. When the gate was closed, Cavanaugh turned to face the Vietnamese strikers and called, "Weapons and equipment check in thirty minutes. Then we'll break for chow."

Tyme watched as the men headed toward their hootches to clean their weapons, even though Cavanaugh was the only man to have fired his rifle. From the direction of the redoubt, he saw Captain Gerber and Sergeant Fetterman coming toward them.

When they were close, Gerber asked, "How'd it go?"

"Pretty routine, Captain. One enemy KIA. We've got the weapon and gear but nothing for Kepler." Tyme stopped talking and looked at Cavanaugh who was standing there, too, listening.

"Who gets credit for the KIA?" asked Fetterman.

"Cavanaugh," Tyme said quickly.

"Good job, Sean," said Gerber. Then he turned to Tyme. "Justin, I'll want a full report in my hootch as soon as you can get there." He looked at Cavanaugh. "Sean, please make sure that the Viets get their weapons cleaned."

"Yes, sir." Cavanaugh took off after the Vietnamese.

"Now," Gerber said to Tyme, "how'd it really go?"

"Just fine, Captain. It went just fine, only..." He stopped talking, looking at the retreating back of Cavanaugh, the darkening of the camp as the sun vanished and then at Fetterman.

"Only?" prompted Gerber.

"A couple of little things bother me. Nothing I can really put my finger on."

"All right," said Gerber, nodding. "Let's adjourn to my hootch." But before he moved, he said, "Either of you care for a beer?"

"Is it cold?" asked Tyme.

"Surely you jest," said Gerber. "Of course it's not cold. Cool maybe, if we're lucky."

"Then by all means," said Tyme, "I would love to have a beer."

As both Fetterman and Tyme headed for Gerber's hootch, the captain stopped in the team house long enough to grab three cans of Oly from the refrigerator, which had broken down again. Then he trotted across the compound to join the two men in his hootch. Fetterman sat in the chair behind the field desk, and Tyme took one of the metal chairs on the opposite side. Gerber handed a beer to Tyme and then set one on the desk for Fetterman.

"I'll get out of your chair, Captain," said Fetterman, rising.

"Don't bother," responded Gerber. "I'll just park on the bunk here." He opened his beer with the church key from the nightstand, then tossed the opener to Tyme. The weapons specialist caught it, opened his can, then slid the opener across the desk toward Fetterman.

"Now," said Gerber, "what's bothering you about the patrol? Cavanaugh fuck it up?"

"No, sir, he didn't." Tyme took a swig of his beer and sat still for a moment as if formulating his answer. "Little things are bothering me. A couple of little things."

"Such as?" asked Gerber.

Tyme looked at the floor and told them about the trip wire. "He just yanked on it without examining it. If it had been tied to a grenade or an artillery round, it could have killed four or five of us."

"But it was a mechanical booby trap, right?" said Gerber. "Maybe he did know. Maybe he had seen something that had clued him about the nature of it. Did you ask him about it?"

"No, sir, I didn't. Not standing there in the jungle."

"Okay," said Gerber. He shot a glance at Fetterman, who was sitting with his eyes closed, listening and drinking his beer. Gerber prompted Tyme. "But that's not the only thing."

"No, sir, it's not. I'm simply not convinced we had to shoot that VC. Sean said that he thought the guy had spotted us and was reaching for a grenade."

"But you don't believe that?"

"I believe that Sean believes it, but I don't see how the guy could have seen us, hidden in the jungle the way we were. The light wasn't right for him to have seen us. Besides, he was standing there calmly. I think he was reaching for his canteen. I think he was going to fill it from the water in the bomb crater."

"So he fired and you didn't," said Gerber. "You think he was wrong to shoot?"

"That's the problem, sir. He may have been right. The VC may have been reaching for the grenades. Maybe he'd planned to grab one and toss it before hitting the dirt. Perhaps Sean was right to fire, although he shot a little faster than I would have."

Gerber nodded and took a long pull at the beer. "Anything else?"

"He took the same path back to the camp. I was wondering a little about him, so I told him to take the point, but I didn't give him a compass heading. He began backtracking on our trail."

Now Fetterman opened his eyes. "You ask him about that?"

"Sure, Tony. He said that we're supposed to be out there looking for the VC. He said that since we'd seen no sign of them, other than the one guy out for a stroll, this way we might be able to draw them out."

Gerber rubbed his chin. "That's a tactic I'm not sure I approve of, but it is pretty standard. I can't really fault his thinking on it."

"No, sir," said Tyme, "but you see what I'm getting at. It's a lot of little things."

"But none of them really mean anything," said Fetterman. "You said you didn't ask him about the booby trap. Maybe he'd seen something that you hadn't and knew what it was going to do. You said the guy might have been reaching for his grenades, and backtracking on a trail is fairly routine practice when trying to draw out the enemy."

"All true, Tony," said Tyme. "All true. I don't know what it is, though. There's something about each of those incidents that doesn't sit right."

"Sergeant—" Gerber put the meeting on a more formal level by the use of Tyme's rank "—is there something more to your concern than your feelings? Did he mistreat the men? Show a lack of concentration? Make any kind of blatant, stupid mistake?''

"No, sir. He moved well in the jungle. He didn't seem overly jumpy or nervous."

"Would you object to going out on patrol with him again?"

Tyme hesitated before he answered. "Ah . . . no, sir."

"You don't seem very sure of that."

"I wouldn't object to going out with Sean, sir." He grinned. "As long as it's not tomorrow."

"I can understand that." Gerber got to his feet. "Why don't you get yourself some hot chow and prepare a written report on the patrol. Leave out your personal observations of Cavanaugh's behavior. Keep it limited to the facts."

As Tyme was leaving, Gerber said, "Tony, I'd like to talk to you for a moment."

"Yes, sir. I had a feeling you would."

"Well, sit down and tell me your thoughts on all of this."

Fetterman dropped into the metal chair that Tyme had vacated. He continued to sip his beer while Gerber reached over to turn on the electric light. There was a single bulb suspended from a rafter in the center of the hootch.

"I think Boom-Boom has reinforced what we talked about earlier," said Fetterman.

"But once again we're stuck with nothing that you or anyone else could point to. A series of incidents that have very natural explanations."

"It seems that we've got a situation here," said Fetterman.

"A very delicate situation, Master Sergeant," said Gerber. "A very delicate one."

"I could set up a little test if you like," Fetterman suggested. "Maybe force something in an environment where it won't matter. That is, here in the camp rather than in the field where a bunch of people could die."

"All right, Tony, I'll leave this in your hands. You let me know how it turns out."

Fetterman stood. "I can have an answer for you in about an hour."

"Don't rush it," said Gerber.

"It's no problem, Captain. It's a simple test."

AS SOON AS HE HAD FINISHED inspecting the strikers' rifles, Cavanaugh headed to his hootch. On entering he saw that Sully Smith was gone and decided that a drink was in order. He leaned his weapon against the wall near his locker, dropped his pack to the floor and then knelt so that he could reach into the top drawer. As he pushed his clothing aside, he noticed that his hands were shaking. Cavanaugh held his right hand out in front of him and watched it tremble.

He grabbed his bottle and sat back so that he was leaning against the side of the cot. For a moment he sat there, puzzling over the vibrations in his stomach, the queasy feelings that rocked him. He tried to figure it out but couldn't. There he was in camp, relatively safe, and still he was shaking, the sweat covering his forehead and sliding down his back and sides. It wasn't that hot out, and the perspiration felt clammy and cold.

Cavanaugh pulled the cork from the bottle, sniffed the opening and grimaced at the strong odor. Placing the bottle to his lips, he drank swiftly, not tasting the bourbon. He felt it in his belly, spreading a warmth through him that seemed to overwhelm and smother the feelings of anxiety.

As the liquor calmed him, Cavanaugh leaned his head against his cot and closed his eyes, breathing out through his mouth. He waited for a few moments, then took another long pull, this time holding the bourbon in his mouth before swallowing it. He concentrated on the liquor, letting it take over, forcing all the other thoughts from his mind.

THE SOUND OF BOOTS on the floor surprised Cavanaugh, and he looked up to see Fetterman standing in the doorway, holding something in his hand that was wrapped in a poncho liner. Cavanaugh had no idea how long he had sat on the floor. The light from the sun had disappeared and had been replaced by the dim glow of the camp's electric lights.

Fetterman's eyes shifted to the bottle that Cavanaugh held loosely. For an instant Cavanaugh thought about hiding it, but the damage had been done. Besides, Fetterman had no idea how much had been in the bottle or how much he had had to drink. To cover his momentary embarrassment, Cavanaugh held up the bourbon bottle. "Care for a snort?"

"No, thanks. The captain just gave me a beer." He reached over and turned on the lights.

Cavanaugh got to his feet slowly, brushed off the seat of his jungle fatigues and then sat on his cot. He picked up the bottle, corked it and set it on the floor near his feet. "What can I do for you?"

Fetterman stood in the doorway and studied the man in front of him. He was still wearing sweat-stained fatigues. His hair hung limply, and his boots were muddy. It looked as if he had come straight from the Vietnamese quarters. The master sergeant's gaze was drawn to a small frame nailed to the plywood at the head of the cot. Inside the frame was the medal that Cavanaugh had won for defending the listening post—a medal that clerks got for doing their jobs well, that officers got for showing up at the office for six months, that was given out during transfers and retirements and that nearly everyone in the Army had received at one time or another for doing almost nothing other than being in the Army. It did not suggest that Cavanaugh's defense of the listening post had been heroic or extraordinary. It suggested that his resistance had been something routine.

Fetterman sat on Smith's bunk. "How're things going for you?"

"What do you mean?"

"You getting settled in okay? Everything as you expected it to be? Any problems that you didn't anticipate?"

Cavanaugh took a deep breath and sighed. "No, nothing. It's just like I expected it to be. Camp's changed quite a bit, but I expected that after I heard it had burned down."

"How do you like the climate? Must be quite a change from hanging around those air-conditioned rooms in Saigon."

"Well, I find it a little hard to sleep at night. I'm not sure how you guys do it. Seems like the minute I hit the sack, I'm covered with sweat and the air stops circulating. I'm trying to get used to the heat and humidity again, but it's going to take time."

"Yeah," Fetterman agreed. "That can be a problem." He stood, moved to the door and stopped. "Oh, I almost forgot. I've got a little present here. A little something I think you'll appreciate having back."

Cavanaugh got to his feet and took a step forward. "What is it?"

Fetterman slowly unwrapped it and held it up. "It's your entrenching tool. The one you had at the listening post. I cleaned and oiled it for you to keep it from rusting. It was badly messed up when I got my hands on it. Watch the edge, it's real sharp. But I guess you know that." Fetterman kept his attention focused on Cavanaugh's eyes.

But there was nothing unusual there. Almost no reaction at all, except maybe some disappointment. Disappointment that the present hadn't been something more substantial, like the replacement combat knife had been. Cavanaugh reached out, took the handle of the E-tool and held it up as if it was a baseball bat. Then he grinned.

"Feels the same, Master Sergeant. Thanks for hanging on to it. I didn't think I would ever see it again." He set it on the floor next to his rifle and picked up the bottle of bourbon. "You want a snort?"

Fetterman reached out. "Yeah. I think I will take one." He grabbed the bottle, drank deeply and handed it back. "Listen, Sean, if there's anything you need, you let me know. We'll work it out."

"Thanks, Sarge. I appreciate it."

"Yeah, I'll catch you later." Fetterman stepped out into the compound and found Gerber sitting on the sandbagged wall outside the team house, drinking a beer while he waited for the ops sergeant.

"How'd it go?" he asked.

Fetterman shrugged. "Test was a flop. No reaction at all. Just took the damned thing and set it on the floor before offering me another drink."

"You think he might have a problem in that area? Drinking too much?"

"I haven't seen anything like that. Hell, Captain, we all suck down the booze pretty good. You've got a beer there, and you've started that ritual where we pass the bottle of Beam's around, taking a healthy belt."

"The difference, Master Sergeant, is that we're not using the booze to drown our emotions. We don't use it to sleep or to wake up."

"Yes, sir." He was silent for a moment. "Cavanaugh took that damned E-tool, looked at it and set it down just like he had ice water in his veins."

"All right," Gerber said. "Maybe we're overreacting here. Maybe we don't have a thing to worry about."

"I don't know, Captain. It's not his veins that I'm worried about."

3

INSIDE SPECIAL
FORCES CAMP A-555

VC were everywhere. Thousands of them swarmed out of the trees a hundred meters away, rushing across the open rice paddies and fields of elephant grass. They were screaming and whistling, urged forward by bugles, shooting from the hip.

Sergeant Sean Cavanaugh jammed a new magazine into his M-1 carbine, locked the weapon against his shoulder and began pulling the trigger rapidly. He could see the rounds strike the enemy. Blood appeared on their chests, spurting from the bullet holes, and dust flew up as stray rounds struck the ground.

But the enemy wouldn't die. They wouldn't fall. Cavanaugh knew that they were hit. He could see it. He could see the impact of the rounds. But the enemy just wouldn't die.

Glancing to the right, he watched Luong fall, his arm severed at the elbow and a neat round hole right between his eyes. Lim disappeared in the explosion of a grenade. Cavanaugh was suddenly alone, the RF strikers dead at his feet. Stuck with a weapon that wouldn't kill.

And then he was awake.

Sweat covered him, dripping from his face as he sat bolt upright in bed. He rubbed a hand over his head, wiped his palm on the OD T-shirt he wore and took a deep breath. If they would only fall when he shot them, the dream wouldn't be so frightening. It wouldn't make him feel so powerless, so impotent. If only he could stop some of them... But he couldn't. They kept coming, thousands of them, springing to life, all of them running directly toward his listening post while the men with him died horrible vivid deaths.

He swung his legs out of bed and put his bare feet on the dirty floor. A chill enveloped him, and he shivered, even though he knew the outside temperature had to be in the eighties. He stood and took a single step toward his wall locker.

From far outside he heard a quiet, muffled pop. Looking at the door, he counted silently, waiting, and a moment later heard the explosion. By its sound he could tell that it was exploding gunpowder that signaled a mortar landing and not the flat loud bang of the 122 mm rockets that Charlie sometimes launched at the camp.

Cavanaugh didn't move right away but knelt by the door, looking out into the moonlit compound, waiting for a second round. He didn't see it land but heard it impact farther away than the first, which meant that the mortar rounds were moving away from him. He got to his feet and waited, watching as some of the men—he recognized Gerber and the new executive officer, Lieutenant Greg Novak—sprinted from their hootches and through the opening in the redoubt, probably heading for the fire control tower.

There was a moment of silence as if the war and the world had stopped, and then the rounds started falling faster than before. Cavanaugh dived to the ground and rolled to his right, stopping next to the sandbags of his hootch. He wondered if it would be safer inside or out. The VC were aiming at the buildings, but they rarely hit anything. The safest place was the commo bunker because it was completely sandbagged and could take a hit from a rocket. Mortars just tore up the sandbags.

There was a brilliant flash as a round detonated outside the redoubt, and Cavanaugh heard the shrapnel raining down on the tin roofs of the hootches. Two more explosions came in swift succession, one at the center of the gate and another at the dispensary, which erupted in a ball of fire.

The moment there was a pause in the firing, Cavanaugh leaped to his feet and started running toward the burning building. He found one of the strikers sitting on the ground, his hands pressed to his ears and blood streaming down the side of his face. Cavanaugh knelt, took the man's head in his hands and turned it so that he could examine the wound in the moonlight. It seemed to be a superficial cut above the hairline, but it was bleeding heavily. The man looked dazed, as if he had bumped his head. Cavanaugh grabbed the striker under his arms from behind and dragged him between the team house and Gerber's hootch.

Satisfied that the wounded man would be protected by the sandbags around those structures, Cavanaugh ran back out and saw that the dispensary fire was spreading. There was an explosion on top of the redoubt, and Cavanaugh dived for cover as it seemed that the world around him was blowing up. Over the ringing in his ears, he heard the whoosh of a rocket engine and then the loud, devastating bang from a rocket detonating close to him. Moments later shrapnel and debris rained down, hitting the ground around him and bouncing off the tin roofs of the hootches. All around him was the odor of cordite, the acrid stench of the gunpowder from the missile's warhead. He glanced to his right and saw that the team house was burning, part of its roof missing. He ran to the door and looked in. One man was lying on the floor, his legs tangled with an overturned chair. Cavanaugh rushed in, threw the chair aside and lifted the soldier to his feet. As he helped the dazed man from the burning building, he noticed that it was Derek Kepler, the team's intelligence specialist. At the door Cavanaugh heard someone moan.

He set Kepler on the ground outside, then looked around, but it seemed that everyone had taken cover. Suddenly aware of the heat from the fire, he turned and ran back into the team house. Cavanaugh stopped at the door and held up a hand to protect his face. Another body. He leaped forward and grabbed the man's shoulders, dragging him away from the flames. This time it was Sam Anderson, one of the camp's demolitions experts. As he pulled on Anderson's shoulders, he saw someone on the floor partially hidden by an overturned table and obscured by the dense smoke.

Cavanaugh pushed Anderson out the door, letting him fall clear of the team house. The young sergeant rushed toward the table as part of the bar collapsed, sending up a shower of sparks. He pushed the table aside and reached down for the last man. It was Sully Smith. Cavanaugh grabbed Smith by the belt and lifted, then began to drag him across the dirty plywood floor toward the door. As they left, he looked up and saw that several of the rafters were burning. A section of the roof over the stove at the back of the hootch fell in. Flames licked across the floor, and there was a series of small explosions as some of the canned foods blew up.

Outside again, Cavanaugh hauled the wounded men away from the burning team house, depositing them near the sandbags and protection of one of the other hootches. He managed to get Kepler to his feet and directed him toward Gerber's quarters. Anderson was semiconscious, unaware of the situation, mumbling something about the church service that should have ended ten minutes ago.

Then, near the dispensary, Cavanaugh saw a shape moving through the shadows and smoke of the burning buildings. He yelled, "Hey, Washington. Over here. Medic! There are wounded."

The man stopped, looked and then began moving toward him. Cavanaugh looked down at Anderson again. The big man seemed to be dazed but otherwise unhurt. There was no blood on his uniform, though it was torn, dirty and blackened where the fire had gotten too close.

When Washington arrived, his medical pack in hand, Cavanaugh ran back to where he had left Smith and picked him up. As he trotted toward Gerber's hootch, Smith over his shoulder in a fireman's carry, he noticed that the mortars and rockets had stopped falling. There was flickering light from the fires in the redoubt, but no one was trying to fight them.

IN THE FIRE CONTROL TOWER, Gerber abandoned the infrared scope and then the starlight because there seemed to be no ground assault coming. Through the eerie green light of the scope, the fields around the camp had appeared bare except for a single water buffalo that had escaped its pen. Using the huge binoculars that Kepler had stolen from the Navy, Novak studied the tree lines closest to the camp, searching for the origin of the flashes as the mortars fired or of the flames as the engines of the rockets ignited.

To the west Novak caught a flash. Turning and leaning forward so that his elbows rested on the sandbags stacked outside the FCT, he studied it and then pointed. "I've got one tube spotted, Captain."

Holding a field phone handset to either side of his head, he called for illumination to the west of the camp, but that only confirmed what Gerber already knew. It was a harassment mortar and rocket attack. He heard a loud, shuddering whir followed by a sharp, distinct crump as a mortar hit near the base of the commo bunker, throwing up a cloud of dust and smoke as it exploded.

Novak called out a couple of numbers, giving Gerber the range and direction of one of the enemy firing positions. Gerber relayed the message to the 81 mm mortar pits, ordering them to fire smoke rounds first. The white phosphorus exploded into spectacular fountains of flame easily visible from the fire control tower. Gerber adjusted for the pits until the rounds were dropping around the enemy's mortar positions. He then turned his attention to the destruction in his own camp.

Inside the redoubt he could see that the team house and dispensary were burning brightly, the flames shooting forty feet into the air. Beyond that a couple of the hootches used by the Vietnamese strikers had been hit, the black holes in the tin roofs evidence of the mortar damage.

Gerber spun the crank on one of the field phones. "Bocker, get a team together to fight the fires in the redoubt."

"Yes, sir."

"Greg, I want you to remain here and keep your eyes open. Charlie might be humping his tubes to new locations before dumping a few more rounds on us. I'm going down to help fight the fires."

"Yes, sir."

Gerber climbed over the sandbags so that he stood on the top rung of the ladder with his chest and shoulders still visible above the sandbags. "See if you can get a muster and damage report. You might have to coordinate a medevac."

"Yes, sir. I understand."

With that Gerber scrambled down the ladder and ran around the outside of the redoubt until he reached the entrance. He stopped for a moment and watched as a group of men, mainly Vietnamese strikers, used their entrenching tools to throw dirt into the fire. Others were running around the burning buildings, darting forward and then retreating as the heat became too intense for them.

Tyme had run out to the helipad and retrieved one of the large fire extinguishers, a huge metal tube on two big spoked wheels, and had pushed it close to the dispensary. The wide foam spray seemed to be smothering some of the flames.

Gerber saw Washington leave his hootch. He ran over to the medical specialist. "What's the status?"

"We've got Smith, Anderson and Kepler wounded. None of them seriously, but I want to get them evaced out of here." He nodded at the dispensary. "Especially since most of my medicine went up in flames."

"How about the Vietnamese?"

"Cavanaugh found one striker sitting on the ground and got him out of the field of fire. Few shrapnel cuts and a little dazed, but he should be okay."

"Any reports from the strikers' hootches?"

"Not yet."

Gerber left Washington and started for his hootch. He saw Cavanaugh sitting on the ground, his back to the sandbags, his hands clasped between his knees. The sergeant was staring at the dirt in front of him.

"You okay, Sean?" Gerber asked.

"I'm fine, Captain," said Cavanaugh, getting to his feet. "Just resting."

Gerber turned and looked at the team house as the roof fell in. The flames were fanned outward, and there was an explosion of sparks that shot into the sky. "Damn," he said. "Just convinced Crinshaw and his accountants in Saigon that we needed new furniture for the team house, got it out here and then Charlie burns it up."

"Yes, sir," said Cavanaugh.

Gerber looked at the young man, shrugged and entered his hootch. He saw Anderson sitting on the floor, Kepler in one of the chairs and Smith lying on the cot. "How are you guys doing?" he asked.

Kepler glanced at the others. "We're fine, Captain. That rocket caught us in the team house."

"How'd you get out?"

"Cavanaugh pulled us out. All of us. Ran in and out of the fire to get us."

"Jesus," said Gerber. "I saw him outside, and he didn't say a thing about it."

"Yeah, well, I've been sitting here thinking about it," said Kepler. "I was thinking that maybe we ought to put him in for the Silver Star on this one. Get the medal that he deserved the last time."

Gerber moved to his desk and leaned over it, pulling open the bottom drawer so that he could get at the bottle of Beam's. There was some shrapnel damage to his hootch—holes in the roof and in the metal wall locker, and his lantern was broken—but the bottle was intact. He jerked the cork free, took a swig and handed it to Kepler.

"I think," said Gerber, "that the Soldier's Medal might be more appropriate. We weren't really under attack, and he didn't have to fight off an enemy force to get into the team house."

"Yes, sir," Kepler said, "but Charlie was dropping mortars on us, and the Silver Star is the higher award." He handed the bottle back to the captain.

Gerber glanced at Anderson, who shook his head. "I'm trying to anticipate problems with the paper pushers in Saigon. The Silver Star might fly, but I think we'll have a better chance of getting him a Soldier's Medal. I don't want to get it downgraded on a technicality."

"That's the last thing we want," said Kepler. "Especially after what happened last time. Fucking brass hats." He looked up at Gerber. "You mind if I take another hit off that bottle?"

Gerber handed it to him, thinking about the discussion he had had with Fetterman about Cavanaugh drinking too much. Gerber shook his head. First thing he did after the attack was get a drink, and the second thing he did was share it. Maybe he was turning the whole team into a bunch of alcoholics. He watched Kepler tip the bottle to his lips and begin to chug the booze. Kepler swallowed several mouthfuls without breathing, lowered the bottle and said, "Yeah, that's smooth."

"Maybe you'd better go a little easy on that," said Gerber.

"Your supply running low?" Kepler asked.

Before he could answer, Novak appeared at the door. "Got a chopper coming in to evac the wounded, Captain. No one in the Vietnamese area was hurt badly. Just a couple of scratches that their medics patched up."

"Anything else?"

"Noticed some flashes near Cai Cai. Couldn't tell much about them though. Might have been grenades detonating or some kind of big fire. I thought maybe we should send out a patrol to see what's happening."

Gerber looked at his watch. "Let's wait for first light. I don't want to put anyone into the field tonight. Nothing they could do until morning, anyway, and a couple of hours won't hurt one way or the other."

"Yes, sir. Just a thought."

4

THE RICE PADDIES
WEST OF CAMP A-555

As the sun came up threatening another hot day, Cavanaugh led his patrol of twenty-five Vietnamese strikers through the gate, then turned toward the village of Cai Cai, which was now marked by a towering plume of black smoke. They had crossed the runway before the peta-prime had a chance to soften in the sun, traversing the field of elephant grass. Mist hugged the depressions in the fields, seemed to bubble from the streams or riverbeds and clung to the trees and along the edges of the swamps.

Cavanaugh kept the pace brisk, skirting the swampy areas and avoiding the jungles by using the dikes in the paddy fields. Normally he would have avoided the dikes, preferring to walk through the paddies themselves, stepping on the young plants to keep his feet from sinking into the dirty, feces-laden water, but they were in a hurry. Airlift, in this case, couldn't be provided in the time it would take Cavanaugh and his men to walk the twelve klicks to the village. The point man and the slack were watching the path on the dikes carefully, looking for trip wires and depressions that suggested booby traps. In this area the farmers usually removed them as quickly as the VC constructed them.

They moved swiftly through the fields, staying as far as possible from the tree lines and the jungle. The patrol crossed unused roads, one of which had been paved in the past but was now broken with jagged pieces of slowly disintegrating concrete. They reached a hamlet of hootches with rotting thatched roofs, decaying fences of woven branches and degenerating wells and water buffalo pens. There Cavanaugh gave the signal to stop and spread out. The group began looking for signs that the VC had been there but found nothing. Fifteen minutes later Cavanaugh had them on their feet again, moving toward Cai Cai.

By midmorning the sun was bright, almost directly overhead in a cloudless sky. The heat radiated down to sap their strength, making them sweat heavily until their uniforms were soaked. The patrol began to slow. The pace decreased to a crawl, each step becoming an ordeal as they chased the column of black smoke that seemed to recede in the distance.

They continued, staying away from the trees, walking on the rice paddy dikes until the fields ended and the elephant grass began again. Fingers of jungle reached out from the Cambodian border and along the canals that crisscrossed the area. Cavanaugh avoided them, moving ever closer to Cai Cai.

Finally they walked into a narrow tree line, spreading out almost on line and then regrouping as they neared the edge. The point man crouched just inside the line of trees. The open ground in front of him was as flat and smooth as a blanket spread for a picnic. Cavanaugh crept toward him, using the cover of the bushes and trunks of the coconuts and palms and the shadows cast by them. He could see the village now but not the inhabitants. For several minutes he remained motionless, his eyes sweeping the remains of the hootches closest to him.

Cavanaugh and his men advanced on the village of Cai Cai, emerging from the trees and into the rutted streets that ran among the burned and smoking hootches. Some of them, constructed of mud walls and tin roofs, showed little evidence of fire. Others, made of thatch, were little more than smoking piles of rubble, and still others were gutted, the roofs missing and a wall or two tumbled into the interior. There were no people near the structures and no bodies among them.

They swept through half the village, checking the hootches, the remains of bunkers hidden behind or beside them. All they found were some dead pigs and chickens. It was as if everything that had any value had been removed and the rest, which couldn't be carried or driven, burned.

On the outskirts of the hamlet, they turned and started back, each of them silent now. Cavanaugh knew that a few of the PF strikers had families who lived in Cai Cai, friends who worked the rice fields and tended the pigs. The strikers were now worried. The villagers, seeing a large group of armed men approach, might take refuge at first, but once the identity of the men was established, they should have come out of hiding.

Cavanaugh stood at the center of the formation, the men spread out on either side of him, looking back toward the west, searching the side of the village they had yet to enter. At the far end was a large communal structure where the villagers congregated during the long summer evenings. A great deal of smoke was pouring from that area, and Cavanaugh was afraid of what he might find there.

Again they began their sweep, finding no evidence of the VC, except for the destruction of the village. On the mud walls of some of the hootches were pockmarks of rifle and machine gun bullets and scars of shrapnel from mortars and grenades. Cavanaugh stared at that and realized that the attack on Camp A-555 the night before had been a diversion for the real assault here.

As they moved through that sector of the village, they found the real horror. At first it was a single body of a village elder who had been shot, his blood staining the red dust a rusty color. His shirt had been stripped from his chest so that several bullet holes were easily visible. His black shorts, soaked with blood that had not yet dried, clung to his skinny legs.

Them men moved slowly toward the fence of woven branches that surrounded the communal building. Lying near the gate was another corpse, one hand missing and most of the head gone so that the brain, a gray mass, had slid to the dirt. Wisps of smoke curled up from the shirt.

Almost as if someone had issued a command, the patrol hesitated. There was a rattling of equipment as the men checked their weapons and fixed their bayonets. It wasn't something that had to be done but something to do to put off the discovery they were about to make. Each of them knew what they would find; the stench being blown at them by the light breeze told them that the villagers had died the night before.

Inside the fence they found the rest of the villagers. Every man, woman and child was there, in some places their bodies heaped in piles. Most of them were charred, and Cavanaugh guessed that the Vietcong had tried to destroy the evidence. Some had obviously tried to run and had been cut down by rifle fire. Those bodies were riddled with bullet holes.

One of the PFs turned his head and threw up violently. He looked up at Cavanaugh, his eyes filled with tears, then was sick again.

Washington approached, holding out his medical bag as if it contained poisonous snakes and he was afraid that it might touch his body. "Christ," he said. "Jesus Christ."

Cavanaugh turned and stared at him, then closed his eyes, his face suddenly pale. He clenched his teeth, trying to suppress a scream of fury bubbling in his throat. He pulled the trigger on his weapon, firing the whole clip on automatic into the mud wall of the closest hootch. When it ran dry and the bolt locked back, he threw the weapon up, one hand on the butt, the other on the hot barrel. He ignored the pain, the cords in his arms standing out. He shouted something unintelligible and then kicked at the brass shells near his feet. He stomped them into the dirt, shouting, screaming, the rage etched on his face as the men stood there watching him, unbelieving and uncomprehending.

Finally he dropped to his knees and whispered, "Why, why, why?" until he saw that the others were staring at him. Slowly he rose and said, "Let's check the bodies. We don't want to overlook someone who might only be wounded." He stood quietly for a moment, waiting for them to react, and then added forcefully, "Let's move it."

Washington came forward. "I don't think there are any survivors. That's why they burned the bodies, to make sure. I'll get onto graves registration and make the arrangements there."

"You know what to do, T.J.," Cavanaugh said. "I'll take half the men and make another sweep through the ville to see if there's anything we might have missed while you do your thing here."

Without a word Washington turned and waved at the RTO. "Over here," he said. The medic then pointed at four of the strikers who were standing at the fence, their faces blank, looking at the smoldering bodies on the ground in front of them.

Cavanaugh stared at the scene for a moment, felt the hate begin burning in his gut again, a physical pain almost intense enough to make him cry out. His vision clouded, a black mass blocking the bright sun, giving the scene in front of him the black and white, grainy look of an old photograph. He clamped his teeth together and breathed through his mouth, trying to rein in his emotions as the bodies of the villagers shimmered and seemed to vanish, to be replaced by the strikers in the listening post and the field of dead Vietcong and NVA soldiers.

He turned slowly, dragging his eyes from the scene until he was looking at the tree line filled with coconuts, teak and palm, the huge broad leaves fluttering in the breeze. He felt extremely hot, sweat pouring from him, and his breathing became suddenly shallow and rapid. Gradually he became aware of his surroundings, the strikers standing near him, staring at him but afraid to speak.

"All right," he growled, trying to mask his emotions, "let's move out now. Search everything thoroughly."

With that he moved along the side of the village where the edge of a canal almost abutted the front of a hootch. The roof was gone, the remains a pile of smoking black debris. Cavanaugh pushed through the door, moving carefully, avoiding the hot spot. He found nothing. Everything of value had either been removed or burned in the fire. He pressed back to the rear and found the hidden entrance to a bunker but was reluctant to pry the top off. He forced himself to do it, even though he was afraid of what he might find there.

It was empty.

For the next hour Cavanaugh and the strikers searched the village. They found more evidence of the VC attack. There was an unexploded mortar shell buried nearly to its tail fins in the dirt. There were casings from AK-47s, the 7.62 mm shell shorter than the American-made version. Someone found a couple of unexploded Chicom grenades lying in the dirt near hootches.

The VC had evidently murdered some of the people in their hootches. Tracks on the ground showed where people had been dragged, and dirty ragged stains on the unburned bamboo mats showed where the wounded and dying had fallen. Clearly the VC had swept into the village for the sole purpose of killing everyone there.

As they completed their second search, Cavanaugh heard the sound of helicopters in the distance and turned to see a flight of Hueys swooping out of the sky. Washington, who was standing near the communal area, moved toward the open field to the west and tossed a purple smoke grenade into the grass. For an instant the breeze took the smoke, blowing it down into the grass, and then a large violet cloud blossomed.

Cavanaugh stepped to the safety of a standing wall of a hootch as the helicopters touched down, the lead ship putting its nose in the middle of the purple cloud. The rotor blades kicked up a whirlwind of dust and swirling grass. Nine other choppers followed, each one sliding to the ground in a staggered trail formation. As each of the helicopters landed, men leaped from the cargo compartments, crouching in the grass, their weapons pointed outward. They waited until the aircraft lifted off, climbing out.

The men from the choppers got to their feet, formed on line and began the short walk into the village, their weapons ready, their heads swiveling back and forth. Cavanaugh headed toward Washington. The sergeant noticed that the big medic was sweating profusely, his fatigues stained a darker color now. He had taken off his green beret, and the perspiration glistened in the curly black hair.

"Called in relief," he said when he saw Cavanaugh approaching. "Hell, there was nothing I could do. Too many people. Way too many. We've got to make sure that everyone gets a decent burial."

Cavanaugh nodded. Washington didn't have to explain it to him. The religion of the people demanded that they be buried, although he wasn't sure how much good it would do. Some of them believed that losing the head forced the deceased to wander the Earth for eternity. That was why the VC sometimes decapitated their victims. Maybe burning away the face did the same thing, Cavanaugh thought. Maybe these people would all be forced to wander the Earth. It was a terrorist tactic directed against the Special Forces camp and the Vietnamese who sought shelter in it.

The new arrivals from the helicopters worked their way across the open grass. Cavanaugh identified the commander by the RTO, who was sticking close to him. The man took the handset, halted and knelt. He snapped his fingers and pointed. Another soldier approached carrying a map and set it in front of the commander. Cavanaugh grinned, thinking that if he was a VC sniper, he could take out the entire group with a couple of well-placed rounds or a single grenade.

Finally the leader gave the handset back to the RTO, stood and folded his map, then handed it back to his sergeant. The line moved forward again into the village. Washington began angling toward the command party. He halted, waited and then turned to walk with them as the new force entered Cai Cai.

Cavanaugh moved toward them, falling in close enough to hear them but staying far enough away so that he wasn't part of the command party, just in case.

"What you want is graves registration," the young lieutenant was saying. "We're a line company."

"Yes, sir, and that is what I requested. But we need someone to stay here until the graves people can get out and take care of it."

The lieutenant stopped walking and turned to stare at Washington. "You want my men to guard a bunch of dead bodies? Bodies already mutilated by the VC? To make sure that the VC don't come back and do more damage?"

"Yes, sir. In a nutshell."

"You're out of your fucking mind, Sergeant. I don't give a good goddamn about what these slopes think. We'd be better off burning everything to the ground and paving it. The whole fucking country. Make it the world's largest parking lot.''

Washington shot a glance at Cavanaugh and raised his eyebrows, but to the lieutenant he said, ''Sir, it's important that we attend to this matter properly. Our strikers won't support us if we don't take care of this, and that means that an all-American camp will have to be built. Better four hundred strikers out here than four hundred Americans.''

The lieutenant unsnapped the straps of his helmet so that they hung down along his face. He rubbed a hand over his clean-shaven chin and said, ''We'll stay the night only because our CO told us to. Tomorrow we're out of here. Now what's the tactical situation?''

Quickly Washington began telling the lieutenant what they had found, using the map that one of the sergeants held out. While that was going on, Cavanaugh walked back toward the communal building.

Washington and his strikers had arranged the bodies so that they were in neat rows along the fence. He had covered the corpses of the children with the poncho liners taken from the strikers, but there weren't enough to cover all the bodies.

Cavanaugh looked at the line of dead. He had seen the same thing a dozen times. After every battle there were lines of dead, and it always seemed more horrible than bodies scattered over the field or lying in the wire or spread among the bunkers. Seeing them lined up for tallying and identification seemed to be the true sign that the people were dead. It was the final act before they were stuck in the ground to disappear from sight forever.

With a trembling hand Cavanaugh reached into the tunic pocket of one of his strikers and took a cigarette. The sergeant didn't smoke, but for some reason he felt the need to now. The striker just smiled at him, exposing a gap in his mouth where his three bottom teeth should have been. He produced an American Zippo lighter with the crest of the First Cavalry Division on it.

Cavanaugh let the man light the cigarette and cupped his hands over those of the Vietnamese as he sucked the smoke into his mouth and into his lungs. He grimaced and coughed violently, bending over with his eyes closed and the cigarette clutched in his left hand. He straightened, wiped the tears from his eyes and smiled sheepishly at the Vietnamese. Then the sergeant sat down, his back against the woven fence and watched the thunderheads building to the west. A shadow fell across him, and he glanced up to see Washington standing there.

"We can pull out now," said the medical specialist. "If you've seen everything you need to see."

Cavanaugh climbed to his feet. "I've seen more than I care to."

"Yeah." Washington stood there for a moment looking at the younger man and then asked, "You okay?"

"Fine." Cavanaugh smiled and dropped his cigarette, grinding it out with more force than necessary. "If you're referring to that little episode earlier, it was just seeing the way the VC treated the villagers. Rage that humans could do that to other humans. A momentary thing. It won't happen again."

Washington nodded, about to say something, then changed his mind. "Okay, then, let's get out of here. I've arranged to leave four of our strikers behind to help and act as scouts. They'll return to camp tomorrow."

"All right." Cavanaugh turned, waving an arm over his head to signal his men. Once they had gathered, they formed a line and began to work their way out of the village and back into the thick grass of the open fields.

They reached the camp about dusk, having stopped once to eat and once for a break. They had walked through most of the afternoon's heat, but as evening approached, the clouds appeared, blotting out the sun. A breeze from Cambodia picked up, blowing away the stifling humidity. They made good time after that, and with the camp as the destination, the men didn't try to think of ways to slow down. They wanted to reach it before dark.

As usual, Gerber met them as they entered the camp. He was sitting on the sandbagged wall, and didn't move as the group arrived, waiting for them to come to him. Washington turned, held his rifle over his head and said, "Weapons check in fifteen minutes. Get them cleaned, and then we'll get a hot meal."

As Cavanaugh approached, Gerber asked, "How bad was it?"

"Really grim, Captain. The VC either killed or carted away every living thing. We found some dead chickens and pigs, but I think the VC took most of them." He hesitated, as if unsure of what he should say next. "There weren't that many young girls around. I think the VC took them, too. Maybe some of the boys."

"Okay, Sean, write a report of everything you witnessed out there and any recommendations that you might have. Don't bust your butt on it, but I'd like it in the next two or three days."

"Yes, sir."

Cavanaugh turned to go, but Gerber stopped him. "How you doing?"

"Fine." He shrugged. "That was quite a sight out there, but I'm fine."

"Okay, Sean. See you later."

After Cavanaugh left, Washington stepped away from the Vietnamese strikers. He held his weapon in one hand and his medic bag in the other. "Captain," he said as he moved closer, "I've got to talk to you about Sean."

"Okay. Let's go to my hootch and you can tell me about it."

They crossed the compound, entered the redoubt and turned toward Gerber's hootch, passing the remains of the team house. The charred debris had been carted away. The concrete slab that formed the foundation of the structure had been cleaned and looked almost pristine in the fading rays of the dying sun. A new stack of plywood and a bundle of studs sat near the slab waiting for reconstruction of the team house to begin.

They entered Gerber's hootch. Washington noticed blood stains on the floor where the wounded men had waited to be evaced that morning. An odor of smoke hung in the air, and the screen above the bunk and over the desk was discolored from the fire in the team house. Gerber gestured at the metal chair and then slipped into his own. Without thinking, he reached for the bottom drawer where the bottle of Beam's was stored and then froze. Maybe they all were hitting the booze a little too heavily. He hadn't really thought about it until Fetterman had mentioned it, but maybe it was time to rethink some of their rituals.

"Okay, T.J., what's on your mind?"

"I'm a little worried about Sean," Washington replied. "Worried that maybe he came back to us a little too soon."

"I would imagine that you have a reason for saying that."

"Yes, sir. First, let me say that I would never do anything to hurt Sean. But if he's—"

"Let's just assume," Gerber interrupted, "that none of us would do anything to hurt him. But we are a combat unit and there are other considerations."

Washington nodded. "Yes, sir." He went on to tell Gerber about the sudden emotional outburst he'd witnessed when they had discovered the dead villagers.

"Was he completely out of control?" asked Gerber. "Could you get through to him?"

"We didn't try, Captain. It was a quick thing, like being called out at home when you know you're safe. A sudden flare of blind anger that burns itself out quickly. It's just something you can't have on patrol."

Gerber stood up. "You're right, T.J. I'll talk to Sean about it. Thanks for letting me know."

Now Washington was on his feet. "No problem, Captain. I do have one other question, though."

"What's that?"

"Where do we eat with the team house gone?"

Gerber laughed. "Well, for tonight I'm afraid we're stuck with C-rations unless you want to eat in the strikers' mess. Minh has invited us to share his facilities until ours are repaired. Either option."

"Thanks, Captain."

"And I'll talk to Sean, but I don't think we've got a problem yet."

"I hope not."

5

SPECIAL FORCES
CAMP A-555

For nearly twenty minutes after Washington left, Gerber sat in his hootch, watching the last of the sunlight fade until he was wrapped in darkness. He didn't bother to turn on the lights, even after he heard the main camp generator start up, signaling that they had all the electric power they would need. Finally he stood and moved to the door, peering across the compound. The work to repair the dispensary had progressed well during the day, and all that really needed to be done was a restocking of the medical supplies. They had been lucky that the damage had turned out to be only superficial.

He stepped into the compound and walked over to Cavanaugh's hootch. He was going to knock, but decided to look inside first. Cavanaugh was sitting hunched over on his bunk, an open bottle of bourbon between his feet. He seemed to be studying it rather than drinking from it.

"Sean, you got a minute?" asked Gerber.

Cavanaugh turned toward the camp commander. "Sure. You want a snort?"

"You drink all that by yourself?"

"Oh, not tonight, sir," replied Cavanaugh, picking up the bottle. "I've had this for a couple of days."

Gerber entered the room fully and looked around, at the metal wall locker with the jungle fatigues hung in it and the dirty clothes and boots thrown into the bottom of it, at the two cots covered with mosquito netting, at the plywood walls covered with pictures torn from magazines. Most of those near Sully's bunk were scantily clad blondes and those near Cavanaugh's were Second World War airplanes. There was a Coleman lantern sitting on a metal folding chair throwing its harsh white light into the room.

"How'd the patrol go today?" asked Gerber.

"You already talked to T. J., so you know what we found," said Cavanaugh.

"Yes, that's true. But I wanted to talk to you about it, too. Get a second point of view."

Cavanaugh snatched the bottle from the floor and took a long pull. He set it down and stared at it. "Come on, Captain, you know what happened on the patrol. I'm sure T. J. told you that I got upset when we found the villagers. Christ, sir, what did he expect? What do any of you expect? We find fifty people butchered and the bodies burned for no apparent reason other than the terrorist tactics of a guerrilla war. Of course I was upset by it. But it was a quick thing."

Gerber nodded but didn't speak. He waited, watching Cavanaugh.

"I know what you're thinking. I know what you all think. You're just waiting for old Sean to flip out again. Waiting for me to go crazy so that you can get me out of here. You didn't want me to come back. I had to ask the doctors. Hell, you didn't get down to see me all that often."

Gerber reached out. "Maybe I will take a drink." As he got the bottle and thought about what he was going to say, he realized that Cavanaugh did have a point. Gerber had been going to say that they were in a war zone where they couldn't hop into the car for a spin down to Saigon to visit a sick friend. But he realized that it wasn't true. They could get rides to Saigon in any of the helicopters that visited the camp daily, and many of the men had been in and out of Saigon dozens of times while Cavanaugh was in the hospital. They could have made a greater effort to visit him.

Gerber shrugged. "You're right, Sean, we could have. But we did have other priorities. That's not an excuse, just a fact. And you might have had to ask to be reassigned here, but that was because of the doctors in Saigon and not anything we did out here. When Bates called to ask if I wanted you back, my answer was yes." He grinned. "Not to mention the fact that we're shorthanded. Even more so now."

"Yes, sir." Cavanaugh took the bottle back and drank from it.

"By the way, I've put you in for the Soldier's Medal for pulling Anderson, Smith and Kepler out of the fire. I think you'll get this one. The criteria say that saving a life is not the only requirement for the award. You saved three and did it during a mortar attack, risking your life. I should have said something about that to you earlier."

"The Soldier's Medal, huh?"

"That's right. It's more of a humanitarian award than a combat decoration, but it seemed more appropriate."

"Yes, sir. Thanks."

"Oh," said Gerber, "I'm sending Lieutenant Novak out on a patrol tomorrow to see if he can find the trail of the VC who hit the village and maybe ambush them. Since we are shorthanded, I wondered if you would mind going out again so soon."

"Oh, hell, Captain, today's patrol was just a stroll through the park. We left in the morning and got back this evening. It's no big deal."

"Then contact the lieutenant sometime this evening and see what he has in mind."

"Yes, sir. No problem."

Gerber got to his feet and stepped to the door. "Sean, if I haven't made it clear before now, let me say that we're all glad to have you back. Probably Smith, Anderson and Kepler more than the rest of us."

"Thank you, Captain. Thank you."

THE PATROL FORMED AT DAWN the next morning at the gate. Twenty Vietnamese strikers stood in a ragged line facing Lieutenant Greg Novak, the big American. He was six feet two and a half inches, weighed about two hundred and seventy-five pounds and had short, dark hair. Although he had shaved before leaving his hootch, he already had a five o'clock shadow. He sported a pistolero mustache, which was against Army regulations, but no one really cared. Next to the tiny Vietnamese, Novak, whose nickname was Animal, looked like a giant.

As Cavanaugh joined them, Novak said, "Equipment check. I plan to stay out two days, minimum."

Cavanaugh nodded and began moving down the line, examining the packs of the Vietnamese, making sure that they carried everything they were supposed to have. He knew that they sometimes threw away or left behind items they could see no reason to carry. Each striker had his small first-aid kit, spare ammo for squad automatic weapons and a couple of spare grenades for the two M-79s. Then Cavanaugh searched through their packs for their personal rations. He moved along the line quickly, also checking the weapons to make sure they were clean and in operating condition, and that each man had two or three canteens filled with water. Novak watched for a moment and then started at the other end to speed up the process.

As they prepared to move through the gate, Cavanaugh with the point man, Gerber appeared from the redoubt. He stopped at the entrance, one foot up on the sandbags, and waved at them. When Cavanaugh saw that he wasn't going to come any closer, he opened the flimsy gate and passed through it. They went down the short road that led to the airstrip, turned to the north, and walked around the end of the runway before turning to the west to enter the fields of elephant grass.

They moved quickly through the field, breaking new ground, avoiding the paths used by the other patrols. The point man was rotated frequently because of the backbreaking nature of leading the men through the elephant grass. With each step the point had to twist his foot to one side or the other, breaking the grass so that the man behind him would have a trail to follow. After only fifty or a hundred meters, the point man's ankles, calves and thighs ached with the strain.

They moved from the elephant grass into the rice fields, stringing out along the dikes, angling toward the tree lines to the south. There were a couple of clumps of trees, tall palms with broad leaves, huge coconuts and teak trees towering above the rest. Tucked in among the trees were farmers' hootches surrounded by pens for chickens or water buffalo and encircled by fences of woven branches, bamboo and elephant grass.

By midmorning, with the sun high overhead baking the ground and sapping the strength of the men, they moved from the open territory into the trees, following the long axis of the tree line and finally moving into a thick silver of jungle that jutted south from the Parrot's Beak to the edge of the Plain of Reeds. They halted as the undergrowth became thicker, the wait-a-minute vines tugging at the clothes, arms and legs of the men. The point was using his machete to open a path through the worst of it, slowing the march. Soon they came to a game trail, a wide path through the thickest part of the jungle, and diverted to follow it, increasing their speed.

At noon Novak called a halt for lunch. The men scattered through the thinning jungle, each watching an area ahead of him as he ate cold C-rations or rice and fish heads, then washed it down with the tepid water form his canteen. The canopy wasn't an impenetrable green sea from either the ground or the air but a splotchy, incomplete roof that let huge patches of sunlight through.

Novak made a routine radio check, joking with Bocker about remaining in the camp's cool commo bunker sucking down frosty Cokes, and then advised him that the patrol would be veering farther south. The only evidence of movement they had found on the game trail was a huge pile of steaming excrement left during the recent passage of an elephant.

When the meal was finished, Novak and Cavanaugh got the men on their feet and pointed them to the south. It was more of the same, except that the jungle had taken on the humidity of a steam bath, and they could almost hear the vegetation baking in the sun. There was a low, quiet hissing, as if it had just rained, and curtains of light mist drifted in the deep shadows. But there was no hint of a breeze that would provide a little relief.

Around them they could hear the chattering of the monkeys, the screeches and cries of the birds and the rustling of the tiny plants as small mammals ran through the jungle. They only saw one snake, a huge, brightly colored reptile that was draped over a branch split from a lightning-damaged tree, warming itself in the afternoon sun. They avoided it easily, none of the men wishing to disturb it.

Cavanaugh had just moved forward, passing several of the strikers as he tried to catch the point man, when he noticed suddenly the jungle was strangely quiet. He could still hear the hiss of the baking ground, but there were no longer the sounds of the animals that inhabited the area. Cavanaugh stopped to listen and then searched the canopy over him, looking for the movement of a monkey or the flash of bright color from the birds.

Puzzled now by the sudden lull, he crouched, one knee on the soft, wet ground. For an instant everything was suspended, the sound and motion of the jungle falling away into nothing—then the world seemed to blow up.

The first explosion was at the head of the patrol. Cavanaugh saw a geyser of dirt kick up near him and heard the scream of the point man as the shrapnel from the Chicom grenade tore into him. The sergeant dropped to the ground as more explosions ripped through the patrol. There was the staccato burst of a machine gun, and he could hear the bullets ripping through the foliage and smashing into the trees.

All around him there was shouting and shooting. The strikers were coming to life, returning fire now. Cavanaugh turned and saw the jungle floor littered with bodies, ten or twelve of his men down, their uniforms dark with blood. Then from the rear of the patrol came a roar like a lion gone berserk, and Cavanaugh saw Novak leap up and rush into the jungle, his M-16 blazing. He was bellowing, the words lost in the crash of the weapons and the explosions of the grenades.

The rest of the strikers were on their feet, running into the jungle, into the ambush, shooting from the hip, screaming at the tops of their voices. Cavanaugh, too, was up, racing off the trail and into the vegetation. He saw a flash of khaki hidden among the shadows and leaped for it. He landed next to an NVA soldier firing an AK at the bodies of the strikers. Cavanaugh slammed the butt of his rifle into the man's head and felt the enemy's skull splinter. He spun and dropped to one knee, his rifle against his shoulder.

For a moment he thought they had broken the back of the ambush. Then there was a bugle call from deeper in the jungle—a single searing note that built and dropped and was joined by whistles and shouts and renewed firing. A dozen enemy soldiers seemed to rise from the ground, coming at him. He fired once, saw the bullet hit, but the man kept coming, and he believed he was in one of his nightmares. His vision seemed to tunnel down until it was just him and the VC at opposite ends of a tube and everything else gone. Cavanaugh aimed carefully, pulled the trigger and saw the man's head disappear in a cloud of crimson as he fell to the jungle floor.

And then Cavanaugh was shouting, a scream erupting from his throat as he began pulling the trigger rapidly. He watched the enemy soldiers tumble into the jungle as his weapon kicked against his shoulder. Turning, he saw more VC and fired again and again, riddling them until the bolt locked back, the magazine empty.

As he hit the magazine release, dropping the empty clip to the jungle floor, he saw Novak rise, a VC in a headlock under each arm. A third rushed at him, but the lieutenant kicked out with a massive foot, catching the enemy soldier in the chest, knocking his rifle to the side and punting the man out of the way. He then slammed the heads together, smashing the skulls of the two VC. He dropped them, yanked his .45 from its holster and began firing at the enemy swarming around him.

Cavanaugh jammed a new magazine into his rifle, released the bolt to let it strip the first round into the chamber. He opened fire, trying to protect his lieutenant. An NVA regular materialized out of the bushes, weaving toward Novak, a machete held high in his hand. Cavanaugh aimed and fired, spinning him and dropping him as the machete flew back, flashing in the sunlight. The sergeant fired repeatedly, hitting enemy soldiers, but there were too many of them. Novak disappeared as they washed over him like a tidal wave. Then, miraculously, Novak was back on his feet. He picked up one of the VC and lifted him overhead, throwing him against the trunk of a teak tree. He grabbed another, one hand on each side of the man's head, snatching him clear of the ground. Suddenly Novak twisted the VC's head, snapping the neck with a popping noise that seemed to penetrate the sound of all the firing. The soldier went limp, and Novak dropped him.

Then Cavanaugh was busy, too, as the enemy rushed toward him from all sides. He emptied his weapon again, but before he could reload, a VC with a machete charged him. Cavanaugh grabbed the barrel of his rifle with his left hand, keeping his right hand near the butt. He thrust it forward to parry the chop as the VC tried to split his skull. The blade hit the rifle with a metallic clang and fell to the ground. Cavanaugh swung the butt around in a tight circle, clipping the VC just behind the ear. His eyes went blank as blood splattered everywhere. There was a crack as the stock of his M-14 shattered. Cavanaugh held it like an oversize pistol and tried to reload, but the enemy was coming too quickly. He then leaped out of the way, seeking cover momentarily behind the thick trunk of a palm. He worked the bolt of his damaged weapon, trying to reload.

To his right he saw Lieutenant Novak for the last time. The burly Special Forces officer was on his feet, punching at an NVA soldier. Novak hit him between the eyes, and as the soldier dropped, Novak suddenly staggered. Cavanaugh saw blood splash the front of the lieutenant's uniform, and then he stood straight up, roared and fell into the jungle.

Cavanaugh opened fire again, shooting at the VC and NVA who stood where Novak had been. He saw them topple over, thrown to the right and left, as his bullets slammed into them. Cavanaugh was grinning but didn't realize it. It was relief. Relief that his weapon was working as it should. Relief that the enemy wasn't able to avoid the effect of his bullets. He kept firing at them until his rifle was empty once more and the bolt locked back, the barrel smoking.

He tossed the rifle aside, grabbed his pistol and began shooting at everything that moved. Another NVA soldier appeared, looked wildly about him, then tried to break for freedom. Using a two-handed grip, Cavanaugh fired five times at the man's retreating back. But he never wavered. Cavanaugh lost sight of him in the thick jungle vegetation.

He spun then, searching for targets, but his surroundings were quiet. He turned slowly, but there was no one moving near him. He could see bodies lying on the trail among the trees and bushes and scattered along the jungle floor. From somewhere he heard a quiet moaning of a wounded soldier that ended suddenly. He crouched, felt the throat of the enemy soldier at his feet, but there was no pulse. On closer scrutiny he saw that most of the man's head was missing.

Slowly he moved through the trees, checking the bodies, searching for survivors. He found the lieutenant lying face-down in a pile of enemy corpses. Novak had been shot eight or nine times through the chest and stomach. One slug had ripped through his cheek to expose his teeth and gums. Cavanaugh checked him carefully, knowing that any of several of the wounds could have been fatal and that Novak was dead. But still the sergeant hoped that the lieutenant had somehow survived. Cavanaugh took the lieutenant's big combat knife, which Novak had bought at Ironmonger Jim's before he left the World for Vietnam. He fastened it to his pistol belt and said, "You got a lot of them, sir."

Cavanaugh surveyed the whole field of battle. He stopped counting the enemy dead when he reached fifty-two. Slowly he began to collect some of the weapons, then dropped them at the foot of a large, smooth teak tree near the trail. The strikers were all dead, too. Almost every one of them had been shot four or five times, and those who died on the trail were riddled with AK bullets.

Cavanaugh stumbled upon the RTO's body. Blood was still leaking from the half dozen or so slugs that had taken his life. The bloodstained radio was useless, having been shot to pieces. The RTO had died gripping the handset, and Cavanaugh wondered if he had lived long enough to get off a distress call. The smaller backup unit, the URC-10—little more than a hand-held survival radio—was missing. Cavanaugh searched the area near Novak's body for it after he discovered the larger radio was ruined, but couldn't find it.

Finally he gave up. He took one of the M-14s from a dead striker, moved away from the ambush site and sat down on the trail to wait. He wasn't sure what he was waiting for, but he knew that something would happen soon.

AT THE SAME TIME the patrol was being ambushed, Sergeant Galvin Bocker was sitting in the commo bunker, his feet propped on the OD green plywood counter. He didn't mind sitting in the dimly lighted, cool bunker while the rest of the team humped through the bush or worked on building the new team house. Monitoring the radios today, as always, was easy duty. Suddenly he caught a burst of static and a shout in Vietnamese over the Fox Mike. The yell was nearly drowned out by firing in the background, then all transmission was abruptly cut off.

Bocker leaped to the radio, grabbed the mike and tried to raise the patrol, assuming that they were in trouble. "Zulu Five, Zulu Five, this is Zulu Base."

He waited, not wanting to cut out their signal if they broadcast, but the sudden silence suggested that the radio had been destroyed. He waited a moment longer, heard nothing, made a last attempt to raise them and then raced from the commo bunker, heading for Gerber's hootch.

As he entered the redoubt, he saw the captain standing with Fetterman near the remains of the team house, the two of them talking to a couple of the Vietnamese who were helping to rebuild the structure. He called out, "Captain, can I talk to you for a moment?"

Gerber turned, waved at Bocker and then told Fetterman, "I'll get back to you." He moved to Bocker and asked, "What is it?"

Bocker looked around, saw that no one was near and said quietly, "I think our patrol has been ambushed."

"You try to confirm?" asked Gerber.

"I couldn't raise them. Thought I should brief you."

"You try to get them on the Uniform? Novak had one of those URC-10s with him."

"No, sir. I thought I'd better advise you."

"Okay, get back and try that. I'll let Tony know, and we'll be over in a couple of minutes."

"Yes, sir." Bocker turned and ran back to the commo bunker.

Gerber turned to face the team house. He called, "Tony, leave that and come over here." When Fetterman was close, Gerber said, "I think we've got trouble. You get a patrol together to see if you can find Novak."

"What is it?"

"I don't know. Get ready to move out and then meet me at the commo bunker. Make it fast and be prepared to leave in about fifteen minutes."

"Yes, sir," replied Fetterman. He headed for his hootch.

Gerber left the redoubt and entered the commo bunker. Bocker was sitting next to the rack of radios, using first the Fox Mike and then the Uniform, listening and trying again. Bocker's Vietnamese counterpart was standing behind the commo sergeant watching him work.

"You get anything, Galvin?" asked Gerber.

"No, sir. Just the one short call with all the shooting in the background and then nothing. The lieutenant might have the URC-10 turned off so we wouldn't be able to raise him, but we should be able to get him on the PRC-10. If something happened to that, I would think he'd be on the URC."

"What's the range on that?" asked Gerber.

"It's an ultrahigh frequency radio, sir, so we should be able to get something. Hell, on a good day you might be able to pick up a signal a hundred miles away. And if all else fails, he can always relay a message to us."

"He's late on a check-in time?"

"Only about five or six minutes, but you know how that is."

Fetterman, wearing his field gear and carrying his M-3 grease gun, entered the commo bunker and walked over to the counter. "What's the word?"

"Not good. Can't get in touch with Lieutenant Novak." He glanced at Bocker. "Let's take a look at the map. Novak and I went over his patrol routes, so I think we should be able to find him."

They moved to the chart of the local area, which had been tacked to a piece of plywood then hung on the wall. Gerber studied it for a moment. "Given the time of day, I would guess that Novak should be in this area." He pointed and added, "Plans called for him to set up an ambush here, unless he found signs that the VC were moving elsewhere."

Fetterman nodded. "So if I come out the gate and turn southwest immediately, I can cut off a couple of klicks."

"That's right. He headed due west before turning south."

"Airlift, Captain?"

"We can try, but I don't think we can get anything out here fast enough to do us any good. Even if there was a unit available this late in the day, by the time they could get here and you loaded, you could walk to the jumping-off point."

"Yes, sir."

Gerber studied the map again. "You know, there are a couple of roads through there. If we loaded your patrol into the trucks, we could be into the area in half an hour."

"Tips our hand," said Fetterman.

"Seems that our hand's already been tipped." Gerber nodded. "Get your squad together, and I'll arrange with Minh to have them trucked out."

"Do we walk back?"

"No. We'll post a guard, and you can drive back once you get an answer. We'll establish a night laager on the road. A forward operating base for this."

"Pretty elaborate plan for something you're throwing together on the spur of the moment."

"Everything is in the manual. All we have to do is put the people into the plan and move out."

"Yes, sir."

THERE WERE four three-quarter-ton trucks and a jeep parked near the front gate. Thirty Vietnamese strikers were tossing boxes of C-rations, extra ammo and additional supplies into the trucks to be stored under the troop seats. Fetterman and Washington were loading medical supplies into the jeep. Mounted on the back was an AN/PRC-25 which would allow them to communicate both with the camp and every aviation unit in South Vietnam.

As Gerber approached, Fetterman broke off and walked over. "We're taking eight M-60 machine guns, a couple of mortars, lots of ammo for the M-79s and enough food to stay out a couple of days. Of course you can have anything else we need airlifted in."

"All right, Tony, you know what you're doing. Just report in every hour, and be careful because we don't know what happened to Lieutenant Novak and his patrol."

Fetterman turned and waved at Lieutenant Duc, who then ordered his men into the trucks. The drivers climbed into the cabs and started the engines. Washington and Duc got into the jeep and started it.

"Good luck, Tony."

"Thank you, Captain. See you tomorrow at the latest."

"Yeah, tomorrow." As soon as Fetterman got into the jeep, Washington spun the wheel, taking them through the gate. They drove along the edge of the runway, then south over a rough road before turning to the west along the path there that passed for a road. The vehicle kicked up a plume of dust that Gerber could see clearly from the gate.

As the dust finally settled in the west, he whispered, "Good lucky, Tony."

6

WEST OF CAMP A-555
SOUTH OF THE
PARROT'S BEAK

Washington pulled the jeep onto an area of solid ground covered with elephant grass that jutted into the paddy fields. He leaned forward and turned off the engine, then sat up behind the wheel, his arm across the top of it as he stared at the trees about seventy-five meters ahead.

Fetterman was trying to locate landmarks on a map that was spread out on his knees. He glanced up and located the angle of the canal as it touched the road and then swung back to the west. There were a couple of black squares on his map labeled Numerous Hootches; farther to the west was a place of Strategic Hamlets. Fetterman folded the map. "Looks like we're as close as we can get on the road."

Lieutenant Duc hopped out of the back of the jeep. Reaching in, he retrieved his M-16, a bandolier of ammo and his pistol belt, which held two canteens and a tiny first-aid kit. He slipped the bandolier over his head so that it hung across his chest and turned to face the trucks that had pulled up behind the jeep.

The men began to jump from the trucks and were scattering; some of them chose to sit in the shade so that they were facing the rice fields where a single farmer was walking along behind his water buffalo. As they trod through the ankle-deep water, neither seemed to notice the trucks or the soldiers.

Fetterman climbed out of the jeep, picked up his weapon and started into the tree line.

"T.J.," he said, "Let's take about ten guys and get moving. We'll sweep through on line, more or less, and see if we can pick up Lieutenant Novak's trail."

"I stay here," said Duc. "Have men set up perimeter and prepare the camp."

"Good," said Fetterman. He moved to the trucks, found a striker NCO and ordered him to pick nine others and get ready to move out. Squinting, he glanced at the sun, still high in the west, blazing in a blue sky. The storm clouds that had promised rain and cooler weather had blown away without releasing a drop of moisture. Now it was hot and humid, and without the wind in his face when the jeep had raced along the road, it was becoming miserable. Fetterman wiped the sweat from his forehead with the sleeve of his uniform.

The men assembled at the edge of the road, facing the trees, each with a pistol belt holding extra canteens and each with either a first-aid kit or additional medical supplies for Washington. They had two of the M-60 machine guns and ammo for it, and two men who were assigned as grenadiers carried the M-79s. Fetterman checked his map a final time, oriented himself with his compass and then stepped into the middle of the dusty road. He glanced over his shoulder, saw Washington follow, and then the Vietnamese. In seconds they were at the trees, where short elephant grass gave way to the dense jungle vegetation.

Fetterman pointed to the left and right so that the men would fan out and enter the jungle all at the same time. They swept forward slowly, some of the men needing to use a machete to hack their way through the undergrowth, some of them avoiding the huge trunks of the teak trees that reached to a height of over a hundred feet. The rest dodged the small thorny bushes or vines that snagged their fatigues and the canvas of their equipment harnesses.

As they reached the center of the tree line where the vegetation was the thickest, masking the sky and the sun, they found a game trail. Fetterman immediately noticed that someone had used it recently. Fresh human footprints covered the soft ground, and he knew that they'd be quickly obliterated after dusk when the animals began using the trail. He could see broken bits of grass or twigs and muddy spots where men had stirred the decaying plants, exposing them to the air for the first time.

Fetterman halted and whistled once, the signal that stopped his men. They took up positions on either side of the trail, their backs to each other so that they could watch the jungle all around them. Fetterman moved to the south slowly, searching for evidence that the trail had been used for travel and not just crossed. When he satisfied himself that he had found his first clues about Lieutenant Novak, he waved the men to the trail. Washington took up the rear-guard position while he took the point.

Before moving deeper into the jungle, Fetterman spread his men out so that they were more than the five or six meters apart, which were normal when patrolling. The game trail allowed them to see twenty or more meters ahead, and Fetterman didn't want the men walking into an ambush. When they were set, he moved off, staying at the edge of the trail, using the bushes, trees and shadows to conceal himself as he worked his way to the south.

They stole forward, each man rolling his foot from heel to toe to try to maintain stealth. No longer did they chop at the vines and branches in the way, but ducked under them and stepped around, pushing them only slightly and then easing them back into position so that they wouldn't rustle. Each man was sweating heavily in the steamy jungle, his breath burning in his lungs as he tried to keep from panting at the exertion of moving quietly. It seemed as though cotton formed in their mouths and it was hard to swallow, but Fetterman had drilled them on the need for noise discipline and the need to ignore discomfort. They moved forward steadily, quietly, knowing that Fetterman would call a halt soon and let them drink their water, wipe the sweat and dirt from their faces and maybe even smoke a cigarette.

It was nearly five o'clock in the afternoon when Fetterman realized that he was getting close to something. The sounds of the jungle had changed slightly, as if the animals and birds had been chased away. He could see a slight blue haze drifting in the shafts of sunlight filtering through trees around him. An odor of cordite hung in the air, seeping toward him, warning him that a lot of weapons had been fired close by. Not a strong smell, just a hint of the acrid stink of gunpowder.

He halted the patrol and turned to watch them scatter from the trail, hiding in the foliage on either side. Then Fetterman crept forward until he could see the remains of a patrol through the gaps in the trees and bushes: ten or twelve men lying on the trail, their bodies shattered by the grenades and bullets of the VC, blood turning their uniforms rusty and staining the ground under them.

He saw Sean Cavanaugh sitting on a palm log, his back against the trunk of a teak tree, smoking a cigarette. He just sat there, his head swinging from side to side, as if he was watching a slow-motion tennis match, occasionally taking a puff of his smoke. There was a strange half grin on his face, as if he was in shock. Lying at his feet was the remains of his rifle, the stock broken and covered with blood.

Fetterman turned to the men behind him, pointed at one of them and then at his own feet, telling the striker that he was to move to the spot where Fetterman was crouched. As the patrol began to leapfrog slowly, silently forward, Fetterman stepped out onto the center of the trail where Cavanaugh would be able to see him easily.

When he heard the noise of Fetterman moving, Cavanaugh looked up, smiled broadly and waved. He laughed out loud. "The stupid bastards missed again. What took you guys so long? You missed all the fun." He stood up, flipped his cigarette into the jungle and laughed again. "Yup, you missed all the goddamned fun."

Fetterman noticed that Cavanaugh held a bloodstained pack of cigarettes in his hand, probably taken from the body of one of the strikers. Fetterman wasn't in a hurry because it appeared as if all the strikers on that patrol were dead. Each had been shot more than once. Limbs had been severed, and bits of white bone poked through bruised and bloody skin.

"They missed me again, Master Sergeant." Cavanaugh laughed. "If Charlie keeps this up, pretty soon the war will be over. He keeps throwing companies at me, and they keep failing."

Fetterman didn't speak. He pointed at his men and motioned them forward so that they could sweep into the jungle and routinely check the bodies to make sure that there were no wounded. He doubted that there were, but he wanted to be sure. He then moved closer to Cavanaugh, who stood empty-handed now, having stuffed the bloodied cigarettes into his pocket.

"Where's the lieutenant?" Fetterman asked.

"Over there somewhere," Cavanaugh said, pointing. He grinned, his face suddenly looking like a cheap mask pulled over a skull, then added, "He took a lot of them with him. Christ, it was fucking beautiful. Just slamming them together, killing them."

"Yeah," Fetterman said quietly. "You hurt?"

"Nah," said Cavanaugh. "I'm fine. Got a bunch of them, too."

"Okay, Sean, sit down and relax for a moment. We've got to look things over."

"Nothing to look over. The sons of bitches jumped us, and we shot our way clear, killing a boatload of them in the process."

"I see that," said Fetterman, "but I've got to check it out, anyway."

Cavanaugh sat down on the log again and fished a bloody cigarette out of his pocket. Fetterman turned away then, moving into the jungle, among the trees and bushes and rotting vegetation, looking at the bodies lying hidden there. Occasionally he scanned the faces of his strikers, observing the shock as they searched the battlefield. They were thinking and feeling the same thing that all men thought and felt as they walked a new battleground—relief that they weren't lying dead themselves, and betrayal that they had somehow let their friends and fellow soldiers down by not being there for the fight. Fetterman had long ago realized that he hadn't betrayed his friends by remaining alive when they died. He felt that he would only betray himself by dying before his time.

He found Lieutenant Novak lying facedown among a pile of enemy bodies, his right hand wrapped around an NVA sergeant's throat as if he had squeezed the life from the soldier as he was dying himself. His rifle lay empty near his feet, and his pistol had been fired until the slide locked back. Cavanaugh was right. The lieutenant had taken a lot of them with him.

When he returned to the trail, he saw Washington kneeling near Cavanaugh, looking into his eyes, his medical bag open beside him. "You check the others?" he asked when Washington noticed him.

"They're all dead," said Washington. "Every one of them. They've all been hit six, seven times, except one guy who had a little hole just above the right ear and Sean here. Sean is fine."

"Of course I am. Like I said, if Charlie keeps this up, the war will be over soon."

"That's enough, Sean," said Fetterman. "Looks like the war is already over for the lieutenant and the rest of the patrol."

"Lighten up, Master Sergeant. It's not my fault I lived through it. Looks like I'll get another medal, but I don't suppose it'll be the CMH for this one, either."

IT WAS DUSK BY THE TIME the patrol reached the trucks, each man carrying a couple of the weapons that had been found on the battle site. Duc had done what he had said he would, setting up a camp that commanded the road and the fields surrounding them. He had placed his machine guns to face the most likely routes of attack, leaving two spots empty so that Fetterman could add his two to the fields of fire. The trucks had been parked in the center of the perimeter, forming a makeshift redoubt in case the attack was too large to beat back easily.

As they approached, Fetterman saw that the rice farmer had given up for the day and was gone, but there was a wisp of smoke from a clump of trees two hundred meters away, suggesting that he and his family were there cooking their evening meal.

Duc left the front seat of the jeep where he had been sitting watching the sun, a flaming ball of orange that seemed to bounce on the horizon. He saw Cavanaugh and the look on the faces of the strikers. "You have found them?"

"We found them," said Fetterman. "They're all dead. I think we should get back to camp as soon as we can."

"I think we can be ready to go most ricky tic," Duc replied.

"I'm going to report," Fetterman said, more to Washington than to Duc. "See if the captain has any instructions for us."

Duc moved with Fetterman, dogging his heels. "Where are the others?" he asked. "You didn't leave them in the jungle?"

"For now, yes. No way we could bring them out. Have to mount an operation in the morning to get them."

"But Charlie come back and cut them."

"I don't think so, Lieutenant," Fetterman told him. "I don't think many of the VC survived the ambush, and I doubt they'll return tonight."

They had reached the jeep, and Fetterman grabbed the handset from the AN/PRC-25 mounted in the rear. "Zulu Base," he said, "this is Zulu Three."

"Ah, Three, this is Base. Go."

"Roger, Base," said Fetterman. "We have located the missing patrol and are prepared to come in."

"Understand you have located the patrol. Say condition."

"Condition is bad. Just about as bad as you can get."

"Understood. Can you wait one for Zulu Six?"

"Affirmative," answered Fetterman. He set the mike on top of the radio and stared to the west. He was remembering the last time he had come upon a scene like the one today. Cavanaugh had been sitting there quietly, clutching an E-tool that had dried blood all over it. He hadn't said a word to them. He had just stared into the foxhole where the RFs lay dead. His position had been surrounded by bodies then, too. Fetterman wasn't sure that Cavanaugh was handling it any better this time. His attitude was different but not really better.

The radio crackled, and a tinny voice spoke. "Three, this is Six. Understand that you want to come in?"

"Affirmative. No reason to remain in place this evening."

"Do you have wounded?"

"Negative. I have no wounded. Repeat. I have no wounded."

"Roger. Bring it on in, and report to me soonest."

"Roger, Six." Fetterman dropped the mike into the jeep. He looked at Duc. "Let's get out of here."

Within ten minutes they had broken camp and loaded the trucks. The convoy moved out, bouncing along a road now obscured with shadows as the last of the light faded. Fetterman didn't like using the same road, but he didn't think the VC would have a chance to get an ambush into place. They hadn't been out that long, and there was too much open ground. Even with the headlights on, shining through the rectangular slits that made them more difficult for the enemy to spot, Fetterman thought they were relatively safe. If they had stayed overnight, Charlie might be waiting, but not now. Not enough time.

Soon the camp came into view, and there was no way that Charlie would hit them. They drove along the runway and pushed through the gaps in the wire. As they passed through the gate, a squad rushed out to close the concertina over the road so that the rings of wire around the camp would be complete for the night.

Gerber was waiting as the trucks rolled to a halt. He confronted Fetterman and demanded, "What in the hell happened?" Then he saw Cavanaugh. "Sean? You all right?"

"Yes, sir. I'm fine. We got ambushed. We—"

Fetterman put a hand on his shoulder. "Captain, they were wiped out. Everyone, except Sean here. Lieutenant Novak is dead."

"Jesus Christ," said Gerber, stunned. "Jesus Christ." He put a hand to his forehead and asked again, "What happened?"

"I haven't debriefed Sean yet," said Fetterman. "They walked into it and, following procedure, charged the ambush and broke it up. I counted over fifty dead VC and NVA there. We brought in most of the weapons but had to leave the bodies. Figured we could get them in the morning. It'll be an all-day job, but we should be able to get them all before dusk tomorrow."

"Sean, how are you feeling?" asked Gerber.

"Just fine, Captain. Little hungry, but fine otherwise."

"T.J.," said Gerber, "want to oversee the cleaning of the weapons and storage of the captured stuff before grabbing some chow?"

"Sure, Captain."

"Tony, I want you and Sean to come over to my hootch and tell me exactly what happened. Sean, we haven't finished the team house yet, so we're still eating C-rations. We can get you some if you want."

Once in Gerber's hootch, they went over the details of the ambush. Between mouthfuls of C-rations, Cavanaugh told them about Novak's actions during the ambush and explained that the unit they ran into was company strength at the minimum, maybe even larger. He had seen no cowardice by anyone. Everyone had reacted quickly, but there had been too many VC.

For the next twenty minutes Gerber quizzed Cavanaugh on the battle and on how he felt. Cavanaugh explained that he hadn't liked sitting alone in the jungle, but given the circumstances, he didn't mind it all that much. He had felt that someone would come by soon.

Gerber tried to press him about his feelings, but Cavanaugh dodged the questions easily, giving flip answers and saying that it had all happened before. He finally asked Gerber if he was going to put the lieutenant in for a medal.

"Of course," Gerber replied. "He'll automatically get a Purple Heart, and I think we'll put him in for a Silver Star. He should get that. I think Minh will put the strikers in for a Cross of Gallantry or something like that. At least that's what I'll advise him."

"And me?" asked Cavanaugh.

"Well, Sean, given the circumstances, I doubt that we could get you the Medal of Honor. Hell, I think you deserve it, especially after the defense of the listening post, but we're stuck again. No witnesses to the action. Just the physical evidence scattered in the jungle. Hell, Sean, we'll try to get you a Distinguished Service Cross."

"Yes, sir! Thank you, sir!" The enthusiasm in his voice was unmistakable.

"Christ, Sean, you deserve it," Gerber repeated as he got to his feet. "Look, I know you've had a rough day. Why don't you hit the sack? We'll talk tomorrow."

"Yes, sir. Say, you get a report on how the others are? I mean Smith and Anderson and Kepler."

"They're all fine. Smith and Kepler might be able to return in a week or so. Sam has been evaced to Japan for treatment."

"Okay, sir." Cavanaugh turned and left.

"Tony," said Gerber, "what do you think?"

"About what?"

"Cavanaugh. You're the one who found him both times. What's your reaction?"

Fetterman rubbed his face as he thought. "He seems to be a little too emotionless this time. No real reaction from him. It's like he was lost in the jungle for a couple of minutes. He seems to be a little too flip."

"Better than being catatonic."

"Yes, sir, if you say so, though I'm not convinced that's true."

"What do you mean by that?"

"Simply that Cavanaugh may be a walking time bomb. I would have liked to see a little more emotion. After all, he had just witnessed his patrol being wiped out again."

"Maybe the difference is that he wasn't in charge this time."

"I think it's more than that. I think we better keep an eye on him for a couple of days."

"I had planned on that, Master Sergeant."

7

THE VIETNAMESE QUARTERS, CAMP A-555

Cavanaugh exited Gerber's hootch, but rather than returning to his own, he left the redoubt and turned toward the Vietnamese quarters. He shuffled around the compound, staring at the small square hootches that accommodated eight strikers or that, sometimes, were divided into four rooms so that a striker who had a family could have a little privacy.

The hootches were constructed along the lines of the Americans': there was a wooden frame, plywood halfway up the walls, the top section screened in and the whole covered by a corrugated tin roof. Most of the structures had been sandbagged, but a few had piles of sandbags in front of them, waiting for someone to stack them around the hootch. There were wooden sidewalks between the hootches, one-by-twelves laid on their edges with planks nailed to them. Wires were strung everywhere, running from poles into the hootches to provide electricity. The smell of nouc-mam was heavy in the air.

Cavanaugh wandered around, searching the faces of the Vietnamese strikers who sat outside, wearing little more than black shorts or their OD GI underwear, shower shoes in a riot of color on their feet, and chattering with one another as the discordant music from a Vietnamese radio station drifted on the light, warm breeze. One group he recognized as men who had either been with him at the village of Cai Cai or who had relatives in it. They were not talking or laughing. They had watched solemnly as Chinook helicopters flew the bodies of their relatives and friends from Cai Cai to be buried in the makeshift graveyard established north of the camp. In their hootches, they had erected little altars and burned incense on them, leaving small portions of food, such as boiled chicken, nouc-mam, fruit cocktail from American C-rations and rice, as an offering for the dead.

Without an invitation Cavanaugh sat with them. They had looked up as the American approached, not acknowledging him but not telling him to leave. They sat quietly for a while, staring at the night sky encrusted with stars and listening to the radio music.

Finally Cavanaugh said, "It's too bad we can't get even with the VC. They sneak in and kill innocent people and run to Cambodia to hide."

A couple of the strikers looked at him, but none of them spoke. They ignored his comment. One of them got to his feet and went into the hootch.

Cavanaugh watched the door for a moment and then looked at the men sitting with him. "We can get even." He waited and then added, "There is no reason for them to get away with their chicken shit tactics of killing the innocent and running away to Cambodia."

When no one spoke, he added, "We can go after them. Just a couple of us, moving at night through the jungle, waiting for them and killing them."

He looked at the impassive faces and wondered what they were thinking, how they were feeling. "You've seen what can be done. You know that the VC are not supermen. They are murderers who sneak through the night and prey on helpless women and children. They kill in a wanton fashion. They are dogs who should be hunted down and shot."

None of the strikers spoke, but none of them left, either. Cavanaugh remained silent for a moment, waiting for what he said to sink in. Then he continued. "We can't let them get away with it anymore. The brass hats in Saigon, both American and Vietnamese, don't understand what is happening out here. We do. We have to do something about it. Show Charlie that he is not safe here anymore and should stay in Cambodia. When he shows up here, we kill him. Quickly."

"How soon?" one of the strikers asked.

"Tomorrow. The next day. Soon." He smiled. "You know that I'm invincible. You all know that. You've all seen the results of that."

"What we do?"

"Okay," said Cavanaugh, clapping his hands together once. "Okay, when Minh or whoever is trying to put together a patrol, you volunteer. We'll just go off and do our thing then."

He looked at the six men there, men who had lost relatives in the VC raid at Cai Cai, Vietnamese strikers who weren't really soldiers but rice farmers and shopkeepers playing soldier. Men who sometimes closed their eyes when they fired their weapons, who liked to fire a whole magazine on full auto and then hug the ground until the shooting stopped.

But something new had been added. They had lost family and friends to the VC. The war was no longer something that happened in the next village or the next province. It was something that happened to them, might be the motivation they needed, if he handled it right.

"Okay," he repeated. "We'll go looking for the bastards the first chance we get. You don't need to say anything to your officers or sergeants, I'll square it with them. Maybe we'll start with some extra rifle practice."

He stood and looked down at them, vague shapes in the night. A little light from the hootches spilled out so that Cavanaugh could see the profiles of the men. He thought there was something else he should say to them but didn't know what it should be. He wasn't even sure that they understood what he had said to them. All he could do was try to form the core of a team that would go out to kill the Communists.

As he headed toward his hootch in the redoubt, he realized that he would need a top-notch NCO to work with him. He doubted that any of the other Special Forces sergeants would understand what he was doing. But Krung would. Krung was like the Vietnamese strikers. He had lost his family to the Vietcong and had sworn to kill fifty enemy soldiers for each member of his family. He would welcome the opportunity to go out hunting the VC. Cavanaugh decided to talk to Krung, then stopped short and smiled. He didn't need to talk to Krung. When the time came, Krung would be ready.

CAVANAUGH GOT his first chance the next day. Gerber had told them that a patrol would be sent out at first light. Cavanaugh volunteered for the mission, but Gerber told him that Tyme would be taking it out. Besides, Cavanaugh would be responsible for leading a company out to where the ambush had taken place.

At first he hadn't been happy, but then the American had realized that once he got into the field, he could take a patrol out to swing through the jungle as if he was looking for any VC who happened to be near. Once he was away from the main body, he could get permission from base to keep chasing the enemy if he happened to see them, and Cavanaugh knew that one way or another he would see them.

He watched Tyme's patrol walk through the west gate and cross the runway before turning north toward the jungle and the Parrot's Beak region. As they slipped from sight, the trucks that would carry his patrol into the field pulled up. The Vietnamese strikers were already loaded. They carried entrenching tools, body bags and lots of water. They also had their weapons with only a basic load of ammo, enough food for a noon meal and little else.

Cavanaugh checked on the six strikers he had talked to the night before and told them to get their full field gear and to carry enough to stay in the field for three days. As they ran off to get the rest of their equipment, Cavanaugh went to find Krung.

Twenty minutes later they were rolling out of the camp, trucks kicking up a cloud of dust as they turned onto the road that would take them to the jungle where the patrol had been ambushed. Cavanaugh rode in the lead jeep with the Vietnamese company commander. He had one foot propped up on the dashboard as the countryside rushed by. It didn't take them long to get to the place where Fetterman had stopped the trucks the day before. The Vietnamese lieutenant had them circle the trucks like the wagon master circling the Conestogas on the western plains. The men jumped out the backs and spread out, finding shade to relax in until someone told them what to do.

Cavanaugh left them alone while he got his private patrol ready, then advised the Vietnamese officer that they had better get going. Within minutes everyone, except a small detachment left to guard the trucks, was moving through the trees. Cavanaugh was on the point, leading them to the game trail and then along it until they had worked their way nearly to the spot where the ambush had taken place. He halted the column and crept back to the Vietnamese lieutenant.

"Sir," he said, "down this trail about fifty meters is the place where we were ambushed. I would like to take six of your men and Sergeant Krung and move through the jungle to the right of that position in case there's anybody still hiding in there."

The lieutenant nodded as if considering the advice and then said, "Very good. I lead men down trail and begin unhappy task of claiming bodies."

"Yes, sir. I would like to take one of the radios with me so that we can maintain radio contact with one another."

"That is good. You do that. I wait here for a while to let you move into position," the lieutenant told him.

Cavanaugh nodded and crawled off, pointing to the men of this hunter-killer team. He assembled them at the rear of the column, checked his map and then moved to the east, through what looked like the thickest part of the jungle. Cavanaugh began hacking at the dense undergrowth with his machete, creating a path for his men. Suddenly they popped into a clearing, a field of elephant grass that sloped gently to a group of rice paddies. Cavanaugh turned the men to the south, moving along the edge of the jungle just inside the trees until he was more than a klick from the ambush site.

He stopped around noon and set up a small perimeter so that the men could eat lunch. Then, before they moved, Cavanaugh used the radio.

"Zulu Base, this is Zulu One Two."

"One Two, this is Base. Go."

"Roger, Base, I have found evidence of VC and am pursuing in accordance with instructions from counterpart."

There was a hesitation and then, "Roger, One Two. Please advise Six on intentions in one hour."

Cavanaugh rogered the instruction, gave the handset back to the RTO and got his men to their feet. They stayed inside the tree line, moving rapidly farther south until they reached a swampy area where the jungle disappeared. Cavanaugh turned to the west again, moving deeper into the jungle, veering slightly to the north to avoid the mushy ground.

At midafternoon, when the sun was at its hottest, Cavanaugh halted his team. They infiltrated the trees, each man finding a good hiding spot. They had come to a trail, a path through the jungle whose width suggested that human beings had made it. It could have been farmers or VC. Cavanaugh decided that they would rest there for the afternoon, and if nothing happened by ten or eleven o'clock that night, he would think about redeploying them.

They passed a quiet afternoon, moving only to take a drink of water, their movements slow, easy and hard to see in the deep shadows and jungle vegetation. At dusk they ate cold C-rations, half of the group on guard while the others ate, then rotated the duty. As the sunlight faded, Cavanaugh moved them a hundred meters farther west in case someone had seen them during the day. Once they were settled, Cavanaugh instructed them that there would be no talking, no movement and no smoking. They were waiting for Charlie and didn't want to tip their hand.

As he settled in, Cavanaugh switched magazines in his rifle, putting in one that was all tracers. He set two hand grenades on the ground in front of him where they could be reached easily and placed a single star cluster flare next to them. Then he crouched, one knee on the ground so that he wouldn't relax too much. He wished now that he had brought a claymore mine or two but had figured taking any would draw attention to his plan.

A dozen things flashed through Cavanaugh's mind. When hunting ducks, you stayed in one place and waited patiently. But he didn't want to wait patiently, he wanted to kill the enemy. He knelt there, his rifle clutched in both hands, waiting, listening, knowing that it would be an hour at least before he could expect any VC. His training reminded him that he should alert the camp about his location and intentions, but he decided against it. The captain would be pissed, but if he ran up an impressive kill record, the captain would get over it.

Far to the right he heard something. A quiet snap and a voice speaking Vietnamese. Cavanaugh tensed, let his finger slide along the trigger guard of his M-14 to slip off the safety. A moment later there was a rustle in the bushes, then Cavanaugh saw a shape loom out of the darkness.

His first instinct was to hose the trail with his M-14, but the American realized quickly that such an action would only identify his location for the enemy. Instead, he reached for one of the grenades, pulled the pin, holding it in his left hand in case he wanted to replace it, and waited. The shape faded into the background again as more men approached. Finally he let the spoon fly, hesitated and then threw the grenade.

Hugging the ground, he watched through the trees as the grenade exploded in a fountain of sparks and flying shrapnel. A second later there was another explosion farther down the trail, followed by two more as the strikers lobbed their grenades. Cavanaugh poked his rifle forward, aimed at a point on the other side of the trail and opened fire, pouring the whole magazine into the shadows.

The enemy, surprised, reacted slowly. There was a shout and then a whistle. One man opened fire with his AK-47, the muzzle-flash extending three feet from the end of the barrel. Two grenades detonated beside him.

From the east another AK opened fire. Cavanaugh spun toward it, watching the burst for a moment, then returned fire, aiming at the center of the muzzle-flashes. He squeezed off a quick burst, dodged to the right and waited. There was no return fire.

The jungle fell silent. Cavanaugh listened intently, his eye flicking from shadow to shadow, searching for movement among them. After five minutes he moved cautiously to his right. He found Krung, and together they moved among the patrol, shifting them another hundred meters to the west again, in case Charlie had identified his location and tried a counter ambush.

Cavanaugh settled down with his back to a large palm tree. There was little vegetation in front of him, and he could see some shadows shifting and dancing near the trail. Slowly he raised his hand and wiped the sweat from his face. Even though the sun was long gone, the heat and the humidity remained. Cavanaugh breathed quietly, ignoring the weather and concentrating on his surroundings, memorizing the positions of the bushes and trees, watching the shadows, searching for any unnatural movement.

After an hour he realized that something had changed around him. He reached up, touched the hilt of the knife taped upside down to his shoulder harness, then felt along the trigger guard of his weapon, checking the safety. He heard a quiet rustling and turned toward the sound. Something was moving slowly through the shadows, along the side of the trail. A hand seemed to snake out, feel its way and then ease to the ground as the weight of the body behind it shifted forward.

The figure pulled even with him, only a few feet away. Cavanaugh rocked forward so that he was on his hands and knees, his eyes never leaving the form near the trail. He moved cautiously toward the enemy and when he was close, he set his rifle on the ground with the operating bolt upward to keep it clean.

Cavanaugh launched himself at the enemy, landing in the middle of his back. The man collapsed to the ground, the air forced from his lungs in an audible grunt. Cavanaugh's left hand shot out and grabbed the man under the chin, snapping his head back to expose the throat. There was a whisper of the knife against flesh that sounded like tearing silk. Cavanaugh felt the warm blood splash over his hand. The enemy bucked once as if he was trying to throw him off, and then the tension seemed to flow into the ground with the man's blood.

Cavanaugh rolled off his victim, scrambled back a pace or two and reached for his rifle. His hand touched the barrel, and he let his fingers ease along it until he felt the rear sight. He picked it up and checked the safety again, making sure it was still off.

Alerted by a sudden noise behind him, Cavanaugh turned around to see a man standing over him, holding his machete high as if preparing to swing it at a thick vine. Cavanaugh rolled onto his right elbow and fired without really aiming. The impact of the slug slammed the man backward, sending him into the dark shadows of the jungle.

At that moment Cavanaugh realized that he and his men were right on the infiltration route the VC were using to try to reclaim the bodies of the men killed in the first ambush. With the need to keep quiet, Cavanaugh had lost contact with his troops. He could only hold his ground, killing the enemy as he saw them moving. He no longer had any good idea of where his men were. If they had slipped from cover in search of VC, they could be scattered through the jungle. The integrity of the ambush was gone, and he was suddenly in as much danger from his own strikers as he was from the Vietcong. It was a mistake that could kill him.

But then he saw another enemy soldier crawling through the jungle. A single man dressed mostly in black, but wearing one of the khaki pith helmets that the NVA regulars favored. Cavanaugh didn't move, watching the soldier as he came closer. When he was three feet away, Cavanaugh reached out with his rifle, put the muzzle next to the soldier's head and, as he turned to look, pulled the trigger. The

VC's body was hurled to the left into a bush, his head blown apart.

Off to his left he heard more movement. His men would be to his right, Cavanaugh guessed, reaching for another grenade. He pulled the pin and waited. Soon a rustling noise broke the silence, and he tossed the grenade in that direction, flattening himself behind the trunk of a fallen tree. He buried his face in the ground and closed his eyes to protect his night vision. Before looking up, he heard the explosion of two more grenades and recognized the flat bangs as the detonations of American weapons.

He heard a new sound in the trees as if someone had thrown a ball or a rock in the forest. It hit something solid, then fell, and a second later it exploded with a dull, subdued pop. It was then that Cavanaugh realized the VC had begun to chuck grenades at him.

For an instant he was consumed by fear. No longer was he the invincible Sean Cavanaugh, survivor of two bloody hand-to-hand fights, but the nineteen-year-old kid who should have been watching his classmates play football on Saturday afternoon. He shifted himself around so that he was lying parallel to the tree trunk and tried to force himself under it for protection. Pressing his face into the soggy, damp jungle floor, smelling the dirt and rotting vegetation, he wondered what the pain would be like if the white-hot shrapnel hit him.

Cavanaugh slipped deeper into cover and felt along his harness to see how many grenades he had left. During the action he'd forgotten how many he'd carried with him and how many he'd thrown. There were two left, and he decided not to use them unless a good target presented itself. Lying there, pressed up against the log, he turned his head so that he was facing the bottom of it, the odor of the damp jungle in his nostrils. The realization suddenly came to him that he was panting, as if he had just sprinted a hundred meters. He slowly moved, turning so that he could look into the jungle.

It was alive with night sounds, and a light breeze rippled through the leaves. Tiny creatures scrambled for safety as they tried to flee the area, sensing the unwanted human presence.

By staring into the gloom, Cavanaugh could see the phosphorescence of rotting vegetation glowing among the deeper black of the shadows. His ears twitched as they picked up the quiet sounds around him, and then they were lost as the blood hammered through his veins and his heart pounded in his chest.

His fear evaporated slowly when he realized that the enemy didn't know where he was. Besides, they were using Chicom grenades, explosives so inferior that they didn't detonate half the time. When they did, they had very little force and almost no shrapnel. He remembered the Army captain he had met once who had been hit on the head by a Chicom grenade that detonated on impact, forcing the man's helmet down so that it had to be cut from his head. The captain had taken some shrapnel hits in the shoulders, but he should have been dead instead of in Saigon joking about the incident.

Cavanaugh rolled clear of the log and crawled backward, toward the tree where he had started. He crouched there for a moment and then lay down, flattening himself on the ground beside the tree. He stayed like that, listening and waiting for the enemy, but it seemed that the grenade duel was over and that the enemy had retreated.

After a long time Cavanaugh moved so that his left wrist was right under his eyes. He peeled the camouflage flap off the top of his watch so that he could check the time. It was nearly 4:00 a.m. The hour surprised him because he wasn't sure whether he expected it to be much later or much earlier.

Suddenly he was uncontrollably thirsty. Cavanaugh tried to tell himself that he didn't need a drink, but that didn't work. It was as if he could hear his body drying out, and his thoughts were focused only on the water in his canteens. He realized that the obsession with getting some water was worse than actually taking a drink. If he didn't, he wouldn't be able to pay attention to what was happening around him. Slowly he reached down and tugged gently at the snaps on the cover of his canteen. They pulled free with an audible pop, and Cavanaugh froze, but no one seemed to have noticed. Carefully he slipped the container out, unscrewed the top, and lifted it to his lips. At first he drank greedily, ignoring the plastic taste of the warm water. It dripped down his chin and onto his sweat-soaked and dirt-stained shirt. Finally he stopped, took a breath and then sipped the water, drinking it slowly until the canteen was empty. Rather than fumble with it further, which could give away his position, he set it near him at the base of the tree, figuring he could retrieve it in the morning.

Then he settled back to wait, concentrating on the jungle around him. The noises that he had heard earlier had faded. Even the buzz of the insects was gone, and it was as if he had become lost in the world of the dead. Glancing upward through a break in the thick jungle canopy, he could see a patch of stars. He watched them for a moment and realized that they were slowly fading, the sky brightening around them.

Cavanaugh turned his head and blinked into the darkness. As he stared, he realized that he could make out the shapes of the trees and bushes near him. The branches became more noticeable against the graying of the sky. Rising to his feet, he picked up his canteen and waited with his back to a teak tree.

Suddenly the jungle exploded with a riot of sound. A screeching seemed to vibrate through the tops of the trees, shaking them so that the leaves rattled. Cavanaugh dropped to one knee and glanced upward. Dozens of monkeys were scurrying along the branches, leaping at one another and shrieking, announcing the morning.

He looked at the trail and saw a human shape lying there— a VC soldier killed during the night. His weapon was near his outstretched fingers. Cavanaugh pulled back, away from the tree, moving to the right, looking for his men.

He found Krung crouched over the body of an NVA sergeant whose throat had been slit. A pool of bright, sticky blood had spread out from the dead man's neck. Krung turned and grinned at Cavanaugh.

Farther to the right he found two of the strikers sitting back-to-back, watching the jungle around them. Each had his rifle across his knees and a couple of grenades near his hands. They were waiting for someone to come and get them.

Not far from the two strikers was a third. He was lying on his side, his hands hidden in a bloody mass on his belly. It looked as if he had tried to push his intestines back into his stomach after they had been ripped from him. His head was thrown back, and his mouth was open in a mute scream.

The other three were huddled near a large bush covered with giant pink flowers. Two of the strikers held their rifles and the third clutched a bloodstained machete. Near them were the bodies of three dead VC soldiers. Cavanaugh could only see two weapons.

The men left their positions and joined him. He looked around, seeing the bodies of the enemy soldiers killed during the fight. A hundred meters away a dozen of them still lay on the trail where the first ambush had taken place. Cavanaugh started toward the site when he saw a couple of bloody trails that disappeared into the jungle. He followed one of them for about fifty feet, then stumbled upon a dead enemy soldier, a half-dozen bullet holes in his shoulders. Cavanaugh stooped to pull the AK-47 from the corpse's fingers. Then he hesitated, drew his knife and cut off the man's trigger finger.

Back on the trail his men were moving among the dead, picking up weapons, searching the pockets for anything worth stealing and taking souvenirs. Cavanaugh knew that he should be trying to determine the enemy's unit and searching for documents that might prove useful for Intelligence in Nha Trang, but he just didn't care. Instead, he was tryng to figure out a way, some trademark or sign, that would identify this carnage as his handiwork, which the VC would recognize. He knew that some units of the First Cav left the ace of spades on the bodies of the enemies they killed, but Cavanaugh felt that was too conservative.

He saw Krung taking a trophy from the body of a soldier that he had killed. Anytime anyone found a body with the penis missing, he knew that Krung had done it. Cavanaugh looked at the trigger finger he had cut from the enemy soldier and remembered a necklace he had seen when he was a kid. The curator of the museum in Cody, Wyoming, had claimed that it had been made from the fingers of soldiers killed by the Sioux Indians during the plains wars, but Cavanaugh hadn't believed that the shriveled, blackened twigs were human fingers. It was, however, just the thing he had wanted—a way to identify himself.

He saw one of the strikers sawing at the left ear of a dead VC. Cavanaugh leaped at him, shouting, "No! Don't do that. Stop!"

The man jumped back and screamed something in Vietnamese.

"No," Cavanaugh answered. He showed the man the trigger finger. "Take these. Just these." He grinned. "It'll strike terror into the hearts of the VC. Take the trigger fingers."

He watched as the men moved over the field then, carrying out his order. They collected the weapons stacking them on the trail. As soon as they had finished, Cavanaugh decided, they would take time to eat a quick breakfast, wrap their dead in a poncho liner and head back to the camp. They would be there by late afternoon. He knew that he should make a radio call, but he had already missed so many checks that it no longer mattered. He could cover that when he told the captain about the ambush. That would make everything all right. He nodded as he watched his men. "Just wait till we get back to camp. The captain'll be surprised."

8

OUTSIDE SPECIAL FORCES CAMP A-555

Cavanaugh halted his patrol in the trees along the road that led back into the camp. In front of him he could see the runway, the heat shimmering on the semiliquid black surface of peta-prime. Across the airstrip men were moving among the strands of concertina wire, planting new claymore mines, checking the trip flares and booby traps. A cloud of dust hung in the air above the center of the compound where some kind of construction activity was taking place. Cavanaugh could hear a power saw as it ripped through plywood and the pounding of hammers as the plywood was nailed together.

After a moment's hesitation Cavanaugh stepped from the jungle onto the road. He blinked in the bright sunlight and began walking slowly toward the compound, waiting for someone there to spot him and his patrol. They were some distance from the wires, and it was late in the afternoon, so anyone who saw them wouldn't think they posed a threat. They walked along the road for a few minutes, but the activity in the camp didn't slow.

Before he had the chance to move very far, he saw a jeep heading in their direction, the driver obscured by dust and the glint of sunlight on the windshield. Cavanaugh suspected that it was Gerber. A second later the jeep slid to a halt next to him and Gerber stared him in the face.

"What's the story here, Sean?" asked Gerber.

Cavanaugh held up a hand to halt his patrol. He said, "We found a couple of blood trails leading from the site where we had been hit and followed them for a while. We discovered another trail that looked like it had seen some fairly heavy use and set up along it. Hit the VC last night, killing at least eighteen."

"Casualties on our side?"

"One dead," answered Cavanaugh.

"Why didn't you make commo checks?"

"We were having trouble with the radio, and once I'd set up the ambush, we turned it off so that we wouldn't alert the enemy."

"What kind of radio trouble?" Gerber asked.

"Haven't really determined it yet, Captain. Figured we'd find out when we got in."

Gerber rubbed a hand over his jaw and stared at the dirty floorboards of the jeep for a moment. "Okay. Get your people into the camp and then report to my hootch. I'll want a full report on your activities during the last twenty-four hours."

"Yes, sir."

Gerber fought the gear knob for a moment, jerking it back and forth until he shifted into First. "I want to see you as soon as possible." With that he roared past the column, made a U-turn, then sped back in the direction of the camp. As he passed the patrol again, he raised a hand in salute and then was gone in a cloud of choking red dust.

Cavanaugh watched him go, grinning to himself. Finally he looked over his shoulder at the men standing there with him. The pole holding the dead striker wrapped in the poncho liner was resting on the ground. The others stood watching and waiting, their weapons held by the barrel and supported on a shoulder or with the butt resting on the ground. They were a dirty-looking bunch. Their uniforms were soaked with sweat and stained with blood, and dirt and mud from the jungle.

Cavanaugh shrugged and waved a hand. "Let's move it."

They picked up the body and their equipment and started for the camp. The column crossed the runway and shuffled through the main gate. Cavanaugh stopped them there and told them to take the body to the dispensary, then go to their hootches and clean their weapons and equipment while he reported to Gerber. He issued further instructions for them to grab something to eat, then wash up after which he would check on them.

He left them at the gate, turned toward the redoubt and walked up to Gerber's hootch. Although the door was open, Cavanaugh knocked on the jamb, staring into the room but unable to see Gerber.

"Enter," came a voice from the left.

Cavanaugh stepped in to see Gerber sitting behind the field desk waiting. "You wanted to see me, Captain?"

"Yeah, Sean, I did. I want to know what's going on. I want to know why you were out of contact with the camp for twenty-four hours."

Before answering, Cavanaugh reached down and unbuckled his pistol belt. The ragged sweat stain around his waist was obvious. He leaned his weapon against the wall and then shrugged, adjusting the shoulder straps of his gear.

"Take it off," said Gerber. "You could have dropped your pack in your hootch."

"Yes, sir. But I thought it was important to get over here."

"Have a seat." Gerber reached toward the bottle of Beam's that was stored in the lower desk drawer, then hesitated, as if thinking about it. He straightened and then said, "Now, then. What happened?"

"Well, sir," started Cavanaugh, "I took the patrol right to the ambush spot so that they could claim the bodies. A couple of us circled the outside perimeter, and I found what I thought was a blood trail. I reported it to Lieutenant Duc and suggested that I take a couple of men and follow it. He agreed. I took six men and Sergeant Krung and we worked our way through the jungle, looking for the wounded soldier."

"Did you find him?"

"No, sir. We did, however, cross a trail that looked like it had been heavily used, so I decided to set up an ambush."

"But felt that you didn't have to coordinate that with either Lieutenant Duc or with us here," Gerber cut in.

"I tried, sir, but the radio wasn't working properly. It was late, and I figured that Lieutenant Duc would have taken the men back to the camp."

"He did, leaving a truck and two men behind. Fortunately, he got away with that because the truck returned this morning," said Gerber.

"Yes, sir. Well, we tried to make radio contact but failed. I figured that since we were set, we might as well remain in place."

"Not thinking about us here," said Gerber. "Didn't you think that we would be wondering what happened and might field a search party?"

"I did think of that, Captain," said Cavanaugh, "but figured that you'd wait until morning since we hadn't indicated any problems. That you'd figure it was a radio problem."

"Sean," snapped Gerber, "that is bullshit, and you know it. You know better than running these renegade operations. When you discovered the radio problem, you should have pulled out."

"But, sir," protested Cavanaugh, "when we learned the radio was out, we were already set and it was nearly dusk."

"Go on."

Cavanaugh described the ambush and then the grenade duel. He explained to Gerber how he had checked the radio the following morning and couldn't find anything obviously wrong with it, but that he couldn't contact the camp.

"More bullshit, Sean," said Gerber. "You're the fucking junior commo man. If a radio isn't shot full of holes, you're supposed to be able to fix it."

"But I didn't have any tools for that, Captain. I didn't take anything because I didn't know that we were going to split up the way we did."

"All right, let's forget that for the moment. It's not that important, anyway. The real issue is the way you handled yourself in the field. I don't think you were using good judgment—out of contact with the camp and you went ahead with the ambush, anyway. If you'd run into something that you couldn't have handled, we'd have been picking up your bodies, if we knew where the hell to look."

"But, sir—"

"Shut up and listen, Sean. I don't like this solo shit. I don't like my men running off on their own. This whole thing, from the moment you left the main body of the patrol, was not thought out."

"What's the problem, Captain?" asked Cavanaugh, grinning. "We got away with it."

"Dammit! That's not the point. The point is your running around in the jungle on your own. There is no way for us to lend support if you don't have a radio and we don't know where you are. Fetterman found the ambush point because we knew where Novak was taking his patrol. With you we only knew that you had been in the jungle east of that point."

"But you hadn't sent anyone out to find us," said Cavanaugh.

"That's where you're wrong again. Fetterman was out with a platoon, and I diverted Tyme into the area to look for you. I've called them off now because you showed up, but they were out looking."

Cavanaugh let his eyes drop to the floor. "Yes, sir. Sorry. I thought I was doing the right thing."

"Well," Gerber said, "you're right about one thing. You did get away with it. Now how are we going to prove the body count? Saigon will want some kind of proof."

"We brought in some of the weapons," said Cavanaugh. "There were too many to carry, so we destroyed most of them, but we do have some weapons."

"How many?"

"Just seven of the AKs. Fairly new ones."

Now Gerber smiled. He shifted through the papers on his desk and said, "MACV just came up with a new guideline. Claims that Charlie doesn't have all that many weapons and lets us count three bodies for every captured weapon. Makes your body count twenty-one if we use that."

"There is something else, sir."

"What's that?"

"Well, I really don't know how to tell you, but the strikers took trophies."

"What kind?"

"Krung was taking his normal ones, you know the dead guys' dicks. I caught a couple of the others starting to take ears."

"And you didn't stop them?"

"Well, I'm really only an advisor, and if the Vietnamese want to cut up the bodies, I can't really order them not to. Well, I can, but they don't have to listen—"

"Sean, you're bullshitting me again."

"I told them to take only the trigger fingers."

"You what? Are you aware, Sergeant, of the MACV directives on atrocities? You can't tell them to take the trigger fingers."

"I was trying to keep them from mutilating the bodies and figured that it was the lesser of the two evils."

"Sean, I'm required by regulations to report this to Saigon. They're quite serious about mutilating the dead and taking trophies. We can't condone it."

Cavanaugh felt the blood drain from his face and his stomach turn over. Suddenly he felt as though he was back in the jungle, grenades exploding all around him. He was scared now, afraid that they were going to take him out of the field. Send him to Saigon to court-martial him for cutting the trigger finger off a dead enemy soldier.

"But, sir—"

"No buts. It just can't be done."

"But the Vietnamese did it. I didn't."

Gerber stood up and walked around the metal chair. He stopped facing the wall, looking through the heavy screen at the redoubt. He turned and said, "Listen, Sean, I'm required to report this." He saw that Cavanaugh was going to protest again and held up a hand. "Let me finish. What I want to say is that we can't always follow all the directives written by the chairborne commandos running around Saigon. I should give you an Article Fifteen for this, dock you some pay and give you extra duty, but I'm not going to."

"Thank you, Captain," said Cavanaugh, the relief obvious in his voice.

"I'm going to be watching you, though, Sean. We're shorthanded and we need every man, but you can't go running off into the field without coordinating it with me, and you can't tell the strikers to take trigger fingers, no matter what the reason."

"Yes, sir."

Gerber moved to the front of the desk. "You've done some spectacular things here. Pulling three men out of the burning team house, surviving that ambush. But you have to use your head all the time. You have to think things through to see how they may affect others. Now grab your equipment and get out of here. I'll see you later.''

Cavanaugh stood. "Yes, sir. Thank you, sir." He turned to pick up his equipment and rifle and left.

Gerber watched his retreating back for a moment and then returned to his desk. He fumbled through the papers on it and read the directive from MACV again. For every weapon captured, it required them to count three enemy soldiers out of action. Since Cavanaugh had brought in seven weapons, he could report twenty-one killed, although they knew the total should only be eighteen. He laughed, wadded up the paper and tossed it at the corner of his hootch. He would ignore it.

He reached down and got out the bottle of Beam's, uncorked it and took a deep drink. He held it for a moment, took a second pull, then replaced the bottle. He was tempted to go out to see how the new team house was progressing but decided against it. Instead, he picked up an after action report that had come with the morning's mail. It had been designed to alert the Special Forces A-Detachment commanders about the actions of the CIDG forces assigned to Camp A-102 during the battle of 9 and 10 March.

The report, in the sterile terminology of the Army, told of Captain John D. Blair's fight to hold his camp under heavy NVA assault. At 3.50 a.m., the first mortars of a devastating attack landed. In the following two and a half hours several of the camp's buildings were destroyed and the communications were knocked out. Two of the Special Forces NCOs were killed in the mortar attack.

An NVA probe on the south was repelled, Gerber read, and with the dawn came air strike support for the defenders. A low ceiling made it impossible for the pilots to see their targets, and the men on the ground directed the firing by sound. Several aircraft were hit and crashed, and attempts to land critical supplies by parachute met with limited success.

Much of it landed outside the camp, and retrieval parties came under constant, intense fire by the NVA.

At 4:00 a.m. on the tenth, another mortar attack destroyed most of the remaining buildings. An hour later the NVA hit the southern side of the camp with a human wave assault and overran the runway and part of the south wall. The 141st CIDG Company defected en masse. The LLDB commander, along with his team, hid during the battle.

In a three-hour hand-to-hand fight, the Special Forces team and their Nung irregulars were pushed back until they held only the communications bunker and the north wall. The NVA tried to take the bunker but were repulsed by heavy firing. The NVA were organizing two battalions to attack, but two B-57s swooped down, dropping cluster bombs that devastated the formation, ruining the assault.

Two Special Forces NCOs, Sergeant Vic Underwood and Sergeant Vernon Carnahan, organized the remaining Nungs into a counterattacking force to drive to the men barricaded in the commo bunker and the dispensary, but the NVA shattered the assault with machine guns and hand grenades. Both men were wounded, and Captain Blair ordered the aircraft overhead to bomb and strafe the camp. One Skyraider was shot down, crashing on the runway. Another landed behind the first to rescue the downed pilot.

The NVA then began destroying the remaining bunkers with machine-gun fire and hand grenades, and Blair ordered the camp abandoned. The camp defenders formed a line, and Marine helicopters landed at 5:20 p.m. on 10 March. As they touched down, the LLDB commander led a stampede that left the wounded lying in the dirt as the LLDB and the CIDG fought one another to get on the aircraft. The Special Forces men fired into the crowd to break it up while the Nungs continued to fight on the north wall.

Two of the helicopters were shot down as they tried to take off. One of them burst into flames, and the crew died. The jets flying cover were all hit by ground fire. The Special Forces men tried to consolidate the position, and Staff Sergeant James Taylor was killed. The camp survivors then exfiltrated into the jungle during the night of 10 March. They were spotted by rescue aircraft about noon on the eleventh. Again the CIDG survivors went berserk, fighting each other to escape and, in fact, shooting each other. The combat ended only when a CIDG soldier threw a grenade into the middle of his friends. Throughout the rest of the day, helicopters attempted to pick up the remainder of the camp survivors, and by dark they were all out.

The last page of the report was a recommendation that camp commanders make arrangements to separate themselves from the locals if they were being overrun. The local Vietnamese population couldn't be trusted and was probably riddled with VC and VC sympathizers. The Nung, the Meos and the Tai, ethnic groups who were hated by the Vietnamese, made steady allies and could be trusted. Plans should include them in the evacuation.

There was a last comment about the LLDB at Camp A-102. The Saigon authorities believed that the lack of assistance provided by them and the display of cowardice was the result of their officer failing to lead them. In fact, the report noted that only the LLDB Operations NCO, Sergeant Yang, had distinguished himself during the fight.

Gerber glanced at the last of it, recommendations that had no relevance to him and his situation. Minh, the LLDB commander, had already distinguished himself a number of times. Most of the Vietnamese strikers were drawn from the surrounding countryside and not made up of jailbirds and criminals as had been the members of the CIDG company that defected at Camp A-102. Very little of what was written in the report affected Gerber and his camp, and he wondered why Saigon would issue it without some kind of classification. It was just the sort of thing that the news media didn't need to get their hands on.

He made a note to show it to Minh and Fetterman and then filed and locked it in the drawer of his desk. Once they had seen it, he would destroy it and pretend that it had never come in. He stood, moved to the door and looked at the compound. The new team house would be ready by nightfall. They wouldn't get a hot meal in it, but they could meet there if they wanted to. Maybe it was time he met with the men again. A lot had happened during the last few days, and it might be best if they discussed it. He felt that something was going to happen soon. He didn't know what it was—he just felt that the pot was about to boil, and the pressure would blow the lid off.

9

GERBER'S HOOTCH IN THE REDOUBT AT CAMP A-555

Gerber sat behind his field desk, his hands laced behind his head, and stared at Sean Cavanaugh. The younger man was wearing a new set of fatigues so green they almost glowed. Although it was early in the morning, Cavanaugh was already sweating, the perspiration staining his uniform.

"Got a problem, Sean," said Gerber. "Need to send out a patrol to check on a couple of things and don't have anyone left to do it. Tyme's out with Washington, I need Fetterman here and Bocker has picked up some kind of rash and low-grade fever." Gerber smiled. "Personally, I think he's gotten used to sitting in that commo bunker of his and doesn't want to go out."

"I don't mind going out again, Captain," Cavanaugh said. "So far, we haven't had to stay in the field more than one night."

Gerber leaned forward and put his elbows on his desk. He wondered again if it was a good idea to send Cavanaugh out on his own. The man hadn't used good judgment when his radio failed, *if* it had failed. Bocker had been unable to find anything wrong with it, but Gerber knew that the moisture in the air sometimes shorted out a radio, and when it dried the next day, it worked perfectly. Still, he wanted someone out in the vicinity of the village, and Cavanaugh was the only man he had left.

"I'd like an ambush set up in the region of Cai Cai to see if we can catch anything," Gerber said. "This would be for one day and one night, two at the most. I don't like sending you out without a medic, but that can't be helped. You'll be pretty close to the camp so that we can get you assistance quickly if you need it."

"Yes, sir."

Gerber reached into the top drawer of his desk and pulled out a map of the AO. He spun it so that Cavanaugh could see it and began to brief him on the operation. Given the facts that his patrols had run into the VC to the south and west of the camp and the VC had raided the village of Cai Cai, it seemed that a clandestine operation into the region, an ambush patrol, might have some success. Since it was a hit-and-miss proposition, Gerber told the sergeant that there shouldn't be any trouble that Cavanaugh couldn't handle. Maybe it was the type of responsibility that Cavanaugh needed to help him work through his problems. Gerber wanted nothing flashy. He wanted a quiet ambush patrol that would disrupt the enemy and take no casualties itself. A simple, by the book operation.

When he finished, he asked, "Think you can handle it?"

"Yes, sir." Cavanaugh nodded. "It's pretty basic."

"Basic and simple," agreed Gerber.

"When would you like me to move out?"

Gerber glanced at his watch and then said, "You could leave soon after lunch. Ambush sites are scattered all over the place, most of them within fifteen klicks or so. Take three, four hours to get there, give you some time to rest and then slide off into the night about dusk. An easy day, as a matter of fact.''

"Who am I going to take?"

"Thought maybe you could get together with Sergeant Hoai and maybe Captain Minh and pull a team from the Vietnamese strikers."

"I'll get that organized." Cavanaugh got to his feet. "Be ready to pull out in a couple of hours."

"I'll meet you at the gate before you leave," said Gerber. He still wasn't convinced that it was a good idea, but he didn't have an alternative.

Once outside Gerber's hootch, Cavanaugh felt like whooping. It was as if God had decided that his plan was right and was taking steps to see that it was put into effect. Cavanaugh couldn't have asked for a better set of circumstances. Only a few team members were still on the camp, so each of them had to take up the extra duty. Since it was only in the commo department that there was backup, Cavanaugh was one of the few men who could be spared. He hurried through the gate of the redoubt and turned toward the Vietnamese quarters.

He found Corporal Tran sitting in the sun, apparently asleep. Tran had lost a sister to the VC in Cai Cai and had been on the last ambush with him. Cavanaugh crouched, shook Tran awake and then pointed into the hootch, indicating that Tran was supposed to assemble the team.

"We begin a new patrol in two hours. Get the men ready, and then meet me at the ammo bunker near the west gate."

Tran put a hand to his eyes to shade them from the sun, blinked and then nodded. Without a word he got to his feet and disappeared into the hootch. Cavanaugh watched him go and then turned to head over to the ammo bunker.

The ammo bunker on the west gate was not the main storage facility. It was a smaller structure, set into the ground and covered over with PSP and several layers of sandbags. The bunker was designed to hold enough ammunition to rearm the men fighting on the west side of the camp in the event of a massive VC assault. It also held all the spare claymore mines because it was closest to the gate. Cavanaugh stepped around the sandbag wall set directly in front of the entrance and descended into the dim, cool interior. Using his flashlight, he located the claymore mines and began setting them out on the floor, which was constructed of thick, rough-cut planks.

A few minutes later Tran and four other strikers arrived. Cavanaugh pointed at the mines and watched as the Vietnamese took two apiece and carried them into the daylight. Cavanaugh grabbed grenades for the M-79s, carrying nearly fifty rounds from the bunker.

Outside, he distributed the ammo to the strikers and then said, "Pack this with your gear. Tran, I want you to draw a PRICK-10 from Sergeant Bocker. I'll meet with you all at the gate in one hour, in full field gear and ready for a two-day patrol."

The men nodded and walked back to their hootches, carrying the claymore mines and the 40 mm grenades. Cavanaugh headed toward his own hootch and, once inside, opened the doors to his metal locker. He took out a set of tiger-striped fatigues and tossed them onto his bunk. Then he sat on the floor, opened the top drawer in the locker and found his bottle. He didn't need a drink but felt he wanted one. Just a short one to take the bad taste from his mouth and light a fire in his stomach—a pick-me-up before a long patrol where he wouldn't have time to think about booze or listening posts or Lieutenant Novak and the deaths of all those strikers.

He closed his eyes and raised the bottle to his lips, letting the liquor set fire to his mouth and throat, swallowing rapidly so that he didn't have time to breathe. He set the bottle on the floor next to his leg and stared at it for a long time. He could almost smell the bourbon in it. Not the smooth stuff that Captain Gerber handed out, not the Beam's Choice but rougher liquor that seemed to sandpaper the throat on the way down. Rougher liquor to give him the edge he needed, get his mind going, his heart started.

He sat there thinking about being in the field with no alcohol. Nothing around except the stink of rice paddies as they baked under the late-afternoon sun, the stink of the water buffalo pens and the open trenches filled with feces. Then he looked at the pistol belt holding his four canteens and wondered why he couldn't carry bourbon in one of them. Oh, he knew of all the MACV and Army directives that prohibited it, but those were designed for the draftees and the clerks, not for the professional soldier who knew his limitations and his way around. Besides, four canteens filled with water seemed excessive. Three would be plenty. The fourth would be the perfect place for his bourbon.

Cavanaugh got to his feet and removed one of the canteens from its pouch and poured the warm water out onto the floor. He watched the water spread, lifting up a film of red dirt that made it look like blood.

Finally he filled the canteen with bourbon. There was a little left in the bottle, so Cavanaugh finished it, figuring that there was no sense in saving one drink. He slipped into his field gear, adjusted the shoulder straps until they were comfortable and buckled his pistol belt. He was about to step into the compound when he realized that the smell of bourbon would be heavy on his breath. He stepped back to his wall locker, took his tube of toothpaste and squeezed some out onto his tongue, working it around in his mouth. Now he would smell like a mint factory, which was better than a brewery. The last thing he wanted to do was inadvertently tell the strikers that it was all right to drink before a patrol. They weren't professional enough to handle that.

Cavanaugh left his hootch carrying his rifle, one of the old M-14s. He liked it better than the M-16 because it was heavier. The M-16 was perfect in the jungle until they got into hand-to-hand fighting. Then it was like being armed with a mop handle. You could hurt someone with it, but it was more likely that you would irritate them. Besides, he wasn't convinced that the smaller slug from the M-16 was all that effective, although Tyme had told him the smaller round was the deadlier of the two.

As he moved to the west gate, he saw that his men were already there, each now wearing tiger-striped fatigues, each with a steel pot rather than the soft boonie hat and each with a large pack holding all the extra ammo and spare equipment that Cavanaugh had requested. Tran had the radio. Krung stood there, dressed and ready to go, too. Krung wouldn't want to pass up an opportunity to kill Vietcong if he could help it.

Cavanaugh moved toward them, nodded at one or two of them and then began checking their backpacks to make sure that they had everything they needed. It wasn't necessary. They had even more than the standard field issue, carrying so much ammunition that it would take a major battle for them to run out.

As he turned to open the gate, Cavanaugh saw Gerber approaching. Cavanaugh stopped and waited, and when Gerber was close, he said, "We're about set to move out."

"Okay, Sean. I just wanted to tell you not to take any unnecessary chances and wish you good luck."

"Thank you, Captain. I'll see you sometime tomorrow afternoon at the latest."

"At the very latest." Gerber shot a glance at the PRC-10 that one of the Vietnamese carried. To Cavanaugh he said, "Remember to make your radio checks, and if you lose contact, you come back in."

"Yes, sir."

"Good luck again, Sean."

"Yes, sir. Thank you." He turned, opened the gate and watched Krung trot down the road, then slow to a walk as he reached the edge of the runway. The rest of the men followed him out with Cavanaugh bringing up the rear. He quickly caught up to Krung and gave him directions across the open rice paddies and empty fields of elephant grass that stretched to the west from the camp. They spread out, five or six meters between them, and walked along the dikes of the paddies, moving slowly, easily, because they had most of the day ahead of them.

At midafternoon they halted for lunch, which took them nearly an hour and a half. They headed out again and approached the remains of Cai Cai near evening. The patrol spread out, swept through and exited on the west side. Cavanaugh stopped at the edge of the village and looked out into the distance. All he could see were open fields of elephant grass, rice paddies and swamps and hills that sloped gently into Cambodia. He could see no point in traveling any farther because the VC and NVA, if they wanted to move into South Vietnam, would have to pass close to where he was.

Under his direction they laid out the claymore mines in a pattern that ranged outward nearly half a klick and would cover the most likely routes of infiltration. They then attached the firing wires and carefully unrolled the cord until they were among the hootches of Cai Cai.

Cavanaugh set up the firing controls in the hootches that dominated the west side of the village, arranging them in a sequence so that he knew in which hootch were the firing controls for which mines. In the hootch farthest to the north were the controls of the mines on the farthest trails; in the hootch farthest to the south were those of the closest. By monitoring movement in the fields with the help of Navy binoculars and a starlight scope, he would be able to ambush the enemy by remote control.

As the sun set, Cavanaugh spread his men out in the village using the decaying hootches as cover. He let the strikers cook their evening meal, using the hootches to conceal the smoke, and then waited. Cavanaugh circulated among them, telling them not to shoot until he passed the word and then to use the grenade launchers. By lobbing the shells, they could conceal the flash of the weapons, and it might confuse the VC. As a last resort, or if the VC attack turned toward them, then they should use their rifles.

When it was dark, Cavanaugh moved to the northern end of the village, worked his way to the west about fifty meters and settled into the corner of a rice paddy where he could watch the fields to the west. He used the binoculars to sweep from the edge of Cai Cai out to near the Cambodian border, looking for movement. He stared through the instrument, concentrating and ignoring the persistent buzz of insects as they swarmed around his head. He ignored the thirst he felt, only occasionally thinking of the bourbon on his hip. He didn't really need it, but the weight of it was a reminder that it was there.

For an hour he watched the fields. The moon came up, bathing the ground in its bright white light and giving the paddies a life of their own. Cavanaugh watched the shadows shifting in the light breeze that did little to cool and thought about his bourbon. Finally, having spotted nothing coming near him, he rolled to his side, tugged at the snaps on his canteen cover and pulled out the bourbon.

The rubber of the canteen retained some of the heat of the day, and as he unscrewed the cap, he was almost overpowered by the smell of the liquor. He held it under his nose for a moment, letting the vapors waft into his nostrils. Then he put the canteen to his lips and took a deep drink. The bourbon felt good going down but tasted terrible. Maybe it was because it had been hot during the day, or maybe it was the rubber of the canteen reacting with the bourbon. Cavanaugh didn't care one way or the other. He sipped his bourbon, thought about it and then took a final deep gulp.

As he put his canteen away, he thought he saw movement in the distance. He put the binoculars to his eyes again and studied the shadows for a moment until they seemed to solidify and take on human form. When he was sure that it wasn't the moonlight, breeze and shadows playing tricks on him, he crawled back to the edge of the village, got to his feet and ran into the first of the hootches. There he grabbed the starlight scope and swept the field with it. In seconds he had confirmed that there were men moving in front of him. Five men spread out slightly but not enough so that he couldn't get them all with one of the claymores.

He tapped one of the strikers on the shoulder and pointed. The man picked up an M-79 and loaded it but didn't fire it. Cavanaugh tracked the VC and then picked up the firing control for the claymores. He watched them closely, excited by the prospect of killing five of the enemy so quickly, so easily. They had been in place for only a couple of hours, and already they were about to score. He grinned to himself and felt excitement twist his stomach. He wanted to take a drink to celebrate the luck but decided to wait until he had made the kill. That was the proper time to celebrate.

Cavanaugh set the claymore control down and dried his sweating palms on the front of his fatigues, watching the five men moving through the night. He wanted to jump and scream but knew that he couldn't. He felt for the claymore controls and picked them up again, his thumb dancing against the firing control, anticipating the action. His eyes were narrowed as if he was staring through a dark tunnel. All he could see were the five men walking along a rice paddy dike a couple of hundred meters away.

He turned to look at his two strikers, then returned his attention to the field. The five enemy soldiers were close to one of the ambush sites. Cavanaugh moved to the wall and leaned forward as if that would help him see better. Then, suddenly, convinced that he had let them walk too far, he fired the first of the mines. There was a flash of light as the C-4 detonated, the explosion quickly following. Four of the men went down immediately, but one of them turned to run. Cavanaugh fired a second mine and watched as the man was blown off his feet.

"You see that?" Cavanaugh demanded, his voice high and strained with excitement, almost too loud. "You see that?" He glanced at the strikers and then peered back into the dark. "Got them all. All five of them."

A sudden burst of machine-gun fire interrupted him. He saw the strikers dive for cover and then saw a stream of green tracers raking the village to the south. There were dull smacks as the slugs hit the hootches. A smaller weapon, probably an AK-47, opened fire, but none of the rounds struck near Cavanaugh's position. Because there was a machine gun firing, he assumed there was a full squad of VC, maybe a platoon of them, that he hadn't seen.

"Tran," he whispered, "use the M-79. Pop a few rounds out there near the muzzle-flashes. High arc."

Tran didn't move immediately, and Cavanaugh reached out to grab the weapon. He snapped the sight down out of the way, aimed the grenade launcher out the window at a high angle but holding it below the sill so that the flash wouldn't be visible. He pulled the trigger and then jumped up to watch for the detonation. The round exploded short of the machine-gun position, throwing up a fountain of sparks and fire.

Cavanaugh increased the angle and fired a second round as more enemy weapons began to shoot into the village. He heard a couple of rounds slam into the mud of the hootch's walls over his head. The VC still didn't know where he hid. They were shooting at the likely locations.

Outside, the round he fired had the distance but was off to the right. He heard a couple of muffled pops as the men in the other hootches fired their grenade launchers. Cavanaugh giggled as he slammed another round into his weapon and aimed it. The firing from the rice paddies and elephant grass increased as more weapons joined in the battle.

Cavanaugh fired, missed and became impatient. He tossed the M-79 back to Tran. "Keep putting out rounds."

Tran took the weapon, moved to the right and then ducked out the door. Using the corner of the hootch for cover, he began shooting as rapidly as he could, using the muzzle-flashes as aiming points.

Cavanaugh crouched at the side of the window, watching the enemy movements. He fingered the claymore controls he held, figuring that he could kill more of them with the claymores than with the M-79. He was just waiting for someone to move so that he could blow them apart with a mine.

He saw a couple of men running across one rice paddy, their heads down as if leaning into a driving rain, heading toward where a couple of the claymores were hidden. Cavanaugh gritted his teeth and mumbled under his breath, "Get them. Get them," because he didn't have the control for those mines. A moment later there was an explosion in the field. Krung or one of the Vietnamese fired a claymore, and the enemy disappeared in the cloud of steel ball bearings from the mine.

That seemed to excite the enemy. Or frighten them. Suddenly there were fifty VC on their feet, running across the open ground. They were shouting, screaming and shooting from the hip, charging into the village. There was a bugle blaring and a machine gun hammering, the rounds pouring into the hootches.

Cavanaugh snatched his rifle, flicked off the safety and aimed at one of the men. He grinned as he pulled the trigger and watched the man tumble to the ground. He sighted on another, fired, missed and fired again.

Around him, from the other hootches, the strikers began shooting, some of them going to full automatic, putting out rounds rapidly, their red tracers bouncing across the fields, and high into the night sky. Those rounds were answered by green-and-white ones from the enemy that raked the village. The sound of firing increased until it was a continuous roar without individual reports. Some of Cavanaugh's strikers used their M-79s, dropping the HE grenades among the men charging at them.

Cavanaugh emptied his weapon, dropped the magazine to the dirt floor of the hootch and clawed at his bandolier, pulling another free. As he slammed it home, three of the VC collapsed as a grenade exploded near them in a mushroom of strobe light and whining shrapnel. Another fell, apparently the result of rifle fire.

Then another of the claymores detonated, taking out half the enemy, the steel balls chopping men off at the knees, or the waist, or the neck. The ground around the survivors seemed to erupt as one of the grenadiers switched to white phosphorus, setting the paddy field on fire. Cavanaugh laughed out loud as he saw the confusion among the enemy soldiers. Some of them had stopped firing or stopped running, and the wailing notes of the bugle faded.

With that the assault broke. The surviving enemy tossed their weapons, some of them throwing their hands in the air, screaming, *"Chieu hoi. Chieu hoi."* Others ran back the way they had come, fleeing toward Cambodia and safety.

Cavanaugh continued to fire, shooting at the retreating men, picking them off one by one, laughing as he watched each fall, cartwheeling into the dirty rice paddy water, stumbling to the ground to lie still or blasted from his feet. From one of the other hootches there was continued rifle fire as a striker did the same. Cavanaugh shot the last of the running men and watched him tumble out of sight in the tall elephant grass just a few meters short of a tree line that promised safety.

Still standing, afraid to move, were seven VC. They held their hands up and continued to shout that they wanted to surrender. For a moment Cavanaugh didn't know what to do. The last thing he needed was prisoners. He looked out the window at them and watched as the men slowly moved toward one another, gathering in a small group as if there was safety in numbers.

There was some shouting from one of the other hootches, the words in a garbled tongue that Cavanaugh couldn't follow. There was a response from the field and another question from the hootch. One of the VC answered, and a second later there was a pop as one of the strikers fired his M-79. The round exploded to the left of the VC. All of them fell, then one started to get to his feet. Cavanaugh shrugged and put a bullet in his head.

For several minutes no one moved. Cavanaugh kept his eyes sweeping over the field, looking for movement, but there was none. He listened carefully but heard nothing. The world around him had taken on the silence of a graveyard. Or maybe it was the silence of a battlefield when the shooting has stopped. Finally he ducked under the window, exited the hootch and checked on the strikers. No one had been hurt, and the closest the VC had come to hitting any of them was when they had put the burst into Cavanaugh's hootch.

He told the men to keep their eyes open, and if they had seen nothing by two in the morning, they could go to half alert. He didn't know whether the VC would try to collect the bodies or if they would stay away, afraid of losing more men. If they hadn't come back by two, he figured they probably wouldn't. Cavanaugh then went back to his own hootch to wait for morning when they could check the dead left on the field, collect the weapons and then celebrate the victory.

10

VILLAGE OF CAI CAI
NEAR THE
CAMBODIAN BORDER

The night passed quietly. Cavanaugh spent most of it in the hootch staring out the window, looking for signs that the VC were trying to recover the bodies of the dead or that some of the enemy caught in the ambush were only wounded. But all he heard were the sounds of the nocturnal animals and insects. Periodically he fingered the canteen that contained the bourbon as it pressed against his hip, reminding him that it was there. Once he took it out and shook it, listening to the liquid slosh around, but then put it away without drinking, congratulating himself on his willpower.

As the sky began to pale, the night sounds outside seemed to diminish, and Cavanaugh could hear the quiet snoring of the striker sleeping on the dirt floor across from him. He took out the canteen, then stood so that he could look out the window. Lumps scattered in the rice paddies and elephant grass were just becoming visible in the predawn half light. He unscrewed the top of the canteen, held it up in mock salute, then drank deeply.

A second later he heard a stirring behind him and turned to see the striker sitting up, staring at the rectangle of gray in the window. Cavanaugh slipped his canteen back into its cover. "We'll eat breakfast and then check the field. Count the dead and collect the weapons."

The striker sat there as if stunned and then nodded. He rubbed his face with both hands and then reached behind him for his pack, searching for his canteen.

Cavanaugh watched him and then left his post at the window. He carried his rifle out the door and checked on the men in the other hootches. He found Tran sitting with the radio, listening to the static, the handset clutched in his left hand, although he didn't say a word into it.

Cavanaugh moved close and crouched near Tran. He took the handset from him, put it against his own ear and pressed the button. "Zulu Base, Zulu Base, this is Zulu One Two."

There was a moment of silence and then, "Zulu One Two, this is Base. Go."

"Roger, Base. Be advised that we have made contact and estimate forty Victor Charlie Kilo Indigo Alpha."

"Understand contact. Any friendly casualties?"

"Negative. Will advise when further information obtained."

"Roger One Two. Understand. Zulu Base out."

Cavanaugh gave the handset back to Tran and then left that hootch. He found Krung sitting outside the last one, his knife in hand, slowly stroking the blade against a whetstone. Cavanaugh grinned at him. "How are you going to know which ones you killed?"

Krung shrugged. "I killed some. I only take a few trophies. That's fair."

"All right," Cavanaugh said. "We'll move out in about an hour. Have everyone eat some breakfast, and post one man to watch the field. We can't assume that the danger is over just because it's now light.

With that Cavanaugh returned to the hootch he had used and dug out some C-rations from his pack. He threw out the scrambled eggs and ham, eating the peaches and a tin of bread smeared with runny grape jelly. When he finished, he organized the men so that they could clear the field.

They swept out of the village, on line, their weapons held at the ready. Cavanaugh ordered his men to check the bodies carefully to make sure that each VC was dead. In some cases it was easy. The wounds were so massive that no one could have survived them. Stomachs ripped open by shrapnel or bullets. Giant holes blown through chests. The head of one corpse was missing; another had lost both legs. The men of Camp A-555 removed the weapons from the bodies, sometimes prying the AKs or SKSs from between cold fingers, and then stacked the guns on a rice paddy dike.

Cavanaugh found one group that had been hit by the claymore mines. There wasn't all that much left to recognize. The seven hundred and fifty steel balls had turned the men into hamburger, splattering the ground with a spray of red that had turned rusty in the early-morning sun. The weapons the men had carried were broken bits of equipment, ruined by the ball bearings. Cavanaugh kicked at the remains of one man, and as he rolled onto his back, he left a pile of entrails on the ground. Cavanaugh grinned at the gaping hole where the chest had been and said, "Got you."

It took them an hour to check the field. Cavanaugh counted forty-four dead men and sixteen blood trails that disappeared into the elephant grass leading back to Cambodia. They had collected forty-seven weapons including a Russian RPD machine gun.

After inspecting the field, Cavanaugh took his Randall combat knife and grabbed the hand of the nearest dead VC. With one swift chop he cut the trigger finger from the hand and held it up for the others to see. Then he nodded at them.

"You get them all. Every trigger finger. But don't do anything else to the bodies."

Spreading over the field again, the Vietnamese cut off the trigger fingers of every dead soldier. The lone exception was Krung. He didn't cut off the fingers but took the genitals. It was a ritual he'd performed a hundred times. He had sworn on the bodies of his dead family that he would kill fifty VC for each of them and kept track by taking the trophies. No one, not even Captain Gerber, had said a word about it.

When they had finished, Cavanaugh summoned the group to the pile of weapons. "I want each of you to take three, and that includes the RPD. We'll destroy the rest of them." He pawed through the captured stock, taking an AK and two SKSs. He knew they made good trading material. Regulations wouldn't allow Americans to take an AK home, but the SKS was a semiautomatic weapon, and it could be taken to the World.

After everyone had been through the weapons, Cavanaugh led them back to the edge of Cai Cai. He turned and faced the pile of stock. He pointed at Tran and said, "One round, WP. Let's see if you can drop it in the center of the weapons."

Tran grinned, broke open the M-79 and loaded the long 40 mm round. He adjusted the sight, aimed, adjusted it again and then fired. The round fell short and to the right but showered the weapons with flaming debris.

"Nice try." Cavanaugh pointed to one of the other strikers and ordered, "You give it a try."

The man loaded his weapon, sighted and pulled the trigger. The round landed in the center of the pile of captured weapons, destroying a number of them on detonation and spreading white phosphorus over the remainder, melting the smaller metallic parts and setting the wood on fire.

"All right!" yelled Cavanaugh. "Excellent shot! Truly excellent." He clapped the man on the back.

The striker laughed. "I did it."

"You sure did," confirmed Cavanaugh. "Okay, let's get out of here. Sergeant Krung, if you'll be good enough to take the point, we'll head back to the camp."

IT WAS THE MIDDLE of the afternoon when they approached the west side of the base. Cavanaugh halted long enough to call Bocker to inform him that they were coming in, but since they had to cross a field that would leave them open to the camp's weapons, Cavanaugh didn't bother to pop smoke. His patrol, because of its size, would pose no threat, and it would be recognized before any damage could be done.

Once they were inside the compound, Cavanaugh halted and turned to face them. He held his rifle up and said, "Weapons check in thirty minutes. I'll expect every rifle, grenade launcher and pistol to be cleaned. Then we'll have a beer. On me. Questions?"

When no one spoke, Cavanaugh said, "Get to it." He watched them head toward their hootches and thought that they looked like winners. They carried themselves erectly and even though they had spent the night in the field, they didn't look tired. Their shoulders weren't slumped. They carried their weapons as if they were still on patrol. They were good men, and he knew that he could rely on each of them.

As they disappeared into their hootches, he turned and headed for the redoubt. Once inside, he thought about reporting immediately to Gerber but then decided that he could drop off his gear and take a short snort. The bourbon wouldn't have the rubberized taste of the booze in his canteen. Upon entering his hootch, he unbuckled his pistol belt and slipped out of his pack, dropping it in the center of his cot. Then, wiping the sweat from his forehead, he opened his wall locker to get out a bottle. He sat experiencing the customary light feeling that one has after carrying a heavy load for a long time. The sensation was that of being able to float to the ceiling.

He took a deep swallow from the bottle, breathed out and took a second. Closing his eyes, he felt the liquor warming his insides, burning his stomach. He could almost feel the fire wash through him, relaxing him, wiping out the memories and the anxieties that had plagued him. He took a third deep drink and corked the bottle, and as he got to his feet, he saw Captain Gerber crossing the compound, moving toward the team house.

Cavanaugh stored the bottle in his wall locker, surprised that nearly a third of it was gone because he had just opened it. He shrugged, figuring that someone else must have taken a drink. Dismissing it, he stepped out into the bright afternoon sun, put a hand up to shade his eyes and called, "Captain Gerber."

Gerber stopped and turned. "Sean. Welcome back."

"You have a moment, sir?"

Gerber turned, stepped several feet closer to Cavanaugh and then gestured toward his hootch. "Let's go into my office, and you can tell me about your mission. Sergeant Bocker said that you reported fifty killed?"

"Yes, sir. That was an estimate. Number of bodies was smaller, but there were a number of blood trails that we didn't follow. And we have quite a few captured weapons."

"Great. Let's step inside and you can tell me about it." Gerber moved toward his hootch. He stopped outside and gestured at the entrance, allowing the sergeant to precede him.

Cavanaugh stepped up and in and took the metal chair that sat in front of the field desk. Gerber seated himself behind it, laced his fingers together on the surface and said, "Give me the outline of your report. You can write something up later to forward to Saigon."

"Yes, sir." Cavanaugh hesitated and then described the firefight of the night before.

Gerber nodded throughout the report. Then he asked, "None of them tried to surrender?"

"No, sir. When they saw they were going to fail, they just turned and ran."

"And you kept shooting at them?"

"What'd you expect?" Cavanaugh snapped. "They were the enemy, and if they got away, they'd just come back another day to shoot at us."

"I know that, Sergeant. I just asked a simple question."

"Then yes, sir, we kept shooting at them until there were no targets left."

"Were they shooting at you at that point?" Gerber asked.

"I don't see what difference that makes, sir. Our job is to kill the enemy, and I don't see why we have to stop because they happen to be facing away from us. Shit, sir, at least they were soldiers and not innocent civilians like in Cai Cai."

Gerber held up a hand. "Listen, Sean, I'm only trying to get the facts. There are some in Saigon who won't understand shooting men in the back."

"But, sir," Cavanaugh protested. "I don't see what difference it makes if the bullet hole is in the front or the back. They were carrying weapons, and they had been firing them."

"Okay, Sean, forget it. Just don't put it in the report."

"Yes, sir."

"Now did your men take trophies?"

Cavanaugh hesitated, staring at his commanding officer. "Yes sir, some of them did."

"And you did nothing to stop them?"

"Captain, I complied with the MACV directives by not cutting off ears, but I can't control the RFs on this. I can advise them but not order them, especially with Krung out there cutting off dicks."

"Goddamn it, Sean, you were in charge. You could stop them if you really wanted to. That's part of your job."

"Excuse me, Captain, but I thought we were here as advisors, so I advised them not to take trophies. They just didn't listen to me."

"I'm sorry, Sean," said Gerber, "but I just can't accept that. We haven't had a problem like this, with the exception of Krung, and we have winked at that given the circumstances, but we can't let it spread. The last thing we need is to let the press discover that we have strikers mutilating the dead."

"What difference does it make, as long as they're dead, Captain? I've never been able to understand that."

"Then I'll explain it to you. The difference is that civilized soldiers do not mutilate the enemy dead. There are rules of land warfare, and we obey them."

"But that's a load of shit, sir. You fight a war to win it, and if cutting up a couple of dead bodies helps you win, then you do it. The psychological damage to the enemy is tremendous," said Cavanaugh. "It's a real advantage to us."

"Then let me explain it this way. MACV Directive 20-4 states that we will not take trophies, and that's the way it's going to be. No more of this John Wayne shit and lame excuses about the taking of trophies."

"We're awfully shorthanded," said Cavanaugh, smiling. "We going to stop patrolling?"

"After tomorrow we'll be in better shape. Smith and Kepler are due back, and we're getting a new heavy weapons man. That way you won't have to go out without a second American on the patrol."

"But, Captain, I don't mind. I've got a good group to work with. We trust each other."

"That's what I'm afraid of. I'm sorry, Sean, but this solo action has got to stop. Too many strange things have happened too quickly."

"Like what, Captain? All the patrols have been successful."

"Come on, Sean, we're not stupid. You've missed check-in times, you've let the men take trophies and mutilate the bodies and you've taken chances that don't show good judgment."

"But, Captain—"

"Sean, that's it. No more hero crap with your hand-picked hatchet teams." Gerber saw that Cavanaugh was going to interrupt and held up a hand to stop him. "Give us some credit, Sean. You've gone out with the same strikers each time. Yes, I notice things like that. You've run up an impressive kill record and have the weapons to back it up, so there is no problem. But I'm not going to let you run loose like this. We're here as advisors, and if we sometimes expand that role, that's the way it is, but it's not a personal vendetta. Once we slip into that, we're no longer soldiers."

"All I'm doing is carrying the war to the enemy."

Gerber slammed his hand against the desktop. "That's bullshit. How many fingers did your assassins bring back this time? No, don't answer that. I only ask you so that you know that we know."

"I don't understand this, Captain," said Cavanaugh, suddenly sweating heavily. "I don't understand at all."

Gerber got to his feet and looked down at the young NCO. "Let's just say that everyone knows what's been happening, and we don't want it to happen anymore. No more missions without a second American. No more of this running off and doing your own thing. No more convenient breakdowns in the radio equipment. I'll let what has happened in the past go because it is in the past, but no more of it."

"Then we stop being soldiers," said Cavanaugh sarcastically.

"Wrong," snapped Gerber. "We stop being rabble and become soldiers—soldiers with a specific mission, and that mission is to train the strikers. To guide them. Not to assassinate the Vietcong."

"I don't understand the difference," said Cavanaugh.

"The difference is we train the Vietnamese to fight their own war. If we must assist, then we assist. But we're not going to take over fighting the war for them because once we do that, then we've lost. If the distinction is too fine for you to grasp, then you are in the wrong place."

"All right, Captain," said Cavanaugh. "I understand. I won't be a problem for you any longer now that I know where we stand."

"Then I'm glad we had this talk. See you tonight at the evening meal." Gerber grinned. "A hot one for a change. We finished rebuilding the team house while you were out."

"Yes, sir. See you then." Cavanaugh walked out of Gerber's hootch.

11

THE HELIPAD AT
CAMP A-555

Bocker had warned Gerber that the incoming supply chopper contained both Kepler and Smith and the new replacement that no one had bothered to identify yet. He was carrying his 201 file with him, along with his orders, and he was a heavy weapons man. He was all that Gerber could ask for.

Gerber had heard the helicopter, the blades popping and the engine roaring, but he hadn't spotted it yet. Fetterman strolled out the gate, turned and looked to the east. The sun was trying to break through the clouds that had blown over the camp about an hour after sunup. He stepped closer to Gerber.

"New man?" Fetterman asked.

"On the chopper," said Gerber without looking at him. "And Kepler and Smith. Bocker confirmed they're on board."

"That's good," said Fetterman, still facing east, a hand over his eyes to shade them from the morning sun. "Especially with Cavanaugh getting weird on us."

Gerber turned to stare at Fetterman. "Cavanaugh's getting weird?"

"You know what I mean. Recruiting that hunter-killer team of his and those ambush patrols. Just a little flaky. Not exactly by the book."

"We do a lot of things that aren't by the book, Master Sergeant. You have a problem with Cavanaugh that I don't know about?"

"No, sir," said Fetterman. "Sure don't. Just glad we've got a couple of the team coming back so that we can put two Americans on each patrol. Help each other out."

Gerber saw the helicopter appear in the distance, looking like a big insect. He said, "If you have something on your mind, Tony, I want to know what it is."

"Nothing, sir. Just commenting on the situation that seems to have resolved itself."

"Then I'll pretend you didn't say anything. It's your job to keep track of those kinds of problems so I don't have to worry about them."

"Yes, sir," said Fetterman, nodding. "I'm keeping an eye on the situation. By the way, when is Miss Morrow due back?"

"Miss Morrow is currently running around in I Corps, interviewing the survivors of Camp A-102. Say, did you know they put the Air Force jock in for the Medal of Honor for plucking his friend off the runway?"

"Didn't know that," said Fetterman. "How about our boys?"

"Haven't heard anything official, but I assume they've gone in for a bunch of stuff. Just not the CMH."

"Well, that figures." Fetterman looked up at the helicopter and grabbed a smoke grenade from his pocket. He pulled the pin and tossed it to the center of the pad where it began billowing red smoke that blew back at them. They stepped to the rear out of the way.

"So," said Fetterman, "you didn't tell me when Robin is going to rejoin us."

"Not really sure." Gerber shrugged. "I imagine that once she gets her story up north, she'll make a pass back by here."

The helicopter had gotten closer, the roar of the engines beginning to wipe out any sound. Both men ducked and raised a hand to their heads to hold their berets in place. Gerber turned his head toward the camp, his eyes closed for protection against the swirling dust and debris kicked up by the blades as the helicopter hovered closer. The noise from the turbine overwhelmed them. A moment later the aircraft settled to the pad, and the whine of the engine decreased as the pilot rolled off the throttle. Gerber looked toward it and saw Kepler leap from the cargo compartment and then reach in to grab his bag. He helped Smith to the ground, and together they began throwing boxes and wooden crates onto the pad.

Behind them a tall, thin man tossed a duffel bag to the ground. He climbed out, reached back for a suitcase and a briefcase. He had one of the new M-16s slung over his shoulder and wore a complete set of combat gear that included a harness, backpack, canteen and a large knife taped upside down to the shoulder straps.

Gerber felt there was something vaguely familiar about the man. He had dark hair that was sweat damp. His face was white, suggesting that he hadn't spent much time in the sun lately. He had dark brown eyes, a long nose and thin lips. He had a solid build. The more he studied the newcomer, the more Gerber couldn't help thinking that he had seen the man somewhere before.

He started to move toward the new arrival, but the helicopter pilot revved up his engine again, lifted to a hover, blowing everything that was light and not fastened down from the helipad, and then rotated the aircraft, taking off the way he had come.

As the helicopter disappeared in the distance, the new man snapped to attention in front of Gerber and reported, "Specialist Fifth Class William Henry Schattschneider reporting as ordered, sir."

Gerber returned the salute self-consciously. "We normally don't . . ." He stopped, looked at the man's name tag and asked, "You related to a Master Sergeant Schattschneider who was once my team sergeant?"

"My dad, sir. When he was killed, I wanted to enlist but finished high school and then got into the Army. I volunteered for the Special Forces and then Vietnam and then for this camp."

"Christ!" Gerber wasn't sure exactly what he should do. Or even say. He remembered the letter he had written to the senior Schattschneider's wife and family, and the last thing he expected was that the son would show up. He wondered about Army regulations regarding the sole surviving heir but figured that someone up the line would have checked on that. He realized that he was standing there much too long and reached for the other man's hand to shake it. "Welcome aboard. You need help with your gear?"

"No, sir. I can manage."

"Okay." Gerber turned to Fetterman. "Sergeant, why don't you take Specialist Schattschneider with you and find him a bunk and then take him to the team house." He looked at the new man and added, "I'll meet with you there, and you can let me see your 201 file."

"Yes, sir."

As Fetterman and Schattschneider made their way up to the camp, Gerber moved closer to Kepler and looked at the pile of equipment and boxes that had been left. "You been doing some horse-trading, Derek?"

"Found a few things I thought we could use, Captain," said Kepler. "Most of it was just lying around, so I volunteered it to assist us." Kepler smiled.

"I'll get you some help," Gerber said. "Anything in that mess I should know about?"

"No, sir. Just routine equipment, including a small generator for the dispensary so that we can take that off the camp circuits. It's big enough to run a couple of small air conditioners."

"Well, maybe on your next trip you can find the air conditioners."

"Oh, no, sir," said Kepler, "you misunderstand. I brought those, too."

Gerber couldn't help himself. He burst out laughing. "Christ, Derek. You're going to get us all nailed."

"Don't worry, the Air Force will never miss them."

"All right, I'll go get a truck to haul this stuff into the camp." He walked back up the short road that led to the main gate, stopped and looked back. Kepler and Smith were organizing the equipment so that it would be easier to load.

In front of him, near the redoubt, Gerber could see Fetterman and Bocker talking to the new man. The captain shook his head in disbelief. Schattschneider's kid here. Now how in the hell was he supposed to react to that? Schattschneider, the master sergeant, had been a damned fine soldier who had died, it might be said, dodging the wrong way. Not a great heroic death defending the camp from the yellow horde battering down the gate, but a small quiet death with a piece of shrapnel cutting the life from his body. If he had been standing six inches to the side, he would have had one hell of a war story. All he got was a pine box, a Purple Heart and a quick trip to Arlington.

Gerber tore his eyes away from the scene. Schattschneider bore a striking resemblance to his old man, and in the bright morning sun it was hard to believe that it was the kid. Gerber had greatly respected the old man, had leaned on him when they formed the team. It was going to be difficult to deal with the kid. To be fair to him. Give him a chance to grow, to learn, and not just protect him.

He moved toward the motor pool, climbed into the cab of a three-quarter ton and started the engine. He fought the gearshift for a moment, then roared out the gate in a cloud of dust and diesel smoke.

He pulled up next to the equipment and sat in the cab staring to the west while Smith and Kepler loaded the rear. Across the open fields of elephant grass and rice paddies were the hills that marked Cambodia. At that moment Gerber wondered just what the fuck he was doing. Sometimes it seemed so worthless. Memories of dead friends haunted him. Hell, he had the living reminders of his dead friends in the form of their children haunting him. And there was Cavanaugh. A young man who seemed to have become completely warped by the horror of close combat. Tyme had been correct when he said there were a lot of little things that didn't seem right.

A quick double knock on the side of the truck broke his train of thought, and Gerber glanced in the rearview mirrors. The equipment had been loaded, and Smith and Kepler were in the back waiting. He started the engine, shifted into Low and turned up the road. He drove through the gate, wove his way up to the entrance of the redoubt and stopped. As Kepler and Smith jumped to the ground, Gerber got out of the cab and walked around the back to help the men unload it.

Just as they were finishing, Fetterman approached alone. He glanced at Kepler and Smith and then said, "Captain, we've got another problem."

"Well, that's great," said Gerber. "I was running out of things to worry about. What is it now?"

"I can't be sure yet, but I think Sean has gone over the hill."

"Over the hill?" Gerber snapped. "What the fuck do you mean by that?"

"I mean simply that it looks like he's taken off. I talked to Minh and his team sergeant, and it seems there are a number of strikers missing, too."

"Christ," said Gerber tiredly. "How many?"

"Minh's getting a muster right now. Said he thought it was about twenty-five. Most of them are the guys Cavanaugh was out with in the last couple of days."

"What about Krung?" Gerber asked. "He still here?"

"Yes, sir. I talked to him briefly. Claimed he didn't know a thing about it."

"Right," said Gerber, shaking his head. "Didn't know a thing. Okay. You checked the equipment yet? See what he took?"

"No, sir. Thought I'd better brief you."

"When'd all this happen?" asked Gerber.

"Nobody saw anything. I would guess they left last night sometime."

"Okay, Tony," said Gerber, "let's you and me head over to the arms locker and see what's missing. We'd better swing by supply and see what's gone from there, too. Have Washington run an inventory on his medical supplies."

"Yes, sir. Then what?"

"I guess we'd better get a patrol together, then go out to find the silly son of a bitch, that's what."

IT HAD BEEN relatively simple for Cavanaugh to get out of the camp, even with twenty-two men and all the equipment they could carry. They had decided to wait until three in the morning, when only a few strikers on the bunker line were alert. The only other American who had been awake was on the north wall, watching the distant flares of artillery as one of the fire support bases rained 105 mm shells on a suspected enemy location. The Vietnamese who had seen them had assumed that it was just a routine patrol, and since that was rarely cleared with them, they let it go. If Minh or his LLDB NCOIC had seen them, it would have taken some fast talking to get out, but neither Minh nor the NCO saw them, so the problem didn't arise.

Cavanaugh had taken them out under cover of darkness, then moved them rapidly through the elephant grass and rice paddies until they had come to a tree line. They had entered it and taken up defensive positions to wait for the sun. Cavanaugh figured that it would be a couple of hours before anyone reported him missing, and another couple before a search party could be organized. By waiting for light, he could make better time. If he forced it in the dark, there was a real chance that someone would get hurt or that they would stumble into a VC ambush.

As the sun came up, Cavanaugh moved among his men, checking their equipment. Some of them were loaded down with C-rations, carrying only a little ammo for a single weapon. Others bore spare ammo for the machine guns, the grenade launchers and the recoilless rifle. And still others carried a couple of rifles and a dozen bandoliers filled with extra magazines. There were enough food and weapons to give him time to build a small base camp.

When he was satisfied with all that he saw, he got them on the move. They swept out of the trees, along the bank of a canal, heading straight for Cambodia. Cavanaugh figured that the best place to put his camp was on the other side of the border. It would keep the Americans away from him because they didn't dare cross into a foreign country. And it protected him from the VC and NVA because they knew that the Americans couldn't operate on that side of the line. It was the last place anyone would look.

With the trees and several klicks separating them from the camp, Cavanaugh moved from the soft, muddy ground along the bank of the canal to the broken pavement of a road that had been allowed to disintegrate. They made good time, forgetting about breakfast and ignoring the growing heat as the sun climbed higher. Cavanaugh checked his map repeatedly, used his compass and, when he was sure that they had crossed into Cambodia, began searching for a place for his camp.

The jungle, a thin, lightly wooded area that reached to the bank of the canal and bisected the road, provided cover. Cavanaugh waved his men into it, and moved along the major axis until he found an outcrop of rock that climbed twenty or thirty feet above the surrounding countryside. The trees, mostly palm and teak, and a light scrub of bushes and a covering of elephant grass combined to conceal the rock. Not far away was a slowly moving stream of clear water and near that were several small ponds, a couple of them resembling bomb craters.

Cavanaugh pointed at the rock and told the point man, "This is it. This will mark our first camp."

GERBER STOOD in the arms locker, a Coleman lantern blazing on the floor beside his foot, and looked at the empty spaces where M-60 machine guns, M-14 and M-16 rifles, M-79 grenade launchers and even a 90 mm recoilless rifle had been. The interior of the bunker was cool. There was a mess in one corner where someone, probably the Vietnamese under Cavanaugh's direction, had opened ammo crates, throwing away the packings that added weight to the ammo. He stood there for a moment, wishing that he had kept better track of the equipment in the arms locker and then wondered why. He knew that a lot of equipment was missing— he could make an accurate guess at the numbers—and decided that a precise count didn't matter. The weapons were gone, and he knew where they went.

He reached down for his lantern and walked outside. He saw Fetterman coming toward him, carrying a clipboard.

Fetterman, who was reading something clipped to it, stopped, looked up and then moved closer.

"Got a list here, Captain. Looks like he grabbed a bunch of C-rations but went through the boxes, throwing out everything that he didn't like." Fetterman grinned. "Tossed out the ham and lima beans, the scrambled eggs, the bread and the like. Kept the pound cake, the fruit, beans and franks. All the good stuff."

Gerber shook his head. "For a spur-of-the-moment operation, this was well thought out."

"Yes, sir."

"Okay, I guess we can assume that he doesn't plan to come back soon. Let's go get him. Find . . ." Gerber stopped and stared at the ground. "Find Krung and a group of Bao's strikers. No, that's no good. Makes it the Tai against the Vietnamese. We'll take Krung as a tracker, but I'll talk to Minh and get a squad of Vietnamese. Be ready to go in half an hour."

Fetterman nodded and headed in the direction of the redoubt. Gerber walked toward the hootch that Minh used for his headquarters in the Vietnamese section of the camp. He stepped into the office. The LLDB sergeant waved him through. Gerber knocked on the door and entered Minh's inner sanctum.

Minh had taken over command of the LLDB after Captain Trang was killed during a ground attack. Minh, unlike most of his contemporaries, had been trained in England and spoke English with a British accent. He was slightly bigger than the average Vietnamese, about five foot seven, and had the typical jet-black hair and dark complexion.

When he heard Gerber, he looked up. "Don't see you here often, old boy. What can I do for you?"

Gerber sat in the old settee along one wall and stared at the screen above the plywood wall. "I've got to take a patrol out and would like a squad of your best strikers."

"No problem, old boy. You've got them." For a moment Minh sat there, seeming to study a paper on his desk. "I assume that this has to do with your Sergeant Cavanaugh and my missing men."

"Yes," Gerber said, not exactly sure what he should tell Minh. He trusted Minh, but this was a new problem, something they hadn't faced in the past. Finally he said, "I think it best if I take a team out to find him. Talk him into returning."

"That would be best," Minh agreed. "I'll go with you."

Gerber got to his feet. "Thanks, but one of us has to stay here. Since it's my man who's gone bad, I'll go get him."

Minh nodded. "Fine, old boy. Where would you like the strikers to form?"

"Have them meet me by the gate in about an hour. Full field pack and be prepared to stay out for two days."

"Airlift?"

"I think not. I don't want Saigon to get wind of this until I've had a chance to talk to Cavanaugh. Besides, we don't really know where he went, so we're going to have to track him on the ground. Helicopters wouldn't be much use."

Minh got up and walked around his desk to the door. He waited for Gerber to step into the outer office. "I'll get my people organized."

"Thanks." Gerber moved out into the late-morning sun and stared up into the cloud-filled sky. Even with the sun screened, it meant that the hike across relatively flat, open ground would be hot, miserable work. It wasn't something that he wanted to do.

Minh had stopped behind him, looked at the sky, too, and then wandered off. Gerber watched his counterpart disappear among the buildings and then moved off toward the redoubt. Two days and it would be over. He hoped.

12

ACROSS THE CAMBODIAN BORDER, SOUTH OF THE PARROT'S BEAK

Cavanaugh supervised the construction of his camp. He wanted to make certain that the place could be used as a rally point and supply depot, not something that would become so comfortable that it would be hard to convince the strikers they needed to patrol.

He helped the strikers set up claymore mines to protect the perimeter. The outcrop of rock, hidden in the jungle, was ringed with the mines, some of them braced against the rock face; a double ring lined the gentle slope on the western side of the rock. Others were hidden at the base of trees, concealed in bushes and even wired to the branches of teak trees, angled downward to rake the game trail that skirted the edge of the outcrop.

On the top he had the strikers emplace their machine guns and recoilless rifle so that they could command the approaches. And when that was finished, they spread the spare equipment out, burying, hiding and stacking some of it out of the way. When he thought they were ready, Cavanaugh stood at the point of the outcrop and slowly turned. He could see the tops of some trees and bushes, others towered over him. To the east, he caught glimpses of the rice paddies and farmers' hootches there. To the south, west and north, he could see nothing other than jungle, which thinned into swamps and open fields. Thirty feet below him was a small clear area and then a rock face filled with cracks and crevices that led up to the point. A hundred meters beyond that clearing was a small stream that would provide a handy source of water.

He didn't want anything that would be easily visible from the surrounding countryside, although he did let the men construct lean-tos of jungle vines, palm leaves and thin branches. Such structures were common throughout the area, so any VC or NVA stumbling on them wouldn't be overly concerned. They might knock the shelters down, but they might not search carefully.

Cavanaugh sat on the rock, staying in the shadows and out of the patches of bright sunlight bleeding through the canopy and thought about that. VC stumbling onto his camp. The last thing he wanted to do was supply the enemy. He got to his feet, sought out Corporal Tran and told him that they were going to booby-trap their equipment just in case.

GERBER STOOD AT THE WEST GATE, binoculars to his eyes as he scanned the fields in front of him. There were so many paths crisscrossing the ash-covered ground made by the patrols he had sent out that he couldn't positively identify one that might have been made by Cavanaugh and his men. Not that it mattered because once they had crossed the killing ground, he was sure that the terrain would conceal Cavanaugh's trail.

"Ready when you are, Captain," said Fetterman, who had come up behind him.

Gerber lowered his binoculars and stuffed them into the case at his hip. "Where's Krung?"

Fetterman pointed, and the two of them moved over to talk to the sergeant. Gerber asked, "You have any idea where Sergeant Cavanaugh might have gone?"

For a moment Krung stared at the ground near his feet. Finally he looked up. "I not kill Sergeant Sean. He good man. He kill VC. I help you find, but I not kill."

Gerber nodded gravely. "We're not going to kill him. We're going out to bring him back here."

"Why?" Krung asked.

"Why?" Gerber repeated. "A damned interesting question. Let's just say because he's not playing by the rules. We can't let him fight the war on his own."

"Why?" asked Krung again. "He kills VC."

Gerber looked at the Tai and shook his head. There was no way he could explain it. To Krung, the whole point of the war was to kill the VC. To Gerber, it was to train the South Vietnamese to kill the VC. A subtle difference.

It was also a question of discipline. He couldn't have one of his men decide to go out to fight on his own. There were other considerations, many of which he didn't know. Treaties with foreign countries, pressures exerted by those foreign countries, subtle and flimsy agreements that could collapse if a renegade American was running his own war.

But to Krung, Gerber knew, none of that made sense. He only saw the war as a means of killing as many of the enemy as possible. To the Tai, it wasn't a giant geopolitical game played with real men and real countries as the pieces.

Gerber decided to reduce his explanation to the basic fact that every soldier understood, even if he didn't know the reasoning behind it. "Because those are our orders."

Now it was Krung who nodded. "And then what do we do?"

"We bring him home and tell him he has to fight the war by the rules." Gerber didn't like saying that because he believed rules had no place in a war. You either fought it or you didn't. The last thing you needed was a bunch of rules imposed by a bunch of fat men twelve thousand miles away who didn't understand the nature of combat.

"Getting late, Captain," Fetterman reminded him.

"I'm aware of that, Master Sergeant," said Gerber. He turned his attention back to Krung. "You find his trail. Show us where he went."

Krung stood rooted to the spot for a moment as if he was thinking it over, and then he nodded. He walked out the gate and down the road, across the runway and into the field of ash.

The rest of the patrol strung out behind him, Fetterman taking the slack and Gerber marching near the rear. They crossed the field, stirring up a choking cloud of ash and dust that seemed to follow them, settling on sweat-damp skin, coating everyone and everything.

Once they were across the field, Krung stopped and surveyed the ground. Ranging right and left, he looked for clues but found nothing. He started off along the bank of a canal that reached westward toward Cambodia and discovered the trail. He pointed it out to Gerber, who told him to follow it.

It was near dusk when they approached the Cambodian border. The last thing Gerber wanted to do was cross into a foreign country, especially at night. Instead, he turned his men around, moving a half klick back to the east, and found a good campsite. It was lightly wooded for cover both from the sun and the enemy, there were good fields of fire in all directions and a source of water was nearby.

Fetterman supervised establishing the perimeter, set the schedules for rotating the guards and then prepared his own meal from C-rations. After he had eaten, he made his rounds, checking on the men. About midnight, satisfied with the guard, Fetterman turned in. He had seen Gerber moving among the men, making his own check.

THE QUIET SOUND of distant firing woke Gerber just before dawn. He came awake suddenly and knew exactly where he was and what had awakened him. Over him was the dark green of the partial jungle canopy and under him the soft wet ground of the jungle floor. He rolled to his side, picked up his rifle and moved to the western edge of the perimeter. There he found Fetterman crouched behind one of the strikers who was lying in a shallow foxhole, his rifle propped on a palm log.

"You have any idea what that is?" asked Gerber.

"No, sir."

Gerber listened carefully and then said, "I can hear a couple of M-16s, maybe an M-60, AKs and one or two RPDs."

"Yes, sir," agreed Fetterman. "Couple of grenades went off a few minutes ago, but I couldn't tell whether they were from an M-79 or Chicom."

"That's got to be Cavanaugh's group," said Gerber. "I know we don't have anything out there that could have walked into it, and since it is our AO, anyone else there would have coordinated with us."

Fetterman turned so that he could look at Gerber. "What do you want to do?"

"Let's break camp and move in that direction. I'll want you on the point because we don't want to walk into anything ourselves. You should be able to find them before they see us."

"Yes, sir. How soon?"

"Make it ten minutes. Half the men. The other half will remain here and guard the gear. Take only weapons, ammo and water."

Fetterman moved off into the center of the perimeter and then around it, waking up the men and selecting the patrol.

He organized them and ordered them to the edge of the perimeter where Gerber waited, his rifle in hand. Without a word Fetterman crossed into the rice paddies, feeling his way along a dike until they were at the edge of a swampy area, the solid ground covered with short bushes and tall grass. Fetterman skirted the swamp, staying on solid ground but angling toward the sounds of firing.

The shooting was tapering off, but by the sound, Fetterman knew that he was getting closer. He searched the ground in front of him, trying to catch muzzle-flashes, but he saw nothing. The sky was beginning to gray as the sun came up, but the ground was still wrapped in darkness.

Travel wasn't easy because it was still dark, but it was a cool morning with a light breeze. Fetterman kept the pace steady, moving toward the battle but not rapidly. He was looking for the rear guards, or maybe a point, if someone had decided to flee.

Finally they were in the immediate area. The noise of the firing had increased suddenly and then tapered. Fetterman held up a hand and waved the men down, telling them to wait. He crept forward along the side of a rice paddy dike, his feet in the water and mud. He moved his feet carefully, trying to make no noise as the smell from the water in the paddy assaulted his nose. He reached out and touched the top of the dike as he moved toward a line of trees. The shooting, sporadic shots now, was quite close. He even saw a muzzle-flash and turned so that he was moving toward it.

When he was fifty yards away and he could see the trees plainly because of the rising sun, he stopped. He watched the palms and saw a lone man break from cover there, but rather than run, the man jogged along a rice paddy dike. Fetterman could tell from the shape of the weapon and the pith helmet the man wore that he was an NVA soldier.

Fetterman slipped down so that he could brace his elbows on the top of the dike and aimed his rifle, looking over the top of the sights because it was still too dark to use them. He led the jogging man and pulled the trigger once. The man seemed to leap to the right, splashed into the rice paddy and didn't reappear. Fetterman crawled over the dike and in the distance could see the body of the man lying facedown in the shallow water. He watched him for a minute, but the man never moved.

Sure that the enemy soldier was dead, Fetterman moved forward, closer to the tree line. He crawled along a dike, keeping to the side, his left hand sliding in and out of the water. He managed to move within twenty-five or thirty feet of the jungle. Within the stand of trees he could see men running and hear the occasional shot, but he couldn't identify the targets. He watched the firefight, muzzle-flashes that looked like lightning bugs on a hot summer night, and waited for an opportunity to contact Cavanaugh.

While Fetterman waited, Gerber brought the rest of the patrol forward, keeping them as far to the south as possible. He used the cover of the rice paddies and the elephant grass until he could turn north inside a finger of jungle. Gerber moved them as close as he could, then spread them out along the forward edge of the tree line as a blocking force in case the enemy broke in that direction. Through his binoculars he could see Fetterman crouched in the distance.

As Gerber watched, Fetterman inched his way forward and disappeared into the trees. A moment later firing broke out to the right of Gerber's position. He spun, dropped to the ground and crawled toward the shooting. A half dozen of his men were crouching next to trees or lying behind logs, firing their weapons on full automatic, their ruby tracers cutting through the jungle fifteen or twenty feet above the ground. There seemed to be no incoming firing.

"Cease fire!" Gerber yelled. "Cease fire!" He waited a moment as the shooting died away and then worked his way up the skirmish line. Looking through his binoculars, he could see nothing other than a light mist and smoke from the gunpowder drifting through the trees. It was slowly becoming lighter.

"Hey!" came a voice from the enemy's line. "Identify yourself."

Gerber continued to stare. He thought he recognized the voice as Cavanaugh's but didn't want to go shouting his name all over the jungle. Instead, he said, "This is Zulu Six."

"Six," came the excited voice. "Advance."

Gerber looked at the men crouched among the bushes and vegetation and then out toward the voice. To the closest of the strikers he said, "Cover me." He slipped the binoculars into the case. He glanced to his right and left, shrugged and then began to slowly inch his way forward.

Gerber stepped around a tree, looked up and saw Cavanaugh approaching him, his rifle held at the ready. "Good to see you, Captain," said Cavanaugh.

"Sean, what the fuck are you doing?"

"I came out here to fight the war. You wouldn't let me do it at camp, so I built my own."

"You know better than that. Get your men together, and we'll head back to camp. My camp. We'll talk about this there."

"No, Captain. I think not. My men and I have decided to take the war to the enemy. You can help us. Leave all your extra ammo and weapons. We can use those. Food, too. And then get out of here."

Gerber took a step forward, but Cavanaugh swung his rifle around so that it was pointed at Gerber. For a moment Gerber thought Cavanaugh was going to shoot him, but then the sergeant lowered the barrel and grinned sheepishly.

"Sorry, Captain. But I'm never going back. I've seen what the bureaucrats in Saigon and Washington do. How they prolong the fighting with their stupid rules and regulations and corruption. How they refuse to recognize the contributions that we make. Or hand the gains we die for back to the VC. We—'' he waved a hand to include the men hiding near him ''—have decided that it's time to take the war to the VC and finish it quickly and cleanly. You can help, or you can get out of here. But we are not going back to the old system and the old camp.''

"Sean, we can't discuss this here in the jungle. Let's go back to the camp. Work this out to everyone's satisfaction.''

"No, sir. You take your men and get out. Leave half your weapons because we can use those. If you don't leave, we'll take them off your bodies. We have you surrounded.''

Gerber took off his helmet and wiped the sweat from his forehead. Suddenly it seemed overly hot and sticky in the jungle. "You know me better than that. You have this group surrounded, but this is not my whole force. Besides, have you seen Master Sergeant Fetterman lately?'' he asked ominously.

"No. No, I haven't. But that won't do you any good. Shit, sir, I just want to fight the Communists, not you.''

"Sean, come back.''

"No, sir. Now please withdraw from the field. And don't come back because we'll be forced to shoot first. I won't ask questions. We'll just assume hostile intent.''

The last thing Gerber wanted was a firefight. In fact, he knew that he couldn't let one break out. There was no telling what the final outcome would be, although he assumed that Cavanaugh and most of his men would be killed. Fetterman had probably slipped into position to take out Cavanaugh if it became necessary. One thing Gerber knew was that there was no way he was going to talk Cavanaugh into returning to camp. It was a stalemate.

"All right, Sean,'' said Gerber. "We'll withdraw, but we are leaving no weapons, ammo or food.'' Gerber turned and called, "Master Sergeant, we move back.''

There was no answer, but Gerber didn't expect one. Fetterman would fall back as ordered but not until Gerber and his strikers were in the clear, and he wouldn't give his position away by answering any questions.

"I'm sorry it turned out this way, Captain," said Cavanaugh. "But this is the way it's got to be. Now please leave, and remember, if you come back, I'll have to kill you."

Gerber retreated to where his men were gathered. As he pulled even with them, he said, "Let's fall back the way we came. Nuong, take the point, please."

Nuong got up, looked around and then moved to the south. The others fell into line and started off. Gerber watched them go and then turned back to where Cavanaugh had been. The young Special Forces sergeant had disappeared. Gerber used his binoculars to sweep the jungle but could see neither Cavanaugh nor Fetterman. Finally he put the binoculars away and started off after the strikers. As they broke out of the trees, Gerber saw Fetterman sitting at the edge of a rice paddy, his rifle cradled in his arms, waiting.

"What now, Captain?"

"We return to camp. Straight back to camp," said Gerber.

"We can't leave Sean out here alone. We've got to do something about that."

"That's right, Master Sergeant, but not now. I didn't understand what was going on." As Gerber moved closer to Fetterman, he shouted, "Nuong, stay on the point. Course one one zero degrees. That'll get us back to where the rest of the patrol is waiting."

Nuong nodded, looked at his own compass and moved off. As the patrol strung out, Gerber said to Fetterman. "We'll have to deal with this discreetly, and I don't think a shoot out between us and Cavanaugh is discreet."

"You know, sir, from what I could tell, that ambush of Sean's was beautifully executed. The VC had no chance to counterattack. The few survivors had to flee for their lives. The VC left a lot of equipment in the field for Sean to use. The longer he's out here, the tougher it's going to be to get him.''

"But right now," said Gerber, "we've got to get the patrol back to camp. Then we can worry about Cavanaugh. I think we can assume that he can take care of himself for the time being."

"Yes, sir," said Fetterman, grinning. "And I think we can assume that he's getting stronger every day, too. Pretty soon he might just come after us."

"That'll make it easier," said Gerber. "That'll make it much easier."

13

SPECIAL FORCES
CAMP A-555

Lieutenant Colonel Alan Bates sat in the cargo compartment of the UH-1D helicopter and watched the landscape slide by beneath him. For the first time in a couple of months, Bates was happy to be going out to Camp A-555 because he didn't have to investigate the camp commander or one of the other Special Forces men assigned to it.

This time he had good news in the form of a Silver Star for Sean Cavanaugh. Unlike the defense of the listening post nearly a year earlier, this award hadn't been downgraded by the chairborne commandos in Saigon. General Hull, because he was a major general, could approve the impact award, which meant that Bates could deliver the medal and citation within days of the action.

Bates glanced out the windshield of the Huey and saw the star-shaped camp in front of him. As the chopper banked to the right and began to lose altitude, Bates instinctively grabbed for the edge of the troop seat to hang on. Looking down from the cargo door, he saw the camp, the redoubt and the helipad. The aircraft straightened and descended rapidly until it was hovering three feet above the pad, which was made of PSP and lined with rubberized sandbags.

As they settled to the ground, Bates grabbed his dispatch case, overnight bag and rifle. He dropped to the ground and stepped away as the helicopter lifted again, creating a whirlwind of dust and debris that hid the surroundings. The chopper turned and climbed out to the north.

"Colonel Bates," said a voice nearby.

Bates spun and saw Bocker. "Yup, I've arrived."

"Didn't expect you in until a little later," said Bocker, reaching for the overnight bag.

"I've got it," said Bates. Then he added, "Got an earlier flight out and thought I'd spend the afternoon in your team house sipping beer and swapping lies with Gerber."

Bocker led Bates off the helipad, around the redoubt and into the team area. As they walked, he said, "Captain Gerber is out on patrol right now. He's due back in a couple of hours."

"Well, I'll let Fetterman talk to me, then," he said, smiling.

"I'm afraid that Sergeant Fetterman is out, too." Bocker halted near the door to the team house, unsure of what to do or where to put Bates's bag.

"That's a little sloppy," said Bates. "With the trouble you've had out here in the last few weeks, I would expect that one of them would be on the camp at all times."

"Yes, sir," said Bocker. "But this was a short patrol and is coming back this afternoon."

Bates looked at the sun and then at the team house. "Why don't we get out of the heat?" said Bates.

"Oh, of course, sir." Bocker gestured at the door. He followed Bates in and asked, "Would you like something to drink, sir?"

"Give me a beer," said Bates. "Oh, and why don't you have Sergeant Cavanaugh stop by, too. I'd like to talk to him since he's the reason I'm here."

Bocker looked uncomfortable. "I'm afraid Sergeant Cavanaugh is out on patrol."

"Uh-huh," said Bates. "Is there anybody on camp? Other than yourself, that is?"

"Yes, sir. Sully Smith is out working along the bunker line, putting in some claymore mines. Sergeant Tyme is in one of the mortar pits. Sergeant Kepler is with the FNG. Sergeant Washington is in the dispensary."

"You mean Gerber's out without a medic?"

"Sergeant Washington had some people to treat here and the captain didn't think he'd be making contact."

Bates slipped into a chair. "Where's that beer?"

Bocker opened the refrigerator and got out a cool can. He handed it to Bates and then asked, "Is there anything else?"

"Yes, there is." Bates pointed to the other side of the table at an empty chair. "Why don't you sit down and tell me exactly what the hell is going on here?"

"I've really got to get back to the commo bunker, sir," said Bocker. "I've only got my Vietnamese counterpart on duty there."

"I'm sure he's capable of handling anything that comes up," said Bates. "I want to know what is happening out here. There are a couple of things that I just don't understand. Thought maybe you could fill me in on the situation."

"I'm afraid you've confused me, sir," said Bocker.

"Let me lay it out for you," said Bates. "There's something happening on this camp that isn't right. You've lost your executive officer and had a fairly large patrol wiped out. You've had three men wounded—"

"Two of them are back, sir," said Bocker.

"You've had three men wounded," said Bates again. "Your Sergeant Cavanaugh has been involved in each of those. Not to mention where he's just come from. Now I arrive to find Captain Gerber, Sergeant Fetterman and Sergeant Cavanaugh out on a patrol. I don't like it."

"Yes, sir," said Bocker. He stood up and said, "You'll have to talk to the captain about that."

"No, Sergeant, I'll talk to you about it. Now you sit back down and tell me exactly what is happening here. And tell me now."

Bocker stood for a moment staring at Bates. Bocker knew that he was one officer who couldn't be bullshitted. Bates was in tune with the Special Forces and the Army. He knew how the enlisted men thought, how the junior officers thought, and he knew how the colonels and generals, so far removed from the mainstream, thought. While Brigadier General Billy Joe Crinshaw, sitting in his office in Saigon, could be convinced of things that weren't true because he was so out of touch with everything, Bates could not be.

Bocker also knew that Gerber had confided in Bates in the past. He knew that Gerber had told Bates the real details of earlier raids into Cambodia or how needed equipment had been obtained. It was Bates who had helped spring Fetterman and Tyme when Crinshaw had tried them for murder. In fact, Bates had even gone into the field with them more than once.

Slowly Bocker slipped into a chair. He didn't know how much he should, or how much he could, tell Bates. Finally he decided that it was somewhere between the complete truth and an out-and-out lie.

"Sergeant Cavanaugh, ah, went . . . I guess you could say AWOL, and the captain has gone to get him."

"AWOL?" said Bates. "Where did he go AWOL?"

"Out into the field. Out on a patrol. Searching for something. I don't know what."

Bates rubbed his face with his hand, aware that he needed a shave and aware that it was damned hot, even in the team house. The tin roof seemed to be absorbing the heat rather than reflecting it. He took a sip from his beer. "That sounds like a load of crap to me, Sergeant."

"Yes, sir," Bocker replied nervously. "But it's true."

"True it may be, but it sounds like crap, and I suspect there is more to it than that."

Again Bocker stood. "I should get back on duty." He turned and fled as rapidly as possible, expecting to hear Bates yell at him, but that never happened.

IT WAS MIDAFTERNOON when Gerber finally saw the camp shimmering in the heat in the distance. A thin cloud of dust and smoke rose from near the center where construction of a new bunker was taking place. Gerber called a halt and sat down on the rice paddy dike, the heat nearly overwhelming him. He could feel the sweat pouring from his body, soaking his already damp clothes. His mouth felt cottony and his breathing was rapid as though he couldn't get enough air. He put a hand to his eyes and with a great effort looked up at the sun.

This was the worst he had ever felt. It was as if he had sprinted a hundred meters, two hundred, and then, without rest, sprinted again. He wondered if it was because he was getting old, if the climate was beginning to affect him or if it was the nature of his last mission. Maybe a combination of them all.

He shot a glance at Fetterman, who was sitting off to one side, looking as fresh as he did the day before. There were sweat stains on his uniform, as there were on everyone's, but somehow Fetterman looked cooler.

Gerber finally managed to glance at his watch, saw that they had been sitting there for fifteen minutes and forced himself to his feet. Krung, who had been on the point since they had left the campsite, leaped up and trotted into the distance. The patrol, taking its cue from that, got up and began to march again.

When they were about fifteen minutes from the camp, Gerber called in on the radio to alert Bocker.

Bocker acknowledged and then added, "Be advised that Crystal Ball is here. He seeks knowledge about our stray chick."

"Well, shit," said Gerber, looking at the radio. Over the air he said, "Understood. Advise Crystal Ball of our location. Zulu Six out."

He gave the handset back to the RTO and muttered, "That's all we need. A surprise visit from the brass."

At that moment Krung turned and looked back. Gerber raised a fist in the air and pumped it twice, telling Krung to hurry. Krung trotted off, reached the field of burned grass and ran across it. He halted at the runway, waited until the majority of the patrol was close and then ran up the road to the gate.

A few minutes later Gerber, Fetterman and the Patrol followed him into the camp. Bates stood there waiting, a beer in each hand. He gave one to Gerber, turned and let Fetterman have the second.

"You boys look like you could use a drink," Bates greeted.

Gerber slipped the can into his pocket. "You don't know the half of it, but you should have brought a case."

Bates nodded. "I understand. My mistake."

Fetterman said, "Let me have your weapon, sir, and I'll see that it gets cleaned." He turned to the men and shouted, "Weapons check in thirty minutes." He held up the can of beer that Bates had handed him and added, "I'll bring the beer."

Gerber studied Bates for a moment and then suggested, "Let's go over to my hootch so we can talk."

"Fine. Lead the way."

As they entered the hootch, Gerber pulled the beer out of his pocket and set it on the tiny field desk. He unbuckled his pistol belt and slipped the harness from his shoulders, dropping the equipment pack to the dirty floor. He picked up the beer, moved around the desk so that he could sit down and opened the bottom drawer. He pulled the bottle of Beam's out.

"You care for a drink of this?"

Bates reached out and took the bottle. He pulled the cork, set that on the edge of the desk and then drank deeply. As he handed the bottle back, he remarked, "That's smooth."

"Yes, sir," said Gerber, reaching for the bottle. He drank, then returned it to the desk drawer. As he opened the beer, he queried, "What can I do for you?"

"Well, for one thing, you can get Sergeant Cavanaugh. I've got an impact Silver Star for him. General Hull signed the paperwork this morning authorizing it, and the reason for its being an impact award is so that we can give it to the man as quickly as possible."

"Yes, sir," said Gerber. He suddenly felt as if an elevator had dropped out from under him. To cover his anxiety, he said, "Sergeant Cavanaugh is on patrol."

Bates glared at him for a moment and then said, "Cut the crap, Mack. I know he's AWOL. You want to tell me about it?"

Gerber rubbed his hand over his face. He leaned forward, his elbow on the desk, his hand over his mouth. "It's a delicate situation. One that we have to be careful with."

"I'm aware of the facts leading up to this point, and you know that the last thing I want to do is nail some guy's ass to the wall, especially one who has been through what Cavanaugh has been through. But there comes a point when we have to draw the line."

"Yes, sir." Gerber picked up his beer and drank. He held the can in both hands, staring at the top of it. "I guess you could say it all started right after we got here. That is, to this camp. It all started with the defense of the listening post and the destruction of the tiny force manning it."

"I'm aware that Sergeant Cavanaugh had some mental problems dealing with that."

"And you probably know that Sergeant Cavanaugh has not reached his twentieth birthday. He is not allowed to vote for the President, he is not allowed to buy liquor, or enter into contractual agreements without a cosigner who can be held responsible. By most standards of our society, he is not an adult. Hell, if he could find a job as a police officer, he wouldn't be allowed to carry a gun until he was twenty-one. This is the man we sent, I sent, out to guard the listening post."

"Yes," responded Bates wearily. "I know all that."

"Then what you don't know is that he was on patrol with Lieutenant Novak when it was wiped out."

"I knew about that," said Bates. "I read the after action report."

"And you know that Cavanaugh was the sole survivor of that, too? Watched everyone with him die in the hand-to-hand fighting, just like the listening post fight."

"Yes, I know."

"Then are you aware that it was Cavanaugh who led the patrol into Cai Cai and found the remains of the villagers after the Vietcong had swept through killing everyone?"

"No, I wasn't aware of that."

"Okay," Gerber said. "Now I know you've seen some pretty raw shit during your career. So have I. But the difference, I think, is the age. Nineteen is just too young to be thrown into a combat environment. Sure, each of us saw some shit when we were younger, but nothing like what Cavanaugh has been through. It took me two wars to see everything he's seen in what works out to only a few weeks in the field."

"You've made your point, Mack. There are extenuating circumstances. You get Cavanaugh back, and I'll have him transferred to my staff. He can finish his tour in Vietnam, and nobody ever has to know about this."

"Yeah, well, there's the problem," said Gerber.

Bates smiled. "You mean there's more?"

"A lot more, I'm afraid. After finding the villagers and the ambush, Cavanaugh organized a team of his own. I guess you could call it a hunter-killer team. Strikers who had lost relatives in Cai Cai. When he went out on patrol, he took these men."

"And you let him do it?"

"Well, sir, it's not quite as cut-and-dried as it appears now. Cavanaugh's idea of an elite team wasn't all that bad. I mean, it gave the strikers some kind of goal. If they were good enough, maybe Cavanaugh would ask them to join. I sort of winked at it because I couldn't see the harm. Then after they had taken the trigger fingers—"

"Hold it right there, Captain," snapped Bates. "Are you telling me that you have knowledge of mutilations of the dead?"

Gerber looked at the floor and took a deep breath. He rubbed his forehead with a finger as if lost in thought. Finally he said, "Yes, sir, I'm afraid I am."

"And you're familiar with MACV Directive 20-4, which governs conduct in the field?"

"Yes, sir. In fact, I briefed Sergeant Cavanaugh on it."

"Mack, you've put me in a real awkward position here. I don't know if I should terminate this interview right now and advise you of your rights under the *Uniform Code of Military Justice*, or just pretend that I've heard nothing."

"In my defense," said Gerber, "let me say that it wasn't my men who committed the mutilations but the Vietnamese strikers. I'll tell you the same thing that Cavanaugh said to me. We're advisors, and we advised them not to cut off the trigger fingers."

"You know that won't hold water."

"Yeah, I told that to Cavanaugh. Anyway, I ordered him to stop it, also any more solo John Wayne shit. I told him the wounded men were returning to camp, we had a replacement coming in and from now on, all patrols would have two Americans on them. That's when he took off."

"Took off?" Bates repeated.

"Yes, sir. Him and about twenty-five strikers—Captain Minh still hasn't gotten a full muster. Went off into the woods to wage their own war."

"Are you sure of this?"

"Oh, yes, sir. I managed to track him down."

"So where is he?" snapped Bates.

"Had to leave him in the field. Couldn't convince him to come back in."

"Christ, Gerber, this is a fucking mess. I saw your patrol come back. You could have forced him."

"No, sir, not without a fight, and the last thing I wanted was to initiate a fight between two elements of the strike force, even if one of those elements was operating illegally."

Bates could stand it no longer. He had to get up and move. He paced across the floor, to the wall, back again and then stopped directly in front of Gerber's desk. "Mack, this is one fucked up mess. I don't understand how you could let things get so far out of hand. You've got a good head on your shoulders, but you let Cavanaugh walk all over you."

"As I said, it wasn't quite as cut-and-dried as it seems now. Sure, I let Cavanaugh have a little more rope than I would any other member of the team, except Fetterman, but given the circumstances, I felt it was necessary."

"Necessary, shit. I'd like to see your medical degree. You should have had Cavanaugh back in Saigon."

Now Gerber was angry. "Fuck that. The man deserved every break I gave him. He earned that much. Now I have a problem to deal with and saying that those pissants in Saigon could do anything about it is ridiculous."

"Captain Gerber!" Bates reprimanded sharply.

"I have a loyalty to the men on the team. We work together, live together and die together, and I'm not about to throw one to the dogs because of—"

"Mack," Bates interjected, "I understand." He held up a hand to stop further protest. "I really do. But we can't have anyone going out on his own. Cavanaugh has to be stopped."

"Yes, sir," Gerber agreed quietly. "I know that. I'll take care of it. Quietly, discreetly, quickly."

"You had better, or else Saigon will have your ass. And mine, too."

"Don't worry, Colonel. It's in the bag." Gerber met Bates's stare. He wasn't sure that anything was in the bag, but he knew that the problem was his to solve.

14

SPECIAL FORCES
CAMP A-555

Gerber stood in the arms locker and studied the weapons that were available to him. In the course of outfitting the camp, he had been given practically every weapon manufactured for the U.S. Army, with the exception of the larger artillery pieces and a tactical nuclear device. He had variations and modifications of those weapons and a few jury-rigged items, such as the flashlight mounted to a rifle stock they had used a couple of months earlier. There were grenade launchers, LAW rockets, a bazooka with a number of 3.5 inch rockets, Fetterman's flamethrower, a mortar and even a Soviet-made RPG-7 with a supply of spare grenades.

He sat on a crate of grenades and stared at the arsenal. In the corner was the one that he needed, but he refused to look at it. He knew it was there, and he knew what it was used for, and once he acknowledged it, he would have to act. By studying all his options, he was ignoring the only one that he had.

Finally his eyes fell on the special M-14, designated an XM-21. It was equipped with a Redfield three-power to nine-power range finder scope. There was also a package that contained a bipod and a sound suppressor, which reduced the velocity of the escaping gases to below that of sound but didn't affect the velocity of the round.

He rose and moved across the rough planking of the floor. In the dim light he stared down at the weapon, which was locked in a rack with a dozen other M-14s. He rubbed the sweat from the palms of his hands, then touched the lens caps over the scope.

"You'll probably need these."

Gerber spun at the sound of the voice. Fetterman stood in the doorway of the bunker, a shadowy shape outlined by the bright sunlight behind him. He held out his hand, and Gerber could see half a dozen M-14 rounds in his palm.

"It's a special round that Tyme and I came up with. We loaded them ourselves, measuring the power. They won't misfire, and they have good long-range ballistics."

"Those what I think they are?" Gerber asked. He moved away from the XM-21 and put a foot up on the grenade case.

Fetterman descended the two steps into the bunker. "Yes, sir," he replied. "Leftovers from when we went after the Chinese guy. They won't let you down."

"Didn't help you much," said Gerber.

"That was because we picked the wrong target, not because the rounds weren't any good."

"Tony, do you realize what we're talking about here?" Gerber kept his eyes on the master sergeant's hand.

"Yes, sir. I know exactly what we're talking about. I came by to offer the tools to do it right and to find out if this is the proper course of action."

Gerber sat down again and stared at the floor for a long time. Suddenly his mind, reluctant to contemplate the business at hand, attached a new importance to everything else around him. He could hear sounds outside, men going about their work. There was a roar of a jet that passed over the camp. A couple of men were shouting at each other in Vietnamese. Gerber raked a hand through his hair, stared at the palm and then wiped it on the front of his fatigue jacket.

"I don't think there's any other choice," said Gerber.

"We could try to talk him in again," Fetterman suggested.

"I doubt that would do any good. Hell, Tony, I tried it when we found him, but he refused to come in. I don't know what all you heard...."

"Very little, Captain. I was too far out to hear anything useful."

"Well, talking won't bring him in. If talking would have worked, it would have worked when we found him. If he was looking for an excuse to quit and a way to save face, it was provided then. But he wasn't interested in it. He's called the shots on this one."

Fetterman leaned back against the wall of green sandbags. He dropped the special rounds into his pocket and folded his arms across his chest. "There has to be a better way, Captain."

"Don't you think I've tried to come up with it?" snapped Gerber. "Don't you think I've analyzed this from every direction? I studied it at length, and I concluded that something happened to his mind in that last ambush. Watching everyone die around him again did something to him. He's not sane anymore. He lays his own ambushes, plays by his own rules, and he takes trophies now. He's not the same man."

"None of which means we should hunt him down," Fetterman observed quietly.

For nearly a minute Gerber was silent. He stared at the floor between his boots. Without looking up at Fetterman, he said, "The only way to handle this is a clean assassination. If we go out with a force to bring him back, it's going to result in a firefight. Many of the strikers will probably die. Overlooking what such a battle would do to morale, we have to consider the lives of those men. They shouldn't die so that we can take the easy road. A single, well-placed rifle shot ends the problem.''

''Then what happens to the strikers who went out with Cavanaugh?''

''When the head is cut off, the snake withers and dies. Without an effective leader they are going to come back here. Maybe as a group, maybe only one or two at a time, but they'll return.''

''You sure?'' asked Fetterman.

Gerber turned so that he could look up at Fetterman. ''No. But it's the only thing that makes sense. Without Cavanaugh they're going to be lost.''

Fetterman nodded and moved forward. He began to pick through the equipment stacked in the bunker.

''Just what do you think you're doing, Master Sergeant?''

''Getting the stuff I'll need on patrol.''

''What patrol?'' asked Gerber.

Fetterman stopped rummaging through the crates and faced Gerber. ''Captain, you can't do this alone. You'll need someone to track Cavanaugh. You'll need someone for a spotter, and you'll need another back to help hump all the stuff you'll want to take. I'm in on this one.''

''It's not necessary, Tony.''

''Don't go telling me what's necessary and what's not. You're going out to take care of the problem. Well, it's my problem, too. Cavanaugh is one of the men on my team, and if he's turned renegade, it's my responsibility to deal with as much as it is yours.''

''Tony, you don't have to do this. I'll take Krung and a couple of the strikers with me. We can handle it.''

''No, sir,'' Fetterman said. ''This is something that we both have to do. It's not something that one of us should face alone. It's a dirty, rotten job, and I'm not going to duck my responsibility in this."

Gerber moved until he was standing in front of the master sergeant. He held out a hand. "I just wanted to make sure you understood that I would take care of it alone. That you were not required to help."

"I understood that from the moment I figured out what had to be done. That's why I brought in those special rounds. So that you would know that I was volunteering."

"Thank you," said Gerber warmly. "I'm not sure I could have done it myself."

"Captain," said Fetterman, "I'm not sure there isn't anything you can't do, once you set your mind to it."

He unlocked the rack and took out the sniper rifle. As he snapped the lock back in place, Fetterman moved to the entrance and waited. Gerber hesitated for a few moments, then walked to the doorway. Exchanging looks that spoke of pain and frustration, Gerber stretched out his hand for the rifle.

He nodded to Fetterman, then walked across the compound, stopping first in his hootch to drop off the sniper rifle. Afterward he made his way to the commo bunker. He found Bocker sitting behind the wooden counter in a pool of light from a single lamp, his feet propped up, reading a paperback science fiction novel. There was a Coke by his hand and a gigantic cigar sitting in an ashtray next to the soft drink. The tiny lights on the various radios glowed in the dim light of the bunker.

"Galvin," said Gerber, "I want you to lay on a recon flight for this evening. Single ship to work the fields west of the camp all the way to the Cambodian border. Have them stop by here before they do anything else."

Bocker dropped his feet to the floor and set his book facedown on the counter to save his place. "Pretty short notice, sir. And those flyboys don't like to run single-ship missions."

"If they can get gun support, that's fine with me, but we'll only need them for an hour or so."

"I'll see what I can do. Are you going to wait?"

"No, I've got a couple of other things to do. When you get an answer and have the mission coordinated, get back to me."

Bocker turned to the radios and said, "Yes, sir."

Gerber left the commo bunker and returned to his hootch. There he examined the XM-21 again. He popped the lens caps and sighted through the scope. He checked the mounting bolts and decided that if he was going to do it right, he would need to zero the weapon. Fire a couple of practice rounds and adjust the scope for his eyes.

Gerber took the rifle and a magazine loaded with regulation 7.62 mm ammo and walked out into the bright afternoon sun. He crossed the redoubt and stepped through the gate. A group of strikers was working in the wire, restringing part of it, checking the firing controls on some of the claymore mines and replacing trip flares that had been in the field for a month or more.

He spotted Tyme working with one of the strikers. Gerber called to him. "Sergeant Tyme, can I speak to you for a moment?"

Tyme looked up and then back at the claymore. He pointed at something and then stood. He patted the striker on the shoulder and then trotted over to Gerber.

"What can I do for you, Captain?"

"You have any of those targets we use to zero weapons?"

"Yes, sir. In my quarters. I'll get you some." He ran up the road and into the camp.

Gerber watched Tyme disappear from view, then turned to survey the empty fields to the south. About five hundred meters away was a clump of trees that had been used as a rally point in the past. Beyond that was nothing other than swamp and river. He considered using one of the trees to hold the target but decided against it.

Two hundred meters south of the camp were the remains of a dike that had collapsed into a paddy. There was a single palm growing from it. The base of the tree was wide, nearly three feet in diameter, but the tree was no more than seven or eight feet tall.

Tyme returned from the camp. "Captain, I've got the targets."

Gerber turned, reached out and took the package. "Thanks," he said. "You have any tacks or nails?"

"In there," said Tyme. "I thought you'd want something like that."

"Yeah. Thanks." Gerber crossed the runway and walked into the open field of short elephant grass. He walked slowly, finding the heat of the afternoon oppressive. He wiped the sweat from his forehead with the sleeve of his fatigue jacket. When he reached the tree, he crouched and opened the package of targets. Using the tacks supplied by Tyme, he fastened one of the targets to the base of the tree, then walked back to the runway.

He sat on the edge, away from the sticky peta-prime, looped the sling of the weapon around his upper arm and braced his left elbow on his knee. Through the scope he had no trouble seeing the target's black square with the notch cut out. He lowered the weapon, jammed a magazine into the well, worked the bolt to chamber a round.

Again he wrapped the sling around his arm, leaned forward, his left elbow on his knee and set the cross hairs on the notch in the black square. He fired once, thought that he could see the bullet hole in the target, centered the cross hairs again and fired a second round. After he fired the third shot, he set the safety and stood. He walked to the tree and examined the target. The weapon was shooting low and to the left. Gerber adjusted the scope and put up a new target.

He ran through the procedure until he was sure that the weapon would put the bullet where he aimed it. He collected his material and walked back to the camp. As he passed through the gate, he waved a hand at Tyme, who was rounding up his work party.

Again Tyme left them. "Yes, Captain?"

"Justin, Sergeant Fetterman and I are going off the camp for the next forty-eight to seventy-two hours. Minh will be running the show, but I want you to watch over our end of it. Just be around to take care of any problems that arise."

Tyme took off his gloves and stuffed them into the thigh pocket of his jungle fatigues. "Yes, sir," he said. "I just—"

"There is nothing we can do about it now. If Animal hadn't gotten killed, he would have been left here. Now there's something that I have to attend to, and I want to be sure the camp is being supervised."

For a moment Tyme stared at Gerber. It was as if he knew what Gerber had to do. He said nothing. "You can count on me, Captain. I'll take care of anything here. Which radio will you take?"

"I hate to leave all our communications to one of the URC-10s, but I can't hump a PRC-10 through the bush with everything else. We'll be on the team uniform. Normal check-in times."

"Yes, sir."

Gerber turned and headed up the road. Inside the wire, he found Fetterman standing near the gate, one foot up on the wall of sandbags. His weapon was leaning against the wall, and his pack was on the ground near his foot. "We about ready?" asked Fetterman.

Gerber was going to shrug but saw Bocker leave the commo bunker, head to the redoubt and then turn. He angled directly to Gerber and stopped a couple of feet away.

"Got a chopper coming in about thirty minutes. Tacked it on to one of their ash-and-trash missions. Said we could have the chopper for about an hour if we need it that long."

"More than long enough. Thanks, Galvin." Gerber waited for Bocker to move off toward the commo bunker and then said, "Tony, let me grab my pack, and I'll meet you back here."

Before Gerber could move, Fetterman said, "I've talked to Krung about this. Figured he could help us find the trail again. He's familiar with the surroundings."

"Good. I should've thought of that myself."

"He'll be here in a couple of minutes. He did go through his 'I will find but not kill' routine again. I told him that was all we wanted to do. Find Cavanaugh."

There was a distant beat of rotors and the whine of a turbine engine. Bocker came out of the commo bunker again carrying a smoke grenade. He trotted past Gerber and Fetterman out to the end of the runway. He pulled the pin on the grenade and tossed it to the center of the dirt and peta-prime strip.

"I better hurry," said Gerber.

Four minutes later Gerber was back, standing at the gate. The helicopter sat on the end of the runway. The last traces of the green smoke were blowing away to the east, drifting over the rice paddies there. Gerber jogged out the gate, handed his weapon to Fetterman, who had already boarded with Krung, and climbed into the aircraft. He crouched near the pilot's seat, opened his map and set it on the radio control heads on the console.

"There's a pretty good LZ about here," shouted Gerber over the roar of the engine as he pointed to a large clearing marked on his map. "Tree lines are a klick apart, but we'd like you to drop us close to the westernmost one."

The pilot picked up the map and examined it carefully. He handed it back and said, "It's getting pretty close to dusk. I don't like being that close to Cambodia so close to dark."

"There's a problem?" asked Gerber.

"No, sir. We low-level in, flare and you hop out. We should be gone before anyone figures out what we're doing."

Gerber refolded his map and jammed it into his pocket. He moved to the troop seat but had to sit on the edge because of his rucksack. He leaned forward, elbows on knees, and took his rifle back from Fetterman.

At that moment the pilot rolled on the throttle, increasing the engine RPM. The chopper lifted in a small cloud of dust and spun until they were facing due west. The pilot eased the cyclic forward as he pulled in some pitch. They began to slip along about three feet off the ground, picking up speed until they were racing across the surface, then climbing slightly to avoid tree lines and hootches. The aircraft turned to the northwest, angling toward the Cambodian border.

As the pilot checked the terrain, they popped up once to fifteen hundred feet, but then dived to three feet. They altered their course, came to a finger of jungle and climbed so that they were flying just above the trees, the skids only inches from the vegetation.

The crew chief leaned around the transmission and yelled, "We're inbound. Get ready."

Fetterman slid across the deck until he was near the door on the left. He put one hand on the pilot's seat and looked out.

Gerber didn't move. As the sunlight faded, he kept his eyes on the clearing below. It was a large oblong area with a single tree growing in the center. He worked the bolt of his rifle, making sure that a round was chambered, and then slipped on the safety.

Seconds later the aircraft flared, the nose coming up as the pilot used the bottom of the aircraft to help slow him. He jerked in an armload of pitch, creating lift on the rotor blades. He leveled the skids and dropped the chopper to the ground.

As soon as they touched down, Fetterman was out the door. Gerber followed him, diving for cover behind a small bush. Krung leaped clear, and the helicopter popped up. It turned, charging toward the trees, using them as cover. When it was two or three hundred yards away, there was a burst of fire, a single line of green tracers stabbing upward, followed by return fire from the helicopter. A flame three feet long leaped from the barrel of the crew chief's M-60 machine gun, the ruby tracers aimed at the source of the green.

Gerber watched the chopper until it disappeared. He then got to his feet and ran toward the trees, Fetterman and Krung following him. He came to a narrow path, a game trail, and crossed it until he was deep in the jungle. Then he stopped and waited for the other two men.

When they crouched near him, he whispered, "We know Charlie is in the vicinity."

"But they don't know we're here," said Fetterman.

"No, but we have to assume they figure someone is. Otherwise, the chopper wouldn't have been here." Gerber stopped talking and then added, "But then, why shoot at it? Gives them away."

"VC close," reconfirmed Krung. "Very close."

"Krung, take the point. Get us out of here, and find us a place to hole up for the night."

Krung nodded, the gesture nearly lost in the last of the fading sunlight. He pushed a branch out of the way, then eased it back into position so that it wouldn't make any noise.

They worked their way deeper into the jungle, away from the trail, angling away from the VC. Moving slowly, stealthily, it took them almost an hour to advance only a few hundred meters. They ducked under branches, dodged trees and avoided bushes. No one spoke, but the trio stayed close enough to each other so that they could see the shape of the man in front. The jungle wasn't the thick, triple-canopy forest that covered much of the Central Highlands. Starlight and moonlight filtered through it, providing some illumination.

After an hour they were tired, soaked with sweat and breathing heavily, as if they had sprinted a long distance in the oppressive heat of the late afternoon. Krung halted near the base of a giant teak tree. Gerber moved to the right and Fetterman to the left, each man watching the ground in front of him, searching for the enemy.

Gerber slowly, carefully, reached to his side and unsnapped the pouch holding one of his canteens. He drank deeply, the water still cool. He then poured some of the water on the go-to-hell rag around his neck, allowing it to cool him slightly.

After a ten-minute rest they were ready to move again. Gerber finished off the water in the canteen because he didn't want it sloshing around as he moved through the jungle. He slipped the empty canteen back into the pouch and waited as Krung surveyed the ground on the other side of the tree. Then slowly the group stole forward.

It was hard work. Walking through jungle wasn't the easiest way to travel, but they had added the strain of not making any noise. The foot had to be lifted high so that it wouldn't snag on anything and then set carefully on the dead leaves, twigs and debris that littered the jungle floor. First the heel. Then as the weight was shifted, the foot was rotated forward so that the pressure was applied slowly. It provided a chance to back off if there was any indication that a twig would snap or the leaves would crumble.

They didn't want to be heard, which reduced the pace to only a couple of hundred meters an hour, if they were lucky. If it hadn't been for the single line of green tracers marking the location of a VC unit, Gerber would have passed the night inside the tree line and then begun the search in the morning. He remembered that only one weapon had been fired, and that could mean there was only a single VC out there, but he couldn't take a chance. He had to get clear of the area.

At midnight, with the moon high overhead creating a spectrum of shadows that danced in the light breeze, they halted again. They spread out in a triangular formation, each man responsible for watching the ground in front of him. They rested there, sweat pouring from them and soaking their clothes as completely as if they had been standing in a tropical rain shower.

Once in position, none of them moved. They didn't bother with their water, didn't brush at the insects that crawled on their necks, faces and heads. There were clouds of mosquitoes that seemed to hover near their ears creating an insistent drone that made it hard to hear anything else and made the skin on the back of the neck crawl. None of them used insect repellent because the VC could pick up its odor from a long distance. To preserve their concealment, Gerber knew they had to tolerate the mosquitoes and hope the malaria pills worked.

The men let their eyes roam the ground, however, looking for signs of the VC. They watched for movement not caused by the light breeze that did nothing to dry their soaked uniforms or to cool them. And they listened to the night sounds of the jungle, waiting for the misstep that would tell them that the VC were near.

Each of them relaxed as much as possible. Gerber was crouched with one knee on the ground and an elbow resting on the other. It was a position that ensured he wouldn't fall asleep easily. He kept his eyes moving. First he memorized the position of everything that he could see, memorized the shapes of the bushes and the trees and their locations. He checked them frequently, looking for a change that would tell him that the VC had arrived, or that an enemy patrol was passing by or had camped nearby.

It was an hour later that he thought he saw movement among the trees. He watched it carefully, staring off to the side, waiting for it to move again. When it did, he knew the enemy was near. He hoped they would pass him quietly and disappear into the jungle. When the point man of the VC raised a hand and dropped to the ground, Gerber knew that he and his men were in trouble.

15

THE JUNGLE WEST OF CAMP A-555 NEAR THE CAMBODIAN BORDER

Keeping his eyes on the VC patrol, Gerber slowly lowered himself to the ground so that he would be harder to spot. He had counted twelve men, each armed with an AK-47. The banana clip, the front sight and bayonet assembly and the pistol grip and short stock gave the weapon a distinct outline.

The VC spread out in a loose ring and collapsed to the ground. None of them moved for ten or fifteen minutes, as if the soldiers were watching the trail behind them, waiting to see if they were being followed. Two then got up and disappeared into the jungle heading south. Another separated from the group, but he didn't seem to have a destination or mission. He strolled casually to where Gerber hid with his face pressed into the dank jungle soil.

The lone VC dropped his trousers and squatted near a small bush. There was a rumbling in his gut and an explosive sound as the odor of rotten eggs drifted toward Gerber. The man seemed to sigh with pleasure but didn't move for several moments. Finally he stripped some of the leaves from the bush, cleaned himself and tossed them away so that they landed next to Gerber's face. Gerber didn't react. His stomach turned over from the pervasive stench, but he didn't move.

The VC finished, stood up and grunted loudly. He bent and jerked his pants up and walked back to his friends, who were now watching him. They were laughing quietly, and there were a few whispered comments.

Gerber waited patiently, the smell from the filthy leaves still hanging near him. With the VC no more than fifteen or twenty yards away from him, he couldn't move. They obviously had not seen him because they had let their discipline lapse.

He had hoped that it was just a short break and that when the two men returned, they would move on. But instead, they seemed to be setting up camp. They dug a small hole, lined it with rocks, then scattered, searching for firewood. A campfire suggested they would remain in place until daylight. Gerber didn't believe they would light the fire at night.

One of the VC came toward Gerber. He stopped and picked up a long crooked stick. He found another larger, shorter one and grabbed it. He stood up, looked at the jungle around him and started to walk directly toward Gerber.

Gerber moved his right hand slowly until he could feel the hilt of his knife. With his thumb he unsnapped the band that held it in place. He kept his hand there and didn't move, didn't breathe. He just waited for the VC to find enough wood and return to his campsite.

But the man kept coming toward him, his arms loaded with wood. He stopped inches from Gerber but didn't look down, his eyes fixed on something else. He began to move again, stepped on Gerber's arm and twisted his ankle. As he stumbled, falling to his knees and dropping the wood, he cried out in pain.

In one fluid motion, Gerber came off the ground with his knife drawn and grabbed the enemy, spinning him. He clamped his hand over the VC's mouth to prevent him from crying out again and drew the blade along the throat from left to right. There was a splash of blood, a coppery odor, and a foul stench as the man died. Gerber felt him jerk in a spasm once, as if trying to kick them both over, and then the man sagged against him.

Gerber lowered the body to the ground and then crouched behind it, waiting for the man's yell and ensuing commotion to draw his friends. For a moment nothing happened. Gerber reached to his right and touched the stock of his weapon but didn't pick it up. He didn't want to move any more than he had to.

There was a whispered call from the VC camp, and then another soldier began to move toward Gerber's position. Behind that man two more appeared. The rest of the enemy were spread out around the wood-filled hole, watching.

As the VC came nearer, Gerber tensed, prepared to spring at him. Suddenly a single report erupted in the gloom. The man's weapon flew upward and outward toward Gerber as he collapsed to the ground with a grunt of pain and surprise.

At that instant more firing came from behind Gerber, a ripping sound as Fetterman fired, the ruby tracers lashing toward the enemy and the strobelike bursts lighting the ground. Two of the VC dropped, hit by Fetterman's bullets. Two more tried to run and were cut down by Krung firing his weapon single-shot.

Gerber scooped up his weapon and fired rapidly. He hit one of the fleeing enemy high, either in the shoulder or the back of the head. The man flipped forward, his feet leaving the ground. He landed on his face, struggled to sit up and then fell.

Firing broke out to the left. Gerber could see the muzzle-flashes in the jungle and could hear the bullets snapping overhead. He watched for a moment, aimed his rifle and fired into the jungle. The return fire, a sustained burst from an AK-47, forced Gerber down. He pressed his face close to the body of the man he had knifed. One hand rested in a pool of sticky blood.

There was a sudden explosion near the point of the enemy firing. Gerber saw a fountain of sparks splash upward as the grenade detonated. There was a shriek of pain, and the firing stopped.

Gerber heard someone crashing through the vegetation. He turned and fired at the sound. Red tracers raked the darkness to his left, but the man kept running.

When the firing died, Gerber moved back to where Fetterman crouched behind a palm log. He leaned close to the master sergeant's ear and whispered, "They know we're here now. At least one of them got away."

"I heard him go," said Fetterman.

"We're going to have to move out. Head closer to Cambodia and then make some good time in the morning."

"I'll get Krung, and we'll take off."

Gerber stared into the darkness where the VC lay. He wanted to check the bodies, see if there was anything on them of intelligence value. He should collect the equipment in order to deny it to the enemy, but he couldn't wait for morning and didn't want to do it in the dark. It was too dangerous, especially with two, maybe three, of the enemy unaccounted for.

Fetterman moved out, heading toward Krung's position. Once the master sergeant had gone a yard, Gerber lost sight of him. He couldn't hear him moving. It was as if Fetterman had vanished in a cloud of smoke. The man was exceptional in the jungle. He could blend into any environment, any terrain, and then spring out before anyone could get near him.

Gerber waited for him to return, watching the VC camp. From somewhere came a quiet moaning sound, as if someone was badly hurt. The moaning rose and fell as the man breathed, sometimes ending with a bubbling cough. But Gerber wasn't going to search for the wounded man. The VC, like their Japanese counterparts in the Second World War, sometimes used the wounded as decoys, getting the Americans to rescue the wounded, or put them out of their misery, and then ambushed them.

Fetterman loomed out of the dark a moment later. He whispered, "Sergeant Krung found the running man and stopped him. Maybe we can hang loose here for a few minutes."

"No, the sound of the firing would alert anyone within a couple of klicks. Besides, two of them left the main body before we had to open fire."

"I find trail near here," Krung said. "We move down it and be far from here."

"No," said Gerber. "Too much of a chance for the VC to set up and wait for us. We can't use any trails for a while, especially after a firefight."

"Then we head off deeper into the jungle," said Fetterman.

"Looks like that is exactly what we do. Krung, you take the point and head due west for a klick. Then stop."

"Sir," said Fetterman. "I probably should hang back a while and see if there is any pursuit. I can catch up later."

"Okay," said Gerber. "Krung, let's go."

Fetterman watched Gerber and Krung disappear into the jungle, moving slowly and quietly to the west. When they were out of sight, Fetterman crawled past the VC camp and found a good hiding place near the base of a large tree. He set his rifle on the ground near it, the operating rod out of the dirt and the barrel slightly elevated. He took his Case fighting knife from the scabbard and settled down to wait.

The moist earth stank with the smell of rotting vegetation. Around him were clouds of mosquitoes that didn't land because his skin was wet with sweat. He could hear some scraping along the branches of the tree just above his head and was sure that it was some kind of snake. He thought he could smell it, too, an odor of ammonia and vinegar. He ignored it because he knew that most snakes would not attack unless cornered. They avoided human beings. The lone exception he knew of was the black mamba, but they lived in Africa, not Southeast Asia.

To the right, hidden by the jungle and the night, was a wounded man. Fetterman could hear his labored breathing. The man seemed to have a sucking chest wound, and the breath rattled in his lungs. It sounded as if the man was quickly drowning in his own blood.

Then he heard the first quiet steps of the returning VC. He knew they would be moving as silently as they could. They would have heard the firefight and would be sneaking back to learn what had happened.

Fetterman shifted slightly. It was an effort to keep his circulation going so that he didn't cramp up at the critical moment. He remained still, glancing right and left, moving only his eyes. He tried not to stare into the jungle.

One of the men came forward slowly, his weapon held in both hands, the bayonet extended. He moved from the cover of a bush to the side of a tree. He passed Fetterman, the hole where the firewood had been dumped and then moved deeper into the jungle.

The second man appeared then. He came forward in a slight crouch. He kept away from the trees where Fetterman hid, looked at the fire pit and then stumbled over a body. He said nothing, put out a hand to break his fall and made almost no noise.

At that instant Fetterman sprang from his hiding place with a catlike motion, clapped a hand over the VC's nose and mouth and drove the blade of his knife up through the man's kidney and into his left lung. Fetterman felt the man's blood spill, covering his hand.

He pulled the enemy backward and slashed the knife across his throat, severing the larynx from the trachea and cutting both carotid arteries. The hot blood spurted weakly, soaking the front of Fetterman's uniform. Quietly he laid the body on the ground, pulled the AK from the slack fingers and set it on the jungle floor out of the VC's reach.

Suddenly the first man appeared almost beside Fetterman but apparently didn't see him. Fetterman stood and turned, driving in his knife to the hilt just above the enemy's web belt, ripping upward until he hit the breastbone. A stench from the VC's bowels rose from the wound to assault Fetterman's nostrils.

The man had tried to jump back at the first hint of pain, but Fetterman held him. The VC dropped his rifle and reached around, feeling his guts spilling from the gaping hole in his stomach. He started to scream, a high-pitched whine that Fetterman ended by slashing the throat. The man fell to the jungle floor and drummed a sandaled foot on the soft ground as he died.

Fetterman quickly moved away from the dead man. He wiped the blade of his knife on his sleeve. He slipped it into the scabbard and then picked up his rifle. As he crossed the ambush site, he wished there was something he could do about the weapons. There were ten or twelve AKs lying in the dirt that could be of use to the VC if they found them soon enough.

He grinned to himself, and moved back to the ambush. He found one of the AKs, depressed the lever at the back of the bolt and lifted off the guard on the top of the weapon. He took the bolt out, released a couple of pins and had the trigger housing in his hand. With an underhand throw he scattered the parts and dropped the AK to the ground. During the next ten minutes he located several other of the weapons and took the bolts, putting them into his pack before tossing the other pieces around. Now even if the VC found the weapons, they would have to be repaired, and if the VC didn't find them for a day or two, most of the weapons should have a terminal case of rust, he thought.

With that finished he headed off to the west to find Krung and Captain Gerber. It didn't take him long to catch up to them.

AT DAWN THEY WERE at the edge of the jungle, looking at a wide expanse of open fields and rice paddies that swept from them into Cambodia. It was broken by a sliver of jungle that dipped into it about half a klick away. To the north was a solid expanse of jungle. A klick to the south was a clump of palm trees that shaded a farmer's hootch. Smoke rose from it, but they could see no one moving near it. Beyond that was swamp. Overhead a jet streaked high, just a flash of silver in the bright blue cloudless sky.

Gerber sat with his back to a tree, eating peaches from an OD C-ration can. Fetterman and Krung were watching for the enemy while Gerber relaxed. In ten minutes he would change places with Krung so that the Tai striker could eat his cold breakfast. Later it would be Fetterman's turn.

When he finished, Gerber buried the can in a shallow hole, threw in the remains of the bread and jelly he hadn't finished, then drank from his canteen. This time he didn't finish the water right away. He would wait until they prepared to move.

Before Gerber could get up, Fetterman was near him. "We've got more company."

"Now what?"

"I think we've got a party of VC spotted about half a klick from here. They're flirting with the edge of the jungle off to the north, so I can't be sure."

"They're not Cavanaugh's men, are they?"

"No, sir, I don't think so. I'm not sure who they are. They could be a bunch of farmers trying to get an early start, although I think that a couple of them are carrying weapons."

"You know," Gerber said, "I can't recall when we've found more people running around this AO. Everyone and his brother."

"Yes, sir."

Gerber got up. "Why don't you show me these guys."

Fetterman led him to the edge of the jungle, but the line of people had disappeared, having diverted into the trees. Krung pointed to the last place he had seen them and told them that the men had turned to the north.

"Then I guess we go to plan two," Gerber announced.

"Which is?"

"Krung, take a break. We'll keep watch," said Gerber.

As Krung eased away from the edge of the jungle, Gerber noticed another group of men who seemed to be following the line of march of the first bunch. Gerber used the scope on his rifle to study them. They wore a mixed bag of uniforms and clothes—some black pajamas, some fatigues, but almost every one of them wore one of the American boonie hats.

Fetterman used his binoculars. He crawled closer to Gerber. "That second group could be Sean's men. I think I recognize one or two of them."

"Christ, Tony, you don't think we've lucked into something, do you?"

"I can't see Sean," said Fetterman. "Wait a minute. Wait a fucking minute. There he is."

"Where?" said Gerber. He flipped the safety off his weapon.

"At the end of the column. There's a big mahogany tree sticking up there. See it?"

"Got it."

"Cavanaugh just passed it."

"Yeah. Got him." Gerber crouched behind a log, using it as a support for his rifle.

"I make the range just over six hundred meters, Captain."

Gerber hit the magazine release. He dropped it to the ground and dug out the one that had eight rounds in it, the special rounds that Fetterman and Tyme had loaded. He jammed the magazine home and worked the bolt, ejecting the round that was already chambered.

"Not much wind, Captain. Light breeze blowing from left to right."

Gerber put the cross hairs on Cavanaugh's chest. He could see the sergeant's face, almost see the color of his eyes. There were sweat stains on his fatigues, and Gerber had the impression that Cavanaugh could use a shave. And the impression that Cavanaugh was very young. That was the thing that stuck in his mind. Cavanaugh was young, not yet twenty years old.

All that through a telescopic sight? Gerber knew that he was letting his mind run loose. There was no way he could get an impression of Cavanaugh's youth through the scope. No way he could tell that the sergeant needed a shave. Gerber's mind was filling in the details.

Cavanaugh disappeared for a moment, stepping behind a tree. He reappeared, and Gerber moved the cross hairs so that he would lead Sean by several feet, gauging the speed of the group's march. He let out his breath, took another, exhaled and began to squeeze the trigger.

The burst of AK fire slammed into the log just as Gerber pulled the trigger. He jerked the trigger, throwing the round off. He had no idea where it went.

Fetterman spun and shot into the sound. He saw a single VC jump to the left, rolling behind a tree. Fetterman slipped to his right, trying to flank the enemy.

There was a single shot from the right, near the location where Krung had been eating. Krung appeared then, holding up the AK-47.

"Captain?" said Fetterman.

"Looks like we've walked into something. Krung, any indication of others out there?"

Before Krung could answer, shooting broke out around them. Bullets clipped the leaves of the trees, showering them. Several rounds slammed into a nearby tree, stripping the bark from it. More shooting came from the right, as if the enemy was moving toward them in a semicircular formation designed to box them in. Gerber couldn't flee across the paddy fields now behind them. It was too open.

Gerber caught a flash and sighted through the scope. He could see the enemy soldier so clearly that it looked as if the man was no more than four or five feet away. He could see the scar on the chin, the light mustache and the thin eyebrows. The man wore a pith helmet pushed back on his head so that Gerber could make out the jet-black hair.

He set the cross hairs on the center of the man's chest and pulled the trigger. A hole appeared in the man's chest and the dust flew from his shirt. He even had time to see the surprised expression on the man's face as he dropped his rifle and lifted his hands. Blood spurted, the stream nearly three feet long as the VC turned and fell.

To the right, Gerber could see part of a VC's head as the man peeked around a tree, firing his weapon without aiming it. He was spraying bullets in Fetterman's direction. Gerber put the cross hairs on the man's eye, a brown bloodshot eye, and pulled the trigger. The side of the enemy's face disintegrated in a spray of blood and bone. He didn't seem to react. He just dropped from sight.

"Captain," Fetterman yelled. "Coming up from behind us."

Gerber turned and saw two dozen of the enemy, dressed in black pajamas, web gear and sandals. Gerber opened fire on them, shooting as quickly as he could pull the trigger. He ran out of ammo, quickly dropped the magazine and slammed a spare one home. He put the cross hairs on a man, fired and saw the VC go down in a loose-jointed fashion.

Fetterman was firing on full automatic. He dropped three of the VC. Two of them tumbled forward into a dry paddy and didn't move. The other fell back, disappearing behind a dike. Fetterman aimed at another man, picked him off easily and fired at a fifth.

To the left, Krung was busy shooting at the shadows. Men would appear, squeeze off a couple of rounds and then dive for cover. A Chicom grenade bounced off the tree next to him. Krung dived for cover as it detonated, the shrapnel burying itself in the trees around them. Krung looked up in time to see two men rushing him. The Tai striker dropped them both with a short burst. One of them fell nearly at his feet, tried to get up and then Krung put a round into his face.

Gerber heard noise to his right. He turned from the rice paddies and saw a man running through the jungle. He snapped a shot at him, missed and tried again. The second round buried itself in the trunk of a tree. Gerber waited, saw the man again and fired. The round again slammed into a tree near the man's head.

"Damn!" Gerber swore. He caught a flash out of the corner of his eye and saw another enemy. Before he could fire, the man opened up, his round smashing into the log near Gerber. Gerber rolled right, fired and rolled again. He heard the man fall into the jungle.

Fetterman reloaded his weapon. Most of the VCs in front of him had taken cover behind the rice paddies. He raked the top of one, the bullets kicking the dirt high in dark brown geysers. There was a shout, and two men leaped up to throw grenades. Fetterman's burst caught one in the stomach as his arm snapped forward. The VC lost the grip on his weapon, tossing it four or five feet in front of him. He disappeared in a cloud of dust and shrapnel thrown up in the explosion.

The other man threw his grenade as hard as he could before he dropped behind the safety of his dike. The grenade hit the ground in front of Fetterman and bounced once toward him. Fetterman fielded it in his bare hand like a third baseman picking up a slow roller. He threw it back and dropped to the jungle floor. As soon as he heard the explosion, he was up again, firing at the enemy as they exposed themselves.

At that moment the area around them seemed to erupt. There was shooting from AKs and at least one RPD. The bullets formed an almost impenetrable wall of lead that stripped leaves from trees, chopped the tops off small trees, toppling them, and shredded the bark from the palms and teaks.

Gerber rolled next to his log. He felt the impact of bullets slamming into it. He listened to the whine and buzz of the slugs as they ricocheted off rocks on the jungle floor. There was a shout from the jungle and an answer from the rice paddies. A bugle call ripped through the noise, a wailing note that built in volume like the siren of a police car. A whistle sounded but was quickly overpowered by the voices of the enemy. They were screaming and yelling at one another as they suddenly left the protection of the jungle trees or the rice paddy dikes, rushing toward the three men.

Gerber looked up and saw four men coming at him. He jerked his rifle around and fired from the hip. One man spun, the round slamming into his shoulder. The head of a second disappeared in an explosion of crimson as the body kept coming at him. The third man was almost on him as Gerber rolled right, braced his back against the log and got to his knees. He fired, but the bullet seemed to have no effect on the enemy soldier.

The man tried to stick his bayonet into Gerber's chest. Gerber parried the blade with his rifle, shoving it to the side. He swung the butt of the rifle around, smashing the man's face. He came back around, the barrel of his rifle pointed at the last VC. The man tried to slam his rifle butt into Gerber's face. Gerber blocked it with his own weapon, shattering the scope. Gerber hit him with the barrel, and as the man fell, Gerber put three rounds into him, the blood splashing over him, staining his uniform.

Gerber spun, saw two men in the rice paddy and fired once. The bolt of his weapon locked back, and Gerber snatched at the ammo pouch on his pistol belt. He let the empty magazine fall from his weapon, slapped the new one home and released the bolt as the two men leaped the last dike before they got to the trees. Gerber fired rapidly, and both men died, blood blossoming on their chests.

The firing around them seemed to peak in a roar that blended the individual weapons into a single continuous explosion. Gerber felt something tug at his shoulder and spin him. He fell forward and threw out his hands to break his fall. He thought he'd been hit but didn't feel any pain. There was no sudden warm wetness and no flare of white-hot pain. He picked up his weapon and opened fire again, ignoring the dull ache.

But the VC were retreating. A couple of them were running to the rear, toward a narrow strip of jungle on the other side of the paddies, north of the swamps. One of them took a round in the back. He dived forward, his arms outstretched, belly flopping into the dirt of a dry paddy. His friend glanced at him but kept running. He tossed his AK away and then unbuckled his web gear, shrugging it from his shoulders without breaking stride.

There was covering fire from one of the RPDs. A grenade exploded in the center of a paddy near them, the cloud of red dust obscuring the retreating men but too far away to injure them. The shooting tapered rapidly until it was only sporadic firing.

Then from the north came the sounds of a sustained battle. It sounded as if the men with Cavanaugh had either caught the VC moving there or had stumbled over them, starting the firefight.

Fetterman moved closer to Gerber. "Captain? You okay?"

Gerber rubbed his shoulder and then glanced down. The bullet had hit him high on the scabbard, which was taped to his web gear. It had shattered the tip of the knife, ricocheted off without penetrating the scabbard or the thick material of the harness.

His shoulder was sore, and he was certain it would be badly bruised, but that was better than having a bullet hole in it. He grinned at Fetterman. "I'm fine," he reassured the master sergeant.

Krung backed up toward them, his rifle pointing at the jungle. He kept his eyes moving, watching the trees, waiting for the VC to come at them again.

"Captain, we've got to get out of here," urged Fetterman. "This isn't the best position in the world."

"And we're going to run out of ammo," added Gerber. He looked at the men lying on the jungle floor close to them. They carried AKs and had extra ammo with them. Gerber and his men could always use that.

"We could try to work our way toward Cavanaugh's men," Fetterman suggested. "Join up with them."

"And then what?" asked Gerber. "Just shoot Cavanaugh once the VC have been eliminated."

"No, sir," Fetterman answered. "But we'd better do something fast, or we're not going to survive until lunch."

16

THE JUNGLE WEST OF
CAMP A-555

Before Gerber could respond, firing broke out again all
around them. Fetterman leaped to the left, rolling for cover
near a palm tree. He opened up as the VC swarmed from the
jungle across the rice paddies, screaming and shooting.
Green tracers, burning dimly in the bright morning sun-
shine, flashed into the jungle or bounced off the ground,
arching skyward.

Gerber dived for the protection of his log, laid the barrel
of his M-14 on it and began shooting rapidly. The smashed
scope was useless, so Gerber aimed by looking along the
barrel. He saw two men go down, but there were so many of
them now. Not just VC in black pajamas, but NVA wearing
full uniforms of deep green and khaki pith helmets. The men
were running across the open ground, leaping the rice paddy
dikes as if they were hurdles in a race.

From the apex of the sliver of jungle, due west of Gerber's
position, an NVA machine gun opened fire, raking the jungle around them with 7.62 mm rounds.

And from behind them came another shout, orders in
high-pitched Vietnamese as the firing there began again.

Gerber heard the flatter reports of Krung's weapon as he tried to stop the enemy from overrunning them.

At that moment Gerber knew it was all over. There were too many of the enemy coming too fast, and even if all three of them had machine guns, they wouldn't be able to stop the Vietcong and the NVA. There was no time to call for artillery or air support because the enemy was too close. If the attack slowed or there was a momentary retreat, he might be able to shout for help. Now all he could do was fight. Gerber tossed his empty M-14 to the side and grabbed one of the AKs near him. He flipped the selector to full auto and pulled the trigger. He emptied the weapon and scrambled over to the body to find more ammunition.

Suddenly another machine gun joined the firing, but this one seemed to be raking the onrushing enemy. A dozen of them fell in a hail of bullets. The others turned, firing at the five men who were attacking them. One held an M-60 at his hip, a belt of ammo across his shoulder, and was running at them, firing short bursts. As he got closer to them, the enemy began returning fire, the bullets kicking up the dirt all around him. He dived for cover in the corner of a rice paddy and started shooting again.

The enemy seemed to forget about Gerber and his tiny party. They turned their assault, attacking the machine gun and the men who supported it, but the machine gunner kept up a steady fire until the bolt of his weapon locked back as the belt broke.

FROM FAR TO THE RIGHT came a single burst of AK fire. Sean Cavanaugh reacted to it by diving for cover among the trees. At that moment the VC patrol that he had been shadowing with nearly three dozen of his men scattered in the trees. The two forces, separated by a hundred meters or more, jockeyed for position, moving toward one another, until Cavanaugh saw one of the black-clad enemy hunched over, an

SKS clutched in his hands, running along a narrow jungle trail. Cavanaugh aimed and squeezed off a round. The man took the slug in the chest, staggered two steps and fell among some small bushes.

Firing broke out all around him. The strikers formed a skirmish line and waited for the VC to rush them. They poured rifle and machine-gun fire into the jungle and punctuated it with M-79 rounds.

Cavanaugh worked his way forward, crawling along the moist ground. He could hear the enemy rounds passing over his head. There was an acrid stink of gunpowder hanging in the air around him. He kept his elbows and knees moving until he was at the edge of the trail, but he could see nothing of the enemy. Their return fire had tapered to an occasional shot or short burst from an AK. They were trying to break contact.

Then to his left he heard more shooting. Machine guns and AKs against M-14s. He pulled back until he was behind his skirmish line and then got to his feet, running to the edge of the jungle. He saw more of the VC and the NVA running across the open ground, firing into the jungle south of him. Some of them fell, hit by the fire pouring from the jungle. The enemy didn't hesitate, but kept the pressure on the unidentified men in the jungle. From a sliver of jungle that stuck out into the rice paddy, an RPD opened up.

The attack seemed to falter as the men trapped among the trees took a heavy toll of the attackers. Cavanaugh watched them fall, tumbling into the dry paddies. He looked at his strikers and changed the skirmish line so that it was covering his back.

The enemy started another surging charge across the rice paddies. Cavanaugh grabbed the handle on the top of the M-60, draped a belt of ammo over his shoulder and shouted, "Let's go."

He ran from the trees, sprinting across the dry paddies, heading toward the flank of the NVA. He fired a short burst that took them by surprise. Several of them fell as the bullets slammed into them. A squad seemed to peel from the attackers, changing direction, firing at Cavanaugh's small force.

Cavanaugh leaped into the corner of a rice paddy, sliding to the ground. He pushed the barrel of his weapon over the top, aimed and began a hammering fire that tore holes in the NVA line. The RPD that had been shooting in to the trees suddenly raked the ground near Cavanaugh, trying to force him to take cover, but Cavanaugh ignored the bullets kicking up the dirt around him. He let the four strikers with him turn their weapons on the enemy machine gun. One of them was lobbing M-79 grenades at the RPD, but the rounds were falling short.

The belt of ammo feeding the M-60 broke as the links separated. Cavanaugh flipped up the top, jammed the rounds back in and worked the bolt, but the weapon failed to fire. He cocked it again and again and pulled the trigger. It fired three rounds, then jammed, and Cavanaugh worked to clear it as the VC and NVA got closer to him.

The strikers fired into the onrushing mass, knocking some of them down, but the enemy kept coming, shooting from the hip. The whole force changed the point of their attack, forgetting about the men hidden in the jungle. Cavanaugh got the M-60 working again, but the enemy was too close.

The sergeant leaped to meet the onslaught. He grabbed the barrel of the weapon, burning his hands as he swung it like a baseball bat. He felt the solid impact as the receiver group crushed the head of an enemy soldier. He swung it back and forth in a widening arc as the VC danced in and out, trying to use their bayonets and knives.

Around him the strikers were in a death struggle. They used their weapons as clubs, hammering at the VC and the

NVA, using the tricks that Cavanaugh had taught them. They screamed at the enemy, trying to force them from their tiny perimeter. One by one they died, a bullet in the head, a bayonet through the neck, or the chest, or the stomach. A dozen wounds that proved fatal and caused their blood to stain the dry ground around them. All went down within a few minutes of one another until only Cavanaugh was left alive.

He threw the machine gun at one of the VC, knocking the man to the ground. He jumped back and grabbed at a handle in the pack belonging to one of the dead strikers, ripping the entrenching tool free. He swung it with all his might. He hit a man in the shoulder and heard the bones break.

He swung again, catching an NVA soldier in the side of the head. The pith helmet flew off as the E-tool opened a gash that exposed the man's brain. The enemy fell, both hands on his head, screaming as his feet kicked spasmodically.

There was a sharp blow to the E-tool, a bullet bouncing off it. In that moment Cavanaugh felt he was invincible. He couldn't be killed because he led a charmed life. He could stand in the middle of a firefight and the bullets would pass him harmlessly. He was a super soldier who would inflict such losses on the enemy that they would quit the war.

He leaped to the top of the dike, challenging the VC. He swung the E-tool downward and clubbed one of the NVA. Blood splattered as the man's head caved in. Cavanaugh laughed as he swung again, missed a man who ducked, leaning toward him. Cavanaugh snapped a foot out and caught the man in the chin, breaking it as the teeth shattered.

Cavanaugh laughed again as the VC and the NVA backed up, almost as if they were in awe of him. As if they couldn't believe the man they were facing, the bodies of their dead ringing him.

Cavanaugh feinted to the left and then came right, the edge of the tool slicing into the belly of a man, spilling his guts.

Cavanaugh swung upward so that the blade hit the man under the chin, dropping him on his back.

"I'm invincible!" he shouted. He stared at the men around him, his eyes blazing with a strange light. "Come on! You can't kill me!"

For a moment he was lost in the half light that had surrounded the listening post. He saw the bodies of Sergeant Luong and Corporal Lim, the remains of the field phone and the PRC-10 that had been riddled by enemy fire. He heard the pop of the mortars as they threw illumination rounds into the sky over the listening post and wondered why the battle went on forever. A battle that he won time and time again but one that he had to fight time and time again.

He grunted with the effort of swinging the E-tool, snapping his wrists as it connected with a man's body. He heard the man groan under the impact.

As Cavanaugh spun, he felt something strike his side. He heard the wet smack as the bullet punched through him and felt a white-hot flare of pain. It didn't bother him because he knew that it was only a momentary annoyance, and then it would be healed. He would continue to crush the enemy until they were all dead, lying in heaps around him, or until they fled the field.

There was a second pain, high on his shoulder, and the bright sunlight began to dim, as if clouds had suddenly obscured it. Cavanaugh didn't realize that he had dropped the E-tool. He thought that he still stood on the rice paddy dike, the makeshift weapon in his hand. He thought that he was still killing the enemy.

Around him he heard shooting and was relieved because it meant that this time the strikers were the ones who had come back to life, the dead soldiers who had been animated by some unseen and unknown force. This time Cavanaugh wouldn't be left alone on the field of the dead. He would have company.

A third bullet hit him in the stomach, and he fell to his knees. He turned slightly to the left and toppled off the dike, landing on his back in the paddy. He was staring up at the sun. It seemed to be no brighter than the evening star. He wondered what had happened to it and what was happening around him. He could hear random firing and shouting in Vietnamese. He felt a tug at his pistol belt and thought that he raised a hand to slap at the man who touched him.

As the blackness closed in around him, he knew that he was the ultimate soldier. He had been born with the world, had fought in all its campaigns and would not die until the last shot in the last war was fired. Then he would grow old rapidly and fade from the landscape.

GERBER CONTINUED to pour fire from his AK into the rice paddies, shooting the VC and the NVA quickly. The bodies began to pile in heaps near the man who, miraculously, hadn't gone down. Cavanaugh had tossed away the machine gun, which had been broken and bent, and was using an entrenching tool to defend himself.

Gerber lost sight of him as a crowd of NVA swarmed over the paddy dike. He saw more of them fall and then heard shouting to the north.

Twenty men rushed from the tree line, racing over the open ground, screaming and shooting until they were mixed with the enemy. Some of them fell as the VC began to return fire, and then the shooting tapered to an occasional shot in the hand-to-hand fighting.

Gerber turned his attention to the VC in the jungle with him. He saw two of them and fired, the rounds slamming into a tree near them. Fetterman did the same, helping Krung drive the VC from them. The sudden increase in shooting pushed the Vietcong back.

As the VC among the trees retreated, Gerber turned his attention to the battle in the rice paddies. The NVA and the

VC there were fleeing, too, forced back by the attacking strikers. The strikers swarmed over the rice paddy where Cavanaugh lay, took firing positions and raked the enemy with a devastating fusillade.

The VC and the NVA raced for safety. Once the men gained the trees, the machine gun fell silent. There was some random sniping that quickly died down. It was as if the enemy was fighting a rear guard action, and once the majority of the soldiers escaped into Cambodia, the rear guard faded from sight.

Gerber spent an hour watching the jungle, the rice paddies, and the men who were crouched among the dikes in front of him. He had contacted his base with the order to have an artillery barrage ready in case the enemy reappeared. They had fired a couple of marking rounds from Fire Support Base Custer and then said they would stand by, but the enemy didn't appear. Fetterman circulated through the jungle around them, checking the bodies of the dead VC, stripping them of their weapons and ammo and searching for insignia, documents and anything else that would be of value to Intelligence.

It was clear that the VC and the NVA had left the field. They had tried for a quick victory, and when that failed, they had withdrawn, fearing that the Americans and the South Vietnamese would use the daylight hours to mount a large-scale assault.

Gerber picked up the broken XM-21. He jerked the sniperscope from the top and dropped it to the jungle floor. He worked the bolt, made sure that a round was chambered and then moved to the edge of the jungle. When he was joined by Fetterman and Krung, he stepped out into the open and walked slowly toward the rice paddy where the strikers waited.

As he neared them, he recognized some of them. They stood waiting for him, their eyes on the ground. He could see that they had gathered the bodies of their dead and covered them with poncho liners. He stopped at the dike and studied the ground around him, staring at the dead men scattered there.

Without a word to the strikers, Gerber moved to the body that had to be an American. He pulled the cover away and stared at the peaceful look on Cavanaugh's face. It was a look of contentment that suggested he knew exactly what he had been doing and didn't care that it would kill him. It was what he had wanted. He had come a long way to find it.

Thoughts swirled in Gerber's mind. Thoughts about Cavanaugh and what he had done. Taking the war to the enemy and fighting them as a guerrilla force made more sense than establishing a line of forts to watch the frontier. That hadn't worked during the Indian Wars, and it wouldn't work now. The hostiles hadn't been subdued until the Army left the relative comfort of its warm forts and chased the Indians across the plains, using the tactics that the Indians themselves used. Maybe Cavanaugh understood on some unconscious level that the VC and the NVA would never be defeated by an Army that built large base camps, then found excuses to stay behind the wire.

Or maybe Cavanaugh's mind had snapped. He hadn't been able to take all the killing, hadn't been able to take all the death that seemed to serve no useful purpose because the accomplishment of yesterday was wiped out by the decisions made tomorrow. No progress was made toward ending the war, but the men still died.

There had been no real reason for Cavanaugh to attack the enemy across the open ground. He could have stayed among the trees and fired on them. The range was long, but it wouldn't have made that much of a difference. His reckless assault had saved the lives of Gerber, Fetterman and Krung. There was no question of that.

Fetterman, who was standing next to Gerber, asked, "Now what?"

"We collect the bodies and move them to a more defensible position."

"What about the strikers here?" asked Fetterman.

"I would think that's Minh's problem. They're his men. If he wants to count them AWOL, then that's his privilege. If he wants to punish them for their part in all this, it's up to him."

"And Sean?" asked Fetterman quietly.

"Sean was involved in two earlier actions that rated the Medal of Honor. There were no witnesses to either of those. I think this one rates it, too, and we both witnessed it. He sacrificed himself to save us."

"Captain," said Fetterman, "I don't think he knew we were here. He only saw the enemy and rushed in to kill them."

"Cavanaugh realized that we were about to be overrun and exposed himself to enemy gunners in an attempt to draw their attention away from us. His heroic act is the sole reason that we survived after being caught in an enemy ambush."

"Yes, sir," Fetterman agreed. "If he hadn't charged from the trees and almost single-handedly turned back a large-scale combined VC and NVA assault, we would have died. Even after being severely wounded himself, he continued the attack. It was a most impressive feat of arms."

Gerber pointed at the bodies, counting rapidly, and then doubled the figure. "When we finally reached his position, there were thirty-two enemy soldiers lying dead around him. In the end Cavanaugh had used his entrenching tool to fight them off."

"Yes, sir," said Fetterman. "An impressive piece of fighting. You think we'll have any trouble getting this one through?"

"I doubt it. And you and I have been around long enough to know *how* to write up the citation. The act becomes secondary to that. It is how it is presented that counts."

Fetterman turned and stared at the captain. "You think this is the right thing to do? Trying to get him the Medal of Honor like this? Won't it cheapen the award?"

"Tony, did Sean deserve it for the defense of the listening post?"

"Yes, sir. He certainly did."

"Then all we're doing is ensuring that he gets it. Maybe he doesn't deserve it for this action, but he does for defending his listening post. Not to mention that patrol that was wiped out."

"Yes, sir."

"Now let's get things organized and get the fuck out of here."

17

THE TEAM HOUSE, CAMP A-555

Gerber sat in the team house, his feet propped on one of the tables, his ankles crossed. He held a can of warm beer in one hand and the *Stars and Stripes* in the other. He had read on the front page that there had been demonstrations in Da Nang, that McNamara had announced the new troop ceiling at nearly a quarter of a million men and that B-52s were being employed in the bombing of the North.

Flipping the paper over to the back page, he found a small story that acknowledged the completion of Operation Blue Star, a body recovery detail that had returned to Camp A-102 about two weeks after the battle there. The North Vietnamese had deserted the camp, leaving two hundred unburied dead scattered across the battlefield. The locals had stayed away, fearing ghosts, and the graves registration party had found that the bodies were reduced to skeletons. They had found watches, still running, attached to the wristbones of the dead Americans. And they had learned that someone, a brave someone, had gotten into the arms room and destroyed all the classified documents before the North Vietnamese could get them.

Gerber stared at the story for a long time. He wasn't sure what it was about it that bothered him. Maybe it was the description of the bodies reduced to skeletons wearing watches that continued to run. Maybe it was the mention of a skeletal hand clutching a .45, grass growing between the bones of the wrist and hand. He didn't know.

He dropped his feet to the floor and drained his beer. He tossed the can at the bin next to the refrigerator that held the empties and opened the paper.

As he looked into the center of the newspaper, he felt his stomach turn over. There was a picture of Sean Cavanaugh, looking as if he had just escaped from high school, smiling out at him. Gerber stared at the young face, short hair and the white shirt and dark tie of a young man who had graduated from high school, evaded the draft by volunteering for active duty in the Army and found himself in Vietnam almost before anyone in the World knew where in the hell it was.

Below the picture of Cavanaugh was another of two people. Gerber had thought of Cavanaugh's parents as elderly, but these people didn't look old. They looked miserable. The woman, who had long, light-colored hair, held a handkerchief to her face as the man, his mouth turned down, the tears obvious on his face even in the black-and-white photo, accepted the Congressional Medal of Honor from the President. The medal, a scrap of powder blue cloth sprinkled with white stars, and a chunk of iron formed into a wreath with a star in the center and the word Valor engraved on it, was certainly not worth a son.

Gerber didn't need to read the story because he knew what it would say. Knew all too well because he had read a dozen, a hundred others. It would mention that the parents of Sean Cavanaugh were presented the medal in a small ceremony at the White House. "Sergeant Cavanaugh, on or about 2 April 1966, did distinguish himself..."

Gerber folded the paper and set it on the table so that he could stare at the photos. Although it was hot outside and the ceiling fan spinning over his head did nothing to alleviate the heat, Gerber was suddenly cold. A clammy sweat dripped down his sides.

Another strange contrast. The death of a Special Forces camp in the A Shau Valley and the death of a Special Forces sergeant near Cambodia. One buried on the back page of the *Stars and Stripes* so that the men who needed the information would have it, and the other featured prominently so that the men who needed the encouragement would have it.

He got up and walked to the refrigerator. He opened it, removed a cool beer and used the church key that was kept on top of the refrigerator to open the beverage. He took a deep swallow and remembered. He glanced over at the open newspaper and remembered.

Remembered Bates telling him, "I don't care what he did out there. He was a deserter, and I don't think he rates the Medal of Honor."

Gerber had listened to Bates explain, at great length, what the medal stood for. Explain that the men who earned it had done extraordinary things that defied the imagination. Men who had risked their lives, who had lost their lives, rescuing their friends, turning back enemy assaults with staggering losses, who had been wounded, two, three, five times and still directed the battle or carried friends to safety. Men who defied the odds.

All through Bates's explanation Gerber had listened and then said quietly, "You mean like defending a listening post when all your friends are dead and there is no ammo. Defending it with the butt of a broken carbine and a bloody entrenching tool. Leaving nearly seventy dead VC around it."

Bates had rocked back in his chair, stared at his desktop for a long time and then said, "Yeah. Exactly like that."

"We didn't do right by Cavanaugh," Gerber said. "We should have pushed for his medal then. We should have visited him in the hospital. The list of what we should have done is so long that it reaches from here to Cambodia. We all stepped on our dicks on this one, and getting him the Medal of Honor now won't make up for it, but it'll make his parents feel a little better. He deserves it."

"All right, Mack, put in the papers. Get the citations written up and signed and notarized, and I'll take them to General Hull. He knows what's going on. He's been around long enough to understand. I'm sure he'll forward it with a recommendation for approval."

And now Gerber was reading that the President had given the medal to Cavanaugh's parents. Held the ceremony in the Rose Garden on a sunny afternoon with a lot of brass from the Pentagon standing around listening and saluting. Gerber looked at the table, at the photos that were blurry now, and took a deep drink of his beer.

"Yeah!" he said. "You deserved it."

GLOSSARY

AC—Aircraft Commander. Pilot in charge of an aircraft.

AFVN—Armed Forces radio and television network in Vietnam. Army PFC Pat Sajak was probably the most memorable of AFVN's DJs with his loud and long "Gooooooooooood Morning, Vietnam!" The Spinning Wheel of Fortune gives no clues about his whereabouts today.

AK-47—Selective fire assault rifle used by the NVA and the VC. It fired the same ammunition as the SKS carbine, which was used early in the war. The AK-47 replaced it.

AN/PRC-10—Portable radio. Also called Prick-10.

AN/PRC-25—Became the standard infantry radio used in Vietnam. Sometimes called Prick-25.

AO—Area of Operation.

AP ROUNDS—Armor-piercing ammunition.

ARVN—Army of the Republic of Vietnam. South Vietnamese soldier. Also known as Marvin Arvin.

ASH AND TRASH—Single ship flights by helicopters taking care of a variety of missions, such as flying cargo, supplies, mail and people among the various small camps in Vietnam, for anyone who needed aviation support.

BAR—.30-caliber Browning Automatic Rifle.

BEAUCOUP—Many.

BISCUIT—C-rations. Combat rations.

BLOWER—See *Horn*.

BODY COUNT—Number of enemy killed, wounded or captured during an operation. Used by Saigon and Washington as a means of measuring the progress of the war.

BOOM-BOOM—Term used by Vietnamese prostitutes to sell their product.

BOONDOGGLE—Any military operation that hasn't been completely thought out. An operation that is ridiculous.

BOONIE HATS—Soft cap worn by the grunts in the field when not wearing a steel pot.

BUSHMASTER—Jungle warfare expert or soldier highly skilled in jungle navigation and combat. Also a large deadly snake not common to Vietnam but mighty tasty.

C AND C—Command and Control aircraft that circled overhead to direct the combined air and ground operations.

CARIBOU—Twin-engine cargo transport plane; C-123.

CHINOOK—Army Aviation twin-engine helicopter. CH-47. Shit hook.

CHURCH KEY—Beer can opener used in the days before pop tops.

CLAYMORE—Antipersonnel mine that fires 750 steel balls with a lethal range of 50 meters.

CLOSE AIR SUPPORT—Use of airplanes and helicopters to fire on enemy units near friendly troops.

CMH—Congressional Medal of Honor.

CO CONG—Female Vietcong soldier.

DAI UY—Vietnamese Army rank equivalent to U.S. Army Captain.

DCI—Director, Central Intelligence. Director of the CIA.

DEROS—Date of Estimated Return From Overseas Service

DONG—Unit of North Vietnamese money about equal to an American penny.

FIIGMO—Fuck It, I've Got My Orders.

FIVE—Radio call sign for the Executive Officer of a unit.

FNG—Fucking New Guy.

FRENCH FORT—Distinctive, triangular structure built by the hundreds throughout Vietnam by the French.

FUBAR—Fucked Up Beyond All Recognition.

GARAND—M-1 rifle, which was replaced by the M-14. Issued to the Vietnamese early in the war.

GO-TO-HELL RAG—Towel or any large cloth worn around the neck by grunts to absorb perspiration, clean their weapons and dry their hands.

GRUNT—Infantryman.

GUARD THE RADIO—To stand by in the communications bunker and listen for incoming messages.

GUNSHIP—Armed helicopter or cargo plane that carries weapons instead of cargo.

HE—High-explosive ammunition.

HOOTCH—Almost any shelter, from temporary to long-term.

HORN—Specific radio communications network in Vietnam that used satellites to rebroadcast messages.

HORSE—See *Biscuit*.

HOTEL THREE—Helicopter landing area at Saigon's Tan Son Nhut Air Force Base.

HUEY—Bell helicopter. Slick. Called a Huey because its original designation was HU, but it was later changed to UH.

IN-COUNTRY—American troops operating in South Vietnam were all in-country.

INTELLIGENCE—Any information about enemy operations, including troop movements, weapons capabilities, biographies of enemy commanders and general information about terrain features. It is any information that could be useful in planning a mission. Also refers to the branch of the military that specifically deals with the gathering of such information.

KABAR—Military combat knife.

KIA—Killed In Action. Since the U.S. was not engaged in a declared war, the use of KIA was not authorized. KIA came to mean enemy dead. Americans were KHA or Killed in Hostile Action.

KLICK—One thousand meters. Kilometer.

LEGS—Derogatory term for regular infantry used by airborne qualified troops.

LIMA LIMA—Land line. Telephone communications between two points on the ground.

LLDB—Luc Luong Dac Biet. South Vietnamese Special Forces. Sometimes referred to as the Look Long, Duck Back.

LP—Listening Post. Position outside the perimeter manned by a couple of soldiers to warn of enemy activity.

LZ—Landing Zone.

M-14—Standard rifle of the U.S. Army, eventually replaced by the M-16. It fires the standard NATO 7.62 mm round.

M-16—Became the standard infantry weapon of the Vietnam War. It fires 5.56 mm ammunition.

M-79—Short barreled, shoulder-fired weapon that fires a 40 mm grenade, which can be high-explosive, white phosphorus or canister.

MACV—Military Assistance Command, Vietnam. Replaced MAAG—the Military Assistance Advisory Group—in 1964

MEDEVAC—Medical Evacuation. Dustoff. Helicopter used to take wounded to medical facilities.

MIA—Missing In Action.

NCO—Noncommission Officer. Noncom. Sergeant.

NCOIC—NCO In Charge. Senior NCO in a unit, detachment or a patrol

NEXT—The man who said he was the next to be rotated home. See *Short-timer*.

NINETEEN—Average age of the combat soldier in Vietnam, in contrast to age twenty-six in the Second World War.

NOUC-MAM—Foul smelling fermented fish sauce used by the Vietnamese as a condiment.

NVA—North Vietnamese Army. Also used to designate a soldier from North Vietnam.

OD—Olive Drab, the standard military color.

P-38—Military designation for the small one-piece can opener supplied with C-rations.

PETA-PRIME—Black tarlike substance that melted in the heat of the day to become a sticky black nightmare that clung to boots, clothes and equipment. It was used to hold down the dust during the dry season.

PETER PILOT—Copilot of a helicopter.

POW—Prisoner Of War.

POGUES—Derogatory term describing fat, lazy people who inhabited rear areas, taking all the best supplies for themselves and leaving the rest for the men in the field.

PSP—Perforated Steel Plate used instead of pavement for runways and roadways.

PULL PITCH—Term used by helicopter pilots that means they are going to take off.

PUNJI STAKE—Sharpened bamboo stake hidden to penetrate the foot, sometimes dipped in feces to increase the likelihood of infection.

QT—Quick Time. It came to mean talking to someone quietly on the side rather than operating in official channels.

R AND R—Rest and Relaxation. The term came to mean a trip outside Vietnam where the soldier could forget about the war.

RF STRIKERS—Local military forces recruited and employed inside a province. Known as Regional Forces.

RINGKNOCKER—Graduate of a military academy. The term refers to the ring worn by all graduates.

RPD—7.62 mm Soviet light machine gun.

RTO—Radiotelephone operator. Radio man of a unit.

RULES OF ENGAGEMENT—Rules telling American troops when they could fire. Full Suppression meant they could fire all the way in on a landing. Normal

Rules meant they could return fire for fire received. Negative Suppression meant they weren't to shoot back.

SAPPER—Enemy soldier trained in use of demolitions. Used explosives during attacks.

SHIT HOOK—Name applied by troops to the Chinook helicopter because of all the "shit" stirred up by the massive rotors.

SHORT—Term used by a GI in Vietnam to tell all who would listen that his tour was almost over.

SHORT-TIMER—GI who had been in Vietnam for nearly a year and who would be rotated back to the World soon. When the DEROS (Date of Estimated Return From Overseas Service) was the shortest in the unit, the person was said to be *Next*.

SIX—Radio call sign for the Unit Commander.

SKS—Simonov 7.62 mm semiautomatic carbine.

SMG—Submachine gun.

SOI—Signal Operating Instructions. The booklet that contained the call signs and radio frequencies of the units in Vietnam.

SOP—Standard Operating Procedure.

STEEL POT—Standard U.S. Army helmet. It consisted of a fiber helmet liner with an outer steel cover.

STORMY WEATHER—Code name for the Cambodian border.

TAI—Vietnamese ethnic group living in the mountainous regions.

TEAM UNIFORM—UHF radio frequency on which the team communicates. Frequencies were changed periodically in an attempt to confuse the enemy.

THREE—Radio call sign of the Operations Officer.

THREE CORPS—Military area around Saigon. Vietnam was divided into four corps areas.

TOC—Tactical Operations Center.

TOT—Time Over Target. Refers to the time the aircraft are supposed to be over the drop zone with the parachutists, or the target if the planes are bombers.

TWO—Radio call sign of the Intelligence officer.

TWO-OH-ONE (201) FILE—Military records file that listed all a soldier's qualifications, training, experience and abilities. It was passed from unit to unit so that the new commander would have some idea of the incoming soldier's capabilities.

VC—Vietcong. Also Victor Charlie (phonetic alphabet) or Charlie.

VIETCONG—Contraction of Vietnam Cong San (Vietnamese Communist Party, established in 1956.)

WIA—Wounded in Action.

WILLIE PETE—WP. White Phosphorus. Smoke Rounds. Also used as antipersonnel weapons.

WORLD—United States. Always referred to as "the World."

XO—Executive Officer of a unit.

ZIPPO—A flamethrower.

"What scares you about North Vietnam?" Gerber whispered

"It truly is my home," Kit answered. "If we are caught, I will be shot as a spy, but not before I am tortured. They have some people who enjoy that work..."

"Kit, if any of us are caught, we're going to be shot as spies."

"Please, do not let them catch me." Her voice was insistent, with a note of terror.

"I can't—"

"You *can*," she interrupted. "You can make sure that I am not captured. Please, Captain. As a friend you cannot deny me this one request."

Gerber sat back, forcing himself into the corner between the side of the truck and the cab. With his free hand he wiped the sweat from his face. He needed a breath of fresh air. He felt hot and his stomach was fluttering because he knew what Kit was asking of him.

If they got into a situation where they might be captured, she wanted him to kill her.

VIETNAM: GROUND ZERO
GUIDELINES
ERIC HELM

A GOLD EAGLE BOOK
London · Toronto · New York · Sydney

ISBN 0 373 62708 4 (Pocket edition)

First published in Great Britain in pocket edition by Gold Eagle 1988

© Eric Helm 1987

Australian copyright 1987
Philippine copyright 1987
Pocket Edition 1988

This OMNIBUS EDITION 1989
ISBN 0 373 57746 X

8911
Made and printed in Great Britain

VIETNAM: GROUND ZERO

GUIDELINES

ERIC HELM

PROLOGUE

OVER THE GULF OF TONKIN

The darkened coast of North Vietnam, painted in a glowing green line on the F-4 Phantom fighter-bomber's radar-scope, was still almost a hundred miles distant. Captain David Bidwell, a lean young man, kept his face pressed close to the blackout hood, his eyes glued to the screen with its sweeping green arm, studying the coastline, searching for the point where they were supposed to cross it. A necessary task for their rendezvous with the Wild Weasel escort.

The pilot, Captain Richard Wornell, a shorter, stockier man than his WSO, began a long slow descent that would bring them closer to the ground. He kept his gaze outside of the cockpit, looking down at the silvery wisps of the cloud deck, which was lighted by the nearly full moon above them. Over his shoulder, the stars blazed like thousands of pin-sized spotlights in the night sky. To his right was the dark shape of another aircraft.

Without a word to either his backseater or his wingman, he began a gradual turn, following the VDI, which had slipped slightly to the left. As the wingman pulled away, they entered the overcast. Wornell now could see nothing other than the blackness around him, broken by flashes of gray from the cloud cover and the dull glow of the red and green navigation lights of the other aircraft.

Bidwell knew exactly where they were. The radar mapped the coast with unerring accuracy. He sat straight up for a moment, his eyes now on the other instruments as he arched his back to relax the muscles. Then he pressed his face to the hood as the coast of North Vietnam slipped under their aircraft. Bidwell told Wornell that they were no longer feet wet.

They broke out of the clouds and continued their descent until they were close to the deck. Wornell squeezed the control yoke until his hand ached, but he couldn't relax. He was nervous, flying at nearly five hundred knots, at night, so close to the ground.

To the right he saw a stream of tracers streaking upward, looking like a string of glowing green baseballs. Moments later a second string was fired, but neither burst was near him nor his wingman. Probably just a North Vietnamese farmer shooting at the roar of the jet engines with his militia issued AK-47.

They raced on, climbing to avoid hills, then dropping back into the valleys. Wornell, moving his head as if on a swivel, ignored his instruments now because he was much too close to the ground. Their response was too slow at this altitude, and he didn't have the time to glance at them, and instead tried to concentrate on the roar of his own twin turbines, waiting for a change in the pitch that would warn him of impending disaster.

There was a buzz in Wornell's headset and the sky around him burst into flame as a 57 mm antiaircraft gun opened fire. Wornell ignored the flashes, tightening his grip on the yoke. His wingman, for a moment nothing more than a shadow in the distance, moved nearer and then fell away.

"Got a SAM low light," said Bidwell.

"Weasel Lead, this is Baron Lead," radioed Wornell. "We have a SAM warning."

"Baron, this is Weasel Lead. We have a radar lock. Going in," came the reply.

"Radar's off," said Bidwell.

Wornell grinned at that. If the North Vietnamese operators didn't keep the acquisition and tracking radars on, they couldn't fire the missiles. And if they did fire, the missiles would be ineffective as they blindly climbed into the dark. They needed the radar guidance.

"More Triple A," said Bidwell.

Wornell glanced to the right. It was as if the ground was carpeted with strobes. The muzzle flashes of the weapons sparkled, sending up fountains of green tracers. The sky was alive with them, swarming upward, trying to knock down the American aircraft.

"Got visual on a SAM Two site," said Bidwell.

Wornell saw the missile site, a rosebud pattern on the ground, the black ribbons of road leading to the missile launch areas. There were revetments of dirt around each missile, making it difficult for bombers to take out all six positions at once. Hidden away were the radar vans, the maintenance trucks and repair vehicles and the command post.

The site was dark and Wornell saw no one on it as they flew by. The radar vans and command posts that were usually targets of the Wild Weasels, were somewhere else, separated from the actual launch complex by as much as a klick.

As they crossed the complex, Wornell relaxed slightly. There were still no warning lights on his panel. The missile radars, the Spoon Rest and the Fan Song, which were needed to acquire the target and guide the missiles, had been shut down. The Weasels had done their jobs.

Then out of the corner of his eye Wornell saw a flash as rocket motors ignited. Before he could react, the missile was off the ground. Helplessly he watched the streak of yellow-white flame homing on the tail of his wingman. An explosion at the rear of the Phantom seemed to lift it up and flip it over. A ball of red-orange flame burst around the aircraft, enveloping it completely. Then there was a secondary explosion followed by a shower of flaming debris raining onto the rice paddies of North Vietnam.

"Jesus H. Christ on a crutch," said Bidwell. "What in the fuck hit him?"

"Missile," said Wornell. The single word nearly stuck in his throat.

"There were no warning lights."

Wornell keyed the mike for the radio. "We're taking missile fire down here."

"Roger," came the reply from Weasel Lead. "We have no warning lights."

"Baron Two is down to missile fire," said Wornell. There was no emotion in his voice. He was merely reporting a fact to the Weasel Lead.

"There's one coming at us," yelled Bidwell.

"Hit the chaff," ordered Wornell as he rolled the jet to the left, diving toward the ground. An instant later he hauled back on the yoke, beginning a spiraling climb that rocked both men, slamming them against the restraining straps of their shoulder harnesses.

"Chaff's no good," said Bidwell.

Wornell rolled the aircraft to the left and then back to the right, finally diving toward the ground again, pulling up at the last moment as the engines screamed and the aircraft shuddered, fighting the stress. As he broke to the left the missile slammed harmlessly into a rice paddy.

"Another one!" said Bidwell. "Where the fuck are they coming from?"

Wornell had no chance to answer. He began a steep climb, rolled the aircraft over into a power dive, twisting back and forth. He couldn't check to see the missile's progress. All he could do was flip from one maneuver to another in an attempt to evade the missile, using its greater speed, which produced a wider turning radius, against it.

As he leveled out, he was smashed forward, as if someone had struck the back of his seat with a sledgehammer. He could feel pain in his shoulders and a curtain of black descended until his vision was like looking down a long, dark tunnel. Around him he was aware of buzzers and bells and the cockpit seemed to be filled with smoke. There was a whining, two-tone warning buzzer demanding attention.

For a moment he couldn't figure out what had happened. The aircraft was buffeting, bouncing around like a speeding car on a rutted road. Glancing out, he noticed that the wings were riddled by shrapnel and trailing a thin plume of smoke.

Wornell tried to initiate a climb. The nose of the aircraft came up, but the shuddering became worse as the jet threatened to tear itself apart. Before Wornell could order the bailout, the canopy was ripped away and the cockpit was filled with the roar of the wind.

Seconds later Wornell ejected, his arms wrapped about his head to protect it. The wall of wind hit him like a brick through a plate-glass window and forced his arms against his helmet. Clear of the burning aircraft, he opened his eyes as the jet began a long, shallow descent into the rice paddies below. A spectacular yellow-orange explosion lit up the night sky as the plane struck the ground, destroying itself in a roiling cloud of black smoke.

The parachute popped, jerking at Wornell. Not far away, the backseater was hanging from his own canopy, drifting down into the night, sliding away from Wornell until he lost sight of the man in the darkness. A single stream of tracers reached out of the dark, arcing toward him, but didn't come close. He couldn't hear the sound of the firing or see the muzzle flashes of the weapon.

Wornell landed with a splash in a foul-smelling rice paddy. He rolled to his right and hit the quick release, dropping his chute away from him. Wet from head to foot, he scrambled to his feet, then rubbed a hand over his face, trying to wipe the excrement-laden water from his eyes. After his vision returned to normal, he reached to his right and drew the .38-caliber revolver from the holster sewn into his survival vest. Slowly he turned three hundred and sixty degrees to survey his surroundings.

The world around him was so quiet that he wondered if he had lost his hearing during the bailout. After a moment or two he became aware of the distant pop of Triple A as the tracers danced skyward. Myriad streams crisscrossed each other like a cheap fireworks display.

Knee deep in the clammy paddy, and with water dripping from the barrel of his weapon, he gazed at the flash and pop of flack as the enemy gunners tried to down more of the American planes. The breath was rasping in his throat, as if he had run a long distance, and he found that he was suddenly quite thirsty. His desire for water nearly overwhelmed him.

Out loud, he said, "It's not fair. We didn't get a launch warning. They can't do that."

1

UBON AIR FORCE BASE
THAILAND

The special meeting had been called for thirteen hundred hours on Thursday, the twenty-fourth. Jerry Maxwell, dressed in a rumpled white suit, stood in the hot tropical sun, sweating heavily. Maxwell was a short man who had lost weight during his tour in Vietnam so that he looked gaunt. His black hair was sweat damp and plastered against his forehead. Dark circles under his light-colored eyes contrasted sharply with his permanently sunburned skin, and the fact that he needed a shave all helped to give him the appearance of a starving clown. He watched the F-4 Phantoms taxiing toward the runways in front of him. The sleek aircraft were camouflage painted and carrying heavy bomb payloads, taking off for missions against suspected enemy positions in South Vietnam, Cambodia and southern Laos.

Maxwell turned, squinted at the palm tree near the door to Operations, and then stepped back into the shade. He drew a handkerchief from his hip pocket and mopped his face, leaving a light brown stain on the cloth. A Jeep with three passengers pulled into the parking space in front of the Operations hangar. Two of the vehicle's occupants were dressed in crisp, starched jungle fatigues topped off by soft baseball caps, and carried M-16s. The other was bare-headed and wore a lightweight, light blue suit, looking as if he couldn't wait to get inside where there was some air-conditioning.

As they hopped out of the vehicle, the man in the suit approached Maxwell and said, "Come on, Jerry. No need to stand around out here sweating."

"Yes, sir." The group moved toward the door and entered the building, running smack into a wall of cold air.

They made their way down a narrow corridor, which was paneled in dark wood about halfway up and then painted a light blue to the ceiling. The floor was waxed concrete, and an unbroken line of fluorescent lights ran along the middle of the ceiling. They took the first stairwell they came to and climbed to the second floor. Not far away was a doorway leading to a conference room.

It was typical of the conference rooms on any American military base. In the center of the room sat a large table. On it was a water pitcher beaded with moisture and surrounded by six glasses. There were a dozen metal chairs around the table, with a high-backed leather one at its head. A bank of windows, partially hidden behind venetian blinds, looked out onto the airfield. On the other three walls were water-colors of jets in revetments, taking off, dropping bombs, shooting down MiGs, and limping home.

Maxwell slipped into one of the chairs and shivered as the cold air dried the sweat on his body. He reached for one of the glasses, decided that he didn't really want a drink, and rocked back, waiting. Within minutes they were joined by four more military officers and two civilians.

One of the officers was an Air Force brigadier general. He wore tailored jungle fatigues with embroidered stars on the collar and command pilot wings above the left breast. He moved toward the leather chair at the head of the table, but instead of sitting, he stood behind it, and placed his hands on the back rest as he surveyed the men around him.

"Gentlemen," he began. "For those of you who don't know me, I'm General Thomas Christie and I'll be chairing this meeting. Our recommendations will be forwarded through the chain of command to both the Pentagon and General Westmoreland. With me are Colonel Edward Kent, Majors Andrew Dillon, Roger Quinn and the Wild Weasel flight leader, Terry McMance. Next to him is Captain Charles Fallon."

Christie then sat down and looked at the civilians. "Mr. Cornett, would you be so kind as to introduce your people?"

Cornett, a short, stocky man sporting a beard that was inconsistent with the clean-shaven ravings of most of the power structure nodded and said, "Certainly, General. To my right are Tim Underwood, Paul Harris and Jerry Maxwell."

"Thank you," said Christie. He picked up a black folder with the Air Force crest embossed on the cover and opened it. "I have a simple agenda for the meeting and would like to stick to it as closely as possible. If anyone has any objections, we'll discuss those in a few moments."

He glanced at the men around him and said, "All right. First we'll get a report from Major McMance concerning his observations over North Vietnam two nights ago. Captain Fallon will supplement that description with his own observations. Colonel Kent will discuss the recent developments of the Soviet SAM force."

Cornett interrupted at that point. "Mr. Underwood has made a recent study of the Soviet SAM threat and might have some insights along those lines. That includes developments of new missile systems that are not deployed outside the Soviet Union. We do have some photographic intelligence available to us."

"Good," said Christie. "Finally, Major Quinn and Major Dillon will discuss the possible tactics we can use to counter this new threat." He looked up from his notes. "That about cover it?"

There was a murmur of agreement and then silence. Christie smiled, "From this point, I think everything we say will be classified as secret. I don't want any of it discussed outside of this room."

When no one said anything, Christie nodded. "Okay, Major McMance, you want to lead off?"

"Yes, sir." McMance stood and moved so that he was near the head of the table. McMance was a tall, thin man with black hair and bushy eyebrows. His face was tanned a deep brown and with his brown eyes, he looked Latin.

"Is everyone familiar with the Wild Weasel concept?" He glanced from man to man and saw a couple of them shaking their heads.

"The short course, then," he said, grinning. "The idea is simple enough. The North Vietnamese, using equipment supplied by the Soviets, are shooting at our bombing forces. Almost all the acquisition and guidance is radar controlled, whether for the SAMs or the Triple A. The Wild Weasels detect the radar signals and, using Shrike missiles that ride the radar beams back to their sources, attack the radar vans and the co-located command vehicles. Knocking out the radar effectively blinds the antiaircraft capability whether it is missile or ZSU-23, S-60 or 57 mm."

"But the missiles themselves are not damaged?" queried Underwood.

"No, sir. The command vehicles and radar vans are normally a couple of klicks from the missile or Triple A site."

"Then the missiles can still be fired," said Underwood.

"Yes, sir. The Triple A also has the capability to be fired through optical sights, but it becomes very ineffective that way. Most of the missiles won't be fired because of the lack of tracking radar.''

''What if they simply turn off the radar while you're overhead?'' The puzzled look that Underwood wore began to disappear.

''That's the beauty of the system,'' replied McMance, smiling. ''If the radar set is off, they can't detect and track our planes. If they turn it on, we attack it. Either way, we've won.''

McMance hesitated and then looked at Christie.

''If no one has any further questions,'' said the general, ''we'll move on.''

''I've seen no figures on how effective this Wild Weasel thing has been,'' said Underwood.

McMance had started back to his seat, but halted. ''After implementation of the concept, our losses to enemy antiaircraft dropped off significantly. Prior to that, losses were running so high that it was becoming suicidal to attack the North.''

''Captain Fallon,'' said Christie, ''do you want to tell us what happened two days ago.''

''Yes, sir.'' Fallon stood, but didn't move away from his seat. Like McMance, he was tall and thin. Reduced body weight of the pilots and electronic warfare officers meant higher payloads. His hair was sandy blond and his face burned pink. He had light, washed-out eyes.

Fallon's voice was high and squeaky. He cleared his throat once and said, ''The thing that bothers us is that there were missile launches from a standard SA-2 site, but no radar indications that we were being tracked. No indications that the site was active.''

''My information,'' said Underwood, ''is that the Soviets are moving the radars and command vehicles off the sites. You wouldn't get the radar detection indications if the radar vans have been moved.''

"I understand that, sir," said Fallon. "We've seen the North Vietnamese following that example. We just flood the whole area with aircraft and hit them when we get the radar detection. Besides, the jets being painted would get SAM lights. No, sir, we believe there has been a drastic change in the Soviet missile technology."

Underwood emitted a laugh that sounded like a bark. "That's quite a conclusion based on a single raid."

"We saw launches off a SAM Two site and there were no radar indications. If they can do it again, we'll have no defense against it. Their Triple A, designed to fire up to fifteen, twenty thousand feet and to use optical as well as radar sights, coupled to the Guideline with a range of up to ninety thousand feet will create a protective umbrella that we can't penetrate. We can't fly under it or over it. The air war suddenly evaporates."

"You're being overly dramatic," said Underwood.

Christie slammed a hand to the tabletop. "Damn it! You don't have to fly those missions, Underwood. You have no idea what it's like flying into a wall of flack and missiles. If we can't counter this threat, you're going to see a reduction in the air war."

Underwood stared at the general for a moment and then looked to Cornett. "Sir, I think this is an overreaction to a perceived new threat. I don't think we have a problem here except one created by the Air Force."

Cornett nodded his agreement and said, "General?"

Christie turned his attention to Fallon. "Captain, can you make your case clearer for these men?"

"Yes, sir. Up until two nights ago, we had no launches from a Guideline SAM site without a radar indication. Now that indication may have been fleeting. The operator turning on his radar, getting a blip and turning it right back off. No matter, because we picked up the warning indications.

Two nights ago, we got no radar indications, but we did get missile launches from those sites."

"Does that make it clear, Underwood?" asked Christie.

"No, sir, it doesn't."

"Damn it, man," snapped Cornett. "It means they've developed a new guidance system for their missiles and we have to come up with a way to counter it."

Underwood nodded, his eyes on the table. He looked like a little boy who had been reprimanded in school. All he said was, "Oh."

"Yes, oh," said Cornett. "Now, are we certain that the launches came from an SA-2?"

"From the site, yes," said Fallon. "There is no question about it."

For the next hour they discussed the state of Soviet missile technology. The CIA representatives argued against a sudden improvement in the Soviets' missile abilities and then pointed out that even if there had been one, it wouldn't be given to the North Vietnamese.

Maxwell listened to it all calmly, never speaking. When they all wound down, he said, "I'd like to add one thing. In May, 1960, Soviet missile technology took a giant leap forward when they knocked down a U-2. Totally unexpected. And not unlike the situation we find ourselves in now."

"Except the Soviets didn't give that technology to an ally," said Underwood.

Maxwell ignored Underwood, looked at the general. "He's right about it. They didn't give it away, but they did use it to knock down the U-2, which told us something that we didn't know. That they could do it. We have the same situation here. A sudden improvement in their technology."

"Then you see nothing inconsistent with their behavior in the past," said Christie.

"No, sir. I think we'd better investigate this further as quickly as possible."

Christie closed his folder. "Gentlemen, I think we've gone far enough for today. We'll meet again tomorrow. At that time I'll want recommendations to take up the chain of command."

Outside, as they walked to their Jeeps, Cornett pulled Maxwell to the side. He glanced right and left to make sure that no one was near him. Then he pulled off his sunglasses and stared straight into Maxwell's eyes.

"Jerry," he said, and then stopped as the scream of a plane taking off drowned out everything he said. When it was airborne, he continued. "I want you to return to Saigon tonight. We're not going to need you here for the rest of this."

"I didn't contribute much to it today," agreed Maxwell.

"You weren't ordered here to contribute to this discussion. I wanted you to listen in. I did that because you've been working with the Special Forces SOG in Saigon, and those guys always have answers."

"Yes, sir."

"Then you can see where I'm going with this. Hell, we can't put a CIA man into the North to look things over. He'd stick out like a sore thumb. And we don't have anyone infiltrated into the Soviet delegation there. Besides we've no one trained to operate in the jungle . . ."

"You want me to come up with someone to go into the North and look at one of these missile sites."

"Yes. You've got the people to do it. Some of those Sneaky Petes you work with would be perfect. Have them parachute in, take a look at one of the sites, steal a fucking guidance system if they have to, and then bug out. Answers everyone's questions and gives us all the information we need to counter the threat."

"I don't know about this," said Maxwell.

Again Cornett looked around, as if afraid that someone was going to sneak up to listen. He wiped the perspiration from his forehead and slipped his sunglasses on. "Don't bullshit me, Jerry. You've had people in the North before. Or if you haven't, SOG has. They've been operating there for years. That's not a problem and you know it."

"No," said Maxwell shaking his head. "No, I guess it isn't."

"Okay," said Cornett. "What I want you to do is catch the first ride back to Saigon and set something up. I want those men on the ground in North Vietnam inside of forty-eight hours."

Now Maxwell laughed. "I can't put something like that together that fast. The coordination, getting the men together and then into the field is impossible that quickly. Hell, it'll take a week to work out the airlift."

"Jerry, you have your orders. I want an answer to this inside the week. We don't have time to fuck around on it. I know that the President will be asking the DCI for some answers and I don't want him to have to say that he doesn't know. I want him to be able to hand the President a completed report on this so that he'll see we have it wired."

Maxwell rubbed a hand through his hair. He looked at the ground and then up at a nearby palm. The sound of the jets on the airfield threatened to drown out their voices. The light breeze was more like the wind from a blast furnace.

"I'll do what I can," Maxwell said. "I can put a team in there, I just don't know if forty-eight hours is enough time."

"You can have whatever you need except extra time. Priorities will be arranged all the way. If you run into trouble, you call me and I'll see to it that the roadblock disappears."

"Yes, sir. I'll get right on it."

"And Jerry," said Cornett, "we have to keep this discreet. The political situation in the States is volatile. We don't want a lot of publicity on this."

"I understand," said Maxwell. It was the same kind of directive that he worked under all the time.

2

MICHELIN RUBBER PLANTATION NORTHWEST OF SAIGON RVN

U.S. Army Special Forces Master Sergeant Anthony B. Fetterman stood in the shade of the rubber trees, one hand on the rough bark, and watched the ARVN ranger trainees sweep through the bunkerline.

Fetterman was a diminutive man with black, balding hair, dark, cold, hard eyes and a heritage that he claimed to be Aztec. The two hundred would-be graduates of the ARVN ranger school were having their final examination in the field with the American Special Forces.

There had been reports of VC operating in the vicinity of Dau Tieng. The Saigon government wanted the ARVN, with the help of the Special Forces, to search for enemy activity.

Fetterman was out there, as was Captain MacKenzie K. Gerber, to evaluate the unit and to coordinate assistance if the rangers happened to find more of the enemy than they expected. He waited as three men explored a bunker, two standing outside it, on either side of the entrance, while the third man dived into it. When the man reappeared, shaking his head, Fetterman relaxed and moved toward the Special Forces captain, checking his watch.

"I make it two more hours," said Fetterman. He wiped the sweat on his face with his sleeve.

Gerber nodded but didn't speak. He was a career officer, and on the promotion list for major. Gerber was a tall, well-muscled man with brown hair and blue eyes. At the moment he looked hot and miserable, the sweat turning his jungle fatigues black under the arms and down the back. He held his M-16 by the rear sight mount, which looked like a luggage handle. At first his attention was on Fetterman and then he glanced at the ARVN rangers as they filtered through the rubber trees.

Unlike the jungle and forests that surrounded the plantation, this was a well-manicured area that looked like an overgrown orchard. The trees were evenly spaced, planted in rows with a thin ground cover. It was almost like a park inside the plantation.

Finally he said, "Let's get them out of here and move toward the west and the base there."

"Yes, sir," Fetterman said. Resignedly he turned and stepped closer to the Vietnamese officer who had attached himself to the RTO. Fetterman had cautioned the man three times that the enemy liked to shoot the people with the radio man, figuring they'd get the officers, but the ARVN wouldn't listen.

Almost as if to prove his point, a single shot rang out in the distance. There was a muffled pop and a snap as the round passed overhead. Fetterman dived to the right, twisting around, looking for the source. A number of the men were standing upright as if they hadn't figured out what was going on. One of them was pointing to the north.

"Hit the dirt!" Fetterman shouted.

There was a second shot and a scream of pain. One of the rangers grabbed his shoulder as he fell to the ground. He spun, rocking from side to side, his right hand against his left shoulder. Blood was welling between his fingers as he continued to scream.

A ripple of firing broke out, the rattling of M-16 rifles. The men had scattered, taking up positions behind the trees, along the sides of the bunkers, or on the ground with nothing between them and the enemy. Some of them fired their weapon by holding it around the trunk of the tree and squeezing the trigger without looking for a target.

Fetterman crawled to his left, where the wounded man was still screaming. He grabbed the man and held him down. With his free hand, he peeled the ARVN's fingers from the wound. It was a clean shot through the shoulder, and the blood was washing it. Fetterman shook out a bandage from his first-aid kit and pressed it to the wound and then let the man grab it again, holding the gauze in place.

In the meantime, Gerber had worked his way to the RTO and the ARVN ranger commander. The ARVN CO was crouched behind a bunker, his hands holding his helmet tightly to his head. Although he couldn't see the man's face, Gerber was certain that he had his eyes closed.

"*Dai uy,*" Gerber said. "You'd better organize your response. You have a sniper, two men at most out there."

"We shoot and they run," the CO said without looking up. He remained frozen in place.

"They won't run away. They'll wait and then shoot someone else the first chance they get."

"We shoot and they run," he repeated.

"*Dai uy,*" said Gerber. "It's your responsibility to get the men up and moving."

This time the man didn't speak. Gerber stared at him for a moment. Around him the Vietnamese were still shooting in ill coordinated and ragged volleys. Bullets were snapping through the thick green leaves of the rubber trees, and slamming into the trunks.

Off to the right, one of the Vietnamese NCOs was suddenly on his feet. Shouting at his men, he pointed deeper into the trees. He ran to one man, jerked him to his feet and shoved him toward the enemy position.

Gerber took a final look at the officer who hadn't moved or spoken since the last fusillade, then leaped up. He raced toward the Vietnamese sergeant and dropped to the ground near him. Gerber wasn't going to say a word to him, unless he did something stupid.

The NCO ran to another of the Vietnamese and snatched the M-79 grenade launcher out of his hands. He screamed at the soldier who then surrendered the spare ammo for the weapon. The man refused to get to his feet.

Gerber shook his head and mumbled, "This is the best they've got?"

The NCO was up and moving from one tree to the next. He stopped, shouted a command. The firing, which had been tapering off, suddenly started up again. A couple of the soldiers pointed their weapons at the sky and pulled the triggers, firing on full auto until the bolts locked back, their rifles empty.

Others were shooting into the trees, firing short bursts and reloading as necessary. The Vietnamese NCO began to move again, dodging from tree to tree. Leaping to cover, he rolled right, and then clawed his way forward.

Gerber followed him, watching his every move. He was grinning, thinking of Captain Minh, the camp commander when Gerber had been assigned to Camp A-555 on his first tour. Minh had been the same kind of self-starter. A soldier's soldier in anyone's army. There were so few of them that it was a pleasure to find one.

The NCO slid into a depression, broke open the M-79 and dropped a round into it. He flipped up the sight, worked it up and down and then sighted on where he suspected the enemy sniper was hiding. He pulled the trigger and waited to see where the round hit. He ducked, his eyes on the enemy position. There was a dull thump and a tiny cloud of black smoke at the base of a tree.

As the NCO fired two more times, Gerber ran toward the wounded man. Fetterman had dragged him to cover behind one of the trees and had dressed the wound. He now held his canteen to the man's lips, letting him drink.

"How bad?" asked Gerber.

"Through and through. I think the shoulder is pretty torn up, but he's not in danger of dying right now."

"Medevac?"

"I'm not thrilled with that idea, Captain. It could be a trap to get us to bring in a chopper and give someone else a shot at it. Could be what they had in mind."

"Yeah," said Gerber. "Get the Vietnamese medic on this guy and then you get a sweep going to the west, toward the LZ there. I'll be checking on that NCO. See what he does next."

Fetterman grinned. "Since these guys are still in school, I say they flunk."

Gerber turned and ran back, dodging around the rubber trees. He dropped to the ground behind the NCO, who had stopped firing his M-79 and was watching the field in front of him. There was the pop and crack of weapons as the troops fired single shots now. A few of the Vietnamese fired tracers, bright burning rubies that bounced across the ground. None of the fire was incoming.

Finally the NCO got to his feet, jogged to the right and fell next to a man with an M-16. The sergeant took the rifle, leaving the soldier with the grenade launcher and spare ammo. Then, on his feet again, he pointed to several men, gesturing that they should move forward. Together, the line of infantry advanced, half of them covering, while the others sprinted among the trees. When the forward line had moved twenty or thirty yards, they fell into firing positions so that the men behind could move up.

They continued that maneuver for a couple of minutes. Gerber followed behind the rear guard, watching them carefully, but offered no advice or help. As he approached there was a burst of rifle fire. A single staccato ripping of M-16 ammo followed it. Everyone dived for cover and shooting broke out along the line.

The Vietnamese NCO was on his feet suddenly, shouting at his men. He ran forward, hurdled a small bush and disappeared behind it. A second later there was a long burst from an M-16, two return shots from an AK-47 and then complete silence. The sergeant suddenly reappeared, the AK held over his head like a trophy.

The Vietnamese rangers lost the little discipline they had. A dozen of them leaped to their feet, running forward toward the sergeant. They were screaming wildly, like rebel soldiers storming the Yankee lines. Gerber followed, yelling at them to watch their security, watch for booby traps, but no one was listening.

From the trees came a shot, followed by four more, all from M-16s. Gerber arrived in time to see two of the Vietnamese rangers firing their weapons into the heads of the dead sniper and his spotter, splattering their blood and brains over the soft decaying ground.

"Cease fire!" ordered Gerber. He snapped his fingers at the NCO who was standing off to the side.

One of the rangers looked at Gerber, the anger on his face unmistakable. Then, in defiance, he spun and put a burst into one of the dead VC's chests. The impact of the rounds caused the body to shudder. Blood had stained his shirt a rusty brown and soaked the ground around him. One of the bullets opened the abdomen, spilling his guts to the earth. The odor of the bowels drifted on the light breeze.

"Knock it off," snapped Gerber. "You might need that ammo later. Don't waste it."

The Vietnamese sergeant who had taken charge said something and then stepped next to the shooting man. He grabbed at the weapon, pushing it aside. Then he slapped the man twice. For a moment it looked as if the man was going to shoot the sergeant. Then he turned and stomped away.

"I get them," the sergeant told Gerber.

"Thank you, Sergeant. Very well done." Gerber glanced at the bodies and then at the man's name tape. Le Duc. "Now, is there something else to be done?"

"Oh, yes, sir. I check bodies for papers and insignia. We find out good things from papers and insignia. That helps us to find more VC to kill."

Gerber couldn't help grinning. Trying to teach the Vietnamese how to fight the war was a futile effort. They couldn't understand that a live prisoner was more valuable than a dead man. They couldn't understand why they should collect papers and insignia and not ears and fingers. But once in a while you came across a Vietnamese who seemed to understand exactly what was happening. Someone who was willing to listen and to learn. Sergeant Le Duc was one of the few who did.

"Get the weapons and anything else you can and then return to the group."

"Yes, sir."

Gerber returned to find Fetterman had gotten a perimeter established with the help of the captain who had finally decided to move. It was a ragged perimeter that wouldn't have lasted long if the enemy decided to attack them. The men were scattered through the trees, facing away from the center, each man with a friend close at hand.

"How's the wounded man?"

"Sooner we get him out of here, the better off we're going to be."

"Got the sniper and his spotter," said Gerber. "Doesn't seem to be anyone else with them."

"But there was a lot of shooting over there."

"Yeah. The Viets riddled the bodies when they found them." Gerber crouched, fingered his canteen but decided against taking a drink. "Let's get the sweep under way and secure the LZ. We'll get a Medevac in here and then a flight to take us out."

"You think the exercise is over?" asked Fetterman.

"Tony, these guys are terrible. They haven't the slightest idea of what's going on. I think some district chief designated them rangers to get some equipment for them. Then, because the chief had influence, no one wanted to irritate them with training. We get into a fight with them and they're going to all get killed."

"Yes, sir," said Fetterman. "I noticed their noise discipline was lax and they didn't have much unit integrity. Not to mention that the leadership by the officers didn't exist. What are you going to do?"

"Write a report and give it to the ARVN command and Saigon so they can file it."

"And then?"

"See if I can't con SOG or Maxwell or MACV into letting me go up to Bromhead's camp for a couple of weeks on a fact-finding tour so that I can hide out while the ARVN command cools down."

"What facts will you be looking for?"

"I don't know. There must be something going on that we don't know about. Maybe follow up on the reports of VC and NVA infiltrating the area in unprecedented numbers."

"Yes, sir." Fetterman got to his feet. "Why don't I get these people moving so we can get the fuck out of the heat?"

"Good plan."

THREE HOURS LATER, Gerber, now in clean jungle fatigues and having showered and shaved, sat in the open air bar of the Carasel Hotel in downtown Saigon.

Within minutes, after Fetterman had ordered the evacuation of the wounded man and then called for the helicopters to take them all out, the dustoff chopper had come and gone, and a flight of Hueys had diverted to pick up the rangers. From their camp at Trung Lap, it had been no trouble to hop a ride to Tan Son Nhut. When they had returned to Saigon, they had taken a Jeep from Tan Son Nhut into the city where they had rooms at the Carasel.

The bar where Gerber sat was eight or ten feet above the street. It was a concrete balcony loaded with tropical plants and ferns that obscured some of the view. A bar constructed from stone and red leather and plastic stood at one end, with a single bartender working there. Several Vietnamese women, wearing skimpy costumes, roamed among the closely packed tables, serving the customers, mostly civilians from the embassy or the news media.

Gerber's table sat in the shadow of a nearby building, a spot carefully chosen so that the late afternoon breeze would dry the sweat from his forehead and face. He sipped the ice cold beer, delivered by the sweating barmaid and thought about the nature of the war.

When Fetterman, now wearing a fresh uniform that didn't show any signs of the muggy afternoon, appeared and sat down, Gerber said, "I think I know what's wrong with the Vietnam war."

Fetterman raised an eyebrow, took a sip of the beer that Gerber had ordered for him. "What's that, Captain?"

"Simply that there is no incentive to end it. None whatsoever."

"Yes, sir," said Fetterman. He set the beer on the table, glancing at a group of civilians who were laughing and shouting. "No incentive," he repeated.

"You see," continued Gerber, leaning back in his chair and lacing his fingers behind his head, "a couple of hours ago we were in the field, hot and miserable, sweating and thirsty. Now we sit in a bar, still hot, but we could be cool if we went inside, sipping beer and looking at the ladies. And if we wanted, we could retire to our rooms, watch TV, order room service, and just relax in the air-conditioning until tomorrow."

"And since we're no longer uncomfortable," said Fetterman, "we have no incentive to end the war."

"Right. Now in World War Two, the soldier was in for the duration. Granted, from the landings in France to the end of the war in Europe was something like eleven months, but the soldier who landed in France might have been fighting in Italy before that, or North Africa. They were uncomfortable and miserable and knew they had to stay until they ended the war. They didn't know how long that would be."

"So you're saying," said Fetterman, "that the year-long tour doesn't provide an incentive to end the war."

"Not only that," answered Gerber, "but look at our surroundings. Not exactly uncomfortable. We spend a day or two in the field and then we're back here in our air-conditioned rooms, watching TV and chasing women."

"There are men in the field," said Fetterman. "Men who stay out there most of the time."

"True enough," said Gerber, "but they're the exception rather than the rule. Hell, Tony, how many guys are in Vietnam now? Four, five hundred thousand? And of those how many end up in a combat environment. One in eight? One in nine? And even those guys know they've only got to survive eleven, twelve months and they're out of it. All the officers are rotated every six months. What's the point in knocking yourself out if you know you'll be free and clear in less than a year?"

Fetterman nodded without comment and sipped his beer. He had heard all this before. It seemed that lately, every time they had come back from the field and sat around drinking beer, the captain got off on his this-is-what's-wrong-with-the-war speech. That was not to say that Gerber wasn't right about it.

Smiling, Fetterman said, "If you'd like, sir, I'm sure we could volunteer for a mission that would get us into the field for a few weeks. We could sweat all day humping through the jungle, be miserable all night sleeping in trees and waiting for the sniper's bullet or ambush to cut us down. No TV or air-conditioning or room service."

"That's not what I mean and you know it," snapped Gerber. Then realizing that he had said it all before, he grinned. "Actually, the real solution for this is to call up the National Guard. Those guys would end it in a weekend so they could go home."

At that moment a group of journalists burst into the bar, shouting at the waitress for instant service, hailing at other news people already there, and demanding that the music be turned up so they could hear it.

"Think we should go?" asked Fetterman, draining his beer.

Gerber nodded and then saw Robin Morrow. She was a member of the press community in Saigon. A tall, slender woman with blond hair and green eyes, who had attached herself to Gerber a year before. She was wearing a short skirt, a light blouse stained with perspiration and a camera bag. She flopped into a chair, crossed her legs and then leaned forward, her chin on her palm.

Slowly she turned her head, saw Gerber and didn't move for a moment. It was as if she hadn't recognized him. There was a dreamy look on her face, making it seem that this wasn't the first bar she had visited that afternoon.

For a moment Gerber didn't move. He thought about the things they had shared, the adventures and the romance and the anger. He recalled the incident not too long before when she had stripped on the stage of a nightclub in an attempt to get his attention. He remembered how she had gotten drunk with them after the big fight in the Hobo Woods. He remembered washing her back in a shower, seeing the thin network of scars from the whipping she had endured at the hands of a sadistic Vietcong officer. They had shared so much over so many months, and yet remained strangers.

Before he could move or say anything, Morrow was on her feet, staggering toward him. She dropped into a vacant chair at his table. "Captain Mack Gerber, officer extraordinaire."

"Hi, Robin."

"Hi, Robin," she mimicked. "That all you can think of Captain Mack Gerber?"

"Can we get you a drink?" Fetterman piped up, smiled and added, "Although you don't seem to need one."

"Sure, I'll drink," she said, turning her head toward him in an exaggerated movement. "Anything with alcohol in it. Except a damned beer. Not enough kick in the damned beer." She leaned her elbow on the table, slipped off and sat up as if nothing had happened.

Fetterman got to his feet and said, "I'll see what I can do for you."

Morrow nodded at him, and then ducked her head as she swiveled around so that she could stare at Gerber.

Her eyelids moved up and down with considerable effort, as if she might fall asleep any second. And Gerber was certain that she wasn't very far from it. "Never called me for that dinner you promised. Let good old Colonel Bates take us to dinner once, but you never called. Went to dinner with Tony, but not you."

"Hell, Robin," said Gerber. "I've only been back in-country a couple of weeks."

"Never called," she repeated. "Promised, but never did. Tony called, but you never did. Probably called my sister, though. Probably called Kari."

Gerber felt his stomach grow cold. He took a deep breath, giving himself a moment to think. Robin and her sister. What a pair they had turned out to be. Gerber had fallen for the sister and when she deserted him, had taken up with Robin. It had seemed a bad idea at the time and it had gotten worse over the last few months.

"I haven't talked to your sister for a couple of months," said Gerber. "She doesn't even know I'm here."

Robin laughed, nearly doubled over, her arms wrapped around her stomach. "Ho, that's good. Bet Kari's so pissed she can't see straight. That's very good."

Fetterman reappeared with a drink in hand and set it in front of Morrow. "You really think you need that?" he asked.

"Hell, Tony," she said. "No one needs a drink. I want it, okay with you?"

"Drink up," he said.

"Drink up," she repeated. She wavered for a moment, as if about to fall from her chair. When Gerber reached over to hold her up, she said, "Oh, you can touch me. I don't have the plague. That's fucking nice."

"Look, maybe we'd better get out of here," said Gerber.

She smiled lewdly and leaned toward him. She pulled at the top of her blouse, revealing her cleavage. "You got some plans, Captain Mack? Going to take the drunk to your room?" She seized her drink, spilling some of it on the table.

"Captain," said Fetterman, "you'd better get her out of here. There's no telling what she might do." He spoke quietly, as if she wouldn't understand his words.

Gerber got to his feet and took her elbow while visions of her striptease in the club in downtown Saigon danced in front of him along with the confrontation outside on the street. He had tried to cover her with a jungle jacket while she had shouted at him and a group of GIs had stood around watching, a few of them clapping.

"Come on, Robin, let's go."

"Where we going, Captain Mack?" She picked up her cocktail and drank half of it. She slammed it to the table, spilling the remainder.

"For a little walk. Give you a chance to sober up," he said, lifting her to her feet.

She fell into his arms and looked up at him. "Okay, Captain Mack. Anything you want."

Almost supporting her full weight, he guided her out of the bar and into the hotel. They crossed the carpeted floor of the cavernous lobby, past the Vietnamese-French bell captain who grinned his approval, and into the elevator, which was a gilded cage that rose through the interior of the hotel.

Once upstairs, Gerber guided Morrow to his room, unlocked the door and helped her inside. While she leaned against the wall, Gerber closed the door. A moment later he heard a thud and turned to find Morrow sitting on the floor, her legs spread and her skirt hiked, revealing her cream-colored underwear.

"Now what, Captain Mack?" she asked innocently. "What you got on your mind?"

"Oh, God," he moaned, knowing that anything he said would be wrong. He reached a hand out and said, "Let me help you to your feet."

"If you insist."

Gerber hauled her up and maneuvered her toward the bed. As they approached it, she turned around so that she faced him. Looking over her shoulder, she saw the bed and fell back, sitting on it.

"What now, Captain Mack?" she asked. Although her speech in the bar had seemed slurred, now it was precise. She held herself upright, in a stiff, unnatural posture, as if to prove that she wasn't drunk or that it had all been an act to get him to take her to his room.

"I think you need some rest," said Gerber, looking down at her.

"Rest," she said, nodding. She looked at her chest and began to fumble with the buttons of her blouse. "Can't sleep in my clothes. Get them wrinkled."

"Robin, why don't you lie down and catch a nap. You need it."

Instead she stood and stripped her blouse from her shoulders. She held it wrapped around her upper arms, barely covering her breasts as she winked at him, her tongue in the corner of her mouth. Then she dropped the blouse, unfastened her skirt and let it fall so that she was standing in front of him in her panties and bra.

She turned slowly, arms on her hips, showing him her body. She stumbled and caught herself. Then she faced him. "What d' you think, Captain Mack. Better than my stuffy old sister, don't you think? Firmer. Smoother. Softer. She's got a big butt." She began to giggle helplessly, sat on the bed hard, and repeated herself. "Got a big butt. Old Kari has a fanny and a half."

Although Robin was giggling, Gerber could detect a maliciousness under her words. He studied her carefully, the light coating of sweat that made her skin shine, the way sweat-damp bangs brushed her eyes, and the sexuality that she exuded right now.

He moved toward her and pushed on her shoulders, forcing her to lie back on the bed. She grabbed his wrists, her fingernails digging into his skin.

"Robin, I think you should take a nap and then we'll talk."

"Sure we will, Mack. You always say that and then you weasel out of it."

"Not this time." But he knew he would, just as he had a dozen other times. That was the thing about drunks. They often spoke the truth. No longer inhibited by the social norms, they felt free to speak things that they would never say if they were sober. Robin was right when she said that he managed to get out of the situations without talking to her as he had promised. He'd done it so often that it was becoming second nature.

He was about to say something when she rolled to her side, tucked her hands between her thighs and let out a ragged snore that might have been a partial sob. Her body jerked once, as if to shake off the effects of the alcohol, or the war, and then she was still.

"Oh, Robin," he said, amused by her. He jerked the bedspread across her curled form to protect her from the air-conditioning. Satisfied that she'd be okay, he went into the bathroom for a drink of water. He sat in the wing chair, watched her sleep for a few minutes. As the sun disappeared and darkness descended on downtown Saigon, he sipped the water and wondered what would happen when she woke.

3

THE CARASEL HOTEL
SAIGON

Robin was still asleep when Gerber woke. Spending the night sitting in the chair with his feet propped on the end of the bed hadn't been the most pleasant he had passed in Vietnam. But then, it wasn't the worst, either.

Robin had wakened during the night, sick from all the alcohol that she had consumed during the day. She had stumbled toward the bathroom, moaning to herself, and calling Gerber's name. A light sleeper himself, he had awakened instantly to find her sitting on the floor, her head resting on the toilet seat. Her skin had an unhealthy pallor to it. He had managed to sit beside her and hold her while she puked. With a damp towel, he had wiped the perspiration from her face and the vomit from her chin.

When she was ready to go back to bed, he helped her to her feet, had gotten her a glass of water to wash out her mouth and silently guided her into the other room. As she climbed into bed she looked at him and mumbled, "So sorry." Her voice was soft, quiet.

In the dim light filtering through the window, he had studied her face. There was a glint of brightness at her eyes, as if they had filled with tears. Gerber sat on the bed, held one of her hands and told her not to worry about it. Everyone got drunk once in a while.

She pulled her hand free and rolled over, her back to him. As she closed her eyes she said, quietly, "I didn't think you'd understand."

Now it was morning. Gerber looked at his watch. It was nearly seven. He padded into the bathroom and shut the door. Quickly he shaved, brushed his teeth and combed his hair. Back in his room, he put on his jungle fatigues, and picked up his socks and boots. From the wardrobe shoved into a corner, he retrieved his rifle. He left the room and finished dressing in the hall, ignoring the amused stares of a couple of Air Force sergeants and their whores.

Fully dressed now, he took the elevator down to the lobby and then dropped into one of the chairs to lace up his boots. He had almost finished when a shadow fell across him.

"Morning, Captain," said Fetterman. "How is Miss Morrow?"

"How would I know?" asked Gerber.

"The two of you left together fairly early and neither of you reappeared. The conclusion is obvious."

"Okay, Sergeant Obvious," said Gerber, "Miss Morrow is asleep in my room where she passed out soon after we got there last night. She was out all night, except for the hours when she was sick."

"And she's there now?" asked Fetterman.

"Still asleep. She's going to wake with a big head. She was bombed out of her tree."

"Well, it's just as well," said Fetterman. "We're due over to MACV Headquarters in about an hour."

"Shit! What the hell for?"

"I don't know. Talked to Maxwell and he has to see us right now. Wouldn't give me a clue, but said it was important."

"Just great." Gerber sat up, looked at his fingernails.

"We've time to eat breakfast first, if you want," said Fetterman.

"Let's just go see Maxwell. Maybe he'll have some doughnuts for us. If not, we can grab something in the cafeteria over there." Gerber grinned. "Besides, with Westmoreland running around MACV, the food should be good. They won't want to offend the general."

"It's still a mess hall, Captain."

"How could I forget?"

Outside the hotel they found a taxi, an old Chevy that was a riot of color, having been partially repainted half a dozen times. The interior smelled of cigarette smoke and vomit. The seats were stained in a dozen places and the floor littered with crushed cigarettes, candy wrappers and a used condom.

The driver was a burly South Vietnamese who sported a stubble and understood almost no English. He grinned at them, showing a gap where his front teeth should have been and nodded vigorously when Fetterman mentioned the MACV compound. Gerber instinctively knew that the man would have a Kamikaze complex.

They roared off, scattering a couple of pedestrians and barely missing a young woman carrying an armload of packages. They weaved in and out of the traffic, sliding into gaps that were almost too small for the car. Once he had the destination in mind, the driver kept both hands on the wheel, using the horn more often than the turn signal or brake.

They raced up wide boulevards, past palm-lined lawns of government buildings, then down narrow streets jammed on each side with squalid hovels. The cardboard and plywood structures were taped and nailed together haphazardly, unable to withstand the first of the coming monsoons; low, dirty buildings with wires strung between them or dangling from poles that looked ready to fall. The streets were muddy and lined with garbage. The open sewers reeked of refuse.

Then they burst onto a wide street, fell in behind a convoy of U.S. Army trucks, driving in the diesel stench of the engines until their driver got impatient. Leaning on the horn, he roared around them, causing a Vietnamese traffic cop to seek refuge behind the middle-of-the-road traffic light.

Finally they slid to a halt in a cloud of gravel dust in front of the MACV complex. The driver turned, one arm on the back of his seat, grinning as if he had won the Indianapolis 500.

"You pay me now!" he said. "One thousand P."

"No good. Numbah Ten Thou," said Fetterman. "One hundred P at most."

"You GI *dinky dau*. You pay me now. One thousand P. Good drive. You like."

Gerber couldn't help laughing over Fetterman's haggling. The driver wanted less than ten dollars for the trip for the two of them. If he had been a ride at an amusement park, he would have been worth the money.

"I give you two hundred. No more." Fetterman looked grim. Determined.

"Eight hundred," said the driver, his face becoming a tight mask.

"Too much. Too much. I give you three hundred and a tip of fifty P."

"Six hundred," said the driver, looking as if he had lost his best friend.

"Five," said Fetterman.

"Five!" said the driver, shouting. "Five hundred P and tip."

Fetterman took out his wallet and counted out the money. He handed it over to the driver who was happy again.

As he got out of the cab, the driver called, "Hey, GI. You numbah one! Good Joe."

Gerber, who was standing on the sidewalk that led to the building, had a smirk on his face. "Come on, Joe. We don't have all day."

"Be right with you, Captain." He watched the taxi rocket off, nearly crippling a couple of MPs who flipped him the bird. Then the vehicle disappeared in a cloud of dust around a corner.

"The man was phenomenal," said Fetterman. He turned, squinted in the bright morning sun and added, "That was a fine piece of driving."

"Then why argue the price down?" asked Gerber as they started toward the building.

"Because the price was too high for here. I pay it and the next guy then has to pay it and we have runaway inflation. Everyone thinks he should have more money. I argue him down to a more reasonable price, then prices remain low and everyone is happy."

They reached the first set of large glass doors. "Nice of you to worry about the Vietnamese economy that way, Tony," said Gerber, bowing slightly and ushering Fetterman through with a sweep of his arm.

Fetterman grabbed the inner door and did likewise for Gerber. The air-conditioned air hit them like a hard November wind. Gerber shivered as he stepped into the building.

"Just doing my bit, Captain," Fetterman said. "If we'd provide our troops with a little cultural training, perhaps teach them a little about the Vietnamese people before they got over here, we could avoid some of the problems we run into. Wouldn't have our soldiers trampling on Vietnamese beliefs and traditions without realizing they were doing it."

"I don't need a lecture on Vietnamese culture, Tony," said Gerber.

"Yes, sir."

They walked along the tiled hallway, looking at the posters on the bulletin boards, the photos of the presidents of the United States and of Vietnam. Pictures of the military chain of command, from the Chairman of the Joint Chiefs of Staff, down to the local men. They didn't speak to any of the men or women who were hurrying along the hall, all looking grimly determined while clutching bundles of paper as they rushed from one office to the next. Some wore starched jungle fatigues, others were dressed in civilian clothing and a couple in Class A uniforms.

They reached a stairway that led down to a lower floor. There, they were barred by a floor-to-ceiling iron gate, which was guarded by an MP who wore a shiny black helmet liner and a .45 on his hip. They stopped outside of the gate, Gerber produced his ID card and told the man that he was expected inside. The guard used a field phone to confirm Gerber's clearance into the restricted area, checked Fetterman's ID and watched while both men signed in. Then he opened the gate and directed them to the proper office. He carefully locked the gate behind them.

Gerber and Fetterman turned down a corridor lined with cinderblock walls that were damp with condensation. Rust spots, where metal furniture or file cabinets had been and later moved, stained the green tile floor. Finally they stopped in front of a wooden door that had no markings other than a small, black number at eye level. When Gerber knocked, the door was opened.

Jerry Maxwell stood there, looking as if he had been up all night. He stepped back and waved them into the office. Inside was a disaster area. One wall was lined with file cabinets, the tops covered with file folders, loose papers and boxes of material. A massive cabinet squatted in a corner, a combination lock on the second drawer. A battleship-gray desk, the top littered with more papers, documents and file folders, was pushed into another corner. One side was lined with a wall of Coke cans nearly two feet high. A small chair sat in front of the desk and a larger one next to it. A single picture with its glass broken hung on the wall. Under it was a stack of framed pictures showing U.S. Cavalry men fighting the Cheyenne Indians in the Hayfield Fight.

The subterranean office had no windows and was therefore lit with fluorescent lights. The air, super-cooled by the massive air-conditioning system on the roof of the building, threatened to freeze everything solid.

Maxwell closed the door and gestured at the chairs. "Please. Sit down." Then he leaped in front of Gerber and plucked his wrinkled suit coat off the chair reserved for visitors.

"Excuse the mess, but I've been up all night trying to get this thing coordinated. We don't have a lot of spare time."

"Jerry," said Gerber patiently. "I've told you this before. First you ask us how things are. We chat for a moment and then you chop us up with your impossible request."

Maxwell leaned a hip against the desk and then shoved some of the paper out of the way so he could sit down. "I'm in no mood for your lectures on manners, Captain."

"Sorry, Jerry," said Gerber, taking the chair vacated for him.

"I told you I've been up all night working on this. We don't have a lot of time to fuck around on it. You've got to have your team ready to go by zero three hundred tomorrow."

"Well, Jerry, I was up most of the night, too, so I'm not impressed with that." Gerber smiled. "Of course, my reason was probably more pleasant than yours."

Maxwell pinched the bridge of his nose. "If you're done, I'd like to get down to business."

Fetterman picked a folder with a bright red secret stamp on it from the desk. He flipped it open and began to read it.

Maxwell grabbed it out of his hands and slammed it onto a pile of other secret material.

"You guys through clowning around?"

Gerber shrugged and looked at Fetterman. "You done clowning around Master Sergeant?"

"I don't know. You?"

"Yeah, I think I am. Okay, Jerry, fill us in on the big project that kept you up all night."

"Are you gentlemen familiar with the air war being flown over North Vietnam?"

"Only that we've got bombers and fighters going in there day after day and that our Secretary of Defense is doing all he can to make sure that the bombing does no grave injury to the enemy," Gerber said glibly.

"Now what in the hell does that mean?" Maxwell appeared to be momentarily distracted.

"It means that the Secretary of Defense has ordered that our pilots avoid certain targets like the manufacturing centers in Hanoi, small though they may be, and the harbor at Haiphong. Heaven forbid we might sink a Russian ship off-loading war supplies for the communist forces."

Maxwell shook his head. When he spoke again his voice sounded tired. "There are good political reasons for those orders. Reasons that the men in the field might not be fully cognizant of."

"Fine, Jerry," said Fetterman. "I'll tell the men who are being shot at with those weapons and ammunition that there are reasons for it that they aren't fully cognizant of. I'm sure it will make them feel better."

"Can we get on with this?" Maxwell was beginning to get testy. "Or are you two planning to play Mutt and Jeff for the rest of the morning?"

"Look, Jerry," said Gerber, "it's very hard for us to sit here and listen to this bullshit. That we can't do something because it might violate some stupid guideline some ignorant politician thinks is a good idea. Not when there are people out there shooting real bullets at us.''

"Okay, okay," said Maxwell. He stood and shuffled over to the file cabinets. He turned, leaning back on them and said, "I have a mission for you two. You'll have to move quickly, and given what you've said, I think you'll go for it.''

"Tell us, Jerry," said Gerber.

"First you have to agree that everything you hear in this room from this point on goes no further than this room. That's the guideline on this.''

"You know that we don't talk out of school," said Gerber. "Go ahead.''

"Okay," he said, and then launched into a tale about the Wild Weasels, the air war being fought over North Vietnam and the sudden development of a missile system that seemed to use something other than radar for acquisition and guidance. He explained the prevailing feeling that because of this new development the balance had been tipped in the enemy's favor and that U.S. involvement in the air war was at a disadvantage.

"The most worrisome thing," continued Maxwell, "is that all indications are the missiles are being launched from SA-2 Guideline sites.''

"Guideline?" said Gerber.

"The NATO name for the SAM missile. SA-2 Guideline. Anyway, prior to a couple of days ago, all these missiles used radar for target acquisition and guidance. We could counter that, but now they seem to be launching missiles that don't use radar and that negate our Wild Weasels.''

"The missiles are coming from the SA-2 sites?" A frown appeared on Fetterman's face.

"Yeah. That's the problem. No indications from the launch site that they're even tracking and suddenly our fighters have a missile flying up their tailpipes.''

"So the assumption," said Gerber, "is the Soviets have developed a new tracking and guidance system and given it to the North Vietnamese."

"Yeah."

"And to defeat this system," said Fetterman, "you need a guidance system to study."

"Exactly."

Gerber took over again. "And since all these missiles are deployed north of the UMZ, you want someone to go north to get you one."

"UMZ?" Maxwell looked confused.

"That's what the grunts call the Demilitarized Zone. UMZ for Ultramilitarized Zone, because of all the heavy ordnance both sides have stacked up there."

"Oh, of course. And yes, we want someone to go north and get a guidance system. But it's not quite the hit-and-miss proposition that you might think. We have identified the sites where the new missiles are deployed so that we put you down close to one."

"Why not just bomb the shit out of them?" asked Fetterman. "End of problem."

"Not really," said Maxwell. "That takes out the site, but doesn't prevent them from using the missiles on a different site or reequipping the old one. If we divert everything to Triple A suppression, then we have nothing left to hit the primary targets, the railroad yards, the bridges, the roads."

"For the little good it will do," said Gerber.

"The point is," said Maxwell, "we need to know what the new guidance system is like. Once we have that data, we can design a countermeasure that will allow us to carry on the air war."

"Okay," said Gerber, passing a hand through his hair. "When does this boondoggle begin and who do we take with us?"

"The composition of your team will be left to you, unless you wish for me to pull in some people. Tomorrow morning you'll take off for Ubon Air Force Base in Thailand, board a B-52 for a HALO into North Vietnam—"

"Now wait a fucking minute." Fetterman's voice cut through like a knife. "You want us to bail out of a bomber?"

"Perfect cover," said Maxwell. "The NVA won't expect something like that. They'll spot the planes, sure, but they'll know they're bombers that will have a real mission. You'll be jumping from thirty-five or forty thousand feet so they won't know you're on the ground."

"Jesus H. Christ on a popsicle stick." Gerber was incredulous. "The air temperature at that altitude will be thirty or forty below. We hit any kind of upper air winds, we could be scattered all over fucking North Vietnam."

"Admittedly there are a few details that need to be worked out. However, you'll have to use the bombers. Just makes good sense. Puts you into the North with no one knowing it."

"Any more little surprises?" asked Gerber.

Now Maxwell smiled. It was an evil smile that said things were going to get worse. "Just one," he said. "You'll have to take a Kit Carson scout. One who grew up in the area."

Gerber shook his head. "You don't mean . . . ?"

"Of course. Brouchard Bien Soo Ta Emilie. You've worked with her before," he said.

"She's not from the North," said Gerber.

"Oh, but she is," countered Maxwell. He moved back to his desk and dug through the files piled there. When he found the one he wanted, he waved it like a banner. "Says right here that she was born in the North. Debriefing was completed by the CIA, so this is the good stuff."

"Jerry," said Gerber, "do you have any idea of how many different stories she's told?"

"Doesn't matter what's she said to the others," Maxwell said. "This was an interrogation conducted by our people...."

"Oh, well," said Fetterman sarcastically, "then it's got to be right. No one would lie to the CIA."

Maxwell ignored the comment. "Okay. You have until five this afternoon to get your team together and get over to Tan Son Nhut. I'll meet you over there at Hotel Three and escort you around to the Air America pad. Once there, we'll get you on a flight to Ubon."

"Are there restrictions on the makeup of the team?" asked Gerber.

"None. Whoever you want, within reason. We don't want to take a company in, but we want you to have everyone you're going to need."

"You going to provide us with someone to look at the missile?" asked Fetterman.

"Meaning?"

"Suppose we get up there and onto the site and discover, for whatever reason, we can't get the system out. Shouldn't someone on our team know what to look for?"

"Jesus," said Maxwell. "I never thought of that. Good point. I'll work on that."

Gerber glanced at his watch. "If we're going to pull this off, we'd better get moving. What about transport?"

"I can get you a chopper out of here in ten minutes. It'll be yours all day, take you wherever you want to go. You have any trouble with local commanders, you call me on the lima-lima and I'll have someone call them back within ten minutes with verbal orders. Anything else?"

"Briefings on the local area. Restrictions on our operations. Equipment we're going to take. Extraction plans because I don't want to have to E and E all the way to South Vietnam. Support we can count on..."

"Once your team is set and we know exactly how many are going, we'll get all that taken care of. Finally, intense briefings will be held at Ubon just prior to takeoff. Extraction is being coordinated with the Navy and final plans will be available at Ubon."

"Codes, radio procedures," said Gerber.

"All will be worked out and available at Ubon. Your task, right now, is to put together the team. Everyone you think you'll need and get them back to Hotel Three. I'll approve them at that point."

"Maxwell, if I go to the trouble of getting someone here, I don't want you second-guessing me. If I say I need them, they have to go."

"Okay, Mack," said Maxwell, holding up his hands in mock surrender. "Whatever you want."

"Tony?" Gerber turned to Fetterman.

"I think we better get the show on the road."

"Chopper's on the pad outside," said Maxwell. "I'll get the crew out to it and you can be on your way."

Gerber got to his feet and moved to the door. As he touched the knob, Maxwell said, "Mack, I'm sorry about that fiasco in the Hobo Woods. That wasn't my fault. I did everything I could for you."

"Yeah, Jerry, that's what you always say. Well, we'll pull the fat out of the fire again." He opened the door and stepped into the corridor.

Fetterman joined him and they walked toward the iron gate. The guard opened it and let them out. Slowly they climbed the stairs, reached the first level and walked to the end of the building. Fetterman opened the door, letting in a blast of hot, humid air. For an instant it was a pleasant sensation after the meat-locker cold of Maxwell's office.

Together they stepped into the bright sun, letting the heat and humidity wash over them like the surf on a beach. Before they had moved more than two steps, they were covered with sweat. Gerber put a hand up to shield his eyes and turned to the single chopper standing on the rubberized pad away from the building. The crew was swarming around it, preparing it for flight. One man was on top, checking the rotorhead, shaking the assembly, looking for mistakes that maintenance might have made.

Gerber stopped short, and watched the activity for a moment. Then he turned to Fetterman. "I don't like this, Tony. They've thrown it together without thinking it through. Seems to me that having someone familiar with the guidance systems of the missiles on the team should have been the first thing they thought of."

"Yes, sir," said Fetterman. "That, and finding such a man who is jump qualified. Don't see how they can do it in a couple of hours."

"That's what I mean. Rush, rush, rush, until we've rushed ourselves out of options."

"How are we going to handle this?"

Gerber wiped the sweat from his face with the sleeve of his jungle fatigues. "You remember that ranger sergeant in the rubber plantation? You know, the one who was so good. Le Duc or something like that. Why don't you see if you can find him and anyone else who you think might be good?"

"Okay. And what are you going to do?"

"I'm going to get these guys to fly me up to Song Be where Johnny has his camp. See if I can borrow some people from him. I understand he's got Glen Mildebrandt as his exec and managed to get Bocker and Tyme assigned to him. Not sure who all he's got there, but I'm going to borrow the people from him. I think we can trust his judgment."

"How many men do you want me to find?" asked Fetterman.

There was a high-pitched whine and the rotorblades of the chopper began to spin. The noise built into a roar so that Gerber had to lean close to Fetterman to hear.

"You talk to them and then take anyone you think necessary. We can cut it down later, but it'll be better to have too many rather than too few."

"So where'll we meet?"

"Hotel Three, like Maxwell said."

"What about Robin?" asked Fetterman. "She still in your room?"

"Yeah. If I get a chance, I'll give her a call and explain the situation to her. She'll understand."

Fetterman looked at Gerber as if he couldn't believe what the captain had said. "Give her a call, sir. She deserves that at the very least."

"Okay, Tony. I'll see you at Hotel Three."

4

SONG BE SPECIAL
FORCES CAMP B-34

The chopper circled the camp once at altitude, giving Gerber a chance to look at it from the air. Like the old Triple Nickel, it was a star-shaped outpost surrounded by five strands of barbed wire and concertina. The interior was crammed with corrugated tin buildings that caught and reflected the blazing sun. In the center of it was a redoubt with very little empty ground. Buildings and bunkers were jammed into the center.

On the east side of the camp lay a long runway, partially paved with blacktop that turned to a graded slash of red dirt. On the east side of the runway was a helipad and south of that a turn around for airplanes. Outside the wire of the camp was a ramshackle village of dilapidated hootches, open garbage dumps and muddy streets. Most of the montagnards assigned to the camp lived there. In the event of an attack, all the villagers would rush into the camp for protection and to help with the defense.

As the helicopter touched down on the pad, kicking up a swirling cloud of red dirt, a hundred kids ran from the village. Before the rotors had stopped spinning, they had encircled the chopper and were screaming for candy or C-rats or cigarettes. When Gerber refused to give them anything, they melted away as quickly as they had appeared.

He climbed out, but before he could move off, the AC shouted, "You going to be a long time, Captain?"

Gerber turned and stepped up on the skid so that he was looking in the window of the chopper. "Don't know. Why?"

"Well, I just thought that if you're going to be a while, I could get my boys inside and find them a cold drink."

"Fine with me. The aircraft going to be safe here without someone to guard it?"

The AC smiled. "We never leave it alone unless we're on an all-American base. Crew chief or gunner will remain behind. Little later we'll rotate that man so everyone gets a chance to relax inside."

"Just keep your eyes open so that I don't have to go searching all over for you." Gerber dropped back to the ground. A tall, thin officer approached him. He recognized the lopsided gait, the freckled face that was tanned a deep brown. He had an M-16 slung muzzle down over his shoulder. It was hard to see the sun-bleached hair under the green beret molded to his head, but there was no doubt that it was Captain Jonathan Bromhead.

As he neared the chopper, Bromhead called, "Ho, Captain Gerber. Good to see you again." He moved closer, held out a hand and tried to look dignified, but a grin threatened his composure. "Good to see you again, Mack."

Gerber grasped the younger man's elbow, squeezing it. "How's it going out here, Johnny?"

Bromhead said quietly, "They call me Jack here."

"Okay, Jack, how's it going?"

Bromhead waved a hand and said, "We've got a good camp. Patrol the mountains to the east, hunting the VC and NVA. Get mortared once a week or so, but no real problem with that. The locals are good in a fight. Only trouble is when they bring in the Viets. They can't get along with the Yards so we have quite a bit of tension."

"At least the VNAF stopped dumping their bomb loads on the Yard villages."

"Yes, sir. You want to stand out here in the hot sun talking Vietnamese politics or you want to come on in and take a look at my camp?"

"Take the tour, of course," said Gerber.

They crossed the runway that miraculously hadn't been ruined by peta-prime and walked up to the gate. Gerber was surprised at how small the camp was. Unlike the Triple Nickel, which had nearly seven hundred soldiers living inside, most of the camp's defenders lived in the village. Since the defense force was smaller, the camp was designed so that fewer men could hold it. From the front gate, Gerber could see into the redoubt. Although there were a couple of large, tin buildings inside, they were almost completely underground with sandbagged steps leading down to them.

"New idea," said Bromhead. "Makes the mortar attacks less effective because the shrapnel goes through the roof without hitting anything."

"What about the direct hit?"

"No problem. We've a layer of sandbags rigged in the ceiling so they absorb everything. A rocket is a different story, but Charlie doesn't fire that many at us and usually misses the camp altogether."

"Looks good," said Gerber.

"Come on. We'll go to the team house. Last time I saw Bocker, he was in there drinking beer and complaining about the heat. He'll probably want to say hello to you."

As they moved toward the redoubt, Gerber asked, "You got Tyme here?"

"Sure. He's out on the perimeter making the monthly check of the claymores."

"I'd like to see him, too."

Bromhead stopped near the door of the team house and searched Gerber's face. "You here on some kind of official business?"

"Uh-huh. I've a mission coming up and I need some help on it."

"So you're going to take my best men and go," said Bromhead.

"That's about the size of it." Gerber stepped down onto the wooden riser that led down into the team house. A wall of sandbags rose on each side to protect the entrance. As he entered he noticed a platform, two feet off the main floor, running around the walls of the team house. There was a series of firing ports near the ceiling so that defenders could shoot at the attacking enemy if they penetrated the wire.

The inside was like any other team house. There were four tables with four chairs around each of them. Red vinyl tablecloths covered each table. A metal pitcher, the outside beaded with moisture, sat on each cloth and place settings in front of each chair. There were bamboo mats on the floors and a few pictures of nude women on the walls, most of them torn from either *Playboy* or *Penthouse*.

The back third of the team house was hidden behind a latticework wall but there was enough visibility to see the stove, sink and refrigerator. Two shadowy shapes moved behind it and there was a clatter of pots and pans.

"Lunch will be served in about thirty minutes," said Bromhead, checking his watch. "You want to join us?"

"Sure. Glad to."

"Why don't you grab a seat and I'll see if there's a cold beer in here somewhere?"

At that moment Bocker appeared through the rear of the team house. He stopped, stared and then yelled, "Captain Gerber!" He rushed forward with his hand out. "Damn, Captain! It's good to see you."

Smiling, Gerber got to his feet and shook hands with the older staff sergeant. Bocker was a burly man, about five ten or eleven and weighed close to two hundred pounds. His light brown hair was close cropped so that the gray invading it would be invisible.

"How you been, Galvin?" asked Gerber.

"Just fine. Captain Bromhead runs a good camp although he's having problems with the Viets, but hell, who isn't?" He saw Bromhead bringing the beers and remembered the old days when Gerber would have beer available at the pre-mission briefings. "What's going on, Captain?"

Gerber accepted a can of beer and jerked the pull tab free. He took a deep drink, rested the can on the table and then slumped into a chair. "Got a deal going on and need some help with it." He shot a glance at Bromhead and then said, "I'm looking for a couple of volunteers. When Justin gets here, I'll let you in on it."

"Then buy me a beer."

"You got it. Captain Bromhead, you heard the man."

"Okay, but I don't want you getting my team drunk."

"I'll keep that in mind."

ROBIN MORROW CAME AWAKE SLOWLY, aware that there was light filtering in through the blinds on the window, aware that her head hurt badly, and not sure of where she was. She tried to remember what had happened the night before, but the only thing that came to her was being hunched over the toilet, throwing up violently. The thought made her stomach flip and her nausea worse.

It was then that she realized she was nearly naked. Involuntarily she pulled the sheet higher up, to her neck as if someone might be able to see her this way. She tried hard to recall what she had done the night before, who she had let talk her into returning to his room.

Cautiously she opened her eyes, saw that she was alone, and threw the sheet off her. She sat up slowly, trying to keep from moaning and wondering why she drank so much. Wobbly, she got to her feet and stumbled to the air conditioner to turn it on. The sudden clatter was almost more than she could bear, but the cold air that blasted out of it made the noise secondary.

She remembered finding Gerber in the bar. Tears stung her eyes. "Damn. Damn. Damn." She sniffed, and rubbed her eyes with the heels of her hands. "Damn you, Mack Gerber."

With a sigh, she stood and padded into the bathroom. She flipped on the light, blinked at the brightness and then leaned forward, studying herself. Her hair was a tangled mess, there were black smudges under her eyes that weren't entirely from the makeup she hadn't removed, and her face looked puffy. With her right hand, she tugged at the skin of her cheek, smoothing it.

"You keep drinking like that," she told herself, "you're going to be old before your time."

There was a rumbling in her stomach and she spun, dropping to her knees in front of the toilet. She heaved once, the muscles cramping and forcing, but there was nothing left in her stomach. She dropped her head to her arm, her stomach heaving and heaving and she wished that she could throw up. When the spasms subsided, she rocked to her haunches with her back against the wall, perspiration beaded on her forehead and upper lip. Tears stung her eyes again and tumbled down her cheeks.

After nearly five minutes she climbed to her feet and turned on the sink water. She found Gerber's toothbrush and loaded it with toothpaste. She scrubbed at her teeth and then her tongue until her mouth felt clean. When she finished, she cleaned the brush, left it on the edge of the sink where she had found it.

Back in the bedroom, she looked for a note from Gerber but couldn't find one. She felt sure he would have left her one and looked again. When she didn't find it, she felt the tears again and fought them back. She snatched her clothes from the chair, scattering them on the floor. Bending to pick them up, she started to cry.

"Damn," she said and then began to dress.

DURING HIS FIRST TOUR of duty in Vietnam, Fetterman had seen many of the French forts that dotted the landscape. They were triangular structures that hugged the ground and gave the defenders the best fields of fire. He had walked by them and flown over them, but he had never been inside one.

Now he stood at the gate, waiting for the Vietnamese corporal to open it and let him enter. The chopper that had brought him sat on the pad twenty yards behind him, the rotor blades slowing as the pilot shut down the engine.

The man was waiting until one of his officers ordered him to let Fetterman enter. An officer approached and shouted something in Vietnamese, and the guard opened the gate. Fetterman stepped through, and studied the interior of the fort.

The walls of the bunkers that made up the three sides of the fort were no more than two feet high. Each was topped with barbed wire, and each connected to another with a trench. A network of trenches split the flat, smooth ground on the inside so that there were clear fields of fire in all directions. The fort had obviously been designed with defense in mind. If one wall fell, the defenders could retreat to the trench or one of the other bunkers and fight from there. Each fort was a complex little island that could be cut and cut again, but without the defenders losing the whole thing. Fetterman wondered how well it worked in practice.

The officer stopped near Fetterman, who threw him a salute that could have passed muster on a parade ground. Fetterman normally didn't bother with saluting in the field, but they weren't technically in the field, and sometimes it helped to grease the skids with a little extra military courtesy.

"Good morning, *dai uy*," said Fetterman.

"How may I help you?" asked the Vietnamese captain. He was a short, skinny man with olive skin and black hair. His face was oval and seemed to contain no trace of beard. His brown eyes held only the slightest slant. His English was good but had a French accent to it, which was no surprise to Fetterman.

Fetterman glanced up at the sun, blazing out of a cloudless sky, and then at the open ground to the walls. He shrugged, wishing the man had invited him into the command post. "I was with your men yesterday, during the mission into the rubber plantation."

"Yes?"

"There was a sergeant on that mission," said Fetterman. "A good man and I have another mission for him. Sergeant Duc."

"Sergeant Duc is busy with his duties here," said the captain.

"Yes, sir, I understand that. But if I might have a word with him."

"Follow me," said the officer. He turned on his heel and strode across the hard-packed red dirt.

Several men were sitting in the hot sun, field stripping their weapons. Fetterman and the officer entered a bunker, moving down into the earth. They came to an orderly room, a sandbag lined structure that was noticeably cooler than outside. There was a couch along one wall, a waist-high refrigerator pushed into one corner and a bookcase with Army manuals in the other. Two green file cabinets, both badly dented, stood next to the bookcase. The floor was made of wooden planks and covered with a thin coating of dust. At the foot of the steps was a bamboo mat that had seen better days. Behind a battered, wooden desk sat an American infantry officer. He was wearing faded fatigues with black insignia sewn to the collar. He was a young man with light skin, a huge mustache that violated half a dozen Army guidelines, and eyes that sparkled with a joke that only he knew.

"Can I help you?" he asked.

"Yes, sir," said Fetterman. He noticed the man wore the patch of the Twenty-fifth Infantry Division. Obviously he was an advisor for this group.

"Yes, sir," repeated Fetterman. "There's this mission, and I need to borrow a couple of your people for a couple of days."

The lieutenant nodded and dropped his pencil to the desktop, rocking back in his chair. It squeaked loudly. He slowly laced his fingers behind his head, his eyes locked on Fetterman's.

"Just like that? I assume you have the proper paperwork."

"Well, not exactly. However, I can provide you with a phone number so that you can receive verbal approval to be followed with the paperwork. Orders will be here for you in the morning, though I have to have the men out of here in the next couple of hours. We have a bit of a time crunch."

The lieutenant sucked in a lungful of air and exhaled. He put his hands on the desk and shoved himself up, grinning. "If you have that kind of juice, then I don't want to stand in your way. I could get myself into some real trouble. Besides, you Sneaky Petes get everything you want anyway. So tell me, who you after here?"

"Sergeant Duc."

"Of course. One of the best. Is this a volunteer mission or is he ordered to go with you?"

"Strictly volunteer."

The lieutenant stepped around his desk. "Well, follow me and we'll see if we can't find Sergeant Duc." He stopped at the steps leading up and asked, "You looking for any Americans to round out your team?"

Fetterman shook his head. "Afraid not, unless you happen to be an electronics expert. We're going to need a good man with that kind of background."

"I can get my stereo to work if that's what you mean."

Fetterman had to laugh. "We've something a little more complex in mind."

"Figured as much." The lieutenant turned and walked up the steps.

As they crossed the center of the fort, the lieutenant pointed out various features like a tour guide in a museum. He outlined the visible defenses and suspected staging areas for the enemy if they decided to attack, but told Fetterman nothing about the hidden weapons, concealed strongpoints, or surprises that had been built into the walls.

They were about to step into another of the sandbagged entrances when there was a shout behind them.

"Sergeant Tony!"

Fetterman turned and saw a small man dressed in tiger-striped fatigues. He had dark hair and oval eyes that were cold and hard. He carried one of the old M-1 carbines with two banana clips taped together.

"Krung!"

The lieutenant looked confused. "Do you two know one another?"

Fetterman did not reply while he waited for Krung, his hand outstretched. When Krung took it, Fetterman asked, "What are you doing here?"

"I train Vietnamese. Teach them to kill VC."

"Why aren't you still at the camp? Where's Lieutenant Bao and the rest?"

"Trung uy Bao killed by VC."

"Sergeant," said the lieutenant.

"Sir, is there a place where Sergeant Krung and I could talk? I know him and would like to take him on the mission, too."

"I'll find Duc for you. Why don't you go back to my office and use it?"

"Thanks, Lieutenant."

While the lieutenant went in search of Duc, Fetterman and Krung walked back to the orderly room. Once inside, Fetterman turned to Krung. "Tell me what happened."

Krung dropped onto the frayed couch jammed against one wall. "Bao on patrol with Vietnamese from camp. We out two, three days. We walk into ambush. VC zap us pretty good. Many die on trail but some of us escape."

Fetterman thought of another ambush that had happened nearly eighteen months earlier. The VC had zapped them pretty good then, too. Krung was one of the few survivors that time, fading into the jungle as the VC overran them, killing everyone in sight.

"We go back two day later. We find everyone. They all dead. VC kill them many times. Shoot them many times. Cut them up." Krung's face darkened as he remembered finding the bodies. "They do things to them. Fill their mouths."

Fetterman knew that Krung was groping for the English words to describe the horror he had seen. From what Fetterman knew of VC terror tactics, he was sure that Krung was trying to tell him that the VC had cut off their penises and shoved them in the mouths of the dead. That was a new wrinkle the VC had added in the last year or so.

"I understand," said Fetterman.

"I decide that I kill fifty VC for Trung uy Bao."

"That in addition to the ones you swore to kill for the members of your family?" Fetterman was referring to the pledge that Krung had made when he discovered the communists had killed his family. Fifty of them for each member of his family. And Krung had had a very large family. He had kept score by nailing the genitals of the dead to a board he kept in his hootch. When Fetterman had DEROSed from his first tour, Krung was within twenty or twenty-five of completing that mission. Apparently he had found another.

They talked for a few minutes, and Fetterman learned of the breakup of the Tai strike companies by the Vietnamese command in Saigon. Krung and a platoon of his fellow tribesmen had been assigned to the Vietnamese rangers. Krung didn't like it, but it provided him with the opportunity to kill VC so he didn't complain.

The lieutenant reappeared with an Oriental in tow. "I have Sergeant Duc."

"Thank you, Lieutenant. I need to talk to them in private." Fetterman hesitated and then added, "The mission is classified."

The lieutenant stared for a moment and then said, "Please call me when you're finished. I have work that I have to complete, too."

"Yes, sir. Thank you."

After the lieutenant left, Fetterman walked about the room, checking it, as if looking for hidden microphones. When he had satisfied himself that they were alone, he lowered his voice. "We've been handed a real hot potato. I'll give you some of the details and then if either of you want out, you get out."

Duc sat quietly, first staring at Krung and then at Fetterman. "Why me?" he asked.

"Because we need at least one Vietnamese on the mission and you demonstrated an initiative yesterday. Are you jump qualified?"

"As ranger it is necessary to learn how to use parachute. I have twelve jumps."

"Good." With that, Fetterman launched into his account of the mission, stopped for a moment and when neither Krung nor Duc asked to be excluded, filled them in with as much detail as they needed. He wanted to let them know what they had let themselves in for by not getting out when they had the chance. He then told them to gather a little of their gear but not to take anything they valued. Weapons, clothing, food and ammo would be provided later. When they were ready, he would meet them at the front gate.

5

AIR AMERICA HANGAR
TAN SON NHUT
SAIGON

Gerber, along with Tyme and Bocker who had volunteered for the mission, entered the corrugated metal hangar. They crossed the waxed cement floor until they came to a stairwell. The door there held a sign warning that the base commander could refuse entrance to unauthorized personnel, and that all personnel were subject to search at the discretion of the base commander.

They climbed the cement stairs, with a metal corner on the edge of each riser painted yellow. A second locked door barred their way. This time they knocked and a civilian peered through a window with a sliding shutter, and let them in. A second civilian led them down a hallway filled with steam pipes, electrical wiring and locked access doors. He stopped and pointed out the briefing room.

Gerber entered first, stopped short and stared at the people around the table. Fetterman sat there looking cool and collected. The uniform he wore looked fresh, as if he had put it on only moments before. Next to him was the Vietnamese sergeant from the Michelin Rubber Plantation, his fatigue uniform stained under the arms and down the front. On the other side was a smaller, darker man, whose black hair was now unkempt. His clothes, the remnants of a U.S. Army fatigue uniform, were frayed, but all the rips had been mended and it was clean.

For a moment Gerber's gaze rested on the smaller Oriental. "Sergeant Krung?"

"I find Sergeant Tony and he invite me to go with you," Krung said.

Gerber moved forward, a hand out. "I'm glad to have you. I think we'll need you on this one." A dozen questions swirled through his mind, from where Krung had been for the last year, to how he was doing with his personal war of vengeance against the Vietcong.

"If you'll take a seat, Captain," said the man at the head of the table, waving at the chairs opposite him, "we'll get this show on the road."

Gerber turned and saw Maxwell sitting at the head of the table. The CIA man was dressed in his usual rumpled white suit with a thin black tie. The knot was loosened so that it hung low. On his right was an attractive Eurasian woman whom Gerber recognized immediately. Her petite form, beautiful face and long black hair attested to her French-Vietnamese heritage. Gerber remembered being entranced by her blue eyes, which appeared to be violet, depending on her mood or her clothing. She wore a flight suit now, with its sleeves hacked off near the elbows. The legs had been rolled up several times so that the cuffs wouldn't drag on the ground.

"Kit?" He had hoped the reluctance he had shown earlier would have convinced Maxwell that she wouldn't be of value on the mission.

"I am going, too," she said, smiling at him. It was something more than just a warm glad-to-see-you smile.

"Maxwell, this is getting a little out of hand." Gerber tried not to stare at her.

"Miss Brouchard was born in the North and will be a valuable asset," said Maxwell, repeating what he had said earlier that day.

Gerber jerked a chair away from the table and dropped into it. He stared at Maxwell. "Miss Brouchard has told so many stories about her background that I'm surprised you accept any of them as fact." He turned toward her. "No offense."

"I understand," she said quietly. "But this time Mr. Maxwell is correct. I was born in the North. You will see that I will be helpful on this mission."

Maxwell glared at him and then gestured at Tyme and Bocker. "If you men will close the door and sit down, we can get this briefing under way. The aircraft, an Air Force C-130, is scheduled for departure in thirty minutes, so we don't have a lot of time—"

"Does the crew have a reason for going, other than to transport us?" interrupted Gerber.

"No."

"Then they're not going anywhere without us, Jerry. Before you start, I want to say a few things about this mission." He looked at Fetterman, then at the others. Tyme and Bocker had slipped into chairs on either side of him, and Kit sat next to Maxwell. Seven people already on the team and not one of them knew what to look for when they got where they were going. Bocker, with his background in electronics and radios, might be trained to understand the guidance system quickly, but that would be at least a ten or twelve-day job, and they didn't have ten or twelve days.

"Isn't someone missing from this group?" asked Gerber.

Maxwell studied each of them again. "No. Everyone's here, unless there's someone you requested and he hasn't arrived yet."

"How about your electronic warfare specialist? I don't see him?"

"He'll meet you in Ubon. Air Force found him and have him there already."

"I assume he's jump qualified. You made sure of that, didn't you?" Gerber turned his attention to Kit. "I assume you are, too?"

"Yes, Captain," she said stiffly. "I have been jump qualified by the Luc Luong Dac Biet. That is the least of your worries."

"And this Air Force puke?" asked Gerber again.

"He is fully mission qualified," said Maxwell. "The Air Force wouldn't have given us someone who isn't mission qualified."

"Meaning you don't know whether he's jump qualified or not," grated Gerber. "Christ, Jerry, I thought after those other fiascos you saddled us with, you'd think this thing all the way through."

Maxwell chose to ignore the remarks. He opened the file folder in front of him. "Final mission briefing will be held at zero two three zero tonight in Ubon. The jump, a HALO mission, is now scheduled to go in at zero four hundred, which should give you over an hour of darkness for cover once you're on the ground."

"Fucking great," said Gerber, sarcastically. Rather than pick up the file folder in front of him, he looked around the conference room. Since it was in the Air America hangar, he had expected something a little nicer than he found, which only proved that the people who fought the war didn't have any of the luxuries of the brass, no matter who they worked for, the CIA included.

The table was scarred with cigarette burns. The ubiquitous water pitcher, this one cracked and empty, sat in the center of it. There were no drinking glasses and the tray that it sat on was dented and stained. Along one wall, which someone had paneled in an attempt to improve the surroundings, was a broken down green couch that was covered with burns, stains and rips. The stuffing hung out in a dozen places. The paneling behind it was warped and nicked.

On the wall opposite Gerber was a recruiting poster that someone had stolen. Under the picture of Uncle Sam pointing out, someone had scrawled in bright red, "I want your fucking ass in Vietnam, now!"

"Actual mission preparation will take place in Ubon," said Maxwell. "I have a few directives that I want to pass along to everyone on the team, and then we'll hustle on down to the airfield."

"I have to make a phone call," said Gerber, suddenly remembering Robin Morrow left behind in his hotel room.

Maxwell looked up startled and then laughed. "You're joking, of course."

"I'm not joking. I have to make a phone call."

"You're making no phone calls, either," said Maxwell. "Now, if you're through with all this other nonsense, I'll finish here and let you go."

When Maxwell finished the briefing, he took them downstairs, through the Operations area of the hangar and out onto the ramp. An Air Force C-130 sat at one end, the doors open and the engines running. One of the crewmen jumped out of the front door near the cockpit, ran around the wing to avoid the propellers, and stopped near Maxwell.

"These the passengers?" he yelled over the roar of the four turboprops.

When Maxwell nodded, the gesture exaggerated, the airman looked at the group and shouted, "Please follow me closely. Watch out for the props."

He led them out of the hot air being blown back at them in near hurricane force by the engines. At the hatch, he helped Kit up the ladder, then waited as each of the men climbed aboard. Gerber glanced up into the cockpit. There was an empty seat across the bulkhead behind the seats for the pilots. When he moved into the cargo area of the plane, he saw the pilots sitting in position, waiting. Neither of them bothered to wave.

Gerber moved to the rear of the plane and stumbled on the rails. These were part of a conveyor system consisting of metal bars with cylindrical rollers between them so that the loaded pallets would slide out of the aircraft easily. Gerber fell, grabbed at the red webbing that was the rear of the seats, steadied himself and moved deeper into the plane. Finally he dropped onto one of the seats and didn't move. The others had already buckled themselves in except for Kit, who climbed over Fetterman and Krung so that she could sit next to Gerber.

The load master circulated, yelling over the noise of the engines that they should buckle in. When he saw they had all complied, he took his seat and buckled himself in.

The roar of the engines increased and the plane began to vibrate. Gerber wiped the sweat from his face. He wanted to talk to Fetterman, to work out the details of the jump and the mission, but the Hercules lurched once and then began moving, sending vibrations through the fuselage. There was a stink of hot oil and burnt jet fuel that made the interior of the plane oppressive.

They stopped moving and the flight engineer came forward with a flashlight, checking the oil levels. A moment later he sat down and the aircraft began its takeoff roll. As the speed increased, the C-130 began to shake and rattle and the hot cargo bay filled with the stench from the engines and heated oil. Gerber tried to keep from leaning with the pressure as the plane rotated and struggled into the air. Kit grabbed Gerber's arm as if wanting protection and squeezed tightly as the C-130 shuddered. There was a whine and a series of bumps as the landing gear came up and almost immediately the flight engineer was moving again, checking various fluid levels.

After a long time it grew cold in the rear of the plane and the heaters kicked in, blowing hot air at them so that their feet froze while they sweated. Gerber unbuckled his seat belt and started to stand. Kit gripped his arm and he leaned close to her so that he could hear what she had to say.

"Where are you going?" she asked.

"Talk to Sergeant Fetterman. I'll be right back. Don't worry," he told her.

He looked at the deck, placed his foot carefully between the rails and the seat and moved to the rear. He sat next to Fetterman and put his lips close to the sergeant's ear.

"Tony," he yelled, "when we get to Ubon, I want you to take charge of this Air Force guy. Find out all you can about him, including whether or not he's jump qualified. I doubt he's HALO-qualified, but who knows?"

"Yes, sir," shouted Fetterman. "Planned on it. You didn't have to come over here to tell me that."

"No, I didn't. Listen, you thought about this HALO out of the B-52?"

"Not much. Just that we'll have to bundle up pretty good so we don't freeze solid and we'll probably have to go out the bomb bay."

"Yeah, that's kind of what I thought. You see any problem with that?"

"No, sir. Just figured we'd drop off the front edge of the bomb bay and free-fall away. I can't see a problem with it, unless they've got a full bomb load and then we'll have trouble, especially if they plan to drop the bombs close to us."

"We'll have to make sure there are no bombs on this one then."

"There's one thing I don't like," said Fetterman. "And that's dropping into a DZ where we've had no scouts and we don't have any photos. The terrain could be real shit."

"Yeah," agreed Gerber, his voice loud so that he could be heard over the engine noise. "Can't be helped. We'll bring that up and see if there's anything they can do for us on that point."

They sat quietly for a moment, listening to the roar of the engines. Finally Gerber got up and moved back to Kit. She smiled up at him and leaned close so that she could shout over the noise of the engine and the heaters. "You haven't had much to say to me."

Gerber nodded in agreement. "But I haven't had much of a chance."

"You didn't want me to go on this mission?"

"No, I didn't, but it has nothing to do with you." After he had said it, he realized it had everything to do with her. He didn't want to be thrown into a situation where he had to rely on her, although he knew he could. He didn't want to spend several days living in close quarters with her. A woman on a combat mission was a complication he didn't want, especially this woman, although he knew she was capable.

He thought about all that and realized he had shot down all his own arguments. It boiled down to the fact that she was a very attractive female, who had previously shown an interest in him, and that was the complication he wanted to avoid.

She leaned close again, her breath hot on his ear. "You promised me a dinner and you never delivered it."

Gerber felt his stomach knot, realizing that Morrow had accused him of the same thing. And both of them were right. He had promised them dinner and hadn't delivered .

She put a hand on his thigh. "It's all right. I understand you have been busy. So have I. But that doesn't mean I didn't miss you."

Gerber leaned against the red webbing of the troop seats and stared at the dull gray of the fuselage's interior. He didn't know what to say. It was almost a repeat of the scene from the night before, except that Kit wasn't drunk and he couldn't escape because he was in an airplane.

He ignored the one comment and responded to the other. "When we get back, I think I should buy you that dinner." He wanted to tell her that they needed to have a talk, but by refusing to talk about it now, he would be adding to her confusion. On a mission like the one they were going on, the last thing he needed was to have any member of the team upset.

Kit laid her head on Gerber's shoulder, looked up at him for a few minutes and then went to sleep. He wasn't sure what he was going to do. He couldn't afford to worry about her emotional state as they prowled the forests of North Vietnam.

He decided he'd have to do something to set the record straight the first chance he got. An airplane heading to Ubon carrying the rest of his team was not the place.

And then he realized that Maxwell had managed to railroad them out of the hangar before he had a chance to call Robin. She was probably madder than hell about that.

ROBIN MORROW STOOD OUTSIDE Gerber's hotel room and knocked. At first, she tapped lightly on the door, almost afraid someone would hear her. Then she knocked harder, slamming her fist into the wood, rattling the door in the frame. When someone across the hall opened his door and stuck his head out, she grinned sheepishly and shrugged at him.

If there was someone in Gerber's room, he wasn't answering the door. She waited a few seconds longer, embarrassed by the stony silence coming from the room. Finally she turned and walked down the hallway, her footsteps muffled by the stained and torn maroon carpet. When she reached the gilded elevator cage, she noticed exactly how shabby the hotel looked. Marked walls, ripped wallpaper and peeling paint. In its heyday it might have been a first class hotel but it had degenerated into a second class apartment building housing soldiers, airmen, and marines, many of whom didn't have the opportunity to stay the night very often.

As she left the elevator she noticed two civilians standing next to the door that led to the bar. Smiling, she approached them, thinking incongruously that their attire, sweat-stained khakis, was becoming the uniform of the American press corps. One of them wore a shirt with loops above the breast pocket. The loops were designed for the large caliber bullets used to kill big game on African safari. But the tunic had become fashionable with journalists in the tropics.

"George. Peter," she said, nodding at them.

George Krupp, the larger and older of the two, pushed at the door, holding it open for her. He had thinning, gray hair and a bald spot on the top of his head, which glowed red from too much time in the sun without a hat. His skin was unusually pale despite the time in the sun, as if he was sick to his stomach, but his brown eyes were clear. A network of red lines crisscrossed his nose, indicating that he spent more time writing his stories in the bar than in the office.

"Care to join us?" he asked, nodding at the bar. "Thought we'd grab a quick one before sallying out to find some food."

"Thank you," she said as she passed him. "Don't mind if I do."

Peter Latham had thick black hair that was fashionably long, hiding the tops of his ears. Robin knew that he thought of himself as some great adventurer, someone who didn't let obstacles stand in the way of the story. Yet his youth, the long hair, thick eyebrows, and almost delicate features suggested something else about him. He was a skinny man whose deep tropical tan stopped at his neck and shoulders so that only his face and arms were brown. Robin knew that he was embarrassed by the lack of muscular development on his body so he refused to wear shorts or go without his shirt.

He held a chair out for her and she took it. "Thank you, Peter."

He slipped into the chair next to her and leaned forward, leering. "The great warrior hasn't returned, huh?"

"Nope. Still missing."

Peter sat back, looked at George, who was signaling for a waitress. "If it was me, I'd be trying to find out where he is."

George had caught the attention of a Vietnamese girl who looked hot and miserable. Her hair, nearly waist long, was sweat damp and there were large stains under her arms and down the back of her skimpy blouse. She slid close to them, smiled weakly because she didn't have the energy to waste on useless flirtation.

George ordered beers for everyone and sent her off with a solid smack on her backside. She didn't react, already used to the crude behavior of the American press and too tired to care.

"Now," said George, turning his attention back to the people with him, "you say this captain left early and hasn't returned. Left you no note or anything."

"I never said all that." Robin felt as if her privacy had been invaded by George. He leaped to conclusions on the barest of information. The unfortunate thing was that he was right too many times.

"Okay," he said, slapping his hands together and rubbing them briskly. "I think your captain left you in the morning, assuming that he would be back before you woke up, or at the very least, before you got out of the room this morning. That's why there was no note."

"I like that," said Robin. She liked it more than she cared to admit to either of the men with her. It was what she herself had thought and it was what she hoped was true.

"Then," continued George, "he planned to call you, but found that was impossible."

"Now why is that?" asked Peter. "Telephones all over Saigon. It's not like we've fallen off the edge of the earth."

George turned to face him. "No. But Robin's captain might have. You're assuming that he's still in Saigon, but there's no reason to assume that. Given the way some of these guys work, I wouldn't be surprised to learn that he's in North Vietnam now." He grinned as if in on some private joke.

"Oh, come on," said Robin.

"Maybe not North Vietnam," said George, "but the point is, he's out of Saigon now, doing who knows what."

Robin was going to protest that, too, but the waitress arrived. She carefully avoided getting too close to George, set beers on the table and tried to retreat, but George was too fast for her. He waved a five dollar bill at her. Not MPC, the military payment certificates that were periodically changed to ruin the black market, but a real American greenback. She moved toward him, endured George's hand on her backside, and then snagged the bill.

As she disappeared into the crowd, Robin said, "Most bases have a field phone connection to Saigon."

George drank half his beer in a hasty, noisy gulp, leaving foam on his upper lip. "Who said he was on a base. Hell, Robin use your head. The poor man could be ass deep in mud, miles from a phone. This isn't like he's an errant husband who hasn't taken the trouble to phone. Besides, that field phone connection doesn't give him a phone from which to call you. It just gives the base commander the opportunity to talk with someone at MACV Headquarters if he has to."

She took a sip of her beer before speaking again. "Why are you going to such lengths to protect him?"

Now George grinned. "All part of the plot, my dear. First I prove what an understanding guy I am. Next, having disarmed you with that, I propose a dinner. You, thinking I'm harmless, agree. We go to dinner and then—"

"Nothing," interjected Robin, laughing. "Nice try."

"Okay. I fall back to my second position and ask, what in the hell is so important that he doesn't even have a chance to call the girl he left? The girl who, the last time he saw her, was puking up her guts—"

"Now how in the hell did you know that?"

"Elementary, my dear Robin. I saw you yesterday, pretty well blitzed. I saw you stumble into work this morning, wearing the same clothes you had on last night, looking as if the world was going to end and pissed that it hadn't happened yet. Now you turn up here, dressed in your fineries, looking radiant, obviously to rub out yesterday's image."

Robin glanced down at her silk blouse. She picked at the shoulders with her thumbs and index fingers, pulling it away from her sweat damp body. "This old rag?"

"Is marvelous," said George.

"Glad someone likes it."

"I think it's beautiful," said Peter, feeling left out of the conversation.

"But more importantly," said George, "is where the hell did your captain get to and what the hell is he doing?"

"I don't know," said Robin.

"Well, my dear, if you'll agree to that dinner, we'll work on that problem for two reasons. One is that you want to find him again, and two, I think he's at the heart of one hell of a good story."

IT WAS DARK when the C-130 touched down on the runway, bouncing high and dropping back in what was probably the worst landing ever made at Ubon. It wasn't totally the pilot's fault. He had to land in the middle of a thunderstorm that hovered over the field with winds in excess of forty miles an hour. The lightning kept blinding him, the radar and ILS had failed and if he hadn't been ordered to get the damned plane on the ground, he would have circled far to the south, waiting for the storm to spend itself.

They taxied through the howling wind and the driving rain, the interior of the plane lighted only by the storm. The aircraft rolled to a stop and the load master opened one of the rear doors, pushing it up and out of the way. The moment he did, the swirling rain whipped in with the hot, humid air of Northern Thailand.

Outside, on the taxiway was a solitary man holding a flashlight. He wore a regulation military rubberized poncho that was trailing behind him like a thick, useless tail. Behind him was a staff car and a three-quarter-ton truck, each with the engine running and the windshield wipers going at full speed. Their headlights blazed into the night, illuminating the slanting rain as it whipped along the tarmac.

Gerber moved closer to the hatch and looked out. There was no way to get to the car or truck without getting soaked. The engine noise died as the pilot shut down the engines so that the pelting rain drummed on the fuselage.

The man with the flashlight walked to the hatch, stuck his head in and yelled, "Let's hurry it up. Everyone's waiting for you."

Gerber shot the man a glance. "Thanks for the invitation." He turned to the load master. "What are your plans now?"

"We RON here and go back to Saigon tomorrow. I'll be in here along with the pilots for only another twenty or thirty minutes."

"Guess we can't leave the equipment then," said Fetterman, anticipating Gerber.

"Okay," said Gerber, "everyone grab everything and let's hustle to the truck. Tony, why don't you hop into the car with me?"

"Yes, sir."

Gerber moved to the hatch, staying to one side, out of most of the rain. He put a hand up to shield his face, saw the dome light in the car come on and leaped through the hatch. He hit the tarmac, slipped and twisted his body to correct his balance. His boots splashed water in the puddles as he jogged through the pelting night rain and skidded to a stop near the rear door of the car. It popped open and he ducked inside and slammed the door.

"Christ, that's a monsoon."

"Close to it, Captain."

Before Gerber could look up, the door was ripped open again and Fetterman dropped in. Rainwater was streaming down his face. He swiped at it, then wiped his hand on his soaked trousers.

"Give it up, Tony. You're soaked through."

Fetterman looked at Gerber, grinning. "Completely, sir."

"Gentlemen," said one of the men in the front, "I understand that you have a number of Vietnamese in your party."

Gerber nodded and stared at the man. "Who might you be?"

"Ah." The man twisted in the seat so that he could hold his right hand out. "Robert Cornett. I work with Jerry Maxwell."

"Well, Mr. Cornett," said Gerber, "we have two Vietnamese and a Nung tribesman. One of the Vietnamese is a Kit Carson scout that Maxwell plants on me every chance he gets. The other just graduated from the ranger's school. Or would in the next few days."

"Yes, well, that presents us with a problem."

Gerber looked at Cornett and then out the windshield. Gusts were rocking the car and the hammering of the rain was making the talk difficult. There was a rhythmic thump of the windshield wipers as they fought the rain. Gerber raised his voice, "Isn't there somewhere else we can talk."

"I have a briefing ready," said Cornett, "but I'm not sure that the Vietnamese should see it."

"Why not?" asked Fetterman. "If you trust them for the mission, there should be nothing in the briefing that they can't see."

"That's the problem . . . ?"

"Fetterman. Master Sergeant Anthony B. Fetterman."

"That's the problem, Sergeant Fetterman," said Cornett. "While you are right about the content of the briefing, it's the source material that I'm worried about."

"Source?"

"Yes, Captain. The information I'm going to give you will have to be disseminated to your men. I don't mind that. Hell, the very nature of the information is so perishable that in a week it won't matter if they're looking at it in Moscow or Hanoi. In a week I'll send it to them myself."

"I wish you wouldn't use the word 'perishable,'" said Fetterman half seriously.

"Ah, yes. Well, hell, in Hanoi they know we're concerned about this new missile. They'd be stupid if they couldn't figure that out."

"So what's the problem?" asked Gerber.

"I have a file of aerial photographs to show you. They were taken by the SR-71, our new spy plane. Taken from nearly a hundred thousand feet and it's like nothing you've ever seen. Like standing on the second floor of a building looking at the stuff. Incredible pictures. I don't want that known in Moscow. That we have that capability."

"My people are trustworthy." There was a finality in Gerber's tone.

"I'm sure they are, Captain, and I have no problem with you telling them everything you know. I just don't want them to see either the photos, or the after-action reports from the pilots on the latest missions."

"I find this all fascinating," said Gerber. "But can we get out of the car and into the building?"

Cornett snapped his fingers and the driver slipped the car into gear. They splashed through the night in silence while wind howled and the rain slammed into them and the windshield wipers shuddered. A few moments later they stopped in front of the Operations building, a sea of light. The leaves of the palm at the entrance were standing at a forty-five degree angle, attesting to the strength of the wind.

"Before we go in," said Cornett, "I want it understood that the Vietnamese are not to see the photographs or the after-action reports."

"I can understand why you don't want them to see the photographs, but how would the after-action reports hurt?" asked Fetterman.

"During World War Two," said Cornett, "the Japanese launched a series of balloon bombs at North America. These bombs traveled on the jet stream, which they had discovered, and were set so that the bombs would release automatically over the United States and Canada. It was a very successful plan. They started a number of forest fires in the northwest, did some property damage and killed six people in Oregon. The point of this is that the Japanese thought the bombs were falling into the sea harmlessly because there was absolutely no intelligence suggesting they were hitting the land."

Cornett stopped talking for a moment, glanced into the back seat and then continued. "Their plans called for biological warfare to be used once they had determined the effectiveness of the weapons. They would load disease-carrying bombs on their balloons and drop those, except they didn't believe the bombs were hitting the ground. They abandoned those plans. If the enemy finds out how dangerous this new missile is, they're going to deploy it all over North Vietnam. If, on the other hand, they think we're not concerned, they might just avoid the expense of it. What they don't know can't hurt us, just as the balloon bombs didn't hurt us because the Japanese had no idea how effective their bombs were. Hell, the remains of some of them were found as far east as Michigan. It was a very good plan, ruined because their intelligence system broke down.''

''The logic sounds weak to me,'' said Gerber.

''Granted,'' replied Cornett, ''but the whole point is that we don't have to hand the knowledge to them on a silver platter, either.''

''Okay,'' said Gerber. ''I want one of my people in on the briefing and then he and I'll brief the others. I'm not going in without the team fully briefed. You'll have to find a comfortable place for them to wait.''

''That's no problem,'' said Cornett. ''We'll stick them in the VIP lounge near Operations here in the hangar until you're ready for them, or they can wait in the break room behind there. They'll be comfortable.''

''If I might suggest,'' said Fetterman, ''I'd like to take a look at the parachutes and other gear we'll be using. I don't want to leave all that to someone who isn't going on the mission. Our weapons man will probably want to see the weapons and have them zeroed.''

''No time to zero them.'' Cornett slowly shook his head. ''These are good weapons.''

''Sergeant Tyme is going to be royally pissed.''

''You can tell him the Air Force had one of their weapons people check each of the rifles. They were selected with great care.''

''Yes, sir,'' said Fetterman. ''Sergeant Tyme is going to be royally pissed.''

Cornett had to grin at that. ''Yes, I think I understand. I wouldn't want to go into the field with a weapon that someone else checked for me, especially some Air Force puke. Unfortunately there isn't time to zero the weapons. Takeoff for your mission is in a little more than three hours. In that time you've got to get briefed, the equipment checked and changed into the new uniforms.''

''Not to mention brief our people, check out the DZ, get the recognition codes for both the ground and air elements, maps and everything else,'' added Gerber.

''I know all that,'' said Fetterman, ''and I say again. Sergeant Tyme is going to be royally pissed.''

6

SAIGON, SOUTH VIETNAM

Robin Morrow was hot and sweaty and had drunk more than she planned to. The night before, when she had been sick in Gerber's hotel room, she had promised herself that she would never drink again. Now here she sat, in the darkness of the outdoor bar, sucking down the beer as fast as either Peter or George would order it for her.

She wiped a hand over her face and then rubbed it against the thin material of her skirt, leaving a wet, ragged stain on her thigh. Her face had begun to tingle, telling her that she was getting intoxicated and even though she had refused the last beer, George had insisted and the waitress had brought it, sitting it in front of her with a smile.

"Dinner," she said.

Peter, who was weaving from side to side while he tried to remain sitting on his chair, and whose eyes refused to focus on the lights of downtown Saigon, giggled and said, "Dinner."

"Yes," said George. "We'll go to dinner in a few minutes. First we must plan tomorrow's attack on the secrecy of MACV Headquarters."

Robin crossed her legs slowly, tugged at the hem of her skirt because it had ridden all the way to mid-thigh. "Why MACV?"

"Use your head, Robin. That's where all the planning takes place, it's where all the secrets are hidden, and it's where we'll find the people we need to talk to."

"You know," she said, leaning forward and setting her chin in the palm of her hand, "Perhaps we should talk to Jerry Maxwell. He's the CIA wheel around here and has been involved in a couple of these messes."

"Shh," cautioned George. "We don't know who might be listening."

"Oh, hell, George, everybody and his brother knows that Maxwell is CIA. The real secret is the name of the Station Chief at the embassy."

"Dinner," said Peter again.

"Okay," said George. "Then we'll go find Maxwell and tell him that we know he's got Gerber on a super-spook mission."

"And tell him that we know Fetterman's been sent on it with him."

"You sure about this?"

"George, if Gerber's on any kind of important mission, then Fetterman is with him. Those two have been together ever since I've known them. They go on R and R together, were assigned to the same base in the States, and were assigned to the same unit over here on their return. Knowing that, we can dazzle Maxwell with what we already know and see what he drops on us."

George clapped his hands and smiled. "My dear, I think you're beginning to see the light. Fuck with their minds and they'll tell you things to try to shut you up. Tell you more because they think they can snow you with just a little bit of the truth, and before they know it, you have the whole story."

"Dinner," said Peter. He picked up his beer, took a swig and tried to set it down. He only succeeded in spilling it. He dabbed at it with the corner of a napkin and giggled helplessly.

"Robin, I really think we ought to pour the poor boy into a cab. You like my play on words there?"

She stood, trying to focus on the bar, which was spinning crazily, the lights blurring and blending until there were only bands of color in front of her. The noise of conversation disappeared, replaced by the driving beat of rock music from a club somewhere down the street. With one hand, she reached out to steady herself, felt her stomach flip over, and promised herself that she *would* never drink again.

"You okay?"

She shook her head gently to clear it, then rubbed her eyes. There was an explosion of colors that slowly faded when she stopped rubbing. When everything focused, she nodded slowly. "Everything is fine."

George helped Peter to his feet and he and Robin supported Peter between them. They walked him into the hotel lobby and out onto the street where they dumped him in a cab, giving the driver instructions on where to take him. George shoved money at him to make sure that Peter got to the right address.

"Now," said George, "that Plan A has succeeded, that is, getting rid of Peter without raising your suspicions, where would you like to eat?"

"I'm not hungry now," said Robin.

George placed a protective arm around her shoulder. "Of course you aren't, but if we don't eat something, the alcohol is going to be absorbed into your system and you'll get sick again. Food will take the edge off, and you'll be ready to see Maxwell early."

Robin only wanted to sit down and rest, but not close her eyes because that made her dizzy and sick to her stomach. If she kept them open, she wouldn't feel nauseous. "If there is something going on, Maxwell will be working tonight."

"Of course, and he'll be there in the morning, tired from a night of no sleep and ready to make mistakes for us to exploit. What we need to do is have dinner and then catch some sleep." He held up a hand and added, "Notice that I said sleep and not go to bed. Wanted you to know that I am as interested in this story as you are."

"I'm not sure how to take that," she said, "but I think it was nice. Okay, let's eat, then hit the sack."

"Right. And trap Maxwell in the morning."

She linked an arm through his, bumped a hip into him and said, "Okay, George. The show is yours. Let's get it on the road."

AT TWENTY-SEVEN THOUSAND FEET, the flight of F-4 Phantoms crossed the coastline of North Vietnam. Slowly, without a command from the lead aircraft, the flight began to separate, each pilot trying to keep an eye on both the jet nearest to him and the instruments in the cockpit. Radio chatter, so much a part of the air war in South Vietnam was unknown in the North. Everyone knew that the North Vietnamese monitored the radio frequencies and sometimes used the transmissions to spot the planes.

Each of the pilots, and the electronic warfare officers in the back seat, knew that the mission was a diversion. They were hanging their butts out for someone else. The Intelligence Officer, giving his portion of the serial lead briefing had known only that they were a cover for another mission. He didn't have any details, but told them that the cover was important. Saigon and Washington wouldn't have risked the flight for some bit of nonsense.

"Of course not," McMaster had said, interrupting. "Those boys in Washington would only risk our lives for important nonsense."

That had brought a laugh from the others, but the Intelligence Officer had only smiled. He shrugged. "I didn't make up the mission profile." He then detailed the known SAM locations, flack batteries, recognition codes for E and E, and gave the SAFE areas. When he finished, he asked for questions, but the men had flown so many missions over North Vietnam that they knew as much about the North Vietnamese capabilities and the locations of those capabilities as he did.

Now the flight leader, Captain Roger Newman, stared through the Plexiglas canopy, watching the flickering lights on the horizon, waiting for them to explode into antiaircraft fire. With a gloved hand, he touched the folded map that was attached to the holder strapped to his thigh and checked his waypoint. They were on time and on course.

A sudden, insistent buzz in his headset made him glance at the instrument panel. The intercom crackled. "Got a high SAM light."

Newman looked out of the aircraft, right and left, and then low, trying to spot the rosebud pattern of the SA-2 site, but even with the bright moon, all he could see was water in the rice paddies and dark stretches of jungle and forest.

"Pods on," he said, telling the aircraft commander of the jet carrying the jamming gear to switch it on. As he spoke, a line of tracers, emerald green softballs, floated upward about a mile away. Nothing to worry about because of the distance.

Almost as soon as he had completed the transmission, the ground in front of him began to twinkle as if someone had set off the longest train of firecrackers in the world. There were flashes of orange in front of him as the rounds detonated. The bursts seemed to be below them, far enough away to be of no threat, indicating the smaller weapons. It would take an 85 mm antiaircraft gun to reach them.

The flight fanned out even more. They began to pick up more SAM lights as the North Vietnamese operators turned on the radar sets. Newman heard the buzz again, but only momentarily as the set was switched on and then off.

More tracers lanced upward, making it look like a second-rate Fourth of July celebration. Cheap fireworks that either burned out quickly, or exploded into yellow-white flashes without the glowing red and green fountains.

"Missile launch," one of the pilots shouted.

Newman looked to the left and then right but the sky was dark. There was nothing on his instrument panel to indicate the enemy gunners were firing at them. To his left the wingman broke down and away, trying to get the missile to follow. At the last moment he would rotate into a rapid climb and hope the missile would slam into the ground before it could turn.

"We have Triple A all over the fucking place," came another radio call. The voice of the pilot was icy calm.

"Roger that. Flight, let's take it up. Begin slow climb... now!"

"Lead, this is Three. I'm hit."

"Roger, Three." Newman turned to look. The single Phantom had shot ahead of him and was climbing rapidly. In the dark, Newman could only see the twin flames of the exhaust, burning a bright blue. The crippled jet seemed to surge forward, bounced once and blossomed into flame. Fire burned on the underside and along the wings. The canopy, now glowing in reflected fire light, exploded away from the plane and then both the pilot and the EWO ejected.

"We have a SAM light," another of the pilots called on the radio.

At that moment the flight began to break up as each of them tried to evade the threats. Newman saw the steady burn of the upcoming missile and turned, diving down at it. He passed it in the power dive, waited and then hauled back on his stick, the G-force crushing him into his seat. A curtain of black rolled down over his eyes, cleared and then returned. He shallowed his climb and then rolled to the right.

Below him there was a plume of yellow-orange fire as the missile crashed into the ground and exploded into a fountain of flame. Suddenly Newman wanted to shout because he had beat that one. Adrenaline surged through him and he felt indestructible. As he stared into the star-studded night sky, he spotted the blazing trail of another missile. In horror, he watched as it closed on the F-4 to his right, which turned and juked, trying to shake the missile's guidance system.

There was another bright flash as the SAM detonated, momentarily blinding him, but as his vision cleared, he saw the Phantom wobbling through the air like a wounded duck trying to remain in the sky. A moment later the canopy snapped back as the crew bailed out and the plane began a slow spiraling dive to the ground.

Newman decided that he had seen enough. On the right was the last of his flight. Together they began a slow turn to the north and kept going until they rolled out on an easterly heading, racing for the safety of the coast and the Gulf of Tonkin.

Over the radio, he called air-sea rescue, giving them the coordinates where his two planes had gone down. He was afraid that they were too far inland to try for a rescue, and he could not stay on station to assist. He reported that all four men had gotten out and that he had seen the chutes, but didn't know if they had reached the ground. There had been nothing on the emergency frequencies yet, but the men could still be trying to get organized.

As they approached the coast they heard the two-tone wailing of a survival radio, indicating that someone, somewhere, had survived the long descent. Newman wanted to turn around and head back, but knew it would do no good.

He couldn't help them by running out of fuel over North Vietnam and having to bail out himself. Instead he reported hearing the homing tone of the radio.

When it faded, the backseater touched the intercom button. "I hope that jerk-off Intel guy was right. I hope this was something important."

"Yeah," agreed Newman. "I'd hate to think those guys get a stay in the Hanoi Hilton because somebody in Washington thought it important that we make a nonhostile statement. See, Ho, we can fly over your country any time we feel like it and you can't do a damned thing about it."

He hoped that wasn't the case, but somehow he doubted it.

AT UBON, CORNETT SAT in a small office with both Gerber and Sergeant Tyme, studying the intelligence photos from the SR-71. As they examined the pictures, Cornett was filling them in on the whole plan.

"We got several flights of fighters, both Air Force and Navy, flying over North Vietnam tonight as a diversion. Want the sky filled with activity."

Gerber was sorting through the photos that Cornett had scattered over the table. There were a couple of deep gouges in the wood that had been filled with paint. Gerber sat in one of the wooden chairs that creaked each time he moved. Tyme sat across from him, and Cornett was at the end of the table, flipping through file folders.

The room itself was tiny, the walls and ceiling covered with soft cardboard tile in an attempt to soundproof it. From the outside came the rumble of thunder and an occasional rattle of rain pelting the sheet metal of the roof.

Gerber pulled the map toward him. "Where are the SAM sites in relation to the DZs?"

Cornett took the map, spun it around and then worked his way through the grainy black and white photos. "Okay, most of the DZs are within five to seven klicks of one of the SAM sites we want investigated." He placed a picture on the map and said, "This DZ is actually about eight klicks from the SAM complex here, at Ke Sat. This is one of the places where we had missile launches but no detection."

"Uh-huh," said Gerber. "That's putting us down close to Hanoi and a good fifty miles from the sea."

"Can't be helped," said Cornett. "The other sites are farther inland. There are three of them, any of which is suitable for our purpose."

Gerber took the photo again and bent over it, studying it carefully. The DZ was a wide open field that might have been rice paddies or tilled ground with only a single structure, little more than a farmer's hootch visible. All four sides of the field were bordered by trees, but from the center of the DZ to the nearest tree line was a good klick.

Ke Sat was on a road that linked Hanoi and Haiphong. There was a major river far to the south and another to the north, but neither presented a problem. A couple of small, slender tributaries cut through the trees north and south of the DZ, but they looked small enough that Gerber and his men would be able to cross them quickly.

"What's the traffic like on this road? Looks like a major highway," said Gerber.

"During the day there is truck and foot traffic, most of it light. Some days, after the off-loading of the ships at Haiphong, it can get heavy, but the Vietnamese prefer to use more circuitous routes and travel at night. The road is far enough to the north that it shouldn't interfere with any of your plans at Ke Sat."

"Yeah," grumbled Gerber. "I'll bet."

Cornett started gathering the pictures and stuffed them in a folder. "I take it that you'll be going into Ke Sat."

"I don't know," said Gerber. "Justin?"

"I can't see where it makes a difference, sir. The enemy isn't going to expect us anywhere so we might as well take the site that's closest to the sea and extraction."

"How close to the coast do we have to get for the choppers to come in to get us?"

"Well," said Cornett, a smile on his face, "the Air Force asked that you get to the beach, but I think they'll try an extraction eighty or ninety miles in, if the situation warrants it."

"Why not have the choppers pick us up on the SAM site once we have the information?" asked Tyme.

"Because if you can get to the coast, there is a better than ninety percent chance they can get you out without drawing any fire. The farther inland they have to travel, the more likely it is they're going to get shot at. If no one's chasing you, what's a couple of days in the jungle?"

"You ever been in the jungle, Mr. Cornett?" asked Gerber.

"No, I haven't."

"Well, the jungle is loaded with all sorts of nasty creatures. Carnivorous cats, poisonous snakes and venomous insects. Mosquitoes that could carry off a child. Leeches— Sergeant Tyme's favorite form of parasitic life. Mammals to bite you and give you rabies. Plant life that can poison you, give you fevers, paralyze you or just make your life miserable. Not to mention that the longer we're on the ground, the better the chance that the bad guys will find us."

Cornett rubbed a hand over his face in embarrassment. "I guess I asked for that. At home I spend weeks in the field camping and hiking and hunting. Doesn't seem to be that big a problem."

"At home, it's not," said Gerber. "But we're talking about the jungle. An environment where a scientist who wanted to discover a new species of animal or plant life could probably waste a week looking for it. What I'm saying is that so very little is known about it that it doesn't resemble your hikes in the friendly mountains or parks in the World. Especially when you throw in a hostile population and enemy army.''

''Well, then, let me rephrase that,'' said Cornett. ''Is it a big problem to try to get off the site before the choppers come in?''

Now Gerber grinned. ''Not really. In fact, it would probably be best for us to get fifteen or twenty klicks off the site before pickup.''

''Good, we can compromise,'' said Cornett. ''If you get clear without pursuit, we'll haul you in before you get to the coast. If the bad guys, as you call them, are chasing you, we'll let the situation dictate the response. If you can shake them on your own, then we'll hold up the rescue. If you're about to be overrun, we'll try to get you out.''

''That's acceptable.''

''Then let's move on. Target is the missile complex at Ke Sat. Now, I have on this piece of paper the radio codes, code words and authentication tables for this mission. Memorize them and then destroy the paper.''

''I'd like my communications man to see that,'' said Gerber.

''Okay, but I want that information destroyed before you hit the DZ.''

For the next twenty minutes Cornett covered the radio frequencies to be used, check-in times, and when instructions or intelligence updates would be broadcast. He explained the coordination for the mission and that while they were on the ground no air strikes or Wild Weasel missions would be directed against any of the antiaircraft defenses around Ke Sat. They would have one week to complete the mission and call for extraction. If they hadn't checked in or been extracted by then, it would be assumed that they were killed or captured and a new mission would be mounted.

"One thing," said Cornett. "I think it is of paramount importance that none of the Americans are captured. The last thing we want is for the North Vietnamese to be able to parade you in front of the world press."

Before Gerber could respond there was a tap at the door. A moment later an airman dressed in damp fatigues entered and handed a sealed envelope to Cornett. "Excuse me a second," he said as he opened it. After he read the contents, he said, "That will be all, Airman."

When the door closed, Cornett said, "You better make good on this mission. The Air Force and the Navy report heavy losses on the diversion missions. Five planes down, and three others missing."

"The crews?" asked Gerber. "Where are the crews?"

"Reports indicate that some of them bailed out. Chutes were seen."

"Just what we need," said Gerber. "All the fucking North Vietnamese in the world out looking for downed aircrew, and we jump right in the middle of it. Nice job on the diversion."

FETTERMAN, DRIPPING RAINWATER, was directed through the Operations area and into a back break room. There were vending machines along the rear wall, the fronts brightly lit, offering everything from cold drinks to hot sandwiches. A toaster oven was on a waist-high counter next to the machines. It was flanked by an overflowing waste can. There were a couple of white picnic tables in the room, pictures on the wall torn from men's magazines and aviation magazines, and a musty odor of heavy rain.

There was one man in the room, sitting on a bench in front of a picnic table, drinking Coke from a can. He wore fatigues, the sleeves cut off short and ragged, and the stripes of a staff sergeant sewn to them. He looked up when the door opened, but didn't stand.

The driver of the car pointed and said, "That's Sergeant Barlett. He's the electronics expert for your team."

Fetterman stepped to the table and looked down at the man. He had broad shoulders but there was a roll of fat around his midriff that bulged over his belt. His arms were thick and covered with wiry black hair, but there was nothing about the arms to indicate great strength. The man's face was white, as if he didn't get out in the sun at all. He needed a shave and a haircut and a bath. He had brown eyes that were bloodshot.

"Barlett?" said Fetterman.

"Yeah, I'm Barlett. Who are you?"

"Master Sergeant Anthony B. Fetterman, the NCOIC for this mission."

Barlett took a drink of his Coke and set the can down carefully. "I'm impressed."

Fetterman looked at the driver and said, "That'll be all. Sergeant Barlett and I have some things to discuss."

"Fine. Captain Gerber will be down in a few minutes. Mister Cornett is briefing him."

As the driver left, Fetterman sat opposite Barlett. When the Air Force sergeant tried to pick up the Coke again, Fetterman's hand snaked out, locking itself around the other man's wrist and holding it against the table.

"Oh, now don't tell me," said Barlett. "You're going to prove how tough you are. Well, go ahead and give it your best shot."

"You have jump training?" asked Fetterman.

"What?"

"Jump training? Have you any jump training?"

"Not formal," said Barlett caught off guard. "Civilian training. Skydiving, when I was in college, but nothing in the military."

"That's something, anyway," said Fetterman. "You know what's going on here?"

"I know that you're going on some fucked-up mission to steal a fucking missile or some dumb thing and everyone would like me to go."

Fetterman's grip didn't loosen. He stared into Barlett's eyes and said, "You're going with us and you're going to pull your weight or you're going to die—"

"I don't think so," said Barlett. "You can make me go, but I'm not going to do anything I don't want to. You need me so you'll just have to look out for me. Everyone will have to look out for me."

Fetterman let go of the man's hand and sat back. He grinned and said, "You got that wrong. Hell, the captain and I could steal the guidance system and get it back here all by ourselves. We don't need you. You need us. Now, once we're on the ground, you had better do as we say or I'm going to put a bullet in your head."

Barlett tried to laugh, but only managed a high squeaky sound. "You wouldn't do that. You couldn't."

Fetterman didn't bother to answer. Instead he got to his feet and headed for the door. Standing in the hallway, looking wet and miserable, were the other members of the team. Fetterman waved them forward. As they approached he said, "Use the machines and get something good to eat and drink because it might be a while before you have the chance again. Galvin, that man is Sergeant Barlett and he's joining our team. Make sure he doesn't get lost."

"Sure, Tony. What will you be doing?"

"I want to find our equipment and check it out before they try to palm it off on us. I'll meet you back here as soon as I'm done. Captain'll be down in a few minutes."

7

UBON AIR FORCE BASE
THAILAND

Fetterman spent nearly an hour checking the equipment, sorting through it all carefully. He examined the parachutes and the reserves, the clothing all dyed black, the boots from West Germany, the Soviet assault rifles that looked almost new, the stacks of ammo and the cartons of C-rations. He searched for signs of rust, tampering, and neglect, but found none.

The combat knives were all brand new, held nearly razor-sharp edges and were dulled to a flat black so they wouldn't catch the sun or reflect the moon. Each of the AKs in the pile had Russian stamping on them, which meant they weren't cheap imitations manufactured in North Vietnam or Red China but quality weapons. It was the best that could be found. Everything looked to be in perfect condition.

He turned, ready to exit the hangar where the equipment was stored, but hesitated. He didn't like leaving it in the open, although access to the area was limited by a security policeman with a roster and a locked door. Fetterman was afraid that someone would sneak in and replace the good stuff with inferior supplies. Once Fetterman and the team parachuted into North Vietnam, who would know the difference.

As he left the hangar he saw Gerber and Tyme coming down the steps from the second floor. He waited until they were close. "Equipment looks good. Checked everything out."

"You meet the Air Force guy?" asked Gerber.

"Yes, sir. We, ah, reached an understanding."

"Uh-huh. He jump qualified?"

"Not by the military but he claims to have been a sky diver, so he's familiar with free-fall. But he probably hasn't made a night jump."

Gerber grinned. "Good. We can scare the shit out of him then."

"Yes, sir."

"And the rest of the team?"

Fetterman looked at Cornett and shrugged. "In the break room having a Coke."

"If you'll have someone watch the door, I'll brief my people in there and then we'll move to the hangar to collect the equipment."

"Fine. And I'll have someone get a deuce and a half into the hangar so you won't get wet on the way to the plane," said Cornett.

"I appreciate that," said Gerber.

"It's to prevent anyone on the base see us moving you from here to the B-52," said Cornett.

They walked from the stairwell until they came to a hallway. Fetterman opened the door of the break room. Gerber stood at the head of the table and looked at his team. Three Special Forces NCOs, an Air Force technician, who didn't look up to a stroll across the airfield, let alone a trip into North Vietnam, and a Vietnamese, a Nung and a woman. Somehow it didn't inspire him with confidence.

"Okay," he said, "here's the deal." He dropped the map on the table, pointed to Ke Sat. "Tomorrow morning we're going to make a HALO infiltration into this area for the purpose of identifying the guidance systems being used on the SAM missiles here."

When the briefing was finished, all of them went to the hangar. Fetterman pawed through the uniforms, finding pieces that would fit the Special Forces men. He found one for Barlett and then they all changed. The Americans were wearing black jungle fatigues with no insignia and no tags. The Vietnamese wore black pajamas and Krung wore tiger-striped fatigues.

Next they divided all the equipment so that everyone would have a load of about equal weight. When the equipment was distributed, Bocker made a radio check, and then they waited for the truck.

Moments later a horn sounded and a yellow light began to flash. An airman who stood at the end of the hangar near the door, pushed a button. The huge doors began to open with a rumble and the breeze, carrying a light mist, swirled in.

Gerber had expected it to be a cold wind because of the thunderstorm that had finally blown itself out, but it wasn't. The mist coated them quickly, and the humidity wouldn't let them dry. Instead of a refreshing evening breeze, they were greeted by an oppressive warmth.

As soon as the door was open far enough, a truck backed in, wrapped in the stench of its diesel engine. It ground to a halt and stood waiting.

"Let's go," said Gerber, shouldering a parachute with one hand and a pack with the other.

Tyme stood still, holding a couple of the AKs by the slings. "This means we're not going to zero the weapons."

"I'm afraid it's a luxury that we don't have time for on this one, Justin."

"Zeroing the weapons is not a luxury, Captain, it's a necessity."

"I understand that, Justin, but there isn't the opportunity to zero the weapons. Besides, we won't be doing any long-range shooting so it's not that critical."

Tyme shook his head and stared at the smooth concrete floor. "I don't like it, sir. I don't like it at all. Maybe once we're on the ground . . ."

"Once we're on the ground," said Gerber, "we're going to be as quiet as possible. The last thing we need is a bunch of people shooting."

"Yes, sir," said Tyme.

Fetterman approached. "Gear's in the truck."

"Then let's go. Once we're airborne, we can sort it out a little better."

They climbed into the rear of the truck. Gerber crawled along the wooden bench and chose a seat next to the cab. Kit followed, sitting next to him. Krung and Fetterman took positions near the tailgate while the rest of the team got into the other side, working their way around the pile of equipment.

As he sat down Barlett said, "I don't like this."

"You don't have to like it," said Fetterman. "You just have to do it."

"I joined the Air Force to avoid this sort of nonsense," Barlett continued. "If I had wanted to jump into North Vietnam and play in the dark, I would have become a fucking Marine."

"Why don't you shut up?" growled Tyme.

When they were loaded, Cornett dropped the back flap so that no one could see into the truck as it crossed part of the airfield. In the darkened confines of the truck's rear section, Gerber slapped the cab to tell the driver they were ready.

There was a grinding from the front as the starter turned over and then a belch as it caught. The vehicle jerked once, then lurched forward.

As they began to move Kit took Gerber's arm, felt her way down it and clasped his hand. She turned toward him but it was too dark to see, other than an almost invisible silhouette against the black of the cab. She leaned close and whispered, "I'm scared."

Gerber squeezed her hand. "What are you scared about? This is nothing new for you."

"I don't like jumping out of airplanes. And I don't want to go to North Vietnam."

Gerber tried to see the others, but that was impossible in the dark truck. He didn't know if they were listening or not. He whispered, "What scares you about North Vietnam?"

"It truly is my home," Kit answered. "If we are caught, I will be shot as a spy, but not before I'm tortured. They have some people who enjoy that work . . ."

"Kit, if any of us are caught, we're going to be shot as spies."

"Please do not let them catch me." Her voice was insistent with a note of terror.

"I can't . . ."

"You *can*," she interrupted. "You can make sure that I am not captured. Please, Captain. As a friend you cannot deny me this one request."

Gerber sat back, forcing himself into the corner between the side of the truck and the cab. With his free hand he wiped the sweat from his face. He needed a breath of fresh air, not the polluted diesel fumes that were blowing into the truck. He felt hot and his stomach was fluttering because he knew what Kit was asking of him. If they got into a situation where they might be captured, she wanted him to kill her. It was something that no one had ever asked of him before and he would refuse to do it, if she hadn't called him a friend.

They were more than that. He knew she loved him, and he had managed to avoid that situation most of the time. She understood his feelings and didn't let that bother her. But beyond that, she was a fellow warrior and a very good one. If that was what she wanted, he was almost honor-bound to grant her request.

He was silent for so long that she thought that he hadn't heard her. "Did you hear me?"

"Yes, I heard." He hesitated before speaking. "No bullshit this time, Kit. You really from North Vietnam?"

"Not far from Ke Sat. A small village on the river. A village called Hung Yen. There they knew my father was French, but they didn't care at first. Then—"

"I'm going to ask you once more, Kit, this the truth? I have to know."

She gripped his hand tighter. "Yes. This time it's the truth. I told those other stories because I thought that was what your interrogators wanted to hear. I told them all what they wanted to hear. I made up some good stories, too, but this time I'm telling you the truth."

"Okay, Kit. I'll make sure you aren't captured." But even as he said it, he wasn't sure he could do it. Fetterman could. Fetterman seemed to understand these things on a level that was below the conscious mind. He understood that sometimes the greatest gift you could give to a friend was death. Gerber knew it, too, but wasn't sure he had the courage to do it.

If he told Fetterman of the request, Fetterman would offer to carry it out, but this was something that Gerber couldn't delegate. It was something he'd have to do himself.

"I'll make sure," he repeated and then resolved to keep that situation from happening.

There was a squeal of brakes and the rocking of the truck stopped. Fetterman threw the flap up and out of the way, then disappeared over the top of the tailgate. Gerber could see the soft blue lights of the airfield's taxiways. Standing there was the B-52, a black shape that rumbled and vibrated as the crew prepared it for flight.

"Come on, people," said Fetterman. "We haven't got all night. Let's get the gear loaded."

Gerber slid along the bench, following Kit. He dropped to the ground as one of the people from the aircraft approached. Over the sound of the engines, or the APUs, Gerber wasn't sure which, the man shouted, "Who's Gerber?"

"I'm Captain Gerber."

"I'm Major Martin," said the man.

In the dark, Gerber couldn't tell much about him except that he seemed to be short and skinny. His voice was deep, though.

"I'm not accustomed to carrying passengers, especially ones who will be leaving early."

"Not my idea, either," said Gerber.

"As soon as your men get their gear stowed on board we can get this wound up." He shook his head. "I don't know how you're going to do it."

"Thought we'd go out the bomb bay," said Gerber.

"Yeah," said Martin, as if he wasn't sure about that, either.

Fetterman joined them, "Sir, there are a couple of questions I need to ask and no one I talked to had the answers for. First, is it possible for us to bail out the bomb bay?"

"I wouldn't think that would be a problem." Martin hesitated before adding, "Probably not the best way to get out of a plane, but it's all I can suggest."

"Okay. We need to have you slow to your lowest airspeed so you don't scatter us all over the place and we need to all get out as quickly as possible."

Martin looked around. "I'm not sure how we're going to do this." He rubbed a hand on the back of his neck. "I suppose I'll reduce the speed, open the bomb bay and out you go. Why don't you get your equipment over to the hatch there and the crew will get it stored for takeoff."

"You've been briefed?" asked Gerber.

"I know what's supposed to happen."

"Going out the bomb bay, we'll need a place to hook the static lines of the equipment pods," said Fetterman.

"Get with the crew chief," said Martin. "There's some handholds in there that might work for you."

"Yes, sir," said Fetterman. "I'll want to get a look at the bomb bay and check it out. Something that should have been done before anyone sent us out here."

A yellow truck with headlights blazing and a flashing light on the roof of its cab stopped near the front of the giant bomber. It sat there for a moment and through the back window they could see the driver twisted around looking at them.

"We're almost ready for takeoff," said Martin.

Fetterman turned and waved a hand. "Grab the gear."

Another Air Force officer appeared and pointed, "Use that hatch there. Spread it out along the bulkheads so that we don't have all the weight concentrated in one spot."

Fetterman moved off to supervise the loading of the equipment. He helped Kit pick up a bundle and together they carried it to the hatch. They hoisted it, and a man there snagged it and dragged it inside. In a few minutes they had the equipment loaded and were handing up the weapons, none of which were loaded.

Martin saw the progress and watched as first Kit, and then the rest of the team, disappeared into the belly of the aircraft. Martin touched Gerber on the shoulder. "Let's go."

Inside, Gerber found that his team was scattered throughout the plane, taking the seats that had been added for inspectors. Belted in and waiting, none of them looked thrilled by the idea of riding in the rear of a B-52, unable to see out and having to trust their fate to Air Force pilots who didn't look old enough to have graduated from high school, let alone find time to learn to fly.

Gerber strapped himself into a chair near the navigator. He tossed a glance over his shoulder and saw Kit sitting with her eyes closed and clutching the arms of her chair.

The engine noise increased as each of the ten engines was started. Gerber sat quietly watching the flashing lights on the panel in front of him, occasionally shooting a glance out the window nearby. He couldn't see much, just light reflecting off the low cloud base that had spawned the thunderstorm earlier.

They started to move with a gentle tug. The aircraft vibrated as they rolled along the taxiway and took up their position on the runway. A moment later the roar of the engines built into a thunder that wiped away all other sound. The vibrations increased until it seemed the plane would shake itself apart, and then they were racing down the runway and finally clawing their way into the sky.

For the first few minutes Gerber was forced back into his seat by the pressure of the climb. He sat there quietly as the aircraft shuddered in the turbulence, telling himself over and over that the pilot would never have taken off if the weather was too bad and that the jolting and rattling were normal.

They leveled out and everyone seemed to relax. The navigator looked at Gerber. "You planning to bail out at thirty thousand feet?"

"Yes. Why?"

"You know a person remains conscious for only seconds unless you're on oxygen."

"Of course."

"And you know that the air temperature is something like thirty or forty degrees below zero."

"Is there a point to all this?" asked Gerber.

"I just wondered if you've done anything like this before."

"Never out of the belly of a bomber, but I have made high-altitude jumps. We've got some gear to keep us warm and some disposable oxygen bottles."

"Oh." He was silent for a moment and then said, "You're going out in the dark. How can you do that?"

Gerber smiled. "Simple. We've got an altimeter on top of the reserve. Besides, you can see the horizon. There's plenty of light to see by."

The navigator shook his head. "Christ, what a deal."

The flight into North Vietnam was short. Within what seemed like minutes, the copilot came back and said, "We'll be in position in about ten minutes."

"Thanks." Gerber unbuckled his seat belt and flipped the shoulder harness out of the way. He stood, ducking his head to keep from hitting it on the low-hanging beams, then moved toward the rear to find Fetterman. He signaled the master sergeant and they all moved to the hatch that led into the bomb bay.

Together they gathered their team at the hatch. They helped one another into their parachutes, checking each other. Tyme passed out the weapons, handing each of them a magazine that he had loaded himself. He still wasn't happy about not having time to zero them, but that couldn't be helped now.

When everyone was set, Fetterman checked them one final time. Gerber stood next to Kit. "You know how to use this?" He pointed to the altimeter and the oxygen bottle attached to her equipment.

"Yes."

"Okay. Once we're outside you'll be able to see this. When the little hand rolls down to the glowing line, you'll be about a thousand feet above the ground. Pull the rip cord."

"I understand."

One of the crewmen came back. "Pilot wants to depressurize. You'll have to go to oxygen. Be about three minutes after that."

"Put on your oxygen masks," instructed Gerber. He tucked the bottle under the straps of his parachute harness, then tugged a ski mask over his face to protect it from the biting cold of the upper atmosphere. He rolled down the sleeves of his uniform, then pulled on a jacket and the gloves that would protect his hands. When he finished, he looked at his team, found them ready, and held a thumbs-up. One of the crewmen used the intercom to alert the pilot.

After the depressurization was completed, Fetterman opened the hatch into the bomb bay. The doors in the belly of the plane were closed and it was nearly pitch black in there. A moment later a light came on and Fetterman stepped through. Using the static lines, he attached the rip cords of the equipment pods to the handholds. Next he arranged the team the way he wanted them to bail out, pointing to each of them. He could feel the cold of the atmosphere seeping into the belly of the bomber. In seconds his toes began to tingle.

The crewman stuck his head in. "When the lights go out, it'll mean the pilot is going to open the bomb bay."

Fetterman held up a thumb to indicate that he understood the instructions.

Over the roar Gerber shouted, "We've got to get out quickly. Even at the reduced speed, if we hesitate, we're going to be scattered over several miles and won't be able to regroup."

At that moment the lights went out.

"Remember. Out quickly."

As Fetterman stepped back, there was a whine of servo motors and the bomb bay opened so that there was a rectangle of gray. The roar of the wind and engines filled the interior of the plane as bitterly cold wind swirled in, buffeting them.

The crewman who had remained near them shouted, "Thirty seconds. Twenty. Ten..."

Fetterman shifted around so that he could dump the equipment pods. As soon as they were clear, Tyme would jump, followed by Gerber, Barlett, Kit, Krung, Duc and then Bocker. If they weren't all out in seconds, they would be widely scattered.

The crewman counted down the seconds and as he shouted "One!", Fetterman shoved the pods. As they tumbled clear, Tyme plunged into space. Gerber was just a gray blur as he dived through the bomb bay. Barlett went out like an expert. Kit hesitated for an instant and Fetterman thought he was going to have to push her. Then she was out, looking like a teenager jumping into the cold water of the neighborhood swimming pool.

As soon as the others had jumped, Fetterman flashed a thumbs-up at the crewman who now stood in the hatch, and dived through the opening. He stretched out in a spread-eagle position to stabilize his descent. Below him, he could see the dark shapes of two of the men and the dark smears that marked the canopies of the equipment pods.

He turned in time to see the three planes in the B-52 flight disappearing from sight, blue-white flames marking the engine pods. Then, on the ground below them were orange-yellow flashes as the bombs from two of them exploded. Another diversion.

From miles away, he saw the muzzle flashes of the anti-aircraft weapons. There were air bursts, but nothing that came close to the B-52s as they turned toward the east, heading for their base in Guam.

He looked down and watched the numbers on the altimeter unwinding rapidly. In front of him was the line of the horizon, a sharp, defined line, easily visible. There was the black of the ground and the dark gray of the night sky. From the angle, Fetterman could tell that he was close to a thousand feet.

He glanced at the altimeter a last time and pulled the rip cord. He felt the chute pull free and heard the whispering sound behind him as the canopy spilled from his pack. There was a single, soft jerk and then a harder one that yanked the harness tight against his crotch.

Seconds later he watched the ground come up to meet his feet and he rolled to his shoulder in a perfect PLF. The ground was soft and damp and cold. He came to his feet and punched at the harness release so that the billowing chute wouldn't drag him across the open ground. Then he moved along the risers, rolling the chute into a loose ball. Finally, he determined a westerly course, where he hoped to find the others, and started walking.

8

THE FIELDS
SOUTH OF
KE SAT
NORTH VIETNAM

Gerber hit the ground hard, rolled into a muddy hole and then scrambled to his feet. He punched the quick release on the chute harness and stripped the oxygen mask from his face. He wiped the back of his hand across his face and realized that he was still wearing the ski mask. Instead of whipping it off, he left it on, using the black material to hide his features from the bright moonlight.

Free of the chute, he crouched on one knee, and felt the cold water seep through the fabric of his uniform. He let his eyes roam the open fields for signs of people moving, of soldiers maneuvering, but saw nothing. He gathered up his chute, rolled it into a soggy, loose ball and then started moving toward the north and the rally point.

At the edge of a tree line—he couldn't tell if it was the jungle or forest—he stopped and listened. Cautiously, he moved into it, staying near the edge so he would see anyone coming toward him. He dropped his chute and quietly worked a round into the chamber of his AK-47. Then he waited, his breath rasping in his throat, wishing that he had a drink. He knew he wasn't thirsty, and that the desire was a psychological effect of the jump and the situation, but that didn't lessen the desire for water. He fought off the urge and kept his eyes on the open ground in front of him.

After several minutes he caught a flicker of movement. He turned toward it and lost it and then looked away. With his peripheral vision, he found it again and watched as the man-sized shape worked its way toward the trees. Gerber didn't feel the need to challenge the man. He recognized the form and the hat and the weapon. Tyme stopped just inside the trees, and let the chute he carried fall to the ground.

Gerber hissed at him, saw him spin at the noise and then grin, his teeth white in the black of the night. He slipped closer to Gerber, dropped to one knee, and put his lips close to Gerber's ears.

"Didn't see any of the others."

"Damn," said Gerber. "I was afraid we'd scatter all over hell and gone."

A voice came from their right. "I'd suggest you two hold it down."

Gerber dropped to his stomach, aiming at the sound, before he recognized the voice as Fetterman's. Feeling foolish, he got up and moved deeper into the trees.

"As you can see," said Fetterman, "I managed to locate Kit, Krung and Galvin while you two played footsie."

"You didn't see either Barlett or Duc?"

"Nope. Did find the equipment pods, though, and managed to get them over here."

"Good," said Gerber. He reached up and pulled the ski mask off his face. There was a rush of cold air that made him shiver. He mopped the sweat from his forehead with the mask, stuffed it into a pocket. He turned to Tyme, "Get this stuff buried. Doesn't have to be too deep or too good because we aren't going to be around that long."

"What about the others?" asked Fetterman. "How long do we wait for them?"

Gerber pulled the camouflage cover from the luminous dial of his watch. "I make it an hour, hour and a half to sunrise. Take us thirty minutes to bury the equipment. They have thirty minutes."

"You going to leave them, then?" asked Fetterman.

"I don't see that I have any choice. We can't hang around here, and I don't want to leave anyone else behind. They know the target, so if they're in the clear they know where to go."

"That's what bothers me," said Fetterman. "Both know where we're going and I don't think it would take much for the North Vietnamese to convince Barlett to tell all he knows. All they have to do is suggest they're going to beat him, and he'll open up."

Gerber wiped his face again. "We can be in place tomorrow night. I can't see how he could compromise us that quickly even if he tries."

"Unless he walks into one of their patrols and starts talking the second they catch him."

"We can't abort now, Master Sergeant," said Gerber. "You want to stay here and wait for them?"

"No, sir, but I will. I think I should give them until midmorning at the latest. Besides, it'll give me a chance to clean up the DZ and spot their bodies in case they were killed in the jump."

"If they're dead, they're no problem."

"Yes, sir. Unless the bodies are recognized as parachutists and not pilots who bailed out. I'll hide them if I find them. I'll wait."

"Okay. The rest of us are getting the hell out of here." He dropped to one knee and pulled his compass from one of his pockets. He sighted a course to the north and pointed it out to Bocker.

"You sure we're in the right DZ?" asked Bocker when Gerber told him to take the point.

"No, and I won't be until it's light enough to see a couple of landmarks. Until that time, I want you to head zero-two-zero degrees and stop when you come to anything big."

"Yes, sir."

Gerber organized them quickly, telling Tyme to bring up the rear. Bocker then slipped deeper into the trees, followed by Krung and Kit. Gerber was right behind her, one hand on her shoulder as they stepped out. He then dropped back a pace so that he could barely see her outline as they moved among the shadows of the forest.

Bocker set a rapid pace because the vegetation was very light, more like a forest with very little undergrowth than the tangled nightmares of the South. There wasn't a canopy overhead so that moonlight and starlight filtered through, giving them enough illumination to see. Bocker avoided the big trees and bushes, using a branch as a walking stick to test the ground in front of him. The last thing he wanted to do was walk off a cliff or drop into a hole.

After an hour, Gerber noticed that it was getting brighter. Trees and bushes that had been little more than dark outlines against a gray background were beginning to take on detail. There were occasional flashes of movement as small animals and lizards scurried through the forest. The sky had paled and some of the stars had faded. As he saw that, he moved forward, passing Kit and Krung, until he caught Bocker. He stopped him and the patrol scattered among the ferns, trees and vegetation.

"I think we need to find a hiding place for the morning," said Gerber.

Five minutes later Bocker found the perfect spot. There was a source of water close by and good cover. They fanned out, with Bocker working his way into the clump of bushes and brush, leading them in. Once everyone except Gerber was inside and hidden, the Special Forces captain checked the ground around them for signs that they had been there. He found a couple of footprints that were rapidly filling with water and located a dozen others that had been made by the locals. There was nothing that pointed to them.

He slipped into the cover, being careful not to bend and snap the tiniest branches of the small bush or crush the newest blades of grass. While Bocker and Tyme took the first guard rotation, Gerber ate some cold C-rations. These had been packaged by the West Germans for the NATO forces, so it was doubtful that it would fool the North Vietnamese about who was there and using them, but it certainly wouldn't point directly at the Americans.

Gerber ate the food rapidly, buried the remains at the base of a small bush, and then drank part of his water. He set the canteen on the ground next to him and rolled over so that he was almost wrapped around the bush. The low-hanging branches concealed him.

Moments later he felt a light pressure along his spine. He turned his head and saw that Kit had crawled into the bush with him. She was now clinging to his back, molding herself to him.

Gerber whispered. ''We've got to spread out.''

''No one will see us.''

''For safety. We can't all clump up like this.''

''I feel safe this way,'' she said. She slid forward and nuzzled the back of his neck and then breathed into his ear. ''I feel very safe.''

''Kit, we've got to spread out.''

She didn't move except to lick his ear. Gerber felt shivers up and down his spine. He wanted to shout at her, shove her away from him, but couldn't. It would make too much noise. Besides, he could see too well. The sun was up, lighting the whole forest, and the bigger animals were beginning to stir. In minutes the local population would be out of their hootches heading to work in the nearby fields. He couldn't afford noise or movement.

"If you insist," he hissed, "you can stay, but behave yourself. Get some sleep."

She didn't answer, but she did stop working on his ear. He felt her face on the back of his neck and then felt the slow, moist exhalations on his bare skin there. She wrapped one arm over him, holding him tightly.

FETTERMAN MADE A QUICK, quiet search of the DZ but had no luck locating either Duc or Barlett. As the sun came up he slipped to the north and found a hiding place in the trees. He waited patiently, scanning the ground, searching for a sign of either the airdrop or the fate of Barlett or Duc. But there was nothing.

To the east he heard a babble of voices and then a lone man wearing black pajamas walked into the field. He turned once and shouted something to whoever was hidden in the trees there. Then he continued across the open field. About halfway to the other side he stopped, staring at the ground. He cocked his head to the right, looked around, then stooped over. He plucked something out of the mud, turned his back to Fetterman and examined whatever it was.

The man stood and put one hand to his forehead to shield his eyes from the rays of the rising sun. He looked toward the woods and it was then that Fetterman saw what he held in his hand. An Air Force combat knife like the one Barlett had worn the night before. Although it was more a survival tool than a fighting knife, it wasn't something that Fetterman wanted swung at him. As the man started toward him, Fetterman climbed from his belly to his hands and knees and then to his feet. Crouching so that he was covered by the dying branches of a fallen tree, Fetterman slipped to the right.

The man looked at the forest where Fetterman crouched, almost as if he had seen the Special Forces sergeant. He took a step forward, looked over his shoulder and then started to walk again. At the edge of the trees he hesitated and then plunged in. He shoved a branch to the side and stopped.

When it seemed that the man was momentarily distracted by something in the forest, Fetterman moved toward him with catlike agility despite the weight of the equipment he wore. He clapped a hand over the North Vietnamese's nose and mouth and shoved the blade of the West German combat knife up through the man's kidney and into his left lung. Then, as he pulled the man backward, he withdrew the knife and dragged it across the throat, severing the larynx from the trachea and cutting both the carotid arteries. A warm flow of blood ran down the man's chest as he died. A foul stench assaulted Fetterman's nostrils.

Fetterman ignored both the sticky, coppery-smelling blood, and the odor of bowel, dragging the man deeper into the trees. He hadn't wanted to kill him, but the man held Barlett's knife and Fetterman was afraid that it would be enough to compromise the mission. A smart enemy officer might figure it out.

He rolled the man over and stared at the face, now waxy looking. The eyes were open and unfocused. Fetterman pried the knife from the death grip of the man and then quickly searched him. In South Vietnam the man would have been suspicious because he was a "military-age male," but in the North, Fetterman wasn't sure that the term applied. Still, he had no choice.

He found a pistol concealed under the black silk shirt. That could only mean the man was an officer in some military unit. This wasn't a weapon captured from the French, but a Soviet-made 9 mm Makarov. Fetterman took the weapon and shoved it into his waistband.

Now Fetterman was certain that the man hadn't been a harmless peasant out for a morning walk, but an officer, possibly searching for the parachutists who had dropped the night before. Maybe a farmer had seen something and reported it. Not enough for the man to initiate a full-blown search, but enough so that he decided to come out to look around for himself.

After Fetterman concealed the body, he hoped the dead man wouldn't be missed for a couple of days. A minor official might not be missed for a week. There was no telling. It all depended on what he had shouted at the men who had remained hidden in the trees.

Fetterman worked his way back to the edge of the forest and peered into the open area. He waited quietly for fifteen minutes, but the only sounds were those made by the animals and the insects. And although the sun had barely cleared the horizon, it was already hot and humid. Sweat from the exertion of the fight didn't evaporate, but dripped along his sides, tickling him. It ran down his face and stung his eyes. But Fetterman didn't move, waiting for the ambush to spring, and waiting for the men to appear in the trees, but nothing happened.

When it was clear that no one had followed the man, and obvious that neither Duc nor Barlett was going to turn up, Fetterman crawled to the rear. When he was thirty or forty meters into the forest, he got to his feet. There was a rough trail leading to the north, a path worn deep by the feet of hundreds of North Vietnamese. The vines hanging from the trees, the lacy leaves of the ferns and the broad-leafed branches of bushes had been trimmed back so that they didn't block the trail. It looked like a green tunnel through the forest. Naturally, Fetterman avoided it.

Instead he worked his way through the trees, moving quickly and silently, slipping around the obstacles. He didn't want to touch anything, afraid that he would leave signs that an astute tracker could read. That slowed his progress, and it wasn't until midmorning that he reached the area where Gerber had taken refuge for the day.

IT TOOK MOST OF THE MORNING for George and Robin to track down Jerry Maxwell. At first he had been out of the office, and each time they checked somewhere, they were told that he had just left. Finally they had caught up to him at MACV Headquarters. The MP at the iron gate wouldn't let them through until Maxwell came out of his office to vouch for them. Then, reluctantly, he let them through, cautioning them not to go anywhere without Maxwell and not to poke their heads into any of the other offices.

Maxwell opened the door for them and let them enter the cold, dim interior of his office. He hit the light switch. "Forgive the clutter, but I've been busy lately. Grab a seat where you can."

Robin entered and fell into the large visitor's chair. She watched George move to the rear near the file cabinets. She leaned to the right, an elbow on the desk, glancing at the labels on the folders that were stamped Secret.

"What can I do for you now?" asked Maxwell, taking the seat in front of the desk. Nonchalantly, he tried to slip the Secret material into the drawer away from Robin.

"I'm not sure that I know how you can help," said George, leaning against the files.

Robin crossed her legs slowly, letting the hem of her skirt ride up. She wanted to smile as she saw Maxwell staring at her legs.

He tore his eyes away and shot a glance at George. "Why don't you just tell me what you want?"

George made a production of pulling a notebook from the pocket of his sweat-stained khaki safari shirt. "We know that Gerber and Fetterman have taken off on some kind of important hush-hush mission."

"So?" said Maxwell, turning. He noticed that the top two buttons on Robin's blouse were open. As he shifted to his left slightly, he could see down her blouse to the gentle swell of her breasts and the white lacy cup of her bra.

"So?" he repeated, distracted by Robin.

"So, we know that Gerber is out of the country."

Maxwell jerked around. "There is no way you could know that."

"Given what we know, we believe he is in North Vietnam," said George.

"Jerry," said Robin quickly, "we don't want you to violate any of your rules on secrecy, but we do want the story. We want it exclusively, as soon as it can be released without jeopardizing the men involved." Casually she reached down, scratched her leg and managed to pull the hem of her skirt even higher.

Maxwell kept his eyes on the pile of paper on his desk and then on the ceiling and finally on the wall about six inches above Robin's head. When he thought she wasn't watching, he looked at her legs.

"There isn't much to tell," said Maxwell.

"Come on, Jerry," said Robin. "I know better than that. Mack was supposed to have dinner with me last night. He left the room in the morning and never even called. That means something big came up."

"Damn," said Maxwell, and then tried to recover. "All it means is that he was sent out to check on the possibility of a Montagnard revolt."

"Wait a minute," snapped George. "What in hell are you talking about?"

Maxwell realized that his attempted cover story had blown up the moment he had pulled it. Inside MACV, he had been instructed to hint at a Montagnard revolt in some of the strike companies if someone missed Gerber or Fetterman, or had a suspicion that something was going on. Outside, he should have just denied everything.

"Robin, George, please. We're treading on ground here that is very shaky. I'm not sure what you should know, but too much of this getting out could be damaging to the war effort and prove dangerous to some of our people."

"You know," said George as he scribbled in his note-book, "I'm getting a little tired of that old chestnut. Every time you clowns make a mistake, let too much information slip, you fall back to national security or the war effort. It's beginning to wear thin."

"Sometimes it's true," said Maxwell. "Too much out now could get people killed."

Robin leaned across the desk and patted Maxwell's arm. "We're not out to hurt anyone," she said. "We just want to know what in the hell is going on."

Maxwell turned back to her and looked down her blouse. He could almost see her navel, but her breasts and nipples were discreetly covered by her bra. Maxwell found the peek-a-boo game to be very stimulating. He didn't want to do anything to end it, yet he didn't want to tell them things they had no need, no right to know.

As a compromise he said, "You forget that about the Montagnards and I'll give you something else. Tell you a little about what Mack Gerber is doing now."

"I'll go along with that," said Robin, rocking back in the chair.

"As long as it's good," said George. "We reserve the right to refuse if it becomes clear that you're handing us a line of shit."

"Okay," said Maxwell, realizing that he had dug himself a deep hole. "Mack Gerber, Sergeant Fetterman, and a small group of Special Forces NCOs are on a trail-watching mission just inside the Cambodian border."

"Oh, Christ," said George.

"Now wait a minute," said Maxwell, holding up a hand. "They're looking for evidence of a massive buildup of enemy forces in this region, including the influx of heavy weapons, like 20 mm and 37 mm antiaircraft weapons."

George shook his head. "Not going to wash, Jerry. That's not nearly as good as a revolt in the strike companies. And you've been using that one for too long."

"I never said there would be a revolt, but publishing a story like that could precipitate one. We just know that some of the Montagnards are unhappy. Our people are working to head it off, but too much information now could foil their attempts and jeopardize some of our people."

"How is that, Jerry? The Montagnards read the American newspapers?" asked George.

"I'm just saying that such a report would be, ah, premature."

"You're talking awfully fast," said Robin. She smiled at him and lowered her eyelids, trying to look sexy.

Maxwell studied her for a moment. She was showing him the long expanse of her leg and quite a bit of her thigh. She kept tugging ineffectually at the hem of her skirt. Suddenly he realized that he was being double-teamed. Her job was to distract him while George fed him the hard questions. He felt sick to his stomach as he realized how easily they had done it to him.

"I'm not going to tell you anything else. Just get out of here. You print anything and I'll call it a lie. I'll see that your press credentials are revoked and that you're both expelled from Vietnam."

"What's this?" asked Robin.

"Just get out," repeated Maxwell. He wanted to say that he had thought they were friends, maybe a little more than friends, but she had violated that. She had changed the rules of the game so that she was using his affection for her against him. She had been leading him along, flirting with him so that he would give out more than he should.

And he had fallen for it like a college boy new to the agency. Fallen for a pretty woman flashing some thigh and letting him look down her blouse. And it wasn't as if she had shown him anything. It made him angry that she would try something like that. And it made him angry that he had been dumb enough to fall for it.

At least he hadn't told them anything they didn't already know. Somehow they had learned that Gerber was off on a mission, but they had no idea of what or where. While they chased around the camps near the Cambodian and Laotian borders, Gerber would be finishing his mission in the North and then it would be too late to do any damage.

Robin watched Maxwell for a moment and then stood, smoothing her skirt over her thighs. It stopped a few inches short of her knees.

Without a word, they left the office. As they approached the iron gate they heard the door slam, but neither looked back. They checked out, walked upstairs and then out into the almost unbearable heat of late morning.

As he blinked in the sun, George said, "He gave us more than he thought he did."

Robin shook her head. "I don't feel good about what we did."

"What's not to feel good about? We went in, used the little information we had to get some more. We now know that Gerber is in North Vietnam and Fetterman is with him. We know that they have a team in there and we know that there might be a Montagnard revolt. Hell, this could keep us busy for a month and get us a Pulitzer prize."

Robin put a hand up to shade her eyes. She felt the sweat bead on her forehead, under her arms and drip between her breasts. "I don't feel good about using my friendship with

Jerry Maxwell the way I did. I was flirting with him to get information.''

"If you feel that strongly, ask him out to dinner. Hold his hand, kiss. Hell, fuck him if it'll make you feel better.''

"George, sometimes you're a real horse's ass." She looked at him and then added, "Not sometimes. All the time."

He touched her shoulder. "That may be true, my girl, but I'm one hell of a reporter."

9

SOMEWHERE NEAR
KE SAT
NORTH VIETNAM

Gerber snapped awake, sweating in the heat of the early afternoon, his black uniform soaked with perspiration. The fact that Kit still clung to his back didn't help matters, and the bush that kept the direct rays of the sun off him trapped the humid air around him. It felt as if someone had dumped a bucket of warm water over him.

For a moment he lay still, quietly listening to the sounds around him. The buzz of insects, the scratching of tiny claws as small animals climbed through the center of the bush, and the calling of birds as they screamed at one another. There was a crashing overhead as a couple of monkeys played in the treetops. He opened his eyes and stared at the rough, thorny bark of the trunk. He didn't want to move and wake Kit and then realized that she was awake.

He pushed backward and felt her shift out of the way. As he crawled from under the bush he listened for sounds of people other than his team. To the left he saw a large black shape that had to be Sergeant Bocker hiding. In the other direction, Sergeant Tyme watched the open ground that led to the clump of trees and bushes where they hid.

While Kit crawled deeper into the bush, Gerber slipped the map from his damp pocket. The map had been printed on thin vinyl to withstand the moisture of the tropics. He unfolded it carefully, and then refolded it so that the patch of North Vietnam where he was supposed to be was on top. Using his compass, he sighted on the landmarks he could see. Once he crawled to the edge of the forest and found a thin, broken streambed that sparkled in the sunlight. He took a compass reading. In the distance, to the northwest, he could hear the occasional rumble of a truck, indicating a road. And there was a swampy area to the southwest. Given all that, he was sure that the Air Force had dropped him right where they had said they would—south of Ke Sat.

With the compass and the map, he figured out a route that would get him to the SAM complex near Ke Sat after dark. It was through light forest and scrub, and barring unforeseen incidents like an American bombing mission, which he had been promised would not go in, or NVA maneuvers, they could get there a little after midnight.

Convinced that he knew exactly where they were, Gerber crawled to Tyme. He touched the young sergeant on the shoulder and pointed to the rear. Before Tyme could move, Gerber leaned close. "Fetterman?"

Tyme shook his head and shrugged. "You want me to look for him?"

Gerber shook his head, then folded his hands and placed them against his head as if he was sleeping. He also motioned to his mouth as if he was eating. He was telling Tyme to get some sleep or to eat something. To take it easy. And that they shouldn't be talking, given the circumstances.

Tyme's face was stained with camouflage paint, which made him look like a green-black nightmare vision in a horror film. He grinned, showing perfect white teeth. He nodded his understanding and worked his way into the trees and bushes, disappearing from sight in seconds. Although Gerber listened intently, he could not hear Tyme moving. There was only the quietest rustling of the bushes, caused by the light breeze.

For nearly an hour Gerber lay there motionless, his eyes shifting right and left as he watched for the NVA and the local civilian population. His left elbow was in a puddle of water, but it wasn't an unpleasant sensation. He could feel water seeping through his clothes to mingle with his sweat. Through the lacy curtain of an overhanging fern, he could watch a trail, and to the right, he could see a clearing carpeted with short grass and wild flowers.

A rustling to his left caught his attention. Kit appeared and crawled to him. She didn't speak. She put her lips next to his ear, as if she wanted to talk, but then blew her hot breath on him.

His first reaction was annoyance because it wasn't the time or place for games and then he realized that it was the time and place. Maybe the only time and place they would have for the next forty-eight or seventy-two hours. Instead of reprimanding her, he glanced at her and grinned, but didn't respond. After a couple of minutes she stopped, withdrawing to the hideout.

An hour later, Krung relieved him. Gerber crawled to the rear for water and food and to plan for the night mission. He found Kit sitting with her back to a tree trunk, her black pajama trousers pulled up to expose her legs to the light breeze. She had unbuttoned her blouse, letting it hang open. When she moved, he could see her small breasts.

He wanted to laugh. That was the last thing they needed on a patrol. A little sex to lighten the mood. He crawled past her and sat facing the other direction so that he wouldn't have to look at her. Besides, it made good sense. Cover all the approaches.

As the light began to fade, Gerber pulled Bocker to the side and whispered to him. "I'll want you on point again to-

night. I don't think Tony is going to find us before we have
to move out of here.''

"Shouldn't we look for him?"

"Why?" Gerber wanted to laugh. The idea that Fetterman was lost was ridiculous. He had thought that Fetterman would find them before dusk. But now Gerber expected
to find him at the SAM site. He said as much to Bocker and
then added, "I think Kit should be right behind you, so she
can help. According to her, this is her homeland. I don't
know if it is or not, but if she has a suggestion, listen to it."

"Do I take it?" asked Bocker.

"Shit, I don't know. Let the situation dictate. If you think
she's slinging crap, ignore her."

Bocker wiped his mouth with the back of his hand. "Do
we—do you—trust her?"

Gerber sighed and looked around toward her. He saw the
swell of her calf and trim ankle. He thought of everything
they had been through together, thought of the hillside in
Cambodia and the opportunities she'd had to betray them.
"Yeah, Galvin, I think I do. But keep on your toes."

"Yes, sir. When do we move out?"

Gerber pulled back the camouflage cover of his watch.
"Thirty minutes, moving slow and easy." Gerber showed
him the map, the compass headings, and the major landmarks. He was going to explain how to go about navigating
in the dark, then remembered that Bocker was on his second tour of duty, too. If he couldn't read a compass and navigate at night in unfamiliar territory, he had no business in
Special Forces or in Vietnam.

With Bocker briefed, Gerber circled the tiny perimeter,
talking to each of the men with him. He detailed Tyme for
the rear guard and told Krung to hang back, close to Tyme,
in case the young sergeant needed help. Both Tyme and
Krung asked about leaving Fetterman behind and Gerber
told them the same thing he had told Bocker.

Finally they shouldered the equipment, checking it to make sure that it was still in good condition or that it hadn't gotten wet during the day, and that there was nothing on it to rattle. Before he signaled Bocker forward, Gerber finished the water in one of his canteens so it wouldn't slosh around as they maneuvered in the forest.

With that, they moved out, leaving the campsite. Tyme would hesitate there for a moment and clean up anything they might have left behind. Their progress was rapid while they still had some light. The group moved through a forest that had little in the way of undergrowth. There were saplings and tiny trees all around them, and a carpet of dead leaves that was decaying so quickly it was a moist, slimy film and not a brittle, crackling booby trap.

When the sun set, the forest didn't turn into the black morass that the jungle did in the South. There was still light, from the moon, from the stars, from the fluorescent decaying vegetation. There were shades of gray and streaks of black with pale areas and ribbons of silver. There were sharp contrasts between the trees and the bushes and open ground. Bocker seemed to have a knack for choosing the path of least resistance and they made good time.

Once or twice they heard the scream of jet engines from passing aircraft, and once, in the distance, the crump of antiaircraft fire. The cry of a large cat slowed them for a few minutes. Gerber hadn't been frightened by the animal, but afraid they would find it necessary to shoot it. Of course, in North Vietnam, many farmers were armed with automatic weapons and were told to shoot at any American planes they saw. Pilots had reported seeing the tracers from those farmers on dozens of occasions. Still there was no point in advertising their presence.

They stopped to rest a couple of times, the men and Kit spreading out in a loose circle so that they would have a view of the entire area around them. Gerber wanted to drink his water. His mouth felt as if it was filled with cotton from the exertion of the night march through the forest. But he didn't want to drain a second canteen, sure that if he did, he would need the water later.

After ten minutes, they were up and moving again. Bocker, Kit, Gerber and then Krung and Tyme. They wormed their way through the forest and out onto an open field. Crouching they hurried across it and then came to a road. Since there was no traffic, Bocker didn't even stop. He sprinted to the other side and disappeared into the woods. When there was no firing, the rest of them hurried to the other side.

Thirty minutes later Bocker dropped to the ground at the edge of the trees. Gerber crawled to him. There was a four-foot-high earthen breastwork about fifty yards in front of him. Sticking up above it was the nose of a missile that was pointed more or less toward the sky. There seemed to be no one moving anywhere near the missile.

"Captain?" asked Bocker.

Gerber studied the moon and stars, figuring it was about midnight. They were supposed to listen for instructions on the radio if they were in a position to do so, but the last thing Gerber wanted to do was break out the radio equipment. There would be more instructions at six.

"We watch for a while."

"And then?"

"We penetrate the missile site and see if you can make heads or tails of the guidance system."

Bocker nodded, the gesture lost in the darkness. "I was afraid you'd say something like that."

NEARLY HALF A KLICK AWAY, Master Sergeant Anthony B. Fetterman crouched under the leaves of a flowering bush and examined the tail fins of a different SA-2 Guideline missile. He was no more than fifty meters from the missile, hidden on a slight ridge that allowed him to look down on it. The earthwork berm that protected the weapon didn't conceal it from him. Even part of the concrete road and the hardstand were visible in the pale moonlight.

As Fetterman studied the weapon he thought there was something wrong with it. It somehow didn't look right. The missile itself, a two-stage rocket with four tail fins, a set of small stabilizing fins about a third of the way forward and then a final, larger set just in front of that, seemed to be real enough.

It was the launcher that wasn't right. Fetterman knew that the SA-2 rested on a metal turret that could be rotated as first the Spoon Rest and then the Fan Song radars acquired and tracked targets. Hydraulics in the metallic base raised and lowered the missile, depending on the range and altitude of the incoming enemy jets. Behind the missile was a thick metal blast plate to protect the site.

Even in the moonlight the whole firing platform looked phony. It seemed to be no more than a training mock-up, to be used by the NVA for their recruits. From the air, it would resemble a real SAM site, especially in a jet traveling at five or six hundred miles an hour.

As a lone cloud slipped in front of the moon, Fetterman crept from his hiding place, and slid down the hillside until his feet rested at the base of a dry rice paddy dike. He crawled over it and then got to his feet. Crouching, he ran along the side of the dike, leaped over another, then dropped to the ground.

Around him, he heard nothing except the night sounds of the rice paddies. Insects buzzing in search of food. A light breeze rustled the grass growing on the dikes. From the missile complex there was nothing.

He felt sweat dripping down his temple but ignored it. Instead he scrambled to the side, up and over the dike and crawled along it until he reached a corner of the paddy. He rested there for a moment, watching and listening, and when he was convinced that he had disturbed no one, he was up and moving again.

In seconds he was at the base of the berm. On the other side of it was the SA-2. Fetterman could see the nose of the missile and the four miniature stabilizing fins on the nose cone. Patiently he waited in case someone, a guard, a technician, a soldier out for a smoke, had seen him working his way to the berm, but no one appeared to search for him. No alarms went off and no searchlights blazed. The site remained dark and quiet.

Slowly, his rifle held in his hands, he used his elbows and feet to crawl up the berm. He froze at the top, expecting to find barbed wire or booby traps, but apparently the North Vietnamese didn't fear saboteurs or guerrilla attacks.

He slid down the berm and found himself sitting on the ground no more than six or eight feet from the side of the missile. It was about thirty-five feet long and slightly over two feet in diameter. It was painted gray with a mottling of green and black to camouflage it from the air. The erector was dark green and looked flimsy. Fetterman moved to it and touched it, expecting to feel cool metal, but instead found rough plywood. For a moment he was confused and then looked again at the missile. It was a fake.

"Son of a bitch," he whispered. He had penetrated a dummy missile site. He slipped forward so that he was in the shadows thrown by the missile. The berm formed a semicircle with a paved road leading into the open end. That was for the trucks that brought the replacement missiles. To one side was a bunker of some kind. Constructed of concrete, it didn't look as if it belonged on the dummy site. Fetterman worked his way toward it.

On the side closest to the road was a metal door with a long metal bar across it. Fetterman lifted the bar and the door swung open with a whisper of well-oiled hinges. He entered the building but too little light filtered through the open door. There was a glint of light off metal and the smell of oil and dust. He couldn't see what was stored in the building. He knew that it wasn't a real SA-2 because the structure was too short for that. When he reached out, he touched a cool metal tube that was pointed at one end. He ran a hand along it and found short triangles of metal at the other end.

Using the available light, he bent close and tried to see what he had found. Compared to the mock-up outside, this was a miniature missile not more than five feet long. The diameter and configuration seemed to indicate an SA-7.

More confused now, Fetterman backed out the door and closed it. He crouched at the side of the building, listening to the sounds around him. By craning, he could see down the road to another of the missile launch areas. The whole SA-2 site would have six missiles and a command center. The thing to do was find the command center and see if it was an active one or another mock-up.

USING THE AVAILABLE COVER and crawling rather than walking, it took Gerber's team nearly an hour to cross the short distance from their hiding place to the berm guarding the missile. When they reached it, Gerber sent Tyme around the outside one way and Krung around the other. After they both disappeared into the darkness, Gerber, Bocker and Kit began a slow, quiet climb up the hard-packed earth.

When they reached the top, they slipped over and scrambled down the side. While Kit covered them, Gerber and Bocker scrambled to the side of the missile. Bocker put a foot up on the erector, heard the wooden thud and dropped back to the ground.

"Something's wrong here, Captain," he whispered.

Gerber moved forward and touched the plywood and then reached up to pat the side of the missile.

"Dummies."

"Sir?"

"Those CIA and Air Force dummies gave us the location of a dummy site."

At that moment both Krung and Tyme appeared. They took up positions at the opening in the berm to cover the team inside. Bocker watched them and then put his lips only an inch from Gerber's ear, "Now what?"

Gerber sat with his back against the plywood and looked at his watch. Twelve minutes after one. There was no way they could get to one of the other sites that the CIA had wanted them to explore. Moving at night with the caution that would be necessary, would take them three or four days to travel the seventy miles to the secondary target.

"Captain?" asked Bocker.

Gerber wanted to shout at him, to tell him to shut up and let him think, but knew it would do no good. Bocker wanted instructions and Gerber didn't have any. He took a deep breath of the night air that now held the hint of a chill.

"Let's explore the whole site. Maybe they erected a couple of dummy launchers to fool the Weasels. Maybe the real missile launchers are somewhere else."

With Kit and Bocker trailing behind him, Gerber moved to the entrance. He fell into a position next to Tyme as the young sergeant watched for the enemy.

Gerber examined the whole site. To his left the rise of a berm ring protected another missile. There wasn't much of anything to the right. An open field that had been planted with crops. In the center of it was a clump of trees and bushes that could conceal the headquarters and workshops, if this was more than just a dummy site.

From the left came a quiet voice. "Captain, I have good news and I have bad news."

Startled, Gerber rolled away, landing hard on his left elbow as he swung his weapon up. Fetterman materialized out of the gloom and shadows at the side of the berm.

"Christ, Tony," whispered Gerber, "I could have filled you full of holes."

"Had faith in you, Captain," said Fetterman, grinning. "You didn't shoot in North Carolina when I surprised you there, so I figured you wouldn't shoot here."

"So what's your news?"

"This is a dummy site. No real SA-2s on it at all. That's the bad news."

"You check the command vehicles and the maintenance sheds?" asked Gerber.

"Haven't gotten there yet, but I doubt they'll be manned," said Fetterman. He stopped talking and looked toward the center of the site. "You know, Captain, I found a bunch of SA-7s stored near one of those plywood Guidelines. That's the good news. I found real missiles here."

"So?" Then it dawned on Gerber. "The SA-7 is a shoulder-fired weapon. There has got to be someone around here to shoot it."

"Exactly."

He thought about that. No SA-2s, only the plywood mockups, but real SA-7s. Something about that troubled him. It made Gerber feel he had the answers he had been sent to find.

However, this wasn't the time to dwell on it. He had other things to worry about. He stared at Fetterman. "You find a sign of either Duc or Barlett?"

"No, sir. Ran into an NVA officer who had found Barlett's knife . . ."

"His knife?"

"I saw him pick it up. It looked like it was Barlett's knife. I thought Barlett might have dropped it while he was in the air. There was no sign of his body anywhere, or that of Duc. I had to kill the officer. I didn't want him running around with that knife."

Gerber shook his head, thinking about what Fetterman had just told him. The missing men were still missing. The only sign of them was the knife that Fetterman said the NVA officer had had. That bothered him greatly.

"That officer was alone?" asked Gerber.

"There was someone with him in the forest that I never saw, but no one came looking for him."

"I don't like it."

"Sorry, Captain, but there was nothing I could do. He had Barlett's knife and was coming right at me. I figured that if he disappeared, it would be more confusing if he disappeared completely for a couple of days."

There was more that Gerber wanted to know, but it wasn't the time or place for it.

"Okay, Tony, take the point. Justin, you've got the rear again. Bocker, Kit and I will follow in the center. Tony, you spot anyone, either take him out or take cover and we'll rethink this thing."

Fetterman glided to the right past Gerber and the opening in the berm. There was another of the concrete sheds that Fetterman was sure contained more of the SA-7s. He passed it and drifted along the edge of the road, a light gray ribbon that twisted and turned, and then stopped. He heard a bubble of laughter and then loud chattering in Vietnamese. Through a gap in the vegetation, he saw a single dim light bobbing like a lantern being carried by someone.

A moment later Gerber joined him and together they examined the tiny camp. There were several trucks, Soviet ZIL-151s that resembled a deuce and a half. They were covered with canvas covers and had wooden steps leading up into them. It looked as if they had been there for quite a while. Grass and weeds grew around the tires, which were low. The vegetation at the foot of the steps was worn away from frequent use. Apparently sometimes the rear of the

ZILs were used as maintenance workshops and repair sheds for the SAM sites.

Beyond them were several squad tents. They were canvas and surrounded by wooden walkways. From the interior of one came a diffused glow. Low voices, men talking quietly came from there. Not far from the tents were the Fan Song and Spoon Rest radars and their control vans. It seemed ridiculous to have those radars on a site that was little more than a fake.

Fetterman pointed to them and asked, "Are those dummies, too?"

"Hidden in the trees? I don't think so. This whole thing makes very little sense."

"What'll we do?"

"Infiltrate," said Gerber. "Slowly and quietly. Take out anyone who is moving around and then use grenades on the tent if anyone spots us. We kill everyone and then examine this site carefully."

"Wouldn't it make more sense to fall back? There's nothing here for us."

"Tony, I don't like this setup. A dummy site would have all fake missiles. There wouldn't be any real ones on it. It would have the berm and the roadwork because each of those can be seen from the air or in photos. Without them, the site is flawed and our Intel people could tell in a minute. But the radar vans are usually hidden. A fake site doesn't need them because they wouldn't be readily visible. I want to find out why they're here."

"Shouldn't we just pull out and let the spooks figure out what is going on?"

"They're going to ask us some very difficult questions. Since we're here already, let's see if we can find some answers. Then we get out." But even as he said it, he realized that he had all the information that anyone could want. The answer was buried in there somewhere.

"Yes, sir."

Bocker joined them then. He glanced at both of them but didn't say a word.

"Galvin, once we've got the site secured, I want you to examine those radar vans. Make sure that the proper electronic gear is in them."

"Yes, sir."

Gerber eased back then, his eyes on the campsite. He located the rest of the team and explained the plan. He told each of them that they would attack quietly from all sides, using their knives. At the first sound of firing, they would each attack the squad tents with automatic weapons and grenades. If no one fired, they would discover what they could and then slip into the night so that the Vietnamese wouldn't know they had been around.

When each member of the team understood the instructions, Gerber told them to fan out and begin the recon of the site. Without another word each member of the group faded into the dark. Gerber watched them and then began to crawl to the trucks parked close to him. As he reached them he listened, but could hear no evidence of anyone working inside. He then crawled under one of them, working his way to the front where he could see the squad tent. He looked at his watch and realized that the assault would begin in less than a minute.

10

SA-2 GUIDELINE
MISSILE COMPLEX
NEAR KE SAT
NORTH VIETNAM

Bocker killed the sentry.

It was a simple thing to do. He waited until the soldier passed him, then he rose quietly, grabbing the man from behind. With his hand over the enemy's mouth and nose, Bocker jerked him backward as he levered his knee into the small of the man's back. As he collapsed onto the fulcrum of Bocker's knee, Bocker cut his throat. There was the whisper of ripped silk as the knife slashed the delicate flesh. The man spasmed as his hot blood washed over Bocker's hand and down his chest.

It took the man a moment to die. He jerked right and left and heaved himself upward, trying to escape from Bocker's grip. Then he stopped struggling and was still. There was no tickle on Bocker's hand as the man tried to breathe. Just a rattle deep in his throat as the lungs collapsed and the heart stopped beating.

Bocker dragged him into the deep grass at the edge of the camp and stripped him of his weapon and knife. Not wanting to be burdened by the extra weight of the dead man's AK, Bocker broke it open and slipped the trigger housing and receiver group from the weapon, dropping the pieces into the grass and mud to hide them.

He moved forward again to the side of the van where the operator of the Fan Song radar would work. He pressed an ear against the thin metal but heard nothing inside. Satisfied that the van was empty, he skirted it and moved closer to the tent. When he was ten or twelve feet away he dropped to the grass and waited. From the inside, he could hear a little noise and the uneven, discordant strains of Vietnamese music. The movement of the men inside threw an ever-changing pattern of shadows on the canvas of the tents.

GERBER PULLED HIMSELF from under the truck and worked his way to the left, along the line of vehicles. He stopped near the last one and watched as one of his people came around the corner of the generator shed. It was a structure with a thatched roof and support poles around its perimeter. The sides were open, giving a full view of the generator that sat inside. It was not running.

The team member, crouched in the darkness at the edge of the shed and waited. Gerber was sure that it was Krung. A solitary enemy soldier approached from the other direction, a red glow between his fingers. When the enemy soldier stopped walking and leaned against the pole of the shed, Gerber's man struck.

There was a flash of movement and then a muffled choke, almost a cough, escaped from the guard who dropped his cigarette. He slid down the pole and Gerber's soldier lost his grip on the enemy. He rolled to the right, his foot drumming on the hard wood of the support. To Gerber it sounded as if he was banging on a bass drum, the sound echoing through the night, but there was no reaction from the men in the tent.

A moment later the team member emerged from the shadows and dropped into the grass, almost disappearing. Gerber followed the movement until his soldier halted a few feet from the squad tent.

The enemy soldier's body was in plain sight at the edge of the generator shed, but there wasn't anyone around to see it. Gerber crept forward then, moving on his belly and keeping his eyes moving. He slipped toward the shed and when he was close, caught the odor of fresh blood. He dragged the corpse into the shadows where it would be found less easily.

He stopped and surveyed the area. A faked missile site with men and radar all over it. Fetterman had found missiles of a different variety. There were questions that had to be answered, but Gerber didn't think he'd find them on the site. The best course of action now was pull everyone back and get the hell out. He figured he already had the answers and didn't know it.

He crawled back to the shed until he was close to the tent, nearly in front of the open flap that served as a door. Here he halted and rolled to his right. At that moment a man wearing a dark undershirt appeared in front of the tent. He held a cigarette between his lips. Fiddling with his fly he turned and began to urinate into the grass at the side of the boardwalk. At the sound of a shout from inside the tent, he looked over his shoulder.

Hastily he buttoned his fly and pulled the cigarette from his mouth. Suddenly he froze, staring into the dark. He took a step forward, off the boardwalk and then spun, leaping for the tent, shouting at the men inside.

Gerber jerked a grenade from his belt, pulled the pin and dropped it. His eyes on the tent, he let the spoon fly, mentally counted to two and tossed the grenade through the flap of the tent.

As it bounced on the wooden planking, there was a single shout of fear. Gerber dropped his face to the ground and the weapon detonated. He heard the shrapnel rip through the sides of the tent, men crying out in pain. Cries of anguish pierced the air as a second and third grenade went off, thrown by others on Gerber's team.

Gerber was on his feet, retreating. He dived for cover near the trucks, his weapon up and ready. A flicker of movement to the right caught his eye. Krung appeared, running across the open ground. He threw himself to the earth and opened fire with his AK, raking the sides of the tent that was beginning to burn.

Now Gerber realized that it was Kit who had killed the guard. It explained why the death of the enemy had been a little sloppy. Krung would have made a clean job of it.

Two men dived from the tent, rolling into the grass. There was a burst of fire and the copper-jacketed rounds slammed into the trucks behind him. Gerber ducked and came up firing. As he ducked, the enemy turned on him. He pushed his face into the soft, moist earth.

From the right there was a second burst from an AK. The ground around the enemy soldiers exploded. They returned the fire, the muzzle flashes lighting them like a strobe.

Gerber was up on his knees, his finger on the trigger. He held it down, aiming at the two NVA soldiers. He saw one of them hit. He flipped to his side, his weapon flying from his fingers.

The other man spun, aiming at Gerber, but caught a burst in the side of the head. He shrieked and dropped into the grass.

There was a wild burst from the rear of the tent, answered by the hammering of more AKs. Green tracers ripped into it. The shooting increased until the night was filled with the sound of it, and then suddenly, it all stopped.

For a moment it was quiet around him, the only sound was the building roar of the fire as it gained momentum, consuming the tent. A lone figure rushed out of the tent, screaming, his body ablaze. He fell from the boardwalk, rolled over, setting some of the grass on fire. The stench of roasting flesh drifted over to Gerber.

A figure came running from the far end of the complex, his weapon held high. He slowed, then headed straight for the burning tent, yelling at the top of his voice. Krung stood in front of him and shouted in Vietnamese. At close range he cut the soldier down, the flame from the barrel of his rifle stabbing out and brushing the enemy's shirt.

Gerber exploded into motion. He skirted the burning tent and ran toward the radar van. Bocker was standing at the foot of the wooden steps that led up into it, staring at the door.

"Anyone inside?" asked Gerber.

"I don't think so."

"Then go."

Bocker leaped up the steps, grabbed the knob and ripped open the door. Gerber followed him and dived through. He moved to the right and collided with a rack of equipment. A metal object dropped to the floor and rolled away with a clatter, but even in the darkness, Gerber could tell he was alone inside.

Bocker closed the door. A moment later there was a pencil-thin beam of light from Bocker's hand. He played it over the equipment, the radio gear and the radar screens and said, "Looks like the real thing. This hasn't been faked."

Gerber climbed to his feet. "Yeah. This is a real van but equipped with dummy missiles."

"And a concrete building with SA-7s," said Bocker. He was on his knees, checking the wiring to make sure it was all there, although he couldn't see any purpose in mocking up the equipment in the van since it couldn't be seen from the air.

"Let's get out of here," said Gerber. "We'll collect our people and get off the site."

The ex-filtration was simple. Gerber's group watched the burned tent collapse and the flames die. There were no further threats from the NVA soldiers. Convinced that the enemy were either dead or had fled, Gerber ordered his men to retreat.

From the command center of the missile complex, they entered the tall grass that bordered a farmer's field, diverted to the left and worked their way between the rows of the knee-high crops. At the tree line, they spread out, waiting for signs of pursuit. But nothing happened. The fire from the tent then spread to the truck park and generator shed and those burned quickly and brightly for a few minutes. Then the glow faded as those flames died, too.

Gerber felt an overwhelming need to get away from the missile site. He told Tyme to take the point and they started toward the east rapidly, using the fading moonlight and starlight to navigate. As the sky paled, Tyme found them a hiding place for the day. It was a thick copse of trees and bushes in the middle of the forest. A clear stream bubbled close to them. Gerber nodded his approval and they moved in, fanning into a loose circle with half the team on alert while the other half ate and then slept.

Bocker crawled to Gerber and whispered to him, "We can make the six o'clock check-in, Captain."

"What do you need to do?"

"Run the wire antenna up a tree and weave it among the branches. Won't be visible from the ground."

"Would anyone be able to get a fix on us because of it?"

"No, sir. We'll only be receiving and not transmitting. If we transmit and someone happens to be set on the frequency, they could triangulate, if they were prepared to do it. If we stayed on the air long enough."

Gerber took a deep breath and exhaled slowly. His muscles ached from the activity of last night. His eyes felt like someone had poured sand into them. The sweat he had worked up during the fight had dried, leaving a sticky, itchy film over his body. At times he could smell his own body odor. His black uniform was stained with mud, kerosene and ripped in two or three places. The very last thing he wanted to do was climb a tree with Bocker's wire antenna.

"You get it up," said Gerber.

Bocker grinned as if he had just been given a three-day pass. "I'll let you know when we're ready."

He turned and scrambled off until he reached a large tree with clumps of pine needles that looked like leaves from a distance. Since the branches hung close to the ground, Bocker could easily hoist himself up into it. He climbed high quickly disappearing from sight. A moment later he reappeared, dropped to the earth and worked his way back to Gerber, detouring long enough to pick up some of his equipment.

When he reached Gerber, he sat and plugged the leads from the wire antenna into the radio. He handed an earpiece and a splitter to Gerber, then, plugging another earpiece into the splitter, he plugged it all into the jack on the radio. He turned it on, adjusted the volume so that there was a quiet buzz from the static as he played with the gain knob and then only the hiss of the carrier wave.

For a while there was absolutely nothing to be heard. Then, quietly, sounding more like an insect buzzing from long distance, they heard their call sign.

"Diablo, Diablo, this is Cheyenne. Stand by for a message in three parts. Diablo, this is Cheyenne. Stand by for a message in three parts. Break. Break."

Gerber put a hand to his ear, pushing the tiny earphone in deeper and holding it there so that he could hear better. He cocked his head to one side and closed his eyes in order to concentrate.

"Part one," said the radio operator. "Aircrews downed in your vicinity. If possible locate as many as feasible and escort out. From original target, bearing one-two-five and one-seven-zero, twenty to twenty-five klicks.''

Bocker shot a glance at Gerber, who nodded. He had understood the message. The paper pushers in Saigon wanted him to try to find downed aircrews and escort them all out of North Vietnam.

''Part two. Target changed to Lima Lima five-eight six-one. I say again, target changed to Lima Lima five-eight six-one.''

That figured, thought Gerber. Send us on one mission and then have us check out something else. With the edge of his hand, he scraped some of the dried grass away so that he could write the numbers in the dirt.

''Part three. Royal Palace asks you to investigate the detention of our nationals at Saigon Sheraton. Code name Involved. Message ends.''

Gerber pulled the map from his pocket and checked the grid references. They had designed their own grid system so that anyone listening in wouldn't be able to plot anything unless they happened to have a map with a similar grid. And only Maxwell and Gerber had them.

He ran a finger down the map and located the new target. It was near Hoa Binh, sixty or seventy miles to the west. Someone in Saigon wasn't looking at the map. There was no way that Gerber could travel south and southeast on one mission, then turn west for a second and back to the north for a third. It would require traveling over a hundred miles in enemy territory while more of the North Vietnamese army joined in the search.

Bocker switched off the radio and asked, ''What was that Saigon Sheraton nonsense?''

Gerber couldn't help grinning. ''An oblique reference to the Hanoi Hilton, I believe. I think they would like us to try to spring some of our people from it.''

"My God," said Bocker, his face suddenly pale. "They want us to infiltrate Hanoi, find the POW compound and try to free the men, and still want us to hike to the coast?"

"If it's not too much trouble."

"What are we going to do?" asked Bocker.

Gerber didn't have a quick answer for that. He was in place and had the chance to do it. But he didn't have the information. No one had briefed him or his team on the Hanoi Hilton. All he knew was that it was on the southeast side of Hanoi, but he didn't know where for sure. He didn't know how many guards there were, what the routine was, or even where inside the Americans were being held. It was a pipe dream thought up by someone sitting in an air-conditioned office in Saigon. Someone who had a bright idea and had the power to see that it was sent down the chain of command.

But there was nothing that Gerber could do, no matter how much he'd like to help the prisoners. If he tried, the best he could hope for would be some of his team surviving to be taken prisoner. At worst, they would all die in the attempt. Nothing would be gained by it. He rejected the idea.

"We'll rest here for the remainder of the day and then head out tonight," he said. "We'll try to find those downed crewmen, but I can't see us trying to get to the other missile site or trying to break into the Hanoi Hilton. It won't work."

"What are you going to tell them in Saigon?"

"That we had to get our butts out of North Vietnam before we joined those men in Hanoi. Besides, we've got some good information for the Intel boys."

THE KNOCKING AT HER DOOR forced Robin awake. She rolled to her side, opened her eyes and stared across the room, but didn't get up. Instead she shoved her hands between her thighs and tried to go back to sleep, but the hammering continued until she shouted, "All right."

She climbed out of bed and slipped on the jungle fatigue jacket she used for a robe. Since it was large, it hung to mid-thigh. Fumbling with the buttons, she stumbled to the door. Before opening it, she ran a hand through her hair, trying to straighten it slightly.

Robin opened the door to find George standing there, his hand poised to knock again. She left the door open and walked back to the bed, her head pounding. She sat on the bed, yawning. When George was inside, she asked, "What in hell are you doing here so early?"

"We've got a noon deadline on the story and we need to find out a few things." He looked at her, staring at her ankles, and then slowly moving his eyes upward until they were on her face. "Christ, you're good looking," he said, the awe obvious in his voice. "I woke you up?"

"What d'you want, a testimonial? Yes, you woke me up."

"You look about ten times better than any woman I've ever seen when she's just gotten up. You looking for a husband or live-in lover?"

"George," she said tiredly, "You've got a wife waiting for you in the States." She smiled. "And for all I know, you've got one waiting for you here, too."

"Not here," said George. "You got any coffee?"

She pointed to the tiny kitchen off the main room. George looked at the heavily lacquered cabinets, searched through a couple of them, and found little except canned fruit and juice. Finally, he saw a tin of coffee. He ran water in the chipped sink and then filled the pot. He added the coffee and plugged it in. That finished, he walked back into the combination bedroom-sitting room and dropped into the only chair that wasn't covered with books, magazines or clothes. He glimpsed a pair of mesh bikini panties that would hardly conceal anything and wished that he could see Robin modeling them.

For a moment she studied George and then stood up. She located a pair of khaki pants and slipped them on without giving George anything to look at. She turned her back to him and let the fatigue jacket fall to the floor so that he could see her bare back.

"Jesus, what in the hell happened to you?"

Too late, she remembered the network of puckered scars that marked her back, hips and backside. Because she couldn't see them, she often forgot they were there. As she pulled on a white blouse, she said, "Something that happened a couple of years ago. No big deal."

"No big deal," said George. "It looks like you were—"

"It's something I'd prefer not to talk about." She spun on him, buttoning her blouse. "Okay?"

"Sure. Fine." He got to his feet. "I'll look at the coffee."

"What's your plan for today?"

His voice, muffled because he was in the other room, was still strong. "Thought it would be nice to talk to the B-Team commander here and see what he has to say. Talk to the folks over at MACV-SOG and quiz them. Let some things drop and maybe we'll have scared them enough to tell us some more."

He reappeared carrying two cups of coffee. He held one out to Robin. "Here's your eye-opener."

George sat down again and took a long sip from his coffee. He let his eyes roam over the clutter in the room. There was a table littered with books and papers. A portable typewriter sat in front of the chair. Beer cans and empty whiskey bottles were lined up against one wall. The shutters were closed and the air conditioner was on, but did little to dissipate the heat of the room. George was sweating heavily now, but Robin didn't seem to notice the heat.

He suddenly felt bothered by this woman. The scars on her back had done it. She'd seen more of this war than he had. He hoped that he'd never see it as closely as she had. Now he was afraid that she was a woman on the verge of a collapse. The way she lived, the haphazard way she pursued her career, the scars, all suggested something was going on below the surface. From the evidence, it was obvious that the captain she was chasing had something to do with it. George wondered if the captain suspected Robin Morrow's mental condition.

As the silence between them broadened and then became uncomfortable, Robin set her coffee cup on the floor and disappeared into the bathroom. She didn't say a word to George. He sat quietly waiting for her, wondering if he should derail the investigation now that he understood some of her motives.

Robin returned a few minutes later looking even better than before. She grinned at George, showing him her perfect white teeth and said, "Ready to go?"

George gulped the last of his coffee and said, "If you are, then I am."

WHILE GERBER AND FETTERMAN discussed the new orders, which they decided were stupid, Bocker was working with the radio, changing the frequencies and listening to the emergency channels, and trying to locate the downed crewmen. He knew that anyone down in North Vietnam would be broadcasting on 242.0, letting everyone know they needed help. If he could pick up the signal, it would make the task of locating downed crews easier.

He had left his wire antenna in place. If worse came to worst, he could leave it there forever and let the North Vietnamese wonder about it if they ever found it. The only thing wrong with it was that he couldn't turn it for a directional bearing on the signal, if he found one. He would have to make voice contact and get directions then, if possible.

With the earpiece in place and the radio set, there was nothing more that he could do. He sat with his back against the trunk of a rough-barked tree and ate some of his C-rations. As he spooned the bland-tasting boned chicken from the can, he listened to the carrier wave telling him that they were receiving, if anyone ever bothered to transmit a call for help.

Of course, the downed crewmen had the same problem that Bocker had. To transmit invited eavesdropping. A clever North Vietnamese, with a radio and a directional antenna, could do a lot for the men searching in the field. Two NVAs narrowed the search zone and a third would be able to pinpoint the transmitter.

But, if the downed men wanted to escape from North Vietnam, they had to transmit. If the air rescue people were running the show properly, the downed men would have been given a time to make contact with the SAR forces. They would make one or two quick calls and then the rescue choppers and the covering fighters would come in.

Finally he heard a two-tone wailing sound. A voice broke in requesting, "Beeper come up voice."

"This is Baron One."

"Say authentication number."

"Zero-six-one-two."

"Roger, Baron One. What was the first car you owned?"

"Ah, Mustang."

There was a pause, then the voice came back. "Say favorite football team."

"Broncos."

"Roger, Baron One. We have choppers inbound. Please come up again in one-five minutes. Do you copy?"

"Roger."

Bocker waited in silence, the white plastic spoon stuck in the forgotten can of boned chicken he held. The whole routine that he had listened to was the Air Force authentication system. Each pilot, crew chief, load master, everyone who was on flight status, had a card filed with all kinds of personal information on it. That card, and that information, was a classified document that would be given to the commander of the SAR forces before rescue. It was a way of ensuring that the man on the ground was not a decoy trying to suck in aircraft for an ambush. If the answers did not match, the SAR forces would refuse to land.

When nothing more was broadcast right away, Bocker shut off the radio to conserve the batteries and then worked his way to where Gerber and Fetterman sat, their heads together as they studied the map.

"Call sign of downed crew is Baron One," whispered Bocker. "Air rescue is trying to get in to him."

"You have any idea where he is?"

"Only that he's fairly close, based solely on the strength of the signal. But hell, sir, that could be caused by skip and he could be down around the DMZ."

"Any other information available? Anything at all?"

"No, sir. Air rescue advised him to come up again about ten minutes from now. I'll see what I can get."

"You going to try to contact him?" asked Fetterman.

"I don't think we should. But I'll keep monitoring."

"Okay," said Gerber. "And keep me advised. You get something a little more definite, let me know."

"Yes, sir."

"Tony, let's grab some sleep. We'll get started again about dusk. Galvin, you'll have to monitor the radio this afternoon, but you can trade with Justin later. I want everyone to catch a little sleep."

"Yes, sir."

Gerber watched the communications sergeant retreat into his hiding place. When he was gone, Gerber said, "I'm going to sleep first shift. You take second?"

"No problem, sir."

"The moment you get tired, wake me up. I've probably had more sleep lately than you."

Fetterman grinned. "That's only because you officers are by nature lazy."

Gerber crawled toward a bush and slithered under it. He rolled onto his back and felt the rough ground, broken twigs and dropped thorns pricking his skin. He rocked right and left, crushing them, and then closed his eyes. Although the sun was hidden by the bushes and the trees, he could feel the heat radiating through the leaves. Sweat broke out now that the early morning chill had burned off, and Gerber knew it was going to be a long, hot day. There was almost no breeze and what there was didn't reach him in the bush.

Before he closed his eyes, Kit slipped in beside him. She laid her head on his belly, her eyes open so that she was looking up at him. Gerber wanted her to find another hiding place, but didn't want the confrontation that was sure to follow. Instead he winked at her, telling her to stay, and then closed his eyes.

As he did, the images from the firefight the night before flashed in front of him. Not much of a fight. They had ambushed the enemy almost as they slept, killing them before they could respond. Not exactly the fairest way to fight a war, but one that the NVA and VC had used many times. Sneak up on a unit and cut the throats of the sleeping men. In fact, some of the more clever VC cut every other throat. It inspired terror in those left alive, and they communicated that terror to everyone they talked to.

He reminded himself that they were fighting a war and that was what happened in war. He forced the thoughts from his mind and briefly wondered about the new orders. There was no way he could carry out all three parts. Given the option, the part with the greatest likelihood of succeeding was to locate the downed crewmen and help them out. Exploring another missile complex or trying to break into the Hanoi Hilton wouldn't work.

As he thought about the dummy complex, he realized there was something that he had seen, or been told about, that should have bothered him. Something about it was wrong, but he didn't know what it was and before he could figure it out, he fell asleep.

11

MACV HEADQUARTERS, SAIGON

Robin sat quietly while George Krupp did all the talking. She had no desire to flirt with Major Richard Palmer. Instead she studied his Spartan office. By MACV standards, it was a cubbyhole, furnished with a battered desk, two old chairs and a bookcase crammed with Army manuals. The walls were bare except for a single picture of John F. Kennedy. The lone window overlooked the parking lot and although the blinds were down, they weren't closed, so that the bright morning sun invaded the room.

"This afternoon," Krupp was saying, "we're putting a story on the courier plane that shows a group of our soldiers are operating illegally inside North Vietnam. Unless, of course, you can show me that my statement is wrong."

Palmer leaned back in his chair and laced his fingers behind his head. "Mr. Krupp, I have no knowledge of any of our teams currently operating north of the DMZ."

Krupp grinned. "A very precise answer."

"And a truthful one." Palmer dropped his feet to the dirty, tiled floor and leaned his elbows on his desk. "Look, we have people running around all over South Vietnam. We're engaged in trail-watching activities, and some of our men have gone into both Cambodia and Laos for that purpose. We've made no real secret of that. However, current regulations prohibit our men from operating in Cambodia, Laos and most especially, North Vietnam."

"Then you're denying the report that a Special Forces team is in North Vietnam."

"I don't know how to make it any clearer to you." A smile creased Palmer's face. "Anything else?"

Krupp rubbed his chin and then flipped through his notebook. He glanced at Robin, then looked at the major again. "Yesterday morning a highly placed source suggested that a mission had been mounted into the North."

"Yes, I'm very familiar with your—meaning the press's—highly placed source. The catchall leak peddler who is never identified, or who can be blamed if the information turns out to be faulty."

Krupp jotted down what Palmer said and then stood. "Our story is going out today. Special Forces soldiers are working in North Vietnam. Anything you say, or anyone says, is going to sound like you're trying to cover up illegal operations on foreign soil."

The smile left Palmer's face. "That's irresponsible journalism. You'll be feeding the fires of discontent that already threaten to cripple our effort."

"Maybe the effort should be crippled," Krupp shot back.

"That's not for you to decide." Palmer slapped a hand to the desktop. "Who in the hell died and left you in charge? When did the press get the mandate to tell all, regardless of who suffered?"

"The people have the right to know."

"That's an old one," said Palmer. "The people's right to know stops where it conflicts with national security or my right to life."

"That, too, is an old one and you argue from your own self-interest on this. You want to make a statement, fine. If not, then the story goes out this afternoon."

Palmer looked at Morrow, who had spent the whole interview staring at the floor. Although he was addressing Krupp, he spoke to Morrow. "Can I say something off the record?"

"I don't like to start an interview and then go off the record," said George.

"And I don't like irresponsible reporters," snapped Palmer. "I'm not going to say anything you'll want to print."

"Then let's stay on the record."

"Fine. Miss Morrow?" When Robin looked up, Palmer said, "Miss Morrow, I know that you have a relationship with one of our officers, so I'm counting on you." He turned to stare at Krupp. "Mr. Krupp, as I said, I have no knowledge of any operations in North Vietnam run by the Special Forces, but that doesn't mean there isn't something going on."

Krupp was about to speak, but Palmer held up a hand to stop him. "No, what I'm trying to say is that by printing your story in the blind, so to speak, you might be compromising security. It's the reason that we tell our men who are captured not to make up lies for the enemy. First, a skilled interrogator will eventually penetrate the lies. And second, by making up something that sounds convincing, you might inadvertently compromise some other mission."

Krupp shook his head. "What a load of shit."

"Believe what you want," said Palmer. "But I do know that we have pilots on the ground in North Vietnam right now, fighting for their lives, and if you print your story, you're going to make it that much harder to get them out."

Krupp was going to protest again and then realized that Palmer had let something slip. "Pilots on the ground. You have names and units?"

"I have nothing. It's an Air Force matter. But right now, those men are trying to evade the NVA. A story in the American press, broadcast all over the world, is going to be heard in Hanoi, and even if your facts about a covert mission are wrong, you're going to damage our chances of getting those men out safely."

"How long?" asked Krupp.

"How long what?"

"How long do I have to sit on this? I put it on the courier plane at noon, it'll be on the morning news tomorrow. I delay until a later flight, maybe the news tomorrow night."

"I could call you when it's safe."

"Not good enough, Major. Then others will have the story, too."

"Then check with me this afternoon. But please don't write your story yet."

George Krupp got to his feet again. "I'll call you this afternoon. Please don't try to avoid me or my call or I write my story. And I'll be expecting a better answer from you about this."

Palmer stood up and extended his hand across the desk. "Thank you for understanding. I'll try to find something to make it worth your while." He glanced at Robin who was now standing, too. "Nice to meet you, Miss Morrow. Hope to see you again soon."

FETTERMAN STOPPED AT THE EDGE of the bush and spoke in a stage whisper. "Somebody's coming."

Gerber was awake in an instant, his hand reaching for the AK near him. He felt the pressure of Kit's head on his belly, but hadn't moved enough to awaken her.

"How many and how far?" he asked quietly.

"At least a dozen at two hundred yards, maybe a little less."

Gerber reached down and touched Kit's shoulder, knowing as he did that she was now awake, too. She rolled away from him and froze facedown, her palms pressed to the ground in case she needed to move quickly.

"What kind of formation?"

"Looks like some type of search party, Captain, but I don't think they expect to find anything. They seem to be going through the motions, and aren't paying much attention to that, either."

"What do you think is our best course of action?" Gerber trusted Fetterman's judgment.

"I think we should spread out a little more and let them walk past us. They're not exactly beating the bushes. If we're quiet, I think they'll miss us."

"Kit, you stay here. Crawl in as deep as you can and don't move. Shoot if you have to, but try to avoid it. We don't want to get into a firefight now."

She nodded her understanding and then shifted around so that she was next to the base of the bush. She snagged her weapon and pulled it around, the barrel pointing out. Gerber slipped forward into the open. He had expected the air to change, but it was no cooler or warmer in the open than it had been under the bush. There was no breeze blowing. Only the humidity settling on him like a warm, wet blanket.

"Where's Bocker?"

Fetterman smiled and pointed. "Climbed the tree with his antenna, reeling it in as he went up. Totally invisible from the ground."

"Tyme?"

"Took Krung and moved to the west to the other side of the stream. There's good cover for them there."

Gerber looked to the west but couldn't see a thing. He didn't like the way the team was spread out. That would make it hard for them to support one another if a fight developed, but then, if one or two were caught, the others might get away. He sacrificed unit integrity for the possibility of escape.

"Okay, Tony," he said. "Let's you and me head to the south and east."

Fetterman nodded and took off quickly. Gerber turned to make a rapid survey of where they had been. Nothing was lying around to give them away. Nothing pointed to the bush where Kit hid, and there were no footprints leading to the stream. Satisfied they had cleaned up after themselves, Gerber followed the master sergeant, dodging among the trees and bushes as they fled deeper into the forest.

Up ahead, there was a slight depression in the ground with a bush and a rock at one end. Fetterman pointed to it and grinned, disappearing into it before Gerber could react. As Gerber went by, he could see no sign of Fetterman. In fact, he knew that Fetterman could extract himself from the hiding place quietly if he had to.

A moment later Gerber found a hiding place for himself. An outcropping of tented rocks with several large bushes that provided good cover. If he was rushed from the front, he could escape through the rear while the stones on the sides would protect him. He crawled in and waited patiently, quietly, for the enemy to appear, or for the sound of gunfire if they discovered part of his team.

Lying there, his face close to the dank earth, he felt his heart pounding. Sweat poured from his face and down his sides and he wanted a drink. He wanted to scream, to shoot, to do something rather than lie there quietly. He shifted around so that he could see into the forest.

It seemed to take them forever. Gerber's back began to itch like he was lying in a patch of nettle. His ears twitched at the sounds of the forest as the animals ran from the men or chased one another. He could hear the buzzing of flying insects and saw a single spider inch its way up the rough surface of the rocks.

Suddenly there was a burst of laughter and a shout in Vietnamese. From the sound of the voice, Gerber knew it wasn't a warning and from the new laughs, that it had to be some kind of joke. An instant later the first of the NVA soldiers appeared.

Unlike those who were assigned to units in the South, these soldiers wore badges of rank and unit identification. One man had bright yellow shoulder boards with a red border. From the single stripe and the two stars on it, Gerber knew that the man was a North Vietnamese first lieutenant. The officer also wore a pistol in a holster held up by a belt with a red star in the center of the buckle.

Next to him was a sergeant. He was a burly man, much older than his lieutenant, with a face that had been scarred badly. He had blue shoulder boards with three stripes on them. Like the lieutenant, he was wearing dark green fatigues with collar tabs.

The rest of the men were scattered too far and wide for Gerber to see much detail. One might have been a corporal from the way he talked and gestured to the others. Each of them carried an SKS carbine, except for the sergeant, who had a new looking AK-47.

The thing that surprised Gerber the most was their boots. He had expected Ho Chi Minh sandals, but instead they were wearing canvas shoes that looked like high-topped basketball shoes. Gerber suspected that the design was stolen from the French since the boots looked like the lightweight patrol shoe used by the Foreign Legion.

As they came closer to him, Gerber saw that the officer wore the collar insignia of the cavalry. Inside a red parallelogram were the crossed sabers and horseshoe that marked a NVA cavalry officer. Gerber wondered if the man was a horseman, if he could actually ride one, or if the North Vietnamese Army had changed the cavalry as much as the U.S. Army had.

One of the privates sat at the base of a tree, his back against the trunk. He lit a cigarette and took a few puffs. Suddenly the sergeant was next to him, almost nose to nose, shouting at him. The private looked startled, jumped to his feet and then handed the cigarette to the sergeant. The NCO took a deep drag, exhaled and handed it back to the private. Both men laughed and then rushed through the trees making enough noise to wake the dead.

If Fetterman's theory was right and these men were a search party, they would never find anything. They made too much noise and weren't looking very hard. When they finally disappeared and Gerber could hear them no longer, he crawled from his hiding place, picked up Fetterman and headed back to round up the rest of the team.

Once they were gathered together and hidden behind a screen of bushes covered with bright orange flowers, Gerber told them, "I think we'd better get out of here. We're still too close to the SAM site at Ke Sat and to the roads leading to it. Apparently no one has discovered the fight there yet because those guys weren't looking too hard." He hesitated, studying the faces of the people with him. They seemed to be waiting for him to give them their orders.

"Galvin, what's the status of the men on the ground?"

"Haven't been picked up yet, sir. Triple A and MiGs have kept our people from getting in. That is, up to forty minutes ago. At that time we were still in radio contact."

Gerber took out his map and studied it quickly. "Justin, I want you up on the point. Sergeant Krung right behind. Kit and I will make up the middle element with Sergeant Bocker and then Sergeant Fetterman in the rear. Compass course of one two five. Questions?"

"You sure we should be moving in the daylight?" asked Tyme.

"No, especially with search parties out. But it'll be dark in a couple of hours and I don't like the proximity of the SAM site. We're still too close to it. We'll risk moving in the daylight, staying to the cover and moving very carefully and quietly."

"Captain," said Fetterman, "we've got a fairly large, known enemy force nearby."

"I know that, Sergeant, but I don't want to risk a firefight with them. We let them roam unharmed and everyone feels safer. If they all suddenly disappear, or we get into a firefight with them, we'll have a division in here looking for us. Right now, it seems to be their second string searching for lost pilots and that's the way I'd like it to stay."

"Yes, sir. Thought I should mention it."

"And that's why you've got the rear guard action. Make sure those guys don't sneak up on us. Make sure they don't find our trail. If you have to, take them out, but I'd prefer that we didn't."

"Understood."

"If there is nothing else, Sergeant Tyme, please move out. Remember, slow, easy and quiet."

GEORGE KRUPP SAT ACROSS THE TABLE from Robin and studied her closely. She hadn't spoken much during the day, avoiding eye contact with him and avoiding attempts to draw her out. Now she picked at the food in front of her and sipped at the rapidly warming beer.

"Robin, what's gotten into you?"

She took a drink and set the glass on the table, watching the bubbles rise in the beer. Finally she looked at George and said, "I'm not convinced that we should be following this story so closely."

"Why not?"

"It's just as Major Palmer said. We might be endangering some men without realizing it."

"You mean your Captain Gerber and his boys?"

She smiled weakly. "Not necessarily. But that doesn't make any difference. Palmer was right. When did we become so knowledgeable that we could make life and death decisions for everyone?"

"When did the Army? Or the government?"

"At least the government has some legitimacy," she said. "It wasn't self-appointed."

Krupp put down his fork and looked at her. "I'm not going to do anything to intentionally hurt anyone, but I am going to get the story. If we don't keep the pressure on, then those elected officials are going to think they're above the law and we'll be no better off than the people in Russia."

"I'm only saying that we should go easy until we're sure that we're not accidentally hurting someone."

"What's really on your mind?" asked Krupp. "This isn't about some unidentified pilots who might have bailed out over North Vietnam."

Robin started to tell him. The words formed in her mind and she could hear herself speak them, but before they got to her mouth, they were gone. She couldn't tell George about her love for Gerber, or how her heart had soared when he reappeared in Vietnam. She couldn't tell him that she knew he was free of her sister because Gerber had left her in the States without even a farewell phone call. There were so many strange twists and turns to the relationship that she had no idea where it was going. All she knew was that if Gerber happened to be in North Vietnam and was killed there, she would not have the opportunity to explore those feelings with him.

Instead of all that, she said, "We shouldn't file our story until we're sure of the facts. Even if someone else beats us, we have to be sure of what we know."

"I can live with that, Robin."

She finished her beer. "Then let's go over to the embassy and see what they have to say. If we hurry, we can still make the evening press briefing."

TYME HEARD THE ENEMY SOLDIER, and dropped to the soft forest floor, the decaying vegetation cushioning him. He slipped to the right until his side was against a hardwood tree. A lacy fern, dripping moisture, was directly in front of him. He could smell the rotting vegetation, the damp dirt and wet bark on the tree.

As he inched toward the sound that he had heard, he was careful not to put all his weight down at once. He moved slowly, cautiously shifting his hands, hips, knees and feet until he was sure he would make no noise. To move silently in a jungle, or forest, required total concentration. It could take him an hour to move fifty feet, but he didn't have to crawl that far.

Then, in a clearing, he saw a single man dressed in a green fatigue uniform. He wouldn't have been concerned, except the man wore a chest pouch that held three AK-47 banana magazines, a rucksack, and an entrenching tool. The noise he had heard was the quiet tap of the tool against the rounded, metal canteen on his hip.

Tyme slipped away and eased to the left. Movement caught his eye and he spotted another NVA soldier. Tyme froze, one hand out in front of him as the enemy pushed aside the branches of a bush, his hands fumbling with the buckle of his belt. As Tyme looked up, his eyes met those of the enemy soldier.

Before the enemy could move or shout, a hand snaked out of a dense bush and was clamped over his mouth as his head was jerked back. An arm flashed and Tyme was sure that he could hear the sound of a throat being cut. For a moment there was only a thin line on the skin and then blood blossomed, bursting from the severed arteries and veins, spilling down the front of the man's uniform, staining it crimson. One hand clawed futilely at the air and then dropped.

An instant later Tyme was on his feet, moving toward the first soldier he had seen. He waited until the man stepped from the clearing into the trees, then swept his feet out from under him. The man hit the ground with a grunt, the air forced from his lungs. At that moment Tyme struck, burying his knife in the hollow of the throat, twisting it savagely as he clamped his free hand over the man's mouth.

The man's hands shot up and grabbed Tyme's shirt, dragging it close to his face. The soldier's eyes were on Tyme. They went wide with fright and then seemed to glaze over, staring into the trees. As his grip loosened and his blood stopped spurting, his eyes rolled up into his head. He died with a dry rattling deep in his throat.

Tyme jerked his knife free and spun. Krung stood near the body of the other soldier. He pointed to the rear and Tyme nodded his agreement. He pushed the body of the dead man under the protective leaves of a bush to conceal it. Then he helped Krung hide the first body. He picked up the NVA's ammunition and the weapon and slung it over his shoulder.

Before they retreated to the rest of the team, they watched the clearing and the forest, but saw no sign that anyone else was there. Tyme was convinced that the two men would not be out on their own. In minutes, an hour or two at the most, there would be more enemy soldiers around, hunting them.

When Tyme was sure that no one would appear quickly, he withdrew toward the rest of the team.

Gerber was surprised when Tyme and Krung appeared in front of him. "What happened?" he asked.

"Ran into part of another search party," said Tyme. "Krung killed one and I got the other. Figured there were more of them, but we didn't see anyone."

"Shit!" said Gerber. "I suppose there was no choice in the matter."

"No, sir. The one guy almost stepped on me. Krung had to take him. That meant I had to kill the other one."

"Damn!"

Tyme was crouched on one knee, his rifle in his left hand. He was breathing rapidly, as if he had run the distance back to the team. With his right hand, he wiped the sweat from his face and wiped it on his blood-stained uniform.

"I suspect there are others around," Tyme repeated.

"I agree, Captain," said Fetterman, his voice barely audible. "There are a lot of people out here looking for those downed flyers."

"We could break for the coast," said Gerber. "Our orders are open-ended."

"Or we could try to find the flyers," said Fetterman.

"If we do find them, we might get airlift out. We provide LZ security for the choppers and then hop on when they come in to rescue the pilots," added Bocker.

Gerber hesitated, his eyes roaming the forest. Small, skinny trees, bushes with broad leaves, grass and vines and ferns. A carpeting of wet and decaying leaves. It was possible to see forty, fifty meters in the forest as they moved through it. Very easy for the enemy to spot them.

"Krung, you take the point. Kit, you're right behind him with Fetterman. The rest of us will bring up the rear. Do not engage the enemy unless it is absolutely necessary. Same compass heading as before."

Krung didn't move immediately. He stared at the group with him and then got to his feet. Slowly he stepped between two trees.

A second later Kit was up and moving, following Krung, her rifle held in both hands. As she reached the two trees, she glanced back over her shoulder and nodded to Gerber.

With that, the rest of the team was on their feet, moving among the bushes and trees of the forest. They spread out in a thin line, moving quietly, listening for sounds of pursuit and the sounds of a search party, hoping that they wouldn't stumble over something before nightfall.

12

THE FORESTS SOUTH
OF KE SAT
NORTH VIETNAM

At nightfall they stopped long enough to eat a cold meal of
tasteless C-rations. Afterward they rested for a moment, and
then were up and moving again. Their path meandered to the
south and east, avoiding the usual peasant and game trails,
villages that weren't marked on the maps, farmers' hootches
and open fields. From overhead came the roar of jet aircraft
as American air strikes against Hanoi and SAM sites were
sent in. They heard the rumble of distant bombs and the
popping of the large-caliber antiaircraft weapons.

And even with all that, each was surprised at how deserted the countryside was. Farmers rode in groups to their
fields in Soviet-made ZIL trucks and returned to the larger
towns at night, apparently afraid of an impending American
invasion. There were no lights on because those would provide beacons for the American bombers and fighters.

They avoided one large group of the NVA who had spread
out in a clearing, drying themselves in the last of the fading
sun. Near the center of the group was a fire under a huge
black pot. Three men stood around it, tossing in vegetables

and hunks of raw meat. They had stacked their weapons near the cooking pot as they began setting up their camp, apparently planning to stay where they were for the rest of the night.

Once, as Gerber and his team began to move after the evening meal, they heard the distant pop of rotor blades. They knew it was one of the rescue teams searching for downed American flyers. Firing had erupted then. Small arms from the ground and cannons from the fighter escort. It sounded as if the rescue craft had been driven off before they had a chance to pick up the flyers.

Krung, who had been on point, fell to the ground again and waved at Kit, signaling her to the right. Gerber saw the activity and hurried forward.

After a short distance, he dropped to his belly and crawled the rest of the way, being careful not to make noise. Again they were at the edge of a clearing where an NVA unit was spread out. In the center of it were three men. Two of them wore the remains of U.S. Air Force uniforms. The last wore black pajamas and looked as if he had been badly beaten. The flickering firelight played across his features, illuminating them. Gerber felt his stomach turn as he recognized the man in the black pajamas.

Somehow, Le Duc had managed to get himself captured and not executed. Knowing that, Gerber searched the faces of the other two prisoners, but couldn't tell if one of them was Barlett or not. He suspected not because both wore flight uniforms, and not fatigues, but there was no telling for certain. At least it answered one question.

At that moment he felt Fetterman's lips near his ear. "We take them?"

Although he hadn't thought about it, he nodded. "Yeah, we take them. We get Le Duc out of there. I count seven, eight, nine. Nine."

"What's the plan?"

Gerber rolled to his side and looked behind him. In the darkness and shadows of the forest, he could only see one shape. If they spread out and opened fire at the same moment, they could probably kill all the NVA before the enemy could realize what was happening. Tyme or Fetterman could be detailed to take out anyone who reached cover. One of them wouldn't fire with the rest.

As he thought of that, Tyme's words hit him like a rock. Tyme had told him that zeroing the weapons wasn't a luxury and Gerber had forced the issue, telling the weapons specialist that they wouldn't be doing any sniping so that if the sights were off slightly, it wouldn't matter. Now it mattered and there was no way he could go back to zero the weapons. It was the first time that the situation had come up. Maybe it was because they had always zeroed the weapons before the mission. Tyme had always insisted, and had always gotten his way.

Gerber touched Fetterman on the shoulder and pointed twice to the rear and then along the left side of the clearing. Fetterman nodded and retreated to find two people to position there.

Gerber moved closer to Krung and instructed him to wait. He was not to fire until Gerber opened up. Then he was to rake the clearing, being careful not to shoot too low because they didn't want to hit the prisoners seated there.

He positioned the team, instructing them not to open fire until he did and for each to try to kill the enemy soldiers directly in front of them. When they were set, Gerber worked his way back to the center and crouched near the base of a large tree.

He thumbed off the safety and aimed by looking over the top of the barrel, not using the sights because of the darkness. He waited for the NVA soldier in front of him to turn so that he would present his back as a target. Gerber didn't have to wait long. He pulled the trigger, feeling the weapon buck against his shoulder. The smell of burned cordite assailed his nostrils and the green tracers flashed outward, some of them bouncing high.

At that moment the rest of the team began to shoot, pouring rounds into the clearing. Their side of the forest twinkled like Christmas lights from the muzzle flashes. The enemy soldiers fell, shredded by the fusillade. One tried to get up, was struck again and flipped to his back.

When the shooting started, the three prisoners fell facedown. None of them looked up, even after the final shot had been fired. They waited for someone to tell them what to do.

As the echoes faded, Gerber got to his feet. He dropped the empty magazine from his weapon and jammed another one home. He worked the bolt, keeping his eyes on the clearing, his ears cocked, watching the dead men. Finally he pushed himself out of the trees. He stepped to the first body and touched it with the toe of his boot.

The dead man was lying facedown, blood staining the back of his khaki uniform in great wet smears. In the firelight, Gerber could see that part of his face had been blown away by a bullet. The skin along his cheek was ripped, exposing his teeth in a death's head grin. Gerber kicked the AK away from the corpse's outstretched hand.

Around him, the others moved forward, checking the bodies and picking up the weapons. Gerber walked over to the prisoners.

Using his knife, he cut the rough hemp that bound the wrists of the prisoners. "I'm Captain MacKenzie Gerber, U.S. Army Special Forces."

One of the Air Force officers sat up and rubbed his wrists. For a moment he said nothing, just stared into the dirty face of the man who had rescued him. Then he grinned. Holding out a hand, he said, "I'm Captain Richard Wornell and I'm happier than hell to see you."

Gerber nodded, looked at the other two men. "You okay, Duc? What the hell happened?"

"NVA got me," said Duc. "They wait for me as I come down. I was all alone and they catch me."

"I can see that. What about Barlett?"

"NVA didn't see him. He ran. They chase and then come back. They say he dead. He fight with them and they kill him. They leave his body for the maggots. But I hear no shooting. Nobody shoot."

"You think he got away, then?" asked Gerber. "You think he's out there on his own?"

"No. I think they catch him and kill him."

"Why?"

"One of them came back with his hat but they don't have him. If they take him alive, they bring him, too, but if they kill him, they leave body."

"What if he managed to get away from them?" insisted Gerber.

"Then they still be out there looking for him, but they came back. I think man dead."

"Captain," said Fetterman, "I think we better get out of here. Someone had to hear the firing."

"Right, Tony." He turned to the Air Force man. "Can you travel?"

"Yes," said Wornell.

"How about your friend?"

"I don't know who he is. We picked him up a day or so after they got me. He hasn't said a word to them. Wouldn't even tell them his name."

"Captain?" said Fetterman.

"Bocker, I want you to stay close to this guy." He pointed to the silent man. To Wornell he said, "Can you use an AK?"

"I know which end the bullets come out of if that's what you mean," he said, his teeth flashing in the firelight.

"Good. Grab a weapon and as much ammo as you can carry. The more the better. Duc, you do the same. As much as you can carry. Tony, let's take some extra weapons with us. You never know when you'll need them. Once we're clear, we'll figure out something else."

Tyme suddenly appeared. "I think someone's coming, Captain. I didn't hang around to get a good count. Sounded like at least a platoon and they didn't give a shit about noise discipline."

Gerber spun toward Fetterman. "Tony, take the point and let's get out of here."

Fetterman grabbed Krung. "Come on."

"Justin, help Captain Wornell and Le Duc. Galvin, let's get going."

"What about me?" asked Kit.

"Follow the rest of them. Go. Go."

Fetterman trotted across the clearing and disappeared into the forest. Krung was right behind him. Tyme gestured at Wornell, pointed him in the right direction and then took off with him. Kit and Le Duc waited for Bocker and the unidentified pilot and followed closely. When everyone was out of sight, Gerber kicked the fire out, spreading the burning embers. Then he, too, ran toward the jungle.

At the edge of the forest he stopped momentarily and looked back. Although he wanted to see if anyone was coming, he couldn't take the chance that he would lose his people. When no one appeared quickly, he spun and ran. A moment later he found his team as they worked their way through the trees.

He joined them, listening to the noise being made by the Air Force men not familiar with the environment. Heavy footfalls and snapping twigs. Once there was a grunt, as if one of the pilots had walked into a tree.

They kept going for nearly an hour, rushing through the forest, tripping over bushes and logs, disregarding noise discipline as they fell, but afraid to slow the pace. They could hear the pursuers occasionally. They were rattling their equipment, shouting orders to one another, slashing at the vegetation. It was as if they were trying to drive Gerber and his team to panic. Force them to run, forgetting everything they knew. It was a plan that might work against downed pilots, but not men experienced in jungle warfare. It only told Gerber where the enemy was and what he had to do to stay in front of them.

Finally, Gerber decided that they had pressed their luck far enough. He caught up to Fetterman and told him to halt. They spread out, facing opposite directions, listening to the night sounds of the forest around them.

Gerber felt tired. His muscles ached and his mouth was full of cotton. He drank water and offered some of it to Wornell who crouched near him. Wornell took the canteen gratefully and at first sipped the warm water and then chugged it. When he realized that he had swallowed most of it, he handed the canteen back to Gerber and said, rather sheepishly, "Sorry."

"Don't let it bother you."

Fetterman came up and knelt next to Gerber. "Now what, Captain?"

Gerber wanted to look at the map and pinpoint their location. Given anything, he knew that they were south and east of Ke Sat. If he remembered the map correctly, due east was a river system and not far beyond that was the coast, no more than thirty or thirty-five miles. With the Air Force pilots, it could take them a week to travel that far. Without them, they could cover the ground in two days.

"Let's move to the east and try to find a place with good cover, not far from a landing zone. We'll try for a helicopter pickup about dawn."

"Don't need an LZ," said Wornell. "They've got jungle penetrators that can lift us out right through the thickest canopy."

"Captain," said Gerber, "how long does each rescue using the penetrator take? Five minutes? Three? And, of course, there are nine of us. Thirty or forty minutes. Will the chopper hover over the jungle that long?"

"I see your point," said Wornell.

At that moment Tyme approached. He leaned close to Gerber. "I think they're still back there. They're moving quietly now, like they want to catch us unprepared."

"You get an idea of who and how many?"

"No, sir. They're pretty good, though. They're moving rapidly, making little noise now."

"You think we can evade them by hiding?"

"No, sir. I think these guys are going to be poking into bushes and ravines looking for us."

"Okay," said Gerber. "Tony, I want you . . . No, get Galvin. I'll have him escort the fliers out of here. The rest of us will stay and ambush the enemy patrol."

"Captain," said Fetterman, "I might suggest that Kit go with Galvin. Give him another experienced jungle fighter and someone familiar with the area."

"Okay, Tony. You get the men deployed, and I'll get Galvin and Kit moving."

"Captain," said Wornell, "I know a little about this. Been through a couple of jungle fighting courses with our perimeter defense teams."

"I rarely turn down a volunteer, but this is a little different than that," said Gerber. "Besides, once we spring the ambush, we're going to be moving very fast. You'll be of more use with Sergeant Bocker arranging for that chopper to get us out of here in the morning."

"Yes, sir," said Wornell.

Together they moved to where Bocker crouched, his weapon aimed into the trees, his eyes shifting rapidly. Gerber knelt next to him. "Going to send you ahead with the Air Force people and with Kit. Find a good location for extraction. We'll need an LZ that can accommodate a Sea Stallion, and I'll want a place nearby with good cover. Don't worry about a water source or the like. With luck, we'll be out of here in a couple of hours. The cover is more important now."

"Shouldn't be a major problem," said Bocker.

"Once you've got it established, I want you to make contact with the air-sea rescue boys and arrange extraction for dawn tomorrow. Wornell can help you. We'll have caught up to you by then."

"Yes, sir. When do I go?"

"Now."

Bocker turned and stared into the darkness. He could see the gray shape of Gerber and Wornell. He wanted to look into Wornell's eyes, but it was too dark. Instead he reached out and touched Wornell on the shoulder.

"Let's go."

As they faded into the dark, Gerber moved to the rear. He found Fetterman. "You ready here?"

"Set in an L-shaped ambush. That assumes that they'll be following our trail. Got Tyme in the rear, watching from that direction so that they don't get behind us."

"Good. Where did you want me?"

"About five meters to the left. Use grenades and once the enemy firing dies down, we'll drop to the rear to wait five minutes. See if they pursue."

"Then all we can do now is wait."

"That's about it, sir."

ROBIN READ THE LAST PAGE of the story, carefully rearranged the papers in their proper order and tapped the edges against the top of the table.

"You can't print this," she said.

"Why the hell not?" demanded George Krupp. "The facts are accurate."

Robin stood and moved across the small room to the window. She opened it and looked out on downtown Saigon. She had taken the room because it was cheap, close to her office and gave her a view of the nightclub scene. A contrast that was almost too stark to believe. The countryside was throbbing with war, machine guns and mortars, people dying horribly in filthy rice paddies and dirty villages, yet the downtown looked like any teeming Oriental metropolis in peacetime. Women in revealing costumes and men, many of them in wild civilian clothes, haggling over the prices and services. The glow of the neon radiated up at her, reflecting from the rain-wet streets and the dirty glass of the bars.

"George," she said, still staring at the scene below her. "I don't want to argue about the accuracy of the story. You can't print it because it will endanger the men involved. It gives away too much information."

"Oh, hell, Robin," he snorted. "That's a load of shit. You going to tell me that the North Vietnamese read the American newspapers? I can't believe Palmer tried to pull that old one on us."

"I just don't see the point in even giving the enemy the opportunity to read about it," she responded.

"I think it's time you found yourself another occupation," said Krupp quietly. "Maybe you've lost your edge here."

"If that means I've developed a sense of responsibility," she said, "then you might be right." She turned to face him. "I've been thinking about this a lot lately. About the role of the press and the power of it, and I think we've gotten too caught up in our own self-importance. Nothing matters except the story and we go after it, claiming the people's right to know, but that's bullshit. We're just after bigger and bigger stories so that we're no longer reporting them, we are them. We've lost our perspective."

"Christ, Robin, those Special Forces jerks have you brainwashed."

She sighed and moved forward to sit on the bed. "No, I don't think that's it. But you know what I mean. I get the big story and suddenly all the other reporters are calling me. I'm interviewed on TV and radio and quoted in the newspaper. I become the source for the story, or I become more important than the story."

"There's nothing wrong with that," said Krupp. "It's merely the recognition you deserve for finding a good story. For ferreting out facts and information that everyone else would prefer that you didn't have."

Robin shook her head. "Not when I decide that I know what's best for everyone. Not when I claim that the people have a right to know while endangering the lives of others. People who have the right to live."

"I still say it's a load of shit." He grabbed his story off the table. "I'm going to file it because the people do have a right to know. They have the right to know that their government is trying to get them involved in a land war with nearly a billion Chinese. One that could easily escalate into a global, thermonuclear war."

"You talk about me slinging the shit. You've taken the story of some downed crewmen and changed it into the possibility of nuclear war." She laughed humorlessly. "You see. You're doing exactly what I've said. Taken a nothing story and changed into the end of the human race. And you don't care about the men in North Vietnam fighting for their lives."

"I have no interest in them. I don't know them and I doubt my story could hurt them."

"And if you knew it would? Then what?"

"That's a ridiculous question, Robin."

She stared up at him, not sure that she liked what she saw. Afraid that she saw herself reflected in the man. Chase the story and to hell with the consequences. She knew that wasn't right because she had withheld one hell of a story to protect the people involved. And then she wondered if she would have done it if she hadn't been in love with one of the principal men in it.

"What difference is a day or two going to matter?" asked Robin. "By waiting a day or two, you might be able to write the end to the story. A much better end."

"In a day or two I will write the end to it, but now I'm going to file this one."

"Somehow I knew you were going to say that."

13

THE FOREST REGION
EAST AND SOUTH
OF KE SAT
NORTH VIETNAM

Bocker found the perfect place in less than thirty minutes. The hilltop, no higher than fifty feet above the rest of the territory, was hidden from the rice paddies and farm fields surrounding it by the trees that grew halfway up the slope. The top was lightly grassed, nearly a hundred feet across, and would easily hold a Sea Stallion. If there were enemy soldiers standing in the rice paddies, they would not be able to see the hilltop because of the trees.

The forest was thick in places and thin in others. There were a few outcroppings of rock, ravines hidden by bushes and grass, and a few trails. From the summit, they could command a view of all approaches. The forest would inhibit the enemy, holding him back if he tried to rush the hilltop as the chopper landed on it.

After climbing partway up, he detoured to the south and found a hiding place there. He put the uncommunicative flier in the center of a rocky fort with Wornell, Kit and himself guarding him. In the half light of the moon and the ground glow from rotting vegetation, Bocker could see remarkably well. It always surprised him how bright the night could be when the moon was nearly full and the stars were blazing.

He slipped into position, checked the likely avenues of attack. Satisfied there'd be no threat, he leaned close to Wornell. "Think you can raise the rescue boys on your radio?"

"I can give it a try. What do you want?"

"Captain said to get a chopper in here about dawn. Land and pick us up. You can arrange that. Tell them about us, too. We don't want to get mistaken for NVA. Tell them that we'll have secured the LZ so they won't have to worry about a bunch of NVA showing up."

"I doubt that'll bother them. They'll have fighter escort to take care of any ground threat."

"You work on getting that arranged then."

"Okay, Sergeant."

With that, Bocker stole back to the man who hadn't spoken. He performed the best examination that he could under the circumstances, and found no obvious wounds. The man's limbs seemed intact, devoid of breaks. As he worked on him he noticed a name tag and leaned close to it. Even in the half light of the moon and stars, he could read the name. McMaster.

Bocker sat back on his heels, looked into McMaster's eyes. "Captain McMaster, I'm Sergeant Galvin Bocker, United States Army Special Forces. You're safe with us now. The enemy won't be able to get to you."

McMaster didn't respond. He stared straight ahead, as if he was catatonic. When Kit approached, McMaster turned to stare at her, but didn't speak.

"Is he all right?" she asked.

Bocker nodded and heard the first burst of firing from the west, a high-pitched, staccato sound that punctuated the night. It sounded like a single AK on full auto. Then came the dull thuds as grenades exploded. One. Two. A half dozen, and then more firing of AKs. In seconds it was over. Silence.

Bocker searched the area to his right, where the sound of the battle had come from, but could see nothing. He wished he could head in that direction to offer assistance, but knew what his orders were. Instead he listened to the growing silence and prayed that the ambush had worked, that it had been Gerber and Fetterman and his men who had been successful. Who had survived.

TYME HAD BEEN RIGHT about the NVA unit chasing them. They were very good. Gerber could hear almost nothing. Only the occasional scrape of a boot against the exposed root of a tree, or a dull, quiet clink as metal touched metal. They were moving slowly now.

Then he saw the first of the enemy soldiers. A dark shape moving among the trees. Even in the night he could see the telltale shape of an AK-47 held at high port, the flattened pith helmet the enemy wore and the chest pouch for spare AK-47 magazines. The man's head swiveled right and left as he searched both sides of the trail, looking for signs of the men they were chasing.

Several soldiers followed that man. They had spread out in a loose triangle-shaped formation. A few had the bayonets on their weapons extended and were using them to prod the bushes as they passed them.

At that moment there was a burst of AK fire. A stream of emerald-colored tracers lashed through the night. Two of the men toppled into the bushes, one of them screaming in pain.

"Grenades!"

Gerber jerked the pin from his grenade and threw it at one of the enemy soldiers. He snatched a second and repeated the performance. Then he dropped flat, his hands over his ears to protect them from the shock waves of the detonations.

There was a series of explosions. Crashes that shattered the night. Fiery bursts lit up large sections of the trail, freezing the action. Shrapnel rattled overhead, smashing into the trees, shredding them and tearing the leaves off the branches. The debris rained down gently, quietly. Gerber rolled to the right and poked the barrel of his weapon out in front of him.

The night was ripped by more firing from AKs. Muzzle flashes winked as the tongues of flame leaped out of the barrels. Green and white tracers lanced outward and bounced high. They crisscrossed in the night. Gerber used his own weapon to hose down the area.

"Fall back!" he ordered. "Fall back!"

With that, he was on his feet, moving rapidly through trees, heading to the rear. He spotted Fetterman and angled toward him. "Take the point."

Fetterman turned and ran into the trees. Krung and Le Duc were behind him. Gerber hesitated, saw Tyme and pointed at the others. Tyme spun, emptied his magazine into the forest where the enemy was. Then he dropped back. As he ran he changed the magazine in his weapon, letting the empty fall to the forest floor. Away from the ambush site, he fell into line. When he was sure that all his men were away safely, Gerber took off after them.

They ran through the forest, popped into the clear and kept on running. They crossed the area, splashing through a couple of rice paddies, and then entered the forest on the other side. As he got to the trees he found Fetterman deploying the troops again.

"Good place to stop the pursuit." The breath was rasping in Fetterman's throat.

Gerber glanced over his shoulder and saw the moonlight reflecting off the dirty water. The area was wide open and would provide little cover for the North Vietnamese. There was a network of low dikes and then the black smudge that was the forest opposite them.

"Yeah," he agreed. "We can catch our breath, but if we see no sign of the enemy in fifteen minutes, we take off. We don't want to wait for them to find us."

Gerber dropped to the ground. Through a gap in the vegetation in front of him, he had a perfect view of the clearing. Sweat popped out on his forehead and dripped down the sides of his face. He touched his forehead to his shoulder to dab away the sweat, afraid to rub it because it might remove the camouflage paint. He worked hard so that his breathing wasn't an audible rasp but a quiet intake of air.

The time passed slowly. Gerber kept looking at his watch and then glancing right and left, at the men with him. Suddenly in front of him, at the far edge of the clearing, he thought he caught a flicker of movement. He studied the black mass of trees, and saw it again. Movement just inside the tree line.

"Here they come," he hissed. "Let them get into the open before firing."

The enemy seemed to hover inside the forest, as if they knew what was going on, and then slipped out of the trees. Two men on point cautiously entered the clearing. They separated, moved to one of the dikes and crouched near it. More men emerged from the trees, moving hunched over, their weapons held at port arms.

As they fanned out, the flankers, separated from the main body by ten or twelve meters, appeared. They approached the point men, slowing down as they did so. The point got up, sweeping forward.

When they were halfway across the field, Gerber used his last grenade. He tossed it as far as he could, aiming for a point beyond the NVA soldiers. There was a quiet splash, like a fish breaking water. A couple of the enemy turned, searching behind them as the grenade exploded into a flash of light that silhouetted them.

Before the enemy could dive for cover or retreat into the forest, Gerber's men opened fire. The night was filled with the rattle of rifle fire, the tracers bouncing as they struck the ground.

The enemy panicked. Two of them ran into the blazing barrels of the American weapons. They were cut down quickly, their bodies disappearing into the filthy water.

The main body of NVA soldiers returned fire quickly. The rounds snapped through the leaves over the Americans' heads and slammed into the trunks of the trees with dull thuds. The strobing lights of the muzzles gave away their locations.

"Grenades!" ordered Fetterman.

A second later there were two explosions and then a third. Return fire from the enemy stopped abruptly. A few random shots echoed among the trees, then there was complete silence. Gerber pulled the empty magazine from his weapon, tossed it away and slammed a fresh one home.

For a few minutes they waited, searching for signs of movement, but there were none. Apparently everyone had either been killed or had managed to reach the trees without being seen. Gerber knew he should check the field, but didn't want to expose his men to enemy fire. He would have to leave things as they stood.

He crawled away from the edge of the clearing, and found Fetterman. Touching the master sergeant on the back, he whispered, "Let's get out of here."

They alerted the rest of the men and then, keeping low, they withdrew. Once clear of the area, they got up and began moving faster. Fetterman remained at the rear, watching and listening for signs of pursuit.

It wasn't long before they came to the hillside. Gerber called a halt, then sent Tyme out in search of Bocker. In a few moments, the whole team was united.

"What happened?" he asked.

"We got them," said Tyme, his voice quiet but filled with excitement.

"I've got a good hiding place over there," said Bocker. Without another word, he led them to it.

Once inside the rock enclosure, Gerber asked, "You have any luck making contact with the rescue choppers?"

Wornell spoke up. "They'll be here at first light. Claimed they got a good fix on my signal and were satisfied with the recognition and authentication codes I gave them."

"Thanks." Gerber moved closer to Fetterman. "After that ambush, they're going to be beating the ground for us tonight."

"Maybe not," said Fetterman.

"We've been lucky," said Gerber. "We got in and out of the missile site with no casualties. We've had a couple of run-ins and left bodies scattered all over but not run into any real trouble yet. They're going to be looking for us."

"Yes, sir," said Fetterman, "but I don't think they'll do anything until the morning. Every time they've gone up against us in the dark we've zapped them."

"I was thinking," said Gerber. "Maybe you and Tyme could slip back along our trail and rig a mechanical ambush. It would slow down their pursuit."

"I'll get Justin and we'll do it."

TYME AND FETTERMAN, carrying several of the spare weapons, extra magazines and the majority of the remaining grenades, worked their way down the hill. They moved rapidly, avoiding the paths as they walked through the forest. They reached the bottom of the hill. Fetterman stopped for a moment, surveying the area around them.

There were a couple of likely approaches from the west. A wide path led toward the crest of the hill and he also noticed a couple of smaller, less well-defined trails. If the enemy was going to approach, he figured they would use the paths because there was no reason for them not to. Ambushes and booby traps were not that common in the North, so the soldiers there had not learned to avoid them.

Fetterman told Tyme to take some of the equipment and rig it to cover the paths. When the younger man disappeared into the forest, Fetterman set to work.

First he took one of the AKs and wired it into the fork of a tree so that it was pointing to the west, covering the path. He looped the wire through the trigger guard and tied it with a slip knot. He then hooked it around the butt of the weapon, fastened it under a forked stick shoved into the earth and played it out across the trail. He anchored it there, tying it around the base of a sapling. Before he left, he made sure that the wire was taut. If someone's boot struck the wire, it would tighten the loop around the trigger, causing the weapon to fire. The whole thirty-round magazine would empty, raking the trail with 7.62 mm ammunition.

That finished, he moved farther to the west and set an empty C ration can on the ground. With his knife, he buried the can and anchored it with a couple of small sticks. He tied the end of his wire around the top of the grenade and stuffed it into the can. Again he stretched the wire across the trail, making sure that it was only two or three inches above the dirt. When someone kicked it, the grenade would be jerked from the can and would explode.

He returned to the can, took the grenade from it and pulled the pin. Carefully he slipped it back into the tin. When the grenade was yanked from the can now, with the pin out, the safety spoon would fly off.

Fetterman spent the next hour rigging other surprises. Some of them were little more than punji stakes, sharpened bits of bamboo hidden in shallow, camouflaged holes or set on traps that would sweep across the trail knee high or crotch high. He didn't have much faith in those, but they would be enough to slow down the enemy, if they were getting close.

A man looking for booby traps in addition to fleeing soldiers moved slower than a man just chasing the enemy.

He rigged a second booby trap with an AK, this set at crotch level. He tied the barrel down carefully so that it wouldn't rise as the weapon burned through the magazine. Finally satisfied with his preparations, he moved to the rear, looking for Tyme.

The young weapons specialist had set up a dual AK arrangement. The first one was set to be tripped by someone walking on the trail, catching the wire with his foot. As it fired, the recoil of the weapon was set so that it tightened the wire on the second AK. If he had calculated correctly, the first weapon would be about halfway through the magazine when the second, aimed lower, would begin to fire. It would appear to be two soldiers shooting from two locations. It would take the enemy several minutes to discover the nature of the trap. Those could be the minutes the Americans needed to escape.

He had also rigged a couple of grenade traps, including one set so that the grenade, as it was pulled from the can, would be jerked upward and explode five or six feet in the air. The burst would throw the shrapnel about head high and none of it would be wasted as it was in a ground explosion.

Convinced that they had done everything they could, they withdrew from the area, trying to cover the evidence of the booby traps, but leaving some sign that they had been there; those footprints, bent twigs and crushed blades of grass would lead the enemy into trap. If the enemy panicked, they could spend an hour trying to figure it out.

Together, they worked their way back to where the rest of the team waited. They were challenged, quietly, but Bocker recognized them and gave them the word to approach. Gerber was waiting there. "You see anyone?"

Fetterman shook his head. "Nothing. If they're moving in on us, they're doing it quietly and carefully."

Gerber pulled back the camouflage band on his watch. "Be light in another hour or so."

"Yes, sir. I would think anyone out there would be following our path closely. That being the case, if they're reading the signs we left, they'll walk into the ambush. That'll warn us they're close."

"And give us a chance to escape," said Gerber.

"But I don't think they'll be looking for us before morning. The night is our ally. They'll probably regroup near that last ambush and then sweep out from there. In the daylight we're at the disadvantage."

"I think you're right, Tony. Let's spread out a little more and keep our eyes open. With any luck, we'll be out of here long before the enemy can get close to us."

Dawn broke quietly. A mist obscured the clearing and hid the trees on the other side of it. Fetterman and Tyme scouted the trees, making sure that no one had sneaked up on them during the night.

Bocker and Wornell crouched among the rocks, the antenna of the survival radio up. For a few minutes they listened to the frequency but heard nothing. Bocker shrugged. "Go ahead."

"Rescue, this is Baron One."

"Baron One, this is Kingfisher Two-Two. Say authentication number."

"Zero-six-one-two."

"Authentication confirmed. Say condition."

"Be advised that there are ten of us now. Condition is good."

"Enemy troops?"

"No contact with the enemy for nearly four hours. LZ is secure."

"Roger. We are inbound. Wait, One."

The radio went silent and Bocker looked at Wornell, who raised an eyebrow in question. Bocker shrugged. He wasn't familiar with the procedures used by the air-sea rescue people this far north.

"Baron One, we will be at your location in one-five minutes. Do you have smoke?"

Bocker nodded his head vigorously.

"Roger, we have smoke."

Gerber moved toward them, "Let's head up the hill. Galvin take the point and don't get sloppy now. We're too close to getting out."

They formed a single-file column with the still silent pilot, McMaster, in the center. Bocker leaped over the rocks, knelt there for a moment as if waiting for someone to start shooting at him and then began a rapid climb up the rest of the hill.

The terrain wasn't bad. They could use the saplings to haul themselves up the hillside. The carpet of decaying vegetation, wet with the early-morning dew, kept the noise down. The slanting rays of the early-morning sun illuminated the forest around them. There were some mature trees and full-grown bushes, but quite a bit of younger vegetation.

In only a few minutes they had reached the edge of the trees at the top of the hillside. Wornell dropped to the ground, his back to a tree, relaxing. Bocker turned, hesitating, waiting for instructions from Gerber.

"Let's not fall apart now," he said. As Fetterman approached, Gerber pointed and said, "Tony. Security right and left."

"Yes, sir."

Fetterman moved to the right and Tyme headed in the opposite direction. Gerber slid down the hillside for twenty feet and found a shallow depression. He lay in it, concealing himself, and kept his eyes downslope, searching for the enemy.

Glancing at his watch, he decided that the enemy wouldn't have time to find them now. In minutes they would be airborne, flying out of North Vietnam, the mission halfway completed. He regretted that he couldn't get into the Hanoi Hilton, but that instruction had been stupid. With his small force he would never have been able to get clear. Perhaps with the element of surprise they could get in easily, but within minutes they would have been trapped. Still, it was an interesting prospect.

The air overhead was split by the sound of a low-flying jet. Gerber looked up and through gaps in the trees, saw the smoky trail of a Phantom. He grinned, knowing that the choppers couldn't be far behind.

At that moment the first of the booby traps in the mechanical ambush went off. There was the detonation of a grenade and then the ripping blast of an AK. Silence fell and then the cacophony rose again as the enemy soldiers tried to return fire. First there was only a couple of their weapons, and then more as all the enemy began to return the fire until it sounded like a company was closing in on them.

Around him, Gerber could hear the stray rounds ripping through the trees over his head, peeling bark from the trunks, and tearing leaves from the branches. He hesitated, watching the slope below, but nothing moved down there. Then, in the distance he heard the heavy pop of the rotor blades of the Sea Stallion. Jet engines roared, nearly drowning out the sounds of shooting.

Gerber got to his feet and ran up the slope. He came to Fetterman and pointed. Fetterman and Tyme took up the rear guard position, their weapons ready, as Bocker and Wornell ran to the center of the LZ.

Wornell dropped to the ground and pulled at the antenna of his radio. He pointed it straight up and said, "This is Baron One."

"Roger, Baron One. Can you pop smoke?"

Bocker took a smoke grenade from his pack, pulled the pin and tossed it to the center of the LZ. A yellow cloud began to billow.

Kit, Krung and Le Duc gathered near a tall tree. At first they watched Bocker and Wornell, and then turned to where Gerber, Fetterman and Tyme crouched. Krung moved closer to the Special Forces men, his weapon held ready. He heard Kit whisper at him, but waved a hand to silence her without turning around.

Through the trees, Gerber caught movement. A shape flashed and then fell. He kept his eyes turned toward it, and saw it begin to crawl forward. Gerber aimed, but didn't fire.

A grenade exploded. Gerber saw the flash and then the drifting cloud of dust. More firing erupted as the enemy soldiers fired into the trees, as if they believed they had been surrounded. More grenades exploded, but these were duller, quiet pops. The NVA were throwing their own grenades, trying to break up the ambush.

Behind the Special Forces men the roar of the jets came again and then the popping rotors became louder. Gerber looked over his shoulder, saw the yellow cloud drifting on the center of the LZ and knew that the chopper was inbound.

"Let's take them," he said.

With that, he let the front sight seek the enemy soldier. As soon as he saw the movement again, he pulled the trigger, felt the weapon slam back into his shoulder. The man took the round in the side of the head. For a moment he was frozen there, a gaping red wound between his eye and ear. Then he slowly collapsed.

Both Fetterman and Tyme opened fire on full auto. They burned through the ammo as fast as they could, changing magazines without hesitation. Their rounds tore through the thin vegetation, shredding the trunks of the saplings and ripping the leaves from bushes.

Return fire was sporadic and poorly aimed. The enemy was thoroughly confused, firing in all directions. They seemed to be pinned down by the mechanical ambush. Gerber watched the shooting, and tried to spot the muzzle flashes, but the rising sun washed them out.

He began to crawl toward the rear until he found Fetterman. Gerber ordered the master sergeant to collect Tyme and follow. Then he located another good hiding position and dropped into it.

Fetterman and Tyme rushed by. Fetterman halted, spun and emptied his weapon into the forest. He dropped to one knee, jerked his last grenade from his pistol belt and tossed it into the trees. Then he ran into the clearing.

Gerber waited for the grenade to explode. When he saw the orange flash and the fountain of dirt and debris raining back to the ground, Gerber was on his feet, running.

As he passed the last of the trees, he saw the chopper coming out of the sun, right at him. It was a gigantic machine, capable of carrying forty troops. Behind it were two jet fighters, patrolling, looking for the enemy, waiting for the Triple A to open fire.

Gerber slipped to one knee and aimed his weapon at the trees. Fetterman and Tyme ran toward him, and fell next to him, but none of them fired.

The noise increased until it was a roar that overpowered everything else. The rotor wash blew with the force of a small hurricane, trying to smash them to the ground. The swirling wind grabbed at them, ripping at them and tearing at the loose grass, leaves and debris in the LZ. It threw up a whirling cloud of dust, sucked the last of the yellow smoke in, and tossed it out.

Behind him, Bocker and Wornell scrambled toward the open door on the right side of the chopper. Wornell leaped into the interior and rolled against the bulkhead. Kit dropped her rifle, stooped to pick it up and then fell to her knees. From the trees, to the right of where Gerber had been, an RPD opened fire, stitching the side of the chopper. Kit snatched her weapon from the grass, spun and emptied the magazine at the machine-gun nest.

Firing around them increased. Gerber was on his feet running. He saw Fetterman shooting. Duc was aiming into the trees where the RPD was concealed and Gerber yelled at him. "On the chopper! Get on the chopper!"

As Duc turned to run, a round caught him in the shoulder, spinning him to the ground. His weapon flew from his hands and he screamed once. It was a sharp, piercing sound that was nearly lost in the roar of the jets and throbbing of the Sea Stallion's rotor blades.

Gerber grabbed Duc under the other arm and jerked him to his feet. Duc took a stumbling step, caught his balance and ran. At the chopper, Bocker grabbed him around the waist and threw him inside.

Both Fetterman and Tyme were shooting now, pouring rounds into the forest, aiming at the RPD. It fell silent as the NVA gunners dived for cover. Then the two Americans were on their feet, running toward the Sea Stallion.

Gerber reached the chopper but didn't climb in. He stood, his rifle at his shoulder, and when two enemy soldiers appeared, he opened up. Both dived to the side. As they did, Fetterman and Tyme reached the helicopter. They scrambled up. Kit still had not entered. She was now next to Gerber, shooting at anything that moved.

"Get in! Go!"

She didn't move. She kept pulling the trigger until the bolt locked back.

Gerber saw that and slapped at her. She glared at him as Bocker grabbed her under the arms, throwing her up into the chopper.

At that moment Gerber tossed his weapon through the hatch. He reached out, grabbed the side and lifted. Bocker held a helping hand out and a crewman snatched at Gerber, dragging him partially inside.

Before he could get fully on board, the chopper lifted off. It climbed straight up while Gerber held on, his feet waving in midair. He felt his hand slip and was sure that he was going to fall, but then others grabbed him, jerking him into the cabin. The chopper spun, dived at the trees to pick up speed.

From below came the sound of the enemy weapons. An RPD, AKs and even SKS carbines. There were snaps and pops as rounds penetrated the thin metallic skin of the chopper. Then came a single, loud explosion as one of the covering jets began suppressing fire. Gerber looked back and saw the edge of the tree line engulfed in flames, black smoke billowing into the sky.

"We get everyone?" shouted Gerber. He looked around, trying to make a head count.

"Everyone's out," Bocker yelled, nodding with an exaggerated motion. "We got everyone out."

Gerber relaxed leaning against the metal of a bulkhead. He looked at the dirty, sweating faces of the men around him and felt his stomach turn over. Those last, hectic minutes had done it. He could feel the excitement bubbling through him, coursing through his veins. He wanted to shout, to scream, but knew he was premature. They were still over North Vietnam.

Then, through the door of the chopper he saw the tan sand of a beach and the blue green of the Gulf of Tonkin. The chopper continued to climb as two F-4 Phantoms shot by, one of them doing a barrel roll.

At that moment, he knew they were clear.

14

THE CARASEL HOTEL
SAIGON

Mack Gerber sat at a table in the corner of the bar outside
the hotel. A copy of *Stars and Stripes* lay in front of him. He
had been back from North Vietnam for nearly a week, but
because of all the briefings and debriefings, he hadn't gotten to the hotel until earlier that morning. His first act was
to take a long, hot shower and then to dress in the wildest civilian clothes he had. A Hawaiian shirt covered with blue
birds and red flowers and purple volcanos. He wore bright
yellow pants and frayed black tennis shoes without socks.

Across the table from him, Robin Morrow sat quietly sipping the beer he had bought her. Her low-cut dress revealed
the tops of her breasts, and the hemline came almost to mid-
thigh. She was uncomfortable, the sweat beading on her
forehead and upper lip, dampening her hair, but she said
nothing about it. She was happy to be with Gerber without
having to worry about the Vietnamese woman they all now
called Kit, or Fetterman or George Krupp or even Jerry
Maxwell and the rest of the CIA spooks.

Gerber folded back the front page of the *Stars and Stripes*,
punched in the gutter to flatten it, and was surprised to se

a story by George Krupp and Robin Morrow that detailed illegal operations in North Vietnam by members of the U.S. Army's Special Forces. He glanced over the top of the paper at Morrow, who was looking over the railing around the perimeter of the outside bar, staring into the streets of Saigon.

He scanned the story quickly, wondering what asshole had leaked it. He figured it had to be Maxwell or one of the civilians in the embassy who refused to understand that the North Vietnamese routinely violated the supposed neutrality of Laos and Cambodia, and who had large numbers of troops fighting in the South.

With that, the memories of the debriefings returned. Gerber, Fetterman, Tyme and Bocker, had sat in the cold conference rooms. An almost endless parade of military officers and civilian intelligence experts had filed through asking questions. They believed that Gerber and his men deserved no consideration and owed the debriefers something other than honest answers.

First there had been the three men, Robert Cornett, General Thomas Christie and Tim Underwood. They had spent several hours going over every detail of the SAM missile site near Ke Sat. They had been appalled that Gerber had not explored the base at greater length, especially when the missiles on the launchers were found to be dummies but the radar and tracking vans had been real.

Gerber had tried to explain that the North Vietnamese Army hadn't been thrilled to have Gerber and his team running around on the site. Besides, the longer he thought about it, the more he was convinced that he had seen everything that needed to be seen. He had all the answers to the questions. It was only a case of analyzing the data to learn exactly what it all meant.

Cornett had been interested in Fetterman's find of SA-7s and as Gerber thought about it, everything began to make

sense. It was what Gerber had suspected all along, but a sus
picion that he had failed to voice.

A jet pilot, seeing a missile launch in the dark from an SA
2 site, while flying below two or three hundred feet, would
assume the missile launched was an SA-2. At night he would
only have the rocket flame and site configuration to give him
a missile ID. With less than two seconds to identify the mis
sile and to evade it, the assumption would be that it was an
SA-2. After all, one bright flash from a missile engine ignit
ing looked pretty much like the next. The split second that
the pilots had to react made their observations of flight char
acteristics of the missile less than perfect.

"Then that's it," shouted Christie. "The SA-7 is an in
frared guided missile. They use the Spoon Rest for early ac
quisition, get a flight heading and then shut it all down. No
SAM warning lights for the aircraft as the North Vietnam
ese soldiers grab their weapons and suddenly the fucking
missiles are coming up at our boys."

Underwood nodded slowly. "And we are led to believe
they've added something new to their inventory. Some
thing we can't counter so we stop the bombing raids." He
clapped his hands. "A marvelously constructed plan."

Bocker looked confused and then asked, "What's going
on here?"

Gerber waited but no one else spoke. "The new guidance
system that everyone was so worried about doesn't exist."
He stared Christie in the eyes and added, "General, I be
lieve your pilots' debriefings need to be a bit more detailed.
The observable characteristics of the SA-7 vary significantly
from the SA-2."

"That's right, Captain," said Christie. "We've done
everything we can, but when you're flying over an SA-2 site
and you have a missile coming at you, you're usually so busy
trying to evade it, you don't have time to study it. The as
sumption is that it was an SA-2."

"I understand that, General," said Gerber. "But it was my butt hanging out in North Vietnam because your people misread the situation."

"Actually, *Captain*," said Christie, stressing Gerber's lower rank, "it was the CIA and Naval Intelligence people who leaped to the wrong conclusions. They followed their guidelines. Before we initiated the activity, that is, your mission into North Vietnam, we would have spent a little more time studying the situation."

"Yes, sir," said Gerber. "But that didn't keep my people out of the North, did it?"

And when the Air Force and CIA had finished with them, Army Intelligence came in, asking for everything that they could get. Unit organizations, uniforms, training, equipment and morale they had seen of the North Vietnamese Army. Did it seem that the NVA was getting ragged, sloppy? Did it seem that discipline was about to break down? Gerber, Fetterman, Tyme and Bocker had told them everything they could remember. In the end the Army people went away very happy.

Finally there was an Air Force contingent that wanted to know what happened to Barlett. This was the debriefing that Gerber had dreaded because no one had a good answer. Le Duc had reported that Barlett had been captured or killed before he had gotten very far off the LZ. Gerber speculated that Barlett, because he wasn't used to the military chutes and all the ramifications of a combat HALO operation, had popped his chute early and drifted a long way from the rest of them. Separated in hostile territory, he had been either captured or killed. But Gerber, knowing that the Air Force would want to protect the memory of their own, told the Air Force investigators that Barlett had been a brave man and had gone down fighting. There was no point in telling them that Barlett had been a big pain in the butt and probably would have compromised the mission within hours.

"And there was nothing you could do for him?" asked the Air Force officer when Gerber had finished his speculation about Barlett.

"We had no idea where he was or if he was alive until we located Le Duc. We were on another mission, which had priority. Once we found Le Duc, it became obvious that Sergeant Barlett had been killed in action."

When the Air Force officer left, there was a final debriefing with the air rescue people about the procedures used. And finally, with a word of caution from Jerry Maxwell to keep their mouths shut about the mission to North Vietnam, they were released. No one asked why they didn't try to break into the Hanoi Hilton or why they didn't make more of an effort to find the downed aircrews. And no one wondered why they hadn't tried to get to one of the other missile sites to examine the weapons there. Gerber assumed that it was because the requests were seen for what they had been. Pipe dreams at best and disasters at worst.

Now, sitting across from Robin, the late afternoon sun beating down on him and making him squint, he felt the anger boil up inside him. They had gone through all that. Men had died for the information they had gotten, and Robin had tried to blow it all. If the story had appeared any earlier, it could have compromised the whole mission, jeopardizing all their lives.

He folded the paper and tossed it across the table at her. "You really responsible for this piece of shit?"

She glanced at the paper. "Not really."

"Your name is on it."

"Right. George thought he was doing me a favor by adding my name to the byline."

"You realize that this kind of irresponsible reporting can get men killed."

She felt the anger flare in her and then burst. After all she had gone through with Krupp, Maxwell and the others, she didn't like his attitude. "I don't need a lecture from you on the workings of the press."

"Somebody sure as hell does. Somebody needs to rein these guys in."

"Not me. I got the story held up for a week as it was. I told George all about responsible journalism and that in time of war some things had to be soft-pedaled. But do you give me credit for half a brain? Oh no. You immediately assume that I've done it again. You don't even have the courtesy to ask. You just assume the worst. After all I've been through for you, after all the crap I've taken as you chase my sister or that Vietnamese whore, I still come back for more. I must be stupid."

Gerber rocked back in his chair and stared at her. The venom of her response surprised him. He had assumed that everything was fine between them when he had gone off on his merry way. Well, maybe not exactly fine. He realized that she wasn't angry about his accusation. It was something more than that and he understood it now.

He had the sense not to try to jolly her out of it. Instead he leaned closer and took hold of one of her unyielding hands. "I'm sorry Robin, I didn't know . . ."

"How could you not know?" she asked, her voice breaking. "After everything, how could you not know?"

"Incredible stupidity on my part. It's not much, but maybe you'll be happy to know that Karen is madder than hell at me." He stopped speaking, his mind running full speed. Suddenly it was important to him that she understand what was going on. "She found out that I sneaked into Vietnam behind her back. Claimed that it was just an excuse to dump her, and pretended that she didn't know that it was coming. Said she never wanted to see me again. She was breaking it off."

Robin smiled weakly. "She was breaking it off? Is that what she said?"

"Well, she was a tad late, but that was what she said."

"You won't go crawling back to her?"

"No, Robin, I won't." He felt her hand soften and then grip his.

"And you understand about the story? That it wasn't my fault?"

"The press is doing more to undermine our effort here than everything the VC and North Vietnamese can throw at us. You have to understand my reaction to a story like that one." Even as he said it, he knew Robin wasn't interested in that. They were talking on two different levels but it was all about one thing. It was about them.

"Yes, but after all we've been through, you should know I wouldn't do a thing like that," she said.

Gerber knew she was right. With his free hand, he grabbed his beer and drained the glass. He set it down, and then got to his feet.

"Come on," he said, "I want to talk about this somewhere a little more private."

For a moment she resisted him, pulling at his hand. "Discuss this? Private?"

"You know perfectly well what I mean."

She stood, knowing perfectly well what he meant and approving of it completely.

GLOSSARY

AC—An aircraft commander. The pilot in charge of the aircraft.

AK-47—Assault rifle normally used by the North Vietnamese and the Vietcong.

AO—Area of Operations.

AP ROUNDS—Armor-piercing ammunition.

APU—Auxiliary Power Unit. An outside source of power used to start aircraft engines.

ARVN—Army of the Republic of Vietnam. A South Vietnamese soldier. Also known as Marvin Arvin.

BISCUIT—Term that refers to C-rations.

BODY COUNT—The number of enemy killed, wounded or captured during an operation. Used by Saigon and Washington as a means of measuring progress of the war.

BOOM BOOM—Term used by the Vietnamese prostitutes in selling their product.

BOONDOGGLE—Any military operation that hasn't been completely thought out. An operation that is ridiculous.

BOONIE HATS—A soft cap worn by the grunts in the field when not wearing their steel pot.

BUSHMASTER—A jungle warfare expert or soldier skilled in jungle navigation. Also a large deadly snake not common to Vietnam but mighty tasty.

C AND C—The Command and Control aircraft that circles overhead to direct combined air and ground operations.

CARIBOU—Cargo transport plane.

CHINOOK—Army Aviation twin-engine helicopter. A CH-47. Also known as a shit hook.

CHOCK—Refers to the number of the aircraft in the flight. Chock Three is the third, Chock Six is the sixth.

CLAYMORE—An antipersonnel mine that fires 750 steel balls with a lethal range of 50 meters.

CLOSE AIR SUPPORT—Use of airplanes and helicopters to fire on enemy units near friendlies.

CO CONG—A female Vietcong.

C-RATS—C-rations.

DAI UY—Vietnamese Army rank the equivalent of captain.

DEROS—Date Estimated Return from Overseas.

ELEMENT—Two aircraft working together. Two elements or more make up a flight.

EWO—Electronic Warfare Officer.

FEET WET—Term used by pilots to describe flight over water.

FIVE—Radio call sign for the executive officer of a unit.

FOX MIKE—FM radio.

FNG—A fucking new guy.

FREEDOM BIRD—Name given to any aircraft that takes troops out of Vietnam. Usually refers to the commercial jet flights that take men back to the World.

GARAND—The M-1 rifle was replaced by the M-14. Issued to the Vietnamese early in the war.

GO-TO-HELL RAG—Towel or any large cloth worn around the neck by grunts.

GRAIL—The NATO name for the shoulder-fired SA-7 surface-to-air missile.

GUARD THE RADIO—A term that means to stand by in the commo bunker and listen for messages.

GUIDELINE—The NATO term for the SA-2 surface-to-air missiles.

GUNSHIP—Armed helicopter or cargo plane that carries weapons instead of cargo.

HALO—High Altitude Low Opening. A type of parachute jump.

HE—High-explosive ammunition.

HOOTCH—Almost any shelter, from temporary to long-term.

HORN—Term that refers to a specific kind of radio operation that uses satellites to rebroadcast messages.

HORSE—See Biscuit.

HOTEL THREE—A helicopter landing area at Saigon's Ton Son Nhut Airport.

HUEY—A UH-1 helicopter.

ILS—Instrument Landing System.

IN-COUNTRY—Term used to refer to American troops operating in South Vietnam. They were all in-country.

INTELLIGENCE—Any information about enemy operations. It can include troop movements, weapons, capabilities, biographies of enemy commanders, and general information about terrain features. Any information that would be useful in planning a mission.

KABAR—A type of military combat knife.

KIA—Killed In Action. (Since the U.S. was not engaged in a declared war, the use of the term KIA was not authorized. KIA came to mean enemy dead. Americans were KHA or Killed in Hostile Action.)

KLICK—A thousand meters. A kilometer.

LIMA LIMA—Land Line. Refers to telephone communications between two points on the ground.

LLDB—Luc Luong Dac Biet. The South Vietnamese Special Forces. Sometimes referred to as the Look Long, Duck Back.

LP—Listening Post. A position outside the perimeter manned by a couple of soldiers to give advance warning of enemy activity.

LZ—Landing Zone.

M-14—Standard rifle of the U.S., eventually replaced by the M-16. It fires the standard NATO round—7.62 mm.

M-16—Standard infantry weapon of the Vietnam War. It fires 5.56 mm ammunition.

M-79—A short-barrel, shoulder-fired weapon that fires a 40 mm grenade. These can be high explosives, white phosphorus or canister.

MACV—Military Assistance Command, Vietnam, replaced MAAG in 1964.

MEDEVAC—Also called Dustoff. Helicopter used to take the wounded to the medical facilities.

MIA—Missing In Action.

NCO—A Noncommissioned Officer. A noncom. A sergeant.

NCOIC—NCO in charge. The senior NCO in a unit, detachment or patrol.

NEXT—The man who says he is the next to be rotated home. See Short.

NINETEEN—The average age of the combat soldier in Vietnam, as opposed to twenty-six in World War II.

NVA—The North Vietnamese Army. Also used to designate a soldier from North Vietnam.

P (PIASTER)—The basic monetary unit in South Vietnam, worth slightly less than a penny.

PETA-PRIME—A black tarlike substance that melts in the heat of the day to become a sticky, black nightmare that clings to boots, clothes and equipment. It was used to hold down the dust during the dry season.

PETER PILOT—The copilot in a helicopter.

PLF—Parachute Landing Fall. The roll used by parachutists on landing.

POW—Prisoner Of War.

PRC-10—Portable radio. Sometimes called Prick-10.

PRC-25—A lighter portable radio that replaced the PRC-10.

PULL PITCH—Term used by helicopter pilots that means they are going to take off.

PUNJI STAKE—Sharpened bamboo hidden to penetrate the foot, sometimes dipped in feces.

RON—Remain Overnight. Term used by flight crews to indicate a flight that would last longer than a day.

RPD—Soviet light machine gun 7.62 mm.

RTO—Radio Telephone Operator. The radio man of a unit.

SA-2—A surface-to-air missile fired from a fixed site. It is a radar-guided missile that is nearly 35 feet long.

SA-7—A surface-to-air missile that is shoulder-fired and infrared-homing.

SAFE AREA—A Selected Area for Evasion. It doesn't mean that the area is safe from the enemy, only that the terrain, location, or local population make the area a good place for escape and evasion.

SAM TWO—A reference to the SA-2 Guideline.

SAR—Search And Rescue. SAR forces are the people involved in search and rescue missions.

SIX—Radio call sign for the Unit Commander.

SHIT HOOK—Name applied by the troops to the Chinook helicopter because of all the "shit" stirred up by its massive rotors.

SHORT—Term used by everyone in Vietnam to tell all who would listen that his tour is about over.

SHORT-TIMER—Person who has been in Vietnam for nearly a year and who will be rotated back to the World soon. When the DEROS (Date of Estimated Return from Overseas) is the shortest in the unit, the person is said to be "Next."

SKS—Soviet-made carbine.

SMG—Submachine gun.

SOI—Signal Operating Instructions. The booklet that contains the call signs and radio frequencies of the units in Vietnam.

SOP—Standard Operating Procedure.

STEEL POT—The standard U.S. Army helmet. The steel pot is the outer metal cover.

TEAM UNIFORM OR COMPANY UNIFORM—UHF radio frequency on which the team or the company communicates. Frequencies were changed periodically in an attempt to confuse the enemy.

THREE—Radio call sign of the Operations Officer.

THREE CORPS—The military area around Saigon. Vietnam was divided into four corps areas.

TRIPLE A—Antiaircraft Artillery or AAA. This is anything used to shoot at airplanes and helicopters.

THE WORLD—The United States.

TOC—Tactical Operations Center.

TOT—Time Over Target. The time the aircraft are supposed to be over the drop zone with the parachutists, or the target if the planes are bombers.

TWO—Radio call sign of the Intelligence Officer.

TWO-OH-ONE (201) FILE—The military records file that lists a soldier's qualifications, training, experience and abilities.

UMZ—Ultramilitarized Zone. The name GIs gave to the DMZ (Demilitarized Zone).

VC—Vietcong, called Victor Charlie (phonetic alphabet) or just Charlie.

VDI—Vertical Display Indicator. A modern term for the old artificial horizon gauge on the instrument cluster in an aircraft's cockpit.

VIETCONG—A contraction of Vietnam Cong San (Vietnamese Communist).

VIETCONG SAN—The Vietnamese Communists. A term in use since 1956.

WHITE MICE—Refers to the Vietnamese military police because they wore white helmets.

WIA—Wounded In Action.

WILLIE PETE—WP, white phosphorus, called smok
rounds. Also used as antipersonnel weapons.

WINGMAN—Pilot whose job it is to protect another fror
surprise attack. The number 2 aircraft in an element c
two aircraft.

WSO—Weapons System Officer. The name given to the mar
who rides in the back seat of a Phantom because he i
responsible for the weapons systems.

XO—Executive officer of a unit.

YARDS—Short form for Montagnards (pronounced mor
tan-yards).

ZAP—To ding, pop caps, or shoot. To kill.

ZIPPO—A flamethrower.